Two-i

The Dog That Talked to God

and

The Cat That God Sent

plus a sneak preview of
Conversations with
Saint Bernard

Jim Kraus

Abingdon Press
Nashville

TWO-IN-ONE VALUE EDITION
THE DOG THAT TALKED TO GOD
THE CAT THAT GOD SENT

15 16 17 18 19 20 21 22 23—10 9 8 7 6 5 4 3 2 1

MANUFACTURED IN THE UNITED STATES OF AMERICA

THE DOG THAT TALKED TO GOD

Jim Kraus

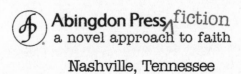
Abingdon Press fiction
a novel approach to faith

Nashville, Tennessee

The Dog That Talked to God

Published by Abingdon Press, P.O. Box 801, Nashville, TN 37202
www.abingdonpress.com

Library of Congress Cataloging-in-Publication Data

Kraus, Jim, 1950–
    The dog that talked to god / Jim Kraus.
        p.   cm.
    ISBN 978-1-4267-4256-9 (book - paperback / trade pbk. : alk. paper)
    I. Title.
    PS3561.R2876D64   2012
    813'.54—dc23

                                                                    2011044545

Printed in the United States of America

1 2 3 4 5 6 7 8 9 10 / 17 16 15 14 13 12

To Rufus, a noble dog

1

Born in the wealthy enclave of Barrington, Illinois, in late autumn, Rufus was the smallest pup in a litter of four—black with white highlights, white eyebrows and chest. The breeder, a precise woman with a lazy eye, said that as an adult, he would most likely remain on the smallish side. That's a good trait for a miniature schnauzer. He had the look, even as a seven-week-old, of a polished, professional dog, holding a practiced dog show stance—legs back, chest forward, eyes alert—all inherited traits, genetics at its best.

But she said nothing about Rufus talking. Not just talking, but talking to God. In dog prayers, I imagine.

Though, in her defense, I would guess that she was unaware of this unusual talent.

And, also in her defense, if she knew of his abilities and had mentioned, "Oh yes, Mrs. Fassler, and the runt of the litter—the dog you want—well, he talks, and he claims he talks to God." I mean, honestly, if she had said that, or anything remotely like that, then odds are that the good dog Rufus would not be sitting in the chair opposite me right now, watching me type.

Perhaps if Rufus had been adopted into another home—a home with an owner who wasn't lost and confused and didn't need to be returned to the awareness of the existence of God—he would not have bothered speaking at all, except to bark at the door to be let out. Even Rufus is not sure of that possibility.

"I don't ask foolish questions, Mary," Rufus answered when I asked him about the odds of him spending his life with me, rather than some other, more spiritually healthy person.

But I digress.

I did not mean to cavalierly hurry past the most compelling element of this story: the fact that Rufus talks to God. And he talks to me—Rufus, that is, not God. Sometimes.

It's hard to be nonchalant or blasé about such an ability, I know. But I cannot leap into this tale without returning to the beginning. You need to know how all this came about. You need to know the origins of the story. After all, what would the Bible be without Genesis and the garden of Eden? Confusing, to say the least, and most likely incomprehensible. Imagine the Bible as a movie you walk into during the middle. You can make up your own backstory, but it would all be just a guess. Admit it: without that opening scene, not much of the rest would contain any internal logic.

As a child, I used to do that—walk into a movie theater whenever, and watch the film, sit through the ending, and wait for the opening reel to start again until I would say to myself, "This is where I came in." It was easier years ago, before the age of googolplexes and corporate theater chains. Back in the day, each theater had one screen and would play the same movie over and over, with only a cartoon and previews to separate one screening from another. Once I got to that point of having seen a particular scene before, I would leave, satisfied that I saw the entire story. I remember doing that to *The Time Machine* with Rod Taylor, a movie star without much reason to be a star. Seems ludicrous to me now. I had constructed my own narrative as to how Rod got to whatever point in the future he started at, which then altered my imagined story as the true narrative unfolded. With that movie, I was close to guessing the actual story and plot. Close, but, as they say, no cigar.

As a child, reconstructing a complicated narrative was child's play.

It is not so easy today.

———✦———

Throughout my youth, my family owned pets. *Owned*, I suspect, is now a pejorative term. I mean, do we really own a dog? Or do we merely cohabit in the same spaces? The latter, I am now certain. My father, an impetuous man with a generous heart, once bought a squirrel monkey from Gimbels Department Store in Pittsburgh, Pennsylvania—when department stores, I surmise, could sell squirrel monkeys.

A monkey proved to be a pretty interesting pet, but if you fed it something it did not like, it would simply heave it out of the cage. Neatness is not any monkey's most endearing trait.

I remember growing up with a mutt, the family dog, a loyal animal who became as much a member of the family as I. As a teenager, I stood beside her in the vet's office when he administered the oh-so-humane and oh-so-lethal injection to a lame, sick, dying dog. I remember her eyes, just as they went dark. I remember weeping all night over that loss.

In my forties (midway, if I am feeling honest) I found myself alone again. I was pretty certain I needed a dog. Christmas was coming and I did not want to be alone.

Before—well, before my current losses and tragedies—the parameters of a dog purchase became the topic of long conversations among Jacob, John, and me. It had been decided that hypoallergenic was a necessity; preferably non-shedding, small, with minimal genetic health concerns, loyal, good with children, non-nippy, benevolent, artistic, and kind. Just kidding about the last three, but we did have a pretty substantial list of preferences. The miniature schnauzer breed met all of our qualifications.

But we, as a family, never had a chance to fulfill that dream.

Alone, now, I decided to take action—and taking action was something I did not do lightly. Unlike me, the schnauzer, according to the breed books, had decisiveness bred into its genes. A good watchdog, the books insisted. A barker, but not a biter. Since I live in a relatively safe suburb, a barker would be sufficient.

I made a few calls; I looked on the Internet.

A friend advised against getting any dog. "They're all the same—stupid, hairy, and only interested in food. Trust me," she had said. "You will get companionship, but it will be stupid companionship. Like a blind date who you find out later cheated to get his GED, and who is five inches shorter than he claimed."

She owned an Irish setter, a truly small-brained animal. I say *she* owned it since she did all the dog upkeep in her family—feeding, walking, feeding, letting out, letting in, feeding, washing the muck off of it. The rest of the household liked the dog, but as is often usual for families, the mother remained stuck with all the dog duties. And to complicate things, her dog could not be described as smart—not even close to smart.

It ran into the same glass sliding door every morning of its life. Like a chicken, it appeared to wake up to a new world every dawn. A pleasant dog, for certain, but, as noted, not very smart. And it often smelled wet. Most of us know that musty, yeasty, heady, nearly unpleasant aroma of a wet dog. Like wet newspaper. What they have in common is beyond me.

"But I'm looking at a smaller dog. Something that I can pick up if I have to," I told her.

It took two people to lift my friend's Irish setter, or a single person using a hospital patient lift—and where was one of those when needed?

"Jacob always wanted a schnauzer. Sort of like fulfilling a promise, you know?" I added.

My friend shrugged, apparently resigned to my choice, to my fate.

After all, how do you argue with one of the last wishes of a dead man?

There were a few AKC breeders near where I live who specialized in miniature schnauzers.

And when I was ready, only one breeder—the precise lady in Barrington with the lazy eye—had a litter with an unspoken-for puppy.

"I have a litter of four. The two females are spoken for. The larger male is going to another breeder in Florida. That leaves one male puppy. He's the runt of the litter. But he's healthy."

I attempted to make arrangements to complete the purchase.

"It's not that simple," she said, a slight note of caution in her voice. "Before you come, I have some questions. Save you a trip. I don't sell my dogs to just anyone."

"Of course not," I said, thinking it was a poor method of marketing puppies, but I played along. "I completely understand."

"Do you live in a house or apartment?"

"A house. It's too big for me," I said, telling this stranger more than she needed to know. "I plan on selling in a year or two, and moving to a smaller house. More manageable. But a house. A house, yes, not an apartment or a condo. I don't think I would do well in an apartment anymore. Odd noises and someone is always cooking with too much curry. So, yes, I have a house. I will have a house. Now. And in the future."

"Does the house have a yard? Will the new house have a yard?"

Don't all houses have yards?

"It does. And the back is fenced. It's pretty big. The land-scapers bill me $40 a week to cut it . . . so there's a lot of room for a dog to run. And if I do move, that house will have a fenced yard. Keeps out the riffraff dogs, if you know what I mean."

Her silence probably meant that she didn't.

"Do you work?"

No . . . I thought I might pay for the puppy with food stamps.

Sorry. That's just me being snarky. Sorry.

"Yes."

"Are you gone all day? Will the dog be alone all day?"

Oh . . . now I see why you're asking.

"No. I work from home. I write books. And I edit some. And I publish a newsletter for writers. But I'm home 95 percent of most weekdays. I do go out to Starbucks sometimes to write. There's something about having to block out other people's conversations that makes me concentrate more effectively. But that's only once a week. Maybe twice, if I'm stumped by something."

The precise lady waited, then spoke carefully.

"I wouldn't sell this dog to a single person who worked outside the home all day. These puppies need companionship.

They'll get neurotic without a person—or people—around. Nothing worse than a neurotic dog."

She said nothing about dogs that had delusions of grandeur. Would I describe Rufus as . . . delusional? Or would that just be me?

"Any small children in the home?"

I waited a heartbeat, as I have done now for these last few years, until that small scud of darkness passed.

"No. No one else. It's just me."

The precise lady must have been thinking "divorced," or "widowed," or "never married." I did not volunteer further information. She did not ask. Often, when even thinking about the past, even to myself—still—I would get teary. Buying a dog is no time to get teary.

"Well, why don't you come up this Saturday? The puppy won't be ready to leave for at least another three weeks. You can see how you'll get on with him. We can talk."

I hung up the phone thinking that I need to make a good impression on this woman, or else I'll have to find another breeder and the next closest—with puppies available—was in Ohio. I did not want to drive to Ohio. Not just yet. Maybe not ever.

I arrived at the breeder's home early—a lifelong trait. To me, being on time is fifteen minutes early. The setting was not exactly rural, but I estimated that I was a good ten minutes from the nearest Starbucks—or a Texaco station selling chilled bottles of Starbucks Iced Coffee. So I sat in the drive and waited. I would have really liked a coffee. Caffeine settles my nerves.

I rattled in the car, more than a little nervous.

The breeder was exactly as I had pictured: precise, wore her hair short, trim, with practical glasses clipped to a gold chain around her neck; with that one eye slightly off-kilter to the other. She may have been wearing Earth Shoes. I was unaware if they had made a comeback; hers looked sensible and organic with a leather strap. I admit that I am far from being style-conscious. I buy good clothes, good outfits, designed to last. I haven't purchased a new outfit in years . . . well . . . since before the accident, I guess.

She extended her hand for a firm handshake, and escorted me to the basement. I could hear scuffling and yipping as we descended. In a large, airy room, with French doors leading to the outside, now closed, two adult schnauzers were in a large pen with what appeared to be a large, single mass of wiggling puppy. The room smelled of dog—but that inviting new-dog smell.

"Sit down," she said, and for that second I was not sure if the breeder meant me or the dogs. I realized that I should sit.

I sat on a plastic chair—one of two in the enclosure.

The two adult dogs sniffed the air, not in fear, but in exploration, in greeting. The larger one trotted over to me, placed its front paws on my knees, and stared hard into my eyes.

Schnauzer eyes are dark, or mostly dark, so the iris in their eyes is all but indistinguishable. They are like cartoon eyes—all one color—so it is difficult to see emotion in them. And schnauzers are not smilers. Some dogs—like labs, for example—can pull their lips back and offer a grin, with a lolling tongue. (I have since discovered that labs aren't that happy. They are simply manipulative.)

The larger dog, apparently satisfied with what it was looking for, hopped down.

The smaller dog walked toward me, with what I took to be deliberate steps. It too placed its paws on my knees and stared.

"That's the mom," the breeder said, not using the word *mom*, but the breeder word for a female dog—a word, incidentally, that I have never liked using, either in anger or in scientific dog-calling. She was Rufus's mother after all, though the name Rufus would not be decided for a few weeks.

She stared deeply, as deeply as a dog can stare, without being distracted by the yelping of one puppy or the whine of another. She stared, just stared, for the longest of moments. Longer than most dogs stare at anything, with the possible exception of an empty food bowl. (This I have learned recently as well.)

I didn't know what to do, so I gently covered her paws with my hands—like offering a manner of assurance that I was a good person who would treat her offspring well.

After what seemed to be a long time, she sort of gave a nod, like she approved, or found me acceptable, or knew her one special offspring was exactly the puppy I needed, then dropped back to the ground, sniffed my leg and shoe for a moment, and walked back to the big ball of puppies in the corner. This was not her first litter, so she obviously knew the routine. Puppies grow up and move on in the wild, and they do the same if they reside in urban domesticity.

The breeder walked over, reached in, and extracted a small furry lump of wiggle, mostly black, with some white. She handed it to me.

"This one will be yours if you want."

I held the small wriggling bud of puppy cupped in my two hands with plenty of room to spare.

"The pup can't see real well yet, so all it sees is your hands."

I stroked the little face with a finger, gentle, but not overly gentle. It was a boy puppy, after all. The puppy seemed to like that, and promptly fell asleep in my hands.

"That's a good sign. Some dogs just stay all riled up—being picked up, carried, strange scents—they'll struggle to get away. Apparently, he thinks you're a safe place."

He was the most beautiful puppy I had ever seen.

And he fell asleep. My heart began to sing, just a little. After such a long silence, it startled me at its ability to do so.

This was indeed the puppy that I needed to have in my life.

More surprises came later.

The breeder gave me a list of things to do, and to have them all accomplished in the three weeks between the initial meeting and the final handoff—Rufus's adoption, as it was. The list was not extensive, but it was twice as long as I had anticipated.

"I can't visit your house, so you have to give me your word that all of it gets done. Okay?"

It was a command that I could not say no to.

"Of course."

I could see why she was good at training dogs. I really wanted to please her.

A dog crate; dog carrier for the car ride home; puppy food— one of two preferred brands—a water dish; collar, two leashes; one retractable, one a strong tether; the name of the dog's veterinarian; a picture of the fenced yard; an appointment set for a puppy class. The list ran on for nearly a full page.

Obtaining all the necessary documentation and supplies was not that difficult. The cage—sorry, the *crate*—fit into the alcove of a desk built into the kitchen layout. (I had been told that *cage* was pejorative, *crate* was preferred by most breeders.) I never used the kitchen desk, except as a temporary storehouse for receipts, mail, and magazines waiting to be evaluated before becoming recyclables. The top drawer held in the neighborhood of a thousand pens and pencils, all halfway to being thrown away because none of them worked, forcing me to take telephone notes with a huge felt-tipped sign marker on legal pads, the ink soaking through four sheets at a time.

I have to get better organized. I mean it this time.

The cage—rather, the crate—fit snugly in the kneehole of the desk. I added two sleeping pads, the top one a leopard print, to ensure a soft rest. I took a picture of it. I would show the breeder all my preparations.

No one prints pictures anymore. All they do is show others the back of their camera or cell phones. I miss passing actual snapshots around, but I didn't think I needed a permanent record of a dog crate and food bowls and the like, so I carried my camera with me.

I'll probably never delete them from the memory stick, though.

I wasn't sure about the crate situation. I never had a crated dog before. The family dog had the run of the house. Looking back, I don't remember where the dog slept. Did we have a dog bed somewhere? My mother, the sole surviving parent, resided in a nursing home, and while she had only begun to wade into the shallow, yet troubled waters of dementia, for now she would resent being asked inconsequential questions like "Where did the dog sleep?"

She would become agitated a little, and wave the question off as if it were a pesky mosquito. "How I am expected to remember foolish things like that?" she would snap, prickly as she had ever been. Some things do not change over the decades.

I would want to say that I did not expect her to recall the details, but that we were simply making conversation. Instead of asking a follow-up question about how the family had decided on a dog name, I would instead sit back, and watch *Wheel of Fortune* with my mother. She could not hear worth beans and had no use for gadgets like hearing aids, so the volume would be turned up to a painful level. Virtually every television in the Ligonier Valley Nursing Unit remained turned to the same level. I don't understand how the nurses and aides tolerated it. It would be like working in a tavern that featured heavy metal music. Or working in a steel mill. Here, all televisions, except the one in the main visiting lounge, had to be turned off by eight in the evening. Then silence rolled down the halls like a tsunami.

The breeder said that the prehistoric dogs lived in dens, so a crate, which she was careful to call a crate, fulfills their ancestral urges of being covered, protected, and easily defended. I draped a thin blanket over the top and sides. I planned to swap the thin one out for a heavier one in colder weather. The door latched easily. The crate provided plenty of turnaround area. The padding looked, and felt, pretty comfortable as well.

I had not purchased the Kuranda Dog Bed—patented, orthopedic, and chew proof. It certainly looked comfortable in the pet store, nearly as expensive as the new mattress I had purchased for myself eighteen months earlier. That was a necessary purchase; a deluxe dog bed could not be considered in the same category.

I had an assortment of puppy food, puppy chews, puppy toys, and assorted puppy diversions.

Even before I handed the breeder a check, this dog purchase had become expensive.

Do friends ever give puppy showers? My initial reaction was a strong no, with a wishful yes right behind.

I was ready. I was prepared.

Yet nothing could prepare me, really and truly, for what was to happen in a few short months.

The breeder actually looked at every picture I took of my purchases, my preparations, my supplies, my complete photo essay of my backyard. She even checked the photocopy of the medical license of my intended veterinarian.

"I've never heard of him," she said, "but he went to Cornell. Best vet school in the country."

"She. She went. The B. T. stands for Barbara something or other," I answered.

The breeder brightened.

"Good. I've always found female vets to be more compassionate—and intuitive. Good choice."

I felt proud of what I had accomplished. It was a feeling I had missed in recent months.

She presented me with the puppy's papers and AKC registration—a thick packet of documents that displayed his lineage back to the *Mayflower*, apparently. I had assured her that I had no interest in showing the puppy, or dog, as it grew. I promised to have him neutered; perhaps breeders do not want more competition from unskilled amateurs like me. "Neutered makes for better pets," she declared. I knew, for certain, that his papers would be filed in my office at home, and then lost in less than six months.

I'm not going to sell the dog for a profit, like flipping a foreclosed house. He's not going to procreate. Why would I need to know his great-great-great-grandfather?

I handed her the check. The dog was now mine.

"What are you going to name him?" the breeder asked.

I shrugged, apologetically.

"I'm not good with names . . . or book titles. I let my publisher pick titles. But with the dog, I thought I might see what sort of name fits him after a day or two."

"Don't wait too long. Puppies get imprinted with whatever you call it—especially if you use it a lot when they're young."

He lay down in the middle of the pet carrier, not frantically trying to escape or cowering in the corner. But in the middle, like that is where he was supposed to be. It did make it easier to carry, since the weight was evenly distributed.

I had been nervous concerning the ride home, worried about a whining, yelping puppy carrying on so much that I would have to stop. I'd imagined him chewing wildly at the door, scrabbling to escape his new and probably evil owner. But there were no histrionics, no puppy on the edge of puppy craziness. Just a very calm puppy, supine, staring out through the wire mesh door.

I pulled into the garage, stopped the car, and carefully took the carrier from the car.

"Show him his bed, his food, and the door you'll use to take him outside. Take him out on a leash right away and start his bathroom training," the breeder instructed, touching on the three most important elements in a puppy's small world.

I followed her instructions to the letter.

He dutifully sniffed at his crate, stepped inside, sniffing, looking at the cushion, then up at the top of the crate—like people do on all the HGTV shows when they enter a new room. I have noted that potential homebuyers invariably look at the ceiling, as if to make sure the house has one. Why do people do that? It's a plain ceiling. Look to see how big the closets are first, and if you have good water pressure. No one checks the water pressure on those shows. I have yet to see a single buyer flush a toilet. There might be a lot fewer home sales if people flushed toilets or ran showers.

The puppy completed his examination of the crate. I led him to his food dish and water bowl—both filled with fresh supplies.

He sniffed at both.

I snapped a leash onto his collar and led him to the . . .

Wait. What door am I going to use?

The back door led to a back deck, a second-story affair. A puppy this small would not yet be able to climb stairs.

I'll have to use the front door.

We stepped outside through the main door, and his sniffing became a bit more earnest. It took him fifteen minutes to sniff his way around the front yard. I was cold by the time he completed his inspection. There were other dogs in the neighborhood, so he took some time getting acquainted with their calling cards.

I am told that dogs can tell the size and sex and temperament of other dogs by the scent they leave. Seems a crude way of doing it—but if you can't talk or write, I suspect it is the only way.

He actually relieved himself out there, by a bush toward the side of the house—a bush I didn't really like, so if his ministrations killed it, I would not be upset. It was some sort of weedy looking shrub that had been billed as the bearer of fragrant flowers. The flowers lasted all of three days; the rest of the time it simply looked weedy. I praised him, as I had been told to do.

We walked back into the house. I unclipped his leash.

"Keep him in the kitchen at first. He'll be overwhelmed if he has too much space to explore."

Two doorways led into the kitchen: one a pocket door to the dining room, easily closed off; the other archway could be cut off by opening the basement door, leaving a gap of only an inch or two. The bigger problem was the wide arch between the kitchen and the family room.

The puppy seemed to be a cautious type, so my initial solution employed two lengths of white clothesline rope, strung at two inches off the floor, and the other at six inches, and affixed to the molding with adhesive-backed Velcro. If the puppy ran into them at full force, which he gave no indication of doing, the ropes would give way. More important, if I ran into them, stumbling toward the sunroom with the first coffee of the day and with my typical morning slit-eyes, then I would dislodge them as easily, without tumbling down and scalding myself with hot coffee.

The puppy sniffed the ropes, and made no attempt to cross the barrier.

It appeared effective. Maybe I could market this idea.

The puppy stared up at me.

No. How hard would it be to duplicate this? Not very.

I sat on the floor, my back to the wall, and invited the puppy to play. He slithered over with a wiggle. I imagined that he looked happy. I couldn't tell. This was the start of a long process, learning how to read the moods of this small animal.

He crawled into my hands and began a gentle nibbling on my fingers. His breath smelled healthy, like milk.

"Don't let him bite you," the breeder had scolded me. "Bad habit for a dog to have—biting."

But chewing is what a puppy does. As long as he did not bite in anger, I would tolerate a dog-to-owner chew every now and again.

After thirty minutes, the puppy crawled down from my leg and sat on his haunches, looking as tired as a . . . well, a puppy.

"Go into your crate," I directed and pointed at the open door to his den.

The puppy stared at my finger for a moment, as if my finger was the object he should focus on. "No," I said, as I pushed my finger forward into the air, gesturing toward the door. The puppy appeared to scowl, or furrow his brow as if in thought, then turned his head toward the crate. He lifted himself off the floor and walked with a surprising deliberateness toward his den, his crate, climbed over the two-inch frame, walked in, circled three times, then laid down, his head on his paws, his eyes facing me.

"Tired?"

He blinked, and let his head fall farther onto his paws.

"Can I get some coffee? Will I keep you awake?"

He did not answer. I am not sure, in the retelling of this episode, if he understood me at that young age, and simply waited to speak until the right time, or if he was in the process of trying to understand my speech. I think the latter, though I have not asked him. It doesn't seem to be that pertinent a question, in retrospect.

I sat in the upholstered chair in the bay window in the kitchen, sat with my coffee, watching The Weather Channel with the sound muted, sipping as quietly as I could manage, watching the puppy fall into a deep, untroubled sleep.

2

I named the puppy Rufus. I wish I had an interesting story behind the name. I don't. There was a King Rufus of England, I think, and a Rufus King, an American politician back in the 1800s (that fact I looked up), a minor biblical character, and Rufus Wainwright, a singer—but none of them had any bearing on my selection. Like with a new baby, I opened the *Baby Names* book to find an appropriate moniker. I had done this only once before, and I had, in the years between then and now, never, ever imagined that I would be doing it again. When I found the *Baby Names* book on a bookcase in the basement, it took me three days to open it.

I scanned the pages, eyes avoiding certain letters, then settled into the "R" chapter. The name Rufus appeared halfway down on a left-hand page. The name means "red." The dog wasn't red, nor would he ever be red, but the roundness of the name sort of fit perfectly. I knew no one named Rufus. I don't think I had ever been introduced to anyone with the name Rufus. There were no Rufuses in the neighborhood, so if I were to stand on my back deck and call the dog's name, there would be no confusion. Nor would I feel foolish—like shouting "Mr. Wiggles."

The puppy sat a few feet away, still in the kitchen, gnawing politely on a very small chew toy. The long rays of an autumn sun streamed through the bay window and the puppy sat in a warming pool of sunlight.

"Do you like the name Rufus?"

The puppy stopped chewing, and looked up at me. I had no idea what was in his eyes, save that it was a wide-eyed look up.

"Rufus. Should I name you Rufus? It sounds sort of dog-like, doesn't it? I don't like when people give dogs a real people name—like Mike or Paulie or something like that. Confusing to everyone, I think."

The puppy waited, the chew toy gripped between its forepaws.

"Rufus," I said with some authority. The puppy's ears perked up, as if he had heard the word and was now trying to remember it.

"Rufus," I said again a little louder.

This time, the puppy laid the chew toy down, stood up, and scampered toward me.

"Rufus," I said again, and by this time he stood at my feet, then on his hind legs, front paws on my legs. That meant he wanted to be picked up. Or to go outside. Or his stomach was empty. This time I interpreted it as wanting to be picked up. I cradled him my arms, not like a baby; that gets weird when an almost middle-aged woman starts treating a dog like a real human baby. No. I resisted that urge and held him like a dog should be held as I sat in the easy chair in the kitchen. Then he sort of stood on my stomach and made a beeline for my face. He did not try to nip at my nose. It had become a favorite game of his. Instead, he stopped mid-chest, and stared up.

25

"Rufus," I said, more softly this time, with as much quiet solemnity as I could muster.

He sat back and stared. I knew he had to be internalizing the sound of the name. I hoped that was what he was doing. No one could have told me with assurance that he wasn't doing exactly that. "Rufus. That's your name. It fits your face. You look just like a Rufus is supposed to look. A little beard. White eyebrows. A perfect Rufus."

He waited another moment, and then leaped at my nose. I caught him mid-jump. His teeth were sharp enough to draw blood and I did not want to spoil this sort-of-almost-hallowed moment of bestowing a name. I held him in both hands, while he squirmed happily.

"Rufus. From this day forward, noble dog, you will be known as Rufus."

Then I held him close to my chest and tried not to cry, remembering too much from the only other naming ceremony I had been party to.

This one was much different. Happy. But so had been the time before.

And as had happened in my only previous naming cere-mony, moments later the newly named fell asleep in my arms, the sun bathing his perfect features, outlining every color and fold, every centimeter of a dog's personal topography in immaculate clarity.

I would remember this day forever, too, feeling a tiny heart beat close to mine once again.

———

I know I should tell something of my past. I have been avoiding that story every time I've felt the slightest nudge to let it unfold. Sometimes, that dark night seems as if it stands decades in the past; other times, it lies within a hand's reach.

I will tell you what I can, what you need to know at the moment.

I am forty-three, nearly forty-four years old. I am a widow. My name was . . . is . . . Mrs. Jacob Fassler. I think that was the proper terminology. Now I sign my name "Mary Fassler."

Obviously, this means that I had once been married. Until three years ago.

I am now living alone. Well, now with Rufus here, sitting in the office chair, staring out the window, watching me from the corner of his eye, I am not quite totally alone.

My house is much too large for one person and a small, well-mannered dog. The house was much too big for my husband and me. It was much too big for my husband and son and me.

I will soon get myself organized. I will clean the clutter out of this office. I will go through their clothes. I will donate them to the church's resale shop. I will find the golf clubs, the very old lacrosse equipment, and the electronic games and give them all away.

My heart is beating faster. I do not want to tell more of this story. I do not think I can.

I am alone. I don't like being alone. I wish things were different. I wish they had never headed east and had never crossed into Ohio.

I have stopped typing. I cannot stop weeping—softly, silently, without tears really—just a heaving of the chest and a near strangling tightness in my throat. I have never before—in the space of the last few years—put any of my story to paper or computer screen. Now that I have, it comes back in a flood and I am forced to stop.

That's when I see Rufus standing at the edge of the chair. He is too small to jump down by himself, but that is clearly what he wants to do. I had to help him up into the chair earlier. I take him down from the chair and he runs at me and attempts to scale my leg, thankfully clad in denim this afternoon. He makes it up my shin before he falls back into a heap. I stop wallowing in self-pity and pick him up. He burrows and climbs and attempts to get to my neck, and once there, in the crook of my neck, he nuzzles against it, pushing his damp, cold nose against my skin. It is almost a shocking feeling, and my tears leave me, my throat unsticks.

And that's when Rufus settles down as well. I sniff once more, and my stifled tears stop, and the puppy is obviously happy that I am no longer so unhappy.

Rufus lived in the kitchen for two weeks. He hid toys under the pair of upholstered chairs in the bay window and circled the bottom skirt, pretending the toys were rabbits in hiding, then lunged under the flap of fabric, pulling a plush animal out into the open. He did not attempt to dismember any of his toys. He nibbled at them ever so gently. He would circle his domain every so often. He would stop at the rope barricade, look out into the family room and the sunroom beyond, never once trying to break through the flimsy and mostly symbolic gating. He slept in his crate at night, with the door closed.

I agonized over that first night. I placed him in the crate, patted him on the head, closed the door, and told him, "Good night." He looked back up at me with those impervious eyes—not with sadness, but something more akin to resignation. Too small to climb the steps to the second floor anyhow, he had to sleep somewhere safe. I expected a long night of whines and barks, but I got nothing. Not a single peep. The next morning, a bit earlier than usual, I hurried downstairs. Rufus sat in the middle of the crate, not smiling, but waiting for me. He jumped out of the crate into my hands and began his puppy-nibbling.

We happily went outside. Rufus needed to know what dogs had come calling during the night. He tried once more to kill the shrub at the corner of the yard. He had found his spot.

At the end of those two weeks, I took down the ropes separating the family room from the kitchen. Rufus waited until I coiled them up and placed them in a drawer, then he took off with a joyful bounce and ran, full tilt, through the family room and into the sunroom, sliding on the polished hardwood floor, and crashing into the pair of hassocks, rolling, paws akimbo in the air, as happy as I had yet seen him. He had been looking at this route for a long time, and now he was relishing his first chance at experiencing in a joyful, headlong charge.

You had to admire both his inscrutable patience and his joyful verve.

He was almost big enough to scramble up into one of the chairs or onto the sofa in the sunroom. I spent little of my time in the family room—the room that lay between the kitchen and the sunroom. The room had seemed to grow too large, too uncozy, despite my best efforts of adding warmth. The acoustics were odd as well; the vaulted ceiling swallowed up dialogue on the television, and I did not like turning up the sound to the volume in my mother's nursing home. So, even on the chilly days, I usually had my morning coffee in the sunroom. Well, with the exception of these past few weeks. I would have felt guilty about abandoning poor little Rufus in the kitchen, all by himself for breakfast as well.

So I sat in the sunroom again, my back to the sun. Rufus snuffed and sniffed his way around the room, then sat at my feet, looking up. We had been outside, and he had noisily eaten kibble for breakfast, so I assumed that he wanted up.

I placed him on the sofa with me and he explored each cushion. Then he placed his paws on the back of the sofa, as if he wanted to climb up. The sofa had a wide back, with plenty of room for him to navigate. I picked him up and placed him there. He paraded back and forth once, then sat near my shoulder, staring out into the back yard, growling ever so slightly when he caught a glimpse of a squirrel in the trees that grew along my back property line.

In the future, that would become Rufus's favorite daytime resting and/or sleeping spot. He could watch out over his world, be close to me, and nap peacefully as the sunlight flowed, diffused by the slats, through the wide wooden blinds.

Friends came over to visit that first month, after hearing I had acquired a dog. They oohed and aahhed over the puppy, picking him up, with some planting kisses on his head. I had determined not to be the sort of semi-crazy pet lady who would do that. I have to say that human-to-pet smooches simply look wrong. Weird. I am pretty sure that Rufus did not like the forced smooches either, but he had no forearm with which to wipe off an unwanted kiss after being bussed on his forehead. Worse yet was the occasional trace of lipstick that remained afterward in his white eyebrows that I had to clean off when the over-affectionate guest departed.

Over lunch at a local fish house (a restaurant I could never go into by myself because it just felt too much like a couples place) one of my friends asked what was going on in my life. I appreciated that; most friends felt uncomfortable delving into my personal life and its tragedies and found it easier to chatter on about gardening or the upcoming house tour for charity or their exercise classes at the YMCA.

"I'm doing . . . okay," I said. "It doesn't get any easier. But maybe I'm just getting used to the way things are now. And the dog helps. Somebody in the house to talk to."

Beth pushed her blonde bangs from her eyes. (The blond was not natural, but then, what in today's world is totally real and unadorned?)

"No . . . I mean how are you really doing? You don't come to church anymore. Or hardly ever come. No one from our Sunday school class ever sees you. I've asked. We're worried about you. Or . . . well, I'm worried about you. You only come out when somebody calls you for lunch."

For a moment, I felt sad that I disappointed so many people. Then a moment later . . . no a second later . . . I grew angry. Why do I have to answer to so many other people about how I spend my Sunday mornings? Is it any of their business? I think not.

I decided to lie. I decided to smile and lie. Once more. It was just so much simpler than the truth.

"I'm fine. Really. It's hard to go to church. I see so many familiar faces, and I keep imagining that they either pity me or are waiting to pounce on me, offering some off-kilter advice. Or set me up with their third cousin on their mother's side who is way into comic books or is a *Star Wars* or *Star Trek* fanatic. Trekkies do not make for good potential dates."

The best defense is a good offense, they say. Put the blame on others.

Beth smiled. I know she knew what I meant about the matchmakers in the church. Then a more serious look appeared in her eyes. "Mary, are you sure? Maybe it's time to find another church, then."

I took a deep breath. Of course I had considered that option. Every Sunday since the accident, I guess. But I couldn't. He . . . Jacob . . . grew up in this church. His father had been an elder for decades. If I left now, people would talk. His parents were still here—for the summers, anyhow. Mesa, Arizona, for the winter. (Cubs training camp was their version of Lourdes.) How would I explain to them why I was leaving the family church? I couldn't. They were not what I would call generously spirited people. They waged a letter-writing campaign when the new pastor started taking his tie off for the summer services. Personally, I don't see how a few feet of expensive fabric makes a man more devout or righteous or reverential—but there it was.

It's where our baby had been baptized.

That's all I need to say. There could be no leaving.

And, at the moment, there could be no going either.

I did attend—maybe monthly. Or thereabouts. I slipped in the back after the service began, and slipped out a split second after the benediction and hurried into the narthex before the final "Amen." I ran into more people than I wanted to even at that.

So I still attended. Just on my own terms. Abbreviated, to be sure, but it was all I could handle right now. Maybe, in the future, in a year or two more, I would start full power again. I would join the Ladies Bible Study. I would volunteer in the nurs . . . no, not there. I would volunteer in the library. I would begin to go back to Sunday school. I would begin to reintegrate my life with the family of God again.

But not now. Not now at all.

"No, that's silly. I'm just healing a little more slowly . . . than I expected."

Beth pushed her hair back again.

Why didn't she get a different haircut? I want to smack her hand every time she does that.

"But you are healing? Right? You're not simply fading away from . . . you know—church and Jesus and all that, are you? I mean, that would be a shame."

"No, I'm fine. Or getting to be fine. Really."

Beth reached over and patted my hand, like an aunt does to an unruly seven-year-old niece. "It will be okay. You know, things happen . . ."

DON'T SAY IT! DON'T SAY THINGS HAPPEN FOR A REASON. DO NOT SAY THAT!

I forced myself to take a deep, cleansing, calming breath. Beth seemed to sense the possible impending eruption.

If I hear once more that "all things happen for a reason" or "God wanted them in heaven" or "You're young—you can marry again—start over" or "Everything works out in God's perfect plan . . ."

My life has not happened according to God's plan! The accident was not part of God's merciful plan to draw unrepentant sinners to him. How could that be? Why take those two people, God? Why? Maybe they are in heaven—no—they *are* in heaven. But I'm here. I'm left here. I'm alone. There is no reason for that. I'm sad and miserable most of the time and alone. There is no part of this that would fit into God's master plan. It does not make sense. Don't say it!

". . . you know that little things happen, like not going one Sunday, and then it happens again, and pretty soon, you don't go at all and it's for no real reason."

Beth smiled as if she had dodged a plummeting chandelier. Or an angry bullet. I think she knew.

"It's not that. Well, maybe it is, a little."

I decided to let her off the hook. She meant well.

I speared the last of my tilapia. It was covered in a lemon *beurre blanc* sauce with a light, flavorful cream, probably made with really good wine, for sure, and some topping made with something crunchy and nutty and extremely delicious. I missed having good fish and refused to smell up my kitchen for days as I overcooked some nearly fresh halibut filet from the grocery store. This tasted much, much better.

"Beth, I know you're concerned. And I appreciate that. I do. You have no idea. I'll tell you what: this Sunday, I'll go to church with you. We'll sit together. Like old times."

Except one of us—two of us—won't be there like old times.

"Well, then," she said brightly, "that's the old Mary I know. Call me on Saturday then. We'll figure out where to sit."

"That's a promise," I said, smiling a bit too broadly, happily knowing that I had three full days to come up with an excuse for why I could not be there.

Three days is a long time.

I once wrote half a novel in three days.

Not my best work, but—surprise, surprise—it was one of my best-selling efforts.

Go figure.

Yes, I'm an editor. And a writer. I know you're thinking, *Well, you certainly couldn't prove it with this book. It goes on and on . . . and those ellipses and em dashes. What's up with that? You think there is any other sort of punctuation you could employ?* But it is true—I am an editor. With a master's degree in English and no marketable skills, it is the career that pulled me into the whirlpool of misplaced commas and horrible, gut-wrenching shifts in narrative voice. I started out as a proofreader, which is the publishing industry's fancy word for underpaid editor. I told friends that I enjoyed it, but not really.

I proofread, correcting spelling and punctuation, and gritted my teeth over horridly florid descriptions of women's clothing and their dramatic, breathy sighs over Bradford, a lost love, who miraculously turns up in Chapter 18 with amnesia, a scar, or rich. For three years I worked at a publishing house whose management team specialized in collecting tales of how they almost signed the next Stephen King or Tom Clancy. I heard the same tales over and over of how they missed signing the latest writer du jour because they offered a measly $100,000 advance, or because our acquisitions editor laughed like a hyena. But the team managed to get a few base hits, and they kept the doors open and the proofreaders paid.

At the end of my first three years as a glorified proofreader (and this years before I met Jacob), I received an offer from another publishing house. They were located in the Loop in Chicago, which meant a longish train ride or a nightmarish car ride or a move, relocating to somewhere closer to downtown. The money was better, but with the added costs, I probably would break even.

I suspected, after the interview, that I would have to start over with my wardrobe. While none of the women at the downtown publishing firm wore expensive couture designer garb, really, they all seemed to specialize in Bohemian Expensive— odd, off-kilter apparel that must have been purchased at eclectic, off-kilter boutiques in Lincoln Park, where the sales personnel wore black lipstick, had multiple piercings, and wore berets indoors without the slightest hint of pretension.

I might have mentioned before that I am semi-unstylish.

I made the mistake (which proved to be a wonderful serendipity) of mentioning the new job offer to my closest work friend—two cubicles down, single, master's degree in English from DePaul, aspiring author of children's books—and she related it to the proofreading supervisor, who quickly became apoplectic. It seems that our corporate culture frowned on losing staff to competition.

The supervisor hurried into my office . . . cubicle . . . sat down, breathless, I guess, from the seven paces it took to get there from his office, and drew the uncomfortable guest chair close to my desk.

"I heard about . . . your situation, Mary."

He said it with such earnest compassion that I thought I might be pregnant or have cancer.

"We don't want to lose you. I like your work. You're really good."

This was all whispered, since, after all, we were in an open cubicle. I had to lean forward to even hope to hear correctly.

He might have been coming in to tell me that people were talking and saying we were having an affair—that's how close and whispery he was.

"I want you to stay. I'll promote you to associate editor. *A little better paid, and you could actually change a writer's horribly mangled syntax now and again.* With an office. And I am prepared to offer you a raise in this amount . . ."

He took a folded slip of paper from the breast pocket of his short-sleeved dress shirt, which he wore with a tie—a fashion abomination if there ever was one. He placed the slip of paper on my desk and slid it forward—all of three inches.

His eagerness and excitement plainly evident on his face, he watched me open it. I was surprised: four hundred dollars a year more than the downtown offer.

"If you need some time to think about it, that's fine," he whispered.

I am a terrible poker player. Or I would be a terrible poker player if I played poker.

"I'll take it. When do I start?"

He looked surprised. He would have stuttered had he started talking right away, which he didn't.

"Next week. Please, let's keep this confidential until HR signs off on who has to move. Or who doesn't get to move."

There was an empty office, smaller than my cubicle actually, but it had a door. The previous editor had a baby and told everyone she would be coming back and then we never saw her again. All the single women in the editorial group wondered if they would do the same. A number of proofreaders were silently vying for the coveted room with a door and a window, jockeying for the most favorable position. I figured that I had no chance, so I had not participated in the maneuvering.

That's how I became an associate editor. A year and two pregnancies later—not mine, of course, but those of other newly married staff—and I became a full-blown editor.

━━━━━∞∞∞━━━━━

I realize that this seems off target based on the title of this book. But I need to tell you a little of how I became a writer and now manage to stay home and do my work in my pajamas.

I never do that—work in pajamas, that is. I hate the feeling of it being 10:00 a.m. and I am still pajama-clad. I can't do it now that I have to take Rufus out for a morning walk, anyway. It's up and change clothes and go out into whatever the weather is. Rain, cold, snow—the dog needs to go outside, and that means I need to go with him. Yes, I could boot Rufus out the back door and let him handle things on his own. But if I did that, when would I get any exercise? So, unless there is lightning in the sky, Rufus and I head outdoors. My neighbors marvel at our consistency.

The neighbor to my right uses a service that cleans up their yard after their dog, so it may be faint praise. A truck comes once a week and the poor serviceman walks back and forth over their lawn, looking for the leftovers from a dog. How I pity that poor man. I know he gets paid fairly well to do what normal people would consider a really, really unpleasant occupational choice. Not much in job prestige, either. "I pick up dog poop for really lazy people and get paid for it," would not be the most effective pick-up line in a trendy singles bar.

So, there I am, an editor. And that role, I must admit, I am born to do. I can see the weeds and chaff in a writer's work, and usually have the kindness and tact to get writers to allow me to prune their work. Or more truthfully, they encourage me to do the pruning.

After editing and helping rework a few novels that actually sold pretty well, several of those authors began to ask for me by name. Our publishing company is all too happy to oblige them. Anything we can do to edge the competition is smiled upon by management—most of whom don't really understand what it means to edit a book. So I get a lot of smiles. I suspect that I should have parleyed those smiles into a better salary—but that sort of savvy horse-trading is not part of my nature.

And you know what was strange in all this? After a few of our authors hit it large—not big, but large—the company's editorial team seemed to take great relish in disliking them and their work. Familiarity breeds contempt, I guess, and a large number of our best-selling writers were not corporately beloved best-selling writers—at least among our editorial cubicles and tiny offices packed to the gills with free books.

We seemed to like them a lot for their first and maybe second books, then they all morphed into being pains in our collective necks. Not so much me, since I have a pretty high level of tolerance for unknowingly sadistic, insecure, and inept writers. And who could blame authors for being needy and requiring constant attention? You slave and write and rewrite and worry and agonize over a book for six months or a year or all your life up to that point, and then you hand it over to a nameless, faceless editor who doesn't tell you a thing until that person sends the manuscript back to you, filled with so many red slashes and cuts and suggestions and deletions and addendums and slings and arrows of outrageous fortune. And then she asks—urgently—for you to make your changes and get it back to her in three days because she has a printing deadline to meet.

The horror, I know.

So, there I am, in my mid-twenties. Well, late twenties, but no single woman ever says she is in her late-anythings. I have many friends at work, some closer than others. There is a group of us single women who do things socially—dinners, movies, even host a party now and again. Some of us attended a large, almost mega-church, whose singles group is large and notorious for being a Christian singles meat market. As much as I pooh-poohed the image before I attended, I discovered that it was exactly that—attractive, stylish single men eyeing the new women with a critical tilt of their heads, and you could see them dismissing the ones, out of hand, who did not meet their criteria. A small contingent of less-attractive men—with less attractive haircuts and who shopped at Target and did so badly, who had a lower standard—looked for women who were at least breathing and if they were lucky, semi-sentient.

And occasionally a woman from work—one of the single ones—would meet a man, start to date, then get married. Go figure. It did not happen for me, and while I was not nervous about it, I did think about such things. I heard the echo of my mother, when not as close to dementia as she is now, telling me not to be so picky. I would have argued with her; I'm not picky at all. There just weren't that many men who orbited about me to be picky over.

That was until Jacob Fassler joined the company. He worked in marketing—smooth-talking, glib, always with a ready smile. You know, one of those marketing types. And he was handsome, in a Bohemian sort of way. He stood a few inches taller than me—and in flats, I was an even five feet, five inches tall. He had an almost dark look about him, dark hair with waves that he sort of pushed back from his forehead with a calculated insouciance that made it look as though he had just stepped away from the beach. I would have wagered that he smelled of salt water. He had dark eyes—deep, expressive, more brown than any other color—in contrast with my Nordic-looking blue eyes, my blond hair in a limp bob. He had a dangerous look to himself, opposite from me and my gingham-and-lace-apron aura. I could wear a leather jacket with leather chaps and studs in my nose and ears, and someone would ask me where the Sunday school social is being held. I have that sort of nice, nearly angelic face. I'm not that way, really. I can be bad. Seriously. I have done bad things.

Sort of.

Well . . . not really bad. Maybe *naughty* is a better word. *Mischievous* perhaps.

So Jacob joined the company, and he became the talk among the single ladies—or shall I say, single girls, or single women—in the company for weeks. He was a safe subject because none of us women had actually talked to him. And I am pretty sure that, in the deepest, darkest, remotest part of our hearts, we all figured that we had no shot at him.

He was that handsome.

Most of us in editorial did not lack intelligence, but we did lack self-confidence.

I would have considered my situation, my chance with Mr. Jacob Fassler, as long of a shot as shots could go—until that one fateful Saturday.

I tend to do my editorial work quickly and usually left work at the official quitting time. There were other editors who always worked late, and my opinion is that they simply worked slower. To me, desk time had always been less important than a job well done.

But, owing to the neurotic behavior of our latest good-but-not-great-selling author, his deadline had been shredded. He had held on to his manuscript six weeks longer than scheduled, the edits were more extensive than usual, he became more anxiety-ridden as he worked through the suggestions, and now it fell to me to get the final manuscript ready for typesetting by the end of the following week.

That's why I worked in my tiny office on Saturday. I was there because I knew I could work faster there than at home, where I would be distracted by my roommates and the availability of cable television and mah-jongg on the computer.

Midway through a particularly confusing shift in voice and tense in the manuscript before me, I heard a voice from the end of the hall.

"Anyone here? Anyone know how to fix this machine?"

There was a copy room at the end of the hall. It used to hold the fax machines as well—and most of those have long since disappeared.

I stood up and sidled around my desk. That's how you had to do it—sidle past it. I told you my office was small.

I stepped into the doorway of the copy room.

There stood Jacob Fassler in all his dangerous glory. He wearing a white T-shirt and worn jeans—actually worn, and not just purchased new and worn. He had on sneakers—white Converse high-tops. I had, up to that moment, considered high tops to be an affectation on anyone but actual basketball players. But on Jacob, they looked good.

His hair was slicked back more than usual; it appeared as if he had just come in from working out.

"How do I fix this thing?" he asked, holding a sheet of paper in his hand. "Is it turned on?"

I nodded. "It is. But it's temperamental."

"Do you know how to fix it?" he asked.

"I don't," I said. "Usually when it stops working, I sneak out of the room and go to another floor, looking for a copier that works. Eventually someone shows up who knows what to do—or they call the service guy."

Jacob smiled at me, a knowing secret smile.

"That's what I'm doing. The copier in the marketing area went down, and I'm wandering about the building looking for another that works."

I liked it that he smiled at me.

"I don't think anyone else is in the office today," I said. "The finance person—Rita, the lady who pays the bills—she came in here earlier. But I don't think she turned on the copier in her area."

"Rats," said Jacob.

"Is it important?"

He offered a half smile, half grimace.

"No. It's just a . . . a recipe that I promised I would get for my landlady. I can do it Monday, but I happened to be in the area."

He cooks. And I don't think he's married. No ring. And married people don't usually talk about landladies. And the temp in HR said he wrote "single" on his employee file—but no one can trust a temp.

"Hi, I'm Jacob Fassler. Marketing."

He extended his hand and I took it. It felt warm and firm, but not painfully firm like some men I have met who make it their mission to cripple others with their Gigantor Death Grip.

"I'm Mary Knopf. Editorial."

"Like the publisher?" he asked.

"I wish. Well, yes, like the publisher, but no relation. At least not that I've been able to ferret out so far. If I turn out to be a long-lost cousin or daughter of Alfred Knopf . . . well, you won't see me again. I'll move to New York and edit books while looking out over Central Park."

Jacob laughed, his laugh melodic and not monkeylike, as in some men I have met.

And from there, I am not sure where the conversation went. *Dreamy* would be a word I would use if I ever used the word *dreamy*—which I don't. All I know is that twenty-five minutes later, we were in the Starbucks down the street, both with small lattes—"I hate ordering a small coffee as a tall"—and sat there and talked for another two hours.

That's when he asked me out to dinner and that's when I accepted.

And that's the night I fell in love with Jacob Fassler.

3

I'm a novelist because of that same Jacob Fassler.

I have always been a writer, I suppose. Back in fourth grade, I wrote an essay about what I did over the summer vacation that so impressed my teacher that she had me read it aloud in the fourth grade class—and after I finished, they all applauded. Of course, that has never happened before or since then—the applause thing, I mean—but that started my writing career. I wrote for school newspapers and the school's overly dramatic "literary" magazines. I, of course, was just as guilty of emotionally overreaching back then as any other pubescent writer. I believe I have matured some since then.

An avid reader, I often blustered at bad novelists, sputtering to anyone in the vicinity that I could do better than what I'd just read.

I blustered that way to Jacob one day, in a Starbucks, my ire fueled by a second small latte.

"Then write something better," he said. "I mean—you do work for a publishing company, you know. If anyone has an inside edge to finding a receptive editor, it would be you."

He was charming when he said that, and I should have reacted differently, but I recall scowling at him. We were at that point in our relationship where one or the other could offer a pretty-much-fake scowl in response to being called on something.

"Well, maybe I will then."

A few sips passed. Silence.

"What do you think I should write about?" I asked.

Jacob shrugged. He was reading the fifth article on the most recent Chicago Bears' loss. Why anyone would need to go into such great depth over a stupid game—a game that they lost by multiple points—was beyond me. You would think that losing would be suffering enough. No, they had to revel in the gory, painful details of just how they lost and who they could hold responsible for the latest loss.

I am not a sports fan. Obviously.

Jacob looked up from his coffee.

"I dunno. Something about somebody who's Amish? Or doesn't want to be Amish anymore? Maybe somebody who wants to become Amish again? Amish seems to be a hot genre."

He resettled into the sports pages, his glum eyes fixed on the grading system for a bad team in a death spiral, I guess.

"Amish?" I replied.

I sat there, mulling over his words, and the story came to me, just like that: a beautiful woman who grew up in a traditional Amish farm family has to leave the faith—or better yet, abandon her culture—to go to New York to be a model because she's so beautiful and models spectacularly well. She makes a lot of money, gets famous and into *People* magazine, finds the modeling/famous people world horribly shallow and degrading, seeks to return to her roots and find a husband, and live a quiet life, but she meets great resistance from everyone

45

on both sides until she discovers the kindness of Kurt Franz, a bachelor Amish who's semi-outcast because he's sort of a rebel. They find love and eventually are reaccepted by their Amish community and everyone lives happily ever after.

Really. That's the story. It came out of my head, that well formed, in as much time as it took to type the paragraph. Her name . . . was Gretchen—uh—Gretchen Stolz. That sounds Germanish.

By the end of the next day, I had written twenty-three pages of the novel, done a two-page synopsis, and the company agreed, by the end of the week, to take a chance and publish it.

Go figure.

It did not sell huge numbers out of the gate, but it got reprinted six times.

And with that, I became an editor *and* a novelist.

Being a mid-level novelist (and I'm being generous with the grading system here) pays about the same as you would get if you worked the same hours at the local 7-Eleven, except at the 7-Eleven, the hours would be better and you probably get benefits with it. And all the Slurpees you care to consume. The company graciously signed me to a three-book contract after the first one came out. I became their go-to Amish writer.

And the truth is, I didn't know all that much about the Amish. I was born in western Pennsylvania and our family visited the Pennsylvania Dutch country several times—before it morphed into a family-friendly tourist attraction. And I saw some old movie on TV with Tony Perkins playing a Quaker a few years ago. And I read a lot. My research may not be encyclopedic, but it has been said that my dialogue was "very believable" and that my characters "face true-to-life problems" and that my plots "keep you guessing to the end." The last praise is both wonderful and quite flawed, because in gentle Amish fiction, one seldom has the hero or heroine dying before they communicate their love for each other. Endings are usually pretty happy affairs for all concerned.

I don't mind writing those sorts of books. I guess I never considered myself a serious novelist. A serious modern novelist is one whose books leave you really depressed at the end. A truly great, modern novelist is one who leaves you wanting to kill yourself at the end of the book. I am a popular modern novelist. People who read my books know pretty much what they are getting, and I deliver a finely crafted, and mostly intelligent, novel. I write believable stuff—the truth, I call it.

Jacob said he loved the cover of my first book. He took me out to a very expensive restaurant to celebrate the publication.

"Did you like the book?" I asked him, just before the crème brûlée arrived.

Jacob seldom looked to be at a loss for words. But at this moment, his tongue appeared to be tied.

"You did read it, didn't you?"

He looked away.

"I will," he said in a very small voice. "I planned on it. I just got busy." We both knew that he was a terrible liar. "I'm not much of a reader."

"But you work at a publishing company," I countered.

"I work in marketing," he replied. "We don't have to read books to sell them."

I narrowed my eyes and said as drily as I could. "Really?"

He squirmed. "Some of us do, I think, read them. Or some of them, I guess. But reading takes a lot of time. We sell a lot of books. Other people said your book was really, really good. Much better than any other Amish stuff on the market. I trust them. I bet it's great. And I really liked the cover. That woman is hot—even in the goofy bonnet and all that."

And that's when I knew I would marry Jacob Fassler. He told the truth when a lie would have been so much easier—and more productive, if you know what I mean.

I knew Jacob would marry me after one particular moment during our first spring together. That's when I knew he loved me. He really, really loved me. I had come down with a cold, or the flu, or dengue fever. My eyes puffed, my nose turned red, I went through an entire box of tissues in one evening. My hair ratted into a Medusa-like do. I felt wretched and looked every bit a wreck.

I awoke, just after 5:00 p.m., to hear my front door squeak open. Jacob called out to tell me it was him. He had an "emergency" key—just for situations like this. He called up and said he would be upstairs in a few minutes. I heard rattling and clanging from the kitchen, but could not rise out of bed under my own power.

The noise stopped. And in my doorway, Jacob appeared, carrying a tray. He closed his eyes.

"Are you decent?" he asked softly.

"No, but I am clothed," I responded with a sneeze.

He carried in a tray with a glass of orange juice. (He must have brought it with him, because I never bought the stuff.) On a plate was a grilled cheese sandwich. And a pot of hot tea, with a freshly sliced lemon.

Jacob had a red beach towel wrapped around his waist. He saw me staring at it.

"These are good pants," he explained. Then added by way of further explanation, "Your stove spatters."

I had to smile, weakly and sickly.

He placed the tray on the bed, helped prop me up, helped feed me the grilled cheese sandwich—overdone on one side (the side he placed face down on the plate) and a bit light on the other side.

"You don't have Velveeta. How can you make a grilled cheese without Velveeta? It's un-American, I think."

He helped me drink the tea, now strong and hearty, sweetened with honey.

He sat beside me on the bed as I nibbled. He scooped the tray away when I finished, came back up—without the towel this time—and sat with me, holding my hand, until I managed to fall asleep.

I staggered out to the kitchen the next morning and found him asleep on my couch.

"I didn't want to leave you alone," he said, wrinkled and groggy.

How could I not marry him after that?

———— ✺ ————

Jacob and I were married by the Fox River, west of Chicago. Neither of us had any strong ties to the river, except that autumn had come and the foliage along the river would provide a good backdrop to our wedding pictures.

The day before the wedding, a storm passed through, with high winds and thundering rain, and when the sun peeked through the following morning, virtually every tree along the river had been denuded of all its colorful leaves. We could have just as easily gotten married in somebody's backyard for all the scenic beauty the river provided.

Despite that, the wedding and reception were lovely— another word I do not use often. Here I was, a plain, semi-attractive woman, edging toward the end of my prime, almost mousy, snagging the best, most attractive man our company had seen in years.

You might be wondering how I managed to do that.

I asked myself the same question. And often.

I didn't do it with a "come-hither" look, nor smoldering sex appeal or sexual antics, I can assure you of that. I mean, I was super attracted to Jacob, in every way, and I mean that both literally and figuratively. But we were both brought up by very strict parents with horribly strict interpretations of the moral depravity that marked premarital relations—thus, we maintained a fairly pure dating relationship.

There were moments, however, when the spirit and the flesh were very weak. Or would that be willing?

But as we edged toward whatever abyss we were edging toward, one of us, or the other, would draw back, take a deep breath, push away, and say something inane, like, "We need to slow down."

And we did.

The waiting and self-denial did make for a wild honeymoon, however. And incredibly satisfying.

<hr />

The wedding was wonderful, but coming back to work, quite problematic. The company had no rule about two married people working at the company, but there were those sidelong glances that followed us—as if what I did could help Jacob's career or vice versa.

I suppose that Jacob could steer more advertising dollars toward my books, but he did not set budgets.

I submitted my resignation a few months after the wedding.

And no, I had not become "with child"—although that would have been more easily accepted and understood as a reason for my departure.

As I think about how we fell in love, which warmed my heart, I also considered the question of why we fell in love.

People have asked that of me on occasion, and I do not think I provided a good answer.

But here's an attempt at the truth of why it all happened.

I have no idea—save for a best guess. I could make him laugh, and vice versa. He's always funny . . . *was* always funny and always game for any adventure. I thought things out more, and acted a bit more analytical, so I guess we balanced out. He said I was pretty. He never said beautiful—except on our wedding day—and other than that day, I wouldn't have believed him if he had said "beautiful." He always said "pretty." And he said it in a wistful, yearning manner, as if he really and truly meant it. He said that he had dated a lot of women, but there was something lacking at their core—the beautiful ones he'd dated, that is. He once said that some really attractive women know, deep down where they hide their own painful truths, that their beauty is always in the process of fading. Of course, beautiful young women sometimes turn into beautiful old women—but for someone who has savored the wine at the acme of its taste, any reduction in clarity and power will be viewed as a slippage, a step into the abyss of looking merely nice, or sort of attractive. It was a slide that some of them did not want to endure; their fight against it made them brittle and hard at the same time.

Me, on the other hand—well, I was a ray of warm sunshine by comparison. I knew that I had not started at the mountaintop, so my personal slide into being a little less pretty was far less steep and nowhere near as frightening.

He didn't phrase it so crassly or harshly, but that is what he meant.

And that was enough.

We did make each other laugh.

And we both believed in God.

He did up to the end.

Me? Now I am not so sure.

---æœ---

This is where the good dog Rufus makes his entrance onto the main stage of my life—the play in motion was the tragedy of my most recent years. I get maudlin at times, and wallowing in self-pity seems to be my second-favorite form of exercise.

Rufus, now in his second year, is full grown, and as large as he will ever get, plus or minus a pound or two and an inch or two.

Even though the breeder said that as an adult, he would be smallish, she had been mistaken. The runt grew up to be a big dog, by miniature standards. We run into another schnauzer during our evening walks—a distant cousin of Rufus, actually, due to the fact that they came from the same breeder. I haven't looked at his papers to see if they actually are related, but they do look alike. Go figure—they are both schnauzers. The other dog is exactly the same as Rufus except for Rufus's size. He is a big miniature schnauzer. Taller than his cousin by several inches and a good half-dozen pounds heavier. I don't mind at all; it simply means that he will never be a show dog. And he couldn't be, actually, since he was "fixed" a few weeks after I got him, and such dogs aren't allowed to participate in dog shows.

I don't know why.

Well, actually I do know why, now that I've looked it up, but it still doesn't make sense to me.

4

I snapped on the leash to Rufus's collar and we headed out-side. The air had grown cutting and brittle, a hint of winter to come, and any wind, at night, found its way through the weak defenses of my coat and hat and scarf and gloves. The complaint from the dog during winter months came from walking in newly fallen snow, the wet kind of thick snow, like chilled oatmeal. It would ball up between his toes. The snow balled up and he would stop every so often to try and chew it out. Or look at me with a supplicant's face and silently request my help. He was small last winter, and we only caught the tail end of winter, and we did not travel as far during our walks. Winter had never been my favorite season. It was to be Rufus's second.

The moon slipped up over the horizon, and the winter moon seemed whiter, more ashen, than normal, the pale light at the bare tree limbs, spiking shadows along our path.

Rufus stopped to investigate a particularly interesting bush. Sometimes, I let him have free rein on the time we're out; other walks, when I am either cold or impatient, I will snick at the leash to get the small beast moving again.

This night I waited.

I pulled a dog snack out of my coat's breast pocket. I buy them in bulk at the local pet store. They look like Styrofoam, in yellow and brown and tan, supposedly representing the flavors of chicken, beef, and peanut butter. Rufus loves them. He considers them almost as desirable as table scraps.

Almost.

I took one and broke it in half, the snap of the snack crackling loud in the cold air.

Our vet said he might be a pound or two heavy for his size, "but nothing to worry about. He's in good health."

I slipped the half-snack back into my pocket and bent down and gave Rufus the other half. He accepted it with gratitude and chewed as noisily as he could.

We both began to walk again. A dozen paces later, Rufus stopped. He did not look at me directly, nor did I look at him. He stops all the time during our walks.

"Why do you break my crunchy in half?"

I heard the voice, his voice, Rufus's voice, as clearly as I have heard anything in my life—maybe clearer than most.

Have you ever seen any of the Walt Disney animated Winnie the Pooh cartoons? Do you remember Eeyore, the sad-faced donkey with a tacked-on tail? Do you remember his voice? A very slow, deliberate, bass voice—not stupid by any means—but as if his words were being very carefully chosen and formed in his mouth, like chewing a large amount of gummy food. The voice, not stupid, just slow, as if each word had to be slowly measured out and scrupulously selected to be the most correct.

That's what Rufus sounded like.

Wait.

That's Rufus I am talking about.

And Rufus is a dog.

Bewildered isn't the right word for how I felt. *Frightened* isn't the right word, either. *Nonplussed*, maybe. I don't know. I never trust anyone who claims that they don't have the right words to describe something. We think in words—right? Use them. But tonight . . . tonight, I really did not have any words to use, no words that could properly describe what I was thinking.

The conversation, such as it was, simply felt . . . normal. Just everyday normal. Sorry, but I did not have a thesaurus handy.

So normal that I remained standing—rational and standing—and slowly formed a reply.

"I . . . I don't want you to get fat," I said, as I would to a friend whom I tried to convince from taking a third piece of pie at an all-you-can-eat buffet after breaking up with her cad of a boyfriend.

At that specific moment, his question and my answer seemed altogether, totally normal. I think I already said that . . . but it all felt . . . normal.

Rufus sort of nodded, as if digesting the information, and began to walk again, only to stop a few paces later. He turned his head ever so slightly toward me like he might be dreading the next question.

"Am I fat?"

What do you do when your dog asks you a perfectly linear, logical question?

In the cold dark of a winter night.

You answer him.

"No. You're not fat. Dr. Barbara, you know, your vet . . ."

Rufus nodded.

"She said that you could lose a pound or two. No big deal, she said. So . . . I thought I would cut back on these treats. Just a little."

Rufus waited a heartbeat or two and then continued on our walk.

"Okay," he said as we turned the corner on Glencoe and headed for home.

———⁓———

Several hours later, in bed, well after midnight, I sat bolt upright, wide awake.

It was 2:15 a.m.—exactly the time I received that phone call three years earlier. The phone call that shattered everything.

Sometimes the night terrors would overcome me.

But this was no night terror.

I had awoken from a hallucinogenic dream—where up was down and light was dark and dogs could talk.

Rufus lay at the corner of the bed. He slept there, not always, but when he did, he positioned himself at the corner, on a diagonal, so he could see the window and the bedroom door at the same time. His guarding instincts were deep in his being.

He must have heard me sit upright, or felt the movement. I snapped on my light.

He blinked, his eyes trying to adjust to the brightness.

"Did you really talk to me, Rufus? Or am I just widow-lady-crazy, with a horribly overwrought imagination?"

He did not speak, but I saw his eyes. The dark color seemed to deepen in understanding. He lowered his head, then looked back up, as if sheepish about not responding.

He nodded. At least I am pretty sure that he nodded.

Then he lay his head back down on the comforter and closed his eyes.

I took a series of deep, cleansing breaths, learned from the three yoga lessons I took at the YMCA until I dropped out because I couldn't stand the soft-talking instructor.

My dog talks to me.
Is that my life now?
It is and was.
Go figure.

The moment Ava touched my doorbell, Rufus both fell and jumped off the sofa in the sunroom, his claws scrabbling for purchase on the polished hardwood floors, his back legs looking like a cartoon, where the animated animal in question spins its legs in a furious circle for a moment until it finds traction. Rufus was like that, at least on the hardwood. On rugs, he took off like a shot, right away.

And the doorbell was the only device I had found that drove him completely insane. I suspect the guarding instincts, buried under hundreds of generations of domesticity and civility, were not so buried after all. Rufus slid through the kitchen, like a stock car on a clay track, his rear legs pumping furiously, barking with every step, barking louder and more frantically as he drew near to the front door, the pitch of his barking escalating with each step, until it sounded like he was nearing an explosion from a paroxysm of the squealy-bark-squealies.

But as soon as I opened the door and deemed the visitor welcome, Rufus would revert, like an iconic Jekyll and Hyde, into a tail and hindquarters wagging machine, with yips of joy and lots of happy whimpers and squirms, reveling in welcoming whoever had come calling. So far, we had never encountered a person I did not want to be there. Some people, Rufus liked more than others. But with Ava—well—he really liked Ava. As soon as she took a chair in the kitchen, Rufus attempted to climb onto her lap. He almost made it, and she grabbed at him to pull him up, only to have him yelp like he was in excruciating pain. A small spot at the end of his rib cage elicited this sort of response.

The vet—our vet, I suppose—Dr. Barb, had found nothing amiss when I told her about it. She had poked and prodded a bit.

"My best guess is that he just doesn't like being touched there," she had said. Now, when I pick him up, I try to avoid the area.

Ava recoiled as if she had caused permanent damage, and nearly dropped Rufus to the floor. But he clawed his way back onto her lap and, with a raised paw, demanded that she pet him.

She obliged, of course, and scratched and petted him for the better part of twenty minutes, until I made coffee and brought out cookies. Rufus could not beg from her lap, so he took his standard position at the foot of the chair, staring at me, then Ava, wondering who would first give in to his plaintive staring.

I usually was the one to weaken, but today, Ava snapped off a corner of a tea cookie and slipped it to a grateful Rufus, who did not chew, but swallowed it relatively whole.

"So, life has been good?" Ava asked.

Ava has been a long-time friend, a friend before Jacob came along. She worked with me, at the same company, for a year. She left to return to teaching and got married—and divorced— all before the accident. Her life was neither simple nor turmoil-free. Now we were both single again. Commiserating with her felt good, sort of therapeutic. We both lived at the same level. Lonely. Addicted to sympathy.

"It's been okay," I replied.

Ava popped most of a tea cookie into her mouth. "You're a bad liar."

She could get away with saying things like that because . . . well . . . she sort of always told the truth. She pushed an errant wisp of brown hair from her face. She had added red highlights to her hair a few weeks earlier, but they came out more purple than red.

"Just like when you lied about my hair. You said it looked 'striking,'" she said, mocking my tone, her self-amusement lighting up her face. She was a pretty woman when she smiled—wide mouth, full lips, with cheekbones that made makeup almost unnecessary.

"It is striking."

"It's hideous. Like it had been attacked by a wine-soaked stylist-in-training, after a particularly trying day. Without her glasses. Or a mirror. Or directions. While I lay deep in a coma."

I laughed, almost spitting out a mouthful of coffee. I didn't because I would have spilled it over the upholstery that I tell other people to be careful of. She was right. As hair goes, it indeed could be classified as hideous, but in an avant-garde sort of way. I don't think Ava considered herself avant-garde.

"Well," I said after composing myself, "the color will fade soon enough."

I really liked Ava. She made me laugh. We made each other laugh—though I know her job of amusing me was much more difficult than mine.

"I do get second looks from the young hoodlums at the car wash and the 7-Eleven on Main Street."

"Ava," I said in my best schoolmarm scolding voice. "You are terrible."

"No. I mean it. They think I'm an older degenerate—just like they want to be in twenty years. Like flies and honey. I could have been asked to the fall dance at the high school a hundred times, if I had wanted to. Just have to pretend to be more accessible, if you know what I mean. Dress the part more. A little more cleavage."

Ava acted as a tonic for me. She lived so far from the traditional suburban woman—if there is really such a person. Her almost abrasive, semi-caustic sort of personality could shock people. I guess I liked that quality in her.

"So how are you and Dr. Tom getting along?" I asked. She was three months into a relationship with Dr. Tom Wakley, a twice-divorced podiatrist with a large practice the next town over. He was fit, bald, and drove a Lincoln.

"He's not a doctor. He's a podiatrist," she answered.

"They go to medical school. That makes them doctors."

She shrugged. "When is the last time you heard of someone dying from toenail fungus?"

I stifled a laugh again, gulping down the last half swallow of coffee.

"I'll call him a real doctor when my TV has a doctor's show featuring a staff of podiatrists," she smirked. "Like that will ever happen."

Rufus trotted off once our cookies were consumed.

"Me and the podiatrist . . . well, we're doing okay." She toyed with her empty cup, tilting it back and forth. "I guess. He's a nice enough guy. A bit of an ego problem. Not a deal-breaker. Not the best sense of humor, but he can be funny on occasion. You know . . . it's okay, most of the time. It is nice to have someone to hold hands with . . . if you know what I mean." She arched her eyebrows, as if unwilling to say out loud what "holding hands" meant. Maybe she didn't want to shock Rufus.

I did know what she meant, which marked a huge difference between myself and Ava. Some things she did, I could never do. At least, I think I could never do.

She poured herself another cup of coffee.

"I would be having a better time if this were wine."

"Ava—it's three in the afternoon."

"So? Wine is illegal in the afternoon? Not like I'm operating on a bunion later today."

I walked to the refrigerator and took out the half-and-half. In all honesty, I had always been relatively addicted to coffee, so multiple cups in the afternoon were pretty much standard operating procedure.

"And how goes it with you, Mary? You're always asking the questions—and never answering any."

"I'm a writer. I observe."

Ava offered a twisted smile.

"You steal truths from other people's lives, that's what you do."

"Do not."

"Do too," she countered. "Remember that character in that book of yours—the rebellious Amish farmer who wanted to move to . . . where . . . Montana or someplace?"

"He wanted to learn to ski."

"Yeah, that's the one. He was the spitting image—a duplicate—of Ronald Weerset. Remember him?"

We both knew Ron Weerset as a single man from our shared work experience some ten years earlier. I will be kind and say that he could be classified as odd. A socks-with-sandals sort of guy, a gentle spirit I suppose, but given to long-winded explanations of just about everything, and hair that looked as if he cut it himself.

"He was not. Ron was not that handsome."

"But his characteristics. His mannerisms. They were like twins."

I hesitated in answering. She was right. I had copied that poor man's characteristics. And I didn't offer him a dime in royalties for the usage.

"Okay. I'll answer a question. Ask away."

Such an offer did not occur often with me. I seldom had ever volunteered to provide personal information—even to a friend.

I am pretty sure that having Rufus in my life had broken down some of my personal walls, my protective shell, just a little. I was getting used to talking to him during the day. After three years, almost, of silence during the day, for the most part, I now yakked—a lot. Jabbered, actually. Rufus would fall asleep sometimes even in the middle of a particularly impassioned diatribe. However, he never talked back during the day—or had not so far. Instead, I would chatter on and on to him.

And I would never admit this to anyone, not even to Rufus, at least not now, but before Rufus came into my life, I would walk about the house, and talk to the various pictures of Jacob that I still had on display. Some of the pictures—pictures of me with my son—I removed, stored safely in a cardboard box, taped shut, securely taped, labeled IMPORTANT PICTURES.

There were still three pictures of my son on display: one in the sunroom, a small one, his face nearly hidden by the hood of his sweatshirt; one in the bedroom that used to be his, a group picture of his friends at a church day camp the summer before I lost him; and one in the formal living room, a horrid picture of the three of us, taken for the church's pictorial directory. Jacob in a tie and a jacket nearly luminescent in the harsh lighting and my hair looking more wispy and flyaway than usual, with John serene and happy between his mother and father.

Jacob was represented in a handful of pictures, spread out over the house.

Furtively, I would walk about, usually late at night, after dusk for sure, and talk to the pictures, asking my husband, my late husband, about things in my life and what I should do about the insurance for the house and if I needed to roll over his IRA into something else. I would ask him about what color I should paint the family room and if I should highlight my hair, and if the plumber who quoted replacing the leaky toilet in the guest bath could be considered honest or not.

I talked and talked and talked and tried not to be a crazy lady. I tried to avoid talking directly to the picture, you know, talking while staring at a dead man's face. I was shy, even circumspect about it. But I did it. A lot. And I waited to hear an answer.

Sometimes, I would get a very strong, nearly visceral feeling. Unmistakable.

Like the question about the plumber. I heard . . . felt . . . and came to the conclusion that the plumber I considered operated on the up and up. And he did the job quickly. There were no leaks. He cleaned up after himself. And he charged me less than he quoted. I think he realized I was a widow and took pity on me.

That's how Jacob talked to me. Not like Rufus. No . . . their communication styles were very much different. One . . . maybe one I made up. The other one was real.

One . . . I wanted. The other . . . came to me, came upon me, without my looking for it.

There is a difference. A big difference.

Since Rufus arrived in my life, I have talked less to the photos of Jacob, though I still do so, once in a while, in a quiet hiss of a whisper, in the fading light of day. I wait for the nudge from beyond.

Sometimes it happens . . .

Ava snapped her fingers.

"Mary? Are you listening? You said you would answer my question."

I blinked.

"What? What did you ask again? I guess I was thinking about . . . something else there for a minute. A book problem, I think."

Ava placed her hand on my forearm.

Funny how much communication is done without words through the simplest of gestures—like one person's hand placed on another person's arm. I have lived now for years with little human contact—skin to skin touching, that is.

Oh, there is the quick, shoulder-to-shoulder hug at church, or at the supermarket. There is the handshake from insurance salesmen and car dealers.

But there is little discretionary touching in my life.

That's why widows go to the beauty parlor every week. It is the human touch they crave, without knowing it. No one needs their hair cut and styled on a weekly basis. With the possible exception of the queen of England, perhaps.

Ava's hand on my arm got my attention. A connection—a physical connection—grabbed me. The intimacy—even that slight touch—got to me like no words could ever do.

"Are you ready to start dating?" she asked.

The words registered, but I think I must have looked shocked, or puzzled, or gobsmacked. (Don't the English have such great words?)

"Well? It's a legitimate question. I waited a year after my divorce. Healing time. And it has been lots longer for you, Mary. It's time, right?"

I struggled to find a word, or words, to answer her with.

(I have discovered recently that most grammarians, the modern ones anyhow, now say that it is okay to end a sentence with a preposition. I don't think I have ever been a stickler for not doing so, but now, when it happens, I no longer worry that an aggressively proper copy editor will flummox my sentence construction to prevent ending my words with a "with" or a "for.")

"No."

"No?"

"No."

"Why not?"

"Because."

"That's not an answer.

"It is too."

"It's time, Mary. You know it's time."

"It's not."

"You're young. Sort of, anyhow. And you—and I—neither of us are getting any younger. You need to. Date. Really."

"I don't. Really. It's too soon. Much too soon."

But I did crave that touch. Not sexual, I think, but just touch. Hand in hand. A hand on my forearm or bare shoulder. How wonderful it would be to be held by a man with strong arms . . . protecting me . . . enveloping me.

"It is not. You know it."

She glared at me for a moment, then tilted her head.

"You're thinking about it, aren't you?"

"I am not."

"Rufus," she said, trying to recruit my best friend to her side, "doesn't she need to go out? It's time, isn't it?"

Rufus sauntered over, looked at me, then put his paws on Ava's knees and looked back at me in a pretty snide dog manner.

They had ganged up on me.

"I'll . . . I'll think about it. That's all I can promise you."

And I was determined to get back at Rufus for siding with my other best friend.

Later that evening, after Ava had left, after she made me promise, again, to think about what she had said, twice, I gathered my coat and Rufus's leash. I was still smarting from his cozying up with Ava, as if he thought that chumminess wasn't obvious to me. He took her side on this dating thing.

I shivered when the word came into my mind.

Dating? Good grief.

Ava was right. It had been a long time. And there were those times when I nearly ached for the touch of a man. I did not admit that to anyone—not to friends, not to Rufus, and certainly not to the pictures of Jacob.

But dating? Another man? A stranger? Kissing some other man? Wouldn't that amount to cheating? Adultery, even?

Yes, there were a few earlier attempts to entrap me into dating—all of them at church. What is it about churchgoers who seem to think it is unnatural for a woman to be alone? I know, there are those verses that say something about "better to marry than to burn with lust."

I wasn't burning with lust, exactly, though I did miss all that went along with lust. In the good, married sense of the word. Please. But what I missed more than all that biology and anatomy was being held, being wrapped up in someone's arms. I missed being connected by touch.

Hugs are hard to do without.

Rufus bounced and wiggled as he always did, making it difficult to attach the leash to his collar.

"Rufus, stop wiggling," I barked at him, my voice not at all kind and gentle.

He stopped and looked back up at me, as if my harsher tone was unfamiliar and unsettling.

We stepped out into the cold. I could see my breath form in the shadowy light of the streetlight at the end of my driveway. Rufus sneezed once. He sneezed a lot. Dr. B. ruled out allergies. "He sneezes. It's what he does. No big deal. He's a snouty sort of dog."

We hurried to the corner, then turned south. We would take the route that included the sidewalk that ran alongside the small retention pond behind the big houses. The pond lay on private property, and one homeowner plastered her fence with stern NO TRESPASSING and PLEASE CLEAN UP AFTER YOUR PET signs. Not a welcoming attitude. The sidewalk was community right-of-way, but we always hurried past the pond. It was darker, not dangerously darker, but it was less traveled at night. Streetlights lit most of the rest of the way.

As we stepped into a pool of darkness, halfway between streetlights, I stopped.

"Why did you side with Ava?" I asked Rufus, and immediately realized how delusional I sounded—expecting a dog to answer me.

"I don't know. What's dating, anyhow?" he replied.

"Dating? Well, it's when two people go out together so they can get to know each other better. Dinner. Coffee. Movies. That sort of thing."

Rufus stared across the waters of the pond. During the summer, a large egret lived along the shore. It swooped over us once, taking off and spooking the bejeebers out of both of us. Now Rufus kept an eye out for it. He was not a dog that liked being spooked.

"Do dogs date?"

How do I answer that?

"No. They don't. But people do. They have to get to know each other before they . . . get married or move in together."

Rufus pulled gently at the leash, the cord ratcheting out, clicking loudly.

"That man in those pictures on the wall. The pictures you talk to."

He meant Jacob, of course.

"Yes?"

"Is he dead?"

My throat tightened.

"Yes. He and the little boy in those pictures died in a car crash several years ago. The man was my husband. We were married. The little boy was my son."

I felt the tears start to form, and I fought to hold them back. I did not want to wander through the dark, my eyes fractured like stained glass from salty tears.

"I thought so. You get sad when you look at them. But I wasn't sure. You never told me. I thought I should wait to ask you about them."

"I do get sad sometimes. I miss them very much."

We walked on a short distance, Rufus's nails clicking on the cement sidewalk. They would need to be clipped during his next visit with the groomer. He did not like the groomer. Too many dogs, a shampooing at the hands of a stranger, rattling hair clippers. It was an unnerving experience for him.

"I think you should date." Rufus had the speaking part of conversation down. His timing was not as solid. A kind and caring person would most likely have waited longer to give me that opinion—especially following on the heels of my unburdening about my husband's and son's deaths.

We turned the corner onto Western. It was uphill until Hawthorn. It wasn't steep, but I never liked this part of the evening route.

"Really? Why? Why do you think I should date?"

Rufus could not shrug, of course, but he nearly shrugged just by using his tone of voice.

"Aren't people supposed to be together? I see that on television all the time. People together. A man and a lady. People talk a lot about getting together."

"But I don't have to be with someone. I have you. I can talk to you."

"That is true. You do."

We walked in silence, the empty branches clacking together in the breeze, like mute, cold, wooden fingers drumming on a desk in another room.

"But I'm pretty sure you need to be with another person."

"Pretty sure?" I asked. I was debating with a dog.

Good grief.

"I think that's what is supposed to happen. Isn't that what he says it should be like?" Rufus asked.

Of course this conversation was already semi-crazy and totally delusional—talking to a dog, carrying on a normal face-to-face, or face-to-muzzle, conversation as it were, asking the dog his opinion on what I should do with my life.

Perfectly normal, right?

"Who? Who says?"

Did he have a secret life that I did not know about? Did he talk to the black lab next door—that stupid, pushy, knuckle-headed beast? What kind of advice could that animal provide?

Rufus stopped to sniff at a leaf that skittered in front of him. When his investigation stopped, he lifted his head and replied. "Why, God, of course."

5

Rufus clammed up for two days. He didn't say a word during our walks, even though I asked him repeatedly about his communication with God. I suspect he meant the God of all, and not some canine deity that I was unaware of. But I couldn't be sure. Could there be a dog god of sorts that all dogs knew about, and about whom humans were clueless?

I did not allow myself to become fixated on Rufus and his talking. I mean, what if his speech was really just my delusional thinking—a manifestation of my repressed desires and grief and doubts and whatever other mental hobgoblins lived in my gray matter? I felt certain it was not. I told myself that I was certain that I had actually heard what I heard, and that Rufus talks. . . . I guess most delusional people are sure that they are sane and rational. But I *was* sane and rational. Or rather, I *am* sane and rational. I have continued to write, and my prose is generally sane and logical. My plots have not begun to include little creatures from the planet Xerlon. I manage to feed myself and find appropriate, if not stylish, clothing. I pay the bills when they come due. I do not hoard aluminum foil or wrap it about my head to keep the federal government from scanning my brain during the day.

So Rufus didn't talk on command. I would wait. And if he never spoke again, I would simply keep his talk a secret and never tell anyone about these episodes. Ever.

Perhaps what complicated my thinking or my receptivity was my wrestling with Ava's question . . . or, rather, demand.

Dating.

I know. I had considered dating, a few times, and only to myself. In the aftermath of the accident, I was too grief-stricken, too paralyzed, too numb, too angry, too bitter, too anguished to even consider the option of trying it all again. Like a small child who takes his first ride on a two-wheeler only to have a terrible accident, ripping a knee apart in the process—well, that young child is not too keen on mounting a bicycle ever again. I was the same as that small, scarred, scared child.

As the months passed, the concept of another man remained horridly strange, but I guess I knew dating did not lie out of the range of distant possibilities—really distant possibilities.

And now, I have to face that fact. If I do not want to die alone, or at least die without human companionship, I have to consider that distant possibility.

Dating.

That night, a cold wind hastened in from the north. I usually pay little attention to the weather. It is what it is. My mother-in-law would watch The Weather Channel for hours on end, letting us know that rain would be coming in four days. The weather forecasters, always helpful, would warn her of impending doom at the hands of the weather. A stretch of below-zero weather? Stay home, make sure that the furnace operated properly, have firewood, stay in contact with family. A stretch of one hundred-plus degree days? Stay home, go to a cooling center if needed, drink lots of water, stay in contact with family.

Weather forecasters did not predict the weather. They wanted to scare people into staying at home, cowering in the basement, watching The Weather Channel all the while—or at least until the dangerous weather passed.

And you know what? The dangerous weather never passed. In Chicago, there are perhaps a couple dozen perfect days during the year. On those days you could safely venture out—but only if you had slathered on sufficient sunscreen to blot out the evil sun. And there is great consternation among the sun-fearers that no sunscreen in existence could prove effective at blunting the sun's evil rays. It was a terrifying, never-ending pattern of threatening weather, followed by terrible weather, followed by downright dangerous weather.

But I digress.

Tonight, well, the weather tonight grew cold enough that my mother-in-law would have stocked up on groceries and ammunition, if she had been in town. No snow yet, but biting wind. I slipped into my well-puffed down parka, tightened the hood around my face, grabbed my bright yellow gloves and Rufus and I headed out into the iced air.

I wear calf-high, superinsulated boots, no lacing required, and a thick, faux sheep-fleecy interior. In fact, I seldom wear socks with these boots, they are that warm and comfortable.

We both walk briskly, movement being the key to staying warm.

We turned a corner. Rufus stiffened and pulled at the leash. Another dog approached, being held on his leash by an older gentleman. Rufus and I pass a number of other dogs and owners during our walks. I know none of their humans' names. We humans know each other by our dogs' names. Gus is a fat yellow lab, who waddles rather than walks. Sometimes Rufus will bounce around the older, fatter dog, both of them offering fake barks of challenge. Sometimes just a sniff and a growl will do.

The other man greeted Rufus by name. I do the same to Gus. We act as our pets' spokespeople. We both comment on the sudden drop in temperature. The other man said it is time to move south.

"Eighteen months and I retire. I'll be out of here in eighteen months and a week."

"Where to?" I asked.

"My daughter lives in Orlando. That's where Gus and I are headed. It will do his old bones good to get out of the cold."

No mention of a wife. Divorced or widowed. I think divorced. There are subtle clues that only the single man or woman can interpret. Rings, of course, are the biggest hint. But it also has to do with how questions are answered. A single man talking to a single woman states things differently. Not suggestive, by any means, but differently. Why? Because he knows he has no one to correct or advise him otherwise. Making an appointment is another clue—married people will always hedge, saying he or she must check with his or her spouse to make sure the date is open. Single people or divorced people never do. And theirs is also an element of need—not pathetic neediness—but a single person often really wants to connect. So conversations are quickly deeper. Married people already have a connection, so dialogue with them often remains superficial.

Rufus and I bid our farewell and continue. The moon has been lost to us, behind a thickness of iced clouds. Despite the streetlights, the night seemed darker than usual, darker than most.

"Do you like Gus?" Rufus asked me, his breath coming in puffs with each word. Out of the blue, he spoke again. I wish it had been a more explanatory statement—preferably about his divine communication skills.

"I guess. He seems like a nice dog. He is very calm. But he is fat."

"That's fat? Really? Gus is fat?"

"He is, Rufus. Maybe twenty pounds more than he should be."

We trotted along. Our chatting felt so right, so calming, the cold disappeared.

"Where is Orlando? What is that?"

"It's a city, Rufus. We live in a small city. Wheaton. A city is a group of people living in the same place. Orlando is bigger than here. And it is a lot warmer. They don't really have winter there. It never gets really cold. Never gets this cold, that's for sure."

Though I could not see his face, I was sure Rufus tried to digest this information. We do watch television together. Maybe he gets some of what he knows from TV shows and news programs and The History Channel and whatever else it is that I watch when I zone out some evenings. It would be a sporadic source of information, for sure, and incomprehensible at times. I mean, how would a stranger, a dog, interpret *Days of Our Lives*—not that I've ever watched it . . . that often. Recently.

"Gus would like the warmth. He says his back legs hurt all the time."

I almost asked Rufus how he would know that. But like taking a watch apart to see how it works would surely render the watch useless, I simply took Rufus at his word, that Gus had arthritis in his legs or hips and yearned to be in a warmer climate. It made sense to me.

Instead of asking him how he and Gus communicate, I decided instead to confront Rufus on his apparent shift in allegiance the other afternoon.

"When I asked you if you thought I should start dating—you said I should . . . right away. Why?"

Rufus did not hesitate. "Because you are ready. To date. I think. If *date* means to be with a man. Then you are ready."

"And you know that how?"

"I can smell it. You are lonely. You need to be with someone. People should be in pairs—like swans. That is the way God has it planned, isn't it? I know it's different with animals, sometimes, but people, well—doesn't God want them to be in pairs?"

I tried to figure out how to respond when Rufus posed another question. "Swans . . . those are those big white things that float, right? The ones we saw at that big water? The ones that wanted to chase us, right?"

We had gone to Herrick Lake in the spring, a bigger lake, and had watched two swans, a husband and wife, I guess, swim closer and closer to us as we walked along the shore.

"They didn't chase us."

"I said 'wanted to.' I could hear them. Another step closer and they would have charged. They scare me. Like that big other bird on the smaller water."

The egret from last summer that had swooped by us, so close I could make out the colors of the underside of its wings.

"So God told you that?" I asked.

"Sort of. Not really. I mean . . . I sort of know what he has said. Instinct, I guess. And you know what he has written—that men marry women, right? Mostly. Not always. But it's better if they were. You are not a pair. And now that I know what dating is, you should try it. You would be a pair, then, right?"

"I guess so."

We walked in silence.

"So God wants me to date?" I asked.

"I guess. That's what's in the Bible. Isn't it? I can't read, but that feels true."

We turned onto our street. "How often do you talk with God?" I continued. For me, well—I prayed, sometimes. Less now. I used to pray a lot. I sort of . . . gave it up for all the good it did me and all the answers that never came. I wanted to know how this dog came to have a direct line to the Almighty.

"Once a week. Like all the animals."

"Only once a week?"

"It's enough for a dog."

Ava's insistence wore me down. I guess I had been ready to be worn down. Her doctor friend—"He's a podiatrist, not a doctor"—had a friend, a few years older than me, divorced, and ready to "get back on the market."

His words, according to Ava.

I was already wary. Like I'm some vegetable on display in the produce aisle? I am pretty sure Ava liked to torment me some, in a good way, in a way that would keep me a bit off balance and unable to retreat into my safe, Christian isolation again.

"So what does he do for a living?"

She shrugged. We were ensconced in two, large, people-enveloping leather chairs at Starbucks. I wondered about bedbugs, since recent infestations were a staple of the twenty-four-hour news shows these past few months. Maybe bedbugs don't like leather. I had no idea if it was true or not, but I felt better for thinking it.

"I'm not sure exactly. Something in sales. Maybe."

"But he does have a job, right?" I said, not fully leaning back into the plush leather.

"Oh, sure. I'm sure that he does."

We both sipped away.

"So what do I do now? Pass him a note in study hall?"

This made Ava laugh so hard that she nearly spilled her triple-named coffee concoction—I only get lattes—and she pushed her napkin at her nose. Once recomposed, she glared at me.

"Stop being funny. I could have choked to death."

"Sorry," I said, not feeling sorry at all. I liked it when I made others laugh. It had not happened all that frequently over the past few years.

"No notes. I'll call the podiatrist and he'll call his friend and he'll call you. Very neat and tidy."

I sat back, the import of what I had just agreed to negating all my bedbug fears.

"So what do we do? Dinner? Dancing? Movies?"

Ava smoothed the folds in her skirt. It was much shorter than the type I would wear. I wore sensible jeans. "It won't be dancing. I've seen you dance before. Better coordination I have seen in marionette shows. So that's out."

I scowled in displeasure. My dancing skills were . . . good . . . adequate. *Uninhibited* would be a better word. Untrained and uninhibited.

Better than a marionette, for sure.

"And a movie is no good either," Ava continued. "Too much time not talking. And if you do eat afterward, it will be late, and you'll be sleepy and yawny."

"I will not," I countered, then remembered almost falling asleep at Denny's, the only restaurant we could find open after a late showing of the what seemed like a five-hour-long movie,

Titanic. Ava had to nudge me awake after she surreptitiously chowed down half of my Grand Slam breakfast.

"So it's just dinner?"

Ava wiped at her mouth with the back of her hand.

"Yes. But you have to pick the place. Don't depend on the man to do it. If he picks, it will probably be at some stupid and loud sports bar that sells 'dynamite wings.' I learned my lesson with the podiatrist. All he eats is fried-somethings. And the fry-ier the better. Sports bars are his default choice. Disgusting venues, and unashamed purveyors of bad American food."

My head started to hurt with the plethora of new—and not welcome—choices this "dating thing" had brought into my life.

"What sort of restaurant, then?"

"How about that Greek place across the road. Carols?"

"I guess that's okay. But the sign out front needs an apostrophe. C-A-R-O-L-S. No apostrophe. I've told the owner and he just smiles at me."

"He's Greek," Ava said. "Maybe he has three sisters, all named Carol. Or, more likely, he probably doesn't speak English."

"He does too."

"Like a dog understands English, Mary. He knows restaurant English."

"Restaurant English?"

"You know. He understands what a hamburger is and what 'chef's salad' means—and that's it."

"You are so jingoistic," I replied. I didn't think she knew the word and I liked using such words when I could—my only edge in our relationship. She had me beat in every other category—looks, skinniness, vivaciousness, and the ability to make me laugh. But I was smarter.

Book smarter, anyhow.

She did not rise to the bait.

"Listen, I know you're not going to do Starbucks. You've already told me the story of when you and Jacob first went out—like a hundred times—to a Starbucks. So that whole chain is out. Caribou is also out, probably, because it sells coffee. As for restaurants, you go upscale and then it feels like you owe him something afterward—and I know you won't be going there."

"Ever."

"We'll see," she said, almost as if she could determine my frustrations on the intimacy front from looking at my face. She couldn't, let me assure you of that. "The flesh can be weak, you know. So Carols is good. The place is nice and safe and well lit. There can't be any unexpected expectations from that sort of meal. And it would be best if the date is just for coffee and dessert, rather than dinner," Ava said, swallowed some coffee, took a deep breath, and continued. "I'm not real fond of the podiatrist's eating habits. How a man can get through elementary medical school eating like an eight-year-old is beyond me. So dessert and coffee is safer. No twenty-five-minute waits for the Greek-style pork chops. No need to chatter away if he turns out to be . . . taciturn."

She used that word in triumph. I had used it on her a few weeks ago and she must have looked it up afterward.

"Or phlegmatic," she added.

I waited a moment, then replied. "That has more to do with attitude, not wordiness."

And for that, Ava punched me in the arm—hard enough to hurt—and maybe to bruise my most sensitive flesh as well.

———— ∞ ————

We had agreed to meet at Carol's . . . or rather, Carols. This saved us both any uncomfortable car rides home in case we thought the other one was a complete jerk, or a stalker, or a terminally mousy woman with no sex appeal.

I waited in the small front lobby. The owners had recycled a few booth seats that they turned into a waiting area. In this restaurant, it was totally unnecessary. A waiting crowd never formed. Not because it was a bad restaurant, but because they turned tables over quickly. I think. Well, to be honest, no one would call it a gourmet place, but it was okay. Dependable. Always edible.

A man came in to the small vestibule. His eyes darted around, so I imagined he was my potential date. Or, now, I guess, my actual date.

"Mary?" he asked.

He sounded nice, his voice a little deeper than on the phone. If Rufus asked me to describe him later, the first word that came to my mind was *average*. And not in the bad sense of the word—I don't mean that I wouldn't call him good or bad, just average. He stood a little taller than me. I found that out when we couldn't decide to shake hands in greeting or exchange an air hug. That's like an air kiss. A hug without really touching. I had my hand extended; he was expecting a hug. We met in the middle of both.

"Brian?"

His grin at the sound of his name grew wider than it should have been—by my standards. But he didn't do it in a Labrador sort of ear-to-ear grin.

"That's me. You ready?" he asked and turned to the Greek owner who obviously understood it when Brian held two fingers in the air, indicating the size of our party. I thought our numbers were pretty obvious without the hand gesture, but that was just me.

I might have guessed that Brian was a few years older than me. I'm a terrible judge of ages. Ava said he was older by a bit. His face looked older than mine, I think, with a few more wrinkles around his eyes. Maybe he had had too much sun. He looked like a golfer.

(I don't like golf much, either. Jacob golfed sporadically. He would watch hours of the game on Sunday afternoon when the Bears weren't playing. Watching golf on TV was akin to watching curling on TV. Why do it? Then he would yell at the screen, for both good and bad shots.) Anyway, Brian looked like a golfer. He wore a golf shirt—though that didn't mean anything, I guess, but it did have a little shark on the sleeve. I imagined only dedicated golfers would spend extra money to get sharks on their sleeves. His hair had thinned, was blond-ish, and, while he didn't do a complete comb-over, it wasn't cut short to expose the thinning, either. He had nice eyes, sort of brown. He was a few pounds heavier than he should be—but who wasn't at our ages? He wore khakis and sneakers.

He waited until I slid into the booth. For a moment, I thought he might slide in next to me. Actually, I think he would have if I had made room, but instead I parked myself in the exact middle and did not move. He waited half a beat, then took the other side.

He smiled. That was a good sign.

"You're not like I pictured you," he said. I thought I heard a hint of relief. "I mean, when I got word that I might be meeting, like, a famous author, I went right to my Apple computer (yes, he said "Apple computer") and looked your books up on the Internet. And they had your picture on the back. At least on Amazon, they did."

I also had a website. It wasn't all that fancy. My publisher made me do it. And there were a number of photos of me there. I guess his Web search couldn't find my name listed. Or perhaps he stopped after the first hit.

"So how do I look different?"

"I dunno. You're taller than I thought."

The photo on the books was a profile, head-and-shoulders shot, making it hard to tell height.

I am being horrible here. . . . I could only describe him as a nice man. He may have been just as nervous as I was.

"And your hair is different. It's shorter now, right?"

He scored points for being observant. I had it cut into what my stylist called "a cute little bob," which I hated and could not wait until it grew out.

The waitress sidled over.

"Ladies first," Brian said.

After hearing my pie and coffee order, he followed suit. I had hoped the instructions about "not dinner" had been passed along. I immediately became worried about it and asked.

"You did know that . . . well, this was just going to be a dessert-and-coffee affair tonight, right?"

I watched his eyes. I think he might have been formulating some sort of feigned surprise, then saw me watch him, and decided against it. Perhaps he was more perceptive than I gave him credit for.

"Sure. I got the word. I mean, that's a good thing," he said. "I bet we're both a little nervous and all. An entire meal is a long time if things aren't clicking."

He was perceptive. And good-natured too.

Maybe I would warm up to him.

Fifty minutes went by quickly. In that time I learned that Brian had been indeed divorced ("We're not friends exactly. We both made mistakes—so I don't spend time saying bad things about her. It's bad for karma. And no kids, which is good, I guess."); had a job selling some sort of medical stent (not the latest technology, but "the cheapest—so a lot of doctors go that route. If you ever have open-heart surgery, let me know and I can get you a deal on medical devices."); that he sold his house after the divorce to handle all his legal bills and divorce settlement, and now lives in the basement of his mother's house—only temporarily ("until I find a good investment-grade real estate place—like a house or something"); and that he has been friends with Dr. Tom for "a gazillion years."

It wasn't horrible.

There were no emotional sparks, not that I expected any, to be sure. There were no sudden flashes of growing old with this man, like there had been with Jacob. I had disabused myself of thinking that this experience would match—or even come remotely close to—the day I met my late husband.

I did feel as if I had been cheating on Jacob and tried my best to smile and push that thought away. Not an easy task— and I was not actually all that successful. I figured, however, that time would make the process less strange and easier to bear.

I ate my cherry pie—with ice cream, the pie not warmed— with coffee, four smallish cups start to finish. He ordered toast. And tea. Only two cups of tea. I didn't understand the toast part of the order, but I desperately wanted to avoid being too critical this evening, or reading too much into insignificant matters.

Brian picked up the check, without hesitation, and put down two dollars as a tip on a ten-dollar tab. He was generous with the waitress. That's a very good sign.

He escorted me to my car. We both said we had a nice time—a pleasant conversation.

He would have kissed me good-bye if I had leaned into him. But neither of us expected that to occur, so neither of us was disappointed. We did the same handshake-air hug like when we met. Maybe that would become our private joke.

I didn't think so—but it could happen.

He told me he would call.

I told him that would be nice.

Perhaps we were both lying. Perhaps we were both telling the truth.

I had no idea of who had done what, or why.

Dating.

Go figure.

——— ∞∞∞ ———

That night, Rufus seemed eager to talk. We had barely gotten to the sidewalk outside my house before he started peppering me with questions.

"Did you date well?" he asked.

I had decided that I would not spend a lot of time correcting his syntax. If I could understand him, that would be sufficient.

"The date went well, I guess. He seems to be a nice man. We talked. It was pleasant."

He did not ask me all that many questions—Brian, not Rufus—as if he had learned enough about me from the two paragraphs on Amazon.com to satisfy all his curiosity. Jacob had been eager to learn every detail about my life and my past and what I thought about the debate between cell phones and smart phones.

But . . . Brian was nice, and he was a man, and it was so comforting to speak to a person with a deeper voice than mine.

"Will you mate with him now?"

"Rufus!" I snapped back, in my best shocked schoolteacher voice. "That's rude."

"Rude?" he replied, the hurt in his voice obvious and palpable. "But . . . how long does it take people to mate? I know dogs don't wait very long. Or so I'm told."

I wondered if Rufus knew what I had done to him as a puppy, to remove all those sexual complications from his life. I didn't need one more thing to feel guilty about. But . . . maybe he lacked the awareness to know what "intimacies" he no longer could enjoy.

And talking to Rufus was like talking to a precocious five-year-old who knew the names of every dinosaur that ever walked the earth but couldn't tie his shoes or make it to the bathroom in time every time. Rufus, like that child, was remarkably poised, and terribly articulate on some subjects, and then, much like the average American five-year-old at times, speaking in baby terms. I could be like that as well. I knew how to write a novel, but balance a checkbook? Well, for me, that seemed as difficult as speaking Russian . . . underwater. In the winter. "Rufus," I said, my voice now under control, "humans have to know each other a long time before they do . . . that. Most humans, I guess. At least, the humans I know. Some go faster. But that's not normal. I guess. At least to me, it isn't."

One of my guilty pleasures was my three-year subscription to *People* magazine. Hollywood types, it seems, bedded and moved on to the next person at an alarming rate. How would any of them keep it all straight, I wondered. And how discouraging it seemed to me to read that a pair broke up because "it wasn't fun anymore." One Hollywood actress in a failed marriage had actually said that. As if it was noble to leave the other person because you stopped laughing and the sex became normal.

Don't get me started.

"I would never do that with someone if I wasn't married to him." I explained to Rufus.

Rufus did not appear to hold onto his hurts or slights much longer than a moment—and he may not have taken any offense to begin with. After sniffing a browning geranium, he looked up and asked, "What is 'married'?"

Well, what is that? How does one explain it to a species that does not mate for . . . well, for any length of time?

"'Married' means saying the other person is so special that you make a promise that you will be with him forever and never be with another person. You get married to someone with all your friends and family watching. So they can share in your happiness."

Rufus gladly accepted a tossed treat.

"And then you mate?"

I sighed.

Rufus wasn't being prurient at all. He was just trying to figure out humans using dog perceptions.

"Yes, Rufus. To me, to people who believe and follow God, marriage comes before mating."

Rufus snorted once, then once again.

"Does God say that is the way it is supposed to be?" he asked.

"He does."

"Okay."

And with that our conversation for the evening had ended. I believe we both had a lot to think about.

6

The next morning, Rufus and I went out for a short walk. He had never talked in the mornings and I did not expect otherwise today. I didn't really pay attention to what went on around me—nothing, I am pretty sure—and Rufus became the beneficiary of my lack of awareness as I thought about the night before.

Dating.

How perfectly weird and abnormal is that? For a forty-plus widow woman, that is.

And here's the rub: I didn't consider what I had done as dating. I had seen one man, for less than an hour, over not-a-dinner. So this had been a semi-date. No one expected anything to follow after the semi-date. There would not have to be any second meetings with Brian, unless we both thought that it wouldn't be horrible. He could call, he might not call, and the world would continue to spin on its axis.

Did I want him to call me?

I don't know. I knew I would have to have an answer before Ava called me the following morning, so I actually had set the alarm an hour earlier and had my first cup of coffee at

5:00 a.m. It was so early that Rufus did not even follow me downstairs. A few minutes later, he did stumble down, but only after he heard the refrigerator door open. That meant his chance of a snack increased exponentially.

I had hoped that the quiet and the early hour and the night's sleep would help me sort things out and put things into perspective.

It did no such thing.

Brian had been very nice . . . and while I did not expect there to be fireworks, they would have been nice.

Maybe it is different the second time. Maybe there can be no fireworks. Maybe it is a different form of attraction, of affection, and perhaps, even a different form of love . . .

I must have tossed a dozen treats to Rufus during our six-block walk. The tossing—done purely out of habit.

Once home, I made a second cup of coffee. I resisted the urge to check e-mails. I could be sure that Brian had not e-mailed me, but . . . there I felt that deep desire to be desired. Like accepting a job offer for a job you really don't want, but you accept it anyway because they wanted you and that felt really, really good. I tried to sort out my feelings, but nothing sorted. Ideas and thoughts flashed about.

The phone rang and nearly knocked me off the chair. Even Rufus jumped up in his crate in surprise.

It was 5:45.

In the morning.

Who calls this early? And it better not be him. Or Ava.

I have this nifty phone system that announces who is calling in a weird, sort of French-accented computer voice.

"Arizona call," the voice announced, with a chopped, dispassionate French tone. "Arh-a-zonuh cahl."

Arizona? Who do I know that lives in . . .

I shut my eyes.

Oh, Lord, no . . .

I walked over to the desk. Rufus cowered in his crate, perhaps thinking I was going to lock him in or something.

I picked up the phone and pressed TALK.

"Hello?"

"Mary? Is that you?"

It was my mother-in-law, or, I guess, legally, my former mother-in-law.

"Bernice? How nice to hear from you."

"Mary?"

Who else would be answering my phone at 5:45? A burglar?

"Yes, it's Mary. How are you, Bernice?"

"What time is it there?"

Bernice is a well-enough educated woman. She always asked the same question when calling from Arizona. Her son, her late son, explained the time difference perhaps a hundred times to her—even making her a map with the two cities listed: Wheaton and Mesa—and what time it would be in both of them.

It made no difference. It never had.

"It's 5:45, Bernice."

"In the morning?" she said shrilly, her tone incredulous. "Are you sure? I called early because I didn't want to miss you."

I never go out. Once, and only once in the past three years, I had missed one of her infrequent calls. She had grown frantic that time, imagining that I lay dead at the bottom of the stairs.

"I didn't wake you, did I?" she asked. Jacob's parents were early risers, but I would have bet that she set her alarm for extra early this morning.

And then I realized why she might be calling.

Lord, please let me be wrong. Please. Oh, please, please.

"Who was that man you were with last night, Mary? You were on a date? Is that it?"

It is why she's calling. Good heavens above, she knows. She already knows.

A thousand thoughts swirled about, as if I were trapped in a windstorm of neuroses—and I could not assemble my thoughts into a string to produce a rational response.

"He was . . . I mean, he is . . . the friend of a friend."

I could hear her sharp intake of breath.

"So you're dating now? Is that it? Already?"

I sat down on one of the stools by the counter. I could feel my face begin to flush, my fingers tremble, guilty over something that I hadn't done, guilty over sinning against my dead husband.

"I wouldn't have called it a date, Bernice. Honest."

"That's not what Lena said. She was there. She saw the whole thing. And Lena does not lie, Mary. She goes to church. She's as honest as they come."

I used my free hand to massage the already-tightening muscles in my neck. If I didn't work on them now, they would start to spasm, and I would have to take to my bed with a heating pad. Or would I need an ice pack? It didn't really matter. When the tightness happened, nothing would help—except time.

"Bernice, all I did was have coffee and a piece of pie with a nice gentleman. And how does Lena know that he's not my insurance agent or financial planner or . . ."

"Is he either of those things?"

"No," I replied, feeling guiltier, like I was trying to find an acceptable alibi.

"Well, then, it's not very Christian to tell fibs like that."

"I'm not. But Lena didn't see . . . what she saw."

"She did too. She's a God-fearing Christian woman, Lena is, and if she saw you on a date, then you were on a date."

I had no reply. I had been on a date. A semi-date, but it would have been too hard to explain the difference.

"Okay, Bernice. I admit it. It was a date. It's been three years. It's been a long time."

Bernice remained silent. Not quiet, but silent.

"We just talked. Honest. It felt good to talk."

Bernice drew in a sharp breath. That I could hear.

"You can't talk at Bible study? Which you don't attend anymore, either. Lena goes. You don't."

I tried to place Lena. The name was familiar, but I could not recall an image. I would have guessed mousy hair, brown, done in helmet style, with longish dresses that could only be the product of a Sew-Rite pattern book, hand-sewn with a few crooked seams—but only where they don't really show.

Stop being so mean, Mary. You're horrible.

"I know, Bernice. I'm struggling with writing a book. It's hard."

I did not like lying to my former mother-in-law, but if she could throw guilt around, so could I. "Sales haven't been as good as they have been in the past. Keeping up with all the expenses is a real struggle. I'll . . . I'll probably have to sell this place eventually. Too expensive for me to maintain."

Actually, I was doing mostly okay, I guess. There had been insurance and all that. Eventually, I would probably sell this house—more because it had become way too big for me, rather than purely for financial reasons.

"Well, if you're running out of money, running to a new man is not the answer. We could afford to send . . . I don't know . . . maybe a hundred dollars a month. We don't need to eat out as often as we do."

We were playing a tennis match of guilt.

"No. I wouldn't think of it. I've been thinking of looking for a job. Have a steady income—rather than wait on royalties."

"Well . . . Mary . . . I guess it has been a while. It's just so hard. You know. It's like I don't want to admit that they're gone."

She is good. She really is.

I bucked up, pinched my cheek, refused to cry.

I am terrible.

"I know, Bernice. It is hard. But we only had coffee . . ."

"And pie. You said pie."

"And pie, yes. I don't think he'll call again. But it was nice to talk. You have George, after all. You have companionship."

I would have sworn Bernice snorted. A derisive snort, at that.

"Sure. We talk. All the time. He's a regular talking machine, George is. Yak, yak, yak. That's all he does is talk. Can't get him to shut up."

I recognized her tone as sarcastic. George, at his most gregarious, was no more than monosyllabic. I never understood how the two of them produced such a wonderful son. Sometimes the acorn gets carried off by a fast-moving squirrel and planted in some other, entirely different, and more humane garden plot, tended to by kind and gentle farmers who till the earth with grace and love.

"I'm glad you called, Bernice. I'll keep you posted on the news. I'll send an e-mail. You are reading e-mails, right?"

Another snort.

"George says there's a virus and I tell him to call that Greek Squad place and he won't because they charge money and George swears he'll get it fixed himself." She drew in a breath, as if she had emphysema, which she didn't. "So no, we're not getting e-mails. Print it out and mail it to me, Mary. Mail, we get."

I promised I would and clicked the phone off, and then stared at Rufus, who had slept through the entire conversation.

92

There would be no asking him questions about it this evening, that's for sure.

———◦◦◦———

Ava called ten minutes later.

At 6:15 a.m.

I don't think she ever woke up that early for anything else.

"So . . . ," she said, drawing out the word long enough to color it up with several sexual innuendos, if I had been that type of person—which, of course, I was not.

The early hour, the odd subject, guilt, an already jittery, caffeinated nervous system—I mean, that all takes its toll on logic, reason, and *The Chicago Manual of Style*.

Blast you, Strunk and White.

"So . . . what?" I responded, feeling all clever and witty.

I am being sarcastic. Or is that ironic? Too early in the day for either, I imagine.

Ava was many things, but she was not a fish that took the shiny, easy bait. She would wait in the cool, deep shadows, before snapping.

"How uncomfortable were you?"

"Not at all, really. That is . . . until Bernice called this morning."

"Bernice? Your Bernice?"

She had snapped at the bait, the shiny lure with a barb.

I related our conversation, and despite the early hour, Ava laughed heartily, not just from the absurdity of it all, but from picturing Bernice in her tattered housecoat—worn because of parsimony, not poverty—and a set of curlers from Woolworth's in her hair. She still had curler sets that dated back to the Eisenhower administration.

After we both stopped laughing (and I admit that I felt guilty for laughing, though I am sure Ava did not), she asked me again, "So?"

"The date went fine, Ava. I liked being out again. I felt grown up and not in a bad way. But I don't know if I'm feeling what I'm supposed to be feeling. I know it can't be like it was, but what happens now? There's no fireworks—that I get. But what should there be, then?"

Ava didn't have any answers for me. I didn't expect them. She once admitted that there were no fireworks with her first husband, and there weren't any with Dr. Tom, either.

Maybe Ava was just not the fireworks sort of woman.

I wonder if Rufus knows what fireworks are.

Oh, that's right, he does. He hates them. Last Fourth of July, we spent most of the evening walk spastically lurching into bushes every time another bottle rocket whizzed up into the warm summer night.

I guess I shouldn't ask him about expecting fireworks then.

∞∞∞

I spent the day sitting at my computer, straightening up my desktop, moving Word documents into folders and folders into other folders, getting thing uncluttered. I even spent nearly an hour just eliminating old e-mails, like the video of the surprised kitten in the shoebox and the monkey that plays the piano. I know I'm too sentimental. It is hard to get rid of the past.

Not that my organizational frenzy extended to my real office. No, the office stayed an undisciplined mess. Jacob had pushed me to be more ruthless. "You use most of your office for long-term storage, sweets. You have an open space on your desk the size of a postcard—and not one of those big ones, either. I don't see how you can produce anything clear and pithy in such disorder."

Of course, I laughed when he said *pithy*. I mean, how many people use the word *pithy* on a regular basis, if ever? I had heard Jacob use it more than once, for sure, and laughed every time.

Okay, so I am an arrested adolescent.

Pithy.

You have to admit it's a funny word.

And the office was a mess. I had scrapbooks and photo albums on the top shelf of the closet, which no one could access because you had to remove the shelf below to get at it. They were lost in plain sight. And the other closet, I filled with all manner of paper that I would never, ever use—like thick, yellow card stock. Why in the world did I buy that in the first place? Might have been for a potential school project by my son. School remained out of the question, but I could not get rid of that thick, yellow paper. It was perfectly good—just not usable to me.

Maybe if I held a garage sale, I could get rid of all the odd bits and pieces that were clogging up my life.

Who am I kidding? That will never happen. It'll take a bomb or something.

That night, after a totally unproductive day trying to plot out the second act of a book that I hoped some generous publisher might buy, Rufus and I went for our walk. The book, in the Amish genre, was a stand-alone novel about a beautiful Amish girl . . .

Wait a second. Didn't I already write this one?

Of course, the plot felt similar to an earlier book, but not identical. In this one, the beautiful Amish girl actually had a twin who had been separated at birth from her sister. The worldly sister gets involved in drug smuggling . . .

I don't know. Maybe it doesn't make any sense at all.

But my desktop was neat and tidy and I felt a small wave of accomplishment lap at my feet.

And now, in the cold, in the dark, with Rufus almost bounding about, I felt normal again, at peace. No books. No dates. No Arizona phone calls. I sucked in great gulps of the coldness, exhaling great clouds of breath into the night air. The air was cold, not too cold, just gloves-cold, not yet mitten-cold with a scarf.

Brian had not called. I truly and honestly did not expect him to call. I knew he would wait at least a day. I am sure both Ava and Dr. Tom counseled him on not acting too eager, not wanting to scare the skittish fawn off into the deep forest.

Fawn? Who am I kidding?

They probably told him not to make the old, grizzled, arthritic doe skedaddle out of the cornfield and into the next cornfield. They were being honest.

So he would not call today, and probably not tomorrow. The third day—that's when he would call. If he called. There were no guarantees. He may have felt no chemistry either. He may not have felt any fireworks.

I may not be hideous—like that actor in *The Elephant Man* who wheezed, angrily, "I am not an animal!" No, my appearance would not be placed in that panic-inducing category, but neither could I be considered a knockout. I could be classified as pleasant looking. I believe I told you how Jacob described me—pretty, not beautiful. Most of what he said still applied. Of course, I was older than that now. There were more wrinkles around my eyes these days. I think, if anything, my face is thinner, more detailed now than it has ever been. My eyes are still clear and focused. My face still lights up when I smile— that is what people tell me.

Yet perhaps the sum of all of me—all of my face and my fig- ure, such as it is (normal, not bosomy, nor svelte, but normal, thank you very much)—had not been enough to get Brian's pulse ticking upward. I could have dressed more . . . pro- vocatively, but that would have been like a butcher slipping his thumb on the scales: cheating. (Do butchers still do that? Did they ever do that?)

No, if Brian called again, he would do so because he saw something inside of me that attracted him, not because he saw down my blouse and saw something there that attracted him.

So how do I explain all of this to a dog? Dogs don't look down blouses.

Unless they think that you have hidden dog treats in your bra. Which I have never done.

"Rufus," I said.

Rufus slowed, then stopped, and looked back up at me, over his shoulder. Is it called a shoulder on a dog? Well, yes, it is. Dogs have disconnected shoulder bones (lacking the collar- bone of the human skeleton) that allow a greater stride length for running and leaping. Thank you, Wikipedia.

He waited. I think that maybe talking proved difficult for him—difficult for him to make the proper vocalizations—so he didn't spend a lot of time chitchatting.

"So, now that I've been out on a date with Brian, what do I do?"

Rufus stared at me, nearly immobile, as if trying to see my eyes.

"Are you asking if you should mate with him now? You said that you don't do that."

I had my hand on my hip in my best "peeved June Cleaver" imitation.

"Rufus, that is not my question. You don't have to worry about me . . . mating with anyone before it is the proper time."

Rufus looked away. A rustling occurred in the tree to our left. It might have been a squirrel, but there were no warning chirps from the branches. And I thought most squirrels were already hibernating—or in their winterized torpor state. (That I knew without looking at Wikipedia.)

"Okay," he responded and began to walk.

"If he calls me, do I go out with him again?"

Rufus did not break stride.

Then I found myself voicing the question that made me sound even more like a lunatic than ever before. "Do you think I should go out with him again?"

Even that question did not break the dog's stride.

"I don't know," he said. "I haven't met him."

"Do you need to meet him?"

Rufus snorted. "What does that funny man say on that funny show—the one with Santa's Little Helper?"

"*The Simpsons?* Homer Simpson?"

Santa's Little Helper is the Simpson family dog.

"Is he fat?" Rufus asked. "That's him, then. What does he say?"

"D'oh?"

I don't think Rufus laughed. Or at least I never heard him laugh. I am pretty sure that he found some things amusing, or funny, or worthy of a smile, if he could smile, which he couldn't. He did like to watch *The Simpsons* with me on Sunday nights.

"D'oh," I repeated and I saw his shoulders, even though they were disconnected, lurch a notch, like he might have been silently laughing.

"So I need to bring him home?"

Rufus did not answer, for the question answered itself. Of course I would have to bring him home. Rufus would have to meet him. And Rufus would tell me if Brian was an honorable man.

Yes.

And now, who sounds like a total and complete lunatic, the grand sort of lunatic who has lost all tethers with reality?

I do, of course, and Rufus and I remained silent on the remainder of our walk. I even stopped tossing dog treats to the poor animal, even though I think he stared at me over his disconnected shoulder, wondering why the treat supply had suddenly gone dry.

On the third day, I was ready.

I admit to having practiced some lines and responses, speaking aloud to the empty rooms, as if he had actually called. I made sure not to do it near any of the Jacob pictures. I would not want Rufus to think I had gone off the deep end again.

Who am I kidding? I had been there and back already, right?

The phone rang at 11:00. I didn't think he would call at 11:00, since he had a job and all. Hard to call for a second date in the middle of a workday, I imagined.

The call came from California.

The only person I knew, or at least knew well enough to be calling me, in California, was my literary agent. It would be either really good news, or really discouraging news. Middle ground seldom existed with Marcella.

Who in their right mind names a perfectly normal child Marcella? I suppose it was unique and memorable. Maybe the odd name became her ticket to being a profitable agent.

"So how is my favorite Amish pro doing these days?"

I was her go-to writer of all things Amish. Over the years, I had pitched a number of different story ideas and different plots and settings and characters and religious backgrounds—from histrionic Presbyterians to gum-chewing Catholics to secular humanists to normal, everyday Christian people like Ned Flanders on *The Simpsons*. But hardly anything other than your standard Amish novel, and the occasional Quaker and Mennonite novel, had sold. I had written two non-Christian books that were published by a small press in Kansas. Both received good reviews yet they both suffered from lack of sales and distribution. Talk about an actor who is typecast—or branded by one role. I became a "branded" author. I didn't mind, mostly, since I was a writer, a working writer, who actually had books published. That is more than 99 percent of the writers in America can say. And I had more than one book published—again—more than most writers can ever hope to say. But I am now typecast as the nice writer who doesn't talk about sex or write about violent things in her books (other than the weather). I had grown tired of it. I wanted to branch out, but no one had given me the opportunity.

"I'm doing fine. And you?"

Marcella did not need a large conversational opening. We didn't talk that often because Marcella talked so much. I let her go on and on, about the weather, her cats, her in-laws, the crazy California politics, and the threat of the next big earthquake.

Finally, she arrived, in a very circuitous way, to me—and to my literary efforts. Marcella had not gotten rich off of me, but she probably made her car payments for the past several years through my book sales.

She did not wrap bad news in gay ribbons and bows.

"No one is buying Amish anymore, Mary. I hate to tell you, but your last proposal received no interest from any of our previous publishers."

"No one?"

This was the bad, drug-dealing twin sister of the good Amish girl who stayed home.

"Nope."

Her reply sat there, like a fat goose in a hunter's crosshairs.

"You have any vampire books? I know that a vampire who believes in God is sort of a contradiction in terms, but they are buying vampire stories."

Vampire stories? I don't do vampires.

"Or werewolves, maybe. They're not quite as sexy as vampires, but I might be able to sell one of those. You have anything like that?"

Usually, I would have snapped at the chance to try something new—but vampires? Or worse yet, werewolves? I just couldn't see how I could make that work.

"Well. Think about it. Maybe you'll come up with an angle on that."

"What about the New York houses?" I asked. "Are they buying Amish? I could make it less . . . less religious, I guess. A little sexier, even."

Marcella laughed, though not pleasantly.

"New York isn't buying anything unless your name is Rowling or King or Turow. Or Clancy. They are playing it safe and no one is paying for unknowns these days."

I took a breath. It felt as though my literary career had entered a new phase: dead.

"I know you're not an unknown everywhere, but you are in New York circles. If you lived under a bridge for a while, then I could sell you as a new writer. An unknown primitive, who has a unique voice that no one has heard yet."

I didn't want to live under a bridge—or even a secluded viaduct. How would Rufus adapt to living in a cardboard box by the freeway?

"No. I don't think that will work," I answered. "Let me think about the werewolf idea, though. Maybe I can come up with something."

"You do that," Marcella replied. "You think about it. Let me know if you can whip up a proposal for some sort of supernatural thriller. I think I could sell that for you. If it's the right concept."

We exchanged some pleasantries and she said she would "keep beating the bushes, but don't hold your breath." She suggested that I might benefit if I took a few months off to think about where I might be heading as a writer—as if it wasn't a concept that didn't occupy all my thoughts anyhow.

She gave me a cheery good-bye and said that I should stay in touch.

I hung up the phone and sat there, almost totally dumbfounded.

Rufus sat in his chair watching me, his eyes narrowed as if he was sleepy, which I knew he was not. I think he felt bad for me and realized that he had no answers either.

Maybe Brian is fabulously wealthy and desires me so much that he'll help me self-publish my next effort—whatever it might be.

Yes, and dogs can talk, right? That will be the day.

I would have to do something. I needed to sell another book. Or find a job. Or have something remarkable happen in my life.

Like maybe my dog could tell me what to do next.

Right?

7

Brian called later that day, at 5:15. At first, I imagined that he had just finished work, and rushed home to call me. He didn't, since he called from a cell phone.

The French-sounding voice on my answering machine said: "cell-uuu-larh cahl."

I was still in a funk about Marcella's call. I spent most of the afternoon wandering about the house looking for direction.

"Hi," he said. "I wanted to tell you that I had a good time with you . . . over coffee. Or tea, I guess, in my case."

I told him that I did too.

"Would you like to try a real dinner? Maybe Saturday?"

"Saturday would be good."

"That's great," he said, his voice full of relief. "I could pick you up this time, okay?"

At least Rufus would have a chance to meet him.

"How about Ki's?" he asked.

Ki's has a reputation as a pretty good restaurant—sort of an older person's place, complete with a bar and not-completely-awful lounge singers, Barbie Jean and the DelMontes, with their glossy eight by ten photos thumbtacked to a wall in the lobby.

Yes, I made that up.

"Okay," I replied. It would be a real date and we could see how things would work out.

"We'll go Dutch, if that's okay with you. No pressure that way."

I wouldn't have felt any pressure if he wanted to pay for my food, but I guess I understood. His "going Dutch" request was not an automatic penalty, not a red flag, but I admit that the ref made a motion to pull the flag from his pocket and hesitated at the last moment and let the infraction slide—just this once.

You don't live with a football fan for all those seasons without some of it rubbing off on you.

No penalty, but the ref would keep a close eye on the game from that moment on.

"Ki's?" Ava asked, cradling the phone to her cheek. "Seriously? Well, it is better than Hooter's."

"He wouldn't have ever suggested Hooter's," I responded, defending Brian for no good reason, shuffling about my kitchen, wearing Jacob's old, too-big, yet luxurious, lamb's wool slippers that I bought for him the Christmas before . . . before the accident. I would have donated them to charity, but I hadn't done that with any of his other clothes, and I didn't have a pair of slippers of my own. His were sufficient. And warm.

"Don't kid yourself, Mary."

"I'm not. But not all men are like Dr. Tom."

"Thank God," Ava replied. "Grease would be our national food if he had anything to say about it."

"But he looks healthy, Ava. You're always on him about his diet—but he looks good."

"Freak of nature, that's all. If I ate what he eats, I'd be like one of those women on *The Jerry Springer Show* in a few months."

I poured a third cup of coffee. I suspect people think I obsess about coffee. I really don't. I just happen to drink way too much of it. Some days—maybe twenty cups. I know, I know—but most of them are small cups. And I'm not overly jittery. Honest.

"Anyhow, Ki's is a good place. Older crowd."

"I know. But you can talk there. I went to that new Italian place in Glen Ellyn with Beverly and her husband . . ."

"You went out with a married couple? How kind of them," Ava said.

"Don't be mean. They are nice people," I replied.

Ava waited a beat, then added, "Did she wear gingham?"

I would have spit out my coffee laughing, had I just drunk a mouthful—which I hadn't.

"She did."

"With lace at the collar?"

"All of her dresses have lace at the collar," I said and then hated myself, just a little, for being mean and gossipy. But the truth is the truth. Beverly dressed as if she stepped out of a J. C. Penney's catalog, circa 1953. She did have an unmistakable style about her. I would have said pre-Beatles, premodern, pre-style. "But I'm talking about the restaurant here. It's too loud, and we had to actually shout at one another to be heard. Most uncomfortable."

"Yep, Ki's is much better. You will call me afterward to tell me all about it, right? I have a vested interest in this love match."

"It's not a love match, Ava. It's just a date."

She waited a second.

"That's not what I'm going to tell Bernice," she said coolly, and then promptly hung up—all before I could shout at her, in mock anger, that if she breathed a word of this date to anyone, I would stalk her down and break her arm.

Keeping secrets. Sheesh.

What am I? Sixteen?

Rufus stared up at me from his pet bed—his usual spot during my morning coffees—narrowed his eyes, and rolled onto his side, evidence of his desire to be left alone and absolved of answering any of my foolish morning questions.

———— ◆ ————

Later that morning, I looked in my wallet. I don't make a habit of looking in my wallet. I guess looking there sort of happens in the course of a day—like when I buy something. But I wanted to check on my cash supply. I tried to pay cash for most of my smaller purchases. It gave me a better feel for where my money was going. That's what the lady financial guru said on her finance show on cable—the woman with the big teeth and even bigger grin. It's easy for her to tell people what they can buy and what they can't; she has millions of dollars and two homes and who knows what else. Even if I did everything she said, I would never become rich. Unless I wrote a financial book like she did. Which I can't, because I'm terrible at finances. Yet I did follow her advice about paying in cash. I think the advice came from her. Maybe it might have been from that other guy, who looked like he dressed in clothing from a Goodwill store. Not that I am anti-poor or anything. Or anti-charity. But if you're on TV, even if it is cable TV, wear something else other than striped polo shirts that look too small on you.

I had nineteen dollars in my purse and way too much change. I took the change out, more pennies than anything else, and dropped it into the large, clear jar, half-filled with mostly pennies, on the far kitchen counter.

One day, I'll take that to the bank and have it counted.

Even though the last time I did that, I got more than a few semi-angry glares from the teller. They count money all day. How hard is it for them to pour a jar full of coins into that machine that does the counting for them?

I would need to go to the bank for actual cash before my date . . . my dinner at Ki's. It would be easier to put down cash on the table—since we'd be splitting the bill—than it would be to figure out how much the waitress should assign to two credit cards.

I knew I should check out my bank balances then. Maybe my checking account needed additional funds. Maybe I would need to transfer money from the larger savings account. I sat at the computer, Rufus followed me back into the office, of course. I am sure he thought that there might be food involved somehow. There wouldn't be, of course, but a dog can hope, right?

I typed in my impossibly long user name and even longer, more complicated password. The password had to be eleven characters long and include at least two numbers. Who can remember all that? I used the state of my birth—Pennsylvania—and the year of my birth. (If you're a hacker, please ignore what I just wrote.) The bank's cheery website came up and welcomed me by name.

The balance in my checking account stood at $783.53. No big bills were coming, so that should be sufficient for a while. I clicked back a page to check the savings account balance. I didn't often look at the number, but when I did this time, the amount shocked me—sort of. It was smaller than I remembered. Much smaller. *Dwindled* is the word that popped into my head. I did have Jacob's insurance money deposited in a separate account—some $200,000. I still had a mortgage on the house. Jacob had taken out a policy that paid off maybe half of the outstanding mortgage when he . . . when he . . .

How do I describe to myself what happened? "Passed away" seems too much like a funeral director's euphemism. "Died" seemed abrupt—and he didn't die. He was killed. Both he and our son suffered the same fate. I guess I seldom mentioned it to myself, so the few times it came up, I stumbled.

So the house had a mortgage. Rather, I had a mortgage. I have more money than many widows, I am sure. I had some retirement money, maybe $50,000, in a 401(k) account that I couldn't get to until I turned sixty-two. But I didn't have all that much cash in savings.

In the western suburbs of Chicago, where I lived, real estate taxes were high enough to feel onerous, and I wrote a check out for just over $10,000 in real estate taxes last year alone. That would be enough to deplete most of my savings—that's how little remained.

All of a sudden, I began to feel afraid again, nervous and anxious—just like I was the days after the accident. At first, I imagined that my royalties and advances from my books would be enough to maintain my lifestyle. But thanks to Marcella's assessment of my literary future—well, that may be wishful thinking at best. The writer's newsletter . . . I enjoyed doing it, but in reality, it broke even at best. Unless I could come up with a way of doubling or tripling its circulation, I suppose I would have to consider shutting it down. I hated to see that eventuality on the horizon. Looming on the horizon would be a more apt description.

So how much money would I need for my date with Brian? Fifty dollars would be the maximum. I would order the

109

chicken, drink water with the meal, eschew dessert, and have more than enough for the rest of the week—provided I didn't do more than a half dozen runs to Starbucks.

Rufus sat up in his chair and sort of snorted and barked, as if asking me to go outside. He did this often. I would let him out the back door, he would run down the steps, run around the bottom deck, then run back up the steps. I blamed myself. I always gave him a treat when we came back home. He didn't have to go out. He simply cadged treats from me.

So we walked to the back door. I went outside with him. The air was cold, bracing, and it helped clear my head. I heard his nails clicking on the bottom deck, shuffling through the leaves that weren't raked from this fall. I looked out over my smallish domain and felt an inordinate wave of sadness, or melancholy, wash over me.

I'll have to give all this up. There's no way I can continue to live here and have enough money to live on. If I stay, I'll have to work. And I don't know if I can do that.

Even now, I hesitated. Not that I was reluctant to work—far from it—I simply didn't want to have to tell my story over and over again. And I would be branded the "widow lady" of the office. I just didn't think I could do that. Not yet, anyhow.

Rufus scrambled up the steps. I gave him his treat and I sat in the sunroom, Rufus beside me on the sofa, staring blankly into space, wondering what was to become of me.

Maybe Rufus might shed some light on my dilemma.

Maybe I should ask God what I should do.

I would ask him—but he and I aren't really speaking these days.

That night, a full moon rose over a very chilled landscape. It had not snowed in Illinois yet, or at least not in DuPage County, but it was cold enough to do so. I bundled up and checked The Weather Channel before we left. No wind. That meant I could make do with just the hood of my coat and not ruin my hair with a thick wool cap.

Not that I had much of a coiffure to be ruined.

Rufus snorted a few times. I should take him to a dog allergist, probably, but after reviewing my finances, odds were good that he would have to learn to live with it.

"Rufus," I asked, well aware of the absurdity of it all, "should I think about selling the house?"

We lived in a big house: four bedrooms—five, really, if you counted my office, which could be legally called a bedroom since it had two closets—and four bathrooms (one in the finished basement, which had its own small kitchen and bedroom.) Two-and-a-half-car garage. Way too much space, of course, for just me and the dog. Big square footage meant higher tax bills and higher utilities and higher insurance.

By selling, would I be admitting some sort of failure?

If the house sold for what I thought it might, I would have maybe . . . I don't know . . . another $50,000 profit? Or does the Realtor take more than 5 percent?

"I dunno," Rufus responded. I have heard that tone before. Dispassionate, maybe. Or uncaring.

I didn't like it.

"So God doesn't care if I need to sell the house?"

Rufus did not break stride.

"I don't know much about houses. You do need shelter, right? We both do."

I nodded, then realized that Rufus could not see me nod.

"But is this a good time to be selling a house? Will I make enough money on it? Doesn't God claim to provide?"

Now, my tone grew snippy. I didn't think Rufus was all that savvy when it came to someone being snarky or mean or insolent. But, then again, maybe he was.

"Doesn't God care?" I asked again, this time nearly to mostly impatient. "Isn't he supposed to care for the sparrows? Isn't he supposed to care for the least of them? Am I not as important as some stupid, insignificant sparrow?"

Why should I have to give everything up? I didn't allow some crash to take the only two people whom I really loved. I certainly did not ordain the accident—for some stupid greater good.

Rufus stopped in his tracks and stared up at me as if he was trying to gauge my mood, looking at me with those dark, expressionless eyes, trying to decipher what I thought. I think I was being pretty transparent.

He bent to nip at an itch on his front paw. Then he spoke.

"I don't think this is a question for a dog. Or God. It seems wrong. Like you want God to help you make money. You need shelter. And you have shelter, don't you?"

I didn't want to answer him. I didn't want to talk to him. And I didn't. And he didn't get another treat during the walk and only one when we got back.

I'm not sure if he knew whether I was mad at him or some-one else.

It didn't really matter.

I spent all of Saturday morning cleaning the house. When Jacob was still alive, we hired a cleaning lady to come in once a week for half a day. It felt marvelous to come home to a recently cleaned house—mopped floors, dusted blinds, scrubbed bath-rooms, gleaming appliances.

Now, all that cleaning was my responsibility.

Rufus followed me from room to room as I worked, often lying down in the doorway, his eyebrows moving back and forth, as he watched me work. Most of the house did not get that dirty. My bedroom and bathroom were the only two rooms upstairs that I used, but I felt obligated to vacuum all the other rooms, and dust when the dust became so obvious that I could no longer ignore it.

Rufus complicated the act of vacuuming. He had determined, early on, that the vacuum cleaner posed a threat as an evil machine, and he did his best to try and protect me from its nefarious ways, barking and lunging at the head of the unit, trying to bite it, or gnaw at it, as I maneuvered it along the carpet. If I stopped and took the head off and approached Rufus with only the silver tube, as the machine inhaled great whooshes of air, he would run off to another room, cowering. But as soon as I put the head back on, he would begin to stalk.

I could just shush him away with a hard word, and he would stop. If I was in a hurry, or feeling unfriendly, I would do exactly that. Otherwise, I would let him feel heroic and a noble defender of our home and hearth.

I dusted the empty rooms upstairs.

John's bedroom was not empty, exactly. The bed remained there, and the desk, the nightstand, the bookcases. But soon after the accident, I could no longer bear to see all the reminders of his short life, so I went to a self-storage facility, bought two large bundles of medium-sized storage boxes, and packed up virtually everything in his room, and—sweating and crying and cursing—had carried each taped box up the rickety, pull-down stairs into the attic. And there the boxes remained, unseen and untouched. I had remade his bed with a neutral set of sheets, and a neutral bedcover. I left his camp picture on his nightstand.

Even now, when cleaning, the room nearly empty and devoid of personality, I would sit on the bed and weep, missing everything about him, missing his smile and his scent and his odd, off-kilter humor.

Today, I just hurried through the room, vacuuming whatever dust had settled on the floor since the last time, Rufus growling and snorting at the vacuum cleaner, making the house a safer place.

I spent nearly an hour in the kitchen; cleaning out the refrigerator required most of that time.

My refrigerator is food purgatory. I make too much of something, or bring home half a sandwich from a lunch out, or deliberately make enough for two meals. What usually happens is that food stays in the cold and dark until I throw it out. I should save a lot of anguish and chilled space by tossing it out in the beginning. I seldom eat leftovers.

I know, I know, I'm not rich and I should use up all that I have. But I can't. Something about the congealed nature of old food.

Rufus would gladly eat it all. I tried that once with three pieces of fish that I had left over from an all-you-can-eat fish fry. (I didn't get extra to take home, honest. They brought me seven pieces on the first go-round, and I had that many legitimately left over.) Anyhow, I fed one to Rufus that first night, which he ate with great enthusiasm. I repeated it the second night; same Rufus result. The third day told another story. I am sure his canine stomach had not been designed to handle processed fats, and the result caused me to scrub floors for another two days. Rufus looked terribly chagrined at his malady, and slunk into his cage after each episode. Of course, I could not be angry. I had been at fault. And he graciously only got sick on the hardwood floors, rather than the few area rugs on the main floor.

Today, I tossed out a bunch of white containers and some condiments whose expiration date lay two years prior to the current year, and disposed of the contents of a few Tupperware containers whose surface had become a seventh-grade biology project on mold growth. I tried not to inhale while doing so, thinking that I may have concocted a lethal strain of blue bacterium that the world has yet to experience.

I'm sure I didn't, but "squeamish" is my middle name.

It isn't, of course, and mold was about the only thing I really find to be disgusting.

That and spiders.

Rufus doesn't like spiders, either. Some bugs he would chase and eat if I didn't yell at him to leave them alone. Not so much with spiders, though.

Then I sprayed all the stainless steel appliances with cleanser, wiped, and sprayed again with Windex. My cleaning lady, when she worked here, said the two-step process was the best technique for doing away with all streaking.

I put the vacuum cleaner away, straightened up the pillows and throws in the family room and the sunroom, and squared up the several piles of magazines that I would one day go through and clip out all the really good recipes, as well as make notes on all the wonderful places to travel to, books to read, and music to experience.

I knew I was kidding myself, but one's ability to delude one's self is infinite.

You know who said that originally? Sandy Koufax, the star pitcher of the . . . . I don't remember what team. Out in California. A Jewish ball player. And he said that about pro athletes hanging on too long. He quit at the top of his game. Yes, I know I said I wasn't a sports fan, and I'm not, but my father and Jacob were both rabid fans. It connected them.

And now I saved magazines that I would never read, and cleaned a house to impress a man whom I would not invite inside.

Crazy, isn't it?

I'll be honest here. I am not sure about that. I did not think that I would invite Brian back to the house. I told Ava that. I would imagine that she told Dr. Tom and he may have relayed the information on to Brian for me.

There would be no "Would you like a cup of coffee?" at the door.

Not now. Not after this date.

But a question remained: why am I cleaning like a madwoman? If he's not going to see the house, who cares if it's dirty or not?

Rufus followed me as I put the bucket of cleaning supplies back into the laundry room closet. He also expected a treat, because that is where I kept them and he had begun to expect a treat every time I went into the room.

I can be a sucker for a sad face.

I looked at the clock in the kitchen.

It was 2:15.

Brian said he would pick me up a little after 5:30. I had told him that would be fine. I had more than three hours to obsess about getting ready.

I hoped that the early hour was not because he wanted to take advantage of the early bird specials.

But I had an uneasy feeling that it was.

The next morning, Ava forced her way into my house.

That may be a harsh description, but it is what she did. She used her emergency key to let herself in before I woke up. Rufus barked and squealed. I heard that from upstairs. Of course I remained in bed. Or rather, had remained back in bed. I had been up at 5:00, had taken Rufus for a walk, came back, and crawled back into bed. That did not happen often.

Never, actually.

And not because I was tired from the night before.

Ava rattled around in the kitchen, making enough noise to wake me again. She called up after a few minutes.

"It's me, the burglar," she said. "You're almost out of cream."

I figured she could navigate the kitchen fine on her own for a few more minutes and I took a shower—a quick shower—but I wanted to be awake for her interrogation.

And I knew that I would be getting an interrogation. Thankfully, I had not seen any church ladies at the restaurant, nor did I see anyone who would have been likely to have known Bernice. Most of the ladies there were much more stylish.

But now I'm being catty.

The hot water on my skin, pulsing against the bare nape of my neck, felt particularly delicious this morning.

Perhaps I was regaining a bit of my sensual side . . . hidden for these last few years.

Who am I kidding? I was never that . . . sensual.

Was I?

Jacob and I had a rich life together, if you know what I mean. Jacob could be so gentle and patient, and . . . well, at times, adventuresome. I mean, I am a literate, literary-minded person who likes words. Jacob could use words with devastating effect on me. Whispering in my ear all sorts of intimacies.

I spun the faucet to cold . . . or less warm, actually.

I allowed myself to be carried away, and I did not want that to happen.

I dressed in shorts, despite the cold. Longer shorts, and a baggy, thick sweatshirt from the University of Pittsburgh, my alma mater—not an original sweatshirt; that one would have faded to tatters years and years ago. This was a replacement model. And I am pretty sure it was at least one size up from the one I wore back then. Time does take its toll.

I brushed my hair back, still wet, put on Jacob's slippers, and padded downstairs.

Ava held her coffee cup up as I entered the kitchen, as if saluting a returning hero.

I did not speak, but busied myself making my first cup of instant-brewed coffee. I had one of those fancy one-cup-at-a-time coffeemakers that was really expensive, with the little tubs of individual coffee that cost ten times as much as my cup of standard grocery store instant. (The fancy machine had been a gift from my agent, when literary fortunes were apparently much better than they are these days.)

Ava remained remarkably poised and patient, sipping little bated-breath sips as I bustled around. Only when I sat in the chair opposite her did she find her voice.

"So . . ." she said, drawing out her words to an almost leer, "how was it? Or should I say, how was he?"

I could have risen to her bait. I knew what she meant, what she implied. And I know that she liked to grab my dainty, prim, golden chain and give it a hard yank now and again, just to see what I would do.

Nothing, apparently, this morning.

"I had a nice time," I replied. "Brian was very nice. And Ki's was very nice."

I watched as Ava's eyes narrowed, like a snake looking at a frightened baby bird abandoned on the ground. Only Ava's tongue wasn't forked.

Ava meant well, I think. She did like prodding and poking. Maybe it made her feel better about herself in some unconscious way. Maybe she needed to feel superior.

"A nice time . . . hmmm."

"I did. We had a very pleasant dinner."

I figured I could derail her train of thought.

"When he picked me up so early, I imagined that he meant to get there for the early-bird specials."

"And he didn't?"

"The waitress offered the early-bird menu, but he said he wanted to look at the 'real' one. He said that if I wanted to see what the specials were, I should feel free to."

"Really?"

"You sound surprised," I replied.

"I am, sort of. I mean, he's buddies with Dr. Tom, and Dr. Tom can be the world's biggest cheapskate at times. Like when he asks for two senior citizen tickets at the movies. I may be older, but I am not that old."

"Really? He does that?"

"He says that what sixteen-year-old ticket seller is going to challenge him on it?"

Rufus rolled over in his cage, snorting twice, rustling and readjusting himself on his stack of cushions. Every day, at least once, I would have to get down on all fours and square up the stack of mattress layers in his cage, so he wouldn't have to endure a thick roll of foam rubber under his rib cage. He would grow immediately nervous when I did this, and try and force his way back into the cage—as if he was trying to prevent me from entering his den.

"And so the date went well? No spinach stuck in your teeth for the entire evening?"

"Not that I noticed."

And in order to circumnavigate any more of Ava's inquiries into the exact nature of the evening, I went ahead and gave her a five-minute synopsis of the date.

Here's my recap: we sat for awhile. He had a glass of wine. I stuck with coffee. We chatted about the weather and the Bears' chances this season (which were not so good; I still listened to the news, so I could be conversant as to their status, on a superficial level), the last movie we saw, the last book we read—and he charmed me by saying he went to the Lombard library and checked out one of my early books. It was an Amish story, and he said he read it only at home so no one would see him reading a romance book. He said the first couple of chapters were quite good.

I would have been happy if the evening had stopped at that compliment. Being complimented was heady stuff. Almost better that having people feel sympathy for you.

And then we ordered. He had the small steak and I had the chicken. (I was being cautiously frugal.) We both agreed that our meals tasted quite good. And they did, really. They make fabulous roasted chicken at Ki's.

He had a second glass of wine after dinner. We both passed on dessert. I had more coffee. He told some funny stories about working with doctors and having to watch actual operations, to see how the stents get placed.

I told Ava that I appreciated his sensibilities. Most men (and maybe this is unfair) would relish the opportunity to make the stories horridly graphic with blood and spurting veins and arteries. But Brian did nothing of the sort. He kept the blood aspect to a mere trace—we were at dinner, after all.

"And you know what?" I asked Ava.

"What?"

"He actually let me talk. He asked me about writing and I talked for a long time—and he listened. Maybe he only acted interested, but if he did, he did a wonderful job of faking it."

"Really? He listened? And there's actually a man who does the faking? Unheard of."

"Ava, you can be terrible at times," I said, trying not to sound like a prudish scold, but letting her know that I sort of mostly disapproved. "He did listen. And asked . . . like follow-up questions and everything. I liked having someone to talk with—and not simply be talked at."

Ava took a deep breath.

"Do you mind if I date him as well? He sounds like . . . like a nice guy."

I smiled, knowing that I had an edge here somehow.

"No," I replied. "You already have one. And that's enough."

8

The following day, Sunday, as cold as it had been all year, dawned with a wind that yowled across the open field behind my house. Winter robbed nearly everything of its color; only browns and grays remained in the muted sunlight, struggling to knife through a thick stratum of bleak clouds, the color of old oatmeal. I nearly froze by the time Rufus and I returned home from our morning walk. There had been no time to talk. The previous night had not been much better. When the wind howled, Rufus often remained mute. Maybe he found it hard to talk over the noise of the wind and weather.

He had his returning-home snacks. I realized I was wide awake and, after seeing that it was only 7:00, I decided to shower, dress, and go to the early service at church. Most of our old friends went to the middle service. Attendance at the first service ran on the sparse side. I could sneak in late and sneak out early and not run into anyone I knew.

I'm not sure why I decided to go that particular morning.

Maybe my date got me thinking. Maybe things were changing in my life. Maybe I wanted . . . I don't know. Maybe I wanted some sort of sign, some sort of divine affirmation.

Where better to get a sign than at a church? Or a mountain-top? We're in Illinois, remember? There are no mountains in Illinois.

I parked down the street, being charitable to those who would arrive later, and the wind, now stronger, whipped and clawed as I clutched my too-thin-for-this-weather coat around my throat. I must have been a sight when I entered, my hair streaming in all directions, my face red, my eyes watering.

I prayed that I would not see anyone that I knew.

I did not. Attendance, by my estimation, stood even lower than I expected, because of the harsh weather most likely. My church's, or any church's, numbers suffer in the cold and nasty conditions.

I took a bulletin and sat in the back, on the right side (not my usual spot, but out of the way). Our church . . . my church . . . or this church, I guess, leaned right and backward when it came to style. Hymns, yes, we still sang them—with a pipe organ as well. Bulletins, yes, we still used them—instead of a projection screen or a Facebook update, or whatever the hip churches are doing these days.

Tweeting, maybe.

I could never do that—Tweet—simply because it sounded stupid to me. Not communicating, but the word itself. Tweeting. Please. It is what birds do.

The first two hymns sounded reedy and fragile as the congregation struggled to match the volume of the organ, whose organist appeared oblivious to the overpowering pipes.

The pastor today, the one delivering the sermon, was not the senior pastor. I was momentarily displeased because I liked the senior pastor's messages. This new guy—well, I couldn't be sure. And then I thought that I may never have heard him before. He was newish, and I had not been attending that regularly in recent months . . . or years, I guess.

Maybe he would surprise me. Maybe this specific conflu-ence of times and events and temperatures and all the other auguries would fall into place in a perfect alignment to bring his message to a needy ear.

Wasn't that what I expected? Wasn't I looking for a sign?

I was. I have been heeding the words of a fifteen-pound dog for the last few months. I wanted to hear from a man of God. Not that the dog of God was leading me astray, but maybe I needed more.

And just how ludicrous do I sound? I am eternally grateful that my thoughts do not become visible, in little cartoon bal-loons over my head.

The pastor strode to the pulpit. He had a lean and hungry look about him, which I did not immediately embrace. I sus-pect that I never immediately warm to anyone who is whippet thin and looks as if he has run twelve miles a day—before breakfast.

He was that sort of person.

Isn't it telling about the frailty of humans that I have, within seconds, dismissed this fellow human being as being cold and inconsiderate? I hope that other people don't do that to me.

He began to speak.

He read a long passage from the book of Job.

And my heart sank.

If you haven't read it, that part of the Bible talks about Job, a rich man who had everything he could possibly want, and how he lost everything—or rather, had it taken away from him.

"Suffering makes us better." I think that's an accurate quote from the skinny pastor. He went on to read: "'The LORD gave me what I had, and the LORD has taken it away. Praise the name of the LORD!' In all of this, Job did not sin by blaming God."

He went on, but after only a few moments, I stopped listening. Not because I chose to, but because I grew angry, the weepy kind of angry that stops all cogent thought.

I fought back tears as well as attempted to quell the anger ascending in me like a helium balloon. The tears acted as ballast, I guess.

I couldn't hear, because of the internal bedlam in my head.

Yes, everything I had belonged to God. And maybe he had the right to take it away.

But why? Why would he do that? Was I not good enough for God that he had to "refine" me in some horrible fire? And after he snatched from me the only two people who were blameless in my life, he wants me to thank him for it?

Well, he has another thing coming if he thinks that will happen. Because it won't. Not now. Not ever. There is no good that can come out of my husband and son being torn apart by a drunk driver and a semi-truck full of blasted, stupid, unnecessary flat-screen televisions from China. There is no good in that. They're gone, and I am here all alone.

I came as close to swearing in church as I ever had in my life.

There is nothing that will ever change that in my life.

I tried to use a tissue and stanch the tears. I was not too successful.

"Job did not sin by blaming God."

And that's it then? That's the sign? That I've been sinning for the past three years? That I haven't been as darn magnanimous and accepting as a "good" Christian should be, smiling bravely in spite of my loss? Well, God, if that's what you wanted to tell me, then message received.

I couldn't stay. I just couldn't.

And I had used angry, almost-swear words inside a church, if only in my head, though that would be marked against me as a sin, too, I imagine. I would have sworn—a lot—if I was a person who used profanity. I wasn't, and wished that I could have been, for just this moment.

I pretended to cough, stood up, and slipped out the back doors, not looking left or right, not hearing anyone call to me, pulling on my jacket as I almost stumbled down the stairs and to the sidewalk, almost running to my car, slamming the door harder than I have ever slammed a door, then pounding on the wheel a few times.

I wiped my face with the back of my hand, inserted the key in the ignition, started the engine, and wondered if I should drive through my tears and ire—though waiting until they passed seemed to be too much pain to endure motionless.

I didn't tell Rufus anything about church that day. When I returned home, he did stare at me for a long moment, as if he had noticed my red eyes. I'm not sure I had ever cried in front of Rufus before—I don't think so—but I imagined that he could not have truly understood the emotion or the reaction.

Dogs don't cry, do they?

Not according to Wikipedia, they don't. They lack the proper moral absolutes for understanding guilt and shame and remorse and unhappiness, the article said, so they have no reason to cry.

I guess that's correct. An animal can easily kill another animal and eat it—for survival—without even a momentary hesitation. I don't think I could do that. Not personally—though I suppose I did pay other people to do that for me.

My usual Sunday afternoon routine entailed reading the newspaper online, watching whatever old movie was featured on Turner Classic Movies, and napping on the sofa in the sunroom, under the thickness of a throw and blanket, with Rufus stationed at the top of the sofa, guarding against roaming packs of hooligan squirrels.

Today, I did none of that. I had two cups of strong coffee for lunch. I went downstairs into the basement, considered bringing up a box or two of Christmas decorations, and then decided against it (too early), went upstairs, opened the linen closet with the idea of reorganizing its haphazard contents, but didn't (too much work for a Sunday), then came back into the kitchen, made another cup of coffee, and sat in the uphol-stered chair, staring outside, over the deck, to the gray sky and bare trees.

It had not proved to be a productive day, by any stretch of the imagination.

The sermon stuck in my craw, being turned this way and that, my inner self trying to come to grips with it and not suc-ceeding in the least.

I know what the man said made theological sense and con-tained theological import—but to me, that was all it had.

I mentioned earlier that I wasn't sure if I still believed or not.

That's why. This is why.

I couldn't get it to make sense.

I just couldn't.

If Jacob had died of cancer or some horrible, agonizing disease—that I could have lived with, horrendous as it might have been. I could have held him and said good-bye. I could have shared in his pain. Even my son—I could have done that for him.

But there were no good-byes. We had no last hugs. The door to their lives had been slammed in my face.

Two closed coffins—that is all there ever was. Closed. Never to be opened. I had no chance at a good-bye. I had to suffer all alone. No one could understand or share that pain. No one. How do you say farewell to a wooden box?

If, in order to be a Christian in good standing, I have to accept, with grace and joy and long-suffering, that pain, then I am turning in my membership badge. I can't live under those rules. I can't be a member of a club that asks for too much sacrifice.

Yes, I am very aware that we live in a broken world and that believers and nonbelievers will suffer—but only the believers are told that they have to have joy in the midst of it. The non-believers can revel in their unhappiness and no one thinks they are weak or lack faith. They are deemed normal. Not me. Not as a believer. I need to put on a cheerful face in the midst of a crumbing, breaking heart. I can't do that anymore. I can't.

So . . . I spent the day, talking to myself and carrying on a very long, heated argument between myself and . . . I don't know . . . that new guy at church—the one with the lean and hungry look.

I ate two blueberry muffins at 4:00, although Rufus ate prob-ably a quarter of one of them. I know chocolate chips are bad for dogs, but I am pretty sure blueberries are okay. They have antioxidants in them, right? And he loves blueberry muffins, licking the floor to make sure every last crumb is devoured.

That was going to be my dinner. Being tied in angry knots left little room for an appetite to develop. And if I lost a pound or two, all the better.

Since I'm dating again, apparently.

And I didn't tell Rufus any of this, not in one of my out-loud monologues to the dog during the day, when I'm not sure he really paid attention to me anyhow. But I didn't tell him any of this because . . . well . . . I was pretty sure he wouldn't really understand. And I didn't want that to happen. And what would happen if he told God all about it. I didn't want that either. What God doesn't know won't hurt him.

That night, the air colder than it had been all fall and early winter, seemed even colder. I checked The Weather Channel before leaving on our walk—31 degrees. It felt icy. I didn't pay attention to the relative humidity—I don't think I really understand the term—but it did feel damp outside and that dampness seemed to have more penetrating power than just the cold.

I promised myself I would look it up on Wikipedia to find out the reason for it. Yes, I know you can't trust Wikipedia. When my son was alive, and in kindergarten, the teachers in the upper grades at grammar school forbade students from ever using Wikipedia as a source for any of their school assignments. What got me is that they would much rather trust a book as a solid, trustworthy source for a second-grade research paper on butterflies. But you have to remember this—I write books (or at least wrote books). I sounded very trustworthy and reliable as I described the cultural mores of the Amish community. I had never included a known falsehood in my books—but I am far from being an Amish scholar. All this to say, for my purposes, Wikipedia always worked fine.

Rufus hunkered down as we turned into the wind on Glencoe. A large open field lay to the south leaving nothing to impede the wind, as it bit and gnashed at us as we tucked into it that night. We both hurried to make the turn, to find some protection from the trees along the private, NO TRESPASSING pond area.

I was puffing when we got there.

"Cold," I said aloud.

"It is. I might need a jacket," Rufus said, "like the one Rusty wears."

Rusty was the schnauzer that might have been Rufus's legitimate cousin—the one from the same breeder. Rufus had scoffed at the idea of wearing a jacket like Rusty's—but he had snorted when it was September and 50 degrees. With the wind and the damp, opinions are easily swayed.

"I could get you one, if you want," I replied.

"Okay."

We walked a ways, and I tossed him a treat, which he chewed happily.

"Rufus," I said, "is my dating Brian okay? Is it okay for me to . . . want to see him again? Is it okay to want to be with him?"

I know. I know. It's crazy doing this. But if I asked any of my female friends or family—well, here's what would happen: Ava would claim that I need to be with a man—in more ways than one. Beth would want to know if he's a church-going man. Bernice would not want to even hear the question. Others would caution about going too fast, or too slow, or at all. Confusing, right? Rufus is the only clear, trustworthy voice I have right now. As they say, he doesn't have a horse in this race.

"Sure," he said quickly, as if he had been considering this question for a while before I asked it. "But I would like to meet him."

"Okay," I responded.

I waited until we got to the end of Anthony Street before I spoke again.

"Does God want me to be happy?" I asked, louder than I wanted, but I wanted the words to be heard over the wind rushing up Western Avenue.

Rufus responded quickly this evening.

"Being with a man is what will make you happy?"

I waited a half a block.

"I don't like being alone."

"I'm with you," Rufus said. And after another moment, he added, "And God is with you, right? I mean, you have asked him about it, right?"

I don't know why, but I immediately grew angry.

"Yeah, right," I snapped back. "I asked. But Brian is someone I can actually hold in my arms. I can actually feel him as he holds me back."

"And that's what you want?"

"Yes," I snapped quickly. "That is what I want."

I wondered what Rufus knew about God, really. He sort of knew what the Bible was—this book-thing that people look at. But he could not read—I felt pretty certain of that. So how could he know so much about God and what he stands for?

I guess I figured it out like this: when I pet Rufus on the head, in a kind, gentle way, more than just touch is communicated. Those gentle strokes must tell him that I care for him, that I will try my best to provide for him, that I will keep him from harm. None of that had been said in words—but instead, communicated through our shared touch. He knew exactly what it all meant.

Maybe good dog Rufus found the same sort of information emanating from God in the same way—nonverbal, but absolutely concrete and real. Maybe God reached down, somehow, and touched Rufus and from that divine touch, the good dog just *knew* God and what he was all about. Maybe that knowledge was all coded into his DNA and instinct.

He knew God because God knows him.

Or maybe I'm just a bit loony these days.

Both could be true just as easily as not.

9

Three weeks before Christmas, Ava and the podiatrist, and Brian and me. How weird is that? A double date.

Well, we did it. Dinner at one of the nicer restaurants in town—a faux French place. Actually, if I'm being uncritical, and I should be, it wasn't faux at all. I think one of the chefs had actually come from France. That's enough to lend an aura of European sophistication to a restaurant in a strip mall. And there's the rub.

The food was superb. The ambiance—well, they tried. My opinion that if you try to re-create some other locale, like a French bistro in DuPage County, then you will succeed in fooling no one at all. People will know that you bought the big French posters and other decorative pieces at Pier One down on Butterfield Road. It's the pretending I can't embrace. Jacob and I went to Epcot in Florida the year before John was born. At the end of the grand loop through a lot of "countries," I came away oddly dispirited. We weren't in Italy or France, or even Canada—we were sweating through an abnormally hot August in Orlando. And while the pasta tasted good at the Italian restaurant in Italy-land, and the waiters (at least ours) actually came from Italy, I still wasn't in Italy—where I wanted to be. "Don't fake it," I said at the time, "just be Disneyworld and try not to put a disguise on it."

I should not depart from my story for these tirades. I am sure you're much more interested in my evening with Dr. Tom et al. than you are of my anti-faux rants.

We had a nice time. The food, as I mentioned, was great. Anything loaded with butter and wine has to be good. And Dr. Tom, whom I had met a few times before, was charming and self-deprecating. I don't think he considered himself a real doctor either.

"But somebody has to do it," he said, "and it pays a lot better than selling shoes."

Brian acted kind and considerate that evening as well, as he had been on our previous few dates.

I should mention that Rufus had gotten to meet him. On our second real date, Brian stopped at the house to pick me up and I asked him to come in while I got my coat from upstairs. Rufus had gone ballistic again at the doorbell. He had calmed down when I greeted Brian with an air hug and had stepped back a few paces to stare at this welcomed stranger.

"I'll be right down," I said as I hurried up the stairs. "Rufus, no more barking. Brian is a friend, okay?"

Rufus turned to look at me, as if to say that I should not be leaving him with a complete stranger like this. Who knows what the man might try to do to a defenseless little schnauzer?

If Brian was put off by a standoffish dog with an attitude, he did not show it. He knelt down and extended his hand, palm open, to the dog. Rufus, in turn, waited a long moment (I could see this from the darkened upstairs landing) then took a very tentative step forward and sniffed Brian's open hand. Brian did not move quickly, and spoke to Rufus in a low, calm voice, and brought up his hand to the top of Rufus's head, gently petting his head. The dog warmed a degree and took another step closer, sniffing and staring intently.

By then, I had my coat and came down the stairs.

"My, don't you look nice tonight," Brian said. He turned to face Rufus. "Doesn't she look nice tonight? I bet if you could talk you would say just that, right?"

For a moment, I grew terrified that Rufus might do exactly that: start to talk. He did not—and obeyed his speech-is-for-outside-only rule.

Later that night, after Brian had brought me home and left, following an air hug at the door, I changed into warmer clothes and Rufus and I went for our walk.

"Did you like him?" I asked.

"Who?" Rufus replied.

I could have easily gotten semi-infuriated at his passive-aggressiveness, but realized that Rufus may indeed not have known whom I referred to.

"Brian. The man who came over earlier. You sniffed him."

"Oh. Him. He seemed nice."

That's it? He seemed nice? That's all the divinely inspired discernment I am going to get?

I waited a half a block until I had to ask a follow-up question.

"But did you like him? Do you think he was a nice man? I mean, do you approve and all that?"

Rufus snorked a couple of times, I guess in an attempt to clear his snout.

"I don't know. He seemed nice. He had a nice voice. Do all men's voices sound that low?"

"Most, I guess. Men's voices are deeper, lower than women. It's the way we're made. Like the big black dog next door. He has a lower bark than you."

"He does? I thought my bark was . . . deep too."

Maybe dogs are like people as well—where our own voices sound so much different in a recording than they do in our own heads.

"It's deep. Maybe he's just louder," I replied, thinking that Rufus might be sensitive to my unintended slight.

"Well, that man seems fine."

"So he's not God's choice for me?"

"I don't know. If you like him . . . But to be honest, I don't think God plans it so there is only one person that a human has to find in order to be happy."

"Really? I don't have to find the only person alive who might be my soul mate?"

Rufus stopped, chewed on his front paw for a moment, then continued.

"I don't know what 'soul mate' is, but I think there is more than one person for every person. I'm pretty sure, anyhow."

I kept quiet for the rest of the walk, trying to digest his take on dating predestination.

At the end of our date, at the end of the meal, thanks were issued all around, and Brian ran off to get his car.

Ava grabbed my arm and whispered into my ear, "Be careful, Mary," she said. I stepped back, trying to look peeved or shocked, or amused, or something. Something worthy of a strait-laced aunt whose purity and moral integrity had just been maligned in a backhanded way.

I waved off her comment.

"I'm fine."

Brian hurried around the car and opened the door for me. There was more waving and thank-yous in the cold night air.

Brian drove carefully. He walked me to my door. Before I could say anything, he volunteered, "I can't come in tonight, Mary. I have a super-early stent surgery tomorrow that I have to attend."

"That's okay," I said. "I'll give you a rain check."

That's when he took me in his arms and held me close, and I felt his face coming close to mine, and I tilted my head just so, like I had done a million times with Jacob (why did his name come up just now?). Brian tilted his head and then I felt his lips on mine and it wasn't unpleasant at all. Quite the opposite. It felt very nice, and I sensed that small electrical rush from the first touch. I found myself feeling the texture of his lips and the pressure—not pushy, but not fish-lipped either—and then I felt myself yielding my body into his, leaning toward him, him leaning into me, our winter coats muffling what might have been a more sensuous engagement, his arms and hands moving up my back and mine pulling him closer.

He was the one who backed away first.

It must have been the wine.

"Thank you for a really lovely evening," he whispered to me, his lips still only inches away from mine.

"No," I replied, "thank you."

And then he kissed me again—or did I kiss him?—quicker, a short press of lip to lip, and another one right afterward, like we had been kissing each other for years.

It felt really, really good.

"Unlock your door," he said softly. "I can't leave until you're inside."

He was quite the gentleman.

I did as he requested, all the while Rufus scrabbled at the other side of the door, hearing us on the front step, not barking, since he heard my voice.

I stepped inside. Brian bowed, not stupidly nor theatrically, but a short little quarter bow, as if he was placing a coda on this first evening between the two of us. The first real shared intimacy. I watched him as he got into his car, backed out of the driveway, and flashed his headlights as a second farewell. It was nice of him to consider the neighbors that way.

I watched him drive off. Rufus waited for me as I turned. I know the dog needed to go out—but did he have to stare at me that way?

—⚬⚬⚬—

I didn't talk to Rufus anymore about Brian during our walk—and beyond. I anticipated what he would say in that regard—that if Brian made me happy, it was okay. Neither did Rufus ask if Brian . . . believed—in God and all that. In Rufus's world, everyone believed. I think they did anyhow. I never really asked him if all dogs believe. Maybe there are good dogs and bad dogs. Good dogs believe. Bad dogs don't believe. I should ask him about that. With good dogs, wouldn't they have to recognize their creation—and by default, their creator? People, well, they are a different breed. When things are communicated in shorthand, the possibility of miscommunication is probable and high. I mean . . . I believe, I guess. Yes, there is a God, a divine God who has put the universe in action, and who keeps it there. But he also can be a cruel God—take a look at my life if you want further proof. So I believe, in God, in a manner of speaking, but perhaps I am not what others might call a true believer. At least not now. Maybe I had been before, but not now. I couldn't say what might happen in the future. I mean, who knows what tomorrow will bring—in terms of people or opportunities or woe. Right now God and I are not speaking. Sometimes those "I'm not talking to you because I'm mad" estrangements become permanent. I couldn't speak for God, but that's how I felt.

And Brian might believe. He might be a believer—just like Jacob had been a believer. I don't know. We had not spoken about spiritual matters at all (although he had said something about "karma" during our first meeting). He was a kind man, and a gentleman, and despite his wearing sneakers too often, I found myself beginning to care for him.

Was God in this situation, in this unfolding, as it were? Rufus said he couldn't be sure. He once said he can't speak for God—but he was probably interested in what happened in our lives. He had said that there is more than one person out there who we can connect with on that deeper, more intimate level. So, if God didn't pull the strings, then he allowed me to muddle my own way through my own life. I think I already knew that.

And I had muddled onto Brian and, to be honest, it began to feel normal and good.

Instead of all that personal and intimate stuff, Rufus and I talked instead about vacations.

—⚬⚬⚬—

I had not been on vacation since . . . since the accident.

I have to stop that—tying every event backward to the date and time of the accident. It made me sad, reminded me of my loss, and did not allow me to move forward, to get on with my life. It was like an anchor, bearing both the good and bad aspects of being anchored—tied firmly to one place, and being held down and back from any forward movement.

But I hadn't been anywhere fun since that horrible day—not that I felt like going anywhere fun by myself. I had continued to make visits to my mother, twice a year, but those could not be remotely considered vacations. I drove from Chicago to western Pennsylvania, spent a night or two at the Wingate Hotel in Latrobe, visited my mother twice a day when I was there, then drove back, in a sour, picklish mood, eight hours alone in my car, filled with the echoes of recriminations and guilt.

A vacation? Please.

I had mentioned to Rufus some weeks earlier that Jacob had always promised me we would live on the ocean at some point during our life together. He never said when—just that we would. He loved the ocean, despite the fact that he spent very little time at the ocean. But those few times, he decided that he had been meant to walk in the salt air every day, with the roll and roil of the waves always a sound in his ears.

We had vacationed one week on Nantucket Island, with most of our time spent on the bay side of the island, yet it was enough to leave him permanently intoxicated by the proximity to saltwater. We had spent a week in Florida, on the water, near Vero Beach. Jacob would have chosen to spend every vacation on the coast.

I had mentioned once to Rufus when we walked past the pond that the ocean was so much bigger than the pond that you couldn't see to the end of it. I said that Jacob loved to walk in the sand at dusk, hearing the wind among the dune grass, and the salt spray stirring into the evening breeze. Rufus took that all in—but I could not be sure if the poetry of the words escaped him, or if their true meanings were not fully recognized by his canine abilities of interpretation.

I did mention to Rufus that night that I had been thinking of going to the beach this spring or summer.

Rufus thought it was a good idea.

Then I told him that I would either have to leave him at a kennel, or take him with me in the car for two days' worth of driving.

He had remained silent for the rest of that evening's walk. He did not like riding in the car, unlike most every other dog in the universe, and after I told him what a kennel experience was, he seemed to furrow his dog brow, as if deep in thought.

And tonight he asked about my plans for this spring.

"If I go to a kennel," he asked, "do I get to pick the dog I stay next to?"

"I don't think so. I think the kennel people put you where they want to."

He remained silent for a long time.

"I don't think I would like that," he finally replied. "What happens if that big, knuckleheaded black dog that lives in the house next to us winds up in the crate right beside me?"

I have to stop speaking ill of the big, stupid dog next door. Rufus is starting to be influenced by my poor evaluation of the beast, and I shouldn't force such bad attitudes on my innocent dog.

"How long do I have to stay in the car if I go with you?"

"It would take us two days. Each day, eight hours in the car."

We walked nearly a block.

"Could we fly there? I see those short stories on the television that say that it is very simple to fly on planes. And fast too. They feed you on airplanes, don't they?"

I did not want to get into a detailed denouncement of the current state of American air travel.

"They do, but, Rufus, if we fly, you'll have to stay in a cage, and be in the cargo hold of the plane—underneath the passengers, in the dark and cold. It is very noisy there."

That was even worse than being in a car.

"Oh."

We were in the driveway.

"I'll have to think about this some more," he said. "I may not like the ocean, after all."

Rufus knew a lot about a lot of things. From the barest sniff he could determine if the scent came from a mouse or a squirrel or a raccoon or a chipmunk, or another dog. And he was really good at the dog scent thing. He didn't know the names of all the breeds, but could describe them well enough for me to guess. And this all from a sniff. He wasn't as good with birds, but knew the difference between a big bird, like a crow, and a sparrow.

Other topics—well, he was not so smart. Things that he had not experienced—like the ocean—he didn't fully comprehend. He saw them on TV, but that's not reality to either him or me.

He claimed to know about God. But he had no direct, two-way conduit to God. He said he talked to God—he prayed. I believed that. But he did not ever speak for God. He knew enough to know that would be entirely presumptuous of him. He knew as much about God as I did. He knew there was a mystery there—as did I. He knew the basics of God and his character—as did I. He talked to God. I did not.

Rufus did not ever claim to be God's spokesman. He did claim to be a dog of God, like some people claim to be a child of God.

So I looked to him for advice. Rufus—not God.

And really now, how pathetic and, well, crazy is that? To trust a savant, a dog savant, with my life.

Pretty crazy if you must know.

But it also felt right.

I met Beth and Ava at the Good Apple Restaurant. I didn't particularly like the place, although they offered a prodigious amount of food for a very reasonable price. Each plate, heaping with eggs or fries, or whatever, besides offering too many calories, presented a dilemma: having too much food to eat at one sitting, meant taking the food home that would wind up in my food purgatory (remember?), or splitting an entrée with a friend, which smacked of weirdness. A husband or a parent could split a meal, perhaps, but not a friend.

So what do you do?

Beth loved the place; Ava was ambivalent.

We sat in a booth by the window and watched the large snowflakes swirl down. It was not yet frigid, just cold, and the snow fell in a most pleasant way, not serious; there would be no noticeable accumulation to worry nervous drivers—like me. That is what the weatherman said this morning.

Both Beth and Ava knew each other because of me—they had been introduced years ago. Beth, I am sure, saw Ava as an evangelistic and/or mission project—that if she could come up with just the right words or situation, Ava would repent and turn back to God.

I don't think Ava was ever "with" God, so walking away from him, or back toward him did not seem part of the equation. Beth always brought her Bible when we had lunch together, the three of us, just in case.

Ava liked to shock Beth.

Talking about sex became her de facto method of shocking Beth, and the best way to fluster her and make her blush. Just the mention of sex outside marriage was enough, which Ava could do because of her "relations" with Dr. Tom. But what moved sex beyond the pale, to Beth, I am sure, was that Ava told tales in greater detail than required, and with a greater emphasis on her satisfaction. Beth would blush bright red at some of Ava's escapades. Well, to be honest, so would I, but I suspect that I felt a little more inured from shock than Beth, a little less capable of being embarrassed by anything my worldly friend wound up doing with her podiatrist. She lived her own life, after all, and my morality did not have to be her morality for us to be friends.

I guess. I know it's not good theology, but at times I grew too tired to recast my worldview.

I ordered a half of a chicken salad sandwich and soup, and figured that I probably couldn't even finish that. I have been eating less recently. I would like to lose a few pounds before the holidays. Maybe Brian is also part of that desire. Not that I'm going to let him see the end result of any weight loss on my part. Well, I guess he could tell if my clothes fit better and all that—but nothing more than that, and I'm sure you know what I mean.

Ava ordered a hamburger and fries and soup and a salad. She claimed that Dr. Tom liked women "with a little meat on their bones." I hated Ava for having to consciously eat more to add a pound or two to her already too-skinny frame. I could accomplish the same weight gain by simply thinking about a milkshake.

Beth ordered a bowl of soup and a grilled cheese sandwich—"hold the fries, please."

We all sort of settled into the booth, relaxed, leaned back, drank coffee (decaf for Beth, of course) and tried to empty the coffee mugs before one of the waitresses sloshed more coffee on top of a mixture that had been sweetened and milked to perfection. It was hard to keep them away from your cup at the Good Apple.

"So, Mary, does Beth know all about your new beau?" Ava asked, not with obvious nefarious intentions—well, maybe just a little.

I had told her about Brian, a little about him, rather than have her hear it from her mother, who had talked to my mother, or the keen-eyed Lena at Bible study. None of that would do, so I had told her straight out that I had seen Brian a few times, that he was nice, and that I don't think I was actually dating him, just seeing him as a friend.

Beth took the news without visible alarm, or even arched eyebrows, but she had looked as if she had been expecting such news for some time. She reacted like you would when a parent goes into hospice—that it's just a matter of time before the inevitable occurs—so you're not really surprised, just taken a little bit aback by the timing of it all.

"I do," Beth answered, nibbling on a bialy. She may not order much food, but she also made good use of the free bread basket. "I think it is fine. It has been some time, you know—a respectable amount of distance and time. Dating a nice man is not inappropriate at all. It is nice to have a man to talk to."

It was interesting to watch my two friends talk about me as if I had just happened to slip away to the restroom, or had been kidnapped by Australian terrorists. Maybe I could learn something. (Please, I am not disparaging Australia. It was the first country that came to mind. It could easily have been Armenia. Now I'm stuck wondering what Australian terrorists might look like. Would they carry boomerangs? Or didgeridoos, like Scots marching into battle with bagpipes?)

"I know for sure that Mary needs a man to do more than just talk . . . if you know what I mean," said Ava.

I am sure Beth knew what Ava meant and didn't like her implication one bit.

And I know that I have, up to this point, been just as adamant about abstention and morality as anyone else when it came to men and dating and sex. Up until Brian, I had no reference point. In the linear path of my life, at first there had been no one, and then there had been Jacob, and now there was no one again. I definitely liked the Jacob part of my life the best, but he was gone. And now I had Brian, sort of. And now temptation entered my life—again. Before, when it was Jacob and me, temptation existed, but I did not know what I was avoiding. Jacob knew a bit more than I did, but had never risked being drummed out of the church or anything. But now I know. I am aware. I knew full well what was missing from my life. I keenly felt the absence of being close to a man . . . in more ways than one. Now it became harder. Now the temptation loomed, more real, and visceral, and, well, alluring and tempting.

I remained steadfast. I told myself I would remain steadfast. I told others that I was steadfast. But . . . maybe I wasn't so steadfast. Or maybe the gates were weakening. Maybe the flesh was becoming more willing.

I was fascinated to see how the discussion before my two friends would end up.

"A woman doesn't need that . . . like a man needs that," Beth replied, crossing her arms lightly.

Ava appeared to be in pain.

"That's just not true. There's the same desires and needs for both. It is for me—as you well know. And our Mary is not getting any younger."

"So? And since she's a little older now, that means that she should have more self-control, more power to resist things that she shouldn't do. And she knows to avoid putting herself into situations where she might be too tempted."

Ava bit into her hamburger, the size of a small house pet, and chewed with great gusto.

"And how is that accomplished? Does our poor, sex-deprived Mary join a monastery?"

"You mean a convent," Beth inserted.

"Whatever. But she's a normal woman. With normal desires. A woman needs to be with a man. For completion. For satisfaction."

Beth chewed at her grilled cheese like a rabbit with a carrot, nibbling at it as if it were going to be pulled from her hands by some unseen force.

"Perhaps. But Mary knows that would be wrong. Outside of marriage, all that is wrong."

Ava slashed a fry through a large puddle of ketchup and inserted the entire piece into her mouth.

"So, tell me, how far can she go without risking thunder and lightning from above?"

Beth almost wandered into the trap, but at the last moment, backed away from providing a list of what I could and could not do with a man. At least in my unmarried state. I wish she hadn't stopped. I would have liked to learn what my parameters were to maintain my "good girl" status.

"That's not the point. Mary knows full well that without a wedding ring, all such . . . shenanigans are off limits to her."

Yes, she used the word *shenanigans*. I never once considered any of "that sort of thing" as shenanigans. Maybe it depended on the way "those things" were done. That I had not considered. I know that I never once pictured Beth and her husband, Todd, as engaging in shenanigans. And I sure did not want to start today.

Ava chewed another large bit of her hamburger, which was rare, with raw onions.

Perhaps the red meat infusion caused it. Perhaps a nearly full stomach had mellowed her. Ava softened, at least a bit, and pulled back from the confrontation.

"Okay. Mary knows what's good and bad."

Beth's face showed a small smile of triumph.

"But if she knows what's good for her, she'll be bad. It does the heart well to exercise that way every once in a while."

Beth's smile turned flat. I saw her hand reach toward the Bible in her purse, but she hesitated, and brought her hand back to her grilled cheese sandwich. I saw it in her eyes. She had no hope for Ava's soul, but would be praying, in earnest, for mine.

And perhaps she had good reason for her fervency.

Ava drove me home after our lunch. She didn't talk much, not until she pulled into my driveway.

"Mary, I know you're a good person."

"A good little girl?" I asked.

"You know what I mean."

I did. I was a good person. I followed the rules. The rest of the world didn't, for sure, but I stuck with the rules.

"I just think you deserve some happiness . . . after everything that's happened in your life. I just think it's time to loosen up a little. Have some fun with Brian. He seems like he would be really kind and gentle and considerate. There aren't many men who I could say that about."

I couldn't be sure how she expected me to respond. I guess I didn't know how I thought I should respond. So I just listened.

"You've suffered a lot these last few years. You've lost so much. You've been alone. You deserve some fun. You deserve to have a good time. Relax, Mary. Have a good time with Brian. You'll be amazed at how much better you'll feel once you get over that hurdle."

She looked like she might be close to tears, and she reached over and gave me a hug.

"Have a good time, Mary. Of all the people I know, you most deserve to be happy again."

Again, how do I respond to that? Or should I even try?

I didn't. I waved as she backed out of the driveway.

I looked up to the sky. A thin wind knifed in from the west—not bitter, but still cold.

I shuddered.

It felt a lot like snow.

And all of a sudden I have become a shaman and sooth-sayer, predicting the snows based on my feelings.

It made me happy to think that, and I went in and gave Rufus an extra serving of dog biscuits.

"So, Rufus, what I am supposed to do? I really liked kissing him. I never thought I would. I mean . . . I thought that having been married to Jacob would prevent me from ever feeling . . . you know . . . sexual with a man, ever again. But that's not true now."

I was pretty sure that Rufus did not really understand kissing—or the reasons behind it. I tried to explain that to him a few nights ago. He understood the mechanics, but I do not think he grasped the implications that lay beneath the action.

And sex, well, he understood that—in the basic, mechanical way—but was pretty much in the dark to all the layers and levels of meaning that accompanied the physical act between humans.

And why did I talk to him about sex and kissing in the first place?

It wasn't like I was going to do anything about it. After all, I am a good girl, and despite the urgings of Ava, I intend to stay a good girl—regardless of the deep and powerful urges that have begun to sweep up and down my body, like miniature tsunamis, hormones and urges and desires, roiling along with no breakwater or dikes to stop their mad rush onto my sometimes willing, sometimes not-willing flesh.

"What do you want to do with him?" Rufus asked. He had stopped to chew out a clump of snow from his front left paw. He did not like snow all that much. I tried to keep his paws closely trimmed, but to no avail. He still wound up with clumps of snow between his paw pads that I would sometimes need to remove by placing him in a few inches of warm water in the laundry tub, which he hated because then he thought I would be forced to give him a bath—despite the fact that I never did and reminded him every time.

"What people do with other people, I guess. I mean what a woman does with a man. Be with him. Hold him. Kiss him every once and while."

"I don't think dogs have the same sort of warm-up activities, do they?" Rufus asked.

"They do not."

He watched several Cubs games with me this past summer and afterward asked why the one man threw so many balls to the other man when no one was swinging that big stick. I told him it a new pitcher had to "warm up" before he started to pitch for real.

Rufus understood warming up.

"Do you think God has some say in this? Dating and all that, I mean," I asked Rufus when he finished chewing at snow on his other front paw. Some snows—wet and damp—stuck more tightly to his fur. This snow fell quickly, wet and damp. "Or do you?"

"I'm sure he does," he replied. "I don't. I don't have any dog sense about this."

"Nothing in your dog DNA or instinct that speaks to this?"

Rufus stopped a moment.

"I don't know what DNA is. Instinct I know. They talked about it on that show with the big dogs. Remember? The white ones that swim."

"You mean the polar bear show we watched?"

"Yes. The big white dogs that eat seals."

The narrator had spoken about the bear's powerful instinct for survival. We walked in silence for a moment.

"What does seal taste like? Could we get some of that?"

"I don't think we can. I don't think people are allowed to eat seals."

"But big dogs can?"

"I guess. Nature takes care of nature, Rufus."

"Oh. Okay."

Maybe I should go on my instinct as well. Maybe. Since there isn't just one special person available to me. Maybe I should muddle through this situation on my own. Maybe I should listen to my body and my heart and my head.

"Don't bother asking God about Brian on my behalf, Rufus."

"Brian? Who's that?"

Rufus had never been good with names. He called Ava Beth sometimes and vice versa.

"The man I am dating. The one who stopped at the house. With the deep voice."

"Oh, him. Was I asking God about something?"

"No, you're not," I replied. "I think I've made my own decision."

"Okay. Instinct?"

"I guess," I replied and we walked the rest of the way home without talking.

After our walk, Rufus stretched out at the corner of the bed. I had the TV on mute with the subtitles on. I disliked the incessant chatter that TV provided, but I did like the company.

I would not talk to God about Brian. Really—what would be the use? To let him snatch away someone else who I cared for? I think I would try and figure this one out on my own. I'm an adult, capable of making my own decisions with my own life.

Ava is right. I do deserve some joy and happiness . . . and excitement in my life. Some satisfaction. I lived by the rules in the past. And where did all of that get me? Pain and loss.

What could be worse than that?

A little guilt?

I could handle a little guilt. I could definitely live with a little guilt if I had more moments of pleasure and joy.

I suspect I stood at a crossroads. When the time came, I wondered what road I would find myself on.

Time would tell.

10

Two weeks before Christmas was a tricky time—for both Brian and me.

Do I buy him a Christmas gift? Will he buy me a gift? How much do we spend? Neither of us could be considered rich, with unlimited capital, but we probably both needed to do something for the other in this time of gift giving and gift receiving.

And what do I get a man whom I don't know all that well? Cologne? Seems like a pretty adolescent gift selection. A shirt? Too intimate. Some electronic gadget? Too expensive—and geeky. A book? I know he reads some, but what genre? I could give a gift card to a bookstore, but that presents two problems: one, he knows how much I spent, and two, I don't like giving gift cards. They're just like money, only a lot stupider. They have to go to the store where you bought it, and I have no idea why a piece of plastic with money on it is more personal than actual money. The gift card industry did a great job of selling a concept.

All that to say, I had no idea what to do. I seriously considered a nice, small gift book of some sort, and a tin with homemade cookies. I wasn't Martha Stewart, but I could make a good batch of chocolate chip cookies.

———⁂———

We had had dinner—at Carols—and afterward had returned to my house. Snow began to fall as we ate and snow made me a nervous driver—almost as nervous as being a passenger in a car in the snow. So this evening, I asked Brian if he wanted to come in for coffee. The snow did not seem to bother him, and he owned a large four-wheel-drive car—as big as two of my small Toyotas put together. It seemed asking a man in for coffee could be considered a symbol or a subtle request for more than just coffee . . . but we were both older, both wiser, and both a bit more removed from snickering innuendoes that the request to "come in for coffee" carried.

This time, Brian had no early operation or doctor's appointment to keep him from saying yes. As I entered the house with Brian, Rufus barking for a moment or two until I scolded him to stop, I felt something new, something not exactly electric— but I felt something. A charged atmosphere, for sure.

It was weird. I never really expected to feel that way again . . . since the accident. Rats. I said I was going to stop that. And I mean it this time. I had felt that way with Jacob—a lot. Before we got married, there were some snuggling sessions that left me jangled and frazzled for hours. And after we were married, the same thing happened. Only then I was jangled and frazzled for different reasons. Better reasons, but still . . .

And the nervy, jumpy feeling was like a warning siren being sounded well before the tornado struck. I could feel the charge in the air, a faster heartbeat, a slight dilation of the eyes, a general tightness in anticipation.

I liked the feeling. I liked being almost electrified.

I made coffee. We talked at the kitchen table. It was early.

He saw the fireplace in the family room. He asked if I had wood. I said I didn't, but I had a box of fake logs in the closet that I have had for over a year because I was too lazy to light a fire on my own, or did not want to appear to be indolent, enjoying a fire all by myself.

Brian laughed at my sweet neuroses, took two logs out, opened the flue, set the logs just so, and lit them with the long-necked lighter I kept on the fireplace mantel—just in case.

Soon enough, the logs were burning nicely, crackling like they were real logs. I poured a second cup of coffee for each of us and brought them into the living room. I turned off the lights in the kitchen. The fire filled the room with flickering, romantic light. Brian sat at the end of the sofa. He would allow me to adjust my seating to him. Did I mention that he acted the perfect gentleman?

I took a seat close to him—not on his lap or anything, but close enough. I could barely feel his leg against my leg. We were both wearing jeans, as if that offered some insulation from the electricity.

Rufus positioned himself five feet away from the fire. He looked at the flames, then at me, then back at the flames. They may have made him nervous. I don't think I've had any fires in the fireplace since Rufus became a member of the family last year.

Brian moved his arm—the one closest to me—out and around and it came to rest behind me, above me, not really touching me, but it was there, nonetheless. For a long moment, I didn't know what to do. Then I gave up thinking about it. I would enjoy myself tonight. I would experience things. I would just go with my feelings. I would just . . . let myself do what I wanted.

I leaned into him, just a little. Not much. But touching, we were, more or less.

I really liked it. My heart beat like crazy. How's that for a literate metaphor? *Like crazy.* The words, the good ones, were all locked up tight in my head, and the electricity prevented any of the smarter, fancy words from escaping.

He kissed me—a kind and gentle kiss. I expected it, and I wanted it. It felt so nice. I put my hand around his neck, offering my silent encouragement.

I felt his hand on my side, and I did not object or move, or try in some manner to avoid it. His hand remained there, on my ribcage, and I enjoyed the delicate and tentative pressure on my body—a place where no man had touched me for years now. At the moment, I felt pretty sure I knew where his hand was headed and I was pretty sure I was not going to do anything to stop him. Kissing him was just too pleasant to think of objections or reasons to slow down. Here I am, a widowed lady in her mid-forties, and I had no reason to slow down. If not now, when?

I liked his hand there on my body. I hadn't been touched there for years. My doctor, maybe, but she didn't make a habit of placing her hand flat against my side like that. I am pretty sure I would not object if Brian moved his hand farther afield on my personal geography.

Good heavens, what terribly infantile metaphors . . . or similes . . . or whatever they are.

Stopping, just for a second, and looking at myself as I sat on the sofa, next to a man I hardly knew, his hand in a more intimate place than any other man other than . . . Jacob . . . I . . . decided to just relax. I had been starved for so long—I could see that now. What harm could there be to finally get to enjoy life, to feel my heart race again—because of pleasure, not terror.

I would let him do with me what he would. Sort of.

And his hand moved, just a millimeter, and I felt fireworks. Well, maybe not fireworks just yet, but as if someone held a match closer and closer to the fuse.

Our actual fire in the fireplace sparked loudly, and I could see, even though I had nearly closed my eyes in pleasure, Rufus jump a bit, and then he turned to me, to the two of us, I guess, and stared hard. I tried not to see his eyes or watch his inscrutable expression. He stood up and ran at us, actually ran the few feet. He sort of threw himself at my leg, his front feet on my knee, his back feet bouncing up and down, like a small boy needing to go to the bathroom.

I knew what he wanted. Either a treat or to go out.

"Rufus," I hissed, not wanting to break the mood, "go away. Later."

That would often be enough to stop him. He would get back down on all fours, stare another moment, then slink away, his task unfulfilled.

But this night, he kept dancing, bobbing and weaving, and making almost inaudible "wuff" sounds, nearly prancing, his nails, which needed trimming, digging into my knee.

"Rufus," I hissed louder. "Later!"

His dance went on undiminished.

I heard Brian chuckle.

"Ignore him," I instructed Brian. "He'll get tired of it and leave us alone."

We both waited, neither of us humans moving. Just the dog moved, bouncing up and down, wuff, wuff, wuff, a breathless sort of bark.

"It's not working," Brian whispered.

"He'll stop," I insisted.

Brian moved his hand.

Don't move your hand! Please! Keep it there!

"If he has an accident, that will be worse," Brian said. I had to agree with him.

"He needs to go out." I sat up, smoothed my blouse, and watched with pleasure as Brian watched me smooth my blouse. "I'll take him to the end of the block. That should be enough."

Brian sat up straighter and looked me in the eye.

"And I should wait here, in the warm house, by the fire, waiting until you bring the dog back? No man worth his salt could agree to that. I will take him out. You stay all warm and toasty."

"No," I replied. "I couldn't impose on you like that."

He placed his fingertip on my lips, a gentle touch, turning my words into silence.

"Please. Just give me the leash. I'll be back in five minutes."

I snapped the leash in place, gave Brian a plastic bag and a few dog treats, a quick recap of instructions, and closed the door after the two of them. As the door closed, Rufus turned around and looked at me. I read his look as nervousness— after all, he stood there, waiting, with a new walking partner. Or maybe I saw something else, something more nuanced than that, a look more akin to weariness, or surrender, or divine acceptance. I was put off for a moment, trying to find an interpretation that fit the dog's appearance.

Divine acceptance? Where had that come from? Yet that is what his furry little face displayed.

I could never have been prepared for the terror I would face in ten minutes.

How could anyone be prepared?

Five minutes passed. I sat on the sofa and watched the fire, contemplating if I should add another pre-fab log to the flames. I closed my eyes and imagined Brian's hand on my side again and wondered if he would resume the position when he returned with Rufus. I wondered what he might do next and if I should rehearse my whispered response.

Good heavens, I had become a seventeen-year-old again, out on her first date.

But with a lot more knowledge than I had at seventeen.

Now seven minutes passed. Then ten. And I became worried. Did Brian lose his way in the neighborhood? I told him to go to the end of the block and come back. Obviously, Rufus had led him off that course. Maybe Rufus had become shy, or obstinate, or fussy that night. I don't know what criteria Rufus used to select a spot. He presented no discernible pattern as far as I could tell.

Perhaps Rufus got loose and ran off. If he quickly backed away from me, his leash could slip off his neck. He never did it intentionally, and when it happened, only once before, he stood there, surprised, not the least bit aware that he had broken free. He simply waited until I slipped the leash back over his head.

What would happen if Brian fell and broke his ankle? Was he carrying a cell phone? He did not always carry one, which I found charming. But he could have gotten hurt.

I got my coat and walked to the front door. The snow came down—great, fat, wet chunks of snow that sounded like a moist kiss as they landed.

Rufus would be soaked when he returned.

I squinted into the snow and looked up the street. No cars were out, the streetlights were nearly hidden in the glittery snow, the neighborhood hushed and still. Then I saw them, coming down Glencoe, from the north. I seldom went that way. Rufus might be scared from the new route.

I saw Brian wave broadly. I think he grinned. I waved back, happy now that my two men have returned safely. Then Brian bent down to Rufus.

Why would he do that?

I think he was unsnapping his leash.

"Go ahead, boy. Run back to Mary," he said, his deep voice catching and faltering through the falling flakes.

I would never do that. I had never done that. Rufus would never run off, but still . . .

Rufus did see me, and broke into what I thought was a grin. Maybe it was my humanizing the little dog. Rufus had said before that schnauzers do not grin, or could not grin, I'm not sure I remember which. I'm not sure why my head filled up with such prattle when I should be terrified instead.

Too many bad things happen when people are untethered from me.

Of course, Rufus saw me, heard me, recognized his home, and took off at a run toward me, down the block.

As he passed by the Turners' house, I saw the faintest of lights, of headlights, and I began to process a terrifying geometry of coincidences, of fate, of God's hand in the rustling and turning of the world, down to the mundane life and death of a dog, his dog, God's follower here on earth.

The car came down the hill, off Wakeman, and did not slow at the stop sign. A driver could see for the entire block in either direction, and if no one was coming—why stop? I did it myself more than once, though I usually slowed a little—a little safer that way.

The snow prevented any rumble of tire on pavement or asphalt; sounds were muted to just the hushing whisper of a car gliding over a thick, wet pack of snow. No sound, just a whispered deathly swishing hush as the car bumped onto Glencoe and continued straight down Wakeman—my street, our street—windshield wipers clacking at the snow.

The car was at the end of the block. Rufus was mid-block, on the other side of the street. Just as small animals and squirrels have no concept of a fast-moving vehicle, neither did Rufus. Maybe some dogs knew of the danger of a speeding car, but if some dogs were aware, Rufus was not. He jumped over the snow-packed curb, a swell of snow left by the snowplow's visit an hour earlier, and slid onto the road, his small black body lit by the harsh swing of the car's headlights.

Oh, God, it was happening again.

I screamed. I think I screamed. I don't know. My world began to crash before my eyes, those eyes already welling up with tears, my throat already swelling shut by grief. It was all so familiar; it was all so foreign.

Rufus had not looked. He had no reason to look. I had always kept him from harm. I had always tugged his leash tight to me when a car approached our path. I had always kept a lookout for the blister of headlights on our path, from behind, from our side.

Rufus had not looked.

Maybe he did, once, a slight turn of the head toward the danger, but he did not stop.

The driver of the car, a neighbor, a nice neighbor with children and a good job at a food brokerage house, slammed on the brakes. But that would do no good—even with the automatic braking systems now in cars. It would slow and eventually stop, moving in a straight line, but even a computer could not override the elementary laws of physics and mass and inertia and slick roads glazed with a thickness of snow.

No, nothing could stop the events about to unfold.

My hand went to my mouth as I screamed and I shut my eyes. I could not bear it.

I heard the yelp, the terrified squeal of a dog, my dog, my sweet and helpless Rufus, as the three thousand pounds of metal and rubber and plastic hulked over the poor, doomed animal.

The car slid into my mailbox with a crunch, the mailbox canting to the parkway, my neighbor jumping out of the car, shouting that he couldn't stop and he didn't see the dog until the last minute and that he's sorry and so very sorry and Brian is sliding and running toward the car and the death and the snow and me screaming and sobbing and sliding down the driveway like a woman possessed and hysterical and Brian running up to me saying he is sorry and that he didn't see the car and that he would never have done that if a car had been nearby and that he would get me another dog to replace Rufus and that I could start over with a puppy for Christmas . . .

And that's when I balled my right hand into a fist. I don't think I have ever struck anyone in my life. I grew up as an only child, so no sibling fisticuffs ever occurred. I was a nice girl and nice girls do not get into catfights at school. I did not excel at sports, so there were no competitive squabbles over a field hockey game.

No, I was nice and gentle and understanding and accepting . . . until this very moment.

Brian, now at my side, prattled on about a new dog, something white and fluffy, and I made a tight fist, so tight that later that evening, I saw little crescent slice marks, complete with half-moons of dried blood, in my palm, caused by my newly manicured nails. With that tight fist, I coiled back and threw the punch. I aimed for his jaw—just to shut him up—to prevent him from already forgetting about Rufus and moving on—but I missed. He stood taller than I thought, and my punch hit him square on the throat and he fell backward from me, maintaining his balance for a moment, then stumbled and tripped, like a pratfall in a movie, onto his backside, and then slid backward several feet.

I turned to my neighbor, who had sprung from his car, his face torn by guilt. "It's not your fault, Mike," I said. "The dog . . . Rufus . . . he ran out in front of you. I know. You couldn't stop. It's not your fault."

A wash of relief came over him, almost like an angel had forgiven him of a sin he did not know he had committed, providing absolution to an innocent man.

Perhaps I could find solace in his peace, in his forgiveness.

But maybe I couldn't. Now I had to retrieve my sweet dog and . . . plan for a burial in the hard frozen ground. I began to sob again.

I gasped for air. I saw Brian struggle to his knees, coughing and holding his throat. I hoped I hurt him.

Then, oh my Lord, and then, I heard it.

A yelp. A whine. And a rustle, swish, rustle, like a broom being dragged from under a car.

I saw his eyes first, wide and scared, but open and responsive.

Rufus was dragging himself out from under the car, on the passenger side, toward the rear. Dragging and whimpering and looking and searching for me.

I dived down into the snow and slush despite the fact that I wore new, expensive wool pants. I dived down and a trembling, greasy, wet, bedraggled dog managed to limp into my arms.

It was the single most clear, pellucid moment of joy I have ever experienced. Giving birth was different—better—and longer. That moment of joy came after ten hours of nasty labor, and the outcome entirely expected.

Being married was joyful—but again—the outcome all but assured.

This moment seemed to transcend all of that and more. I fully expected to retrieve a mangled dog carcass from under the bowels of the car.

And I didn't.

Rufus was alive—injured but alive. If he died, at least it would be in my arms. He would be held by someone who loved him, cared for him, and would mourn for him after he was gone. But Rufus did not seem like he was about to die. His body was unmangled, uncrushed. He was alive.

Mike came over beside me.

"I must have missed him. I mean—the tires—he didn't get run over. I didn't run him over. He must have slid under the car."

Brian stood up now, coughing and trying to speak. He croaked, froglike, whispery and thick. I paid no attention to him.

I unwrapped the coat from my shoulders, wrapped it around Rufus, and cradled him to me. He whimpered loudly when my hand touched his right front leg, but that was all. I saw no blood. His eyes remained clear and focused. His breathing seemed normal.

I stood up and hurried to the garage door, punched in the code and the door clattered up.

"Get your keys, Brian, and go home. I'm taking Rufus to the vet."

"Nonsense," he croaked. I think that's what he said. "I'll take you."

"No," I replied, my voice steady and clear, angular and ice sharp. "I will. You go home. Get your keys and go. Now."

He must have seen my eyes—the deadly, cold resolve in my eyes—and nodded.

"Help Mike get his car off my mailbox and go home," I said sharply, and laid poor Rufus on the front seat, bundled thick into my coat. My keys were already in the ignition. That's where I leave them. I know—it may not be the safest place, but in the last three years, I have never once misplaced my keys. So who's the foolish one now?

The car rattled to a start, Brian came out of the house with his car keys, I backed out of the driveway, and opened the window.

"You'll be okay, Mike?"

He shrugged. "I don't think I even dented my bumper. I'll come back tomorrow and try and fix your mailbox."

"Thanks," I replied, and did not look at Brian. I pressed the gas and slowly left the scene of my Christmas miracle.

The wonderful thing about living in a metropolitan area is that your choices in services were multiplied. Not only did I have a hundred vets to choose from, I also had two vet hospitals within ten miles that were open all night and offered emergency walk-in services.

Forced to drive slowly because of the snow-packed roads, I found it easy to put a hand to the face of the scared dog, trying to reassure him.

"It'll be okay," I said. "We'll be at the vet's in a few minutes."

I could not watch Rufus. The snow made it imperative to really, really pay attention to my driving.

"Dr. B?" Rufus asked.

This was the first time he spoke in an enclosed space. His voice, richer and deeper than I could hear at night, out in the open, surprised me a little.

"No, not Dr. B. I have to go to the all-night emergency vet up on Roosevelt Road."

"Is she nice?"

"I'm sure she is," I replied, not knowing if it was indeed a she, or if the doctor was indeed nice. Regardless, though, Rufus would be tended to; he would be repaired.

He would not die! He would not die!

"My leg hurts," Rufus said.

"It might be broken."

"Is that bad?"

"Lots of kids break arms or legs. Doctors fix them all the time. Does anything else hurt?"

Rufus must have run a quick check on himself.

"My neck hurts a little. Not much. My leg hurts a lot."

"The doctor will fix you up," I replied. "Hang on. We're almost there."

I pulled into the vet's driveway. Before I undid my seat belt, Rufus spoke again.

"Is the ocean a warm place?"

I could have told him about Maine and Canada and the snowstorms there, but I didn't. Instead, I replied, "Yes, the ocean is warm."

"Then, okay. We should move to the ocean. God says I should move."

I saw his jaw move. I did not imagine his speech. He talked. He talked to me.

"God said to move?"

Rufus couldn't lie—or at least, not well. And why would a dog lie?

Rufus looked away. It was a guilty turn of the head.

"No. I made that up." His words were thick with apology.

"When? Why?"

"While I lay under the car. I wanted God to say that I needed to be warm."

"Why?"

"Because my leg hurts and I want to be warm."

"And you think we should move?"

Rufus licked at his injured leg and whimpered.

"Now I do."

"Rufus, why did you run out in front of that car?"

"Mike's car?"

Sometimes, even in moments like this, Rufus could drive me batty.

"Yes, Mike's car."

"You were going to make a bad mistake. You said that you would never mate before being married, because God says not to, and you're not married and I knew I had to stop it. So I did the only thing I could."

"Get run over by a car? You did that to stop me?"

"It stopped you, didn't it?"

My eyes filled with tears again. I had grown tired of crying, but these tears felt different.

"You risked death to save me?"

"I guess. That's what members of the pack do, don't they? You're in my pack, aren't you?"

I placed my hand on his head, as gently as I could.

"I love you, Rufus."

He did not need to reply.

"The ocean? Really?" I asked.

"If it's warm."

I parked right out front of the vet's office. I hurried around to the passenger side of the car. Just as I scooped the dog up in my arms, I heard him ask, "It is warm at the ocean, isn't it?"

"It is, Rufus. It never snows at the ocean."

Dr. Bartles was on call that night.

"Like Bartles and Jaymes," he said when he entered the examination room. "The wine coolers—remember?"

Everyone under thirty has no idea of who either of those people are, and I only had a vague recollection.

Dr. Bartles gently prodded and probed Rufus. His temperature was normal. "That's good. Sometimes an internal injury will cause temps to spike."

Rufus yelped when he touched his front leg.

"This is broken. No doubt about that," he said. "We'll X-ray the leg, and the rest of him too. But he looks in good shape. No cuts. No lacerations. Eyes are good. No spinal damage from the looks of it. That's what kills most of the animals hit by cars—the spine is broken and then that's that."

He poked a bit more.

"You have one lucky dog on your hands. Went right under the front wheels, you say?"

"Yes. He crawled out from the side."

"Well, he's a bit greasy, but let's get him X-rayed. You can wait in the lobby. Shouldn't be that long."

A sleepy technician came out with the news.

"It's broken. The right front leg. A clean break. The doc is setting a cast on it now. Everything else checked out fine. That's okay, right? You do want to keep the dog, right?"

"Of course."

The technician shrugged. He had the name Tony stitched on his shirt pocket, but he did not look like a Tony.

"What else would I do?" I asked.

Tony waved it off. "Some people hear that it costs $400 to set a leg versus $50 to put a dog down . . . well, they opt for the cheaper choice."

I could have said that such a dilemma posed a terrible and inhumane choice . . . but I didn't. I just nodded. What if you didn't have $400 or what if $400 was all you had to support your family for the next month?

Animals caused tough choices. I guess people did as well.

"The doc will call you when he's done."

———— ❧ ————

Rufus stood on the exam table, his right front leg encased in a white cast. His face glowed with relief. The leg hair had been shaved up past the cast. His skin had a pinkish color at the top of the cast.

Dr. Bartles held what I know is called an Elizabethan collar.

"He'll chew the cast off if we don't use this," he said.

Rufus looked at the collar, then at me. We had both seen the movie *Up*, where a bad dog had to wear a collar like that.

I looked at Rufus. I could read his eyes.

"He won't chew at it. He promises. I promise. If he does, I'll bring him right back."

The doctor did not look assured.

"You won't chew on the cast, will you, Rufus?" I asked him.

The dog looked up at the vet and offered him the most convincing face I had ever seen.

"Okay. If he does, you bring him back," the vet replied.

The doctor turned away, then back again.

"I almost forgot. His leg will hurt. I gave him a localized shot while I put the cast on. Do you think a few pain pills might help?"

I looked at Rufus.

"Yes. He would like enough for a few days," I replied.

"Okay, I'll give him one now. Help him sleep tonight. Could you hold him and I'll get the pill down?"

"I don't have to. Just give him the pill. He'll swallow it."

"You're kidding, aren't you?"

"No. Hand him the pill."

The doctor took one pill out of the bottle and held it out to Rufus, who lapped it up and swallowed a second later.

"You have one special dog there, Mrs. Fassler. Most dogs will fight a pill like that."

"I know. He is special. Very special."

Late that night, near midnight, I heard Rufus rustle and stir in his crate. I sat and watched him from the comfy chair in the kitchen, with a thick blanket over me, thankful that he had been spared—and that I had been spared. He had to sleep in his crate, since climbing stairs would be out of the question for some time.

I tried to push the me-and-Brian-what-might-have-happened-if thought from my mind. I would think on that later.

I saw Rufus's eyes as he struggled to stand.

"You have to go outside, don't you?"

His answer would have been yes. I could see that.

I carefully picked him up and carried him to the front lawn, placing him down on the snow as gently as I could. The mailbox canted backward. The tire tracks and the skid were obliterated by the freshly fallen snow. Snow had continued to fall, in dusts and fits, the wind gone, a quiet blanketing of the area.

"I don't want to do it here," Rufus said softly, almost in a whisper, as if he did not want any neighbor to hear him. "I live here."

"I know. But until your leg heals and the cast comes off, this is where you'll go. Understood?"

"Okay," he grumbled.

He slowly walked through the heavy snow when he finished. He managed to get to the small wall that separated the lawn from the driveway and stopped.

I had been watching the snow and did not see him standing there.

"You're sure the ocean is warm?" he asked again.

"It is. Always warm and it never snows."

He nodded.

"That's good," he said. "The ocean. Where it's warm. He didn't say anything about the ocean. But he did say we need to trust him."

Trust?

"God said that? Trust? In what?"

"I don't know. I mean, I think he said that. That is a good word, right? Even if I said it?"

"Yes," I replied. "It is a good word."

I picked Rufus up from the snow.

Who am I to argue with a dog?

11

I know. I shouldn't have punched Brian in the throat. I know that physical violence is never the answer. And, yes, I did take his call early the next day—the morning after the accident. His voice, hoarse still, was audible enough. He inquired about Rufus. His rasp—it made me feel good. I know, I shouldn't have felt that way, but I did. And I forgave him for letting Rufus off his leash. I apologized several times for hitting him. He apologized many times to me. But, a few minutes into the conversation, I knew that I had to tell him that we had no future together. At this point in my life, I think honesty trumps feeling awkward.

He took it well. . . . I guess he took it well.

After all, it would probably be difficult to remain involved with a woman who reacted as I did. And how many men would feel good about getting punched out by a mere slip of a woman? (I may be more than a mere slip—but you know what I mean.) And I was not still mad. I did forgive him. I did. Holding grudges and anger is a cancer on the soul. I think that's sort of a famous quote by someone noteworthy. Nor was it an issue of Brian being spectacularly negligent. I'm sure he didn't see the car or understand the implications of what could—and did—happen. But to react so cavalierly, so indifferently to what could have been a horrible tragedy—well, that I could not abide. How do you simply pick up and move on after the death of someone—even a dog—whom you loved with all your heart? Did he expect me to do that?

At that moment, I knew that I could never "be" with Brian. He might be able to move on from tragedy and loss with nary a second thought. I could not. And what may look like a small fissure to some would always be a chasm, an abyss, to me— always dividing us. It was a gulf that could not be bridged by desire or good intentions.

So I thanked him for all he had done, and for being nice to me. And I told him, in no uncertain terms, that we had no future together.

And, after wrapping up that entanglement to my life, I set about unwrapping and then cutting every other entanglement that tied me to this place and this house and this life.

The neighbor at the end of the cul-de-sac was a Realtor—a very good one if you trusted her signs posted all over town. I called her and told her that I intended to put the house on the market and would appreciate her advice on what to do to make the place more attractive to buyers. I sent an e-mail to all my subscribers to the writer's website, stating that I would be closing the newsletter and website and I would promptly refund any unused subscription liabilities. (It was not a huge sum—somewhere just over four figures.) I made a list of all the people I would need to call to inform that I planned on moving, all the things I would need to accomplish before a move could take place.

I gave Rufus his pain medication, which I am sure he had begun to associate with his pain relief. He took it gratefully, hobbled over to his crate, scooted around as best he could, laid his head down, and easily shut his eyes.

I knew he would sleep for several hours.

I made a quick trip to a self-storage place near where I had once worked, and bought four large bundles of medium-sized boxes, three bundles of book boxes, and one bundle of larger, lamp-sized boxes. The empty boxes filled the back of my car.

"Moving, you are?" the self-storage person said, very Yoda-like.

"Moving, I am," I replied and immediately regretted it, since the young man's expression did not change, indicating he was totally unaware of being in on the joke.

He hesitated a moment.

"Where to?"

I shrugged.

"I have no idea," I said, feeling at that moment a huge chasm of liberation open up inside of me.

"Really? Most people know. I'm pretty sure most of them know. Don't they?"

I imagined that most people did know. So did I, I guess, in a very generalized way—a macro-knowledge of my moving.

"Well, someplace near the ocean."

He nodded, sagely, as much as a clerk in a self-storage facility three days before Christmas can be sage.

"That's nice. I like the ocean."

Validation.

———❦———

I let the phone go to voice mail that morning.

Ava called, asking about the date. Beth called. Brian called again and left a long message saying that he understood and there were no hard feelings and that we could still be friends.

Mike called asking about Rufus. That call I picked up in the middle of his taped message.

"He's okay, Mike," I said, and explained the doctor's diagnosis and the cast and how grateful I was that the dog had been spared.

"That makes a lot of us. The whole family worried themselves sick. My kids would have been crushed if Rufus had been really hurt."

I once again gladly offered Mike absolution.

I tried to be quiet as I assembled boxes, but there is no way to dispense packing tape quietly. The tape squeals and protests at being unrolled. Yet even the adhesive squallings did not wake Rufus. Those pain pills must be pretty potent.

Soon after, I had assembled every box I had purchased—at least the bottoms of them—using three rows of packing tape along the bottom joints. (I tend to over-tape everything.) The pile became unmanageable in the kitchen, so I started tossing them into the dining room and then the formal living room—two areas that I seldom used. I imagined that I would fill up the boxes with all the "important" material from my life. When I was finished with the taping, I switched on the coffeemaker, and made a cup of instant-brewed coffee—strong, with two sugars this time. I tried to unwrap a package of Girl Scout cookies (Trefoil shortbread cookies) silently. Even the slightest crinkle of cellophane would normally get Rufus excited, charging toward me from wherever he had ensconced himself. But he slept on.

Powerful pills, those pain meds.

Maybe I could use them when we traveled to the ocean. Rufus would sleep—a blissful, unworried sleep—and would arrive at our night's destination in peace.

But then he would be up all night, unless I gave him another pill, and that seemed to put us on the slope of dog drug addiction.

I discarded the plan as quickly as I reviewed the potential downsides.

I ate my four Girl Scout cookies, drank my coffee, then decided that I should call Ava back. She may now have heard about the accident. She may be frantic with worry. Maybe. I looked at the clock. It was only 9:45. I would have sworn it was later.

"Ava," I said calmly, "I'm leaving."

She sputtered, not really offering a cogent response.

I launched into my story, tragic and miraculous, marked by my epiphany, an exclamation point, as it were, summing up my life to date, and the necessity of my forward movement to some oceanfront, or near oceanfront, somewhere.

Really, I have gotten paid to write words in succession. People paid me to do that.

So I finished my story (not telling her about Rufus saying that we should move to the ocean where it's warm) and said that I was now beginning the process of packing up my life.

"And starting over?" she asked.

"No. Not that. I loved what I had. Before I lost everything. So it's not a negation of that. But it is a new beginning. Or a rebirth. Or . . . well, okay, starting over."

I heard her inhale. She did that when she was thinking.

"I'll miss you," she said, her words calm and matter-of-fact, as if she had been expecting this sort of news all along. "But it will take a while, won't it? You will wait till the house sells, right? We'll still have time for lunches and coffee, right?"

I assured her that nothing was going to happen quickly.

"Have you told Bernice?"

"No. I'm going to send a letter. I would e-mail, but I think her computer is still down. She'll get the letter, be able to process it a bit—then we'll talk. I mean, it is not like we live close now."

I heard another inhale.

"I can help you pack, right?"

"Sure, I would love that."

"It also means that I get everything that you're leaving behind, right?"

I laughed—the first time in the conversation that either of us laughed.

"Sure. You're welcome to the detritus of my life. What you don't want, I give to charity."

I heard Rufus stir. His eyes were slits. He stared for a moment, then slowly lowered his head again and closed his eyes.

Those were some wonderful pills.

I wonder if they come in human dosages.

I'm sure they do.

My Realtor neighbor came, gave me a checklist of things that I needed to repair, repaint, toss, clean, close, or hide. The list ran two pages long.

"But nowhere near as long as most, sweetie," she said. "Your house is hospital clean in comparison to most of my clients." She had emigrated from Israel and called everyone "sweetie."

She did not mean it as faint praise. I have been in other people's homes and while I was cluttered, at times, and only in a few rooms, other people's clutter made me look obsessive and manic, in terms of cleaning and organization.

I had a roll of contractor's fifty-five-gallon trash bags—thick, green, huge bags. I discovered them tucked away in Jacob's basement workshop. Inhabiting many of the dark nooks and corners of the basement were items that no one would want. Broken things with cords. I read somewhere that people find it very difficult to throw away an item—even if badly broken— with an electrical cord on it. I admit to that problem. I found radios, iPod speakers, alarm clocks, irons, waffle irons, mixers, camcorders more than a decade old, VHS tape players that would eat any tape that was inserted, fans, heaters, frying pans, toasters, and lamps—all broken, all never to be repaired, at least by me. There were more, and I felt more and more like a hoarder as I assembled my dusty, broken finds. Those I stuffed into the big green bags, trying to keep the combined weight under forty-five pounds. What does forty-five pounds feel like? That was the limit that our garbage collectors set on any single bag of debris. I didn't think they carried scales with them in their trucks, but nonetheless, I attempted to stay vigilant to the limit.

Speaking of scales, I found three scales under the bed upstairs. I had forgotten all about them, the three of them unhappily living with a thickness of dust bunnies.

I also stuffed bags full of clothes—my husband's, my son's. These I would give to the church's resale shop. Someone would make use of them. I tried not to think about much at all as I packed them into bags. I did not caress or hold any item to my cheek. It would serve no purpose other than making me very sad.

I would make a clean break, and this was no time to hold up a diminutive T-shirt of my son's and begin to weep. I had his memories, and they were better and more powerful than any swatch of fabric. I had wept enough over the size and scents of old clothes. No more. Not now.

I'm not sure why it felt easier to do this today when I hadn't been able to do it for years—packing up the remains of my old life, that is. Perhaps I had to come to that "clean break with the past" time. And now, here it was. Time to move on.

I'm not sure why today felt different from a thousand other days—but it was—and I began the process of moving on.

I packed a bag full of men's shoes—just shoes. I had no idea that my husband owned so many shoes, and all very well cared for, albeit dusty at the moment. These items would provide money to the church's charity, and good attire for someone less fortunate. And not one of them would grow teary-eyed when looking at an old T-shirt from a Cubs game. (I was more a Sox fan—but not a very faithful one. I only followed them, barely, if they were in contention at the end of the season.)

I emptied the drawers in the kitchen desk. Of course, I tested every pen to see if it would produce a legible line. Maybe a third of them did. The rest made me feel so wonderfully free and alive when I tossed them into a discard bag. I should have started this process much earlier. I had no idea that throwing away worthless things could bring about such contentment and . . . well . . . joy. Maybe that's true in life too. Get rid of the worthless things that tied you down and held you back. That's what I was doing. That's what was making me feel whole for the first time in a long time. Well, perhaps not totally whole, but closer to whole than ever before.

Ava came over later that afternoon. She made a big fuss over the injured Rufus, who appeared to revel in the sympathy, rolling onto his side, displaying his broken leg like a toddler holding a scrawled crayon picture to his mother. She made herself a cup of coffee, and wanted to go through the bag of useless pens I had already discarded. I refused to let her do that, insisting that I could tell if a pen had indeed run out of ink.

What is it about pens that resist tossing? In the old days a pencil became short or it wasn't. A fountain pen had ink or it didn't. You could tell when things were done. Now, no one could tell if there was still some recalcitrant ink left in the barrel of the pen. Life is more complex and ambiguous these days.

∞∞∞

That night, after a long day of packing and discarding, and sharing a few tears with Ava when she left, Rufus clumped about in the front yard, his cast protected by a plastic grocery bag held up by a small strip of duct tape. I did not turn the front porch lights on, knowing that Rufus did not like doing what he had to do in full view of the neighbors. He stood out there, in the cold, sniffing the air, obviously, I thought, wishing he could take one of the normal routes on our walks. He could not, of course.

I huddled in my puffy coat, hunching deep inside the folds, trying to stay warm. The weather felt so different when we were not walking—colder, more boring, actually.

"Rufus," I asked in a soft winter voice, "why did you decide so quickly that going to the ocean was the right thing to do?"

"Gus said it was warm there. He went there once. He liked it. I like warm. I'm tired of being cold."

I nodded, then added, "I am too," not certain if Rufus understood the meaning of a nod.

"Will that man come back?"

"What man?" I asked, pretty sure who Rufus meant. After all, he did not know that many men.

"The man who let me off my leash."

"Brian."

"I guess, if that's his name."

179

"It is. I don't think you will ever see him again."

Rufus snorted in the cold, a puff of breathy vapor visible in the frigid air. "I never liked him."

That, of course, was a revelation to me. The most I had gotten from Rufus was that he "seemed nice."

"Why didn't you tell me?" I asked, the wonderment, or better yet, bewilderment, hopefully, apparent in my voice. "You could have said maybe God didn't like him or want us to be together or something. Then all of this could have been avoided."

I bet Rufus would have shrugged, had he been able to shrug.

"I don't know. I didn't ask God about him."

I furrowed my brow as visibly as I could to show this dog that I was getting close to being exasperated with him and his reticence.

"Why not?"

Rufus snorted again, this time, I thought, in a nonverbal way of answering me. Rufus did not do ironic or cynical well.

"People have free will. Right? I think I heard you say that. Or maybe it was God who said it."

"Free will? Really?"

"Yes," Rufus replied, frustratingly calm. "So it was not my place to say anything. And I'm not a biter. So I couldn't very well bite him . . . that man. And a dog in the pack does not bite the leader of the pack."

"But Brian wasn't the leader."

Rufus paused a moment, then spoke softly. "Oh. Yes. I guess he wasn't the leader, was he? Him, I could have bitten, couldn't I?"

"You could have. Maybe you should have."

Rufus turned back toward the front door, snow already clumped about his three good legs.

"But . . . Then, I'm not a biter. I said that already, didn't I?"

"You did."

"So the decision was up to you."

Sometimes knowing who was ultimately responsible for a bad decision was not all that comforting.

Not at all.

The next morning, still dark and cold, we stumbled outside, Rufus stretching and yawning. I never feel quite civilized during our early morning walks—but no one in their right mind is out at 5:00 a.m. in the dead of winter. Other than the lady who delivers the newspapers.

I stopped getting the newspaper a few years ago. Up until then, I could be counted among the most loyal of readers, scanning every headline, reading nearly all the opinion pieces and editorials, feeling virtuous at remaining a solid citizen and dutifully informed over everything that was happening in the world. Then my eyes started to go. Not that they were great before. I had begun squinting years earlier, but newspapers were using such tiny fonts. Seriously. And it became harder and harder to read the newspaper in the faint light of morning. Plus, I could get the same material—for free—on the Internet. What are those editors thinking? "We'll give the news away for free and expect people to pay for it as well." Like that makes a lot of sense.

Anyhow . . .

So Rufus and I were out in the cold, and I was obsessing about packing and when to hold the estate sale to sell all the material that I didn't want, couldn't use, or didn't know what to do with.

"Do dogs pack?" Rufus asked, looking up from a dark corner of the front yard.

"No, Rufus. They don't."

"What about my bed?"

"Well, that I will bring with us. And your crate. I'll take both of those things in the car with us."

Rufus snorted as if he was in agreement.

"And what about my crunchy treats? Do you pack those? Will you remember to pack those?"

"Of course, I will."

"That's good," Rufus replied, and began to hobble toward the front door.

"Can you buy crunchies at the ocean?"

"Yes. They sell them everywhere."

How wonderful to be a dog with such simple needs, so few necessities.

12

The days surrounding Christmas were somewhat of a blur to me. As usual, at least usual for the last several years, I did not go anywhere on Christmas morning. In the past, Bernice had begged me to fly to Arizona.

"Being alone on Christmas . . . well, that's just not right," she'd said. "Only communists ignore Christmas."

I didn't think she was accusing me of being a secret, suburban communist, but she meant well. The first Christmas alone had been terrible, but it would have been more terrible had I been around people who were enjoying it. The second time became easier, and I actually did agree to go to a friend's house for dinner, later on, late in the afternoon on Christmas Day.

This year, the holiday came and went, and I had reheated Chinese food on Christmas day, amid a flurry of boxes and packing and feeling overwhelmed.

Beth came to visit two days before New Year's Eve. If there was one day worse than Christmas to be alone on, it was New Year's Eve. This year, I thought, would be easier. I would be busy, not watching a cadaverous Dick Clark announcing the ball drop in Times Square. I mean—really—what kind of person goes to Times Square on New Year's Eve? Any sane or rational person? I don't think so.

Beth arrived with a plate of homemade cookies. Call me a scrooge, but I don't like homemade cookies. I mean, I know how dirty my kitchen can be, and I'm a clean person. What happens in other people's kitchens is best to remain a matter of conjecture. But these were lemon bars and I like lemon bars and Beth said she made them herself and I usually trust Beth to maintain a modicum of proper sanitary procedures. So I made her a cup of decaf coffee. I made a cup of real coffee for myself and we sat in the cluttered kitchen.

Rufus did his now-usual dance with a broken leg, seeming to revel in the sympathy it aroused. And Beth gave him a bite of her lemon bars. He likes lemon bars too.

I nudged a box, half-filled with plates that I would not be bringing with me. Why anyone needs five versions of dessert plates is beyond me. Yet I had five sets. I would bring with me only two.

After a long pause, Beth drew in a deep breath, pushed the hair from her eyes, and tucked it behind her ears—again. It was a habit I would not miss.

I knew she was working on the best way to broach the subject, and I even knew what the subject was: am I making a rash decision?

"Mary . . . You are one of my oldest and dearest friends . . ."

I don't think I am, but it still made me feel good, in a weird sort of way, to be valued by someone. I mean, I knew that we were friends and had been friends for nearly a decade now. But I would have sworn there were other people in Beth's life who were dearer to her than I was. Still . . .

"I know what you're going to ask," I said, preempting her, and saving her a bit of anguish of bringing up perhaps a touchy subject. "And I am not being rash. I've thought this out pretty thoroughly."

Beth looked both surprised and relieved.

"Are you sure, Mary? I mean, really sure? I know that God doesn't want us to do foolish things just because of our emotions. Or just because your dog got hit by a car."

Beth might have been the only person who made that connection, and in a sense, she was the only person with the right answer as to my reasons for going. Or partly right, anyhow.

"Doesn't God seem to reward people who move slowly and cautiously?" Beth asked. I would bet that she had no evidence from the Scriptures, but slow and cautious reflected her take on the proper evangelical path to heaven.

"Emotions can't be trusted," she went on. "They can make us do things that we maybe shouldn't do. You have to be careful."

"But don't emotions help us do the right things sometimes?" I asked.

"I don't think so," she responded. "Well, maybe sometimes. But not usually. We sort of tell ourselves what we want to hear and the more we do that, the more we begin to agree with ourselves—and maybe get fooled into thinking what is wrong is actually right."

Beth is a wonderful person, but not a student of logic. Yet Beth, like so many other people in my life, did not truly understand my life, and just who I wanted to be. So now I felt like a teenager again, complaining that my parents didn't understand me, since neither one of them, obviously, had ever been a teenager. In one sense, though, I was correct. None of the people in my life right now had suffered as I had suffered. Sure, people lost aged parents, and aunts or uncles or grandmothers passed on, but no one I knew had suffered as I had.

And that suffering allowed me to act in a way that made sense to me—even if it did not make sense to others. Not only did it allow me to do so, it forced me to do so.

"Maybe . . . maybe you're running away. A little. From the past, I mean." Beth grew more uncomfortable, as if she were accusing me of using the death of my husband and son to rationalize my irrational desire to leave this place and head to an ocean. With my talking dog.

"So what if I am?" I replied. I was not angry, not at all. I simply wanted to know how she viewed this decision as a bad decision.

"Well, I'm not sure," she said, a little flustered. "But maybe you leaving is . . . well, I mean . . . maybe you have to stay and face the past. Face it rather than run away. That's what I'm saying."

I still did not get angry, and am not angry even now, even though I could have been. I could have let the ire rise and snap back at her and slam my palm on the table scaring both her and Rufus. It might have felt good to me to do that, but it would serve no useful purpose. Instead, I remained calm and collected. Impassive, almost.

"Beth, I know you mean well. I do. But . . . I have lost everything. I have been alone these past years and people still think I am not facing the past. What have I been doing all these years? I have faced it. I have dealt with the loss. I know what it is to be alone. I have lived with that reality every day of my life since the accident. There is not a single hour that passes that, somewhere in my thoughts, that terrible day intrudes on my reality. I am done facing it. I can't face it anymore. I can't deal with it anymore. It has been dealt with. I am ready to move on. And I don't think I need to prove anything to anyone. Or even explain it. I know that I am doing the right thing."

Beth offered me a half-sideways pickerel smile, looking like a fish that bumped into the unseen glass wall of an aquarium. "Well, I don't want you to do anything rash. Patience is a godly virtue. It is. Make sure what you're doing is God's will."

I looked around at the small mountain range of boxes—some packed and taped, some half-filled—that littered my interior landscape. It was too late to urge caution against making rash decisions. The die had been cast. The page had been turned.

And my dog wanted to go to the ocean.

"Beth, you are a dear friend, but moving to the ocean, I think, is the first positive thing I've done in my life . . . since they died. It's right, Beth. It is."

She kept her wary smile.

"Are you sure? Have you prayed this through?"

I lied to her. Lied right to her face.

"I did, Beth. I really did."

Lying about praying. How far I had fallen.

"I have prayed so much about this it's not even funny."

❧

February clumped over Chicago, cold, gray, windy, bone-chilling, marrow-draining, and filled the weak with the numbing dread of an endless winter. I inured myself to the brutality of the midwestern variety of winter, hoping, praying (not really) that it would be my last. Snow fell and stayed, fingers of drifts edging onto homes and streets and mailboxes. Snippets of snow clutched about Rufus and me as we walked. His cast had been removed, his leg was healed, his pain was gone (so he said), and his hair became scraggly and withered, as it slowly regrew on the shaved portion of his leg. Because it did not have protection from the cold, I cut off the end of a child's sock and slipped it as a legging over his foreleg, and held it snug, not tight, with a length of Velcro. His paw remained exposed to the cold, but his pink and wrinkled leg remained warmer.

Both of us had had enough of winter.

Bernice called me several times. She never once tried to talk me out of moving. In fact, she said that she wondered why it had taken me so long to decide. "Our house back in Wheaton had become much too big for two people, Mary. I get winded just thinking about vacuuming the place."

She asked one important question: "Can we visit you when you find a place and get settled? I do like the ocean."

Of course I said yes.

Validation.

And then I decided to buy a new car. Or a car that would be new to me. I had been driving around in a small, nondescript car for years. There was nothing wrong with it, but if I was going to head east, and be on the road for weeks and perhaps months, I needed something bigger.

After all, Rufus would be with me. He needed space.

I decided to buy a used Volvo station wagon. They are safe cars, right? Volvos are for thinking people. Right? Nothing flashy or pretentious. But bigger. Roomier. I could carry with me enough stuff to start over again—once I found a place. Until I could have the rest of my furnishings shipped to me.

I had some money set aside that I could use. Plus I'd have the trade-in dollars, even though that wouldn't be all that much. A car could not be considered a luxury, but a necessity.

I found a Volvo wagon at that used car franchise that has locations all over the country. It was eight years old, a XC something or other, with low mileage and a luggage rack on top—not that I would use it, though it might come in handy. One huge plus: it had cruise control—a luxury I had never enjoyed on any of my previous cars. And leather seats. With seat warmers. What decadent people we have become, needing our tender bottoms gently warmed as we make our way through a frigid environment.

I felt rich.

And the Volvo had plenty of room for Rufus's crate.

February slipped past, a blur of gray and cold.

I began to get nervous about the selling of the house. Only a handful of potential buyers had visited, and none of them had been interested enough to make an offer.

Maybe God, if he actually got involved in petty matters like house sales, would use this as a means to get me to stay put. Maybe that's what the Divine wanted of me. Open doors and closed doors. Isn't that what people often include in their prayers? Really now—some people boldly pray for open doors, and some people are too polite or righteously humble to come out and ask for them directly.

I hadn't asked God about this—or anything else. I had felt guilty about lying to Beth, but it stilled her concerns. And that's what our "pretend" prayers often do—offer a balm to the nervous and timid. And make us look more spiritual than we are.

I can be terrible, can't I? I am sorry for being such a horrid person at times.

But I needed to get out of this cold and this bleakness and this avalanche of memories that kept threatening to engulf me, to bury me forever beneath the suffocating folds of the past.

I would have asked Rufus to speak to God about the lack of buyers, but he already said that house values were not a subject he felt like addressing with the Almighty. So be it. I did not press him. He appeared to be very interested in the daily temperature at Hilton Head. He had no idea where that was; he had no knowledge of distances and geography. He knew that Hilton Head lay on the ocean. I told him that it was one of the places we would explore. I would have showed him a map, but it would have had no meaning to him. I could trace our intended route to the ocean, but it would be all but gibberish to him—funny squiggles on paper that had no meaning. He remained happy to know that I knew the way and how to get to our Eden. He found contentment in that. But he did seem to like the sound of Hilton Head. I think he liked things with two names. He would ask if I saw the weather report on my computer for Hilton Head.

"What is the temperature at Hilton Head today?" he would ask.

I would relate what I had found . . . let's say it was sixty-five degrees. It was often sixty-five degrees in the dead of February. How delicious that would be—to wear a sweater instead of a full-length parka with Everest-level insulation.

"What is the temperature here?" he would then ask.

"Fifteen degrees." It was often fifteen degrees in Chicago in February.

"Is sixty-five better or worse than fifteen?"

"It is much, much warmer," I would say. "I wouldn't need gloves or a coat. I could just wear a shirt outside."

Then he would almost smile. As I said, schnauzers are not physically equipped to do much smiling, but I think he tried. It appeared that his steps were a bit bouncier when he discovered that it would be so much warmer.

"And when will we move?"

"When I sell the house."

"And when will that be?"

"When someone decides to buy it from me," I would say.

"Oh. Then I hope that person decides soon. We are missing out on warm weather, aren't we?"

We certainly were.

———— ∞ ————

During the first week of March, my Realtor brought me the news of an offer on my house.

"That young couple from a couple of weeks ago. They really liked the house, but were afraid that they couldn't afford it. They're going to make an offer."

I wondered if that meant they would be making an absurdly low offer, hoping that I would be desperate.

I wasn't. Not yet, anyhow.

The offer came in lower, but not absurdly lower than my asking price. I know, I know, I should have negotiated tough, played hardball with these people. But I wanted it sold. I wanted to start my life over. And the offer was close to what I wanted.

My Realtor neighbor brought the offer in for me to sign that afternoon. I signed it.

That night Rufus and I stopped by the pond, still a thin, reflective slab of ice. He stretched his front leg. The broken bone had healed, and the fur had grown back, yet he remained a little tentative at times, as if his muscles were still adjusting to the repaired bone.

"You sold the house, right? Is that what that lady from across the street said?"

"I did. I signed the papers. Unless something happens, I move out by the end of the month. We can move out."

"Did you make money like you wanted?" he asked as we started walking again. He limped now, ever so slightly. I could see the hitch in his step. No trauma goes forever unnoticed.

No break or injury goes away without leaving a scar, a limp, a hitch, some reminder of the pain in the past. Perhaps the poor dog would always limp a little. I suspect we could never enter any dog agility trials in the future. We hadn't done so in the past, so it was no great loss. Limping is better than disabled—and much, much better than dead.

"Did you make money? You talk about money a lot."

I scowled. I did not talk about money all that much. Maybe it just seems that way to a dog. Money is a worry—especially for someone now no longer gainfully employed.

"I sort of broke even, I guess. I didn't make any money. I didn't lose any money."

We went another block. Then he asked one more question that night. "But will you have enough money to buy my crunchies?"

⊸⊸⊸

Early the next morning, my Realtor neighbor returned with a book's thickness of papers, all relating to the contract and the expectations of sale and liens and taxes and mortgage approvals and who knows what else. I signed them all, thinking that no one reads any of it. Or do they? Perhaps I should have. But I didn't.

"Listen, sweetie, I know that I shouldn't ask . . . an inconvenience, but . . ."

"Ask what?" I replied.

"Well, the couple who are buying your house are outside in my car. They wondered if they could come in and take some measurements of the rooms. To plan out furniture. That sort of thing. You don't have to say yes. They can come back later."

Mounds of boxes still populated most rooms. I had packed up three-quarters of what I needed, but that was all. There remained a shambled, hillbilly-ish, as-seen-on-the-*Cops*-TV-show quality to the house. I remained a shambles as well, in well-worn sweatpants and a mismatched sweatshirt, my hair pulled back with a band, no makeup, a loose fuzziness of slippers on my feet.

I know what I would have said two months earlier.

"Sure. Let them come in. They do know I'm packing, right?"

"They do. They have their little boy with them. Rufus is okay with little people?"

I stopped for just a moment, just a fraction. I felt a cloud over my heart. I felt the familiar, and almost welcome tightness about my heart and throat.

"Sure. He's fine with them. He may bark some when they come in."

Rufus did not bark once. He did not jump or bounce or get excited at all.

The young couple—a pretty couple, or should that be a handsome couple?—came in, excitement and fear and joy and anticipation radiating from them, like the northern lights.

"Are you sure it's not an imposition us being here?" the wife asked. "We don't want to intrude." I had been told their names, of course, but I did not want to know their names. I had been introduced, but I did not want to know who these people are or were or will be. This would be easier. "No problem," I said. I smiled. "I hope you can overlook the packing supplies and the mess. It'll be cleaned out when I leave—that I promise."

She was blonde, tiny, with deep-set blue eyes. Like a perfect Swedish princess, her eyes wide, her smile quick. He was darker. Taller. Handsome.

The little boy . . . "This is Tyler. He's four."

"Four and a half," Tyler said, holding up four fingers.

He had perfect blond hair like his mother's and had her eyes and her easy, welcoming smile. He had tiny, little-boy jeans on with a sweatshirt and tiny, perfect black sneakers. He had his hands in his jean jacket pockets, as if his parents had instructed him not to touch anything and keeping his hands involved would help him obey.

"I'll stay in the kitchen with Maya. We can talk about the neighborhood and who's putting their house up for sale. Take your time measuring."

"It's really just the bedrooms. We don't have that much furniture and . . . well, we want to figure out where it goes."

Tyler saw Rufus standing in the kitchen. The dog just stood there. This was most unlike him. He usually reacted vigorously, energetically, to visitors. Today, he remained impassive. He just stood there, like a perfectly positioned statue.

"They have a dog," he said, pointing to Rufus.

"That's Rufus," I said. "Would you like to pet him?"

Tyler remained solemn, but nodded in earnest. His mother said, "If it's okay with you."

Tyler sat on the floor with Rufus, in the kitchen, as Maya and I sat in the two upholstered chairs and chatted about inconsequential things, like snow removal and lawn services and where I might be heading.

Rufus had never been a fan of small children. He tolerated the few he had met, but would quickly make himself scarce after only a minute or two. Not so today. Tyler carefully and respectfully patted him, stroking his back and head, very gentle for a four-year-old. He was smiling, and I think Rufus might have tried to smile as well.

It took my buyers nearly twenty minutes to do all their measuring. I was happy to let them have the time. The woman glowed with expectations of the future—here at this house, inside these walls, expecting to build a future, holding onto a golden promise of a shared life.

"Tyler, are you ready to go?"

Tyler obediently rose, patted Rufus once more, then walked to his mother, who took his hand. He leaned up to her and she leaned down to him. He whispered into her ear. She stood up, offered an odd smile, and said, "No, honey, he doesn't."

She must have seen my expression.

She looked at her firstborn son, with his perfect blond hair and blue eyes, and then back to me.

"He wanted to know if the dog comes with the house. He loves dogs."

I saw the look in Rufus's eyes—as if he had been afraid that he might have been a condition of the sale.

I knelt down to Tyler and looked him in the eyes.

My heart was breaking and I could not show that pain to anyone.

"Tyler, Rufus and I have to stay together. Rufus has been with me since he was a little puppy. And he tells me things. We need to be together. But maybe, when you move in here . . ."

I looked up at his mother before continuing. She shrugged as if to say "maybe—go ahead."

". . . when you move in here, maybe you can get your own little dog."

Tyler brightened.

"Really?"

"We'll see, Tyler," his mother cautioned. I already knew the answer. So did Tyler, I am sure.

I asked the perfect little boy one more question before I stood up.

"What would you call your dog?"

Tyler scrunched his face, deep in thought. Picking a name would be a big assignment for a perfect little boy.

"I would call him Johnnie."

"That's the name of his best friend at preschool," his mother explained.

I took a deep breath, then another. I would remain composed. I would. I looked square in the young boy's eyes.

"That's a very good name, Tyler. A very good name."

Validation.

13

Estate sales should be held in the summer, when doors can stay open and no one tracks mud into the house. But I had to move now, and we were in the gray month of March—sleet in the morning and the air grew raw and angry by noon. The good thing about an estate sale in the winter is that you have so little competition. All the estate sale and garage sale addicts out there—and you know who you are—have been inactive for months and months now, at least in the north. Down south, I don't think you face the same deprivation, but in Chicago, only the insane hold garage sales in the winter. So I knew I had a lot of pent-up demand going for me.

I sold virtually everything that I had decided not to take with me. Two weeks earlier, I rented a pack-it-yourself storage container that a nice man dropped off in my driveway. I filled it with boxes, one sofa, two chairs, one table, four kitchen chairs, one bed frame, one relatively new HDTV, a few end tables, a wardrobe of clothes, and not much else. I would buy a mattress and box spring wherever I ultimately landed.

People bought everything else that made up my previous life. Old framed artwork. Desks. Odd tables. Two complete silverware sets. Dishes. An overflow of books. Rugs. A leather sofa. Three televisions—one an ancient analog model. A display cabinet. A full set of furniture from the basement. Tools. Cans of old paint. (Really—a nearly full gallon of off-white sold for a dollar.) Wrapping paper. Towels. Sheets. Pillows. Bed frames. Bookcases. Candles. Lamps. A large dining room table. Fans. Another desk. Tell you what: walk through your house. Everything in your house was something that I sold in one form or another. Mixers. Mixing bowls. Measuring cups—I had collected three sets somehow. Place mats. Napkins. Candle holders. Vases. (I did keep one vase for myself—a Mother's Day gift.) A box of scarves. A box of mittens and gloves. More glasses and mugs and plates than I could count. A full set of Waterford tumblers and wine glasses (which I had used perhaps six times in ten years). Serving plates. A toaster oven. Three coffeemakers. (I kept one.) A huge bag of Tupperware and Tupperware-like containers. Five plastic bins filled with Christmas decorations. An old camp stove that I had forgotten I had. An artificial Christmas tree. Three Christmas wreaths and one springtime wreath. Three bicycles. Two animal carriers—now too small for the adult schnauzer in the family. Shovels. Rakes. An electric tire pump (which I did not know how to use). Two garbage cans. Two large armoires. An exercise bike (which I never used). A treadmill (which I used once last year). An old cedar chest.

I am certain that I have forgotten more items than I remembered.

My head spins at trying to remember why I bought these things, when I bought them, and if I ever used some of them.

I made enough money in two days of estate selling to pay for my new-to-me Volvo wagon.

I began to feel lighter and more unencumbered as each person walked out of my house clutching some new addition to his or her life—and a subtraction from mine.

Rufus had been sent to the Realtor neighbor's house for the sale. It would do him no good to have to face the hundreds of customers who tromped through the house.

That night—the second night, after the estate sale had ended, and after the house had been emptied, and after I got Rufus's leash and supply of crunchies—he stopped at the corner as we walked and asked, "What happened to all your things? The sofa thing that I sleep on in that sunny room is gone. What do I do now?"

I had explained to him earlier how an estate sale worked, but I am pretty sure some of our human endeavors were simply beyond him.

"I sold them all. We're moving, remember? I don't have room in the car for a sofa."

He walked along for a while, obviously digesting the information.

"My bed is still there, isn't it? I didn't notice."

"It is. We're taking that with us."

Another long pause.

"Okay, then."

I gave him a treat, which he crunched up happily.

"But where will I sleep in the sunny room? The sofa is gone."

"On the floor, if you want to sleep in there."

The room stood empty.

"The floor? Really?"

We turned the corner of our street.

"Yes, Rufus. The floor. But we are leaving in a few days. Then everything changes."

He remained silent until we arrived at the driveway.

"I don't like change," he said. "Change is bad."

————∞∞∞————

Walking through the empty house was not as painful or emotional for me as I once feared. Stripped of all the mementos and trappings of my previous life, empty rooms were just that: empty. There were no ghosts of memories, no emotional trauma from seeing a reminder of my husband or my son. It was simply architecture, simply shelter. Nothing more than walls and floors and ceilings and windows and doors.

The people who conducted the estate sale had come in and done a thorough sweeping and cleaning job as part of their process. They even filled all the nail holes in the walls with Spackle. Both the cleaning and spackling were codicils in the contract. (How often have you heard the words *Spackle* and *codicil* in the same sentence? Never, I bet.)

Rufus and I walked through every room. I felt like I was leaving a hotel room and making one last sweep to ensure that I had not left a sock under the bed or my cell phone charger still plugged into the wall.

I hadn't done any of those things.

Rufus sniffed about, checking corners and windowsills. I knew he would not talk to me during the day. (I kept promising myself to ask him why he remained silent in the sun, and I kept forgetting. Perhaps it is not important.) Yet I knew he could listen and understand most of what I said.

"So that's it, Rufus. Everything is gone. The car is packed up. The things I am keeping will be shipped to us once I . . . when we find a place to live."

He looked up at me.

"And yes, I have a bag of your crunchies in the car. And your bed."

I knew that satisfied him.

A door had been closed on what had been my life. It was a door that I had chosen to close and not one that had been slammed in my face. I had some control over this, some degree of personal choice. It had not punched into my gut in the middle of the night, leaving me without breath, without hope, without a real life for so long.

Now, I got to do the inventing. I got to do the creating. A new life, my new life, would rise from the ashes of this one, like a phoenix of sorts, a great bird arising from the detritus of an old life that no longer worked.

The car was packed. I had two large duffle bags filled. I had a smaller computer bag—I now owned a very small laptop—which also held my cell phone charger and e-book reader. I had a small, unimpressive digital camera. Perhaps I would need to document some of this trip, but I didn't plan on making it a scrapbooked adventure. There were three boxes, taped securely. I carried a set of sheets and towels, a minimum of dishes, cups, plates, spoons, forks, and an open box containing a toaster, an electric kettle, and the ingredients for making coffee. I had stayed at . . . well . . . less-expensive hotels in the past and the "coffee service" that is often included with the room is coffee in name only. There is always too much sugar, not enough coffee, and the "coffee lightener" only changed the coffee from a mud-black to a mud-brown. From the first moment, I knew I would bring my own coffee accoutrements with me. I would have packed them in their own suitcase, but I had sold all the rest of my luggage in the estate sale. A cardboard box would do just fine.

I debated what to do with Rufus in the car for what might be weeks of travel. There are some who say a dog should be put in a halter and fastened to the seat belt, ensuring the animal's safety. There are others who argue against it. Whenever he rode in the car before, Rufus would lie on the front seat, his head down, his eyes nearly closed, looking as if he expected to die at any moment—not from a crash or my terrible driving (which wasn't true) but from his general heightened anxiety over being in an automobile in the first place. I did not want to put him in a harness and fasten him to the seat belt. I am pretty certain he would not have liked that. Instead, I placed his crate in the back of the car. Since it was only the two of us traveling, I had folded down the back passenger seats. I placed his crate snug up against the back of the front passenger seat and used a cargo belt to secure it to the floor, so in the event of an accident, the crate would remain secured. Rufus could see me from the crate, and I could turn and glance back to him as I drove. I hoped that being slightly confined would ease his anxieties. There was more than enough open space for a bowl of food and water to be placed down when we stopped.

I laid a road atlas on the front seat, a traveling mug for coffee in the cup holder, and my iPod securely plugged into the car's audio system. I had sunglasses in the door compartment, a baseball hat to wear if I rode with an open window, and a bag of hard candy hidden in the glove box. (Rufus has long ago decided that he expects to taste whatever it is that I am eating. I don't think he should be eating candy—and if I keep it out of sight, so much the better.)

I had filled up the gas tank the day before, had the oil changed a few days before that, had all the fluids checked and filled, and had the tires properly inflated. I had the owner's card and the insurance card in a little leather-like folder in the glove box. I had the emergency kit my husband had given me years ago—flares, signs, a flashlight, tools, bandages, blanket, jumper cables, tow rope—tucked away in a small storage nook at the rear of the car.

Every item on the exit list had a "go" status attached to it.

I put the key in the door. I had my hand on the key. I looked up at the house that once held my hopes and dreams and my life and my husband and my son and I could not stop it—the tears began to flow. I sobbed and sobbed. My heart tightened. My throat tightened. My cheeks grew wet. I began to sniffle as I sobbed, the tears just flowing, unexpected, unbidden. Rufus had been lying down in his crate, his head nestled between his front paws. He raised his head, startled, I imagine, at my outburst. Then he stood up and pressed his little snout between the thin bars of his crate. His impatience or anxiety was marked by his slight movements, shifting his weight from side to side, raising one paw, then another. Then he growled. And then he barked. I am pretty sure I mentioned that he did not tend to bark, so his bark came as a surprise to me. Then he barked again, more emphatic this time, and again, trying to get me to pay attention.

What if I was doing the wrong thing? What if all this turned into a huge mistake? My friends are here. My life had been here—is here still, right? The remnants are still here. Why am I running away from it all? I should find a small apartment here. I could stay here. I could do freelance editing work again. I could go back to church again, and I could join the singles group. I know people here. I have a history here. What am I doing, really? Maybe Beth was right that I am simply running away from my past. Am I doing that? Have I not accepted what happened yet?

All this raced through my thoughts at a million miles an hour, amid my sobs and wailing and tears.

Rufus barked again, louder this time, more heartfelt, if a dog's bark can be described as heartfelt. I turned to him and placed my fingers through the opening. He stuck his nose against my flesh. Then he backed away a little and just stared at me. His eyes were worried, but not really. Concerned, perhaps. Wondering what had upset me so much.

Then he did something he rarely does. He licked my fingers. Rufus, unlike other dogs, other slobbery and obnoxious dogs, did not lick much. He just did not do it. Maybe people tasted bad to him. He would sniff, but not lick and slobber, like the big knuckleheaded dog we were leaving next door. But this time he did, gently, delicately, as if he were trying to reassure me somehow by doing something completely out of his character.

I sniffed loudly. I wiped at my face with the back of my hand. I took a deep breath.

At least I wore no mascara that would run and make my face look like a zombie-woman.

"Is it okay, Rufus? Will it be okay? We are doing the right thing, aren't we?"

Rufus pushed his forehead against my fingers, still wrapped around the bars of the crate.

I took another deep breath.

"I guess we're doing the right thing. We are."

I switched the engine on and backed carefully out of the driveway. As I began to drive away, an unfamiliar car approached. The car held the handsome couple and their son. The boy saw me, I guess, and pressed his face to the window and waved. I waved back. I could see the excitement and happiness radiate from his parents.

This adventure I embarked on, this exit and entrance—it was the right thing to do.

In the rear view mirror, I saw little Tyler jump from the car and literally hop toward the front door. He was home.

Validation.

Note to readers: you can skip the next six thousand words or so. Really. I won't mind. And maybe you should. The next few days in my life are a pitiful, wallowing, depressive maelstrom, awash with doubt, anxiety, seller's remorse, mover's remorse, self-recrimination, depression, and more regret and self-pity. I became paralyzed, certain I had made a mistake. I was certain that I would or should move back to Illinois. The only amusing and interesting event that occurred during these few days of gypsy-like travel is that Rufus became terrified by a horse, and then became fixated on the potential threat of horses invading our new home. For a dog that once stood nose-to-nose with a barking Great Dane, that surprising streak of fear surfaced in my good dog. But other than that, it was all bad. But I have to write those words. I really do. It's the only way the story is complete. But skip ahead if you like.

Things get better. They really do.

14

From my childhood, I remembered Bedford, Pennsylvania, a stop on the Pennsylvania Turnpike, being advertised on billboards beside the highway as the "City of Motels." As I neared the exit, I wondered why that would be so. Bedford appeared like a pleasant small town, with a fort or a tavern or something or other dating back to before the Revolutionary War. But that would not explain the plethora of motels in the middle of that state. Perhaps, back when cars went slower, when people traveled slower, a few hundred miles out of New York City brought you close to evening and a need to stop and sleep, and by then, you were in Bedford. Traveling times have diminished over the years. I could leave Chicago early in the morning, stopping only for coffee and gas, and be in Pittsburgh in time for an early dinner. If I pushed, I could make Philadelphia while restaurants were still open for dinner. I had never done that, but knew that I could, if pushed, and if I didn't get too nervous at setting cruise control at seventy-six miles an hour. Or maybe seventy-nine, and taking a chance at being stopped for speeding.

So, I imagined, Bedford did not have the same stopping power it once had. But still, there were a lot of motels right off the turnpike. I had Googled the place before I left and found one motel that advertised itself as "pet friendly." I had made reservations, just to be safe, just for the first night. From then on, I would be fancy-free and let the highways take me—us— where they would.

Rufus made a show of stretching and shaking when I opened the crate door. I carried his food and water into the motel room, and told Rufus I would be right back, since I feared he might get nervous in the new surroundings and start to bark, then I went to retrieve my smaller suitcase and cardboard box with coffee-making supplies. I went back to the car for my pillow. I have always found it difficult to use strange pillows. They were either too soft or too hard or smelled odd.

I led Rufus out of the room and down the hall and outside, to the large field behind the motel. One could hear the muted rumble of the turnpike only a block or two away. Perhaps that's why this motel was more than reasonable.

"Is this our new house?" Rufus asked as he sniffed a thicket of tall grass. "It smells funny out here."

I anticipated his question. He had no frame of reference. He could live in a hotel room, as long as he got daily walks and crunchies.

"No, Rufus, this is just for tonight. We have a ways to go to get to the ocean."

"The ocean is far."

"Did you mind the ride? You slept for a while, didn't you?"

"I don't know. Maybe. The car wiggles . . ."

"Vibrates."

"Yes, that. It makes me sleepy."

"So the ride wasn't as bad as you thought, was it?"

He scratched at the dark Pennsylvania soil with his back legs.

"No. Since I'm in my crate and all."

We walked back to the Johnson Motor Court and Lodge in silence, the hum and thrum of the turnpike just audible as the breeze carried it along, a constant backdrop. Rufus stopped more often to sniff and examine. It was all new to him. Every morning and every night for a while would be new to him.

I looked up at the stars, only a handful visible through the ground clutter of neon and sodium vapor illumination that pocked the area around the turnpike exit. And I tried to prevent the soft, insistent rise of a nameless dread that slowly unclenched its fist under my heart.

I am doing the right thing. I know I am.

We walked across the parking lot, Rufus's nails clicking with each step.

Then why am I so terrified?

I used the keycard to unlock the hallway door. A faint odor of disinfectant and cigarette smoke lingered.

I'm making a mistake. I am making a mistake. I should have never sold my house.

I attempted to push the thoughts from my mind, but the more I tried, the louder their thump and drumbeat became. Rufus circled around a dozen times at the foot of the bed, sniffing and nosing at the orange blanket. He looked up at me several times.

"I know. It smells funny. But it is only for tonight. We keep going right after breakfast." He settled in a small coil of blanket, rested his head on his paws, and stared at me.

I knew what he was thinking. Or maybe . . . I just projected my fear onto him.

Why did you bring me to this terrible place?

I felt certain that I could not bring Rufus with me to the motel's breakfast room, though I bet some owners do, their yappy, fussy, scrabbling mini-dogs tucked in their purses or coat pockets. I had a yogurt, a glass of what might have been orange juice, a banana, a toasted bagel with two packets of strawberry jam, and two cinnamon rolls (they were on the small side). I had two cups of coffee, which actually tasted quite good, surprisingly. I toasted one slice of white bread and layered on two slabs of butter. Rufus liked toast. I took a third coffee with me in a cardboard cup and presented the toast to Rufus, torn in four pieces on a small paper plate. He ate it eagerly.

The sun had already risen when I took Rufus out for our morning constitutional. He may have questions or observations about the trip or the motel or my rising anxiety, but he did not speak, as is his norm. Just as well. I didn't think I could answer any of his questions without developing a hitch in my voice, some tremor that would lead him to other questions— and further worry for both of us.

No, silence was good. Especially for today, for this morning.

We got back on the turnpike and headed east. I planned on turning south at Harrisburg, toward Baltimore and then Washington, D.C. From there I would drive to Richmond and perhaps a little further for today. Then I would stop somewhere for the night. It wasn't that far, but much of the route went through or around populated areas with lots of beltways and route changes and decisions to make every few miles. A spiderweb of decisions. Decisions made me nervous—or at least driving decisions did. My new Volvo had a built-in GPS system that I programmed first for Baltimore. I would stop there and tap in a new destination. The problem lay in the fact that there were multiple ways to arrive at my final destination, perhaps dozens upon dozens, and the GPS may have picked the short-est, but not the easiest or the one with the fewest turns. All I could do was select the option for "Maximize Freeways."

I suppose if I were being an astute, observant writer, I could use this GPS method as a metaphor for my life—multiple paths to one specific goal—without a clear "Best Route" as an option. There are many ways to reach paradise. Not the Christian par-adise—there's only one way there—but a temporal paradise . . . you know what I mean, right? Find personal satisfaction and self-worth through working—or not working. It's the same destination, satisfaction, but there are two very different routes to take to get there.

To get to Baltimore and beyond, I had reviewed the route I intended to take on my road atlas and marked down, on a four-by-six card, every highway I thought I would need to be on to get there.

South from Harrisburg, it would be I-83, into Maryland, and to the north side of Baltimore. Then take 695—either west or south—around Baltimore proper, to 95 South. A second road paralleled that route that didn't seem to be a labeled as an interstate, but was marked with 295, and a different color than 95. Was this route faster? It might be, since it angled more to the east of Washington.

How do you know what's best? Unless you live there, there is no telling what route works better.

Like life. That's the GPS metaphor again. Maybe I could write an article about that for some magazine. Maybe. I would need to remember all the nuances I was considering now, yet at the moment, I was getting more nervous about my choices, even though they were miles and hours distant.

From Washington, it would be 95 around the city and on to Richmond.

Rufus had settled into his crate nicely, hardly stirring when I took the ticket at the start of our turnpike segment. We drove on, into the sun, into a chilly but clear day in Pennsylvania.

I wondered when it would be warm enough to drive with the window down.

∞

I stopped for lunch at a McDonald's somewhere west of Baltimore. Rufus stirred and stretched as the car came to a stop. He sniffed the air. I am sure that he could smell the grease, thick in the air around the fast-food restaurant. I know I could, and I'm not a dog with a sensitive nose. I put some water in his bowl, a handful of kibble in his dish, let him out of the crate, and left both front windows open a crack. It was still very chilly and quite cloudy—so, please, no hate mail from readers telling me I am a negligent pet owner for leaving poor Rufus in a sweltering car. Besides—I was going to eat quickly, keeping the car in full view the whole time. It's probably not enough for my more militant readers, but when you're alone and with a dog, you do what you have to do.

I ordered the two cheeseburgers meal. I bought a third burger on top of that, which I would share with Rufus. I timed my lunch. From start to finish: fourteen minutes. I know, it's barbaric to wolf down any meal that quickly, but when they hand you your food even as you finish ordering it, that's not a fast time.

I came back to the car, split the third burger with the good dog Rufus, and then took him out into the field behind the restaurant.

"We are not going to live here," I said, knowing he would have asked if he were to speak, which he wouldn't do—that I could be sure of. "We're going to get back in the car and drive a few more hours until we stop for the night. Okay?"

Rufus looked up at me like he understood.

Even if he didn't, it was what I intended on doing.

I reset the GPS for Richmond, studied my road atlas for a long time, got gas, and continued on my trek.

In the past—while a widow, not when I was with Jacob—I liked driving to Pennsylvania to visit my mother. I had a destination, I knew the route, I knew where I would get radio reception for the NPR stations along the way, I knew to wait to stop for lunch until Ohio. So the drive to Pennsylvania—some ten hours in length, depending on the weather and how fast I felt like driving—was . . . like going on a silent monastic retreat for me. No talking. No arguments. No instructions on the proper technique of passing or staying in the right-hand lane. There was no one who would look askance at my stopping for Starbucks every forty-five minutes or so. And since the route and all the environments were so well known, I could switch off my conscious thoughts and set my mind to autopilot. I loved that feeling of letting my mind go free, reliving incidents from the distant past. (Like my senior prom. That came up often. Go figure.) Solutions and options to current situations would appear in my thoughts, almost miraculously. I could daydream a hundred different scenarios and no evil inner voice would interrupt, saying that I had a deadline to meet, or a floor that needed vacuuming. No, I really enjoyed the long, desolate stretches of driving alone. A solitary road trip became great therapy, and inexpensive—only dependent on the price of gasoline, I guess.

I looked forward to that same carefree drive this trip.

It was not happening. Not in the least.

At first I blamed the newness of the route, then the newness of the car, then the fact that good dog Rufus traveled with me.

None of that mattered, I decided, somewhere to the southwest of Baltimore.

The unsettled feeling, the dislocated feeling, I think, all stemmed from the fact that I had nowhere to be. I owned no home now—no more home base. I had no real destination waiting for me. I had become a ship adrift—and even worse. Eventually, even a wayward ship is blown by the prevailing winds into some place, some rocky shoal, some barren island. I was not like that ship. I could go anywhere and everywhere. Yes, we headed toward the ocean, but the east coast of America is like . . . well, like one long piece of possibilities. I could spend years looking and never find a home. True, I had narrowed the choices down—a little—by starting in Virginia Beach and heading south. I may not have mentioned that decision before. I did tell Rufus, I think, even though Virginia Beach meant nothing to him. It did have two names, which he liked.

If one went further north from Virginia Beach, one could experience real winters, with gales and blizzards and snow tinted with salt. I wanted to escape all that, I think. Going south would not make one immune from storms, just the low temperatures of the dreaded nor'easters.

But after eliminating a long swath of northward shoreline, I had a still-too-large path of potential waiting for me. How would I find the "right" place to live? How would I find a house in a nice neighborhood? It took living in Wheaton for years to know what areas might be considered less than desirable. Now I would have to make a decision in the matter of a few hours or days.

So my thoughts remained jumbled and unfocused, unable to rest on any topic, any event, any incident for long.

I did not like the feeling.

And every moment that I remained unsettled became another moment when I had time to almost regret the decision to leave Wheaton and head into a much more unsettled future. I mean, I could be making things worse by moving, rather than better.

I suppose I could go back to Wheaton. I mean, I could tell people that I just didn't like the East Coast. They would welcome me back. And they wouldn't think ill of me for returning. People do it all the time—admit that they made mistakes. It's not irrevocable.

Then those thoughts would leave me for a while.

But never for good. At least not during these first few days.

─────

We made it to Williamsburg, Virginia, that day. I was tired of driving. Baltimore and Washington were like one big suburb with lots of traffic, all the time.

Rattled would be a good descriptive term for how I felt. Just rattled—emotionally as well as physically. Rufus seemed none the worse for wear. That evening, as we walked around the hotel, he admitted that he had slept most of the day.

"I liked that place with the food," he said. "We could stay there."

He meant the McDonald's. He was trying to be helpful.

We were staying at an Embassy Suites Hotel, a few miles from Williamsburg. Rufus appeared impressed when we entered the suite, sniffing it very carefully.

"No, we are not living here," I explained again. "We are only staying for one night."

I had room service deliver a hamburger. Room service can be expensive and I wasn't all that hungry. Rufus had a third of my burger. These were not great dog-feeding habits, but my stressful situation made it hard to keep to a healthy routine. For some reason, in a hotel, I lose the willpower to deny him a bite or two when he stares up at me while I eat. I'm a wimp, I know, but I was also tired. Very tired.

———— ∞ ————

The next morning, I felt much better. I helped myself to a very large breakfast. I brought Rufus back a small serving of scrambled eggs, which are supposed to be good for his coat.

Since we were only a few miles from historic Colonial Williamsburg, I decided to stop and walk the grounds. I had never been there before. Apparently, you have to buy a ticket to enter some of the locations, but you can visit the stores and restaurants without a fee—other than facing the lure of souvenirs.

I packed up the car, parked in a city lot, snapped on Rufus's leash, told him to be on his best behavior, and began to walk down the main street of Colonial Williamsburg—a terrifically impressive collection of old homes and shops and government buildings from the time of our nation's founding. I had already explained to Rufus that we would just be visiting and we would drive to the ocean later in the day.

Early April brings about a beautiful spring in Williamsburg, I observed. A scattering of trees and shrubs had begun to blossom and I could smell the early sweetness of bayberry bushes. Their scent feels historic. The skies were clear and the sun warmed my shoulders.

Then, all of a sudden Rufus stopped cold and scurried behind my legs, almost tripping me in his haste. A half a block away, turning the corner, and coming toward us was a roan-colored horse, his rider in Revolutionary-era garb. As they came closer, Rufus pulled away further, and found himself at the farthest limit of his retractable leash. Rather than risk his slipping out of his collar, I went toward the side of the street and bent down to the frightened dog, putting my arm around him, and held him as best I could.

"It's a horse," I whispered to him. "I bet it's a real friendly horse too."

Rufus would have none of it and tried to claw his way out of my grasp. I held tighter and the horse and rider slowly walked past us. Rufus's eyes were wide in fear and his heart thumped, almost audibly to the unaided ear.

"He won't hurt you. He won't step on you. I promise."

He eyed the animal as it made its way down the street and turned a far corner.

I hadn't expected encountering any horses today, but since this was a historical site, I suppose I should have expected it.

We walked around for another thirty minutes or so, Rufus never more than a foot or two away from my legs. His closeness made walking difficult, and nearly dangerous.

I enjoyed what I saw in Williamsburg. But when something is not shared, it is never as poignant, or as meaningful, or as beautiful as it might have been if it were shared with someone.

I gathered Rufus, still apparently nervous and concerned about the possible reappearance of the big animal, and got him into his crate in the car. He did settle down somewhat, protected in a familiar environment.

I headed south and east, and plotted the route so I would come into Virginia Beach from the north side. There were some bridges to cross to get there. I did not like long bridges. I never have. Consider it an unnatural fear. I suspect I was afraid of twisting the wheel of the car and launching myself into space. Unnatural, I know. But the fear lay there, hiding deep in my subconscious.

I managed to find the route through the city that roughly ran past the ocean. I tried to rouse Rufus to look at the water, but he didn't want to stand up as I drove. Maybe it made him feel unsettled as well. Virginia Beach is probably a lovely city, but I wasn't sure where I was going, and between the ocean and me was a wall of condos that only let me see the ocean in short gaps as I drove. On the other side of the street were restaurants, stores, and jungle mini-golf places with volcanoes and wrecked pirate ships with Jolly Roger flags fluttering in the afternoon spring breeze.

This isn't what I wanted. Not at all.

At a red light, I stopped to turn around and look at Rufus. His head was resting on his front paws, and his eyebrows went up as I turned. I tried to read his eyes—always a difficult task. I thought I saw discomfort, or some sense of impending doom. He looked like he did whenever I had to take him to the veterinarian or groomer: scared, resigned, dark, and morose.

I didn't want to see him this way.

A horn behind me sounded. The light had turned green. I drove farther down the street, hoping that as I left the city behind, I would find something that resembled home.

I didn't.

We made it as far as the south end of the city, several miles from the main drag of hotels and condos. I saw a Holiday Inn on the other side of the street—meaning it would cost a lot less than if it were really on the ocean. Still only early afternoon, I felt more tired than I had been in months and months. I didn't ask, as I checked in, if the place considered itself pet-friendly or not. Rufus would be a quiet guest, quieter and cleaner than many human guests. I asked for a room away from the street on the first floor. When it's not summer at the ocean, hotel guests can be more selective.

I carried Rufus into the room, dragged my suitcase in, pulled the decorative bed cover off the bed, and lay down, feeling most exhausted. Rufus clambered up onto the bed and lay down beside me, his head on one of the pillows. He didn't look all that comfortable that way; maybe he simply mimicked what I did every night.

When I woke up, the sun had been down for a long time. I looked out and the darkness had descended. I hurried outside, retrieved my box of coffee-making supplies, and made a large mug of very hot coffee, with three spoonfuls of powdered creamer. I sat in the lone upholstered chair and sipped. Rufus sat close by me, closer than he ever did when we were back home—the home I no longer had or could ever go back to.

I had imagined all those validation points, hadn't I? None of them were really validating my stupid choices right now.

I had three packets of cheese crackers "Made with Real Cheddar Cheese." (How much real cheddar cheese could there be in these tiny snacks?) I ate those, sharing them with Rufus, who didn't seem to like them any more than I did.

I was so tired already. Tired of traveling. I felt sure I had made a mistake, but did not know what to do to rectify it. Do I simply go home and look for an apartment for me and Rufus? But what of my . . . our plans to find a warm place to live? Do I turn my back on that?

I gathered up the leash and Rufus and I walked down the well-lit sidewalk that ran along the street. A cluster of lights glowed farther south. Maybe there would be a soft-serve ice-cream stand there. I felt a desire for a chocolate cone dipped in chocolate topping.

"What was that big thing? This morning. The big thing that scared me."

"That's called a horse, Rufus. I told you that already. Before people had cars, they rode horses everywhere."

"Do horses live at the ocean?"

"Some do, I guess. But no more than anywhere else."

"There weren't any horses at home. I never saw a horse there."

"I am sure there were horses in barns nearby—we just never went to any of them."

"If there are horses at the ocean, I'm not sure I want to live there," he said, more firmly than usual. "I don't like horses at all. They smell funny. And they could step on me."

"They wouldn't step on you. I promise."

"I don't like them."

We walked on another block. The lights grew brighter. I think it was a 7-Eleven and a gas station. Maybe I could get a Slurpee instead of a cone. I wanted something bad for me, something unnourishing. I wanted . . . I don't know what I wanted. I didn't know what I wanted at all.

Rufus stopped and sat down.

"I want to go home," he said.

I could have asked him if he meant home as in Illinois, or back to the hotel, or back in the car and his crate. I didn't want to ask him. I didn't want to know what he meant, even though I was pretty sure he meant home in Illinois. I hope he knew that we couldn't go back to that life. That life did not exist anymore. We needed to find a new life.

"Did you ask God about this?" I asked Rufus. "About wanting to go home?"

Rufus remained sitting.

"No."

"Are you going to?"

"No."

"Why? I thought you talked to God a lot."

"I do."

"Then are you going to ask him?"

"No."

"Rufus," I said with a note of exasperation in my voice, "Why not?"

"I don't like horses. Not at all. You said that some of them live at the ocean. I don't want to go there, then. You never told me about horses before. Trusting has nothing to do with horses. Nothing at all."

I bent down to him. Both his sitting and talking and my bending close to him were unusual. We always talked as we walked. Neither of us made a fuss about the process.

"Rufus, there are a lot of big animals out there. Cows, for one. They're almost as big as horses."

"Do cows live at the ocean?" He looked over his shoulder, toward the ocean, toward the muted sound of the waves.

"I don't think so. Maybe somewhere, but not around here."

"I don't want to be here. I want things the way they used to be. I want my bed down by the kitchen. We don't even have a kitchen anymore. Nothing is like it was. I don't like that. And now, you tell me about horses and cows. I don't like surprises like that."

I stood back up. Talking to Rufus at close range felt abnormal.

"I'm sorry, Rufus, but we can't go back to the way things were. We can't go back to the old house. A new family lives there now. We have to find a new place, with a new kitchen and a great place to put your bed—where maybe you could lay in the sun during the day."

"What about the horses?"

I sighed. Rufus made me sigh often. How do you calm the heart of a dog—an intelligent dog—but one that just can't grasp enigmatic complexities of the world, like horses and cows and the threat of being stepped on.

"Rufus," I said in my best parental voice. "We have to keep moving. Maybe we'll find the right place tomorrow. Wherever it is, there will not be any horses around. I promise you that. But we can't go back. We have to go forward. We have to give up what we can't have anymore. I think you can understand that. You said we have to trust God. Right? You said that."

Rufus stared at his front paws.

"I guess. Maybe. But I don't like this change. I liked the way things were. Except for the cold. And the snow. And getting run over by cars. Other than that, I liked it. And there were no horses there at all. None at all."

This time I bent to him, not to hear him, but to hug him tight to me.

We were both lost and alone and dislocated and we wanted what we had before and would never, ever get back.

"God did say to trust him," Rufus added, his voice soft, almost a whisper. "I don't know what that means exactly. But I think he will show us what he wants us to do. Right? He does that sort of thing, right?"

"He does, Rufus. I'm pretty sure he does."

I was too tired to tell Rufus that I am still not on speaking terms with the Almighty. Once you stop talking, starting up a conversation is all that much harder. Silence begins to solidify, like concrete. Once it is set, it is terribly difficult to break up. But Rufus talks with him. God will protect Rufus, right? And if Rufus is safe, doesn't a little of that spill over onto me? I think it might. I hope it does. I guess we'll see . . .

I stood up, and then we walked back to the Holiday Inn, both of us quiet. I felt better. I felt tired, but I felt better.

Just before we got to the hotel parking lot, I said to Rufus, "Tomorrow will be a better day. And there won't be any horses at all. I promise."

It was a promise that I hoped I would be able to keep.

15

I had to drive back west, toward Norfolk, to go south again, into North Carolina. A very thin, red line ran down the sliver of land—the Barrier Islands. At the end of a very long stretch of land, a dotted line crossed a blue expanse of Pamlico Sound. It indicated a ferry, and I checked with the desk clerk at the Holiday Inn and asked if that ferry ran all year. He assured me it did. It had better. If it didn't, it would mean a long ride back north, to get to a bridge that crossed the sound as it narrowed, close to land.

I guess it really didn't matter. I had nowhere I had to be. But I sure hoped that the ferry was operating.

I wonder how Rufus would take to a ferry voyage—even a short one. Would he treat it as an unwelcome surprise—like horses?

Using my handy road atlas, I found my way to the two-lane road that ran down the center of the barrier islands. I passed Kill Devil Hills and Nags Head and the site of man's first powered air flight. I drove past lots of small towns with homes that I knew, without stopping or asking, were so far out of my price range—multistory places with lots of glass and cedar siding and swimming pools and a great expanse of sea-shore and palmetto grass and endless views. I suppose if I was rich, I might have stopped and looked at some of the places that featured FOR SALE signs, gently clapping into the strong Atlantic breeze.

But I wasn't rich. Not even close.

I drove through the Cape Hatteras National Seashore. My stomach reminded me of the time—lunchtime—but there were no McDonald's along the pristine seashore. Nor had I expected any. I arrived in Ocracoke and found the ferry.

It did operate, and the last ferry of the day would be depart-ing in less than a half hour. The ferry, the brochure claimed, would hold fifty-three cars. Upon departure, there were twelve autos and one small truck on board. The very nice young man who took my ticket said I could take the dog out on deck, as long as he remained on a leash.

I decided to let Rufus decide.

"Rufus, we're on a boat that will take us across the sound, which is sort of like the ocean, but not quite as wavy or bumpy. You can walk around with me out on the deck if you want. I'll open up your crate. If you want to come out for a walk and look at the ocean, come out. If not, you can stay in your crate."

He looked at me, then peered out the side window. He looked at me again.

"It's very safe. No horses. No cows, either. And all the cars are stopped."

Gingerly, he stepped out of the crate. I snapped the leash on him and led him from the car. The ferry started with a loud whooshing sound, as the propellers bit into the water. Rufus snugged himself against my leg, but did not try to retreat to the car. He tried his best to be brave, I guess.

I led him up the steps to the top deck and an open deck space, with a scattering of benches that looked forward, facing

the wind and the sun. The ferry rolled and swayed a bit, even
though the waters of the sound were calm—at least to my non-
nautical eyes.

"Rufus, the boat will bounce a little bit. The water is not as
smooth as a road. But it is nothing to be afraid of."

We walked a little closer to the rail, Rufus sniffing loudly.

"That's salt water you smell. And maybe some fish."

He snorted once, then again, then he sat down, facing the
wind, his ears slightly back, half-flapping in the breeze. I could
plainly see he enjoyed it. At least that is what it looked like to
me. His eyes were half-closed as well, as if he were deliberately
sunning himself.

You could see where we were heading: a small green thickness of land some miles to the south. From there we would
continue south, past Morehead City and on to Wilmington.
From there we would travel on to Myrtle Beach. I knew people
who disparaged Myrtle Beach as the "Redneck Riviera," but
perhaps there was a patch there of cute little houses, and a
home waiting for us.

Perhaps. That would be validation . . . right?

I am not a gypsy. I don't like traveling. I just decided that
I don't like this at all. I've been in three hotel rooms . . . and I
don't like it.

So if I find a place . . . how will I know that I found the right
place? How will I be able to tell?

I pulled my sweater a little tighter. A sliver of crispness in
the air kept everything fresh and clean smelling.

Maybe there'll be some sort of sign.

Rufus snorted again.

Yeah, that's what I figured too.

We made it across the sound. Rufus appeared to enjoy the ferry ride. I know I did. We got into the car and drove on, now into the early afternoon. We had skipped lunch today. Well, I had skipped lunch. At home—which doesn't exist anymore, I know, I know—Rufus had food available to him all day. He would nibble on it now and again. But I needed more definitive and better-timed feedings than that. I wanted food. Rufus had already eaten a few bites from his bowl of kibble in the car.

After a short distance, I noticed a sign that read WELCOME TO ATLANTIC BEACH. (Weren't all the beaches I had been seeing Atlantic beaches?) Under that was listed a population count of just over 1,800. I liked the sound of that. Pretty small for a town, but the idea just appealed to me. I pulled over for just a moment to check my map. A larger city lay across the sound—Morehead City—connected by a long bridge. That meant a place for grocery stores and merchandise all well within reach.

Hmm . . .

I drove slowly. There would not be a lot of impatient beach traffic this early in the year. No wall of condos faced the ocean. Just homes. Some duplexes, I think. The tallest building I saw could only have been two stories high—three if you counted the parking area underneath—since most of the homes were up on pilings or stilts or whatever they were called. Spider leg construction. To be honest here, I felt certain that I could not afford oceanfront regardless of the number of stories . . . but a street or two back from the water? Maybe. The houses were smaller, more modest—some obviously rental units, some looking lived in, with current residents.

Hmm.

Okay, this was the first possibility I had encountered so far on my trip. I know I was anxious to find a place I could label as a "possibility." I turned down a street a block off the ocean, a street of modest homes—some on stilts, some not, some cottages, some more substantial places. And a few with FOR SALE signs in front as well.

But my stomach growled again. That always proved to be a very bad influence on my decision-making abilities. Never go grocery shopping when you're hungry, right? I never did shopping of any type hungry. I would buy things just to get out of the store so I would be able to go elsewhere and find food.

A few blocks further on, I saw a sign for the Shark Shack. There were picnic tables out front—a restaurant perfectly suited for a dog if I've ever seen one.

I sat at an outside picnic table, under an umbrella, and ordered the grouper bites and the shrimp. Rufus sat on the ground beside me, sniffing and squinting in the sunlight. For April, it was nearing T-shirt warmth. I liked that. A lot. Rufus liked the grouper bites. I know—I'm a bad pet owner. But he was hungry. And I am sure he had never tasted grouper before.

The waitress—Cindi, her name tag said—came out and asked if I wanted anything else.

"Coffee, please, with cream and sugar."

"What about the dog?" she asked and smiled.

"I think he's had enough for today. And he doesn't drink coffee."

She returned with a large, thick mug.

"Do you live around here?" I asked. I seldom engaged in conversation with strangers. But here, well, I played the role of the stranger.

"I do. Well, across the bridge. Over in Morehead City."

"Is it a nice place to live?" I asked. Then I added, "I'm thinking of moving . . . well, I am moving . . . and wondered about what this place is like."

I didn't want to appear like a stalker or anything weird. I wanted to sound normal.

"Yeah, I guess it's okay. I've only lived here for five years. My husband is a drill instructor at Camp Lejeune. You know—the marine base."

I had heard of it, but I didn't really know where it was— until now.

"You don't live on the base?"

"No. Base housing is pretty awful. We rent out a condo over there. That's why I'm working here. Help pay the bills and all. But this is a nice place to work. I'm outside a lot. Get a good tan in the summer. People are nice. It's pretty much okay. For now."

I smiled back. Not a ringing endorsement, but she didn't say it was terrible either.

"What about hurricanes?"

She put her hand on her hip. "Well, the way I figure it is that every place has something terrible about it. We lived in Kansas when we were first married. Really hot. And flat. With a regular sprinkling of spring tornadoes. My sister lives in New York City. There you have . . . well, New York City to deal with. Rude people—or maybe they're all just in a hurry. And it's really, really crowded. Here . . . I guess we get hurricanes every now and then, but doesn't every place get something? And if it doesn't, it's either too expensive or there's too many stuck-up people that live there. Everyone around here is pretty normal, you know. Some pickup trucks and all that. But otherwise normal. I like normal people. So, I guess this place is pretty much okay."

I thanked her, sipped at my coffee, and stared out at the street. Not much traffic in April. I am pretty sure that during the summer it would get really jammed. But then again, there weren't any huge resorts for people to come to. Even if all the houses filled up, it wouldn't be that bad.

Hmm.

Validation? Sort of. Maybe a little.

I drove down the road a bit further south. Rufus fell asleep. I passed another Holiday Inn—this one on the beach. I stopped, reserved a room, and then continued my drive. I doubled back and drove down the side streets. Atlantic Beach was not more than five or six blocks wide and a few miles long, with the standard beach resort apparel and accessory stores along the way. I need to ask someone just how many bamboo beach mats could one place possibly sell?

It was late afternoon by now. I went back to the Holiday Inn, and Rufus and I settled into our room. Standing on the balcony of our third-floor room, I could see the ocean. When I left the sliding glass door open, I could hear the ocean. I liked that. The beach wasn't a mile wide, but neither was it a narrow strip of sand. Fifty yards across? I'm no good at distances like that. But the distance was comfortable. With sort of a sand dune-like area, spotted with shrubs and sea grass, dividing the beach from the houses, I'd call the view pretty. Not Hawaii pretty, but . . . well, I liked the view. Very pretty. The beach, flat and level, would be good for walking. Some beaches have an extreme slope to them, so you need to have one short leg and one long leg to walk comfortably—but that would only be good in one direction.

I lay down on the bed. Rufus jumped up and snorted around, moving the pillows with his snout. He does that a lot. It's not like dogs had pillows way back when; his behavior is just instinctual—like he was moving grass around with his nose and wallowing out a place to lie down. After a moment or two, he felt settled and flopped sideways on the bed. He stared at me, looking like he wanted to talk. He didn't. I surmised what his conversation might be: he wanted to know if we would live here and that he had grown tired of traveling already, and do any horses live here.

I knew the answer to one of his questions—the horse question. And I had grown very tired of traveling too.

When I began planning for this trip, when I made the decision to uproot Rufus and me from everything we had known and loved, I thought it would be easy. I thought it would be fun. I thought that I would spend a month or two or three exploring all the small seaside towns between here and Florida. I thought it would be enjoyable. I thought I would be okay with traveling—like that guy on the public broadcasting channel who is always traveling all over Europe. He seems to enjoy it. I thought I would too. But I didn't. Not at all. And what made it more uncomfortable is that I thought that this is probably what Jacob would have wanted me to do—after he was gone, that is.

Now, less than a week into it, I wanted it to stop. I am sure Rufus wanted it to stop.

What could I have been thinking? Did I really think that I would be magically shown where I was supposed to settle? Did I think that God would have neon signs pointing out MARY'S NEW HOUSE? Did I really think that life worked that way? And I sort of expected, at least a little bit, that the Almighty would swoop in like a superhero and point me to my new Eden. After all, isn't he in the business of protecting Rufus? If Rufus had protection, wouldn't that mean that I would be protected by default? I can't believe how stupid all this now sounded. I can't believe I had listened to a dog. How could he really help me now? And what alternative do I have, now that I started in on this journey?

I switched on the power on my cell phone and dialed.

Ava picked up on the third ring.

"How are you? Where are you? I miss you so much."

I explained where I had landed for the day. I told her about Rufus and the colonial horse.

"That is just so adorable. It really is. Poor Rufus. You should have been filming it. Doesn't your camera have a video record option?"

As if I knew. And if I had known, as if I also would have figured out how to use it.

And then I told her of our drive down the barrier islands and our ferry ride.

"I am so jealous. It snowed here last night. In April. Snow. Can you believe it? I can't stand it here any longer. Find a place quickly, so I can visit. Some place where college boys go to for their spring break, okay? I could come down for spring break. We could have a really good time, if you know what I mean."

I knew what she meant.

"Spring break is over, Ava, isn't it? I think it's already happened this year."

"Well, then find a place with a college nearby. That will ensure a beach filled with potential."

"I don't think there is a big college anywhere near Atlantic Beach."

"I bet there is a branch of some big school nearby. That'll be good enough for now. When can I come?"

I took a deep breath. I tried not to sigh.

"What's the problem?" she asked. Ava knew me well.

"I don't know. I'm tired of traveling."

"Already? It's only been a few days."

"I know. I'm not a gypsy, I guess. I want to be somewhere already."

Ava did not answer.

"I shouldn't have done this."

No response.

"Maybe . . ."

No response.

I had to pose the question. I had to have her take on my situation, on what I felt "Maybe I should come home. Back to Wheaton."

No response.

"It would be the sane thing to do . . . right? Back to my friends."

No response.

"Ava, are you there? Can you hear me now?"

I heard the sigh. I think she practiced at sounding exasperated—perhaps more perturbed than exasperated.

"Listen, Mary. I gave you a going-away party three weeks ago. You don't get a welcome home party until you've been gone . . . I don't know . . . two years. You're not coming home."

"Why not? If I made a mistake."

"You didn't make a mistake. You're just scared. And maybe a little lonely. Maybe that's a good thing. To be lonely for a while. By yourself lonely. Without friends to supply you with the drug of sympathy. Sympathy is the most addicting drug there is. You need to be away from that. And you've never been on your own."

I wanted to shout at Ava to shut up. But I didn't, because I was too nice. And, in that moment, I sort of realized that she might have been telling the truth. I had been alone—but not by myself. Maybe I needed to be alone. And by myself.

I did like sympathy as well. How did she know that?

"So, is this Atlantic Beach a nice place?" Ava asked, changing the subject, having given me all the advice she had to give.

"I guess," I said. A little tacky in spots, but mostly nice."

"Hey, every place by the ocean is a little tacky. Unless you move to Hawaii—and you can't afford to move to Hawaii. I am right, aren't I? You can't afford a place on Wakawakawaka Beach, right?"

"Yes. I can't afford Hawaii. But I think I could live here. I think. I picked up one of those free real estate catalogs at the Shark Shack."

"Shark Shack?"

"A restaurant that I had lunch at. Fish bites. They were good."

"See, what did I tell you? Every place by the beach is a little tacky."

I scowled at Ava and ignored her snideness.

"If I buy a few blocks off the beach—then I can afford it. A small house. It would cost a lot less than what my house in Wheaton cost."

"Are there places to eat there—besides the Shark Shack?"

"Yes."

"Is there a Walmart nearby?"

"Yes. I saw the sign for it on the highway. Three miles, it said."

"What's the beach like?"

I described it to her.

"Then buy a place there already."

I swallowed.

"Really? Here? Just like that?"

"Mary, you picked up and moved. You were my best friend. Still are, I think. But I knew you had to go. It was time. You need to start a new life. I don't think you could do that here. Too many people thinking that they had you figured out. Thinking that they knew what you needed. Thinking that you had to fit into some sort of preconceived idea of a person—like go back to church and marry a deacon."

"Elder."

"What?"

"They are called elders at the church. The church I went to."

"Former church, then. And I don't care what you call them. It wasn't who you were. Trust me."

"Then who am I?"

"I don't know. But you don't know either. I love you like a sister." She laughed. "I take that back. I have a sister and we don't get along at all. But I love and care about you, Mary. You need to do this. You do. Forge a new life. You have to trust me. Atlantic Beach sounds like a good place to do that. If you look up and down the coast, looking for a more perfect place, you will never settle down. Make a choice, Mary. Make a choice and live with it. Your new life will find you there. In Atlantic Beach. It will find you."

Is that validation? I couldn't tell anymore.

"Okay. I'll look around some. But if I don't find the right place . . ."

"You'll find the right place. A little cottage with a picket fence and a screened porch, and when the wind is right you'll be able to hear the ocean. Trust me, Mary. You have to do this—even if you don't want to."

"Really?"

"Yes. Really. And call me tomorrow. The good Toe Doctor is due here in five minutes and I'm not dressed—which he would like, but not tonight."

"I'll call you."

"Trust me, Mary. Things will look better in the morning."

I hung up and listened to the ocean.

What's up with all the "trust me" stuff. Is that some sort of sign?

That night, I drove down to Mosquito Amos's for take-out ribs and chicken. I got the ribs, which I brought back to the hotel. Rufus danced about once he got a sniff of the meat—the puppy-food dance, I called it. The ribs were excellent—huge and juicy, with amazing barbeque sauce. The coleslaw just sweet enough, and the baked potato was as large as Rufus's head. Everything tasted great.

Maybe this is a good place.

I gave Rufus two rib bones. He thought they were delicious, too.

After darkness had settled in, and after I washed the barbeque sauce from my fingers and hands, I snapped on Rufus's leash and headed to the ocean. A small wooden walkway led over the sand dune, through a thicket of brush and sea grass and down onto the beach. The moon was full, and the beach as well lit as any of our walking paths back in Wheaton. The heady salt air washed over us as we climbed down the steps and onto the sand. The wind had gone soft now, the waves a gentle lapping at the shore. Rufus stopped at the edge of the beach and looked out over the water, a million stars reflected in its calm surface, like diamonds dancing on slow-moving Jell-O. (Yes, I used to be a writer. Slow-moving Jell-O? Please.) The moon hung at my shoulder, nearly full, gibbous, offering enough light to read a book—if the type was large enough, that is.

He looked down at the ground.

"What is this?" he asked.

"Sand. It's what beaches are made of."

He took a few tentative steps.

"It feels funny on my paws. Like warm snow."

We walked north along the beach. A trio of pelicans came by, flapping more noisily than I thought they would be.

Rufus stopped and stared.

"What are those?"

"Pelicans. They eat fish."

"Not dogs?"

"Not dogs. Just fish. They scoop them up from the water in their beaks."

He turned to watch them fly on, courting the edge of the sea and shore, glistening in the moonlight.

"I don't like them," he said with finality.

I walked us closer to the water's edge. We stood, just beyond the farthest reach of the waves.

"Does it always do that?" Rufus asked. "The water at home never did this."

He meant the pond behind our house.

"They're called waves. I think it has something to do with the moon and the wind."

Rufus looked up at the moon, and then back at me, as if I was toying with him, trying to make him feel stupid or foolish.

"But I'm not sure," I added. "Sometimes the waves are bigger. Sometimes smaller."

Rufus took one step forward. At home, or, rather, back in Wheaton, he avoided puddles. Some dogs seemed oblivious to casual water. Not Rufus. He didn't like it. He let the wave roll in and wash over the edge of his front paws.

"The water is warm."

"Because of the Gulf Stream, I think," I said, then realized that it would be too much of an explanation for a dog.

He bent down and nosed at the water. I guess he stuck his tongue out.

He snorted.

"This tastes like those pretzels you tried to feed me once. I didn't like those pretzels at all."

"That's okay, Rufus. You don't have to drink this water. You shouldn't drink it. There is salt in it."

"Why?"

I hesitated. I might have known that once, in eleventh grade Earth and Space Science class taught by Mr. Riggens, who had just graduated from Indiana University of Pennsylvania. He was . . . Mr. Riggens, that is . . . how shall I put this politely? He was a pompous jerk.

"I . . . I don't know why there is salt in there, exactly. But it is salty. Most of the water on the earth is salty."

We continued our walk, at the water's edge, where the sand felt firm and the walking became easy.

Twenty minutes later, and perhaps a mile from the hotel, I stopped.

"Time to turn around and go back."

Rufus looked up at me. At home . . . back in Wheaton, I mean . . . I guess we never turned around. We always walked in a long, loopy circle, bordered by blocks and streets. We never just stopped and reversed our course. I wondered if I had to explain this as well, but Rufus only slowed a minute when he turned, then continued walking.

"I like it here," he said. "It smells good."

"I like it here too," I replied.

"Are we going to live here?"

"Well, not at the hotel."

"I know that," Rufus said. Even he had the exasperated tone down. "I mean . . . here."

"I don't know. Maybe. It is warm. And we are by the ocean."

"I like the ocean."

He stopped and looked over his shoulder, a furtive glance.

"There aren't any horses here, are there?"

"I am almost positive there are no horses on the beach."

He snorted again.

"I like the beach too," he said. "We could live here."

Maybe I should pray about this. I hadn't prayed about it. That was not unusual. I hadn't prayed about anything for so long. I didn't think it would be appropriate to start praying now. That would feel disingenuous and hypocritical—like I would call on God only when I found myself in trouble or confused or both. He and I weren't talking and I felt pretty certain that that silence was fine with both of us.

But not so much with Rufus. God and Rufus still talked. If you could believe Rufus, that is. I had a sudden rush that Rufus might merely be making a pretense of his piety and spirituality. But then again, he was a talking dog. No, that had to be something special, something out of the ordinary, something ordained . . . or something like that.

"Did God say anything about this place? Did you ask him if this would be a place that we could live in?"

Rufus bent to sniff a large clamshell, wedged into the wet sand.

"That's an empty clamshell, Rufus. Or oyster. Of some sort of shelled animal."

Rufus sniffed again and looked out over the darkening expanse of ocean.

"I did ask God, actually. I didn't think I would, or should, I guess. But I did."

I waited. I don't think Rufus knew the power of a long, pregnant pause. But this pause proved most effective.

"And?"

"Well, he said it was a nice place. He said there are nice people here. And he said something about being victorious. Something like that."

"Victorious? What does that mean?"

"I don't know. But I am sure that God likes the ocean. He made it warm and salty and beautiful. I like that. I think we should live here. He said we need to trust him again."

"Does that mean I need to trust you who is trusting him who said to live here?"

Goodness. I do sound delusional, don't I? But you know what I mean.

Rufus hesitated, then snorted.

"I guess. If that means we should live here, then yes."

"Really?"

"Sure. As long as there are no horses."

"They don't allow horses on this beach, Rufus," I said. I had looked it up on my phone earlier. "And no ATVs either."

Rufus snorted in affirmation.

Victorious? Validation?

16

The next morning, after our early stroll on the beach, both of us enjoying it even more than the previous evening's stroll, we came back to the hotel room. I took a shower and at 9:00 a.m., I called a local Realtor, Janet Stout, from "The Star Team." Janet might have been the senior member on the team. She had silver hair in a very sophisticated, upswirl flip, and looked every bit like a woman who stepped out of *Southern Living* magazine— at least as much as I could tell from her one-inch-square photo on the back of the free real estate listing catalog.

When you are absolutely new in town, how do you start? I took a chance on a postage-stamp photo. Seemed like a plan to me.

Janet's accent dripped southern honey—the accent that northern people make fun of—but on the phone, it sounded natural and welcoming, and sounded just perfect.

I took that as a sign.

I told her I wanted to buy a house . . . today.

Music to a Realtor's ears, I would imagine. A symphony would be more like it.

She had several properties in Atlantic Beach that could work for me, she said, and all in my price range. She would meet me at Robin Avenue, just a block off the beach. She gave me directions. It lay no more than five minutes from the Holiday Inn.

Janet drove up in a black Lexus, I think. I'm not that good with car makes. She must sell enough houses to keep her in nice cars. And she wore a very stylish outfit, out of *Town & Country*. A Peck and Peck woman. Is Peck and Peck—or would that be, *are* Peck and Peck—still in business? They sell stylish, expensive outfits, from what I recall. I had never read a copy of *Town & Country* either, but her outfit is what I imagined them featuring. Fine, aristocratic women on a fox hunt. Or planning the charity ball at the country club, sipping frosty mint juleps. She extended a hand and the warmest of welcomes. Her entire face turned into a smile, her eyes almost vanishing when she did.

"And what a darling dog," she exclaimed, bending to Rufus. He turned his head, just a little, and sniffed, then allowed her to pet his head, which she did enthusiastically (for a well-dressed woman) for a long moment. "My lands, he is such a gentleman. A real sweetheart, he is. Terriers aren't known for their sweet dispositions, now are they? He is a sweetie."

She stood back up, straightened her blouse, and grew taller somehow, then grandly gestured with her left arm. "This is it."

I loved her accent. I wished my mother had had that accent. No, I wished I had that accent.

"It's been a rental unit for two years," she said. "The couple who own it moved to a condo over in the city and . . . well, the husband passed on last winter and she wants to sell both properties and move to California. She has a daughter there."

The address had a Cape Cod cottage located square in the middle of the lot. I think it's Cape Cod. I'm not an expert on

architectural styles. The Amish had simple homes—no ornamentation, no frills. Their houses were easy to write about.
Amish styles . . . well, they didn't have any. I mean, none that
changed over time. They had bonnets and long dresses and I
had their fashions down pat. But—back to the task at hand—
the house on Robin, a small Cape Cod, faced east, with two
dormer windows, a screened porch, green shutters on the windows that looked like they really closed, and a picket fence
around the yard. The house and fence were mostly white, but
faded white, and chipped. It all needed painting—but I knew
that painting was a comparatively cheap fix. (I watch home
improvement shows on TV. A can of paint and voilà!—a new
look.) From the front of the house, you could actually see the
ocean peeking through between the oceanfront properties.
Perfect.

We walked up a half-dozen steps to the screen door. It
squealed a welcome as the Realtor shoved it open.

"The listing sheet says that the roof is four years old, and
the mechanicals, furnace and air conditioning, are five years
old. That's good." She looked around. "You'll have to paint, for
sure, and repair the screens, of course. I'm not sure if I remember what it needs on the inside. TLC for sure. Maybe it's the
bathrooms that need gutting. I think that is it. But that's not
too bad."

We entered the front room.

"A bit musty. I don't think anyone has been in here since
the fall, other than the rental company's caretaker. I called him
before I came. Just to make sure that the place was in showing
condition. No raccoons taking up residence without paying
rent," she said, enjoying herself.

The front room ran the width of the house, and appeared
more than spacious with lots of large-paned windows and
hardwood floors. One side featured two mismatched sofas; a

few end tables; a coffee table; and a huge, old, analog television set. On the other side, was a dining room table and chairs. I liked the openness of the space.

Janet sniffed, but not an entirely dismissive sniff. My mother could dismiss an entire year's worth of writing with a well-timed and well-toned haughty sniff.

"Not horrible. You could do something with it."

She assumed that I had a sense of style. Sheer flattery—and it worked so very well.

Rufus walked at my side. He sniffed discreetly, perhaps to spare me any anxiety.

The rest of the first floor consisted of a kitchen—smallish, but quite serviceable and in need of new counters, new cabinet doors, and appliances; a nice-sized bathroom, which did need gutting—ancient tile and fixtures, clean as a whistle, but not "good" old, not good retro old, just plain old and ugly; and a master bedroom, a large airy room big enough for a king-size bed, dresser, and sitting area.

"There's hardwood floors under this old carpeting," Janet said.

The upstairs was one large room, with wide, pine planked flooring, that had eight single beds lined up in it, and a second bathroom.

"Snow White could have lived here," Janet said, laughing as southern ladies are reputed do, with a sense of decorum and grace. I loved this woman already.

I lifted windows, tested doors, flushed toilets, turned on the water, switched on the gas range, flipped light switches, stood in the kitchen and tried to imagine if my cooking style would adapt to the new layout.

"Does it flood? Has it ever flooded? Like during storms. Or hurricanes?" I asked and tried to sound neutral. Rufus looked up at me when I said the word *hurricane*. His eyes showed a new level of concern. We both watch The Weather Channel. He knew what hurricanes were. Darn that all-knowing Jim Cantore. Now, besides horses, Rufus would have to contend with the threat of hurricanes. "That you're aware of, I mean."

"Sweetie, if a hurricane hits here, everyone floods. You just pay your flood insurance every year. Get good insurance. I can help you get the right coverage. You live near the ocean, you have to live with what the ocean brings you. But you can be victorious over Mother Nature, if you've a mind to, and if you plan ahead."

Victorious?

"I've lived here my whole life. We've had a few hurricanes over the years. Topsail Beach down the way gets washed away because they built it on a sand dune. Atlantic Beach has always held its own. They built it on higher ground. On the ocean, a few feet makes all the difference. But here is what you have to do: you listen to the radio. If they send out a warning, you pack up your sweet dog, make certain that your insurance policy is paid up, and drive to Raleigh to wait it out. Do some shopping while you wait. Get a manicure. Go to a spa. That's what I do."

That's the most sensible response to a hurricane evacuation that I had ever heard. Even the good dog Rufus seemed to be assuaged by her answer.

"Now, let me show you the yard."

The house sat on a quarter-acre lot, which Janet said was large for this size house. The grass, such as it was, was flat sea grass, she called it, and didn't need mowing much.

"You can get a service to do that for you."

The fence ran the perimeter of the property. It was bigger than my lot back in Wheaton.

"Of course, the fence needs to be repaired. Or taken down—your preference. A thousand dollars should be enough to get it fixed. Add some painting costs, of course. Fifteen hundred. Two thousand, tops."

Labor must be less expensive in the south.

We had made our way back to her car. I looked at the house from there. I could imagine myself on a porch swing, on the screened porch, with an iced tea in my hand, listening to the surf. I could just hear it, if I listened. And there were patches of blue water visible from the porch. The sun would be behind me in the evening—no squinting. A sidewalk ran the length of the block. I could see people strolling by, offering a genteel wave, perhaps. Rufus could keep guard from there. We could take our walks under the glow of streetlights, walk to the ocean, only a block away, stand in the breeze and put the day to rest—or greet the dawn.

It felt right. I looked at Rufus. He offered his best, and most practiced, serene, untroubled look, as if he foresaw no problems or concerns with my decision.

"What about the neighbors?"

She nodded. "The houses on either side are owner-occupied. They're full-time residents here. Maybe half the homes on this street are full-timers. That's good for home values. There are a few summer homes, used all summer and some weekends the rest of the year. And a few rentals. Nothing too rowdy. Families. No swarms of boisterous college boys from Duke, if that's what you're concerned with."

"A little."

I wondered what the right decision would feel like. In the past, I had a husband to ask. In the past, I had prayers to offer. I could wait, back then, for divine revelation, divine reassurance. I didn't have those options now. Neither of them. Rufus may have. Perhaps that's why he appeared serene. I could take a chance on my own human free will. Rufus said I had free will, right? Rufus said God wasn't all that concerned with my housing situation. Something like that.

"Is the price a fair one?" I asked.

A serious look came over Janet, a member of The Star Team. She pursed her lips and leaned closer to me, conspiratorially.

"I would offer 10 percent under the asking price. Maybe even 15 percent. Trust me. The market is slow here. I think she would take it."

I waited a moment, waited to feel something. Trust? Victory? I don't know anymore. Trusting in a dog to help guide me on my odd pilgrimage?

"Okay. Let's write up a contract. How soon could we close? I'm staying at the Holiday Inn and let's just say that the charm is wearing off quickly."

We met later at a Starbucks on Highway 70 in Morehead City. "They have an outside patio so your sweet little dog doesn't have to wait in the car," Janet had said.

I signed the paperwork for the offer, and asked about a home inspection, suggestions for contractors, and where to change my driver's licenses—all manner of Welcome Wagon queries. (Do they still have Welcome Wagons?)

"As for a closing date, the owner is very flexible," Janet said. "I called her agent on the ride over. She also said that since the place is a rental, and if the closing gets held up for any reason, well, you could move in today and pay rent until the closing date. I'm sure whatever the rental amount is will be less than the Holiday Inn charges."

I could move in today.

"Do you have enough supplies to do that? Sheets and towels and things like that?" Janet asked.

"I do. What I don't have, I can pick up at the Walmart. Does Morehead City have a place that delivers mattresses?"

Trust. Is that what all this was? I couldn't be sure, but I simply moved forward and that felt right.

———∞———

My offer was accepted twenty minutes later—no bargaining back and forth. I signed the paperwork—lots of paperwork—and met the owner's agent at Janet's office for the keys to the house.

"Listen," the seller's agent said. (She wasn't anything like a southern belle. I would have guessed a Boston accent, if any.) "The owner is just glad to sell it. She's not going to charge you rent or anything like that. She just wanted to be sure you weren't bringing in any Picassos or rare art since she said her insurance wouldn't cover that."

I assured her that there were no Picassos under the dog crate in my car.

While at the Star Team Realty office, I called for a mattress delivery, trash removal service (since I wouldn't keep any of the house's furniture), a contractor to remove the old carpet in the master bedroom, a cleaning service to do a thorough cleaning (including windows and gutters), and two contractors—both recommended by Janet to meet me at the house later that day for estimates on painting, redoing the bathrooms, updating the kitchen, refinishing the wood floors, and replacing the screens on the screened porch. While there, I took some quick measurements of the windows and ordered wide white wood blinds for all the windows.

By the end of the day, everything had been arranged. Janet had been right when she said that contractors in the area are really hungry for work. Thanks to a bad economy, I would have a livable house in seven to ten days, bathrooms and kitchen included, if everything went as planned. I could camp out at the Holiday Inn for seven to ten more days and enjoy the beach.

I stopped at Walmart and bought enough towels and two sets of king-size sheets, a four-piece dish set, and soap. I stopped at an appliance store and priced washers, dryers, and kitchen appliances.

I kept a running total in my head for all my purchases and potential purchases and scheduled services—and it added up to tens of thousands of dollars less than I had estimated spending on a new home when I had done my original budgeting back in Wheaton.

I would still need to get a job. That I had anticipated from the outset. I guess I could apply at the Shark Shack. I had spent two months as a waitress between high school and college and in all honesty, I was terrible at it—shy, insecure, with a bad case of jitter-induced short-term memory loss. I forgot to return to tables with water, or ketchup, or more napkins, or the check.

Perhaps since I've matured, I might do better.

Perhaps.

That first night I told Rufus about buying the house. I had been pretty sure he understood what I had done. But I could never be sure how much language he had paid close attention to during the day. He became a regular dog during the daylight hours. He became sort of a literate vampire canine by night.

"I know. I paid attention today. You seemed excited," he said, as we walked, skirting the edge of the night's waves. The wind grew a little stronger, a bit more robust this evening, so the waves charged at us a little faster. Rufus would jump out of

the way when they got too close. I think he took my admoni-
tion about not drinking the water to heart.

"What about hurricanes?" he asked right off. "That lady
with the silver hair said there were hurricanes here. I don't
think I like hurricanes."

I told him that he needn't worry, that hurricanes don't
sneak up on anyone. I told him that if one comes, The Weather
Channel knows about it days in advance and we could get
out of the way. I said hurricanes are not at all like horses that
sneak up on dogs.

"Then, that's good," he said, his words firm and solid.

I wanted to ask him if he had spoken more with God, if
he had prayed about this house, or this town. I wanted him
to tell me that I made the right decision. I wanted God to pat
me on the back and tell me that I had passed the test and my
life would be getting easier from here on in. I wanted Rufus to
tell me that everything would be fine and I would no longer
feel alone and abandoned. I wanted to feel whole again and I
wanted God to tell me that I was whole again, that he would
heal the split in my heart, that he would patch the terrible gash
that felt like a permanent affliction on its muscles.

I wanted all that, and none of it came.

I didn't ask the poor dog any of these questions. I knew
what his answer would be, or at least surmised what his
answer would be. He would say something about free will and
us making our own choices and trusting God—providing that
we prayed to God and had a relationship with him.

I don't think I had that. No, I take that back. I know I didn't
have that relationship with God. Even now. Even after moving halfway across the country on the merest nudging of the
Divine—as interpreted by a dog, of all creatures. I hoped for a
symbiotic spiritual relationship—that the person, or creature
that I now lived close to . . . that he lived, spiritually speaking,

close to God and in order to bless and protect him, I would gather at the edges of that protection and be protected myself. I figured this was a logically foolproof plan. In order for Rufus to have a stable home and environment, I would have to have the same things. I would warm myself on the edges of Rufus's celestial protection and blessing. How could it not work? If I were to have made the wrong choice—and everything here went horribly wrong—then Rufus would suffer. God wouldn't let that happen, would he? He sees the sparrows fall . . .

Like a wayward husband basking in the spiritual strength and calm of a believing wife. That is the way it works. At least, that is the way I hoped it would work.

17

Ten days later, the house stood complete and ready for occupancy. Well—almost complete. The granite countertop for the kitchen hadn't been cut yet. The granite people planned to install it in a week, and promised they could do so with a bare minimum of disruption and hardly any mess.

The house turned out glorious. The newly refinished floors gleamed, and the bathrooms, all fresh and white, with new tile and fixtures, smelled of adhesive and grout. The paint on the wood trim glistened, the walls were renewed, and the new stainless steel appliances in the kitchen shined in the afternoon sun. I purchased one small sofa at a warehouse store, one area rug for the bedroom, a pair of chairs for the eating counter in the kitchen, a wicker sofa and chair with summery-striped cushions for the screened porch, and an antique wooden bed frame from a consignment shop in Morehead City, and filled my car with groceries.

The cable people came and installed my Internet connection and I sent an "all" e-mail to every friend and relative I could gather on my e-mail list, telling them of my new address and phone number. I sent a postcard to Bernice, just to be sure she got word. Their e-mail might still be down.

I left the upstairs empty. With just one large room, I could eventually place a few beds up there. I might, come summer, when guests arrived. But for now, I just loved the barrenness of the large, empty, clean space. I made a vow with myself never to allow this house to become cluttered with anything. "Keep things sparse and simple" became my new mantra. Or motto. "Mantra" may imply some oddball Eastern religious sect—and heaven knows, we can't have that.

I called the moving/storage company in Wheaton and told them where to ship my crated possessions. I almost wished I could have said to simply dispose of them all, that I intended on starting over from scratch, that I wouldn't need three boxes of sweaters and winter coats anymore. But I couldn't do that. There were some possessions—pictures and mementos—that I wanted to keep. That I needed. A good thing about living in Atlantic Beach is that the cost of taking away unwanted furniture and assorted detritus of life appeared to be very inexpensive.

Rufus and I sat on the screened porch that first night, enjoying the warm spring evening. The screen door allowed Rufus to lie down on a new sisal rug I'd bought, and watch the street. He'd never had that opportunity back in Wheaton. Most of the windows in the front of our old house were blocked by furniture, or the view obstructed by bushes. Here he had a clear sight line to the street and the sky over the ocean beyond.

I felt settled. Mostly settled. Mostly to partly settled.

That night, Rufus said again that he liked the house, he liked the beach, and he liked the warm water (he once walked in up to his knees). His happiness made me happy—though I was not completely settled. Almost.

I dialed a number on my cell phone. Ava answered on the first ring.

"Congratulations," she said. "Now, I have a place on the ocean to stay at for free."

"You do. And you're welcome anytime."

I gave her the rundown of all that had transpired—the work on the house, my purchases, my being pleased with what had occurred, being happy that I found an affordable place so quickly.

Ava waited.

"Then what's wrong?" she finally asked.

"Nothing's wrong," I countered. "Everything is hunky-dory."

I thought I had learned how to lie well, to hide my true emotions behind a mask of cheeriness. A few years of widowhood and you get good at it.

Ava would have none of it.

"Don't lie to me. There's a hitch in your voice. Something's going on. Rufus hates it, right?"

"No," I replied. "He seems to really like it. He likes walking on the beach. He wades in the water and looks happy."

"Then you hate it, right? Like those $400 shoes you lusted after for months and then bought and when you wore them for the first time on a date, they hurt your feet and made your calves look misshapen."

"I never bought $400 shoes."

"Oh, yes . . . that happened to me, didn't it? But the principle is the same. You want it until you get it, right? Then you don't want it."

I sighed. I don't like sighing.

"I don't know. I think everything is fine. But I don't feel like all the pieces are in place. Like I'm still missing something. I can't explain it."

"Well, when you start making friends, maybe get a job, things will be better."

"I don't know. Maybe. But I don't think friends and a job are what I'm missing. I don't know. Maybe you're right. Maybe it will pass. It has been a pretty hectic few weeks. Things will get better, right?"

"They will. Trust me on that," she said.

I didn't trust her at all.

My granite guy/kitchen contractor made arrangements to install the countertop—mostly black, with some greenish-gray veins—on Friday.

"You'll be there Friday morning to let us in, Miss Fassler?" asked Billy B.

"I will. I get up early, so any time after seven is fine with me." I was eager to have everything totally done. I don't understand how anyone could put up with months and months of interior remodeling while living in the house. I had one item left to do and it bothered me to the point of distraction.

Billy B proved himself a man of his word. He and his crew showed up at a few minutes past seven. Rufus made a point of barking loudly, bouncing up and down at the door to the screened porch. I opened it, and it still squealed.

"I'll put some oil on the hinges, Miss Mary. Or sand off the bottom sill a bit. Fix that for free, if you'd like."

"I would. Thank you so much."

He touched the brow of his baseball cap, which had Billy B William Interiors stitched on the crown.

His team of workers heaved and strained as they carried in the massive, polished sheet of granite. It looked spectacular, if I have to praise myself for a fine job of selecting interior finishes. The old countertop came off with a minimum of fuss, and the new one slipped into place. A new stainless steel sink with new faucets was installed.

Half the crew took off, and the remaining three workmen tidied up while Billy B supervised.

I stole a glance at him. I had to—he wasn't married—and I gathered that he and I were about the same age.

I'm pretty sure he wasn't married. He wore no ring. But perhaps he wore no ornamentation because of work hazards, like getting the ring caught in some sort of machinery.

"Looks very nice, Miss Mary," he said, as the crew packed up.

"Thank you."

Billy B stood thin as a whippet. Maybe a middle-aged whippet. A few pounds north of a whippet. But sinewy. Like he worked hard all his life. He was blond. He might have been bald, but I had never seen him without his company baseball cap. He had features . . . I want to say chiseled, but that is such a cliché. Yet they were chiseled. Prominent cheekbones. Angular jaw. Warm, green eyes. Broad shoulders . . . for a whippet. And a permanent grin. He may not shave every day, but when you're hauling five hundred pounds of granite countertop, you don't really require a close shave, do you?

"I wasn't sure when you picked this stone at the yard. I thought . . . well, I thought it might be too dark for a small kitchen. But no, you were right. It just works in here with the white cabinets and stainless steel appliances, doesn't it? You have a flair for this, Miss Mary."

"I think it does work well, doesn't it?" I replied, proud of being praised for my immaculate sense of design, my flair.

Billy B took off his cap. He was not going bald. Not at all. He had a thickness of blond hair, appearing as if it had been styled under his cap, askew in just the right way, tufts and peaks, looking very, very chic.

"Miss Mary, I hope you don't think I'm being too forward here . . ."

How do you answer a statement like that?

"But I was talking with Miss Janet over at Star Team Realty. Well, she did tell me a little of where you all came from. And why. And all that. Sorry to hear about your loss. I know that must have been hard on you."

He said it, not in a sympathetic manner, but simply acknowledging the truth of my past. I liked that. It hadn't happened quite this way before. Not that I could remember, at any rate.

"Thank you, Billy B. I appreciate that."

He gave me the wryest grin in return, like he knew that it had been the right thing to say, and that he said it just at the right time, and that I would be almost charmed by his down-home charm and innocence.

And, darn it, he was absolutely right.

"Can I ask you a question, Billy B?"

"You can ask me anything, Miss Mary."

Again, his answer did not sound smarmy, or sexual, like some men would sound, leering ever so slightly to see if I reddened at all, seeing if that flirt . . . worked.

"What does the *B* stand for?" His company name appeared as Billy B William Interiors. I had already figured that it might have been a family name. If Billy was a nickname for William, then he would be William B. William. Odd. His lead carpenter was named Ransom.

"Well, funny you should ask, Miss Mary. Folks usually ask right off, or they never do. You waited a good while before asking. Polite, you know. I like that in a woman."

I wanted to blush, just a little, but I don't think I did.

He likes that in a woman. Well . . . he noticed. That's a good sign.

"Well, Miss Mary. I could drag this story out. But I have another job to head to after here. The *B* is a nickname for William. You know, Billy gets turned into a *B* because a *B* is simpler for a baby sister to say when learning to talk."

I nodded, as if I understood, but I didn't.

"So . . . why Billy B?" I was confused.

He looked down at his shoes.

"The first Billy is for William. The *B* is for William as well."

He looked up, and he waited.

I suspect he saw my face drawn up tight in confusion, then slowly open, like a flower blossoming.

"So . . . you're William William William?

He grinned again. This time it was knowing and playful. He must have been used to it.

"Yes, ma'am. My parents had one odd sense of humor, I guess. My mother joked that she always had to call me three times until I listened to her. So that's another reason for their choice. But all my life, I've been Billy B, so no one has paid much mind to it."

I could not help laughing. A little.

"It is funny, in a weird southern gothic way, isn't it, Miss Mary? Something out of Faulkner. Or maybe James Dickey."

"It is. But I love it."

He obviously is well read. And very intuitive. I like that in a man.

He waited a short moment.

"I know this might not be all proper and everything, Miss Mary, but would you like to have dinner with me sometime? Maybe next weekend? I know a great shrimp place up by New Bern. Off the beaten path, as they say."

I tried not to look surprised. Or pleased. I was both. A lot.

"Billy B, I would like that," I replied. "I would like that a lot."

He slapped his hat back on his head.

"Well, capital then, Miss Mary," he answered, in the best North Carolinian interpretation of an English accent I have yet heard. "Capital indeed. I shall call you midweek with details."

"And I shall wait, anon," I said, wondering if I used the word *anon* in the right way. I probably didn't, but Billy B was too much a gentleman to pay heed to my possible gaffe.

<hr />

The shrimp tasted fantastic. They must have caught it that day, or even as I ordered them. I don't think I have ever tasted shrimp quite as fresh as these.

And Billy B had been right. The restaurant, Captain Ratty's, was a place I never would have gone to—probably from the name alone. But it proved to be delightful. Billy B seemed to be a well-known customer. At least they all treated us with great charm.

I took easily to calling Billy B just that. It sort of rolled off one's tongue, didn't it?

Yes, I was on a date. With a man. After Brian, I thought in my darker moments, that such things would never happen to me again. But within a few weeks of moving to Atlantic Beach—well, there was a man.

And I liked him. He was funny and self-deprecating and very, very intelligent. He said he had graduated from North Carolina State University here in New Bern with a degree "in nothing useful" and started working on remodeling to pay off his student loans. And twenty years later, he surprised himself to still be doing remodeling, still enjoying it, and doing "pretty good."

Of course, I told him a little of my own story as well. You already know it, so no need to repeat any of it.

After splitting a piece of Key lime pie (I would have preferred the whole piece for myself, but I tried to look like a lady) Billy B drove along the coast, on some back roads, toward Atlantic Beach. Much of the drive went through the Croatan National Forest. Billy B remarked that this was the only coastal forest park on the East Coast, and magnificent stands of pine lined the road. I would have called it romantic, but romance remained a bit farther away. We would have time to get there . . . later.

We pulled into my gravel driveway. I could hear Rufus from inside the house, scrabbling up on the one chair that faced a front window and afforded him a look at the street. He barked—not an angry, warning bark, but one of recognition.

Billy B escorted me to the front door, the door to the screened porch.

Do I turn and face him here . . . or at the inside front door?

"Well, it is late, Miss Mary."

He called me Miss Mary. I think southerners have a thing for two names. I liked his calling me that. Respectful and playful at the same time.

"Are you sure? I could make coffee. I am good at making coffee."

He smiled.

"I am sure you are good at lots of things," he said, and I did not read even the remotest reference to sex into his comment. How does he do that?

"But I need to get up early. Church and all tomorrow."

"Oh, sure. I understand."

I hoped he did not read into my response that I had no intention or plans to get up early tomorrow and look for a church.

"I had a real nice time. I'll call you this week. Wednesday, probably. Not too soon, and not too late, right?"

I laughed. That is what I was thinking.

And then, as natural as can be, he bent in toward me, loosely slipped his left arm around my waist, and kissed me. It didn't last long enough to be considered a long kiss, nor a short peck. It was just long enough to leave me wanting more, and beginning a mental countdown to Wednesday evening.

"I would like that Billy B. I really, really would."

And I meant that.

Rufus stayed mostly quiet during our walk that night. He asked me if I had a good time, and I said I did. He always asks me what I ate. I told him shrimp and Key lime pie. And he asked me if I brought any home to him. I had to tell him I didn't.

"Have I had Key lime pie before? Is it sweet?"

"It is sweet. And I am pretty sure you haven't ever eaten it."

We walked along, and just as we returned to the house, he asked, "The next time you have Key lime pie, could you bring me some? I would like to try that. It has three names. I don't think I have eaten anything with three names before. It sounds really tasty."

And I assured him that I would.

We fell asleep, in our tidy, snug little home, white with green shutters and a picket fence, and the faint hissing of the surf as it rolled into shore and receded back again.

I think I was happy.

18

True to his word, Billy B did call on Wednesday. He proposed a Friday night date. Dinner, he said. Someplace local. Since I hadn't been here all that long, he suggested that I might appreciate going someplace I probably wouldn't go by myself.

He seemed to be intuitive that way. Maybe he faced the same single person problems that I did. Maybe not, since men can get away with a lot more than women can in that department. No, I am not being a feminist, but a man can more comfortably go into a restaurant by himself. A woman by herself—well, I just think that some people will have the wrong idea of what sort of woman she is. For a woman to walk alone into a tavern, let's say—people will think she's on the prowl. A man does it and no one thinks it odd or unusual at all.

It's the way of the world. And no, I'm not angry about it. I'm not going to picket taverns here to raise the consciousness of the culture. And besides, I never go to taverns. Unless they have really good ribs.

Since a second date was planned, I asked Rufus what he thought about Billy B. We were on our nightly walk along the ocean. We walked down a block to a public access point on the beach, and walked down a small wooden walkway and up the beach for about a half mile, where another public access point cut through the dunes to the beach. So Rufus and I were back on our large circle-walking pattern. I liked walking by the beach. The sound of the waves simply washed any cares from my mind—at least while we were walking. The hush and flow of the waves would be great therapy, if doctors could make money on prescribing it. Perhaps when the weather turned stormy, I might have a different opinion. But now, in the calm, in the warmth, I loved it.

Rufus did too. He treated the narrow spit of sand at the edge of the water as the only probable route. He still avoided water when he could, but if it washed onto his paws, he made no complaint. "I like it here," he said more than once. "I'm glad you moved us here."

Back to Billy B.

Rufus must have trouble with remembering men's faces, because at first, he could not recall Billy B. I had to explain the baseball cap, the man who brought the large piece of stone, and he still could not place him.

"The man who ate the Key lime pie with me," I finally said.

"Oh, that man. I know him. Will you have Key lime pie when he comes next?"

"I don't know," I answered. "But do you like him? Is he a nice man?"

Rufus stopped and walked very deliberately around the small carcass of a jellyfish. I told him to avoid the blobby things because they could sting him. He had been stung by a wasp back in Illinois. He had yelped at that, and had licked the bite area incessantly for two days. I told him it was like a wasp, only that jellyfish didn't fly. After that, he kept his distance from all beached jellyfish.

"Well, I don't have special dog ability to tell if someone is nice or not. I don't think I do, anyhow. He is nice to me. He bends down to pet me. And he's careful with my ears. Some people are not. He is careful. He smelled okay. A little like sweat."

I took that as an endorsement. And it made me feel a little giddy at the same time. I could imagine myself with this man. And that, in itself, felt like something entirely new. Perhaps Brian, back in Wheaton—the man who I punched in the throat—had opened the door a bit to the possibility of another man in my life. After the accident, I couldn't even imagine being with a man. I felt I could be accused of cheating, or committing adultery. Now, time had passed, and distance. I could now think of a future in which I did not live alone. And not just with Rufus. With another human being.

And that made me giddy, a little. Sort of.

Egads, to think I once made a semi-pro living at using the right words in the right way. Perhaps that skill has vanished as my ability to think of men arose, like a phoenix, in my life.

───※───

The rest of my possessions arrived from Wheaton, placed flatly in my driveway in a large blue-and-white container. The delivery service offered assistance in unloading. I knew furniture had been packed inside, so I took advantage of strong men who knew how to heft a sofa up stairs and through doors.

I set up a second sitting area upstairs. The sofa from Wheaton went there, along with the two upholstered chairs that had been in my kitchen. That was the big stuff. I had them pile all the boxes in the dining area of my first-floor living room area. The stack intimidated me. Having only a smattering of possessions had felt liberating, and now this influx of stuff seemed constricting. It made me feel claustrophobic almost.

They emptied out the container in less than thirty minutes. Now I faced the task of either finding a place for everything or reducing the pile through giveaways.

I hung the pictures in short order. The few photos of John and Jacob were hung in the master bedroom. Somehow, I didn't want them more shared than that. The lamps were really needed. This house did not have recessed lighting as did my house in Wheaton, so dark here was darker than there. I quickly went through the clothes, and filled three medium-sized boxes with items that I knew I would never wear again. The next-door neighbor had told me that she has one pair of long pants, and the rest of her wardrobe consists of shorts. I would recycle five of the six pairs of wool pants I had packed.

Rufus sniffed and nosed about the boxes, as if he was look- ing for some item misplaced. He did find his favorite squirrel plush toy. He did not destroy toys like some dogs. He chewed off the eyes, but the rest of the animal remained intact. For the rest of the afternoon, he sat on the sofa, watching me, with his head resting on his old squirrel.

A few boxes were filled with personal items, photos, and memories. I did not want them on display, nor did I want them discarded. Upstairs, I had access to an enclosed attic area, about the size of two large closets. I had that filled in short order with all the too-meaningful-to-toss items, which I could close the door on.

After I finished, I had marked for charity perhaps one-third of the items I brought with me to North Carolina. I felt a bit more burdened, but not overwhelmed. I called the Salvation Army and asked if they would be interested in picking up my unwanted items. They were, and two days later, my place returned to being clear and sparse again.

And then Billy B called and the world was a good place again.

⸺⸻⸺

Friday evening came and Billy B arrived, on time, in a button-down shirt, a very well-fitting blue sport coat, and slim-fit khaki pants. He had warned me that he would be dressed in "business casual."

"I know women get nervous if they feel over- or under-dressed. And I don't ever want to make you uncomfortable."

He had made reservations at Shepherd's Point, in Morehead City, across the sound—another restaurant I would not have gone to by myself. Too nice, too romantic, too much a couples place.

They had Key lime pie listed as their signature dessert. Rufus would get his wish after all.

As I had the waiter box up a two-bite section of the pie, Billy B stirred his coffee.

"It's for the dog, right?" Billy B asked.

"Maybe. If he's lucky. If I don't eat it on the way home."

"Don't worry. Every once in a while I have to stop at McDonald's and get a cheeseburger for my old basset hound. He loves their cheeseburgers. And fries. But not often. He's old and you have to watch their cholesterol."

The dinner was so nice, the conversation so natural, it felt as if we had known each other for years and not weeks. Billy B seemed to have friends all over town. Three people stopped by our table to say hello. Of course, he introduced me, as a proper gentleman should.

"It's a small town, Miss Mary. You live in one place long enough and you're bound to know a whole lot of people."

265

I decided to ask the question that had been at the back of my mind since the first time I had considered accepting a date with Billy B.

"So tell me—how come you're not married? I know, I know, I don't have to know . . . and you don't have to tell me anything . . . but when you pass a certain age, that question sort of sits out there, waiting to be asked. You know what I mean?"

If the question rattled him, he appeared adept at hiding it.

"No. I mean, I do know what you mean. And no, there's no problem answering it. I guess I am surprised that you didn't hear about it from someone else."

I braced myself—mentally only, I hope.

"Who would I have heard it from? I'm new here, remember?"

"Your next door neighbors. The Phillipses. They knew all about it."

Alarm flags were flapping in the storm, but I forced myself to remain dispassionate and calm—on the outside.

In jail? Arrested? Embezzlement? Something really horrible?

"I was married. To my high school sweetheart. We were great for fifteen years."

I waited. I didn't want to seem like I was prying. But now I was desperate to know. Not desperate. Well . . . maybe a little desperate. And more than a bit scared, I guess.

"We had a wonderful marriage. We did. Everything was great. Never had children; that bothered both of us. But it didn't overwhelm us."

He took a sip of coffee.

I really wanted the express version of the story.

"Then, five years ago, she fell in love with the pastor of the church we were attending. I didn't suspect a thing. I really didn't. Then all of a sudden she left. Packed up all her clothes and moved out. While I worked on a job. She called me that night and said it was over. She planned on starting a new life with him. She said he was her true soul mate. And she wanted a divorce."

I started to breathe again. A divorce, I could handle.

"I didn't want to let her go. So I put up a fight. And this went on while the pastor still preached at the church. The congregation started to take sides, and some blamed this one or that one. Some of them thought I should accept it and move on. Some wanted me to leave, like it was all my fault. Some wanted the pastor excommunicated—or whatever Bible churches do. But I didn't want any of that. I wanted my old life. I liked my old life."

The waiter came to our table, a little reluctant to break into our conversation, though he did have the bill in his hand. I apologized, and ordered coffee, after declining it before. It is not that I needed to be awake, but I needed something to do with my hands.

This isn't a deal-breaker. It doesn't sound like it was his fault. I mean, every relationship has ups and downs. Is any divorce absolutely one-sided?

"It went on for six months. Finally, I had had enough. I knew she was never going to change her mind. I relented and allowed the divorce to happen. Fighting costs a lot and doesn't change the way people feel."

I added three sugars to the coffee, two more than I normally do.

"Is the pastor still there—at that church? Did they get married?"

He sighed—a painful sigh. I didn't enjoy watching him relive what must have been a horrible time, but I did want to know.

I had a sudden and small epiphany. I understood why people wanted details of my husband and son's accident. Not because of morbid curiosity, but because they needed to feel some manner of closure as well.

"He is still at that church. And they are married. The church almost fell apart. Went down to a handful of supporters. But the man is a good preacher. Very charismatic. Very dynamic. I hear people say that the building is almost full again on Sunday mornings. I guess a sinner attracts sinners. People can empathize with him. Maybe that's it."

I didn't know what else to ask. He must have been devastated. Disillusioned for sure.

It seemed as if he had heard my thoughts.

"The funny thing is—you would think that my faith in God would be challenged or shaken. But it wasn't. I came through this all feeling more protected and more loved than I ever had before in my life. God provided for me when it mattered."

He leaned across the table.

"What about you, Miss Mary? We haven't talked about church before. You know . . . the things you never discuss on the first couple of dates—religion and politics. I know you suffered a great loss. Mine was bad, nowhere near as bad as yours. How are you with God? Where's your faith?"

I tried to speak, but I couldn't find the right words. But I had to say something.

"Okay. I guess. I . . . God and me . . . well, we don't talk much anymore. After the accident. I didn't see why those two innocent people had to die. I still don't. If it is a lesson I am supposed to learn, I don't want to learn it."

Billy B did not look shocked or discouraged or anything. He simply listened, impassively. That was so kind of him. To listen without judgment.

"So . . . I don't really know about God anymore. I don't know if I still believe. I don't know if I want to believe."

Yes, I know all about Rufus and my pathetic attempts at thinking that he really talked to God, and my attempts at manipulating a Divine being that I was pretty sure didn't really exist, and if he did, didn't really care all that much for me. After all, he saved the life of a dog, but couldn't, or didn't, spare the lives of two innocent people.

So I decided then and there to be honest with Billy B.

"I'm not against religion, Billy B. But for me, it's simply caused a lot of pain. Promises never delivered on. So, as much as I might want to believe, I can't anymore. It's easier and safer this way."

He smiled at me. He understood. I know he understood. He cared about me. He took my hand in his, for the first time, and gently squeezed it. "I understand," he said. "I do."

He gave me a kiss when he walked me to the door, and a gentle, chaste hug. He again promised to call me.

I was sure that he would. I was sure.

And Rufus loved his pie with the three names. On our walk, he made me promise to buy an entire pie if they sell them in the big food stores. He made me promise twice.

I did. I promised.

And he asked me if I liked this man.

And I told him that I did. A lot.

I assumed that he remained silent during the rest of my walk because he was remembering how good the Key lime pie tasted.

I was wrong.

Billy B called on Thursday. Not Wednesday. I worried a bit on Wednesday, but a day . . . well, that isn't cause for great concern, now, is it?

My optimism shows how wrong I can be. And was.

"Miss Mary . . ."

"Billy B," I said, cheerful and happy.

He called. Just like he said he would.

"Listen . . ."

I don't think I really paid attention to that word. Who starts off a conversation with the word *listen?* Wasn't I already listening? And besides, I now felt like this is the place I should be, that Atlantic Beach is just the place that God had in mind for Rufus . . . and me, by default. The perfect house, the perfect neighborhood, and now, maybe a perfect man. Of course, he was not perfect. Just like I was not perfect. But we seemed so well suited for each other. We had the same dreams and the same temperament. And he was wickedly handsome. Isn't that what kids today say? "Wicked good"? Anyhow, he called and now we would see each other this weekend. Maybe I would cook him dinner on Saturday. We could . . . you know . . . snuggle on the sofa as we listened to the waves. Or if it was warm enough, we could sit on the porch, in the new porch swing I would buy tomorrow, and we would swing gently and he would put his arm around me and the moon would come up over the beach . . .

Perfect.

"Listen . . . Miss Mary . . . I am not good at this sort of thing. But it has to be said. Even if I don't want to."

Well . . . that's not how this conversation should start. This doesn't sound perfect at all anymore.

"Listen. I can't see you anymore. After we talked last weekend . . . I rolled it over and over in my mind. And I just can't do it. You don't believe, Miss Mary. In God. You more or less said so right out."

Wait. This is all wrong!

"I sort of figured that after my wife and I divorced, that if I ever found another woman that I felt attracted to, she had to be a committed believer. She had to really know God. She had to be on the same page as me. I'm not a teenager anymore. I don't want to break anyone's heart—nor do I want to be hurt. Nor do I have the luxury of lots of time."

I sat down, the world around me gone gray. Not black, but gray.

"It was only a conversation, Billy B. I didn't really think about what I was saying. Maybe I was just mistaken."

I could hear him take a deep breath and probably run his hand across his chin.

"No, Miss Mary. I heard that certainty in your voice. It's unmistakable. I heard it in my wife's voice too. And faith in God . . . well, I may not pass out tracts on the street corner or raise my hands and yell 'Praise the Lord!' all the time, but God is real to me. And believing in him is a huge part of my life. When she left, I promised myself that I would forever remain true to God."

"But Billy B . . . "

That's all I could think of to say.

"I am sorry, Miss Mary. I truly am. You are a really nice person. You are. But if I keep seeing you, then I would be more and more tempted to forget that promise I made to myself and to God. It would be so easy to do that, and I would wind up hating myself—and you. Neither of us has the time to play games. Neither of us is good at charades. And both of us would have to do so much pretending if we stayed together."

"But Billy B . . ."

"I'm sorry. But I can't see you anymore. I hope you'll understand. If not today, maybe someday. I wish you all the best."

And then he hung up.

I had nothing to say, other than another mumbled, "Billy B?"

I sat on the sofa for a long time. It might have been hours, just trying not to think, hoping that that phone call did not really happen, that I had just imagined it, and pretty soon Billy B would call and life would go on.

Yet I knew that would not happen.

I cried some. I cried because I felt stupid about being too honest with him. I should have known better. I could have said that I was still searching. That would have been enough to keep him around. But I had to be honest, now, didn't I?

Stupid.

Stupid and honest. Maybe they go together.

After sniffling quietly for a long time, Rufus jumped up onto the sofa and stared at me, wondering what was wrong. I did not cry often. Hardly ever with Rufus watching.

I might tell him about what happened during our walk tonight. But somehow, I had the feeling that he already knew. I knew I didn't want to talk to him now. I just wanted to hug him and feel something live close to me. He was only a dog, but that was all I had, and that would be enough.

———— ∞ ————

I did not speak a word to Rufus on our nightly walk. It had started to drizzle, just a little, and we hurried along. This was no time for explanations or conversations.

Tomorrow would be time enough.

———— ∞∞ ————

I woke up early and had three cups of coffee before 5:00 a.m. It remained dark and the beach was windswept as Rufus and I took our morning walk. His ears kept getting lifted up by the wind. I wondered if he disliked that feeling. The surf crashed higher than it had been since we arrived. We stayed farther back from the water on the beach. A low, gray scud of clouds hung over the waves. Even the cawing gulls were all but lost in the overcast. The wind was not cold, not even chilly. Storms and threatening weather were almost always cold back in Wheaton. Here, warm could threaten, just as easily as could cold. Perhaps even more so, because a warm threat was more unexpected.

I thought again about telling Rufus what happened the day before, that Billy B said he would not see me again. But he is a dog, and dogs don't have the same romantic impulses as we humans. He understood loyalty and respect, and love, of a sort. But I don't know if he could understand what I had been feeling for Billy B, nor did I think I could adequately explain it to him. So I didn't really try. I steeled myself and swore that I would learn something from this. I don't know what.

Instead, I asked him a question.

"Does every dog know God?"

Rufus sniffed at a shell.

"Yes. I think. I don't know every dog, but the dogs I know, they know God."

"Did Gus know God?"

Rufus perked up, almost jumped.

"Why, yes, he did. Gus lives near the ocean. Could we visit Gus? I would like to see Gus again."

I couldn't tell Rufus that I never knew Gus's owner's last name—or his first name for that matter—and had absolutely

JIM KRAUS

no idea of how I would find that information. I decided to take the coward's way out.

"We'll see Rufus. We'll see. It depends on how close he lives. Florida is a big place."

"He said Orlando. Is Orlando big?"

"It is, Rufus. And very far away. But I will try to find out where he lives."

"Okay," Rufus said, walking with a jaunty air now, even in the wind and sputtering rain. "He is a good dog. He knows who God is. Gus is a good dog."

I thought for a moment.

"Did the big, black, knuckleheaded dog next door know God?"

Rufus stopped when he heard my question. If he was pondering some deep question or working through some deep thought, he would often stop or slow, as if the thinking and contemplating part of it became so intense that walking could not continue while he engaged in the other two actions.

"I think so. I think all dogs know God. But not all dogs are good dogs. If a dog is a good dog, that means they know who God is and do good things. Some dogs that do bad things do bad things because they have bad people around them. But, deep down, all dogs know what is good and bad. Good dogs do good things. Bad dogs . . . they do bad things, even if they know better. But all dogs know what they're doing. I'm pretty sure of that."

Now it was my turn to remain quiet, trying to understand what Rufus said. It sounded clear and concise. It sounded logical. It almost sounded divine.

But that would mean that I knew right from wrong and if I had been doing bad things, the bad things were being done on purpose. Of course, I am not a dog, so perhaps the rules for dogs and people are quite different—at least to God, that is.

"Do all dogs talk to God?"

Rufus did not slow, or even turn to me.

"The good ones all do. The good dogs I know all do. Maybe there are some good dogs that don't, but I am pretty sure that there aren't many of those. Good dogs talk to God. That's how it goes."

Rufus accepted a dog treat and chewed it with great gusto. I gave him another one, and we turned our backs to the wind and headed for home, the rain becoming more of a squall now.

Warm or not, neither of us liked getting wet.

I'm still not talking to God. I don't know how to break the silence. I don't know how to start a conversation. "Oh, by the way—the one responsible for the deaths of the only two people in the world that I truly loved—how are you today? Time to worship you and offer praise . . ."

I can't do that. I can't. And right now, I won't even attempt it.

And if God is using loss to teach me—well, he's doing a horrible job with the lesson plan. I know all about loss and pain—my husband, my son . . . Right now I didn't need a refresher course in feeling alone and lost and miserable.

19

Gray, windy, squalls, high waves, a thickness of salt mist in the air . . . it could not become any more dreary and depressing. I decided that this day would be a perfect day to start my job hunt.

What's a little more rejection at the moment? Can't hurt any worse. The day can't get any more bleak.

I would start at the county job center in Morehead City, just to get the lay of the land. I could probably do most of what I would do there on my computer at home, but I had to get moving. I had to do something, go somewhere. I could not stay alone in the house any longer.

The job center was closed.

A sign had been taped, at an askew angle, on the inside of the front door, at waist level. Written in pencil were the words CLOSED DUE TO BOILER MANFUNCTION. WILL OPEN TOMORROW. NORMAL TIME.

That's what the sign said, word for word.

The rain picked up a bit, splattering big warm drops on the driver's-side window. I felt safe in my Volvo. It featured some magic traction device on slick roads. I never drove fast in the rain, but it felt good to know it was there in case I had to do so.

Going back home was not an option. Not yet. I didn't need groceries, or gas, or anything new for the house, or clothes.

I could use another cup of coffee.

I just saw a study on Google News that linked high coffee consumption—more than eight cups a day (which is me)—with a lowered risk of prostate cancer.

Oh joy. I found out that I am very well protected from a disease that I can never catch. Just my luck, I guess.

I stopped at a Starbucks, treated myself to a short latte, with one Splenda, and sat by the front window, ensconced in a comfortable leather chair, looking over a downtown block of Morehead City. It was not the quaintest old town I had ever seen, nor the best preserved, nor the liveliest—but it was still alive and attractive. That counted for something. A few good restaurants. A few antique stores. A few women's boutique shops. Two hair salons. A deli. Not bad.

I watched people scurry in and out of the rain. Some folks looked amazed that they were feeling raindrops, others perturbed that they ran the risk of getting wet, others all but oblivious to the rain. I liked those people the best—wearing slickers, or not, they walked slowly, window shopping, apparently not caring one whit about the conditions around them.

By the time I finished my coffee, the rain had slackened. I drove down the main street, only slowing when I noticed an old, two-story, brick building, with windows trimmed in white. I think the ornamentation might have been Victorian. But it could have been Federal. My readers would have known the difference. So let's just say they were Victorian frames. Simpler that way. An author's trick. The building looked old, but not decrepit—not at all. More like someone either had been keeping it up for decades, or spent a lot of money recently restoring it. In a sleepy town—I would have bet on the maintained-well-for-decades scenario.

The sign above the front door read CARTERET COUNTY HERALD.

I like newspapers. I always have. Putting together a publication with probably as many words as my first book—everyday—was a feat that boggled my mind. I liked to read them, peruse the ads, read over community calendars, figure out the Jumble, and do the crossword puzzle as well.

I think I knew that the county had a newspaper, but I don't think I had yet seen a copy. I don't think I looked for a copy either, so that may be why.

There was a sign taped to one of the two front windows. I wondered if there had been a rash of "manfunctioning" boilers in town that day.

No. The sign read HELP WANTED.

Really. A sign in the window of a newspaper office. Don't newspapers have classified ad sections for that? On a personal note, I had found all my jobs—remember that had been in the dark, pre-Internet age—through the Help Wanted sections of newspapers. Maybe the job market has come full circle. No, that's not the right term, but you know what I mean. (And I appear to be saying that a lot, as well.)

Downtown Morehead City in May was not the busiest place I had ever visited. An empty parking place opened up in front of the office. In fact, I could have chosen between a half-dozen empty parking places. I couldn't see a phone number on the sign from the street, so I parked and walked up to the front door.

On the sign, written in pencil, above the printed words HELP WANTED were penciled the words REPORTER/CLEAN-UP/ DELIVERY PERSON. Perhaps they needed someone to do all three tasks at once. Everyone knows that newspapers are having money problems these days.

I stepped inside the newspaper office, thinking that I could ask a receptionist for a job application or find out more about the jobs listed or get a copy of the most recent newspaper. Something.

No receptionist sat behind the counter. A stack of newspapers was on the counter. I glanced at the front page. The lead story covered the school board election. Not bad. They probably didn't do much national news on the front. They published the newspaper three times a week. Not bad. Publish once a week and a newspaper becomes easy to ignore.

To my left was a closed door marked with the words ADVERTISING DEPARTMENT.

Then I saw the small tent made from a folded four-by-six note card standing on the desk where the receptionist must normally sit.

"Gone. Be Back."

Simple declarative sentences tell a powerful story.

I felt better now. The caffeine jolt may have had something to do with it as well. I always feel better after an infusion of a couple of real, double shots of caffeine. Much more than a cup of instant-brewed coffee—no matter how strong I make it.

Off to the side, I heard someone talking loudly—a one-sided conversation—so I assume that either he was speaking to a mime, or was on the phone. I would guess it was a phone call. He spoke loudly, and maybe sounded a little upset. Maybe that is what newspaper people do on a regular basis.

In another moment, a large man—large, but not tall—came from around the corner. He was not bald, not yet, but on his way, and wore a rumpled white shirt, khaki trousers, and suspenders. I would bet he was a man who woke up rumpled and stayed rumpled all day. He did have an inviting smile, though, and knowledgeable eyes—you know, eyes that indicated he knew . . . stuff.

Egads. Could I write or what?

"I thought I heard someone come in. Our trusty receptionist, Lucinda, is out back having an affair with another cigarette. I'm often stuck doing her job. Curse the addictive qualities of nicotine. And I don't say that loudly, because tobacco is one of the area's big cash crops." He took a deep breath. "I'm Kistler Hibbs. I'm the editor here. Managing editor, if you want to know the proper title—which impresses no one except my mother. So I'm in charge. That's what they tell me, anyhow. You are applying for a job, correct?"

"I . . . I . . ."

"How did I know? Well, you look like you're not from around here. There's a look. I don't know how locals are different, but they are. You're a recent move-in. I know you're not trying to sell anything or else you'd have a briefcase. You're not here to place a classified. You would use your computer to do that, since you are young enough to certainly have a computer and know how to use it. You're not related to anyone who works here—as far as I can recall. So . . . you must be applying for a job."

He was right. Must be a good reporter. Observant. A quick study.

"I saw the sign in the window," I said, hoping that I didn't sound enormously pathetic.

"Yes, I know it's odd that a newspaper hangs out a Help Wanted sign. But our publisher is like 150 years old. That's the way they did it back then."

I knew already that I would like Mr. Kistler Hibbs.

"He's not really 150 years old. More like 140. And you are inquiring about the job, correct? Please tell me that my parlor guessing game and prowess were spot-on today." He lowered his voice. "On occasion, I have been known to make a mistake in identification."

I told him that I was new to the area. I told him that I was applying for the reporter job.

"Have you written anything before?"

I should have brought a resumé with me. I should always travel with a résumé at the ready.

Do I even have a résumé? A new one, I mean. The last one I recall using had been written . . . a decade ago.

"I have. Well, yes. I have written . . . books."

Kistler Hibbs took a theatrical step backward, and clasped his hand over his mouth.

"You're Mary Fassler, aren't you?"

This time I was amazed. And I am sure that my face indicated just how amazed I had become. Very, very amazed.

"I've read some of your books. My wife loves you. I just read the one about the Amish cowboy. I wanted to head off into the West after I finished the last chapter."

"*Lariats of the Divine.*"

"Yes, that one! It was so marvelous. I loved it. Of course, I hated the cover. That ungainly man did not look at all like Stephen from the book. It didn't. I'm sorry. Horrid illustration."

I really liked Kistler Hibbs.

"I know. I didn't like it either. But a publisher has the right of way," I said.

He leaned toward me and looked around, to make sure no one listened in on us, in a most theatrical way.

"I hate publishers."

I went back to being amazed, after a short stint at being totally pleased at the recognition.

"But how . . ."

"Janet . . . down at The Star Team. She's our neighbor. She said she just sold a place in Atlantic Beach to a famous writer. And she mentioned your name. I anticipated sending a reporter over to do a story on you. I really did. If I had a good reporter, that is. Which I don't. Hence the sign in the window."

I remained amazed.

"Listen, Mary Fassler, Morehead City is a small town and we love our gossip, so be prepared to have no secrets here. Unless you do something really horrible. Then no one will ever talk about it—above a whisper, and behind your back to be certain, anyway."

I had no idea what to do next. It was one of the few fan encounters I have ever had—other than at poorly attended book signings, that is, or at conventions when one of my books was being given away for free. Free books meant that I had fans.

"Mary . . . may I call you Mary? I thought so. Listen. I know you can write. And I know you could do this job in your sleep. Human interest stories, mostly. Some news pieces. Beauty queens. Nurse of the Year awards. Political spotlights. Business stories—on business owners mostly, not business. Heavens. No one understands business. Or wants to read about it either. Odd collectors and their collections. Artists. Visiting person-alities. Spotlight on a teacher or some other unsung public servant. High-achieving students. A day in the life of someone or other in town. Maybe the odd county or city council meet-ing when someone is on vacation. People who are one hundred years old."

He scrunched his face into a prune, trying to think of other topics, but apparently had exhausted his mental list.

Then his features unscrunched.

"Maybe write a personal column or two whenever. 'Notes from a Newcomer' or something akin to that. What do you think? Do you want the job?"

My amazement knew no bounds. I am certain my jaw was slacker than it had ever been before.

"I know. The offer is out of the blue. And you may ask why. Why so quickly?"

"Well, that did just cross my mind," I replied.

Kistler Hibbs smiled. "Allow me to elucidate. First off—you can write. Your books are ample evidence of that fact. The value of that ability cannot be underestimated. I've had graduates of college journalism schools who could barely string three coherent sentences together. And heaven forbid you want the story done on time. They need time to think and compose—to find their muse. And when they do find it, they can't spell it. I hate spell check. It has ruined an entire generation of spellers. Now, as a writer of novels, you're used to deadlines. You must have a good work ethic or you couldn't have done all those books. And you're new to our pleasant town. A good way to meet people—and make a few dollars."

He stepped close to me and put his hand on my arm in a most fatherly way.

"Janet told me about what happened. I am so sorry for your loss. And I know that a few extra dollars—and work—is often what God wants for us. Keeps us occupied and focused on others, not ourselves. And the money can't hurt. What do you think? Start on Monday? The pay is adequate. Better pay than working at some horrid Quickie-Mart or an abominable warehouse store, regardless of what they sell. We offer benefits. Vacation time, 401(k), dental. Wait, do we have dental? I think so. Some dental, anyhow. Flexible hours. Mostly flexible. Work from home some of the time. You know, Mary Fassler, I have made the position sound so nice that perhaps I'll apply."

For twenty seconds, I tried to formulate a cogent reply, or consider different options, or think of questions to ask, or something.

Instead, I simply said, "Yes. I'll take it. I can start Monday. Can I bring my dog to the office on any day I have to work late?"

Kistler Hibbs smiled.

"As long as it doesn't have rabies—or at least as long as it doesn't show, then it is okay with me."

<hr>

Before our walk, I treated Rufus to a half slice of Key lime pie. So far, his enthusiasm for the dessert had not waned a bit.

As we walked to the end of the driveway, I decided to turn away from the ocean this evening, and head toward the small retail area of Atlantic Beach. I had driven through the area a few times, but never seemed to really see what stores were there. Walking would let me really explore.

I turned toward the sound, part of the Atlantic Intercoastal Waterway, divided from the ocean by the narrow spit of land that Atlantic Beach had been built upon.

"You seem happy," Rufus said as we walked along a dark stretch of sidewalk.

"I am," I replied. "I found a job today."

I'm not sure if Rufus knew what a job really encompassed. I suppose I could have explained it to him, but it would have taken a long time. I cut it as short as I could. "That's a very good thing. It means that I will have enough money to buy a Key lime pie every week."

"Well, that is good news," Rufus said, his stubby tail wagging as much as it could, given its shortened arc. "Very good news."

The first time I took him to the newspaper office, he would have questions. I would wait until then to answer them.

We turned south, down the short business district. The area, bright and well lit, had several dozen pedestrians and walkers strolling about. An independent coffee shop stood on one corner—Sandy Sandy's Coffee Shop. As we walked past, the warm, enveloping, velvet odor of roasted coffee and steamed milk filled the night. Rufus lifted his head and drew in deeply. I would have stopped, but all the outside tables were taken, and I had had a lot of coffee today and I mostly didn't feel like sitting.

Across the street was a smallish beach accessory store— bamboo mats, swimming suits, Boogie Boards, suntan products, and endless rows of vacation stuff that no one needs but buys only when on vacation. A drugstore was part of the mix of stores, along with a convenience store with gas pumps, a restaurant that looked like a mom-and-pop affair, a real estate office (not The Star Team—think more modest), a resale shop that looked as if it sold higher-end items, and at the end of the block, a store with a neon sign that glowed RENT-A-SCOOTER.

We crossed the street and I looked in the darkened window. A row of scooters stood against one wall, lined up on the diagonal, looking all gleamy and polishy in the reflected neon.

(I really did write novels before this. Really.)

Rufus sniffed at the door.

"Smells like the smell your car makes."

"It does. But this store has scooters, not cars. They're sort of like motorcycles."

"I don't like motorcycles. They make a lot of noise. They scare me."

"I know, Rufus. But scooters are much smaller and slower."

"Like a bicycle?"

"More like a bicycle than a motorcycle. And not scary."

He sniffed again at the door.

"I think I'll come back . . . maybe tomorrow. . . and rent a scooter for the day."

Rufus turned his head sideways and offered me a very odd look, as if he had just imagined the most ridiculous image in the world.

"Really? You?"

I didn't take kindly to being sneered at by a dog's preconceptions of what I could or could not do—or worse yet, what I should or should not do. I would bet that Rufus did not mean the comment in a snide way—but that's how it came out.

"Yes. I could ride a scooter. I did it in college. Once or twice. I liked it then and I might try it again."

I wanted to add a snotty "You have any problems with that?" but felt pretty certain that the sarcasm would go over the poor dog's head and he would simply think I was angry with him— which I was not.

Maybe I will. Maybe it's time to try out my wings . . .

This time I snorted.

Sounds like a bad country and western song title.

As we turned the corner on Robin, Rufus asked me the final question of the evening: "Can I have more Key lime pie when we get home?"

20

On Saturday—a warm day, not hot, not sunny, but pleasant—I walked over to Rent-a-Scooter. I had decided to show Rufus that I could be impetuous if I wanted to be, and that I could drive a scooter.

I hoped that I hadn't forgotten how to do it. College lay decades in the past, and I had forgotten everything I learned in freshman English composition, so maybe my scooter skills would be a little on the rusty side.

A bell tinkled above me as I walked in. Rufus had been right. It did smell of gas and motor oil, and car wax. Or scooter wax, I guess.

Some scooters in the line I had seen that night were gone—rented out, no doubt. It was still preseason, and the crowds had not descended on the beach yet. I wondered what that would look and feel like, and if I would begin to resent the tourists after a time, the traditional scornful native, wishing all these strangers and interlopers would simply go home.

After a moment, a door to the back end of the store opened and a tall man, about my age, with dark hair and dark eyes, wearing a gray mechanic's shirt, came out.

For a moment, his dark features reminded me too much of Jacob. I swallowed hard. As he drew closer, the resemblance faded, except for the coloring—I would guess Italian.

"Hello. Welcome to Rent-a-Scooter."

I smiled back. "I'd like to rent a scooter, please, for the afternoon."

He wiped his hands on a shop towel. "You've come to the right place. For a scooter, that is. We have them." The name Viktor was stitched above his breast pocket.

He, Viktor, I guess, asked me where I wanted to go.

"Just around town. I'm new here and I would like to explore the area a little."

He asked if I wanted to go fast. I gave him my best school-marm look and replied, "Do I look like I like to drive fast?"

He agreed with me, but added, "Looks can be deceiving."

He pointed to a blue scooter. "This Vespa is easy to ride. Not fast, but not slow, either. And I have a helmet that matches it. You said for the afternoon, right?"

"A couple of hours."

"Back by five?"

"Before then. More like two hours."

"We can do that. I need a driver's license. And you need to fill out a waiver release form. Once we do that, I can go over the controls. You'll be on the road in no time at all."

He smelled of oil and freshly laundered clothes—an odd combination. Intriguing.

The Vespa featured the simplest of controls. The right hand twisted the throttle for gas, and both sides had brake levers. It was like sitting at a desk, with both feet flat on the floorboard. Not much different from a bicycle, the Vespa was quick and responsive. It also ran quietly. Rufus wouldn't be scared. I felt much younger as I cruised about. Incongruous, improbable, and a little unnerved, but younger.

I drove past my house, and onto the driveway. I beeped the horn. It sounded like an Italian horn should sound.

Rufus's head popped up in the screen door. I waved. "Rufus, it's me," I shouted. He did not seem convinced. I would not go get him—he couldn't, nor would he, ride on the scooter with me. I pointed at the machine. "I like it. Can I buy one?"

Rufus took that opportunity to turn away from the door, like a parent obviously disgusted by an offspring's actions. I took it as his mild disapproval.

I so enjoyed my two-hour ride that when I pulled into the garage area at the rear of the store, I knew I had to have a scooter of my own. Viktor waved hello.

"Enjoy the ride?"

He was handsome in a down-home sort of way. Striking almost.

I'm not really obsessed by men. Honest. Viktor did not wear a wedding ring. I notice these things. That's all. And he was handsome.

"I really did. Like riding a bicycle. You don't forget. And I kept it on the slow side."

"That's good. Being safe."

I handed him the helmet. I am sure my hair looked like an exact impression of the inside of a helmet. Not my most striking look. Not anyone's striking look.

"Do you sell any of these scooters? Are any for sale?"

Viktor slipped the helmet over one of the handlebars.

"I do sell a few, Miss Fassler. But not until the end of the season. I buy a dozen new scooters at the beginning of the year, and at the end, I sell off a few that are a couple of years old. Still in good shape, but customers expect new models. Are you in the market?"

"I would love to have one. I had a blast."

"Can you wait until Labor Day? I'll have some to sell then. I'll make sure I keep a good one for you. A lot cheaper than buying new, that's for sure."

"I can wait. I'll come back at the end of summer."

At that moment, a young girl came through the back door, curly black hair a circular buzz around her face as she ran. "Daddy!" she shouted and leapt up at him from a few feet away. He caught her and swept her into his arms, where she snuggled against him. A horn sounded in the alley. Viktor waved and the car drove off.

"The end of summer will be fine," Viktor said. "I'll see you then, okay?"

Why are all the good ones taken?

⸺∞⸺

I sat at the Shark Shack, enjoying my second order of grouper bites. Rufus had three of them, so I did not feel overly indulgent at the second order. I had french-fried sweet potatoes as well, another decadent southern delicacy. I don't know if it was really a southern dish or not, but a few restaurants offered them and they have since become my favorite greasy side dish.

Rufus sat, panting. He acted odd in the warm weather. Dogs pant when they are hot. We all know that. It helps dissipate heat, since they don't sweat. But Rufus gave the impression that he didn't like to pant, or found it undignified. He would pant for a short moment, close his mouth, swallow, pant, close his mouth, as if the act of panting made him self-conscious. He seemed healthy enough. I asked him during a walk if the heat bothered him.

"No. No. Not at all. Why do you ask?" he replied.

So I let the subject drop.

The waitress came out and sat next to me on the picnic bench. She patted Rufus's head, which he gratefully accepted.

"Thanks for the story on Marine wives," Cindi said. "Everyone on the base said it was one of the best stories they had read on the subject."

Cindi had been the first person I had talked to when we came to Atlantic Beach.

It seemed like a long time ago.

She was one of the Marine wives I interviewed for the story on military spouses—the trials they face, the separations, the anxiety, their often nomadic existence. She was a pleasant person to talk to—and very self-aware. That made for a good story. That made the paper as my first story. Well-received too.

"My husband usually hates things like that, yet he thought it was really good."

"Thanks, Cindi. I appreciate that. Sometimes stories turn out different from what you expected. But I liked working on that one."

"I've got another couple of tables to work. How about if I treat you to a Key lime pie for dessert?"

Rufus nearly fell over turning around and getting into position for a handout.

A reporter for a newspaper in a small city was as close to a media personality as a person could get without being anything close to a media personality. Besides the newspaper, there was one local TV station that offered a local newscast. So together, we were "the media."

Armed with my clip-on name tag: Mary Fassler/Reporter/ *Carteret County Herald*, I could probably go anywhere, unchallenged, throughout Carteret County. I usually carried a large, older, digital camera with me as well, so I looked the part of a journalist. People assumed that you were on the job, and doors opened almost automatically. In truth, how often does the ordinary person's life show up in a newspaper? Rich and famous people might grow tired of their notoriety, but the average person never made it into print unless he or she was in a traffic accident, got arrested, or died.

Not the best way to get noted.

So when I, as a reporter, showed up at someone's office, or place of work, or home, I generally received a warm welcome. Maybe the fellow who covered city hall has a different take on the subject, but for me, the job proved to be an all-access key that opened doors and caused people to talk freely. Someone was interested in what he or she had to say. And, of course, I would not be going all "Mike Wallace" on them. I would write a nice story. That made a difference too.

I did a story on what public school teachers did over the summer. The pay in Carteret County is not the highest in the nation, so most of them worked: painting houses, running a Sweetie-Freeze soft serve stand (all the good names had been trademarked), tutoring, doing lawn service, serving as a lifeguard, and the most unusual—pig wrangling. On a pig farm, someone has to get the pigs onto trucks and to market. Phil Kerl was the only pig wrangler I had ever met.

I did a story on a day in the life of one of Morehead City's oldest doctors who still made house calls. I decided then that he would be my doctor, only to find out that he wasn't adding new patients. "At eighty-four years old, I need to slow down a little. Smell the roses. Take Sundays off." He was a peach of a southern gentleman.

I did a story on a policeman who served on the New York City Police force for twenty years and retired to Carteret County. His was a typical story. He wound up bored stiff within six months, applied for a patrolman's job, and has been on the local force for twelve years. "I love it down here. It took a couple of years to get used to the pace. I found myself getting everywhere a half-hour early."

And now I was working on a piece about a local man, a twenty-four-year-old man, a rising star in the ranks of the world's top professional surfers. Atlantic Beach is not a noted surfer's beach, but this is where he got his start. I had to stop him at least twenty times to ask for a definition of one odd phrase or term after another. I mean, who knew what an "ankle snapper" meant or what a "rhino chaser" was?

With this job, I even had my own desk at the offices of the *Carteret County Herald*—in the far corner, next to a window. I think other people used the desk in my absence, so I kept the personal effects to a bare minimum. I had a fake ivy plant, a picture of Rufus, and a clear glass jar filled with seashells. Hokey, yes, but I thought it looked pretty.

Kistler Hibbs entered the newsroom with a flourish. He did most things with a flourish, making it nigh onto impossible to ignore him. And everyone called him "Kistler Hibbs." Never Mr. Hibbs. Never Kistler. Never Sir. Just Kistler Hibbs—like it was all one word.

I liked him even more now than I did the day we first met. He was a generous man, a great editor, and a stitch.

Friday afternoons were empty times at the office. The Friday edition went to the printer the night before, at midnight. The Monday edition remained . . . like a week away. People who had the time, or the ability, or the nerve, made themselves scarce on Friday. Except for the sports department. Friday was a big high school sports night, but during the slow summer months, the Minor League Baseball team, the Morehead City Marlins, garnered some time, attention, and ink.

But all in all, Friday afternoons were quiet afternoons. I liked working in the office, more than I liked working at home. Rufus didn't seem to mind. When I asked him if it would bother him if I was gone for a few hours during the day, he simply asked if I intended to come back before our walk. I assured him that I would. "Okay, then. I can take a nap until you get home," he answered.

Working at the newspaper office gave me a new sense of belonging, of having a place that I could go to. I began to feel at home here—at the office, in Atlantic Beach, by the ocean. Despite the fiasco with Billy B (and that's how I began characterizing it—as a romantic fiasco) I started to feel as if this was the home and the job and the location that I was meant to have.

Could this have been God-ordained? Like I said before, he and I aren't talking. But Rufus seems happy and content. Maybe that's all the sign I needed. Or all the sign I will ever get.

Kistler Hibbs spread his arms wide when he saw me and shouted, in a nice, but very loud voice: "Mary Fassler—my Brenda Starr reporter!"

I waved back at him, and continued to type. In the old days, I imagine, a newsroom had been a noisier place, with clacking typewriters and paper being yanked out of the reels, and phones jangling, and the staccato tapping of hot-lead linotype machines in the back room. Now all you heard was the soft, nearly mute digital clicking of keyboards and the unearthly warble of cell phones.

I sound like a cranky old woman, don't I? And a little of me is cranky. But not old. Not yet.

By the time I finished the ninth paragraph, Kistler Hibbs had sidled up next to me and nearly reclined on the desk opposite mine. His proclivity to lie about was another reason the staff kept breakables and crushables off their desks. He propped up his ample head with his ample forearm. It looked so totally uncomfortable that it would make strangers wince when they saw him. But he could maintain the position for upward of thirty minutes. Maybe he did yoga in his off hours. Or Pilates. Yet he didn't seem to have off hours. He was always here when I worked in the office.

"Miss Mary Fassler. My soon-to-be award-winning reporter."

I must have appeared quizzical.

"I entered your Marine wife story in the North Carolina Newspaper Editorial Excellence Competition. Or contest. Or judging. I forget exactly what they call it. But it's a big deal if you win. The publisher comes out of his cave and hands you the award and grins at you like a Disney version of the crypt-keeper. You'll find it all so fascinating when you win."

All of this was news to me. That phrase takes on a new level of irony if you actually work in a news organization.

"But I never entered anything."

Kistler Hibbs waved me off.

"Of course you didn't. I did. You wouldn't have known about the competition, and probably wouldn't have wanted to enter even if you had. You're just too nice, Miss Mary Fassler."

Southerners seemed to have a predilection for things with three names.

"And besides, if you win, and I am pretty sure you will, that makes me look better—like a smart editor, rather than a slothful one."

He went on about the award ceremony two months away.

"It's up in Raleigh. At a deluxe hotel. Like a Ramada Inn. Big banquet with real chicken and real waiters and everything. No catering from the Waffle House for this affair. You can bring a date along. The paper would even pay for his entire $10 dinner ticket, I bet."

I must have made a face or looked like I intended to make a face. I thought that I kept most of my emotions—when it came to dating and all those romantic entanglement questions—under check. I remained impassive. I walked above the fray.

Apparently not, at least when it came to Kistler Hibbs.

"I'm sorry, Miss Fassler. I didn't mean to touch a sore point. Truly."

This time, I simply waved him off.

"It's no big deal. I've dated. Once or twice. But at my age, it's not easy. Things have a way of happening, I guess, that make relationships difficult. The older we get, the heavier the baggage."

We could hear Lucinda dealing with a customer out front. Her raspy, deep-toned growl was unmistakable. Something about a classified ad running for two weeks, which offered a much less expensive rate, or just one week. Lucinda was not our most skilled communications expert.

Kistler Hibbs unwound himself from his prone position.

"I am not one to give advice," he said, seriously, and then barked out his punchy laugh. "Oh, who am I kidding? I love to give out unwanted advice. It's my hobby, isn't it?"

I held up both hands, submitting to the obvious.

"Let go, Miss Mary Fassler. Let go of whatever holds you back from living now. I won't say that I understand how you feel, because obviously, I don't. But if there is something you're holding on to—a grudge, a hurt, unexpressed anger—then you need to let it go, or deal with it. It's a lot of work to hold onto hurt. Takes so much energy to keep hidden things cooking away at a simmer. Too many things simmering, and you don't have room to start a new meal. So . . ."

I widened my eyes, as if expecting more.

"So, I came close, right? I know I came close to the problem. Please tell me I did."

Kistler Hibbs behaved more like a clutchy, old, gossipy woman than most clutchy, old, gossipy women could ever hope to be.

And he was sort of on the right track.

I sighed. "You are close. I'll think about it. Maybe you're right."

And with that, he brightened as bright as a ballerina, and headed off to the front counter to undo whatever customer service damage Lucinda had done.

I won the award. I was surprised. Kistler Hibbs had been sure of my win all night. I heard others say that it truly is a prestigious award, and that I may even be offered a raise because of it. The banquet and the official presentation were not until the beginning of October, so I had time to not find a date for the affair.

Ava and Beth came to visit in August. I had invited them both to come at any time and they took me by surprise when they both agreed to come and decided to travel together.

Politics, as well as expensive rental cars, make strange bedfellows.

I set up two beds in the large room upstairs. The room filled up, much to my chagrin of my earlier impulse to leave it empty.

Since I had to work, at least some of the day, both women were happy to take their beach chairs, books, and suntan oil to the beach, only two blocks away. Ava won the award for the best and quickest overall tan. Beth's bathing apparel was much more modest. And she used up two full tubes of sunblock.

We had a wonderful time together. We went to the Shark Shack three times. Beth found the local grocery store and made dinner twice. Ava ordered pizza for our last evening together.

"They can't make pizza down here," Ava declared as she picked up her fourth piece.

"It's all right," Beth countered, thus ensuring that their point-counterpoint dialogue remained in place for virtually every topic we discussed during their stay. "It's actually quite good."

"Ketchup on bread dough," Ava countered, and claimed that Chicago, and perhaps New York, were the only places to find edible pizza in all of America.

Her disdain did not preclude her eating more than a fair share of the two large pizzas delivered from Luigi's Pizza and Subs down the road from Atlantic Beach.

Ava bought a six-pack of local beer from a small brewery in Beaufort, just up the coast. I knew of them only because I was scheduled to do a story on the two brothers who opened the business a few years ago. On my own, I seldom, if ever, partook. Now that Ava was here, perhaps I would relax—just a little.

Beth all but sneered at the offer.

"I'll stick with Diet Coke, thank you," she said, as crisp as starched linen.

After dinner, we had some Key lime pie, and yes, Rufus had a small sliver. "That dog is getting fat," Ava said. "I like that in a dog."

Rufus looked hurt by the accusation. I knew he would ask me about it on our walk tonight, unless all three of us went, which is what had happened all week. Except for the morning walks. Then we were alone.

The three of us retired to the screened porch while Rufus slept on the sofa. Evenings could be warm and humid, but tonight, a breeze off the ocean cooled the air and kept the humidity at bay.

Ava brought it up first. I was surprised that the subject had not come up before.

"So, are you dating? What's the manpower situation like down here? There were a lot of cute beefcakes on the beach."

Beth responded as expected.

"Honestly, those boys were all in college. You're old enough to be . . ."

"You can stop right there, Beth. We were just talking. No one asked me out on a date."

"But you said you would have gone. That blond boy in the baggy blue suit looked to be only nineteen, right?"

She surprised me by paying such close attention. She surprised Ava too, apparently.

"Well, then, you seemed to be watching quite closely."

Beth blushed. She is not a blusher by nature, since she doesn't do anything to blush about. In a clam-sized voice, she said, "He was awfully cute. I'll give you that."

Ava all but slid off her chair. Beth hid her face in her hands, not really ashamed, but maybe a little. "Too much sun does that to me," she said aloud into her cupped hands. "I can't help it."

Later, after Beth had gone upstairs to pack (their flight from Raleigh departed early, and that meant leaving Atlantic Beach at 5:00 a.m.) Ava cornered me, figuratively speaking.

"Is there a man down here? You mentioned that one—the one who worked on your kitchen. Is he still around?"

I tried to describe, without emotion, the relational fiasco that Billy B had become. Ava listened, without comment, but her face did narrow, and her eyes grew harder, like a stern teacher, or a disapproving mother.

I knew that would be her reaction, and was happy that she had waited to the last day to scold me.

"Mary," Ava said, with some tenderness, "we love you."

I waited for the sympathy shower that had to follow.

"But you drive both of us absolutely crazy."

I'm sure I looked shocked.

Maybe a little hurt.

"Listen, Mary, I don't care about you praying, or not praying. I bet Beth does, but even she thinks all this is nuts. I don't care if you believe or if you don't believe. I mean that. I don't care if you talk to God, or if you never talk to God again."

I wanted to say something, to lash back at her, to be mean in return, but I couldn't think of how best to return her angry volley.

"Just get over it. Please," she said and crossed her arms over her chest. She winced. "Too much sun."

I broke ranks and smiled.

But she continued to scold. "Make a decision, Mary. If you don't want to talk with God, then don't talk to him. But don't keep agonizing over the fact. Don't drive the car while staring in the rearview mirror, trying to fix the past. You're going to get killed that way. You want to give up your faith, just do it. Give it up. If you want to believe in God . . . go ahead and do it. And that probably means that you have to pray. So quit feeling sorry for yourself. It's like you're wallowing in the mud pit of self-pity."

"I am not," I said, skillfully opposing everything she said and cleverly refuting her intricate denouement of me and my personality and my behavior over the last few years and everything I believed in. Or didn't believe in. "I'm not, either."

I am such a clever debater.

Ava snorted. "It's the fence-sitting that drives people crazy, Mary. And it drives men even crazier. Commit to one side or the other. You want the shoes? Buy the shoes. Don't expect me to talk you into the purchase."

Ava shook her head. "Now, I'm quoting the foot doctor as a relationship expert. But he's right. He said that to me after we got into a big fight at Nordstrom. I had forty pairs of shoes spread out all around me and I really, really wanted these wonderfully expensive, red, strappy things. But I couldn't pull the trigger. I wanted him to talk me into buying something that I wanted that he could not care less about. For a foot doctor, he doesn't care about shoes in the least. Go figure."

I hadn't followed her logic. I don't think she followed her logic either.

"All I'm telling you, Mary, is that you can't spend the rest of your life saying how bad God is, and then turning your back on him. If you think he doesn't care, then act like he doesn't care. If you want to 'talk' with him—then just do it. But don't play games with the process. It'll tire you out before it tires God out."

And then she did something that surprised me. She hugged me. Ava had never been much of a hugger. But she hugged me. And whispered in my ear, "Mary, you're miserable. Talk to him."

When she released me, she obviously felt better, relieved.

"I feel like I'm in sixth grade reporting to Bobby Deletora that May Ellen Fisher really does like him and that he should talk to her."

I sniffed a few times.

"Did Bobby talk to her?"

Ava grinned. "He did. They dated like forever. They eventually got married after college—and divorced three years later. What do I know about relationships, really?"

There were a lot of hugs, and a few tears, when the two of them left the following morning. Even Rufus seemed more animated than normal, bouncing about, nosing about their luggage.

Maybe he was making sure they weren't secreting away his favorite squirrel back to Chicago or concealing a stash of crunchies in their bags. We promised to call and to write and to visit. There were hugs all around, twice, and Rufus even got his share of hugs, though he did growl a bit when Ava squeezed him.

"Take care of her, Rufus," she said. "Bite her if she keeps on complaining about God not listening. Okay?"

I could have sworn that Rufus nodded. He later claimed that he didn't, but it sure looked like it. And then they were gone, driving off into the early morning dark. We were up, so Rufus and I decided to take to the beach before the crowds descended.

I could have let Rufus off the leash when we walked on the beach. I had tried it once. Rufus didn't like it.

"What if a wave comes in and sweeps me out into the ocean? How will you get me back to shore?"

I tried to explain that would not happen.

"I saw a big wave on television."

I believe he referred to the tsunami in Japan.

"So you want the leash?"

"I do. I am safer with a leash."

So we always used the leash. He seldom pulled on it, except for the occasional times when he saw a squirrel or another dog.

As soon as we reached the water's edge, Rufus turned to me and asked, almost confrontationally, "Am I fat? That lady said I'm fat."

I knew that question was coming.

"No, Rufus, Doctor B said you have big bones and are not fat. Besides we walk a lot. And she just said that because you had Key lime pie. I don't think she ever met a dog who likes pie like that."

"Are you sure?"

Rufus was certainly more insecure about his weight than I had ever imagined. I didn't think a dog would care. Maybe he thought fat was something else entirely, something all good dogs should avoid being.

"I am sure, Rufus. You are a good dog. And you are not fat. Not at all."

We walked along, the waves hissing a good morning, a few scats of gulls careening in the faint light of false dawn. I really did like the ocean. I really was glad that we had moved here. I really did think that this new life was the one I was meant to have.

Now, if I were able to dismiss Ava's comments as easily as I wanted to, everything would be perfect. I decided there was no time like the present to ask Rufus about it.

"Do you think I should start to pray again?"

Rufus looked up at me, confused.

"What? I don't understand."

"I mean, like praying. I sort of stopped talking with God . . . a long time ago. I told you about that."

"No. I don't think you did. That's not right—not talking to God."

"I did tell you that, Rufus. I am sure I did."

He stopped walking. He did that when confused or deep in thought.

Then he slowly spoke. "I thought you meant you didn't talk with him when we were walking. I think that's what I thought. I never once thought you stopped altogether. That is wrong. I think I already told you that, didn't I? Just now?"

"You did. So I should just forget about everything that happened and pretend that everything is hunky-dory and start including God in my conversations?"

Rufus made a wide half circle around a dead jellyfish, keeping his eyes focused on it in case it jumped at him. "Sure. You can do that."

"Just like that?"

"I don't understand. What is God supposed to do? Things are what they are. You start from here. You can't change what happened in the past, to what you want. I don't think it works that way. I know it doesn't work that way with dogs."

We walked on. The sun edged up onto the eastern horizon. I wanted to yell at somebody. Ava had been right. I think Rufus had been right, as well.

Rats.

The earth did not shake. The sky did not fill with lightning bolts. I had no soul-shaking epiphany. The logic piled too high for me to dismiss any longer. What could it hurt? No, that's not right. That's being snarky. I knew Atlantic Beach had been the right choice. Sometimes you just know. And there is no buildup, there is no crescendo. It just is. And that's what this was.

As we turned away from the ocean, I simply whispered aloud, my words carried off by the breeze, no doubt, "Dear God . . . it's me."

21

If I had been expecting rockets, or earth tremors, or a choir of celestial beings, all carrying amplified harps, I would remain disappointed.

Nothing happened.

I reintroduced myself to God, and said I hadn't talked to him for a while, then I ran out of things to say. And by that time, we were back at the house. Rufus took his early-morning nap, and I had to shower and fix breakfast. I had an interview at the office at nine.

Places to go, people to meet.

Maybe I felt a little looser. Maybe I felt a little less down.

I'm not sure. I once had a friend who first tried selling diet supplements, and then she tried selling dried blue-green lake algae, and finally, capsules filled with ginko biloba. She would insist that I try a week's worth, or a month's worth free of charge. Then she would call me every three days to see how much better I felt.

I hated to tell her that I never felt any better after taking whatever it was she was selling. I mean, I never felt run-down or fatigued or particularly dull-witted and forgetful in the past, so perhaps the effects of the drugs or algae or whatever were more subtle. Every time, I would have to tell her that I didn't think I felt anything. And she would respond with an ever-increasingly depressive, "Ohhhhh."

Maybe talking to God is similar to taking dried blue-green lake algae. Maybe it took a while to kick in.

The interview went well. Kistler Hibbs asked how my recent visitors "from up north in Yankee land" liked Atlantic Beach and my new house. I said they really enjoyed themselves, and I enjoyed having them, but if I told the truth, I was happy to see them go because I liked having quiet evenings.

"Don't get too used to the quiet, Miss Mary Fassler. Pretty soon you'll become that crazy old lady shaking your fist at the teenagers who walk down your street playing their music at all hours and much too loud."

I stifled a laugh. We had one of those ladies in our neighborhood growing up. We avoided her house, even on Halloween.

"I won't. I promise. But two people, all at once, all the time, expecting to be entertained—I guess I'm just out of practice."

Labor Day proved to be a bust in Atlantic Beach. I had been told there would be one big party up and down the beach, all weekend long. The rain started Friday morning, and by Saturday fell horizontally. To make things worse, thunder and lightning boomed and flashed sporadically all three days. The rain kept coming, but it was warm. I almost liked warm rain. It felt like you were taking a shower.

Thunder has a way of unsettling Rufus. At the first rolling boom, he runs to the front door first, then to the back, then, using his front paws, lifts himself up to stare out one of the windows. When it booms again, he heads off into the bedroom, coming out every few minutes—as if checking to make sure I am still there.

I had nothing planned for the weekend, so I sat on my sofa, under a throw, reading old newspapers, magazines, and a stack of books I had gathered for just such a time, drinking coffee, and eating shortbread cookies—the real good ones from Scotland. Eventually, Rufus came out and joined me on the sofa, nestling in close to me, lifting his head in surprise at every lightning flash, his eyes darting from the window to me and back to the window as if I had been causing all the terrible commotion. I had explained to him last year what happened during a thunderstorm, but all The Weather Channel explanations in the world did not settle his nervousness. It did not matter that I assured him that he would be safe inside. He even stopped begging for shortbread, a clear sign of his nervousness.

The weather settled down on Sunday. The air, because of all the nitrogen oxide released by the lightning bolts, smelled fresh and clean and wonderful, containing a thick layer of promise you could almost see.

I leashed up Rufus and headed toward the downtown area. The beach would have been strewn with washed-up seaweed and jellyfish and the occasional dead fish from the storm. Rufus loved the smell of dead fish and would roll on top of them if I didn't stop him. I learned that lesson the hard way, staring out to sea one day while Rufus coated himself in Eau de Dead Fish. Downtown would be safer. Despite the rain, a modicum of people walked about. Sandy Sandy's was filled. I didn't feel like coffee right now. We walked past the Rent-a-Scooter store. The "closed" sign hung on the front door. Rain is probably terrible for the scooter business. I looked in and saw the same row of polished scooters waiting for riders.

I had promised myself that I would buy one. And with my literary/reporting prize, a raise had been promised. So the purchase wouldn't cause a big dent in my finances—unless the scooters were really expensive. I had no idea how much they cost.

"I'm coming back this week and I'm going to buy a scooter, Rufus. Remember when I told you that?"

"I do. That's okay with me."

Then he stopped.

"I won't have to ride on it, will I? They look dangerous to me. Do they have a helmet that fits a dog? I don't think they do. Then it's even less safe for me."

"No, Rufus, you will never have to ride on it."

"Okay. Then everything is okay."

As we strolled east, toward the ocean, I realized that I did feel better. Not fabulous. Not on top of the world. But I felt lighter. More free.

Maybe my first steps back toward God were paying off.

Yes, I know that sounds terrible. I know that God is not some sort of cosmic, celestial gumball machine that starts to pay off after you put in a quarter's worth of praying. I knew that prayer and God do not work that way. And that's not how I felt inside, in my heart. These first few days of me praying— well, none of my prayers would be featured on the religious television stations. I didn't really know what to say at first. I still don't. I said I was sorry for being silent for so long. I said I felt lost. I tried to explain how I felt—lost and abandoned. I said I blamed God for what happened. I didn't hold back. I didn't try to fill the prayer with thees and thous. I can't say for sure that God had listened to the prayers of such a wayward one, but I can say for sure that it felt like he had listened. The dialogue was choppy and stilted and angry and contrite and apologetic and meandering and curt; it contained everything that I had held inside for all these years.

I prayed aloud, at night, as we walked. Rufus heard, of course, but did not say anything.

Except, at the end, when I stopped talking, he would add an emphatic "Amen."

His coda, his final word, felt so right—like he put the right postage on my awkward words, helping me know that the words were actually being heard by the Almighty, were actually being posted to their heavenly address.

It took a dog.

Go figure.

Tuesday at noon is when I decided to walk over to Rent-a-Scooter. Rufus fussed and bounced and whined more than normal. In fact, he hardly ever asked to come with me during the day. But today, he all but insisted.

So I leashed him up, and we set off.

The bell sounded as the two of us entered the store. Rufus sniffed the air like he was on the CSI investigation team.

"Hello. Welcome."

Viktor was as handsome as I remembered. Maybe more so. He had a touch of summer tan to him.

"Hi. Remember me?"

His face brightened and he greeted me with a wide smile.

Why are the good ones off limits?

"I do. Mary, right? The last name . . . starts with an . . . F. Right?"

"You are correct. Mary Fassler."

"Yes, that's it."

"So do you have a scooter to sell? We talked about you selling a few scooters at the end of the season."

"Of course I remember that. People rent. Not many buy."

He pointed to the last four scooters in the line. "These four, I'll sell. The blue one is probably the best one. Never had a problem with it. A few minor scratches here and there, but in the best shape of the four. Mechanically, it's A-One. You like blue?"

At that moment, the young girl I had seen at the shop some months earlier bounced out from the rear of the shop. She skidded to a stop when she saw us, her black hair a beehive halo around her face and shoulders. She stared at me, then really stared at Rufus. She looked up at her father.

"There's a dog in here," she said.

"Yes, Molly, that is definitely a dog," Viktor answered, smiling.

She looked at me, then back at her father.

"Can I pet him?"

Rufus had the gentlest of souls, but small children . . . well, they could give him a case of the willies. Sometimes. Not always. Once, back in Wheaton, when Rufus was younger, I had a visitor with a three-year-old son. I wasn't watching, but I heard a bark, a loud snippy bark, and the little boy started to cry in surprise.

At first, we thought Rufus had bit him—but he didn't. He just barked. That's what the little boy said. "He didn't bite, Mommy. He just barked."

Later on, Rufus told me the child had pulled on his ear, and added, "A bark is better than a bite, right?"

This little girl was older, and judging from her asking her father if she could pet him, better behaved.

"You'll be very gentle?" Viktor asked.

The little girl nodded solemnly.

"Is it okay, Miss Fassler?"

"Sure. I think he'll be fine."

The little girl took three very deliberate steps to Rufus's side and knelt down beside him, looking as if she had practiced the movements. Slowly, she reached out, and patted his head, then began to stroke him down the neck onto his back. He actually nudged closer to her and looked up at her wide face, his eyes clear and kind and accepting.

"So, do you like blue?"

Viktor's question snapped me back to the present.

"Sure. I guess. I mean, I never really had a favorite color. But the blue one is very nice."

Out of the corner of my eye, I saw the little girl reach around Rufus to hug him. With a hug, she might have been walking on thinner ice. But Rufus remained stoic and leaned into her as she hugged him. I could tell the hug remained loose, not tight, but soft and gentle and little-girl tender.

"His name is Rufus," I said.

"And her name is Molly. I don't think I introduced her before."

We watched the two of them for another moment.

"The blue one will be fine. Is it the one that I rented?"

Viktor thought for a moment.

"I think it was. Did you like the way it handled? Fast enough for you?"

I told him that it ran perfectly back then. I didn't try to go very fast, but it went as fast as I needed it to go.

"You can get it up to 60 miles an hour, but around here, you don't need all that speed."

"I would be scared, I think, going that fast. But maybe when I get used to it."

"Maybe. Getting used to something new takes time. But you just keep at it. Then it becomes second nature."

"Sure. How much will it be? And when can I come to pick it up?"

Viktor rubbed his chin, thinking. I could hear the rasp of his whiskered skin. He named a price, then said, "Friday. I'll have it ready by Friday. New oil. Cleaned. Buffed. All the paperwork. Would that work for you?"

"I'll see you Friday, then."

As we walked away, from a half block away, Molly ran out onto the sidewalk and waved good-bye. Rufus turned as she did, making eye contact with the little black-haired girl.

—⚬⚬⚬—

The Labor Day holiday meant a short week—except for the newspaper's sportswriters. Guy Wilson and Todd Grossman were "as busy as two cats in a rocking chair factory." That's how Kistler Hibbs described them. Kistler Hibbs's version made no sense and we all knew it, but it felt off-kilter yet deftly appropriate somehow. High school football had begun, and the *Herald* always did a feature on every local high school team in the county, complete with individual pictures of the players. I had nothing to do with any of it. And for that I was glad. As I mentioned before, sports is not my native language. I had been assigned to do a feature—a few weeks away—on how the wives of high school football coaches coped with the pressures of the game. I had been looking forward to that. It would be interesting.

Friday afternoon, I excused myself early.

Well, I didn't actually ask if I could leave early. I had no deadlines, so I sort of got up, sidled out of the newsroom, and pretended to head to Starbucks down the street. Instead, I headed to my trusty Volvo, got in, and drove home.

I would pick up my scooter today. In the back of my house stood a large shed, complete with a cement floor. It had white siding that matched the house, with a green door, so it wasn't unattractive. I suspect that previous owners used it to store gardening equipment. Since I neither had any gardening equipment, nor planned on getting any, I could use it to store the scooter, out of the rain and out of sight. The shed had a large, very-secure-looking lock on it. No sense in tempting fate.

I parked the car, and ran in to change into jeans. I didn't think I had the élan to pull off riding a scooter in a skirt. I'm sure it could be done—just not done by me. I would hate to have it on my tombstone: "Crashed while trying to hold her skirt down on a scooter."

The scooter store was only a few blocks away, so the walk would only take a few minutes. I planned on heading there by myself, but Rufus put up such a fuss, jumping and barking, actually barking loudly, and nosing at the door, that I relented finally, and took the leash off the peg in the back entryway. Once I had snapped on the leash, he settled down, as calm as a kitten.

That doesn't make sense either, as a metaphor. Kittens are not necessarily calm, are they? I think Kistler Hibbs and his nonsensical alliterations and metaphors had begun to corrupt my impeccable sensibilities.

The day was fine, bright, warm, with only the slightest breeze to stir the leaves. If this was the beginning of autumn, I knew I would learn to love the winter here.

My new scooter stood gleaming in the middle of the shop. Viktor must have waxed it, because it glistened in the sun. He greeted me with a warm "Hello."

I waved at him, then I asked him the question I had been meaning to ask him since the first time I saw him.

"Why Viktor with a *K*? Is it a family name?"

His pained yet cheerful smile indicated that it was not the first time he answered the question.

"You'll have to ask my parents. I did once and all my mother said is that she liked how it looked with *K*. I always thought it looked pretentious. I guess I could change it—but at this point in my life, I would have to relearn how to sign my name. And that seems like a lot of trouble."

I handed him the check—actually a cashier's check. He didn't ask for one, but I wanted to assure him that I had the money, and he wouldn't have to call in the check to the bank or whatever people do to check checks these days.

He handed me a thick packet. "Registration. Title. Owner's manual. Service record. Bill of sale. Everything you need is in there."

Molly bounced out from the back of the shop.

"Rufus," she said, loudly, with great cheer. "You brought Rufus." She hurried to his side, knelt down next to him, as before, and started petting him, just as gently and tenderly as she had done before.

Then it dawned on me.

"I don't know what I could have been thinking. I can't take the scooter now. I have Rufus with me."

Viktor realized it at the same time. "That's right. I don't think he would like the ride, would he?"

"He would hate it. Well, I can walk him home, then come back. Will you still be open?"

Viktor checked his watch.

"Sure. But . . . you don't have to do that. You take the scooter home. We'll follow you to your house. I'll take Rufus with us. It's almost closing time anyhow."

"No. I couldn't impose on you like that. You probably have to get home to dinner. Your wife will be worried."

Something dark crossed his face, just for a second, dark and foreboding.

"No. No one will be waiting."

He must have seen the concern in my eyes, or anxiety, or whatever flashed in my mind. I would be horrible at poker.

"My wife . . . I mean . . . she passed away four years ago. Molly's sitter is a college girl and she's gone back to school for the year. Molly doesn't start school till next week, so she's here with me."

I didn't know what to say. Now I knew why all the people I told about my husband were silent.

"I'm sorry," I finally said, soft as I could. I don't know if Molly was paying attention. "I didn't mean to pry."

Viktor did not appear angry or upset or concerned—just resigned.

"It's okay. Really. It's been four years."

We both were silent for a long moment. I could not tell you how long the silence lasted—even trying to remember it now. The time span is fuzzy, hazy, like a dense fog at the beach.

I have to say something. I have to.

"The same thing happened to me. Five years ago. My husband and my son. He was Molly's age."

I looked over at the little black-haired girl and felt that tightness in my chest and the heat in my throat and the wetness in my eyes. I turned away and wiped at my eyes with the back of my hand. I hoped I did it so no one really noticed what I had done.

"So . . . we both know how hard this can be, don't we?" Viktor said, his words at a whisper, not because of sadness, but to keep them from his daughter.

I nodded. I didn't trust myself to speak.

Molly spun around and lay on her stomach, put her head in her hands, and peered up at Rufus. He lay down on his stomach and stared back at the small girl. Rufus never interacted that way with me.

She was talking to him, her words only a whisper, her words only to be heard by Rufus and Rufus alone. He would be trusted with her words and no one else.

I sniffed loudly, then turned to him, with as big a smile as I could manage.

"Are you okay to drive?" he asked.

I sniffed again.

"I am. This sort of moment is old hat. Hard for a second or two, then it passes."

"I know. You get better at it as time goes by. Like shifting gears, isn't it?"

"Exactly. Sometimes you have to do it in an instant. That's when it's hard."

We both looked at the dog and the girl, and then we looked at each other. Neither of us spoke for a while. Again, I don't know how long we stared.

"Here's the key," he said, breaking first.

"I'll drive slow. I live over on Robin. Halfway down the block."

"The little white Cape Cod with green shutters? The one that was just painted?"

"Yes. I just moved here from near Chicago. Well, in April."

"I love that house. I've driven by it a couple of times. I like the picket fence."

I put the helmet on my head. I didn't snap the chin strap. That made me look like I was wearing a deranged party hat. And I only lived a few blocks away.

"Rufus, you will go with Molly and Viktor, okay? You'll ride with them and they'll take you to our house, okay?"

I knew Rufus understood perfectly. He followed at Molly's side, as they headed out to their red truck in the alley. Viktor pushed the scooter through the shop and outside for me. It started right away. I sat down and watched as Rufus slowly climbed up into the cab of the truck. Molly helped him at the last. It was a long stretch for a small dog, and Rufus could never really jump high. I heard the door slam, and I slowly pulled out and headed for the main street.

I thought back to what Rufus said about being victorious. Is that what he meant?

I dismissed it as crazy talk and made a long turn onto Robin, puttering along on my new scooter, happy. I pulled into my driveway and stopped at the back of the house. I switched off the engine, pulled the helmet off, then yanked the scooter up on its stand.

Viktor pulled up behind me.

"Ride okay?".

"Beautiful. I love it."

Molly opened her door and I expected Rufus to bound out. Normally he would have. He didn't take to cars well and the less time he had to spend in them, the better.

Molly kept petting him and whispering something to him.

I don't know what came over me. But something did. Some power. Or courage. Or foolishness.

"Listen," I said to Viktor, "I know this is really forward. But I have a big bowl of spaghetti planned for dinner. Well, I do now, anyhow. I'll tell you upfront that the sauce is from a jar. But it is good sauce—for being out of a jar. And the cheese is imported. That's what makes it good—wonderful cheese. Would you like to stay for a quick dinner? Molly and Rufus seem to be becoming fast friends."

I could practically see inside Viktor's mind. His eyes gave his thinking away. He wanted to, but did not want to be forward either. He wanted to, but he had to protect his daughter as well. He wanted to talk about his wife with someone who really understood, but was afraid to.

I was afraid too. When was the last time I invited a man for dinner? Like never, really.

I was thinking everything he was thinking. Do we have too much of a shared background? Am I—or is he—a nice person? Or perhaps quietly and dangerously crazy? Would there be too much pain?

Then he smiled. And I smiled back.

We both knew the answer.

"Sure. I would love that. I'm pretty sure Molly would love it too. She's a big fan of spaghetti."

"It's not gourmet spaghetti. It's just me doing the cooking."

He leaned toward me, speaking softly.

"I am positive that Molly's grandmother uses ketchup in her spaghetti sauce, so anything will be better than that. All the pressure is off, okay? Sauce from a jar, to me, is gourmet."

After dinner, Viktor and I sat on the screened porch. Rufus and Molly were inside. The music from the introduction of *SpongeBob SquarePants* could be heard through the screen door.

"Is it okay if she watches that show? It's been a long time since I had to monitor children's TV. I mean, I know what the show is, but kids' media is confusing."

Viktor held his coffee cup away from the sofa as if he was afraid of spilling.

"It's okay. Some of it is over her head. But I don't think any of it is bad. I don't think so. Maybe it's borderline, but it's hard to keep up with everything."

Dinner had gone well. I had the spaghetti done quickly. I had French bread slathered in garlic butter to serve with it, and I made a small mixed-green salad as well. The adults ate the salad.

Conversation flowed easily. I asked Viktor about his business. He asked me about my work. I didn't mention my book writing. I will, but to drag out books right now felt a little like bragging. He knew all about the *Herald* and had known Kistler Hibbs back in high school, though Kistler Hibbs had been four grades ahead of Viktor.

"That's what everyone called him back then too. He would correct people. 'It's Kistler Hibbs,' if you please."

I offered to make more coffee. Viktor accepted, but added that after the coffee they would go. Molly's bedtime during the summer was later, but they were getting into practice of going to bed earlier each day to get prepared for school hours.

We could hear the ocean tonight, a gentle thrumming, plus crickets. The occasional car drove down the street. I could hear music from my next-door neighbor's house. They were an older couple who were partial to classical music. I had no idea of the composer.

"Mozart," Viktor said. "Clarinet concerto in . . . something or other. B-flat, maybe."

"I'm impressed," I replied. Seriously. I was impressed.

"The result of a wasted childhood. I never played ball, just listened to classical music."

"Really?" I replied, already angry at his parents.

He laughed quickly. "No. My mother taught music. That sort of music filled our house. I grew up with it. I got to play ball too."

"That's good. I was ready to be mad at them—your parents, I mean."

We sat for a minute. Viktor sipped.

"This is nice," he said. "After my wife . . . I was angry for so long. Maybe still am, a little. Angry at the doctors. Angry at myself. Angry at God. You know—angry at everyone."

I knew exactly how he felt.

"I know exactly what you mean," I said.

"But I realized, over time, that it was nobody's fault. It happened. The world is a broken place at times. I guess we all want God to keep us alive forever."

"I know. I know what you mean," I said.

"Eventually, I found peace in the pain. I had to. I have a daughter to raise. That peace keeps me solid now. I thank God for that."

"So how did you get the peace?" I asked.

"I guess it came when I could finally acknowledge that God has a plan, that everything happens for a purpose, even if we don't like it and don't want it, and that he is still good—even when I don't understand it all."

I smiled at him, in the dark, and hoped that he saw me.

After a long moment, Viktor stood up.

"We have to be going. I don't want to, but Molly has to have a schedule. If not, she doesn't do well at all."

I took his empty cup.

"This was very nice, Mary. It was very pleasant."

We walked in on Molly and Rufus sitting on the sofa. Molly's arm wrapped around Rufus, who sat upright, as if he was absorbed in the SpongeBob cartoon. He might have been. He understood more on TV than I gave him credit for. But cartoons might be hard to explain to him.

Rufus and I stood at the screen door, waving as they left.

I felt both more solid than I had in months, or years, and more nervous as well. The nervousness I understood. The solidity, I did not.

Rufus and I walked the beach that night, the tiniest hint of cooler weather in the breeze. I must have had a hundred questions in my mind, but did not feel like giving any of them voice.

Rufus did ask me one question though.

"How old is that little girl?"

"Molly. Her name is Molly."

"Her name is hard for me to say."

"Not much different than Mary."

"I know. Mary is hard to say too."

"Molly is five years old. Maybe six. If her mother has been gone for five years . . . yes, she's probably six."

"Her mother died," Rufus said. "She told me she died."

"Yes. I don't know how. But she doesn't have a mother now."

"Oh."

And that was all.

I sat on the porch by myself that night, and wrapped a throw around my shoulders. Rufus gave up on sitting beside me, or else he wanted to leave me alone. He might have been that caring. I found it harder, sometimes, to process emotions with his sad face staring at me.

Maybe this praying has done something to me. Maybe it has torn down a wall.

I felt . . . I want to say free . . . but that's not it. I wanted to believe God is still good, like Viktor said. To feel lighter. And more solid. If God could do that for Viktor . . .

I looked up at the dark sky.

Dear God, I am sorry for being so . . . foolish. I am sorry for not talking to you. I am sorry for blaming you for what happened. Can you forgive me? I need your peace. Can you . . . ?

And that's when I felt something break inside of me, something bad and harsh and cold and saw-edged and raspy and mean. It broke, it snapped, it started to crumble and splinter and dissipate.

And that's when I started to cry. Not a sad cry, not a cry of pain, but a cry of release and relief. The tears fell for what I had lost, not only way back then, but in the years between then and now. I had lost me. I had lost my heart. My soul was damaged and broken and hidden.

And now, it felt as if light was entering into my very being for the first time in years and years and years. I sat there, my shoulders hunched and my lungs gasping for air, and then it was gone and then I felt . . . normal again. Like I felt alive once more. Reborn, almost. No, it felt really like being reborn.

And that's when Rufus slowly edged out onto the porch and stuck his cold nose into my calf and made me shriek like I had fallen into a vat of crystal-clear ice water.

We both jumped upright.

And I felt as good as I had ever felt in my life.

"Thank you, God. Thank you."

22

The next day, just after lunch, my phone rang.

I should have invested in caller ID, but I remained in my frugal mode when I signed up for local, landline service.

I picked it up.

"Hello?"

"Hi. This is Viktor . . . from the scooter shop."

How many Viktors does he think I know?

"Hi," I replied, as cheery as I could make a one-syllable word.

"I called to see how the scooter is running."

We both knew he lied. Not bad lying, but he didn't care about the scooter at all—at least not for this call.

I knew why he called, but I would not make him squirm.

"Great."

He paused. If we had been teenagers, I would have thought he frantically looked at his penciled sheet of handwritten conversation starters. I listened intently for the crinkle of paper. But all remained silent. .

"Listen," he finally said, ". . . uhh . . . maybe we could . . ."

I decided to jump in.

"Viktor, would you like to come over and have dinner here tonight? I know it's hard to get babysitters at the last minute. I would love to cook for someone other than just myself. I could make hamburgers. You could bring the chips and soda and maybe some potato salad?"

He paused again.

I prayed that I did not anticipate his positive response in error.

"I . . . I don't know how to make potato salad."

I managed to inhale.

"I don't think I can either. I always buy mine. And maybe dessert? Key lime pie is a personal favorite of mine."

I could see him smile through the phone.

"Mine too. Even Molly likes it."

───

I own a grill the size of a paperback book, but if you're only cooking four hamburgers, it works just fine. One each for the ladies, one and a half for the gentleman, and the remainder for the dog.

We sat around the kitchen table, passing chips and potato salad, Rufus going from Molly to me and back to Molly, trying to beg table scraps.

I only had to tell Molly once that Rufus should not be fed from the table. I know, I know, I do it all the time, and I would let Molly do it, eventually. But right now, she would probably give him her entire hamburger. My telling her once seemed to be enough. Every time Rufus sat beside her and stared up at her, Molly would slowly shake her head, her gloriously curly hair flowing like a cloud, and say, with great sorrow, "I am sorry, Rufus, I am not allowed to feed you."

I am not sure what we talked about that night. But I do remember Molly laughing, her little girl giggles making us giggle as well, which made her laugh even harder. Laughter of a child—I had forgotten how magical it can be. Laughter both wondrous and bittersweet at the same time. I hid the bittersweet part deep in my heart, like a hidden treasure that was only for me.

After dinner, Molly and Rufus were dismissed to watch television. Viktor and I cleared the table.

"It is so good to see her laugh," he said as he handed me a plate. "She doesn't laugh much. Or hasn't since . . . you know."

I waited. I waited a bit more. Then I decided to ask.

"Can you tell me what happened?"

He shut his eyes. Kept them shut.

Then he said, "This is the short version. Molly was a year old. Karen cut her finger while cutting Molly's birthday cake. Didn't think anything of it. Didn't heal quickly. Looked infected. Waited to go to the doctor. She was stubborn. A week later, I forced her to go. The wound developed a septic infection. She died three days later."

My hand went to my throat.

"I am so sorry. I really am."

"I know. I know you are, Mary. I could tell that the first time I met you."

I had to hug him then, and he hugged me back. And all the pain that I had carried for so long seemed to flow out of me. I rested my head on his shoulder. He stroked my hair. I felt his arms around me. He felt solid and muscular under my arms. And warm. And tender. And gentle.

After a moment, he relaxed and let me go.

He looked into my eyes.

"Can I call you again?"

"Yes, Viktor. You can."

⸻ ∞ ⸻

The end of autumn brought some storms through Atlantic Beach, and a bout of chilly weather. Chilly in Atlantic Beach was T-shirt weather back in Chicago. At night, the beach felt nearly barren, save the lights of the homes that faced the ocean, and the occasional bonfire, with sparks flittering skyward and shadows dancing on the waves.

I had a sweatshirt on that night. I do not remember packing Rufus's coat. He never asked about it, since it had never been that cold.

We walked north along the beach. It was our favorite route, the beach access easier because of sidewalks. The air stayed still, the waves made small catlike lapping noises on the beach, and the moon floated above the still water.

Rufus spoke first that night.

"Are you happy?" he asked. I'm sure he knew, but perhaps he felt the need to make sure.

I tried to be as honest as I could in my reply.

"I am, Rufus. I am very happy. Thank you."

We walked up to the ruins of an old fishing pier. The city council had been discussing rebuilding it. Our newspaper reported that this round of discussion seemed to move the project much closer to a resolution.

Rufus stopped walking. He stared out over the ocean for a minute. A long minute. Dogs don't stare much.

"I'm going to stop talking now," he said, his words firm and solid.

I waited.

"You mean tonight? That's fine," I answered. Sometimes he talks a lot. Sometimes not much.

326

"No. I mean forever."

I didn't hear that correctly. I was sure what I heard was not what I heard.

"What?"

"It's hard to do this," he said.

"Hard to do what?"

"To talk. Most dogs don't talk, you know. I need to be a dog again."

"But you are a dog," I replied. "A very good dog. You're my best friend."

"You have a new best friend."

He was referring to Viktor.

"Are you going to marry him?"

I knelt down to Rufus.

"I don't know. He has to ask me."

"The little girl needs a mother, doesn't she? You would be a very good mother. She needs a mother."

"She does," I said, trying not to cry.

"I like her a lot. She is very kind to me and very gentle. She never pulls on my ears. She talks to me. She tells me secrets. You should marry him."

"He has to ask me to marry him."

"Will you marry him if he asks you?"

"I will," I nodded.

"He'll ask you. I think that's what the 'victorious' word was. It might have been Viktor. Maybe I heard it wrong."

We both stared out to sea.

"I'm going to stop talking now."

"But you're my best friend, Rufus. In the whole world. You're . . . I need you . . ."

"Not so much now. But I will always be your best dog, won't I? I'll be your best dog even if I don't talk anymore? I like being your best dog."

I hugged him with a fierce love.

"You will always be my best dog. Forever. I will always love you. You helped bring me back to God."

"And I will always love you the best," he said with a closing finality that broke my heart and healed my soul at the same time. "Forever."

"Thank you, Rufus. Thank you."

———⁂———

And the breeze ruffled along the ripples in the sand, causing just the faintest hiss, and the moon glowed bright, lighting their way home. Rufus, a dog once again, a very good dog, walked home with his best friend, Mary.

23

Rufus stood to my side. It was early afternoon, in the spring, and the ocean reflected a gunmetal gray, quiet and gray, and the warm wind gently clattered the sea grass on the dunes. Clouds hovered above us, providing a white, comforting canopy.

Rufus wore a natty, striped bow tie around his neck, held there by a length of black elastic, which almost disappeared into his newly groomed coat. He did not want to wear it. That was obvious—even without words. He shook his head at first, trying to rid himself of the fashion accessory, until I took his jaw in my hands and stared into his eyes.

We were in my bedroom in my little house on Robin Avenue. He hadn't talked in a long time, and I'd stopped expecting it. But I still talked to him. A lot.

"Rufus," I said with some solemnity, "you have to wear this. Every member of the wedding party has to be properly dressed. That means bow ties on every dog in attendance."

Rufus would be the only dog in attendance, but that was beside the point.

He looked back at me, then slowly settled, knowing, understanding.

"I know you won't speak. It's okay."

He nuzzled into my neck.

"You listen to Molly, Rufus. You be her friend."

He pushed into me harder.

"I am happy, Rufus. Viktor and Molly are so very happy. And . . . I know you are happy too."

A small crowd gathered with us that Sunday afternoon. Everyone wore sandals or went barefoot. Ava had come. Beth had come. Bernice sent a beautiful bouquet. Viktor's mother-in-law was there, hugging, crying, and hugging more.

Molly and Rufus walked down the imaginary aisle together.

Viktor and I followed them.

Molly stood on one side, Rufus on the other, as we said our vows . . . before God.

Oh, yes—and God was there as well.

Discussion Questions

1. Come on now, a dog? Really? A dog talking to God? Seriously, though . . . do you think that God could, or would, use such a method to reach a person who was lost?

2. Mary shows her anger at what happened to her by turning away from religion, the church, and God. Do you think what happened to her when she finally returned to church and heard the sermon on Job could be an accurate retelling of the message—or was she just too hurt to hear the truth?

3. Besides her pain, what other obstacles did Mary face in finding her faith again?

4. Perhaps Mary's mother-in-law meant well when she called to find out about the new man in Mary's life—but she instead sounded scolding and accusatory. How might we be guilty of the same sort of attitude if we try to "exhort" someone who seems to be sinning?

5. Suppose Mary was only hearing Rufus's voice in her head—can that sort of inner voice be the sort of nudge we need to turn back to God? And could the nudge from an inner voice be of a divine nature?

6. Mary gave up her nice, sort-of-safe life in suburban Chicago—and that change defined the rest of her life. Is that sort of dramatic move ever required to effect change? Could she have, or would she have made the same changes even if she had stayed where she was?

7. Do you think Billy played fair when he curtailed his relationship with Mary because of her faith—or lack of it? Couldn't a case be made that he should have at least witnessed to her and tried to bring her back to faith?

8. Many people get stuck in a situation or an emotion because of a tragedy or dramatic event in their lives.

What sort of advice would you have given Mary about dealing with her tragedy? Would that advice change over time—would the advice you offer a month after the funeral be dramatically different than the advice offered a year after the funeral?

9. Mary knows what an intimate relationship feels like—and what it all means. Does that make resisting a new intimate relationship easier or harder?

10. If Rufus really talked, and really gave good advice, wouldn't it make sense for Mary to share that secret with someone else? Wouldn't a person want to tell others about something miraculous in his or her life? Does it make sense that she kept it private? After all, Rufus never tells Mary to keep his talking a secret.

11. The fact that Mary had insurance money and some financial resources made it easier for her being a widow. Many widows may not have such an easy time, comparatively. Does Mary having resources prevent her spiritual growth and maturity, or does it make it harder for her to come to grips with reality?

12. Do you think that Rufus will ever talk—really speak—to Viktor's young daughter? And how important is it for us to have someone to talk to who will never offer a judgment on what we are feeling and experiencing?

Plan your escape.

For more information and for more
fiction titles, please visit
AbingdonPress.com/fiction.

The Cat That God Sent

THE CAT THAT GOD SENT

Jim Kraus

Abingdon Press fiction
a novel approach to faith

Nashville, Tennessee

The Cat That God Sent

Copyright © 2013 by Jim Kraus

ISBN-13: 978-1-4267-6561-2

Published by Abingdon Press, P.O. Box 801, Nashville, TN 37202
www.abingdonpress.com

The persons and events portrayed in this work of fiction
are the creations of the author, and any resemblance
to persons living or dead is purely coincidental.

The words to "Just As I Am, Without One Plea" were written in 1835
by Charlotte Elliott, 1789–1871.

Library of Congress Cataloging-in-Publication Data has been
requested.

Printed in the United States of America

1 2 3 4 5 6 7 8 9 10 / 17 16 15 14 13

To Petey, the noble cat who has deemed us
suitable hosts.

"God made the cat in order that man might have
the pleasure of caressing the tiger."
—Fernand Méry

1

Jake pulled to the side of the road, stopped the truck, then slid out into the chill of the dawn. He flexed his back, left and right, hearing the bones pop. He slowly rotated his right arm, in a windmill fashion, like a relief pitcher warming up. The muscles hurt most at the top of the arc, when it was closest to heaven.

"Think I'll get a sign today? That would be nice. Some sort of sign that this is the right move. That I'm doing the right thing. How about it? Even a little, bitty sign would be okay, too. A sign that doesn't look like a sign—okay as well."

He waited and heard nothing. He held his forced smile for a long moment. If God really were listening, he would know that Jake was only kidding—or at least mostly kidding.

"Well, the proverbial doors were open, right? That was a sign, right? An open door—or rather, an open road to Coudersport?"

The road between Kane and Coudersport remained empty with only sounds of the few birds that made north central Pennsylvania a stop on their early spring migration. To the east, the sun lit the top of a tree-covered ridge, illuminating the still-bare trees with a golden backlit glow.

"Now, here's the thing, though. Those preachers on TV get signs all the time. You talk to them. Why not me?" Jake knew he was being snarky and he was pretty sure God did not like, nor quickly answer, snarky prayers.

He took a deep breath, massaging his right shoulder with his left hand.

"Well, at least my shoulder feels better today."

He tugged on the ropes covering the tarp that held down all his earthly possessions. He checked every rope. By nature and temperament, Jake was a most careful person.

He felt a twinge.

"Almost better."

He started the engine, looked both ways twice, and pulled out onto the road. He had one more hour until he reached Coudersport.

"And that's where I'll start over. That's where I'll show everyone that I can do this. Right? Where I'll find my faith again."

He hoped the words would become his reality.

He reached into the glove compartment of the truck and pulled out one of a couple dozen eight-track tapes.

One of these days I'll get a new truck or put a CD player in this one.

He did not bother to look at the title. None were current.

Do they still sell eight-track tapes?

He popped the tape into the slot and turned up the volume. It was a compilation of Christian camp favorites. The first selection was "Onward Christian Soldiers." Jake could not help smiling and began to sing along. Loudly and off-key. Then his shoulder twinged again, sharply, as if giving him an omen of what was to come. However, the troubling thing about omens is they are open to interpretation.

The dried seed husks at the top of the tall field grass rustled together, stirred by the spring breeze with its hint of warmth. Green tendrils poked about at paw level. The cat stopped, sat down slowly, carefully, and sniffed.

A fecundity in the air.

He sniffed, his nose twitching.

I heard that word on that radio station that talks all the time and is always asking for money.

The cat would have smiled if he could have smiled. If he had the correct muscle structure.

Fecundity. That's a weird word, isn't it? Fecundity. Funny sounding. I know, I know . . . I can be a bit pedantic at times. That's where I heard that word, too. On that radio station that never plays music. They just talk. About needing money, mostly.

The feline snapped back to his task at hand and breathed in again, deeply. Not large by cat standards, perhaps the size of a football, with a thick silvery coat and black markings like a striped lynx. Gold-green eyes, wide set and deeply penetrating, a white chin and nose, and a thick feathering of white fur covering his ears. A thickly furred tail. The dark perpendicular lines scoring his forehead made it appear he was in perpetual deep thought.

I really am, most of the time.

He watched as a white truck pulled into the gravel lot. He tried not to put pressure on his right paw. He tried to ignore the agonizing tightness that raced up his forelimb when the paw scraped hard against the ground. He smoothed his whiskers with his other paw. He watched, showing no outward indication of pain. That is what cats do.

A truck. An old truck. And not very clean.

Then he crouched lower, protecting his right front paw, hidden, perfectly camouflaged in the grass, still as a rock, only his eyes, now slits in the bright sun, moving. The cat slowly tilted his head and looked up, into the pellucid sky, his vision staying on the thin clouds for a long moment. He tilted an ear toward the heavens, as if listening intently.

That looks like the man I heard God talking about. I think that's what I heard. It is hard to identify people. Most of them smell the same. A lot of them look the same. This human looks like he needs company. People need company. That's in the Bible, isn't it? A man without a cat. That's not right. He must be lonely.

The cat's eyes moved back and forth, just a little.

Well, I can say this much for sure: he needs a cat. A good cat. A smart cat. Like me. I am a good cat. I am a smart cat.

He flicked an ear, almost distracted by a soft, leafy rustle nearby. Soft and tender and whispery.

You know what? Maybe he needs a mouse. Everybody could use a fat mouse now and again. People get so excited when I bring them a mouse. They shout. They dance. People must like mice. They shoosh me away and in an instant, the mouse is gone. I guess people are always hungry. However, they are not very good at sharing their mice.

And as the cat thought about it, his stomach growled. It had been a few days since he had eaten. He stiffened, imperceptibly, hearing again the soft, furtive rustling in the grass a few body lengths to his left. He knew what small rodent made the rustle.

He would wait.

And maybe later, he would have something to give the man that would make him happy.

It's why I'm here. I need to give that lonely man a mouse. I need to help him. I am good at that. I can be a good, intelligent, helpful cat. God only uses good cats, and I am a very good cat.

The cat blinked and smiled to himself with a certain light in his eyes that gave evidence of his good humor.

The mouse dance. I really like it when humans dance the mouse dance.

―――∞∞∞―――

Jake Wilkerson pulled into the driveway of the church, an old church that was his new church, his new assignment, his new job—only his second real, adult job. Jake was nearing thirty, tall, thin, with a narrow face, an easy, gentle-to-arrive smile, and wide blue eyes. Some people called him striking. He did not call himself that. His unruly thatch of thick brown hair made *striking* the wrong adjective to use to describe him.

The church's exterior, weathered to a faded, chalky white, featured a scalloping of brown water stains, the residue from lawn sprinklers squirting iron-rich well water on the bottom rows of its clapboards. The building was perfectly centered in the middle of a large grassy and partially graveled two-acre lot at the southwest corner of Route 44 and Dry Run Road—a short ride south of Coudersport, Pennsylvania.

Loose gravel crunched and growled beneath the worn tires of his pickup, a slow, welcoming, rural sound, loud in the quiet of the most pleasant spring morning.

The church sign, ninety degrees to the highway, leaned a few degrees off perpendicular.

CHURCH OF THE OPEN DOOR
11:00 SUNDAY SERVICE
, PASTOR

The space before the word *Pastor* must have been recently painted over, with only a faint ghosting of the former pastor's name remaining.

Jake relaxed, stepped out of his truck, and stretched, breathing deep, twisting at the waist and rolling his shoulders. The right shoulder popped, almost audibly this time, and he felt a ripple of small creaks in his back. He tried to smooth his hair and realized that he needed to find a barber before Sunday.

This isn't so bad, is it? This is good. Really. It is.

He breathed in, filling his lungs, feeling his ribs complain. The ominous twitch in his shoulder still spoke, a hesitant pulsing.

I'm too young to feel this many aches. I need a new mattress.

He squared his shoulders.

I can do this. I can. I can make this work. I know how to do this.

He took a few small steps toward the church, stopped, then stared up at the steeple at the rear of the church roof.

Is that my imagination . . . or is the steeple tilted?

The cat remained still, hidden in the grass, only the very tip of his tail twitching. His ears pivoted and moved, following the sounds of the man's steps on the gravel lot.

He has firm footsteps. Solid. Like he knows where he is going. Some people take little, halting steps, which mean they seldom get where they are going. Not this human.

The cat sniffed, his small nostrils flaring almost undetectably.

And I like the way he smells. Safe.

He heard the rustle again.

I have time. I will wait. Never pounce before the prey is within the space of a leap. My mother taught me that.

Within moments of his arrival at his new job and residence, Jake watched as a pickup truck, even older than his and of an ill-defined paint color, bounced into the parking area and all but slid to a stop. The engine plinked and coughed and continued to sputter even as the driver hopped out, slammed the door, and made his way closer to Jake, his right hand extended.

"T. James Bennett," he declared, shaking Jake's hand enthusiastically. T. James Bennett looked like an inexact, off-center, tattered copy of Willard Scott—the morning weatherman who wished people happy birthday, but shorter and wider, with a genial smile. "We met back when you preached here, but you met a lot of folks that weekend, so I bet not many stand out. Am I right?"

"You are, Mr. Bennett, but I do remember you," Jake said. "I remember wondering about the 'T' in your name."

Mr. Bennett almost frowned, but didn't. "It's been T. James since I learned how to write. I hated the 'T' name, even as a little kid, and I told myself that when I grew up, I would never use it again. That's one promise that I kept to myself. Good to keep promises, you know. The problem with a bad name is all the stuff your name gets put on these days. I figured it was too much trouble to change it. People learned. And besides, they all call me Jimbo. Everyone does, including the Missus. Jimbo. Says it's a proper name for a fellow like me. Been called Jimbo since grade school."

"Well, then, Jimbo, I'm happy that you took time out of your day to meet me here. I appreciate it."

Jimbo drew a step closer. "You know why I'm the elder in charge of meeting you today?"

Jake hoped he looked puzzled. "Seniority?"

Jimbo cackled and replied, "Nope. It's 'cause I don't have a job. At least not one at the moment. Got time to burn, as they say. And I had a spare set of keys for the church. Two good reasons."

Jimbo stepped off toward the rear door of the church. "We did show you the living quarters here, didn't we? When you came and visited? The parsonage part of the church, right? Plenty of room for a single fellow like yourself."

Now a few months past, the day of his candidating had been more than a bit hectic. The drive from Butler should have taken only three hours, but Jake had been on the road for five, his sense of direction not strong. There was no direct route that led door-to-door. The trip involved multiple turns and changes in route numbers and Jake's nervous and constant referring to the map. And, being that he "auditioned" in the early winter, snow had begun to fall while he spoke that cold morning, amping up Jake's nervousness about the return trip.

"I did see it, but I didn't spend much time looking. I guess I was a tad nervous that day."

"Have to say, Pastor Jake, that I didn't think you were nervous at all. You preached good."

Jimbo pulled a fist-sized ring of keys from his coat pocket, jangling like a jailer, and thumbed through it until he found the correct one. He slipped it into the lock on the six-panel door, pulled at the handle while he turned the key, and shouldered the door open.

"Weather makes this stick sometimes," he said, then eyed his new pastor. "You handy around the house? Fixing stuck doors and all that?"

Jake lied.

"Not bad. I don't have as many tools as I would like, but I guess I'm handy enough."

The truth is, besides a hammer and a screwdriver, I don't have any tools. And if it can't be fixed with either of those tools—then it's broken.

Jimbo grinned, satisfied. "Not that this place needs much of anything . . . but the whole building is getting up there in years. Sometimes it takes a hammer to get things going."

Jake wasn't sure he knew what Jimbo meant, but nodded in earnest agreement. "Sure thing."

Jimbo slapped at the wall and switched on the light—a bright overhead lamp ensconced in a white, imitation carnival glass globe. Jake squinted for a moment. The light was much too bright for the room, but the interior was more pleasant than Jake had remembered, especially now that the soft light of spring had begun to arrive. The furnishings might have been from IKEA, even though the nearest IKEA was probably in Philadelphia: matching upholstered chairs in a gray corduroy fabric, a comfy-looking sofa, a stand for a TV. The walls were off-white, maybe a light classic gray, even. The kitchen, visible from the entry, had newer stainless steel appliances, a square wooden table by a large window, and more cabinets than Jake could possibly fill. Wide wood flooring planks. Shiny. Probably original but refinished.

"Bedroom's back there, of course. Bathroom too. That's new as of last year. New shower and tub and . . . all the other facilities as well," Jimbo said, with a guilty smirk, like saying "toilet" in front of a pastor was somewhere midway up on the list of almost-sins. "And the office is over there," he added, pointing, as if he were a lazy real estate agent.

That office Jake remembered. It was a large room, much bigger than he had been used to. Big wooden desk, well used, with great character and patina, wall of bookcases, a large wooden table (looked handcrafted) with a half-dozen chairs— for elders' meetings, no doubt. Three large windows, almost floor to ceiling, matching the Gothic style windows of the church. A smallish door led toward the church itself, buffered by a small office/anteroom that may have once held a secretary, but not in the last few years.

"You need help unloading?" Jimbo asked. "My back ain't quite up to snuff these days, but I could make a call or two."

Jake demurred. "No. I don't have much. Clothes. Books. Towels. Sheets. A few pots and pans. Mr. Coffee. Easy stuff. I'm just so glad that the parsonage is furnished. A great help for someone like me."

Jimbo fiddled three keys off his ring and handed them to Jake. One was marked FRONT DOOR, one BASEMENT DOOR, and one PARSONAGE.

"Pastor Wilkerson," Jimbo said, his words a little softer, "I gotta tell you . . . thanks for taking over here as pastor. Really, thanks a bundle. We don't have much in a small church, I know, and we're on the smallish side of small . . . but . . . well, it is what we got. Ever since Pastor Mokley quit the God business and left to sell insurance in Kane—well, we all have been without. We need a man of God, all right. An honest man. Like you."

He had to say an honest man. He had to go there. Like I'm going to be reminded of that forever. Honesty is not always the best policy. Just ask Barbara Ann. But that's water under the bridge, right?

Jimbo offered a happy grin, hoping to put the new man at ease.

"Well, it is an honor to be called," Jake replied, being totally truthful.

"So, I'll leave you be, if that's okay with you. And you remember that we got an all-church potluck this Wednesday. In the basement. Fellowship Hall, if you'd like. Folks want to meet you, see what you eat. Stuff like that. And you and the elders will meet later on. Talk things over. Answer any questions you might have."

"Should I bring anything to the potluck?" Jake asked. *Maybe pastors in small churches cook things for these occasions. Or bring the rolls or something.*

"Nope. Just yourself. One of the perks of the job. Just stay away from the Missus' Swedish Stew. She ain't Swedish and it ain't stew."

Jake stuck out his hand.

"Jimbo—forewarned is forearmed. Thanks." And as he shook the elder's hand, Jake felt that familiar twinge in the right shoulder, as if the heavens were trying to tell him that something was about to happen. Jake didn't like that twinge. The twinge was there just before he was fired from his previous church in Butler. He definitely felt it just before his former almost-fiancée-waiting-for-a-ring informed him that if he were no longer a pastor, she was no longer his girlfriend. The twinge was there when his former senior pastor and boss said there would be no letter of recommendation—"Because of all that has happened. You do understand, don't you? My niece feels terrible about all this." And he felt the twinge today—clearly and strongly.

Maybe it's a good twinge this time.

Omens.

Jake never liked omens, even though, if there was one, regardless of its portent, he would find it comforting.

———❧———

The cat waited and the prey came to him. It was easy and quick. He circled around at the edge of the field. He could wait. It looked like that other man, the round man, was about to leave.

Then I'll introduce myself, the cat thought to himself. *I don't want to intrude on their conversation. If there is one thing a good*

cat needs to understand it's that good manners are very important.
I will simply wait here until he is available for introductions.

———∞∞∞———

As they walked back outside to the trucks, Jimbo zipped up his work jacket, threadbare at the elbows and cuffs.

"You call me if you need anything. Bobby Richard—he's an elder, too, who you met, of course—got the phone connected last week, so you can call me. But maybe you have one of those new cellphones, I bet. They don't always work up here, though. Anyhow, all the elders are on the list taped to the desk—phone numbers and the like."

"I'll do that, Jimbo. But I'm sure I'll be okay."

At the far edge of the parking lot, where the gravel met the grass, sat a tall, silver-and-black cat with white accents. Jake noticed it first.

"That anybody's cat?" he asked. "Looks a little like a lynx, doesn't it? A small, skinny one."

Jimbo looked over, stared for a long moment, then snorted.

"Don't know. Never saw a lynx up here. But it's just a cat and it's not from around here. No houses nearby. Not within a mile. Maybe even farther than that. More like two miles—and that would be the Jenkinses and I know Old Man Jenkins, and well, he hates cats, so it can't belong to him. That one is just a stray. Might even be one of those feral cats. You know, raised in the wild. If that happens, they're really no good as house cats anymore. And people dump animals out here in the country all the time."

"Really? That's terrible."

"It happens," Jimbo said. "Some people got no feelings, do they?"

"I guess not," Jake replied.

"I got my shotgun in the truck. You want me to get rid of it for you?"

Jake could only manage a surprised, "Wha-what?"

"If you let it stick around, it could be a pest. And, look, it looks like it's got a lame foot there. Be a kindness to end it for it, you know?"

Jake recovered and knew he did not want to sound too surprised or shocked. What Jimbo said was probably true, but he could not cotton to a random killing of a cat—not just like that.

"No. Maybe he's just lost."

"It ain't lost. And it doesn't belong to anybody. Too skinny. It's just like getting rid of a varmint. It'll be okay."

Jake held firm.

"No. Let him be."

Jimbo looked askance, just a little, then shrugged.

"Suit yourself. But if it gets to be a pest, I'll take care of it for you."

"I'm sure he won't."

Jimbo stroked his chin and grinned. "You pastors are in the saving business, aren't you? I guess that goes with the job description, doesn't it? Saving things that are lost and lame and hurting and all that? That's a good trait for a pastor, ain't it?"

And with that, Jimbo heaved himself into his old truck; the engine sputtered to life after the third ratcheting try, and he backed out onto the main road without looking.

"See you Wednesday, if not sooner," he called out, as the truck wheezed into a forward gear and pulled away.

Jake turned back to the cat. It had not moved all the while, but instead, just stared impassively. Then it looked down at the ground beside it, and then back up to Jake. Jake thought there was an air of pride in the cat's stare, but could not imagine why.

⸺⸺⸺

Please. I am not a "varmint." That was insulting. He didn't know a good cat when he saw a good cat. No time for that now. We have more important things to deal with. Like me being sent by God. That should take precedent, don't you think?

And what sort of name is Jimbo? For a grown man. We are not in the funny papers, are we?

A varmint? Really?

⸺⸺⸺

Jake watched the cat watch him. Neither of them moved. Jake relented first and walked to the cat. The cat looked to his left, toward the ground.

Jake's smile dropped, replaced by a squinched expression, complete with pursed lips, a lemon-induced-lips pursed squinch.

Lying next to the cat was a mouse, a perfectly dead mouse, laid out with feline precision on the gravel.

⸺⸺⸺

People are simply terrible at catching mice. I'm very good at it. I know that sharing a mouse is not what cats usually do—so that will prove to this man that I am a very good cat.

A good cat on a mission.

A mission from God.

That was in a movie, wasn't it? Where they wrecked all those cars. I saw that on television.

———◈◈◈———

For some reason, and Jake was not sure what that reason was, he restrained himself from reacting like he wanted to react: dancing away in disgust and dismay and alarm. The cat all but smiled up at Jake, beaming, as if Jake had recognized the mouse, the gift, for what it was—a great sacrifice from a skinny, hungry cat.

"Is that for me?" he asked, then wondered why he asked.

The cat kept his almost-smile and offered a meow, a self-satisfied, happy meow. Almost not a meow, it was more like an explanation, or a statement of accomplishment. Not a meow. More than that. Or less. Nearly humanlike.

Why would this cat do that? Give me his . . . food?

Jake felt another strong twinge in his shoulder. Either he would have to get used to the twinges or find a chiropractor to locate the source and fix it.

"Okay, then," Jake replied. He reached into his coat pocket and pulled out a rumpled receipt from a gas station, smoothed it out, bent down, and picked up the mouse by the tail using the receipt to keep from touching the dead creature. "Thank you," he said.

The cat looked up, seemingly very satisfied that Jake received his gift with gratitude.

Jake looked down and thought he saw an expression in the cat's eyes that seemed to suggest that he expected Jake to eat the mouse then and there. Instead, Jake knelt down and petted the cat on his head, which the cat accepted gracefully, almost regally, and he said, "I'll save this for later. But thanks so much for the mouse. I appreciate it."

Jake had no idea of why he was being so solicitous of this stray, skinny, lost cat, except it felt as if it were the right thing to do. Like the cat understood somehow. The cat really appeared to understand.

Jake walked toward the main door of his new living quarters. He laid the mouse down on an exposed ledge of the building's cement foundation. He would dispose of this particular "varmint" later when the cat wasn't watching him.

Good grief. I'm worried about what a cat thinks of me? It's like being back in Butler again . . . worried about what everyone thinks. That has to stop.

Jake's stomach growled, and his first move was toward the kitchen. The cat looked famished, and Jake could use a cup of coffee. Then he stopped short and realized that there was nothing in the kitchen—no food, no instant coffee, no nothing.

"You're hungry, aren't you?" Jake said, not really expecting an answer from the cat.

The cat had followed him to the door and now meowed plaintively, low and rumbly. It was an obvious yes.

"Well, then. We both need to eat," Jake said, and again the cat meowed, softly this time, in reply.

In that brief, single moment, Jake realized he could use a cat. For company. So neither of them would be lonely. Jake had grown up in the complete absence of animals—allergies, his mother claimed he had, and from his father's side, not hers. But he was pretty sure that the absence of all things furry was simply because his mother just didn't like "wild animals."

Animals are outside for a reason, young man. Jesus didn't have a dog. And you think you're better than Jesus?

"You're not a wild animal, are you?" Jake asked the cat.

The cat meowed in return.

"You agree, right? You must be hungry. You look skinny."

He had no food in the back of his truck. When he had left Butler, he had brought no perishables—nor packed any food of any type. "There's a store just down the road. I think." He dug the keys out of his pocket and opened the door. The cat followed him to his truck.

"You have to stay here," Jake said.

The cat sat and responded with a long meow.

"Good," he replied. "I'll be back. You wait here."

He opened the door to his truck, and the cat, as agile as a squirrel, scurried and limped into the truck and settled on the passenger seat, staring at Jake, waiting for him to get in.

"You can't come in the truck," Jake said. The cat turned from facing him and looked out through the windshield. "Come on, now. Cats don't like trucks. Come on out. Come on. You go back to the house."

The cat did not move.

Maybe off-center is the way things are supposed to be today. He shrugged, and slid into the driver's seat, closed the door, put on his seatbelt, and started the truck. *No sense in struggling with a cat that may have some virulent cat disease and scratch me.* The cat did not move. If the unnamed cat was anxious or afraid, he did a wonderful job of hiding it.

He liked the mouse. That's a good sign. A very good sign. That has never happened to me before. He didn't dance. He just wasn't hungry for a mouse right now. He'll eat it later. That's okay. At least he liked it. He didn't dance. I miss it when they don't dance. People should dance when they get a mouse. Cats don't do that. But then again, I've never tried to dance. I would not be good at it. You need to be a human to dance. Or a dog.

The cat, who didn't call himself anything, who had no name, at least not now, sat up straight on the right side of the truck's bench seat, putting most of his weight on his left front

23

paw. He knew something was wrong with his right paw but, as with most animals, did not consider complaining or obsessing about the pain particularly worthwhile. It was easier to ignore it and complete whatever tasks needed to be completed. The pain would take care of itself. It would go away or it wouldn't. A cat's job is to do a cat's job, regardless of pain.

The cat moved its eyes and watched the man as he drove.

That other, round, rude person—Jimbo—called him Jake. I assume that is his Christian name. Jake. That sounds nice and sturdy. A man's name. Jake. I remember a boxer called Jake. A boxer dog, not a boxer boxer—though there was that movie about a Jake who was a person and a real boxer. But the Jake I remember was a dog. Jake happened to be a very stupid dog. But he could dance, sort of. More like a St. Vitus dance. (I know. I know. You can blame the radio.) And that Jake could smile. That's an ability I envy. Only a little.

The cat saw Jake glance toward him. While animals, especially cats, hid their pain from others, people were not good at it. Not to cats, anyway.

He does look a little lost. It's his eyes. He's here—but he's not here. He knows that something is true and he won't admit that it's true. Not even to himself. A good cat can see these things. Or a smart cat. And I am both of those things. In my experience, half of all cats don't like people. The other half think they could do very well without them. But there are a few cats, like me, who are smart and are sure we can help people find their way. I am not going to speak for God, but I will help Jake see what God wants. What God wants him to do. How to be. That is my job. I will be very good at it.

The cat took his position in the world very seriously.

Humans puzzle me. They spend too much time thinking about how things should be or how they want them to be instead of seeing things as they are and accepting them. People spend too much energy trying to be something they are not. Cats never do that. A cat is a cat is a cat. I never would want to be a dog. As I said, I am a smart cat.

The cat shook his head. The man looked over, then back to the road. He appeared to be a very safe driver. That was a good thing, too.

Who would want to be a dog? Disgusting creatures. All slobbery and loose fur and burrs and snorting. Clumsy. They just don't have enough bones, I guess, and they can't even curl up into a ball. Stiff, they are, like boards. And they stink. Have you ever been near a wet dog? Even dry dogs stink.

The man slowed the truck down. The cat could see a store on the side of the road ahead. Stores meant food. The cat knew that food comes from the inside of stores. Except for mice. They come from fields. The cat took pride in his intelligence, though he tried not to show off because of it. Not too much, anyway.

Did you know that the Egyptians worshiped cats? They did. Really. They have statues of cats. I saw that on the television show that talks like the radio show but with movies and always asks for money. I can understand why those people did that, of course, but they shouldn't have done that. Cats aren't divine. We are imperial, or is the word . . . imperviable . . . impervious? Unaffected. Above the cares of the world. But we're not that, really. We're just serene. We're calm and we listen very carefully. God doesn't always shout. Jake might not know how to listen. To others. To himself. To God. That's it. Listening. Lots of people don't know how to listen to God.

He needs to hear himself—to listen to what is inside. He is exactly the way that God intended him to be—except for the sin part, of course. That's what God would say to Jake. I'm pretty sure, anyhow.

The truck stopped.

I hope they have that food in the gold square cans. I like that food. Maybe I can get Jake to buy some.

2

Jake and the cat had come to a stop three miles south of the church, just across from a shallow wideness along the Allegheny River. It was crossed by an abandoned railroad bridge that looked like it would offer good fishing. The sign read BIG DAVE'S STORE, a ramshackle gas station, bait shop, convenience store, six-pack shop—an all-in-one sort of store. Jake stopped the engine and opened the door. The plastic pennants, hung from the overhead awning by the gas pumps, flapped their plastic welcome in the breeze. He was about to tell the cat to stay put, when it bolted out of the truck and ran, limping, toward the front door, darting inside when another customer exited. Jake hurried after him. "You can't go in there."

Jake hurried inside. "I'm sorry. My . . . the cat ran in. I'll get him out. I'm sorry."

Behind the counter sat a grizzled-looking man in a red plaid shirt, with a beard looking like a swarm of bees hovering about his cheeks and chin.

"Don't worry. We sell leeches and minnows and fox pee for deer hunters. A cat won't be bothering any of my customers, for sure."

He pronounced "for sure" as "fer shore."

An old black-and-white television hung from a wall, most of the picture obscured by bands of snow and static. The clerk peered from behind the counter. The cat stared back at him and meowed loudly.

"Skinny guy. Homeless?"

Jake shrugged. "Don't know. He showed up at the church just now and followed me into the truck."

The man in the red shirt brightened. "I thought you looked familiar. You're the new pastor, right? The church on Dry Run Road?"

"Yes, I am. Jake Wilkerson," Jake said, and extended his hand.

A pastor has to be outgoing, right? I need to turn over a new leaf. And be friendly. I need to remember that. Friendly. Outgoing.

"You can call me Big Dave. That's the name on the sign out there. Actually, my Christian name is Lawrence, but when I bought the place it was named Big Dave's. Changing my name was easier than paying for a new sign. And I guess I sort of grew into the name after all this time. I've been going to your church for a couple of years. Good potlucks, for sure."

The cat began scrabbling at a lower shelf at the end of the aisle.

"The cat looks like he likes Fancy Feast. Not much of a selection. But I do got beef 'n' liver."

"I need a few cans of cat food," Jake said. "Do you have any people food as well?"

Besides the store's entire stock of cat food (six tins), Jake bought instant coffee, half-and-half, sugar, no-name Oreo-style cookies, two frozen cheese and sausage pizzas, a box of glazed donuts, a box of generic corn flakes, a small box of tea bags of a brand of which Jake had never heard, a half-gallon of milk, a loaf of white bread (fortified twelve ways), peanut butter, strawberry jam, a jar of "local" honey, and two Snickers bars.

"Your cat got a limp, you know," Big Dave announced as he rang up Jake's selections.

"I think he's got something in his paw. Any vets around here?"

Big Dave scowled, thinking.

"A couple of clinics, 'animal medical centers' they call themselves, on Route 44—east side of town. Expensive, I bet, by the looks of them. Then there's a lady vet in town . . . Emma . . . something or other. On Broad Street. Big crooked sign in front of her house. She comes in here once in a while. Really pretty. But odd. Opinionated. I think she might be one of them Democrats. Large coffee, lots of sugars, two packages of Drake's Crumb Cakes."

Jake nodded, slowly translating Big Dave's words in his head and trying not to think about how "purdy" the lady vet was. He gathered his purchases, and the cat stood up and followed him to the door.

"I'll see you Wednesday evening then, Dave?"

"It's Big Dave. And you betcha. Wouldn't miss a potluck. Good luck with your cat. Seems to be a keeper, if you ask me. Hard to find a special cat. Ordinary ones are easy."

———— ✎ ————

The town of Coudersport was not that big and Broad Street was not that hard to find. Jake drove slowly, looking on both sides of the street, looking for "Emma . . . something, Vet."

And he found her, or rather, her sign. It stood in front of a large, rambling, ornate, two-story Victorian house, with large front porches on both floors that wrapped halfway around the structure, and abundantly fussy filigree work. It looked freshly painted—whites, greens, darker greens, and ochre accents.

Maybe it's the weather up here. All the signs seem to be at either more or less than ninety degrees. Freeze and thaw, perhaps?

EMMA GRAINGER, VET.

That's what the sign read—simple and declarative and tilted. There was a phone number at the bottom and nothing else. It did not indicate her political preference.

Jake looked to the cat. "Do you think she's open?"

The cat appeared to look at the sign carefully, then meowed.

"Okay. You want to walk in, or should I carry you?"

The cat stiffened at the suggestion of being carried and carefully made his way out of the truck, now lifting his paw cautiously with nearly every step.

Jake stepped up on the porch and tried the front door. The handle turned, the door opened, and a small bell sounded.

"Hello?" Jake called out modestly loud.

The cat followed him into a small reception area and stood next to Jake, holding his right paw up and close to his body.

"Be there in a second," came a voice from the back. Jake thought the voice sounded pretty.

A woman emerged, wearing a doctor's white coat. She was almost very tall, Jake thought, maybe an inch or two under six feet. Blonde hair, most likely natural, though Jake was far from expert in those matters, blue eyes, looking almost Nordic. Her hair was disheveled in a professional, careless way, with two pencils sticking out from above her left ear. She had penetrating blue eyes. Precise, sharp features—almost chiseled, yet attractive in their arrangement. Her nametag read: Emma V. Grainger, Vet.

Jake tried to offer a welcome, safe smile but wasn't sure he managed to pull it off.

"Who's sick?" Dr. Grainger asked, eyeing them both.

Jake could not think of a witty reply, or any reply at all, and instead pointed to the cat who now sat calmly a few inches from his feet.

"I think he might have something in his paw . . . or something."

Very clever.

"Name?"

"Uhh . . . Jake Wilkerson."

"Nice to meet you, Jake, but I meant the cat's name."

Jake was seldom speechless, but was almost speechless now.

"Ummm . . . I don't . . . he just showed up this morning. He looked skinny, abandoned, and he's limping, holding up his right paw."

The cat held up its right paw.

"Well, he has to have a name for me to treat him," the vet said with a medical firmness, crossing her arms and pursing her lips to one side, staring at Jake, almost testing him.

"He doesn't have a tag or a name," Jake replied.

Maybe she's just being quirky.

"I'm not good at names," he continued. "What does he look like to you?"

Emma the Vet came around the counter, a few steps closer, bent down, and stared hard at the cat. She rubbed her chin, as if this naming was a standard part of her normal examination. The cat stared back with interest.

"I would say . . . that he looks like a Petey. Or P. D. . . . P period D period. Either of those would suit him fine." She knelt down. "What do you think, big guy? P. D. or Petey?"

The cat appeared to be mulling the choice over.

"P. D.?"

The cat stayed silent.

"Petey? As in Petey, the normal name?"

And with that, the cat meowed loudly and pushed his head into the vet's knee.

The vet picked him up carefully. "From now on, this noble feline will be known as Petey. Now, follow me," she said with a doctor's authority and led Jake to a very white, very clean, very well-lit room, with a long stainless steel table and a row of cabinets on one wall.

The vet set the cat on the table, carefully, and ever so gently lifted his right paw, bent close to it, and stared for a long moment.

"It's a thorn in the pad. Imbedded pretty deep."

"Like Andromeda and the lion, right?" Jake volunteered. "You know, that old Roman fable."

The cat, now named Petey, turned to Jake and narrowed his eyes.

It's Androcles. And Aesop was Greek. I saw that on the television. It was a movie. I think. Did they make movies when Aesop was alive?

Then the cat stared up at the doctor, his eyes wide and almost pleading.

Emma the Vet kept on with her examination and simply said, "It's Androcles."

Petey the cat began to purr in agreement.

If Jake was embarrassed by his lack of knowledge, he did not show it.

"Can you hold Petey?" Emma asked Jake. "I need to give him a shot to deaden the pain. I'll need to cut the paw open, a little, to get the thorn out."

Jake held Petey while Emma administered the shot. The cat did not flinch.

Jake thought he smelled lilacs as he and the doctor stood side by side, holding onto Petey.

"Hold him like this," she instructed, and Jake did as he was told. He saw the glint of a scalpel and turned away. Jake was most unfond of needles, knives, and other unpleasant medical devices. The vet hummed as she worked. Jake heard the metallic plunk of either a scalpel or forceps. Out of the corner of his eye he saw the sewing motion of stitches being added. Then he heard the cutting of the thread.

"Stay there. He needs an antibiotic. I can administer that with a shot. Hard to give pills to a cat."

Jake did not watch that shot being given either and only turned back when he heard the hypodermic's plastic clatter when Emma laid it on the counter.

"Stay. I'll be right back."

In a moment she returned with a small bootie-shaped bandage and a roll of medical adhesive tape. She slipped the bootie on the stitched paw, then proceeded to tape it securely to the foreleg.

"You don't shave the hair?" Jake asked.

"No. Most animals hate that more than a shot. You just soak this tape in water for a while and most of it comes off easily. And a little bit of alcohol. Less trauma. And easier for me. And for Petey, too."

She stepped back to admire her handiwork.

"Let me scan him for a computer chip," she said, and waved a small wand, the size of a TV remote, around his neck and shoulders several times. "Nothing," she said. "I didn't expect it, either. Him being lost and all. Or abandoned, like you said."

She looked at the cat again. "He's neutered, too."

"You can tell that?"

Emma Grainger narrowed her eyes this time. And this time Jake did seem embarrassed, just a little.

"Oh . . . yeah."

The vet reached into a cabinet and extracted a large white plastic cone.

"I should put an Elizabethan collar on him so he won't chew off the dressing."

The cat looked up, a frantic look in his eyes. He meowed loudly, nervously. And then again, even louder. She stared back, then softened.

"But I don't think that this one will chew at it. Will you, Petey?"

Petey meowed, and anyone could tell he was in full agreement.

"If he does chew on the dressing, bring him back right away. Okay?" Emma the Vet said with a voice that made obedience all but imperative.

Jake nodded.

"I will. Promise."

Petey meowed, obviously agreeing to the terms of his care.

"He's a talker, this one."

"A talker?" Jake asked.

"Some cats are quite verbal. They meow and chatter all the time. I think Petey will be that way. It's almost as if they are actually trying to talk to you. If you listen closely, they'll repeat certain sounds, almost like a chirp, that means 'I want food,' or 'yes,' or 'I want out.' They really are quite intelligent animals. But you have to pay attention to them."

"I guess I'll be learning a new language then. Thanks for the heads-up."

Emma picked up Petey, placed him carefully on the floor, and led him and Jake back to the reception area. Petey chirped and churred as he followed her. She sat down at the computer behind the counter and began typing out the invoice.

"You new in town?" she asked. "I don't think I have ever met you, have I?"

"I am new. I'm the new pastor at the church on Dry Run Road. The little white one."

"With the crooked steeple?"

Jake leaned in. "I thought that was just me."

"Nope," the doctor answered. "Drives me nuts every time I drive past. I want to climb up there and give it a shove—either upright or off."

Emma hit PRINT.

"You don't look like one of those," she said, eyeing him carefully.

"One of those whats?" Jake replied.

"Those church people. Narrow-minded. Judgmental. Bad haircuts. Hypocritical. Wearing suits that don't fit. Like most of the people in this town—churchgoers or not. It's in the water, I think. And don't say I'm being judgmental. I grew up here. I know these people. Just haven't gotten up the gumption to leave."

Jake was almost used to getting odd, sometimes angry responses to his profession.

"Maybe I'm not like all those people. Though I do admit I need a haircut."

Emma the Vet smiled, a wry smile, knowing, almost inviting.

"We'll see. And the only barber shop worth going to is Jeff's—on Main Street. I have a cousin who goes there. And they don't butcher him."

Emma pulled the invoice from the printer.

"You married?"

If Jake was surprised by the question, he didn't show it. He was almost used to bold, intrusive questions from total strangers—or almost total strangers. "No." He didn't think the vet would be interested in how Barbara Ann Bentley broke his heart nine months ago.

"That's a surprise. I thought you church-pastor people had to be married—sort of like the reverse of Catholics."

Jake's day began off-kilter and had stayed off-kilter.

"Well, maybe in some churches. But I'm not married. The church didn't make it a condition of hiring me. So I haven't been frantically looking for a mail-order bride."

Emma folded the bill and handed it to him.

"I gave you the clergy discount. It's the same as the AARP discount. It was a slow day and you made it more interesting. Pay me when you can. My overhead is pretty low here seeing as how I live upstairs."

"Well, thanks so much. I do appreciate it. I bet Petey appreciates it, too, right, Petey?"

The cat, content to wait by the door, meowed patiently.

"Well, it's not every day that I get to name a patient," Emma said with a grin. "You knew I would have treated him without a name, right?"

"I assumed as much. It was nice to meet you, Dr. Grainger. I hope to see you again."

"Hey. It's a very small town. You will."

"Maybe at church?" Jake asked, already knowing the answer. *Friendly. Outgoing. Starts now and starts with me, right?*

"Well, stranger things have happened, but I wouldn't take a bet on that, Pastor Jake."

And as he reached for the door, the twinge in his shoulder went off like an alarm clock. As they walked to the truck, Jake thought that he should have asked her if she knew of a good chiropractor.

Next time.

And she was probably a Democrat.

———— ∞ ————

Jake pulled into the church lot. The cat stepped out of the open truck door cautiously, nursing his bandaged paw. Jake glanced to where the mouse had been. It was gone.

That's good. No disposal problems. Must be coyotes or foxes or possums around here that noticed the free meal. Or a crow. Or a hawk. Something.

He grabbed a cardboard box marked DISHES from the truck, then shouldered the door open—he hadn't bothered to lock it—and Petey followed him in. Jake had tossed his groceries from Big Dave's in the kitchen before heading to the vet, making sure the pizza was in the freezer and the milk and half-and-half were refrigerated.

He found a saucer in the box and a cereal bowl that Jake knew didn't match any of his other cereal bowls. He filled the bowl with cold water and emptied an entire tin of beef 'n' liver onto the saucer and placed them both at the far end of the cabinets, in a little alcove. The cat watched him as he prepared his meal and slowly made his way to the food. To Jake, it was obvious that the cat was famished, but it was also obvious that this cat had a special sense of dignity and decorum about mealtimes. No mad rush to the food, no caterwauling at the sound of the tin opening.

Petey walked, with deliberate steps, to the food, limping, holding his bandaged paw aloft. He sat and sniffed at the dishes for a long moment. First, he took a long drink of water, tiny little lap-lap-lap swallows. Then he set into the food, eating slowly, chewing thoroughly, taking time between bites to look around, often looking back at Jake, who was watching him eat.

"For someone who looks malnourished, you certainly have good table manners. Or floor manners, I guess."

Petey pivoted his head to face Jake and meowed in explanation, as if to say that hunger does not, or should not, supplant proper manners, or feline civility. Then he meowed again, as if to reinforce what he had just said.

Jake had first planned on baking the pizza, but that would take fifteen minutes, plus waiting for the oven to preheat, and even he couldn't eat a microwaved pizza. And he was hungry now, so he made a large cup of instant coffee and unwrapped the donuts.

Not the healthiest of lunches . . . but it will do. Just for today.

It took Jake two and a half donuts for Petey to finish his one full can of beef 'n' liver. Jake figured Petey would eat more if he put it out, but that might make him sick. A can was more than enough. No need to try and fatten him up all in one day.

Petey stepped back, sat down, and used his good paw to clean his face—but only for a few minutes. Then he rose, walked to the living room, and looked around. One large chair stood in a corner, lit by a bright shaft of afternoon sun. That was the one he chose to jump up on. He circled a few times, then coiled himself into a ring, laid his head on his good paw, and watched Jake walk about the room.

I should unpack now. It won't take long.

Instead, he sat on the couch, nursing the last of his second cup of coffee. He leaned back, trying not to wonder if the decision to move to Coudersport and assume the pastorate of this church would prove to be rash or misguided or monumentally shortsighted. He tried to put all those thoughts out of his head.

History does not have to repeat itself. It doesn't. I can do this. I can. Faith will follow works. I think somebody famous said that.

And if they didn't, they should have. Sometimes just doing good things brings about a heart change.

And that's when his shoulder did not twinge but wrenched with an intensity he had not yet encountered. Not painful, exactly, but just prominent, pronounced, and impossible to overlook—like a sore thigh muscle after a marathon.

No more shoulder omens, please. No more pain alerts, okay? Just a burning bush. Something that is easier to interpret. Maybe a letter in the mail. That would work.

Petey looked up, his head up, his ears pitched forward, as if he had heard some rustle in the distance, a prewarning.

"No. Not you, too," Jake said. "Please. No seeing things that aren't there. Okay?"

"So, Winston," Emma Grainger asked, "What did you think of Pastor Jake and his cat?"

Winston was Emma's bulldog, now eleven years old, semi-arthritic, with more than a slight weight condition, and a wicked snore that would put a chainsaw to shame. Winston must have hoped Emma was talking about food, because he began shifting his weight from side to side, anxiously antici-pating some manner of sustenance that would be forthcoming. He was most fond of his cheese crunchies.

Emma, of course, who was on to his anticipatory behaviors, shook her head, "No, Winston. No food. No crunchies."

Winston appeared crestfallen and sat back, heavily, on his haunches, and snorfed his disappointment.

"Winston, I have to tell you that he was the first single man I've met—in years—who wasn't wearing camouflage clothing or a stained baseball hat or chewing on a wad of tobacco. Good teeth, too. All of them right there in his mouth. That in and of itself is reason enough to swoon. And he even realized he needed a haircut. Amazing self-awareness, right, Winston?"

Winston let his tongue loll out of his mouth. Bulldogs, not the best designed dog in the canine kingdom, were chock-a-block full of idiosyncrasies that only the most tolerant owner would put up with, let alone find endearing. Emma, a lover of all things four-legged, was that sort of person. She would readily admit to being more taken with four legs than with two.

"A prime catch—that's what my mother would call him. Right, Winston?"

Emma asked Winston to agree to a lot, and Winston would do so, as long as there was a treat somewhere near the end of her questions.

Winston snorted and seemed to try to smile, which was a cross between a snarl and a grimace in a bulldog. Emma knew the dog had almost given up hope of a treat now. The longer she talked, she knew, the less likely she was to remember that he was near starvation most of the time.

"Of course, there are at least a dozen mothers of Coudersport's most eligible spinsters who will be doing the same thing, right, Winston? A man who probably doesn't have a record for petty crimes and misdemeanors. A man whose truck actually includes a functioning muffler system. And he was wearing an honest-to-goodness, real belt—not suspenders or a tool belt."

Winston let himself fall on his right side, and a rumbly woof escaped.

"I will admit that he was sort of cute. In a boyish, naive, lost sort of way."

Emma leaned back in her chair and stared out the back window. The copse of aspens at the far end of the yard had just started to green.

"But I don't know about him being a preacher. Didn't seem the type. Like he wouldn't be the type to ask hard questions. Something about him suggests that. Do pastors have to believe it *all* in order to get the job, Winston?"

Winston closed his eyes. One of his behavioral tics was the ability to fall asleep at the drop of a hat. No hats had dropped, but the bulldog was already asleep, snoring louder than a dog had a right to snore.

"Preachers are supposed to be tolerant, right? Live and let live. Accept everyone. Love and forgiveness, right? Big tent people, right?"

Emma leaned back in her chair and put her feet up on the desk. She had eight appointments this afternoon, and decided that a short rest now would give her the strength to be her normal, cheery self.

With eyes nearly closed, Petey watched Jake as he drank his coffee.

Coffee. I don't understand how anyone drinks that. Smells like a raccoon. Worse.

Petey saw Jake stare out the window and into the field beyond with a faraway look in his eyes.

He's looking for something that he can't find or doesn't know is lost. He looks like a dog. Well, like most dogs. Some dogs are better at finding things than others. But most dogs are simply simple-minded, small-brained woodland creatures. And lost much of the time.

Petey laid his jaw on his good paw and his eyes fluttered to half-closed.

He's here and doesn't know if he's here. He's in this place, but at the same time, he's not here. Humans can get that way. Dogs are always that way. Yes, I know they cover it up by being all cute and snuggly and pretending to be so loyal. They're not. They would leave one human for another human who offers better food. In a heartbeat, they would leave. Cute and innocent? It's an act. Smart? Please. Put them in a room behind a closed door and they'll whine and whimper and cry, and probably try to gnaw and claw their way through the door. Put a cat in a room and close the door—a good cat, of course—and the cat will just take a nap until you open the door again.

The cat began to vibrate softly, a purr forming in his chest. Petey wasn't sure why the purr started now, but he realized that this was the safest and most comfortable he had been in many weeks, or months, or had it been longer than that? He shook his head, just a bit.

I know that if I talked to him—that would make my job easier. But I don't do that. I know that some animals might. I recently heard a story about a dog that talked to its owner and told her all about God and what he wanted for her life.

The cat adjusted his back paws and let his tail coil around them.

To be honest, that's the most ridiculous story I've ever heard. First of all, I'm not sure if there are any dogs anywhere near intelligent enough to actually speak. I know I've never met one who is that smart. And even if the dog were smart, why would the dog bother? Humans don't learn from words; they learn by experiencing things and finding truth from that. Truth, to humans, does not come from words. I suppose I could tell Jake what God wants him to know—or what I am pretty sure God wants him to know—but that wouldn't work. Jake wouldn't believe it. He has to find the truth on his own. With some help. Obviously. From me. I am a smart cat, after all.

The very tip of Petey's tail began to twitch. It did that when he sensed something was about to happen. Either a mouse was going to show up, or something was going to happen—maybe to Jake.

I know some humans don't believe that God ever uses an animal like a cat to do things. Some cats don't believe it either. However, I am not like that. There are cats that are delusional—like they're really in charge. But I'm not a megalomaniacal cat. I'm not. I'm a good cat. I listen. I hear things. Whispered things. Almost silent nudges. Things only a good cat can hear. I heard what I was supposed to do—or more precisely, what I was needed to do, so here I am—with Jake now. I am certain that God uses small things at first, like a cat, instead of resorting to thunder and lightning first thing. I am nearly positive that I have been sent. Nearly so.

He does use cats. Good, smart cats. I'm sure he does. Cats like me.

Wouldn't it be better for a cat to lead a lost person to the truth rather than that person getting struck by a bolt of lightning tossed by God? I am not delusional. I'm not an angel—I know that—but cats can be like angels. We can help humans find the truth, and then they can feel like they found it all by themselves. It's better that way. It's the way of the cat. God uses cats because he likes cats. He protects them. He protected me. He found a way to fix my paw, didn't he? God cares for me, and he cares for Jake. Maybe I can get Jake to see that.

Petey closed his eyes but would not fall asleep just yet. The sunshine did feel wonderful on his back, and it was nice to have the pain in his leg begin to ebb, like melting snow on a warm day.

I need to be here. I don't need to talk. After all, God whispers at first—and I am just a little louder than a whisper. A heavenly cat whisper. That's me. I think. A cat sent by God.

And with that, Petey almost fell asleep, a seminap, his tail twitching every fifteen seconds or so, as if giving off a silent warning about what was soon to transpire.

⎯⎯∞⎯⎯

Jake slid into a slouched position on the couch.

Comfortable.

He balanced the empty cup on his stomach. Back in Butler, in his little apartment, there were end tables at both ends of the couch. Not here. Not even a coffee table. Jake knew he would have to buy a few pieces.

Does Coudersport have a furniture store? It is spring. That means garage sales. I guess it would be okay for a pastor to look for bargains at a garage sale.

He took a deep breath and watched the cat as he closed his eyes.

A nap. That sounds great.

But there was all that stuff in the truck. It had taken him a week to pack it up. A careful packer, he saved up a month's worth of the *Butler Eagle* newspaper and wound up using only a few issues. A careful packer, yes—but a packer with few breakable possessions.

He closed his eyes, just for a moment.

If this is the most I'll have to deal with here . . . then I'm in pretty good shape. An injured, orphaned cat. A pretty veterinarian who doesn't like church people. A sticky front door. Not bad. I can handle that. No need to call faith into question. Like I said: works can begat faith. Works will begat.

Begat. Now there's a funny word.

And the shoulder again. Sharp. A dig into the muscle.

I'm going to have to have this looked at. That much I know.

He put his hand around the empty cup.

That much I am sure of.

⎯⎯∞⎯⎯

Jimbo pulled the TV tray closer to him. If he didn't, bits of tuna fish would fall on the floor and the dog would go ape trying to find them and probably knock the tray down before Jimbo finished lunch. He didn't want that to happen. Roscoe, the dog, sat two feet away, staring at Jimbo as if he were the most beautiful creation in the entire dog universe, his dog eyes never wavering from the sandwich as it moved from plate to mouth.

Jimbo's wife, Betty, sat in the recliner catty-corner to Jimbo's. She had already eaten—in the kitchen, like a civilized person. She hated eating in the living room but refused to bring the television into the kitchen. Besides, she had argued, they would have to get a longer cable for the TV and neither of them knew how to do that. Eating lunch separately was a compromise she decided she could live with.

"It's not easy having your husband underfoot all day," Betty had complained to her neighbors, often several times a day, often when Jimbo could hear her.

Jimbo had been laid off from the Coudersport Well Drilling Company for the last seven months. New construction was down, and when construction was down, so was well drilling. The owner, Lloyd Cummins, said business looked like it was picking up, and he promised Jimbo a call as soon as he had enough work lined up. Betty was a praying woman and told everyone she prayed for Jimbo getting work every evening.

"So what's the new pastor like?"

"You met him," Jimbo replied, mid-mouthful.

"I heard him preach. I shook his hand. I wouldn't call that meeting him."

Recently, for the last seven months actually, Jimbo and Betty lived at the very edge of a permanent tussle, at the verge of a dust-up, a tiff, a spat. With spring coming, hopefully work would pick up and Jimbo could get out of the house. While she prayed for that every evening, Jimbo did the same.

"Well, he seemed nice and all that," Jimbo replied, selecting a single potato chip and chewing it noisily.

Betty winced. It was obvious she considered the way he ate potato chips to be so disconcerting that she would often have to look away, or turn up the volume on the TV, just to drown out the whole process.

"And?"

Jake remembered that their old pastor went on and on about communication between couples. That was right before he quit.

"Well," he said, picking up one more chip and examining it, "he didn't have much stuff with him. Just filled the back of a pickup truck. You know, clothes and sheets and books and stuff."

"Well, he's not married. Single men don't have much. Remember when we got married? You didn't have anything."

Jimbo chewed. "But I was living at home with my parents. I didn't need anything."

Betty crossed her arms.

"A single man. And the elders were okay with that?"

Jimbo tried not to sigh audibly.

"Yes. We all knew it. So did the whole church. You knew it. He didn't keep anything secret, you know. He said he was single when he came to visit. It was on his resumé. And the whole church voted—that means it was okay. And to be honest, since I am the church treasurer, it's much cheaper this way. Only one mouth to feed. Saves a lot on insurance, let me tell you. The old pastor and his wife—that was expensive. She seemed to get sick every week."

"But no wife means not having anyone to play the piano or teach Sunday school or anything."

"Verna Ebbert plays the organ and piano. She'd be more than a bit tussled if you tried to take that away from her."

"I'm just saying, that's all," Betty said. "You know he's from a big city? He's not used to small towns like Coudersport."

"Butler ain't a big city."

"Bigger than here. We're country folk. Simple people, you know."

Jimbo shrugged. It felt like she was trying to pick an argument, so he backed off some. He wanted to watch *Wheel of Fortune* in peace.

"All I know is that he preached a good sermon. He was funny, remember? You were laughing."

Betty uncrossed her arms.

"Okay, you got me there. He was pretty funny. I do like a preacher who can tell a joke now and again."

"Me, too," Jimbo said as he crammed the last quarter of the sandwich into his mouth. He wanted to be done eating before the show came on, and the theme music was just starting.

Jake jangled awake, tipping over his coffee cup, still on his chest, which he thankfully discovered was empty. He blinked his eyes several times and rubbed his face with his free hand. Within seconds, he realized where he was. He sat up straight and took a deep breath.

He stood up. Petey looked up, only moving his eyes.

Well, might as well unload the truck.

He left the door open and began to bring the boxes in, one by one. Clothes and sheets he took to the bedroom, books to the office, pots and pans and dishes to the kitchen. Still, he wound up with a waist-high stack of boxes that resisted an obvious destination.

Just where do knickknacks go? Does my diploma go in the office? What about my stereo—the office or living room? Fake plants? Throw rugs?

Petey stayed coiled, lying in the chair, content to watch. Apparently he knew he had plenty of time to investigate all of these things later, Jake thought. To investigate now was to run the risk of being stepped on. And for a cat with a bandaged paw, being stepped on was not a pleasant thought, Jake was sure.

As Jake hefted boxes to one room or the other, he watched the cat watching him. Never having had an animal, he could not be certain if the cat's calm observation was normal behavior or not. Jake felt pretty sure it wasn't all that normal. He also felt as if the cat were judging him, as to his possessions and his amateur unpacking technique.

During the afternoon, the phone rang three times, each time scaring Jake and causing Petey to raise his head and point his ears forward. Each time the caller was one of the church's elders, welcoming him to the area, to the church, and asking if he needed anything—anything at all. The last call was from Chester Sawicki, who nearly insisted that his wife "carry over" some stuffed cabbage rolls. Jake was pretty sure he didn't like stuffed cabbage rolls, not being certain if he had ever eaten one, but they did not sound all that appetizing, and Jake ate within a narrow range of acceptable foods. Cabbage rolls lay far outside his accepted range.

Jake lied and told him he was cooking a pizza in the oven and it was just about to come out. Chester accepted the statement as true, and Jake then felt morally obligated to turn the oven on and pull out one of his frozen pizzas—just in case Chester, or his wife, would show up, unbidden, with a casserole dish filled with cabbage and whatever it is they are stuffed with.

The bedroom was done, for now. Sheets were on the bed, clothes from the large wardrobe box were hung in the closet, each on its own separate wooden hanger. Jake liked wooden hangers. He could be precise in some areas of life.

He set up the stereo in the living room, on the large bookcase near the fireplace. He put the speakers at either end. He placed his diploma in the office. It would wait until he found his hammer and the small package of nails that he was sure he had packed in one of the boxes. The box that held his diploma also held the picture of his mother. He had no idea of what to do with that too-large picture. He placed it in the office as well, since that is the one place he was sure his mother would want to watch him.

He ate the pizza, standing at the counter, staring at the assortment of half-empty boxes between bites. His dishes were mostly unpacked. His forks, spoons, knives, and utensils were mostly unpacked. By the fourth slice, he realized that he could easily finish emptying out most of the boxes marked KITCHEN but didn't. Something felt final about emptying the last box, something that felt too permanent.

Tomorrow would be soon enough.

Even then, don't some families take weeks to fully unpack? I can take a day or two, right? I don't have a time clock to punch.

By this time, night had come to Coudersport. Jake stepped out on the front steps of the parsonage and stared up at the dark spring night sky. The heavens here in north central Pennsylvania were much darker, deeper, and encompassing than the skies in Butler. Here, no ground lights cluttered the darkness. There was no intrusion of streetlights or houses or stores. Just the stars and the dark.

He sat down and looked up.

Petey joined him on the step and stared up with him, as if the cat noticed a nocturnal bird flying by.

"Well, Petey, that's the first day. It wasn't so bad, was it? If this is a portent of things to come, then I think I'll be all right. Omens have been positive, haven't they? The people seem nice and friendly and not judgmental at all."

Petey pushed his head against Jake's arm. Jake scratched behind the cat's ears.

"This will work out, Petey. Here, I am sure I will find my faith again. I'm sure of it. It's just a dry spell for me, isn't it? Just a dry spell. I'll be okay. This will all work out. Nothing to worry about. Ebb and flow."

The cat meowed quietly.

"We'll be okay, Petey. We'll be fine."

Petey meowed in agreement.

"Petey?"

Petey meowed.

"It seems like you understand what I'm saying."

Petey meowed.

"Do you really understand?"

Petey meowed again. This time his meow was longer and lower and more nuanced, as if saying, "Of course I understand you. I am a good cat."

"Are you a good cat, Petey? Really a good cat?"

With that, Petey stood, and carefully made his way onto Jake's lap, taking care not to bang his bandaged paw. He growl-meowed.

"So I can talk to you and you'll understand?" Jake asked. Even Jake wasn't certain how serious he was.

Petey answered with a meow that sounded a lot like a yes. Or felt exactly like a yes should feel, Jake thought.

Jake petted the cat's head and scratched behind his ears. He had assumed that a cat liked that sort of attention. Petey seemed to enjoy it. After a few minutes of silence, only the early crickets sounding in the chill, Jake asked, his voice low and careful, "Petey, are you the sign I asked for? Does God do that? Send cats?"

Jake knew he was being way too snarky for north central Pennsylvania.

With that, Petey stood in Jake's lap, balancing skillfully on his back legs, and faced him, their noses only a few inches apart. Jake could smell a hint of beef 'n' liver on Petey's breath. Jake had smelled worse, but not recently.

Petey stared for a long moment, staring directly at Jake's eyes. Then he meowed, a calm, assured, songlike meow, as if telling Jake that he was absolutely correct and Petey was congratulating him for being so perceptive. Perceptive for a human, that is.

"Okay. You're the sign, Petey. Just so I have you to talk to, okay?"

Petey chirped a reply.

"Good. That's good."

And Jake smiled up at the darkness, feeling better than he had in weeks and weeks, pushing away the caustic thought that he had now sunk to the level of taking advice and comfort from a cat who brings home dead mice.

"Oh, how the mighty have fallen, right, Petey?"

Petey chirped a reply, obviously understanding Jake's misguided attempt at humor in a mostly humorless situation.

"That's assuming I was mighty in the first place."

⸜∞⸝

Startled, Jake sat up straight in bed. It was the middle of the night. He must have felt something out of place, something unusual.

Petey, on the floor between the bed and the doorway, stared hard at something, in the darkness, in the hallway. His eyes fixed on it.

Jake squinted hard and did not see anything move or hear anything move. "What is it, Petey?" he whispered. "What do you see?"

Petey did not move, just kept staring at some hidden spot, lost in the darkness, just beyond human sight. He did not move. He appeared to be hardly taking a breath.

Jake tried to slow his rapidly beating heart. He did not want to get up and face whatever it was that was out there. After a long moment, Petey softened, and the tension in his shoulders appeared to melt away in an instant. He turned to face Jake, then meowed, as if to say, "What are you doing up at this hour?"

It would be the first of many such discoveries that Jake would have—learning the intricacies and the secrets of the domesticated cat. Some of them completely inexplicable to humans.

The discoveries would never end.

And Petey was far from an ordinary American domesticated cat.

3

Tassy Lambert, short for Thomasina, a name she had disliked intensely from childhood, watched the silver Camaro as it sped off northward, on Route 44, heading toward the New York state line. She would have shouted out some choice words as Randolph tore off, but he wouldn't have heard her above the static-filled din of the radio, nor did she have the energy to battle with him one more time.

"Good riddance," she muttered, then shouldered her backpack, trying to get comfortable with the weight. "Jerk."

She did not want to follow him and didn't want him to follow her. She knew that she should not have trusted him, but she had had little choice. So instead of heading north, as they had planned, through New York and maybe Niagara Falls and stopping at all the outlet malls along the way, she instead turned south and began walking. A road sign a hundred yards farther along pointed due south, with an arrow, and in bold, block letters, it read: COUDERSPORT: 5 MILES.

It's as good a place as any, she said to herself. She was used to talking to herself, since Randolph was not the most scintillating or prolific conversationalist. As she walked, she gathered her longer-than-ever mass of glowing, dark brown curls and slipped an orange scrunchy around it.

People told her she had beautiful hair—an assessment that she never agreed with. She did have deep-set, large brown eyes. Liquid. Those, she considered an asset. She hoped, one day, someone would call them "penetrating." So far, at least in the last nineteen years and four months, no one had.

A slight girl with a slight frame, she nearly bowed under the weight of her backpack, carrying with her nearly all of her earthly possessions. Hitchhiking was out of the question—especially on lonely and desolate roads of central Pennsylvania.

She would walk. Five miles was not that far.

"Maybe Coudersport will have a cheap hotel. For a day or two. To get my bearings."

Her money, all $267.45 of it, would not last all that long.

A semi whooshed past, carrying a load of TrueValue hardware. The wind pushed at her back, almost making her stumble. But she caught herself at the last moment, running for a few steps. She straightened up, readjusted her backpack, and once more, refused to cry.

Actually, she thought, *I feel really good today. And for no reason. Strong. Solid.*

She looked up to the cloudless blue pellucid spring sky. *Everything happens for a reason*, she thought, then remembered it had been Randolph who had last said that to her. And instead of crying, she smiled, beamed, almost. *He was right about that. He was right about one thing—and that may be the only thing he was ever right about.*

She hitched the backpack again, feeling it dig at her shoulders.

The jerk.

Jake woke with a start again. The room, the bed, the windows, the chest of drawers—they were all strange and new and slightly off kilter. He glanced at his watch.

What time do the stores around here open?

He shook his head, clearing the sleep from his thoughts.

And where are the grocery stores around here?

Petey stood and stretched on the bedroom chair, one of several nighttime sleeping spots.

I need to get a litter box . . . right? A cat needs a litter box.

Jake did not have a litter box, and instead, let Petey go outside. Petey slowly meandered toward the back of the graveled lot, still limping, but much improved from yesterday. Jake was certain the cat would return on his own, and in short order. While he waited, he fixed a cup of coffee and made some toast.

Maybe I'll use honey instead of jelly and peanut butter. Experiment a little. Be brave.

He wondered if there was a local morning newspaper in the area. In Butler there was the staunchly conservative *Butler Eagle* and the Pittsburgh papers if he wanted them. He followed the news, not religiously, but he wanted to know about the culture of the day. It would be important to know about cultural events, famous people, Hollywood, and the rest, if and when he encountered non-churchgoing people, so he would have some knowledge in common with them. He seldom, however, encountered non-churchgoing people, unless you counted the few people he interacted with in stores and gas stations.

He drank his instant coffee and tried to clear his thoughts. Big transitions often caused this sort of thought turmoil in Jake. The cat's insistent and loud meow moved him from his daydream. Jake opened the door. Petey was walking up the sidewalk to the kitchen door of the parsonage. The second that Petey saw Jake and the open door, the cat slowed down, as if walking through molasses. Each step carefully considered, each sniff, perfectly timed.

"Come on, Petey," Jake called, not impatient, not yet, but not willing to watch a cat walk in slow motion either.

The cat moved even slower, and Jake found it hard to imagine that Petey's slowness was nothing short of intentional.

Maybe he's trying to teach me patience.

"Come on, Petey. Get inside."

The last three steps were the slowest yet—as if the cat was part tree sloth. And once inside, Petey sauntered past, back to normal speed, meowing in a most friendly and conversational manner, almost as if he were asking, "Where is breakfast?" Jake responded by opening another can of food and letting it slop out in a single, semi-gelatinous clump onto Petey's plate. The cat made a deliberate move to first sniff at it, carefully, then to taste it with a delicate lick of his tongue, all before deciding to eat it.

Jake watched him eat and had a second cup of coffee.

When he was finished, he found a light jacket in the closest, and when he went to the door, he turned to the cat and said, "I'm going to the grocery store. You have to stay here. I'll be back in an hour."

He opened the door, and Petey set off like a scared rabbit, running fast on three legs, scrabbling at the door of the truck, waiting for Jake to open it.

"No. You have to stay here."

The cat cried, and if Jake had been asked, he would have described the cry as a practiced, pity-me cry.

He took a ride yesterday. I guess he likes riding in cars.

The cat scampered up onto the passenger seat and situated himself perfectly in the middle, with room for his tail, his four paws neatly fitting into the rounded depression in the bench seat.

Jake drove toward town. Coudersport was a small town, but it still was a town. He was certain there would be a grocery store nearby. Doug's Surplus Food looked like it was a viable business and would be open this morning. Jake told the cat to stay in the truck while he shopped.

"Maybe Big Dave will let you shop in his store, but I don't think they would be so understanding in there—you know, at a regular store."

Petey appeared content to remain truck-bound, and Jake lowered the windows enough for air circulation, but not enough to allow an escape. He didn't really think the cat would attempt to leave, but Jake was always happier being safe than sorry.

Jake grabbed a cart and headed through the automatic doors. As soon as he stepped in, he imagined himself in one of those cheap, and badly made, 1960s horror movies, where some mutant alien virus took over the townspeople and they would glare virulently at any newcomer or stranger. Virtually every person in the store pivoted to face Jake when he entered, mouths agape. The only thing they didn't do was gasp in fear and point.

Maybe I'm imagining this a little.

A short man in a green apron who stood at the first checkout lane waved at Jake.

"Pastor Jack, we wondered whose grocery store you'd go to first. And I guess we won."

Jake waved back and veered his cart a little closer.

"It's Jake . . . Pastor Jake."

"Oh, that's right. Jake. Not Jack. I have a cousin named Jack. Lives in Port Allegheny. He's on disability. Got his foot run over by a bulldozer. The two names must be confusing me. And I'm Doug. Doug Olmer. I work here. I own this place. And I work here. I guess that is pretty obvious, isn't it?"I don't go to your church, but I know a lot of people been expecting you. So welcome to Coudersport and all that."

"Thanks. Nice meeting you, Doug."

Does everyone know about me coming to town?

"And how's the cat doing? I heard you got a cat with a bum paw. Doing okay?"

Of course he would know about the cat.

"Much better. He's actually in the truck, waiting for me."

"You made a cat ride in a car? You're a brave man, Pastor Jake. I had a cousin in Smethport—Tilly, that's her name—and she tried that with her cat—Mr. Wiggles or Mr. Snuggles or Mr. Softee or something like that, and then she wound up with twenty-three stitches on her face. Twenty-three. The plastic surgeon had to work overtime to get her to look normal again. And she kept the cat. If that ain't crazy, I don't know what is."

"No, actually, this cat seems to like being in the truck. He just sits there and looks out the window."

"Don't that beat all," Doug replied, ignoring the two people who were standing in line, waiting to check out. They didn't seem to mind the wait, since they were both intently eavesdropping on the conversation.

"You're calling the cat Petey? That's what I heard. That's a good name for a cat. I had an uncle named Pete. He got killed in a car accident back in '84 down near Johnstown. Where they had the flood. He was a drunk, so everyone expected it to happen sooner or later. Ran into a concrete wall."

The two ladies waiting in line nodded at this fact. Obviously, Uncle Pete had been a well-known figure in Coudersport.

"Well, I need to get busy and buy some food. Again, nice meeting you, Doug."

"Okay. You have any trouble finding anything, let me know."

Jake headed into the first aisle, trying to compose a list in his head. He knew he should have written it down, but for a first shopping experience, whatever he purchased he would need.

He made his way through the store, and by the time he was in the next to the last aisle, his cart was near to overflowing with all manner of groceries and canned goods and paper towels and salt and pepper and crackers and condiments. He looked at the bewildering display of spices and wanted to buy a bottle of mace because it had an interesting name, but he had no idea of how to use it, so he didn't.

A tiny woman, dwarfed by a large floral scarf and a long blue coat with what might have been a fur collar at some point, stopped him between the pasta noodles and the pasta sauce, grabbing onto his forearm with a bewildered, amazed look in her eyes.

"Pastor, how do you know what to buy? You're a man."

It was mostly an amazed look. Jake had heard the question, or variations of the question, before.

"I've lived on my own for a while. I have to eat, so I learned."

The tiny woman shook her head, as if in disbelief.

"If my husband were to come to a grocery store, first off, I'd faint dead away, and second off, all he would buy is beer and pretzels."

She leaned in a little closer.

"He's not a churchgoing man. I hope that's okay with you."

Jake had not been prepared to offer dispensation so early in the morning.

"Ma'am, if you two get along and love each other, then it must be working."

The tiny woman offered a knowing smile and smirk in reply.

"Well, I'll guess that's it. Pastor, glad to see you. I go to another church in town, so I'm pretty sure I won't hear you preach. But you seem like a regular fellow. Any man who knows how to get around a grocery store is special in my book.

And you have a cat, so I've heard. And that's a good thing. I like cats. I have three of them, Daisy, Susie, and . . . and well, another Susie. They don't mind the names. Don't listen, anyhow. Like my husband."

And with that, she released his arm, grabbed her shopping cart with both hands, veered around him, banging off one side of the aisle, almost dislodging a box of mostacciolli noodles, and rattled down the aisle, past the beans and the canned fish.

In the few short hours Jake and Petey had been together, Jake had discovered that cats have an entire vocabulary of sounds. It was not just a simple, plain meow. There was that, of course, but much more. Jake had already heard Petey's chirps—like a mouse chirp; churrs—like the sound of a small motor; the growl—like the rumble of a small lion; a curious chattering—where his jaws would vibrate with a vibrato sort of meow; softer chirps—spoken to himself; a low meow-growl combo; a high-pitched whine—like air escaping a punctured tire; and a sharp, staccato sort of chirrup—vocalized when Petey was walking with a hurried purpose.

Jake wondered if Petey actually determined what sound fit which activity, or if he was simply toying with Jake and amusing himself.

It could easily be a little of both.

Tassy trudged on, estimating that she must have traveled at least five miles. Growing up in inner-city Philadelphia offered her no experience in guessing distances out in the country. Mentally, she still estimated distances in city blocks.

She was walking along the Grand Army of the Potomac Highway. Why it had that name, Tassy had no idea. The whole thing sounded old to her and history was not her favorite subject in school. On one side of the road was a small stream. Though she saw a sign reading Allegheny River Public Launch, she didn't believe it was really a river.

Rivers have to be bigger than this, don't they?

Tassy wondered where the town of Coudersport might be. She passed a few buildings and even one hotel—the Hotel Crittenden—that did not appear to be a going business. The front windows were empty and dusty. But none of what she saw and passed appeared to be a real, proper, honest-to-goodness town. She turned the corner and a few blocks down, she spotted a familiar sight: bright yellow arches. Even though she had eaten two cold strawberry Pop-Tarts this morning, Tassy felt her stomach grumble.

An Egg McMuffin sounds really good. And orange juice.

She reached for her cell phone to check the time, then remembered that it no longer functioned. The phone bills had not kept up with her travels, and even if they had, she wouldn't have had the money to pay them. She looked to the left. The sun stood halfway up the eastern sky.

It doesn't feel late. I bet they're still serving breakfast.

She hitched her backpack again, wish again that she had one with a frame instead of one that was just big. It would have made it easier to carry so much. These narrow straps were not designed to hold a heavy load. Inside she carried three pairs of jeans, two pairs of shoes (sneakers and black flats), two sweaters (one green, one black), a dozen T-shirts, a sweatshirt from the Community College of Philadelphia (which she attended an entire semester before running out of money), the second of the Twilight books (a paperback), three tubes of lipstick, an assortment of makeup, two bottles of nail polish, lip gloss, a toothbrush, a travel-size tube of Crest toothpaste, a round hair brush, a handful of underwear, a handful of socks (some matched, some did not), a down jacket scrunched tight at the bottom of the pack, a Phillies baseball cap, a knitted cap with blue and green stripes, a half-empty bottle of Paris Hilton perfume (that Randolph either bought or stole from a CVS drugstore), three long scarves, a gold necklace with a cross stored in a tightly knotted velvet bag, a small flashlight, an address book, a very wrinkled white blouse and a navy blue skirt (in case she had to interview for a job or something), a windbreaker, a short fold-up umbrella, a black polo shirt (that she bought for a quarter at a Goodwill store in Reading), $1.87 in assorted change lying loose underneath it all all, plus a half-used tube of lip balm, and two packs of Wrigley's spearmint gum.

She had a half-empty bottle of water in a side pocket and a handful of hair scrunchies and hair bands in the pocket on the other side.

Everything she owned. She pushed the thought away. No time to be sad.

She stepped inside the McDonald's and blinked. The sun was shining outside but it was twice as bright inside the restaurant. She ordered her Egg McMuffin and orange juice and was then persuaded to get the meal package "because the hash browns come with it—like you're getting them for free," the young man behind the counter said.

Tassy considered asking him about a motel in the area, but he looked all of fourteen.

He wouldn't know.

Instead, she took her tray, slid off her backpack, sat in a booth in the far corner, overlooking the street out front, and wondered what she should do next. She was hoping for some sort of sign, some sort of divine revelation as to what her next move might be. But apparently there would be no signs today. Instead, she simply ate very slowly and debated if she should also get a cup of coffee.

A cup of coffee is good for at least an hour in here. And it's a lot more comfortable than walking to someplace I don't know exists.

I should get a haircut . . . but I have frozen corn in my bag and frozen waffles . . . so maybe tomorrow.

Jake loaded up the back of the truck with his groceries, using bungee cords to hold the load in place and prevent blow-aways. He was used to doing this, not having a trunk to safely transport his purchases.

But I am sort of hungry. Maybe if I see a coffee shop . . . I could get a croissant and a latte or something. I didn't look for a Starbucks on my first visit; I hope there is one in town.

Petey sat with a contented look on his face as he watched Jake load up. Jake had purchased a litter box and litter and kibble-type cat food and a dozen extra cans of the beef 'n' liver variety, plus a few other varieties. The litter and litter box were probably more expensive than they would be in a large pet supply emporium, but Jake was more than certain that Coudersport could not boast of having a large pet supply emporium.

There's probably a lot that Coudersport doesn't have. I wonder where people go to really shop? I wonder if there is a Walmart around here? Probably in Bradford. But that's at least fifty miles away.

He backed out onto the highway.

I'll head toward town. For just a minute. There's got to be some sort of coffee shop.

———⟡———

Tassy decided on a cup of coffee . . . and as she stood at the counter, she changed her mind and ordered tea instead.

I don't even like tea. But it's like . . . healthier, right?

The purchase would guarantee her a comfortable seat for a while longer.

When you have nowhere to go, having a place to sit for a while is nice.

She opened three packets of honey and poured them into the cup, dunked the tea bag a dozen times, up and down, and tried to squeeze it dry with the plastic lid and without burning her fingers.

She wondered if Randolph would come looking for her. He'd never said he would. She did not think he would. Once done with something, he would simply look away and move on. No, he would not put the Camaro in reverse and come searching for her, tears in his eyes, admitting that he had made a hideous, stupid, jerk-faced mistake in tossing her out of the car.

No.

Randolph was not that sort of person.

She actually did not know what sort of person he was. Five months together and she had no real idea who he was on the inside. Most of the time, he was more blank than filled in. And she had no choice—she had to get away from her disastrous home life and her crazy, leering new stepfather. But she had no money and no tuition, and Randolph just happened to show up, with a smile and a car and an attitude that was tailor-made for a would-be runaway.

I think if you're older than eighteen you are not a runaway. I think that it's just making a decision to leave.

And that's what they did, staying at Randolph's brother's house for a month, then at a cousin's house, and then at a house of a friend of that cousin. To Tassy, it felt nomadic and romantic and free—"like we're poets or something," she had said to Randolph's blank stare.

At their last residence, they had their own room and bathroom. At least they did until Randolph's cousin's friend went and got arrested for resisting arrest.

I think that was why he was arrested. Resisting is a great way to wind up in jail.

Randolph's story about the arrest had changed over time— from being all the cousin's fault to the current interpretation that the police just had it in for him . . . since the friend was such a free spirit, and the police hate free-spirited people, who use drugs, but only once in a while.

That meant there was no longer room in the basement for them. So Tassy packed up one more time and they headed west. "California," Randolph said. "It's warm in California. Like in that oldies song. By that group—you know the ones— that old group. With the two guys and the two chicks in it. You know the one. California something or other."

Tassy didn't know the group. But she did sort of remember that song. And Randolph did head west for a while.

Until the final argument. It had been one of many. And they had been escalating in pitch and venom.

Now Tassy, on foot and alone, had a long journey ahead of her if she ever wanted to get to the warm California sun.

As soon as I'm done with this tea. Then I'm moving on.

She watched the traffic roll past.

Maybe I'll ask for a refill. For tea, this tastes good. Maybe it's because of the honey.

———∞∞∞———

Jake drove through town and out of it again and saw nothing that resembled a coffee shop. He noticed a restaurant or two, but no in-and-out, grab-a-latte sort of establishment.

Maybe on a side street somewhere.

On his way back toward church, he saw a McDonald's. He sighed, slowed down, and pulled in.

They do have that new coffee bar thing. Better than instant.

"You stay here, Petey," Jake warned. "I'm just getting coffee. Be back in a minute. Okay?"

Petey meowed in reply. He remained seated and calm, giving no indication that he planned on bolting for freedom at the first opportunity.

"Good cat," Jake said. Petey's face indicated he felt he warranted the compliment and perhaps had anticipated it as well.

Jake stared at the coffee menu, then ordered a medium latte.

"What flavor do you want?" the young man behind the counter asked.

"Flavor?"

"Flavor. Like hazelnut or caramel or mint or whatever. We have like a dozen of them."

"Do I have to add a flavor?"

The young man, now a bit confused, replied, "Well, I guess not. But everybody gets a flavor. It's like, free."

"But I just want the coffee . . . or latte."

"No flavor?"

"Just the coffee," Jake reassured him.

The clerk took his money, apparently quite certain that Jake was both foolish and overlooking a large dollop of free syrup to boot.

As Jake took the coffee, he heard his name called out.

"Pastor Jake."

He turned and there sat Emma the Vet with an older woman who had the remnants of an Egg McMuffin meal spread out in front of her on a smoothed-out sheet of yellow wrapper.

"How's the cat?" she asked.

"Much better," Jake replied. "He's in the truck waiting for me. Seems to like going for rides."

"Cats are most curious creatures, aren't they? It's almost like they can understand what we're saying."

"I think so, too—but this is the first cat I've ever owned."

Jake looked at the other woman, just for a second. There was a resemblance.

"Jake, this is my mother, Rebecca Grainger. Mom, this is the new pastor of the church on Dry Run, Jake Wilkerson."

Her mother smiled, a crackling of wrinkles deepening at the corners of her eyes.

"You're the single one, aren't you? Betty told me about you."

Jake ran down a quick mental list of all the folks he'd met since his first interview, searching for Betty. "Betty Bennett? Jimbo's wife?"

"The same," she replied. "Small town, you know."

"I guess. Everyone in the grocery store already knew I had a cat."

Shaking her head, Emma said, "It is so sad how starved we are for news up here. I figured the cat story would get around, but it should have taken longer than twenty-four hours."

Emma's mother almost stood, but didn't. "Emma isn't married either. You know that, Pastor Jake? Just like you."

Jake had never been good at reading people's expressions. It was a big reason he had sometimes felt inadequate as a pastor. But this was one instance where he was sure what both women were trying to say—both nonverbally as well as verbally.

Emma's mother appeared so earnest and hopeful, as though she expected Jake to ask her daughter out, right then and there.

Jake thought that Emma probably wanted to either die right then or simply melt into a puddle on the floor—of embarrassment, of course.

"I didn't know, Mrs. Grainger. But I guessed at it. Neither of us is wearing a ring."

"Mother, could you be any more obnoxious right now? Seriously. Or more embarrassing? Why don't you start measuring him for a tuxedo right now?"

Emma's mother appeared wounded.

"I was simply making conversation, honey. Pastor Jake wants to get to know people in town. Right, Pastor Jake? And I know you wouldn't mention it. Like it's a crime to tell the truth now. Put me in jail, why don't you?"

Jake could tell that it was a familiar argument or discussion between mother and daughter.

"It's okay, Dr. Grainger. Don't worry about it. But I have to get home before my waffles defrost."

And with that, he waved and stepped away.

As he did so, he heard the older woman remark, a little too loudly, "He's cute." Then she added, "What does waffles defrosting mean? Is that some sort of new slang thing?"

A perfectly nice day for a walk, Tassy thought. In the past, like even a few weeks ago, Tassy would have scoffed at the thought of walking farther than from the car to the door of the restaurant or mall. But today felt different. Today, Tassy felt energized. Maybe it was the tea. Maybe it was the honey. Maybe it was the bright sunshine on her face after several weeks of gray, end-of-winter weather. *Today feels good. I feel good. Energized. Like I could walk to California. Maybe it's because I'm free from that stupid jerk, Randolph.*

She walked another mile or so, thinking that Coudersport must lie just up ahead, or just around the next bend, unaware that she had already walked through Coudersport. The Grand Army of the Potomac Highway skirted the very southern edge of town and if you did not look closely, you would miss it all.

Tassy had not looked closely.

Up ahead, perhaps a little less than a mile away, Tassy noticed a small stand of billboards.

Maybe that's Coudersport there. I can walk that far easy.

She hitched the backpack again, adjusting the straps a bit, bunching the shoulders of her light jacket to provide more cushioning.

The air, with still a hint of chill, felt clean and Tassy thought that whatever toxins were still in her lungs from Randolph's smoking were being scrubbed out of her insides. She felt cleaner and stronger than she had felt . . . since forever, maybe.

She was on her own, with very few resources, yet she felt more whole than she had ever felt.

It's as if something is about to happen and I just have to pay attention to it. Like life is changing and I need to catch it just right. Like a surge . . . or something. A surge? Is that the right word? I think it is. A surge, like a rush.

She stopped and held onto a speed limit sign, slipped off her left shoe, and shook out a pebble.

Or something like a surge.

And as she readjusted her shoe, a truck motored past her, honked its horn, heading upriver, east, and she smiled and waved back, something she had never done . . . well, at least not since she was a little girl hoping to get a semitruck driver to honk his horn.

This time it was simply enough to wave.

It felt good.

———∞∞∞———

A second food dish had been placed in the cat's dining alcove—a deep cereal bowl that Jake filled with the "original flavor" Meow Mix kibbles.

I wonder if they made a new and improved kibble and got complaints from cats, so they had to go back to the original formula?

Petey carefully investigated the new food source and delicately chewed on a few of the newly added kibbles, making a very loud crunching noise as he ate. Jake installed the litter box in a pantry/mudroom space by the back door to the kitchen. The space would be out of sight and allow the cat a certain amount of privacy. Jake was pretty sure that cats didn't really need privacy, but he felt better about not having any of it in plain view.

Then he went to work on unpacking the groceries. Some food destinations were obvious. Perishables went into the refrigerator. Frozen whole kernel niblet corn went into the freezer. Cereal went into a tall cabinet next to the refrigerator. Pretty sure that he wouldn't remember all the locations, he tried to keep storage relegated to two cabinets and the pantry.

Jake looked at his watch.

11:30.

He had decided early that a peanut butter and jelly sandwich and a bowl of soup would be a great lunch. It took all of five minutes to prepare. He sat at the kitchen table and ate slowly. This time, Petey sat on the floor and watched him eat. Occasionally, the cat would lick a paw and comb it against his face. But mostly, the cat simply watched.

I need to come up with a sermon for this Sunday.

Jake had a file folder filled with previously given sermons, none of which now felt anywhere suitable for a first-time-as-the-pastor-in-the-pulpit sort of message.

I should start to work on it soon. It is already Tuesday afternoon, almost.

His shoulder twitched again. Sometimes carrying things made it sensitive. Perhaps the groceries were cumulatively heavier than he thought.

He put the dishes in the sink and walked into the living room, the cat a few steps behind. He sat on the couch and stretched out.

Just for a minute. I'll relax for just a minute.

———∞∞∞———

Perhaps ten minutes passed. Perhaps it was longer. Jake had not paid attention to the time when he first shut his eyes.

Petey was up, standing on the chair, eyes alert, ears back.

Why did I wake up?

Then he heard it. A soft rapping at the door. A soft feminine rapping, he imagined. He wasn't sure what a feminine knock sounded like, but somehow this knock sounded like it came from the hand of a woman. Petey carefully jumped from the chair and made his way toward the door, then sat and waited, a furry welcoming committee.

Jake pulled at the doorknob, but it stuck, just like it had for Jimbo.

Maybe there's an easy fix for this.

He used two hands and pulled harder and the door squealed open. Standing there, shouldering a very large, and apparently heavy, backpack, was a young girl—or rather, a young woman, with a thicket of wavy brown hair framing her delicate face. Sort of angelic. Pretty. Innocent and pretty.

71

The two eyed each other for a moment. Or, really, the three of them eyed one another. Petey walked a few steps into the living room, and peered at their visitor. His tail stood up at attention.

The young woman spoke first.

"You a preacher?"

Jake had asked himself that same question many times.

"Yes . . . I am a pastor. I'm the new pastor here. Jake Wilkerson."

If the young woman had been aware of the conflict in his response, she paid no mind.

"Hi. I'm Tassy Lambert. I heard somewhere that if you were ever in trouble, a church would be a good place to go if you needed to find your way."

Jake's agreed with her statement, but he had no idea if she was expecting a response.

She continued, "Where am I? And is there a cheap motel anywhere around here?"

And the twinge went off in Jake's shoulder once again. This time he blamed too much coffee.

"Jimbo, you have to call him and tell him Vern is coming. What if he's out buying groceries or something?"

Jimbo didn't want to call the pastor.

"No. He'll think I'm checking up on him."

"He will not," Betty insisted. "If it was me and Vern was on his way over, well, mister, I would want to know about that. Vern can be . . . cantankerous, you know."

Jimbo sighed and wished he were drilling a well right about now.

"And his wife is coming as well. Her . . . I don't like, even if she is old."

"Okay. Okay. I'll give him a heads-up. You're probably right."

And he took the phone as if it had recently been on fire and just now extinguished.

"A hotel . . ." Jake's thoughts were in a whirl.

I didn't stay overnight last time . . . the only time I've been here. I don't think I saw any hotels. There has to be one in Bradford but that's an hour away.

"You know, Miss . . ."

"Tassy."

"Tassy, you know, I don't really know. It's . . . well, it's only my second day on the job and I'm not from around here originally."

Tassy's face darkened. No, not darkened; she looked more crestfallen.

Do I invite her in? Jake wondered, his thoughts in even more of a whirl. *She's not wearing a wedding ring. I'm a pastor. This is a church. What's proper here? What do I do?*

Such decisions never reached his desk as an assistant pastor in a very large church with twenty staff members . . . His responsibilities seemed mostly to entail getting a full complement of ushers lined up for the services. This young woman posed a new problem to Jake—one he was not prepared to deal with.

Friendly. Outgoing. Works turn to faith.

Petey stepped toward the girl and rubbed against her leg, purring and meowing softly.

"What a cute kitty," she said. "What happened to his paw?"

73

She bent and picked him up. The cat made no effort to stop her. In fact, he more or less snuggled into her cradled arms.

"He had a thorn in it. And he showed up at church the same time I did yesterday. So I guess we've both started at the same time."

Tassy smiled.

Jake decided to err on the side of hospitality.

"Come on in. At least for a little bit. I guess I could make a few calls. Maybe there's a place in Coudersport. Would you like a cup of coffee?"

She hesitated with her answer.

"I do have some tea," he said. "I just bought it. I never heard of the brand before, but the box looks nice."

"Tea would be great," Tassy said. "Do you have any honey?"

She dropped her back pack, switching Petey between her left and right arms and took a seat at the kitchen table as Jake boiled water. He poured it into a mug, offered her a teabag, and put the honey on the table. He made himself coffee while Petey chirped, happy, content.

"There might be a hotel in Coudersport—on the east side. There are stores that way."

"Are they on this highway?" Tassy asked, pointing to the highway in front of the church. "The Grand Army of the Potomac Road."

"Yes," Jake replied.

"And is Coudersport that way?" Tassy asked, pointing in the direction she had just walked.

"Yes. If you followed the highway, then you saw the town."

Tassy sighed and put the used teabag in her spoon, with a tired, world-weary look on her face.

"Well, then Coudersport doesn't have any cheap hotels that I could see, because I walked that whole way and didn't realize that I passed through a town. And I would bet that they don't have any . . . like, homeless shelters, either."

Jake wanted to nod, but didn't. He was pretty certain that Coudersport did not see many homeless young women just walking through. But he was not positive.

"Tassy, how did you get here? This church is sort of in the middle of nowhere."

"I was with someone," she explained. "We left Philadelphia a while ago and were sort of making our way to California. We had a fight. He said, 'Out of the car.' And he called me a name I don't think preachers want to hear repeated. Several names, each worse than the other. Then he threw my backpack out on the road and drove off. I guess that was where he and I called it quits. So I started walking, ate at McDonald's, and now I'm here . . . and I don't really know what to do next."

Her bottom lip quivered, just a little, and Jake could tell that she was doing her utmost to make it stop.

Petey meowed softly to Tassy, then turned to Jake and stared at him—hard. He then offered a long, low, rumbly meow, almost insistent, that grew louder each second.

Jake hoped some sort of cogent answer would come to him. For a year now, maybe longer, Jake and the Almighty had not shared a common wavelength. Oh, Jake would readily admit that he was a believer and knew all about God and the Bible and all that, but never really felt at home, never really felt listened to. The gulf continued to grow wider—even as Jake pretended to be a pastor. It was hard work, pretending to be faithful without faith.

No. I wasn't pretending. I was a pastor. And I am a pastor now. That's the job I was born to do. Right? There is an ebb and flow to faith. Weak then strong. It will return. Like day follows dark.

He pursed his lips, as if in thought.

It will come back.

Remembering the start of becoming a pastor brought him back to when he was twelve-years-old and his father left without ever saying good-bye to anyone, and his mother took to running the house and his life. It was better to let her have her way than to try and construct an alternative. She wanted her only son to be a man of God and that is what she got. Inevitability. Set in stone. Immutable. As if commanded from on high. From his mother.

I have no idea what to do right now. I could call the elders. Maybe this sort of thing comes up all the time. I could call . . . who? Social Services? I bet the closest office is in Bradford. Or maybe Kane.

She needs help. I don't think she's making up her predicament. How do I help?

I know I don't have the experience that I should.

He looked up, subtly, to the heavens.

Maybe you could drop me a hint about what I should do next?

A person without faith, Jake thought to himself, had no business praying, feeling more than a bit hypocritical going through the motions. It wasn't that he was hedging his bets. It was that he felt as if he were simply pretending.

Please, Lord.

Jake had not shut his eyes while he almost prayed, and worried, a little, that not shutting eyes might invalidate the prayer or further weaken its effectiveness. His former pastor was very good at praying and often would go ten minutes without once looking at notes—just off the top of his head. Jake knew he could never do that.

His prayers all too often included a lot of "justs" and repeating what was obvious to God and everyone else in attendance.

The cat looked up at Jake and meowed. And again, it wasn't a normal cat's meow. It had more to it, like the cat was trying to tell him not to be nervous. And by meowing like he did, Petey was trying to tell Jake that Tassy was a nice person, a person to be trusted, and that something would work out.

That is what Jake thought the cat was saying.

That is what Jake hoped the cat was saying.

I'm depending on a cat for my spiritual guidance now. What next?

———

Well, this is a surprise. I was not expecting this person to be here. I heard nothing about a young girl with curly hair. I listened carefully. I am sure about that. No one said anything about a girl with curly hair. She has a very soft lap. Like a cat is soft. I bet she has a lot of bones. Not like a dog. Maybe she isn't supposed to be here. Maybe this is a test. For me. I'm good at tests. First, Jake helped me with my paw. Now he should help her. I could get her a mouse. There are a lot of mice in the field outside. She looks like the kind of person who would really like a mouse. Like Jake.

———

Jake knew he had to say or do something, but he wasn't sure of what that might be. The phone rang, saving him from thinking on his feet, an unpolished skill. A phone was mounted on the wall in the kitchen.

"Jake Wilkerson . . . Pastor Wilkerson here," he said, trying to sound like a pastor.

"Oh, hey there, Pastor Jake. This here's Jimbo calling. Jimbo Bennett."

"Hi, Jimbo. How are you? Something I can help you with?"

Jake could almost hear Jimbo thinking of how to phrase what he was about to say next.

"I'm fine. But, Pastor Jake, well . . . the Missus said I had to call. Sort of warn you."

Jake felt a coldness in his face.

Already? They've found out why I was fired. I knew it.

"I got a call from Vern. Vern Waldorf. He was—or is, I guess—like a founding member of the church. Been around forever."

And he wants to take back his vote?

He called Pastor Gust in Butler—I knew it.

"Well, last year it seems like Vern went and bought this giant RV in Bradford. It is one big unit, let me tell you. Long as a city block, or just about. We all tried to talk him out of it, but he said he wanted to see the country. But the blamed thing is, well, huge, and sort of tricky to drive, and Vern is not the best driver in the best of times, and since he had his hip replaced this winter his driving has gotten way worse. His neighbors are trying to get the city council to ban RVs in town 'cause it's on his lawn and makes it look like he's got two houses on the lot."

Jake waited.

What does this have to do with me? Or the church? He didn't call Pastor Gust?

"So Vern doesn't want to sell it or anything and he doesn't want to pay a fine or go to a city council meeting seeing as how he and the mayor don't get along at all anymore—ever since the Fourth of July fireworks fight back in '94. Holds a grudge, Vern does."

Okay. But why are you telling me this?

"Anyhow, Vern's wife called Betty to tell her to tell me, sort of warn me, and she said Vern was climbing in the RV carrying the keys and claimed he was heading to church. She says I should warn you. He wants to park it at the back of the church lot. Now, I don't think there's any harm in that. Maybe the elders have to vote on it or something. I don't know about that—the rules and the constitution and all. But I wanted to let you know he was coming . . . and I guess I'm telling you that he can park it there. At least for now. The RV, I mean."

"Well, okay, Jimbo. That's fine . . ."

"And his wife is following him in the Buick. She can't see all that well, so if she pulls in, make sure you're well out of her way, okay?"

"Will do. Vern's on his way. I'll be ready."

That's when the cat issued a low, rumbly growl, almost doglike, and stared out the small window above the kitchen sink, watching as a shadow moved across the opening, like a planet stepping in front of the sun.

The RV was as large as Jimbo said. Massive. Like a semi-truck. Maybe bigger. Jake could only see the crest of a head behind the wheel, covered with wisps of white hair, like a tiny, well-worn doll wedged into a toy truck. The unit rumbled to a stop at an angle to the church and creaked and groaned as the engine shut down. The driver's side door opened with a pneumatic swoosh, and the old man who must have been Vern shuffled out, taking each step individually, holding on to the railing with both hands.

He blinked in the bright sun. When he laid eyes on Jake, he called out, "You there—you the new guy?"

Jake said, "Yes. I'm the new pastor. Jake Wilkerson."

Vern scowled. "I know your name. Couldn't tell if you were the same fellow. You're not wearing a suit. In my day, pastors always wore suits. And ties. You don't have a tie on."

"I . . . I . . . I'm still unpacking, sort of. I arrived yesterday. Still have a lot of work to do." He didn't, really, but he hoped it was a good excuse for a pastor wearing jeans in the middle of the week in Coudersport.

Vern craned his head around and spotted the white pickup.

"And in my day, pastors drove Buicks. Or maybe a Chevy. They didn't drive trucks. You look like a carpenter driving a truck."

Jake had dealt with prickly people before. After all, he had worked at a church. He wasn't all that good at it, but he had learned that it was best to say very little and nod a lot. Jake nodded.

"Yes, sir," he said, hoping he sounded differential and not peeved.

"I told Jimbo's wife that I was parking this here. She said he said to go ahead. So here it is."

At that moment, the parsonage door opened and Petey stepped out into the shadow of the RV, graceful on three legs.

Vern heard the door and stared.

"That a cat? You got a cat? In my day, pastors didn't have money for pets. And it's not a dog."

"No, sir. And I don't really have a pet. It sort of showed up here yesterday morning."

Vern pulled his face into a grimace that was even more prunelike than what existed naturally. "Two days on the job and he's taking in strays. That's what's wrong with the church these days."

The door creaked open again and Tassy stepped out, her arms folded across her chest. She smiled at the two of them. "The cat was crying by the door. I let him out. Is that okay?"

Vern triangulated the three of them, then scowled, as only a small, white-haired old man can scowl. The scowl was nearly as big as he was.

"You're not married," Vern declared.

"No, sir, I'm not."

"Then who's that? The cleaning lady? Cats. Trucks. Blue jeans. Women. I tell you, Sonny, I don't like the looks of this one bit."

Jake remained calm, like a proper pastor should remain.

"Mr. Waldorf, that girl is Tassy—she's homeless and needs a place to stay."

"So you're taking her in?" Vern sputtered. "Sonny, you got a lot to learn about what it is that a proper, moral, law-abiding, God-fearing pastor does. Taking in women off the street is not one of them. What does that look like? Like sin, if you ask me. This church will become the laughing stock of all of Potter County. This is not the big city. Maybe big city pastors do that, but God-fearing people out here—they don't. I don't think we even have any homeless people in Potter County. They know better than to come through here."

Vern wiped at his face with a leathery hand and muttered to himself, knowing that Jake could hear him, "I knew I should have been there to vote no on this guy."

And as Vern muttered, a large, old, gray Buick, with a series of dents in both front fenders, veered off the main road and aimed itself at the parking lot. Jake could not even see the driver of this vehicle. The steering wheel eclipsed the driver. The car missed the drainage ditch by a matter of inches, bouncing through some half-hidden ruts and furrows at the edge of the gravel. Momentarily, it hissed to a stop. A very tiny, white-haired woman emerged from the car, clutching a purse that was nearly as big as she was.

"Vern!" she all but shouted. "I said I wanted to follow you, you old goat. But no, you don't listen, do you? You take off and leave me at the red light, you driving like a bat out of . . . you know where the bat is out of, Vern. I told you to drive slow!"

Vern waved his right arm in the air, palm facing her, as if it were batting away the charges of reckless driving like batting away a swarm of gnats.

"Listen, Eleanor, if I was going to make sure you were following me, we'd still be on the road. Keep up! I was shouting out the window. Keep up! But you poked along like we got all day or something. Speed limit is fifty out here. Five-oh. Not oh-five."

By this time, the tiny, angry woman was within arm's distance. An angry glower lighted her wrinkled face, her eyes flashing. Then, like switching off a light, her demeanor changed and softened to a grandmotherly glow. Deep lines formed around her eyes, as if she had spent a fair amount of her life smiling.

"Pastor Wilkerson," she said, extending her hand, "I'm Eleanor Waldorf. We met when you preached. It's a pleasure to see you again. And you have to excuse my husband, the old goat. He thinks the whole world revolves around him and him alone. I keep telling him, 'Vern,' I say, 'the world is changing and you're still stuck in 1930.' And back in 1930, he was already old and cranky."

"Glad to see you again, Mrs. Waldorf."

Eleanor caught sight of Tassy and the cat, both standing at some distance, both bathed in the bright spring sunshine. Tassy's hair illuminated her face like a thick, curly halo.

Eleanor's eyes went back and forth like she was attempting to solve a particularly difficult word jumble.

"She your girlfriend?"

"No, ma'am. She's homeless. Tassy. She just showed up at church asking if there was an inexpensive hotel in the area. She needs a place to stay. Her boyfriend tossed her out of the car and left her out here."

Vern was about to sputter again, and then Eleanor narrowed her vision to laser slits and aimed them right at her husband. "Not a word, Vern. No more. I'm tired already. I'm tired of you ranting on and on about the Democrats and Episcopalians and the mayor and the Irish. I'm done with you for now. You hear me? No more. Not a word."

Vern raised his arm as if he was about to point a jagged finger in the air, then he thought better of it, and slowly deflated. "I hear you, Eleanor. Loud and clear, okay? Like anyone in the county couldn't hear you."

The last sentence was said almost under his breath, but everyone heard it, including Eleanor, who glared in response.

She called to Tassy, "Young woman, please come here. I'm old and I don't like to walk more than I have to."

Tassy and the cat hurried closer. Tassy offered the assembly her best and most innocent smile. "Yes, ma'am," she said.

"Where are you from?"

"Philadelphia," Tassy responded.

"Did you leave home?" Eleanor asked. "Did you run away?"

"I had to leave," Tassy said, her voice just a whisper. "I couldn't stay there anymore. I have a new stepfather, and . . . well . . . I had to go. It's complicated."

Eleanor must have been a grandmother, because she reached out and took Tassy's hand. "It happens, dear. It's okay. Really."

Petey looked up at the old woman, then at Tassy, back and forth, following the questions and answers like a tennis match. *I like this old human. She smells like vanilla pudding.*

⸺∞⸺

"You don't have a place to stay?"

"I don't. But I have some money. I was looking for an inexpensive hotel. For a few days. Until I figure things out."

Eleanor waved her hand in the air, a smaller, more feminine version of Vern's whole body wave of dismissal. "Nonsense child. I'd invite you to our house, but all we have is two bedrooms and one of them has all of Vern's junk piled in it, so we only have one bedroom. And no one should have to be around this old goat more than necessary."

Petey stood up and walked to the old woman and rubbed against her leg. She looked surprised and looked down. "Is the cat crippled?"

"A thorn in his paw. He'll be fine," Jake said.

"Runaways and cripples," Vern muttered. "We might as well move to Philadelphia. Fit right in. With all the other degenerates."

Eleanor hissed, "Hush, Vern."

She squeezed Tassy's hand. "Listen, honey, there's a giant RV right here that we'll never use, as in never use in a million years. I can make a few calls. The women of this church love helping out. They can get some food for you. Extra sheets and towels and the like. Maybe some clothes, if you need them."

She eyed the young woman.

Vern looked like he was doing long division in his head. "Wait a dog-blamed minute. You're saying that she can stay in my RV? Just like that? I don't know this . . . this . . . person. Maybe she's running from the law. Maybe she's a criminal—

like on those TV shows. Do you think it's smart for her to be right next to the church? We best talk to the elders. She might just drive off with my RV."

Eleanor spun around and faced her husband.

"Vern, I would be happy if she did drive off with it—but she won't. And there will be no calling the elders. She needs a place to stay and we have a place. It's settled. You go around calling the elders and trying to stir up trouble, I'll do my utmost to make the rest of your life truly miserable. You hear me? You know I can do that."

Jake could tell she was dead serious. And he could tell that this couple was inordinately accustomed to resorting to nuclear warfare with each other.

"Yeah. Okay. Okay," Vern said after a long moment of consideration. "She can use it. A couple of days. Then we'll talk."

Tassy beamed.

"You mean it? Really? I could stay there for a while? Really?"

Eleanor smiled back.

"Yes, you can. And there's an extension cord in there that you can run to the church for power. Lights and the TV and the refrigerator."

"Hunert feet," Vern said. "So you gotta park closer than a hunert feet."

"You know, honey," Eleanor said to Tassy, "we had three boys. All moved away from Coudersport a long time ago. See them once a year or so. I always wanted a little girl. Never had one. So . . . you take your time here, okay?"

"Okay," Tassy replied. "Sure."

4

As Jake made his way down the back basement steps of the church, he became enveloped in a thick scent cloud of barbeque, fried chicken, and beans, plus a breeze of aftershave and hints of cologne—the good kind from the drugstore. A battered coffee urn, the size of a small garbage can, wheezed in the corner, steam puffing out from under the lid in little snorts. Two folding tables, the long kind, covered with white plastic tablecloths, were held down firmly by a garage sale assortment of Pyrex casseroles, Tupperware containers, and almost-new square and oblong aluminum tins. Three banks of fluorescent lights beamed down, bathing everyone in a flickering glow.

Jake took the final step, the last stair creaking like a desperate bullfrog at the end of a long, flyless evening. As his foot hit the painted cement floor, like pressing a mute button, all conversation ceased, and the entire congregation simply took a slight breath, pivoted in their seats, or turned to face Jake.

The silence lasted for a long three or four heartbeats, then a tidal wave of Hellos and Howdys and Hey theres cascaded like a roll of friendly thunder.

He managed a wave and a broad smile and then was descended upon by a quartet of members of the women's auxiliary prayer group and Christian Aid Society, each bearing a special plate reserved for the pastor, each pointing out their particular specialty and whispering which ones to avoid.

"I heard that what she brought came straight from Doug's Foods. Out of a package. For a potluck. Can you believe that, Pastor?"

The quartet soon enough became a quintet. Jake trailed the anxious, plate-bearing ladies on a tour of the two tables, which were groaning with all manner of central Pennsylvania delicacies.

Jake found himself washed ashore at the head table, surrounded then by four—no, five—plates containing large servings of white and brown and red and yellow food, mostly hidden by puddles of white or brown gravies. Two glasses of iced tea appeared—one sweetened, one unsweetened. It became difficult to respond, with more than one question being asked at a time. Jake nodded a lot, smiled as much as he could while chewing, and took small bites from each colored assembly of food, smiling more broadly as he did so, then pointing to each, wordlessly, nodding in agreement with whatever it was that he was eating, giving each dish his approval. Jake knew it was not the time to show partiality—or dislike. He gave a lot of silent, smiling, thumbs-up evaluations of the cuisine.

The noise level rose as he ate.

People talk loud up here.

Bursts of laughter punctuated the eating.

Jake did wave to Big Dave, who sat with a plate of food stacked amazingly high. Big Dave pointed to his stomach, then gave a double thumbs-up back to Jake.

Immediately after Jake politely plowed through perhaps half of the food presented to him, another two plates of desserts appeared, as if materializing from the mother ship of potlucks circling overhead.

Three large slabs of cake, two cookie bars, two slices of pie, a cobbler, a pudding, and some fruit that looked like it was simply mixed with Cool Whip—blueberries, maybe. And two cups of coffee—one black, one with cream (whole milk, actually, but it was closer than the white powder that stood in a warped cardboard canister next to the urn.)

Jake managed to try a little of everything, but by this time, his taste buds had retired for the evening. The desserts might have been an epicurean delight; he truly couldn't discern.

As he finally stopped eating and sipped at his coffee, someone behind him stood up. He could feel the shadows from the fluorescent lights.

"Listen up, everyone," a man's voice crowed. "Listen up!"

Then the man put two fingers in his mouth and let out an ear-rattling whistle that came close to being aurally dangerous.

Everyone grumble-mumbled another few words, then silence enveloped the room, except for the coffee pot, which wheezed on, liquidlike.

The coffee was strong for church coffee, Jake thought.

That must be why.

"We here on the elder board want to welcome you all to this here all-church potluck."

Rudolph Keilback, an almost enormous man, as wide as he was tall, swayed back and forth on his heels as he spoke. "Let's give all the ladies a round of applause for their good food. I know I appreciated it," he said, patting at his stomach. There was a lot of territory to pat.

Jake joined in the enthusiastic response.

"Always a pleasure to break bread with the church family."

Someone toward the back shouted out an "Amen."

Jake tried to see who it was.. He felt pretty certain there weren't a lot of charismatic tendencies in the church; at least when he had candidated, no one shouted out encouragement during his sermon.

Maybe they just get spiritually excited about food.

"Since this here is the first time we got Pastor Wilkerson with us, be nice if he said a few words. Maybe warn us about Sunday's sermon—or whatever. Hey, there, Pastor Jake. Get up and say hello to your new family."

Jake knew he would have to say something corporate this evening—he had thought about it all day. He stood up to a loud round of clapping, and the basement was filled with smiling, hopeful faces. Maybe it was a full stomach talking, but Jake sensed a truly warm greeting.

Afterward, he could not recall exactly what he had said. Something to the effect that it was an honor to be called to come to their church, he was happy to be here, and he looked forward to earning his place in this wonderful family. He also said he looked forward to exploring God's word with them.

And finding the truth. I should say that on a personal level . . . but not tonight.

He had practiced his remarks that afternoon and was pretty sure he sounded honest and sincere.

Whatever the words were, they went over well. Elder Keilback slapped him on the back when he finished, and the welcoming gesture nearly knocked him to the ground.

What does he do for a living? Jake wondered. *Professional wrestler? Bear wrangler?*

Jake returned to his seat where a fresh plate of new desserts awaited him. He offered a weary smile and tried to manage to at least try a forkful of each one. Off in the corner, Jake noticed Tassy sitting next to Eleanor. On the other side of Eleanor sat a very dour Vern, who apparently had a permanent scowl etched onto his face. Yet Tassy and Eleanor seemed animated, smiling and whispering to each other. It was comforting to see a stranger so accepted.

Earlier that day, Jake had talked to a few of the elders, explaining who Tassy was and how she came to be at the church. He had been right: Coudersport did not see many homeless folks passing through. The closest drop-in shelter was in Bradford, and no one had suggested that as a solution.

"Seeing as how nobody is using that RV, don't seem right to let it stay empty if there's a need for it," said Jimbo earlier that day. "We been talking and sort of said if it's okay with Vern, I guess then it's okay with us as well."

Jake noticed a few people sitting nearest to him smiling, then pointing toward the back steps. He turned and saw Petey, three steps from the bottom, almost hidden in shadow.

"Is that your new cat, Pastor Jake?" someone called out.

Jake held his hand up and most of the room grew a little quieter.

"One more thing. I forgot. Has anybody lost a cat? Or does anyone know anyone who lost a cat? Petey showed up at church on Monday, and I would like to find his real home."

Petey stared hard at Jake as he spoke, then very deliberately, without pausing, headed straight for Tassy and jumped up into her lap.

A chorus of oohs and ahhs followed.

I am not lost! I am not lost! That's even worse than being called a varmint. I am right where I am supposed to be. I know humans can be dense, but Jake—come on, now. I am supposed to be here. This is my real home.

The cat snuggled into Tassy's welcoming lap yet kept his withering gaze on Jake.

I'm doing what I am supposed to be doing . . . protecting.

Almost with a jolt, Petey sat up straight, then craned his neck backward to peer at Tassy's face. He meowed loudly. Tassy took it as a request for her to pet the cat, but that wasn't it.

Okay, okay, pet me all you want. That's fine. But I'm here to protect. I just heard that. Or felt it. Protect. That's a new task. I didn't hear anything about protecting before. But . . . what I don't get is what to protect.

Petey relaxed as Tassy scratched his neck, and then he lay down, still, forming a tidy, coiled ball.

No one said anything about protecting . . . but then who am I to argue?

He closed his eyes as she massaged his ears.

Well . . . I am a cat, after all. That's what we do sometimes.

Big Dave—Lawrence—pulled into the parking lot of his store. He lived in the attached quarters behind the store. He had four rooms and more living space than he really needed.

Charles, a wire-thin high school senior from the Coudersport High School ("Home of the Falcons") stood behind the counter, his eyes glazed from staring at the little TV. It was tuned to "Dancing with the Stars." Big Dave knew the only reason Charles was watching it was because it was the only channel that came in static-free.

"Busy tonight?" Big Dave asked.

"No. A few gas customers. A loaf of bread. Couple gallons of milk. That's about it."

Big Dave's did not get a lot of evening traffic. It would be busier after the bars closed on Friday and Saturday.

"How was the potluck?"

Big Dave patted at his stomach.

"It was real good. Real good. The new pastor guy brought out a lot more meat dishes. Three different kinds of meatloaf. One had an egg in the middle of it. I kept wonderin' how they got that egg in the middle. Did they freeze it first or what?"

Charles scratched at his chin. "Maybe it was already hard-boiled or something. That could work, couldn't it? Bake the meatloaf around it."

Big Dave liked Charles because he was smart.

"Maybe that is it. I should try that sometime. It was real good."

Charles put on his letterman's jacket—track and field, long-distance relays.

"You know, maybe you should come to the church sometime, Charles. You would enjoy it."

Charles made a face that was somewhere between like biting a lemon and stepping on a nail.

"No, thanks. Too many rules. Old guys yelling at you for having fun."

Big Dave brightened.

"No, the new guy is sort of young. No more than thirty. And he don't seem like the type that yells much."

Charles shrugged.

"Maybe. If they have like a coffee house or a dance or something. Maybe then. If there's girls there. Maybe."

Big Dave kept his smile. "Well, I'll make that suggestion to Pastor Jake. I bet he might try something like that. A coffee house, that sounds good. I'll let you know."

Jake attempted to help clean up afterward and actually managed to wash a few spoons and forks. So shocked were the women observers that they did not respond immediately. But when they did, Jake's actions had set off a small feminine tsunami: at least six women rushed to supplant him at the tub of sudsy water.

"No, no, no, Pastor. You don't wash dishes. That's our work," one of them said, scrambling to the sink.

Jake wondered how they thought the dishes in his kitchen got washed. He allowed himself to be elbowed away from the sink, though he did realize he had made the first small step in establishing a new standard of male behavior in the Coudersport religious community.

Later, Jake stood outside by the basement steps and waved as the last few cars rumbled out of the parking lot. He sighed deeply, grateful that the evening was over. His watch read 9:15.

Most of these people have jobs. No late meetings for any of them.

Tassy appeared at the basement door, Petey a few steps behind her, and she wrapped her sweatshirt around herself, crossing her arms.

"I had a good time," she said.

"I did too," Jake replied.

Petey meowed in agreement, though it sounded like he was still smarting from being called "lost."

"I haven't eaten that much in months," Tassy said.

"I have never eaten that much," Jake answered. "They all seem like nice people," he added.

"That's what Eleanor said, too, but she said that you can't always trust the first impression. She said there have been a lot of people talking about me being here. Some said they thought it was nice that I can use the RV and others said that it sets a bad . . . you know . . . a bad precedent. That only problems can come out of it. But Eleanor said not to worry. A lot of people have nothing better to do than gossip about stuff, she said."

Jake hoped she could not see the pained look on his face.

"She said that you seem like a nice pastor. And she said that you should do what God wants you to do and not listen to people who complain."

"Well . . . I try to do that, Tassy. You know . . . follow God and the Bible and all that."

"She said that was the right thing to do, Pastor Jake. She said that if you do that, everything will be fine. Once you leave that path, she said, then you'll get into trouble."

Neither spoke for a long, dark moment. Their breath frosted in puffs in the air. He could hear an owl hooting off in the woods to the east. Only a sliver of a moon could be seen, but it was as bright as a streetlight.

"Follow God," Tassy repeated. "She said that to me, too. It's just . . . well, it's just that I don't think I can do that, Pastor Jake. That's okay, isn't it? For me to stay here for a little while. I don't know about this stuff about following God or anything. That's okay, isn't it? You won't tell on me, will you?"

Jake tried to offer a reassuring smile but was pretty sure Tassy could not see his face in the dark.

"Sure, Tassy, that's okay. Take your time. Sometimes it does seem like God is far away. That's okay. That's okay."

He could see Tassy smile back at him. The moon caught her face, making her look like an angel.

"Thanks, Pastor Jake. Thanks. And good-night."

Petey meowed a good-night for both of them, then followed Jake back toward the parsonage.

Emma sat in her upstairs office, her face lit blue by the glow of the computer. Winston snored, sleeping on the thick rug in the hallway. There was no carpeting in the office and Winston was a glutton for comfort.

Just as well, Emma thought. *Hard enough to concentrate with him snoring out there in the hall.*

She had debated on what she was about to do for a while, first considering it intrusive, almost stalkerlike, then rationalizing it.

Looking someone up on the Internet isn't a bad thing. Why would Facebook be so popular if it was?

Emma started there. Thirty-seven Jake R. Wilkersons had accounts on Facebook, but not one of them was the Jake Wilkerson who was new to Coudersport.

"Seriously? He doesn't have a Facebook page? What decade is he living in? Even Winston has a Facebook page."

Typing Jake's name into Google returned more than a million hits.

Adding "Butler, PA" to the search narrowed it considerably.

A few more refinements in her search found Emma a short, archived article in the *Butler Eagle* records regarding Jake's hiring at the East Side Christian Church in Lyndora, a neighborhood on the east edge of Butler.

Graduate of the Bible Seminary in Hatfield. Where is Hatfield?
She looked on Google Maps.
Sort of between Allentown and Philadelphia. Never heard of it.

Then she stumbled across another article in the newspaper, written by a senior pastor, Reverend Gust, talking about preparing for marriage.

"I even have a staff member going through my marriage preparation course—Jake Wilkerson. He's not engaged yet, but he and his girlfriend, Barbara Ann Bentley, thought it would be a good idea to get off on the right foot, as it were. I think it's wise as well,

seeing as how Barbara Ann is my niece and a former second-runner up in the Miss Pennsylvania Pageant. Might as well start early," Pastor Gust declared, "and set a healthy groundwork for the future."

Emma did not surprise easily, but this surprised her.

He was "almost" engaged? He didn't say a word about that to me. But then . . . why would he?

She found one more puzzling bit of information. It was a small notice in the electronic version of the church newsletter of the East Side Christian Church.

We are sad to say good-bye to one of our associate pastors, Jake Wilkerson. Jake is heading off to a new opportunity. We wish him well in his new endeavor.

The dates didn't match up—that's what puzzled Emma. The newsletter notice about Jake's departure was dated more than nine months prior. If he were headed to Coudersport after leaving his position in Butler—well, it wouldn't have taken him nine months to pack.

She thought about it and came to the only conclusion that made sense: the church fired him.

Fired? Do they really fire preachers?

Leaning back in the chair, Emma exhaled loudly, causing Winston to snort and almost wake up.

"Well, Pastor Jake, I think there is more here than meets the eye."

She turned off the computer.

"Not that it's any of my business. And not that I care. Really."

She stood up.

"Do I Winston? I don't really care."

Vern parked the Buick in the garage, banging the front end, just a little, into the workbench that no longer served as a workbench in the front of the garage. A rusty gathering of old paint cans and coffee tins filled with loose nails and odd nuts and bolts rattled and jumped, but only a little. He had banged it much harder on former occasions.

"We're home," he declared, thinking that Eleanor had fallen asleep during the ten-minute ride.

"I'm awake, you old goat. Who can sleep with the way you drive, speeding and weaving like that? You make it sound like you climbed Mount Everest or something, getting us home without causing a traffic accident. That's normal, Vern, you know. Driving without dying."

He waved off her reply like he was batting at an angry moth.

It was obvious that this was a routine they had practiced for years and years, neither one really meaning what they said and neither really paying close attention to what was said in between the rehearsed lines.

"House looks so much bigger without the trailer sitting there."

"RV."

"RV, trailer, monstrosity—whatever, Vern. It just looks nicer with it gone."

Vern extended his arm for Eleanor to hold on to. In the dark, she was much less stable on her feet.

"You know what? I think I agree with you on that."

If Eleanor was surprised, she did not show it.

"You think the dead grass will come back?"

"Probably. I got some seed in the garage. I'll put it down tomorrow."

They shuffled along toward the house.

"That would be nice. Maybe we could stop at Smolka's Greenhouse and get a couple of geraniums."

Vern snorted.

"Too early. We can get a freeze up here on the Fourth of July," he grumbled. "Maybe next week, though."

Vern unlocked the deadbolt and the door lock. He was a firm proponent of never being too careful. He switched on the round fluorescent bulb in the kitchen, then helped Eleanor with her coat. "She has a bum shoulder," Vern would say to others when they saw him being chivalrous.

"So what do you think of the new guy? Seems like a kid to me. Way too young to be a pastor of a real church."

Eleanor pulled out a kitchen chair and sat heavily. Long walks tired her.

"I don't know, Vern. Seems like he's fine. But . . ."

"But what?" Vern asked. "He say something stupid that I didn't hear? The elders gunning for him already?"

Eleanor gave Vern a very familiar, peeved look, almost angry, but not quite.

"No, it's not that at all. I just get the feeling that he's not sure if he has it in him. Like he doesn't really believe that he's a pastor. That comes out, you know, Vern. Pastors have to be sure. And I don't know if he is. Of course, he's only been here a few days. Maybe he'll grow into it."

Vern took a Vernor's Ginger Ale out of the refrigerator, held it down in the sink, and pulled the opening tab on it. It hissed, just a little.

"Well, if I know the elders, he won't have that long of a honeymoon."

⸻

Petey had not yet made up his mind where to sleep tonight. He tried the chair in the bedroom. He tried under the small table in the hall, just outside the bedroom. He tried on top of the dresser, but there was some sort of aftershave bottle there that smelled like a dead flower. And he tried the windowsill, but it was narrower than the one in Jake's office.

None of them felt just right.

He looked up at the big bed and decided he would audition that. He tried not to think about that place where he had once lived, a place where there would be punishment for a cat being on a bed.

But Jake isn't like that, Petey told himself. *God would not allow that to happen to me twice.*

So tonight, Petey waited until Jake settled into bed, then jumped up and stayed at the far corner of the bed, waiting.

"Hey, Petey," Jake said as he looked up. "You can stay up here. It's okay. It would drive my mother crazy—but I don't mind."

So Petey took him at his word.

Petey made his way to the center of his side of the bed and circled several times, then lay down, tucking his legs underneath him. He kept his eyes on Jake as he did so, not wanting to be surprised if he changed his mind.

"Good cat," Jake said, and switched off the bedside lamp.

Petey would have smiled, if he could smile, which he couldn't.

Stupid dogs have all the luck. They always get to sleep on beds.

5

Thursday.

I should have finished this sermon by now, so I'd have a couple of days to work on the delivery—and make it exceptionally good.

Jake hadn't even started his first message to his new church.

He did have a three-ring black vinyl binder—not one of the real big ones but a slim, one-inch binder—filled with his past sermons. Some of them were part of a series, a series that someone else started and then required an emergency stand-in. Most were summer sermons, when attendance was down and when the sermons were all "one-offs," nothing in a series.

Jake thumbed through the book a number of times. A few of the messages he felt proud of, but the majority, while theologically sound, did not rise to the level where the congregation would rise as one and applaud, or better yet, cheer.

Instead, he took three volumes from the bookcase behind him—three thick commentaries. An open Bible lay in the middle of the desk, waiting, almost taunting Jake.

Find something worthwhile—I dare you!

He thought he might start by looking at Romans. It was a popular book, lots written on it, lots of uplifting messages could be taken from it.

The hard parts—well, he wouldn't preach the hard parts just yet.

Get a feel for things, the lay of the land and all that. No sense stirring up deep waters first thing. Right?

Petey sauntered into Jake's office, sputtering to himself, little cat chirps, as if he were talking to himself as he walked, reminding himself that he was due for his midmorning nap. A cat person for all of three-and-a-half days, Jake had already noticed the fact that cats seem to sleep a great deal.

He looked it up on the Internet: eighteen hours wouldn't be abnormal for a house cat.

What I would give to sleep eighteen hours a day, Jake thought.

The cat walked to Jake, sniffed at his chair and then sniffed the air, and headed to the window. The window, nearly as tall as a man, featured a wide sill—wide enough to sit on, and wide enough to sleep on if you were a cat.

Petey jumped up with ease. If his bandaged paw was causing him any pain, he did not show a trace of discomfort.

"Hello, Petey," Jake said.

Petey churred a response, acknowledging the salutation.

"So, Petey, what should I preach on this week?"

Petey chirped a short reply, then looked up and hesitated a moment, jumped down from the sill and walked to the desk, and effortlessly, it seemed, launched himself to the desktop. He looked at Jake clearly, as if he had understood his question, then with feline gentleness sniffed each of the three open commentaries. Finally, he sniffed at the Bible, carefully pawed at the pages with his good paw, then looked hard at Jake and simply fell onto his side, covering, very nearly, both open pages of the open Bible.

"Well, Petey, that doesn't really help me at all. Kind of hard to see the Scriptures through a cat."

Petey responded with a low growl—not an angry growl but a warm, knowing growl, as if that was his original intention: to hide the Scriptures for now.

"Really?"

Petey rolled onto his back, inviting his stomach to be rubbed. Jake did, still mostly unsure of what a cat might be asking for. But this time he was correct. Petey responded with a loud purring and lifted his front paws as if signaling for a touchdown.

"So I don't need the Bible this time?"

Petey chirped loudly.

"Was that a yes?"

Another catlike chirp.

"Then what do I do? That's sort of my job here, isn't it? To talk about the Bible and all that? That is what pastors do, you know."

Petey responded by rolling again, stood up, and head-butted Jake's chin, purring even louder. Jake scratched behind the cat's ears.

"What? What are you trying to tell me?"

Jake knew that all of this sounded patently ridiculous, but it actually felt almost-to-sort-of normal. Expected. Like Petey knew what he was doing.

It can't hurt to ask. Maybe he does have some answers. He seems like a pretty smart cat.

Petey sat back and with his good paw, reached out, claws retracted, of course, and tapped at Jake's chin. Then the cat moved forward and butted his head into Jake's chest.

"Me? Is that it?"

Petey meowed loudly.

"Really?"

Another loud meow. And it wasn't for food, because Petey had consumed an entire can of beef 'n' liver for breakfast.

"Talk about *me*?"

Petey sat on the Bible and stared, as only a cat can stare, deeply, with conviction, as if he is seeing something, deep and hidden and hardly moving, that only a cat can see.

"I guess I could do that. Talk about how I got here. I would imagine that most of them are wondering why this church and why me. Myself included. That might work. I guess that would be a good way to start. Everyone on the same page. I could add a few verses to make it less about me and more about the Bible—but it would still be a lot about me. I think that could actually work."

Jake smoothed the fur on the cat's head. He could feel Petey move against and into his open palm as he petted him.

"I could do my testimony."

Petey stood up again and walked back to the Bible, circled three times and lay down, keeping his eyes partially open, watching Jake as he turned to the computer and started to type.

I'll just leave off the last few months.

⤬

See. The way of the cat. Let a man discover what he needs to discover and he'll embrace it. If I told him to talk about himself, he wouldn't have believed me. It's not that God wants him to do this or that, specifically. At least not this Sunday. I would like to hear his story. I know the people in the basement would like to hear it. They like stories. Family stories. Jake should just tell his story.

Petey began to purr softly, as if he were self-congratulating a little.

That's the way cats work. Make people think it was their idea.

Symbiotic.

He closed his eyes to the sounds of Jake tapping at the keyboard.

I think that's the right word.

"Tomorrow is the day, Petey," Jake said as they both sat outside on the steps leading to the parsonage part of the church. "First sermon. First time to really start this job."

Petey meowed, obviously in a most reassuring tone.

"I know. I think the sermon is fine. It is a lot about me, but in a small town—family stories are really important."

Petey chirped.

"I know you thought of it first. Thank you, Petey. I appreciate it. A lot."

Petey rolled onto his side, purring, and gratefully accepted Jake's rubbing of his belly.

I think our relationship is starting off just fine.

Petey looked skyward.

Thank you.

Following the second hymn, as the ushers gathered, each with their offering plates at the back of the sanctuary, the door that led from the pastor's office to the platform slowly opened, just a few inches, as if by magic. Despite the small movement, it managed to catch most people's attention.

From that narrow opening, Petey slipped out onto the platform, stared for a moment at the congregation, as if he were not surprised to see them all there—but maybe a little surprised. He then looked at Pastor Jake, neat and tidy in his best suit and tie and newly polished shoes, chirped twice, and sauntered to one of the three padded high-back chairs on the right side of the platform.

Jake had wondered what the chairs were used for. None of the elders mentioned sitting on the platform with him, and so far, during his inaugural service, none had attempted to join him. The cat jumped up onto the middle chair, then sat, regally, as only cats can do, mostly staring at Jake, but keeping a cautious eye on the congregation as well.

A nervous, amused, small roll of laughter followed.

The giant-sized elder, Elder Keilback, made everyone laugh out loud when he announced from the back, "You planning to give that cat his own giving envelopes, Pastor? If he sits up there, I think you should."

Jake, at first, felt a crushing tidal wave of anxiety seeing Petey stroll in, but the laughter—good-natured, it sounded like—quickly diffused that jangly feeling.

"I might," Jake replied. "We'll see what he says about the sermon afterward. Either envelopes or I make sure that door is locked next Sunday."

Another small roll of laughter followed and in that instant, Jake felt his nervousness ebb . . . not disappear, but lessen. Now it was manageable. Earlier, Jake had worried if he would be able to get through the service without making some horrible, unforgiving gaffe.

———⊗⊗⊗———

Well, it was a pretty good sermon, Petey thought as he watched the people slowly make their way out of the church. *Not deep, but heartfelt. That's good. And it sure looked like they all liked it as well. I only saw two people sleeping, and they were old people. I think old people sleep more than others. Like old cats. I once knew*

*a very old cat who slept all the time. Only got up to eat, basically.
And the litter box, of course. But he seemed content. Maybe I'll sleep
more when I get old.*

Jake stood in the back, shaking hands with all who wanted
to shake hands as they left, nodding, speaking a few words
with everyone.

He seems comfortable. Petey wondered if he should wait for
Jake or slip back into the parsonage and wait for him there.

*Here is better. He'll want to know how he did. He'll ask right
away. That's part of his problem. He should do what God says and
not worry about what others think. We'll work on that. That is, if
he's listening to God. I do sense that he doesn't listen all that well.*

After a long interlude, Jake came back up the center aisle,
loosening his tie as he walked.

When he got to the platform, he stopped.

"So how was it, Petey? Did you like it?"

Petey meowed loudly and reared up on his back legs, his
front paws scrabbling in the air, as if pleading to be picked up.
Jake obliged and Petey began to purr loudly.

"It was okay, then? The sermon? Do you think it went well?"

Petey could not purr much louder than he was, but he tried.
He chirped once and then laid his chin on Jake's shoulder.

That should reassure him.

For now, anyhow.

In the absence of another mouse.

———— ∞ ————

The rule had been written into the church constitution three
decades earlier: "Pastors should have every Monday free from
work and free from any particulars related to official church
business, if they so prefer. Another day may be substituted for

Monday, but should not become a regular occurrence unless approved by a three-fifths vote of the elders."

Monday suited Jake just fine. He had had Mondays off at the church in Butler as well.

A few minutes past nine, Jake let Petey outside and walked to the RV. He listened and could hear the television from inside. He tapped at the door.

Tassy opened the door a crack, a pink chenille bathrobe clutched around her neck.

"The robe's from Eleanor," she said before Jake spoke a single word. "My grandmother had one exactly like this. Isn't it a scream?"

Jake wasn't sure if *scream* meant funny or tragically hip and ironic, so he nodded and smiled. "I'm going into town. You want to come along?"

Tassy shook her head. "No, I'm not feeling real well this morning. Maybe a touch of the flu. Or one of those stomach bug things. I'll stay here and have some tea."

"You need anything? Aspirin? Flu medicine?"

Tassy shook her head again. "I don't like to take medicine. I'll have tea and honey. That will help."

"Are you sure? I don't mind stopping."

"No. I'm fine. It's sweet of you to ask. Thanks."

Petey followed him to the truck and hopped up to the seat when Jake opened the door.

Jake didn't really need to go to town, though he was a little low on half-and-half. His coffee consumption had increased since arriving in Coudersport. And he thought he might pay a visit to Emma the Vet, so she could check on Petey's wound.

That's all. Just a checkup. No other reason than that. He was worried about the cat. As any concerned pet owner would be.

The sign outside her office appeared to be at an even steeper angle than it was a week ago. As far as Jake knew, there had been no freeze/thaw cycles in the last seven days.

Maybe someone backed into it.

He looked at the ground around the sign as he got out of the truck, but there were no recent tire marks.

Maybe some local hooligans pushed it, he thought. That's what Pastor Gust had called most everyone under the age of twenty: hooligans. He was not a man to suffer callow youths with much grace.

Petey climbed out of the truck, sniffed the air, and made his way, quite deliberately, up onto the front porch. He sat and meowed loudly. Jake hurried behind him, opened the door, and was greeted by a rumbling series of barks from the rear of the house. At least, he thought they were barks, though they sounded more like "woof-snarfle-woof-cough."

He then heard Emma's voice.

"Winston, pipe down. You keep barking at patients and we won't have any patients, and then you'll see. No more crunchies for you. Out on the street—that's where you'll be."

Emma swept into the waiting room, wearing her doctor's coat, unbuttoned, with a blue T-shirt underneath, her blonde hair pulled back into a ponytail. She may not have been wearing any makeup. The "natural" look often appeared to be totally natural, meaning Jake usually could not tell the difference between none and natural.

Back in Butler, when he was still one-half of a couple, Jake assumed that Barbara Ann Bentley always wore makeup. She would not leave her apartment without carrying a large nylon bag she called a "clutch," which seemed to be jammed with all manner of small jars and tubes and cylinders filled with powders and gels and ointments. The bag rattled when she picked it up. Barbara Ann always looked pretty, even more so when she kept Jake waiting an hour for a dinner date.

"Well, well, well. Petey and the pastor. Another injury? A barber recommendation?"

Jake reached and smoothed his hair flat. He had skipped the haircut last week, and now he was sure his hair had reached the semiscraggly stage, as Pastor Gust often described it. "Get that scraggly hair cut, Wilkerson. This is not some television church where people don't get their hair cut so they can look all hip and cool to the audience. This is a church, okay? A real church. Not some stage version of a church."

"Actually, I'm on my way for a haircut. Are they open on Monday?"

Emma scrunched up her face. "You know, I don't know. Let me call Jeff. Even if he's off, he'll open the shop for you. You are a paying customer, right? American money?"

"I am. No Canadian dollars or euros."

"Good. And I see you brought Petey with you."

Jake had almost forgotten.

"Oh, yes. Sure. Petey. Maybe you could look at his paw. The bandage is getting sort of raggedy, and I thought either it should come off or be replaced."

Emma smiled at him, as if she assumed that Petey's paw was pretty much an excuse for the visit. But Jake couldn't tell for sure, and he was pretty sure that Emma couldn't know for sure his intentions, so Jake may very well have been in the office with a semivalid reason.

"Sure. I'll take a look. C'mon Petey. You know the way."

Petey and Jake followed Emma into the same examination room as before. Petey jumped up onto the table and sat down, holding his bandaged paw up.

JIM KRAUS

"A special cat you have here, Pastor Jake," she said, and took out a small pair of bandage scissors and began to snip away. She swabbed what remained of the bandage with alcohol and it slipped off with ease. She took a towel, then squirted his paw down with water. She bent to look closely at the bottom.

"Healed up very nicely. No infection. No swelling. Hardly even a scar. So if Petey wants to get into paw modeling, there won't be anything holding him back."

"He'll be relieved to know that . . . Emma. Or should I call you Dr. Grainger? What's the proper protocol?"

"Emma is fine. I have never really gotten used to being Dr. Grainger. Makes me sound stuffy. Or old. Or both."

"Okay, then. Emma."

Emma scratched Petey's neck and he began to purr.

"I hear Petey made an appearance at church this week."

Word does travel fast in a small town.

"He did. He pulled open the back door and sat on one of the chairs and watched me talk."

"I heard the congregation liked it."

"Well, they all laughed. I hope it went okay. It's hard to know if the message was appreciated or not."

"I'm sure they all loved it. Your predecessor at the church was no ball of fire, if you ask me."

"Did you ever hear him? Did you ever visit the church?"

"No. But he tried to sell me insurance just before he left town. I know insurance isn't the most exciting subject, but he even seemed bored with it. I know I was."

"Did you buy any?"

"No. I have a cousin who's an agent. Have to buy from him or I would be drummed out of the Grainger clan."

Jake stopped talking. Often, he felt at a loss for words or subjects. This was a long conversation for him, and since the other participant was an attractive woman, the right words felt more distant than ever.

Petey broke the silence with a loud meow. He then flopped onto his side and rolled onto his back.

"He does that a lot," Jake said.

"A sign of being comfortable. When a cat shows its stomach, it means that it is feeling very much at ease and there is no threat nearby. It's a sign of trust."

"So . . . he trusts me, then? Or you? Or us?"

"I guess. He does seem like a very intuitive cat."

Jake liked being trusted—even if it was by a cat.

"Jake . . . Pastor Jake . . . what do I call you? What's protocol?" Emma asked.

"Jake is fine."

"Okay, then. Jake," she said, her hand gently scratching Petey's stomach. "I know you will think this is horribly forward—and maybe it is. But would you like to see a movie this weekend? Friday? Your church doesn't have any rules against movies, does it? And please don't think I'm doing this to appease my mother—who, unfortunately, you already met."

Jake was indeed surprised, very pleasantly surprised, almost shocked, really, and he hoped that his face did not register just how surprised.

"No. No rules against it. It's like, a regular movie, right?"

"Sure. We actually have a movie theater in town. I think it's the only functioning theater within fifty miles, so you're in luck."

"Okay. That would be nice."

"Okay."

That's when Petey rolled over, stood up, meowed once, jumped off the table, and headed toward the front door, as if to say his work here was done.

"I guess we're done," Jake said as he followed the cat. "What time on Friday?"

"Every movie starts at 7:30. Come around 7:00?"

"Okay, then," Jake said, feeling a lot lighter than he did when he entered.

⸎

As Petey exited the examination room, he stopped, all but sliding on the polished wood floors. Standing in the middle of the waiting room was a large, snorfling, heavy-breathing, overweight bulldog with unappealing breath. Petey's nose wrinkled as he caught a good whiff of his scent, or odor, more appropriately.

Egads, dog, don't you ever bathe?

He could hear Jake and Dr. Emma talking in the room that he just left.

Are you a mean dog? Or just a stupid dog? Those are the only kinds of dogs I know.

Winston sniffed loudly, as if he had adenoid issues. He attempted to grin.

A good-natured dog. As long as you know your place—and your place is . . . out of my way.

The dog lurched backward and sat heavily on his haunches, his back legs splayed out in multiple directions, or so it seemed.

Why would an obviously intelligent woman person like Dr. Emma be associated with a . . . dog? No offense, dog, but you two do not seem to go together. She should have a cat. A good cat.

Then Petey tilted his head, as if truly puzzled.

Maybe there aren't enough "good" cats to go around. That means humans, even smart humans like Dr. Emma, have to settle for a dog. That has to be it. There are so few smart cats that there are not enough to go around.

112

Dr. Emma came out of the examination room first.

"Oh, I see you've met Winston."

Winston? That's much too refined a name for such a slobbery dog, Dr. Emma. Maybe something like Puddle Accident or Smells-like-Raccoon. Those would be more appropriate.

"Winston's been with me since I graduated from college. I got him just before I started veterinarian school. He had been abandoned."

No wonder.

"He's sweet and very harmless. And it seems like he and Petey get along famously."

Petey stared up at Jake and meowed. It sounded like a warning.

If you and Dr. Emma start something—like a relationship—the dog has to go. Okay? Promise?

Jake bent down and picked Petey up.

"Petey, I don't know what you want, but you're not going to stay here and play with Winston. We'll arrange a play date later, okay?"

No! You're not listening! No!

———⟨⟩———

Jimbo whistled as he measured out coffee for the Mr. Coffee. He was in a good mood this morning. Lloyd Cummins had called him on Sunday afternoon and asked if he could come to work on Monday. "I got at least three or four weeks of work signed up. I can't promise anything, but I bet we'll have work through the summer, anyhow."

Betty came into the kitchen, also whistling. It appeared that she was in a better mood than her husband. She filled the toaster oven with four slices of white bread, and gathered the jelly jar and the slippery yellow tub of almost-butter from the refrigerator. "Doctor says to stay away from butter, Jimbo. You gotta listen to what he says."

Betty took two plates from the cabinet. "You make enough coffee for your Thermos?" she asked.

"I did. But the job's in town today, so I could always run to McDonald's if I run out."

"Where's the job?"

"Mondock's Garage. I guess they been losing water pressure. We're going to drill deeper and put in a new line. Couple of days."

The toaster oven dinged, and Betty spread each slice with a fat, thumb-sized glob of the almost-butter. "Doesn't taste like butter unless you use a whole lot of it," she had once declared.

The two of them sat at the kitchen table, the dog staring at Jimbo, and ate in silence.

"So did you think the new pastor did okay?"

Jimbo was reluctant to commit until he discovered how his wife felt about the sermon and the pastor's demeanor on the platform.

"Okay, I guess. The cat was funny. I got a kick out of that."

"Yeah, that was funny. But . . . I don't know. He should have locked that door or something. Shouldn't have cats in the service. I think that might start something. Like people bringing their dogs to church. You know who would bring their dog if the pastor said it was okay? Alice Kamarski. That's who. I swear she would adopt that dog legally if she could."

Jimbo narrowed his eyes, as if thinking deep and hard.

"I bet he won't say it's okay for animals to be in church. It was kind of an accident."

Betty stirred her coffee for much longer than necessary. "I don't want animals in my church. That's all I'm saying. And somebody should do something to make sure it isn't the start of something. Don't want people laughing at us. Bad enough he needed a haircut. No sense in starting up with animals. Next thing you know, we'll have drums up onstage with some sort of rock guitar music. That I can't take. That's all I'm saying."

Jimbo was just about to remark that whenever his wife said, "That's all I'm saying," it was never all she said. He looked at his watch and smiled. "I have to get going. Don't want to be late."

⟨∞⟩

Big Dave added three sugars to his coffee, already pale with two French Vanilla cream packets. The trio of unwrapped Drake's Crumb Cakes waited, so his breakfast was nearly complete.

The electronic bell chimed and Big Dave looked up. Carl Miller, one of his regular customers, hurried in and mixed two kinds of coffee together in a large plastic cup. He snapped on the lid and laid a five-dollar bill on the counter.

"Heard your church was interesting yesterday," Carl said as he wadded up his change and stuffed it into his pocket.

"It was kind of interesting," Big Dave said with a grin. "Never had a cat in church before. And you know what? That cat just sat in that chair during the whole sermon and looked like he was listening to every word. It was the dog-blamedest thing. Or cat-blamedest, I guess."

Carl sipped at his coffee.

"When he starts inviting dogs up front, let me know. Maybe I'll bring old Cutter with me. That dog could use a dose of manners, you know?"

"I do know that, Carl. I do. And I'll take you up on that. You should come and check it out. I bet you'd like this new guy. Seems real down-to-earth. Like a normal fellow, you know?"

115

"You can't be serious. Me? In church?" Carl said, his hand on the door. "Your church got insurance for getting hit by lightning?"

"I'm pretty sure we do. Let me know, and you can sit next to me. Okay? I like living dangerously."

Carl stopped, then looked back.

"Maybe. We'll see. If a cat can go. Maybe."

The field of plastic pennants flittered in the wind, a combination of hissing and crinkling, amplified by a thousand multicolored triangles. When the wind was just right, the pennants nearly blotted out the sun on the western side of the car lot.

Dan Rummel had his arm around the shoulder of a potential customer of Honest Dan's Used Kar Emporium.

"This is one honey of a car. Nearly mint. I had the new pastor of that church down on Dry Run Road come in, and he was giving it a serious once-over."

"The one with the cat?" said the customer, who might have been named Smet or Smote—Dan wasn't that sure he heard correctly.

He brightened. "One and the same, sir. I tell you, he was pretty interested in it. So if you're thinking of making an offer . . . well, no time like right now. Get a jump on the competition."

"And the cat just sat there and listened the whole time? Like he knew what was going on?"

Dan steered Mr. Smet or Smote toward the office. "He did. Like he was some sort of angel watching over things, you know? That's what I thought. Like a cat angel."

The three bells from the door sounded as Dan and Mr. Smet/Smote entered the small office.

"Would you be interested in financing or buying it outright with cash?"

———⊗⊗⊗———

Petey slipped out of the parsonage and stepped into a dense layer of early morning fog. He stood for a long moment, on the top step, just sniffing.

I smell a fox. They stink worse than dogs. Must have gone through the field last night. A lot of mice there—that's why.

Jake had busied himself that morning with a third cup of coffee and buried himself in a commentary on Ephesians. Petey thought it wise of him to now focus on the Scriptures, kind of like those TV preachers do. The church now knew his background. They felt comfortable with his story. That's what Petey surmised. He wasn't a mind reader, but the people of the church appeared satisfied and happy, most of them. There were a few that Petey could not tell how they were feeling. Angry? Maybe. Concerned? Maybe.

His repaired paw remained tender but not painful.

He walked to the big house on wheels and stood on the steps that led into the middle of it. He meowed as loudly as he could while tapping at the door with his right paw—not scratching really, but tapping.

The door opened just an inch or two.

"Petey! What are you doing out there? You want to come in for a while?"

Petey chirped three times and slipped inside.

This is big. Real big. Like a house. With wheels. And a thing to steer it with. That is so cool.

———⊗⊗⊗———

Tassy watched Petey as he walked around the living room. He jumped up on the sofa and stared out the window, back toward the church.

He chirped softly, looking directly at Tassy.

"I know. It's really nice, isn't it? This is the nicest place I have ever lived in. Absolutely the nicest."

She carefully carried a half-cup of tea to the sofa. She had been extra, extra careful since she first stepped foot in the RV not to spill anything, not to damage anything, and to keep everything picked up and as clean as could be. She realized this was an unforeseen opportunity and something she did not want to damage by being slothful and unkempt.

"Now, Randolph, he was a perfect slob," she said to Petey. "Never picked up anything. His idea of cleaning a room was to take a snow shovel and shovel away the empty cups and food wrappers. The jerk."

Petey waited until she was settled, with her teacup within reach. He scrambled off the back of the cushion and made his way into her lap.

She's very soft. And she has small hands. Very gentle. I like that in a person. Jake's good, but this person is better at petting.

"Aww, Petey, of course, I'll pet you."

And she commenced to doing just that as Petey settled in and closed his eyes.

I didn't anticipate this person would be here. Maybe I wasn't supposed to know about her. But she is nice. The funny thing is, every time I'm with her, I want to protect her. Not usually a cat thing. Dogs protect better. They are bigger and stupider and bark louder. But cats can do almost anything. Right?

Tassy hummed as she petted the cat, an almost tuneless melody. But a pleasant tune, nonetheless.

I wonder how I am going to do that? If that fox shows up—well, to be honest, I'm not sure I can beat a fox. They look like scrawny dogs. With big teeth. But I would try. I would have to try. That much I know.

Tassy took another sip of her tea.

"Do you think they'll let me stay here, Petey? It is awfully nice of Vern and Eleanor to let me use this. Eleanor is so nice to me. Like I wish my mother would have been. But I'm not sure about all this church stuff. I guess there is a God and all that. But if there is, he hasn't done me all that many favors. Well, that is, up 'til now. Is that what this is, Petey? Like God doing me a favor? Do you think he'll keep it up? Or will I have to . . . go to church and sing those weird songs and all of that? Does God want me to do that? I guess I could if it means staying here longer. You know, just 'til I figure things out. Does that sound normal to you, Petey?"

Petey opened his eyes and looked back at Tassy. He hadn't been paying all that much attention to what she was saying, but she seemed to calm down as she talked on.

He meowed back to her in his best reassuring cat voice.

I'm pretty sure she'll understand me. She appears to be more intuitive than most.

"You mean that, Petey?"

He chirped again.

"Well, I guess I can hope for that, then. I can hope."

Jimbo felt awkward pushing a grocery cart. He had felt awkward pushing a baby carriage—when his kids were small and that was more than twenty years ago—and a grocery cart felt the same way. He didn't like it when Betty sent him to the store. He didn't like grocery lists. He didn't like trying to remember where everything was. And to make it worse, each grocery store in Coudersport was arranged differently. So the olives in aisle four of one store would be in aisle six in another. And then if Betty just wrote down olives, Jimbo would be in a real pickle. What kind of olives? Green? Black? With those little red things in them?

Too confusing by half.

And since he was told that he had to go to Doug's, it made him even less happy. The Doug inside, Doug Olmer, who always seemed to be there, would talk his ear off. And Jimbo had heard most of the stories before.

But Betty said they needed milk—the BigValu brand, 2% type, a gallon—which she wrote down on the back of a used envelope from the bank, and cookies. She said that Jimbo could pick out the kind he wanted since she didn't eat cookies and he needed them for his lunch. Now that he was working, he went through a lot of cookies.

Doug Olmer was there in the front, leaning on a broom, when Jimbo wheeled his grocery cart inside. He thought about just carrying the groceries in his arms, but he had tried that once. It hadn't gone well at all. He'd dropped a dozen eggs on the floor, and while they didn't make him pay for them, he felt embarrassed for a long time afterward. So he had to use the cart.

Doug waved to him as he entered.

"Hey, Jimbo, the Missus send you shopping tonight?"

Jimbo tried to smile in return. "Just a couple of things. Now that I'm working again, I need to be packing lunches."

"Well, we have a sale on ham salad this week. Make it right here in the store. You should try a sample. On the house, of course."

"Maybe I will."

Jimbo couldn't remember if he liked their ham salad or not. He would have to try a sample to make sure.

"I hear your new pastor is doing well. You know he shops here, too."

"I didn't know that."

"He does. He came in the second day he was in town. Nice fellow, it seems. Personable. Very pleasant young man. He preach good?"

Jimbo wasn't a good one to evaluate preachers. He would never admit it to anyone, but he did not pay much attention to the sermons. If they told a joke or said something about themselves, that he would listen to. But once they started with the "thees" and "thous" and "shalts," well, Jimbo started to count the number of windowpanes in the sanctuary.

"He does preach good, Doug. I think so. He can be funny. I like that. He tells a good story. Keeps your attention, you know."

Doug had a faraway look in his eyes. "I wish our guy would tell a joke now and then. Liven things up."

Jimbo stopped walking. "Maybe you should come and hear him sometime."

Doug looked around, as if their conversation might be overheard. "His cat came to church, right? The one he drives around in his truck."

"I guess. Seems to like to listen to him preach."

Doug walked the few steps closer to Jimbo.

"Maybe I will. Visit your church. Just don't tell anyone, okay? Maybe I'll slip in and check it out. Like going to another grocery store to check out their specials."

"You do that? Really?"

"Sure. Every grocer does it. How else do you stay up-to-date?"

Jimbo didn't know an answer to that, and wheeled his cart away, heading straight for the deli counter and a sample of the ham salad. All of a sudden, he was hungry for a ham salad and American cheese sandwich on white bread with extra mayonnaise.

6

The second Wednesday of every month marked the official elders' meeting at the Church of the Open Door. The church had functioned under three different names since its founding in 1932, starting off as a member of a small group of Anabaptist churches, then as a member of a small group of German Reformed churches, and for the last two-plus decades, as an independent church with no affiliation to any specific denomination.

The church printed and professed a Statement of Faith, but the document was generic enough and broad enough that virtually anyone who called themselves Christian might be comfortable with it.

And Jake knew, from his time in the church in Butler, it was not the big theological statements that usually divided churches—it was the infighting about who was in control of selecting the carpet color and allowing, or not allowing, "rock-and-roll" music in church. Those were the real divisive dilemmas facing an independent church these days.

After the first seven minutes of his first-ever elders' meeting at this church, his new church, Jake realized there was a three-way power sharing, of sorts, in the church. There were three long-time church families, dating back to when the cornerstone was laid, and those families represented the majority of the church members who had at least some tangential longstanding familial relationship to one of the elders.

Jake also determined that, at least for now, there did not seem to be any simmering, mine-laden issues that would blow up and lead to fistfights at the elders' meetings. Whenever Jake read through magazines aimed at pastors, he was amazed to read of the battles in some churches—much like one is startled to see a car accident on the side of the road. Or a hot air balloon flying overhead. Or both. At the same time.

Jake also learned, at the very outset, this specific elders' meeting would not go late.

As Wilbur Brookings, head of the elder board, gaveled the meeting to order, using a metal travel-size coffee cup, he announced, "We're going to keep this short, right? Bass and trout season starts tomorrow, and I plan on getting to my spot by sunrise. Okay? Any questions about that? And no, I am not telling any of you where my secret fishing spot is. So don't ask."

Jake watched a lot of nodding and murmuring, but no one dissented, or pressed for directions.

"We have any old business?"

The rest of the elders looked back and forth at each other, as if they were expecting someone to speak up. No one did.

"Okay. Any new business? Jimbo, what about a treasurer's report?"

Jimbo squirmed a little.

"There's no report, Wil," Jimbo replied. "I left the bank stuff at home. But the last time I looked—'bout a week ago—we had nearly three thousand dollars in the bank. And the fund to fix the roof and steeple had a couple of thousand in it. Bills been paid for the month. I got the new pastor on that automatic deposit thing from First National. Don't have to make out a check or anything. Everything is okay, I guess."

"Good. Any questions?"

There were no questions.

"Hey, Pastor Jake, did you meet with the Sunday school people? They've been talking about doing some sort of summer thing out here for the kids. Been talking about it for a couple of years."

Pastor Jake cleared his throat. "We're supposed to meet tomorrow evening. I think a VBS would be something we should try. It appears that there are enough kids that age in the church."

"You take notes and let us know. We're bound to hear about it. But take notes anyhow. Okay?"

Jake nodded and scribbled a line in his notebook.

"You get the list of sick people?"

"I did," Jake said. "Nobody in the hospital, but I'll call those on the list—ask if they want a visit."

"Good. I hate visiting sick people," Wilbur announced. "They give me the willies. Coughing and shivering and all that. Old people with skin like paper. Tissues all over the floor. Yuck. You don't mind going, do you, Pastor?"

"No. I enjoy visiting. Honestly. It will give me a chance to connect with people."

"Good."

It was obvious to Jake that everyone around the table agreed with Wilbur on this one—that none of them liked being around sick people.

"You gonna let that cat come to church next Sunday?"

Jake had been ready for the question. "No. I'll make sure the door is locked. I don't know why I didn't do it last week."

"Pastor, the cat being here was okay. I heard a lot of people in town yakking about that cat during the week. I would bet, if I were a betting man, and I'm not, 'cept if the lottery gets more than $100 million, but I would bet that we get some visitors next week. I heard one lady say . . . well, it was my cousin, Irene . . . but still, Irene said that if our church was open to having a cat on the platform, it just may be worth her making a visit. And this from a woman who hasn't been inside a church since her dad passed, and that was nearly forty years ago. Some pastor said something about how her dad drank too much and she never let it go. So . . . if the cat shows up, let it show up. It would tickle her pink if she saw that. She just might come to see if it happens."

Jake took a quick glance around the table. The pro-cat sentiment looked like it was shared by three-quarters of the group. The other one-quarter looked pained, as if they were getting just about fed up with these one-man pronouncements by the head elder, and when they got elected, things would change, by George.

But in the meantime, no one said anything to the negative.

"Well, I won't chain the cat up, but I will lock the door this week."

"Okay by me, Pastor. And by the way, we all liked your sermon. Nice to know about you. You say your mom is a single mom. She still around here?"

"She lives in Meadville now, with her sister."

"Well, if she ever visits, you let us know. We'll plan a meal or something. A barbeque, maybe. She'll visit, won't she? She can travel and all that, can't she?"

"She can. And I'll let you know. She said she would wait a month or so 'til I get settled in."

"Good. I'll have a freezer full of trout by then. She like grilled trout?"

"I . . . I don't know. I do, though."

Jake wasn't sure if he'd ever eaten grilled trout before, but he was certain he had trout in a restaurant once, and he must have liked it, so grilled would be acceptable. "Well, we'll see what the weather is like when she comes. I really like grilled trout."

Wilbur sat there, his face showing that he was imagining a plate full of fresh trout, and maybe roasted corn on the cob dipped in butter.

He shook his head.

"Anything else? Anybody got anything else to talk about?"

No one spoke.

"Okay, then. Pastor, you pray and we're done. You're not one of those twenty-minute pray-ers, are you? Two pastors ago—that Green fellow—remember him? He prayed once for forty-five minutes straight."

There were smiles and murmurs of agreement.

"No. I'll be brief."

"Good man, Pastor Jake. Good man."

—⟋∞⟍—

Later that night, Petey lay down on the center of the bed, in his spot, with a sigh, as if he, too, were glad the evening was over. Jake reached and patted his head a few times.

"Petey, it is nice to have you here. Really nice. I never knew what having a pet was like."

Petey bristled, just a little, at the mention of the word *pet*, but settled back down again.

"So thanks for showing up," Jake said. "I appreciate it."

Petey closed his eyes.

As if you don't know who sent me.

—⟋∞⟍—

Petey tugged hard at the kitchen door with one paw. He'd noticed recently that most of the doors in the house didn't close all that tightly. Unless the door was slammed hard, the latch didn't really set solidly—so a hard head-butt would force open most of the inside doors. A good tug with one paw would pop open the outside ones. Jake was already up, puttering around in the kitchen, so he must not have noticed when Petey tugged the door and slipped out.

I love mornings like this. A chorus of birds, the breeze rustling leaves against each other, the scrabbling of mice in the field. A glorious creation, indeed. And since I have had my breakfast, I am most content. Jake seems to be doing fine so far. Maybe he doesn't need me as much as I thought he did. I suppose I could have been wrong. But that doesn't seem right, does it? Me being wrong, that is. That doesn't seem right.

Petey sniffed about the steps carefully.

No foxes last night.

He sniffed again.

Raccoons. Those animals I don't like. They're always fighting with each other, and their squalling gets my fur standing on end. I don't see what they have to fight about, and if they can't get along with each other, then they shouldn't travel together.

Petey made his way to the house on wheels and meowed outside the door.

He waited for a long time, then meowed again.

That's odd. She usually lets me in right away.

Petey eyed a narrow ledge under the window.

I think I can make that. Maybe.

He bent down into a crouch, wiggled his back hips a few times, mentally gauging the effort and the jump that it would take. He laid his ears flat against his head. After a moment of preparation, he pushed off mightily and landed, with inches to spare, on the narrow sill.

He meowed louder, his best let-me-in meow. He heard rustling from inside, then saw Tassy, holding her robe together with one hand and a tissue in the other.

"Okay, Petey," she said, "I heard you. Come on in."

She slid the window open and Petey hopped in, appearing a bit annoyed he had been forced to take such drastic action to visit.

Tassy sniffed and dabbed at her eyes, then sort of folded herself onto the couch, hugging her knees to her chest, offering Petey no place to sit. He jumped up beside her and sniffed at her hand.

She's crying. Women humans do that more often than men humans, I think. Cats don't cry. I know I can feel sad, but I can't cry like that. Crying. That is a very odd manifestation of emotions. I think I heard that on that radio station.

He reached up and put his paw on her forearm.

Why is she crying? Humans are so complicated. She has food and water and a place to stay. I should ask her.

He tried to form his meow as a question. He wasn't really good at asking questions, since there wasn't all that much he didn't know. But in situations like this, a question was in order. He tilted his head at the end of the meow. He had seen people do that when they were asking about things.

"I don't know, Petey. All of a sudden, everything seems to be wrong. What am I doing here? I should just go back to Philadelphia and make the best of it. No one seems to care that I'm gone, apparently. My mother sure doesn't. Randolph doesn't. No one here really knows me. So what am I doing here?"

She sniffed very loudly and wiped at her eyes with the sleeve of the pink chenille robe.

Petey moved closer and placed his front paws on her arm and extended his face closer to hers.

What would an angel do in this situation? Petey wondered. *I would imagine he would say something comforting. Or do something comforting.*

Petey tried to climb into her lap, and Tassy uncoiled herself and let the cat sit on top of her.

This always makes people feel better. A purring cat.

Tassy began to pet Petey, stroking his back and head just the way he liked it.

And they feel better when they pet a cat. That's a proven medical fact. They said it on the television. It makes blood pressure go down. I'm not sure what blood pressure is and why it should go down, but if the people in the television said so, it must be true. And they said it's a good thing.

"Petey, what am I going to do? Pastor Jake has been so nice. Eleanor has been so nice. Even Vern seems nicer."

Petey purred louder, his front paws making little kneading motions on Tassy's stomach. He was very careful not to extend his claws very far. He did not want to inadvertently hurt the young woman.

"I don't have any family here. I don't know what to do. I shouldn't stay here . . . should I?"

Petey was still mulling what it was that an angel could do that he couldn't. When he heard the pain in her voice, he simply acted and did not think about it. He stood up on his rear paws and placed his front paws on Tassy's shoulder. He then nuzzled against her neck, his cold, wet nose against her skin.

She has to hug me back. That will make her less sad.

And after a moment, Tassy did indeed hug the cat in return, and leaned her head onto his.

"Well, maybe I can stay a little while longer. But's that's all. Okay, Petey? That's all."

Petey did not move even though hugging a human was an odd position for a cat.

A little while is all I need to convince her to stay here longer.

He heard her sniff once more and then lean back. Petey also leaned back and returned to that soft spot on her lap.

There are times I really wish I could smile.

Irene gestured with a wide sweep of her left hand, the phone firmly clenched in her right.

"He said it was a CAT, Mom. Not a rat. THE PASTOR'S CAT!"

Talking with her mother, Norma Mahon, grew more and more exhausting. Norma had been a resident of the Sweden Valley Manor in Coudersport for more than a decade, but her hearing had been failing for even longer than that. She refused to even consider a hearing aid. "They make you look like an old person," she would shout back when it was suggested. Irene, at least for the first few years of Norma's fading audio abilities, would shout back, "But you *are* old!"

Irene had been attempting to tell her mother about the cat and Pastor Jake and how funny she thought it was. She was actually going to go to church there Sunday just to see if they let the cat in again.

"I would love to see that!" Irene shouted. "Maybe this pastor is a regular person. A REGULAR PERSON."

After ten minutes of shouting, Irene had gone hoarse, and told her mother that someone was at the door, just to get off the phone.

Maybe this new guy could visit her and talk some sense into her about a hearing aid. If he lets cats into church, he must be different.

Jake broke from his work on the sermon a few minutes past 11:30 a.m. He thought he had the passage well in hand, but the more he worked on it, the less comfortable he felt.

It's not because I'm not trying. And it has nothing to do with faith. It just takes work.

He decided a change of scenery would help clear his thoughts. Petey was sound asleep on the windowsill in the office and did not wake up when Jake grabbed his keys from the hook in the kitchen.

He stopped at the RV and tapped at the door.

"I'm going into town for lunch," he said. "Would you like to come along? Get out for a while."

"Where to?" Tassy asked. "I don't have a lot of money."

"I was thinking McDonald's. And I can treat you to lunch."

"No. I don't like to do that. I have enough for McDonald's. And that sounds good. But let me make the bed first. If Eleanor stopped by and saw a messy bedroom . . . well, I just wouldn't want to disappoint her like that."

Soon enough, Tassy climbed into the truck and fastened the seat belt.

"What about Petey? Doesn't he want to go?"

"He was sleeping. Let sleeping cats lie, I always say."

Tassy scrunched up her face.

"I've heard that before. What's it mean? And isn't it with dogs instead?"

Jake nodded. "It is. Usually. But I don't have a dog, so I have to use a cat. And it means that if there is possible trouble out there—like a sleeping dog—you don't wake it up to find out for sure. You just let it sleep."

"Oh. Now it makes sense."

Tassy rolled the window down and the wind tousled her hair, a hundred delicate wisps dancing around her face like a spherical halo. "Do they have a newspaper in this town?"

"They do. The *Potter Leader-Enterprise*."

"That's a funny name for a paper."

"Because of it being Potter County, I think."

"Oh. That makes sense. Does it have ads for jobs and stuff like that?" Tassy asked.

"I'm sure it does."

"Could we find a copy? I need to look for a job. I can't stay in their RV forever."

"Probably have a newspaper stand at the McDonald's," Jake said as he pulled in. Jake ordered a Big Mac meal; Tassy ordered a single burger and a small fry. Plus a cup of tea with lots of honey.

They found a booth and as Tassy unwrapped her food, she looked up at Jake. "Can I ask you a personal question?"

"Sure. I don't have any secrets," Jake responded, hoping he told the lie well.

"You're not from around here, are you? Where did you grow up?"

"No. I grew up in Pittsburgh. Not downtown, but east of the city. In Shadyside. A nice place."

"Then why are you here? This is sort of out in the middle of nowhere, isn't it? That's what you told me when we first met, wasn't it?" Tassy nibbled at each fry carefully and precisely.

"They needed a pastor."

"I bet lots of churches need pastors, don't they?"

"Maybe," Jake replied. He hoped he did not look uncomfortable. "But I guess I see this as a challenge."

"Did . . . like, God tell you to come here? I heard other people talking about how God told them to do this or that and then they do it and everything works out or they get healed or some sort of miracle happens. You know—those church pastors on television. So what I'm asking is, did God tell you to come here? To Coudersport and all that? Did you hear his voice or see a sign or have a dream or something like that?"

Jake took a large bite of hamburger and held up a finger indicating that he had to stop talking and chew. And he hoped he could come up with a coherent answer.

"Well . . . he didn't really do that. Not like a voice from the sky," Jake explained.

"Then he didn't make you come here? You picked it out on your own?"

He dragged a trio of fries through a dollop of ketchup. He shrugged. "I don't know. Though I am sure that if God didn't want me here, he wouldn't have let me come."

Tassy tilted her head, like she was hearing an odd ratcheting noise.

"Okay. I guess. I'm here because I got tossed out of a car by a really stupid ex-boyfriend. I just wonder how other people get to where they're going and how they know once they got there if it's the right place to be. Because I don't know if I'm supposed to be here or not. I can't tell. I keep thinking people will find out the truth about me and make me leave. I'm afraid of being . . . you know . . . left on my own. And without knowing what to do next. Not having hope is hard. You know what I mean, Pastor Jake?"

Jake nodded.

More than you will ever know, Tassy. More than you will ever know.

As Jake and Tassy sat in McDonald's, having a most unexpected existential discussion, in a booth across the restaurant perched a clutch of older ladies: one of them the mother of Emma Grainger, Veterinarian. Without being obvious, she kept glancing at them, noticing how the young woman ate with the delicacy of a songbird and how Jake laughed and tilted his head back when he did.

She then slipped out her old flip phone from her purse, which was resting in her lap as she ate, and dialed a familiar number. She leaned in closer to the table and turned her back to the rest of the room.

"Do you know who's having lunch at McDonald's? Yes. In the middle of the day. And do you know who's with him?"

She waited a moment.

"Well, I don't either," she said with exasperation. "That's why I'm calling you."

∞∞∞

Wilbur Brookings sat in his office at the very back end of the Tri-County Rural Electric Cooperative. It was the biggest office in the building and the only office without a single window. Wilbur tacked up a series of outdoor posters, along with maps indicating the electrical grid as well as the major transmission lines that snaked across Potter County.

He had gotten through half the pile of incoming reports from the weekend.

As general manager, Wilbur had many job responsibilities, very few of them he actually enjoyed. He started out as a linesman, working on transmission pylons. That was a job he loved, but he was promoted out of it after only a few years.

He stirred his coffee, in a blue Tri-County Co-op mug, and stared at one of his posters—a large trout, leaping out of the water in pursuit of a small mayfly. He put his chin in his palm and his elbow on the desk.

What did Pastor Jake say Sunday? I told myself I was going to remember it. Something about working.

He wondered if his wife would remember. He wondered if Jimbo might recall it—he seemed to have a good memory. He tried to remind himself that at the next elders' meeting he should bring up the possibility of taping the sermons.

Up until now, I wouldn't have bothered. But the new guy has something to say. And I haven't taken notes since high school. But I might listen to a tape. How much could that cost? A couple hundred bucks for a tape recorder? Do they still make tape recorders? Maybe it is all on digital stuff now. So it should be even cheaper. We should look into it.

Oh, now I remember. He said it was from Matthew, I think. Something about doing small things well, with great love—and that would please God.

Well, I'm doing small things well here. I hope God is pleased with the work. Maybe I just need to change my attitude. Maybe that's what he was trying to get us to understand. Could be.

He drew in a deep breath, and then began to work through the second half of the weekly reports.

"If I get done early, I'll take a walk down to Kaytee's for lunch. That will be my reward."

Jake pulled up to the veterinarian's office a few minutes before 7:00. He prided himself on his punctuality. Actually, his on-time standard was at least ten minutes early. He had never liked to hurry, not even as a child. He would always be the first child at the bus stop for school. Always.

He was also early getting ready for this evening.

Not the most fashionable dresser, Jake spent an inordinate amount of time this evening standing in front of the mirror in the bathroom. He had tried on, and had discarded, three shirts, and had settled on a sort of quarter-zip-up sweater-shirt that Barbara Ann told him he looked good in. And he wore a pair of dark, almost-black jeans, with a relatively new pair of black slip-on shoes.

Petey had watched it all while lying in the short hallway that led to the bathroom, carefully observing Jake and his pre-date ministrations. He'd chirped softly every now and again, as if making kind but condescending comments on Jake's obsessiveness. He sat on each shirt, in succession, as Jake discarded them.

"It has been a long time since I've been on a date," Jake explained to the cat. "Even if this may not be as much of a date as most dates are. I know. I know. Emma is being friendly and knows I am new in town—so it's sort of like a Welcome Wagon date. Not a real, potentially romantic date."

Jake tried not to think about that aspect of his life. The last romance did not end well, and that brought out his cautious, anxious nature.

"You open yourself up, Petey, and bad things happen, you know? I shouldn't have been so candid with Barbara Ann. I knew it was a mistake when I started talking about all of that. But I expected her to understand, not to tell other people."

Jake had run his hand through his hair. People with thick hair didn't always need a comb or a brush. Jeff the Barber had done a good job with it, and the result was a cross between tousled and controlled—just the right amount of both.

He'd smiled at himself in the mirror.

"This is as good as it is going to get."

He parked in Emma's driveway, making sure the passenger door was even with the sidewalk.

Do I just go inside and call for her? Is there a private entrance? Do I have a cell phone number for her?

Emma appeared at the side of the house, making his worries for naught.

"Hi!" she called out as she walked toward him. "I forgot to tell you to ring the bell on the side door. Unless you have Petey along and need a quick checkup."

"No, it's just me tonight. I gave Petey the number for Domino's Pizza and a twenty-dollar bill. He should be fine."

Emma stopped and laughed with gusto. She was in jeans and some sort of silkish, white blouse, with a paisley scarf around her neck, her hair pulled back with two gold pins.

"Does Coudersport even have a Domino's?" Jake asked.

"No," Emma replied. "Closest one is in Port Allegheny, I think, and that's like forty miles from here."

Jake thought Emma looked very nice.

"So what's the movie tonight?" Jake asked. "I was going to look but forgot all about it until this evening. I wasn't sure if the theater had a website either."

"They do. And the movie . . . I forget the title. The latest explosion-filled epic about mutant machines taking over the earth. I think. Someone said there's a lot of action, and all the dialogue could be written on a three-by-five note card."

"Oh, so this is an intellectual movie? I don't like to think that much at the movies."

For a second, Emma took him seriously, but then realized he was being funny and she smiled back at him.

"Jake, you had me scared for a second. I have known guys who would have said just that without the slightest hint of irony."

Jake opened the truck door.

"And they would have no idea what *irony* meant, either," she added.

The Coudersport Theater was a small jewel box of a theater, appearing much like it must have looked back when it was built in the 1920s.

"This is amazing," Jake said as they walked to their seats. "I had no idea it was this beautiful."

"'An unexpected pleasure,' some travel critic wrote. And they use real butter on the popcorn," Emma added.

"Then it doesn't matter what the movie is," Jake replied. "You had me at 'real butter.'"

<hr/>

Petey nudged hard at the kitchen door and after the third tug, it squealed open.

I wonder if I can get Jake to install one of those little doors for animals.

The door closed behind him, and Petey made his way across the graveled lot to the house on wheels. He walked slowly on the gravel; there were lots of sharp angles that hurt if he stepped hard.

He meowed at the door, and Tassy hurried to open it.

"Petey," she cried. "How did you know I needed company tonight?"

I know these things, Petey said to himself. *I am a good cat.*

Tassy retreated to the couch and patted at the cushion next to her.

"Come on. Come on up."

I'll take my time, Tassy. I like you, but there is no reason to be doglike here and rush into things. Cats are deliberate creatures, and good cats are even more deliberate.

A flat-screen television was mounted to the wall opposite the sofa, but because the RV did not get cable, the television only received a few channels and none of them very clearly. Instead of watching television, Tassy found herself reading more. She borrowed books from Pastor Jake, and Eleanor brought a paper grocery bag filled with mysteries (hers) and

Westerns (Vern's). On her last trip to town, she bought the most recent copies of *People* and *Us* magazines. Those she doled out sparingly, reading only a story or two at a time. She knew her money was extremely limited, and without a job she would have to ration out those sorts of luxury purchases. Midway through this week's *People*, she picked the issue back up and began to finish the latest story on the Kardashians.

"Suit yourself, Petey. If you don't want to be petted, that's all right with me."

With that, Petey jumped up on the sofa and headed straight for her lap.

"I could swear you actually understand me."

Petey meowed in reply. Tassy tossed the magazine to the side and began to pet Petey and he responded by purring loudly.

"Petey, can I ask you a question?"

Petey churred softly and tilted his head as if expecting a tough query.

"Well . . . here's the thing. I don't know if I should be here. I told that to Pastor Jake. He said it was okay to have questions. He said answers to some questions are long in coming, but that I should never give up hope. That sounds right, doesn't it?"

Petey meowed.

"So do I tell people the truth? Is that what they want to hear? What if the secret you have is really, really big, and sooner or later the truth will get out? What do I do then? Do I tell people?"

Petey rolled onto his back and stared up at Tassy.

I'm not sure what she is asking. And I'm not a mind reader. God sent me here, sure, but he did not give me any super powers. She's seen too many superhero movies. Or those horrid vampire ones. Gack. Who thinks a deathly pallor is attractive?

He knew he couldn't give a concise answer to a nebulous question, so he decided to take action instead.

Maybe she'll get the metaphor here.

He grabbed at her hand with his front paws, using no claws, of course, and pulled it close, then mimed biting her hand, but instead, at the last minute, licked the back of her hand, gently and tenderly.

You know . . . sometimes the fact that you can do something doesn't mean you should do something. Some things you are able to do will cause pain in others.

"I'll think about it, Petey. I'll think about it. Pastor Jake said to be truthful . . . but I don't know. I'll think about it."

—— ⚬⚬⚬ ——

Both Jake and Emma were smiling as they walked out of the Coudersport Theater.

"Not exactly at the Noel Coward level of urbane, witty dialogue," Emma remarked.

"What?" Jake almost shouted, "I couldn't hear from all the explosions."

She playfully pushed him on the shoulder.

"It was loud, wasn't it?"

"I bet there weren't more than fifteen seconds of quiet in the whole movie. Maybe when that one robot died."

Emma tucked her purse under her arm.

"No Academy Award for scriptwriting, but it was entertaining—in an explosive way."

Jake opened the truck door.

"It really was. I couldn't do a steady diet of these movies, but once in a while they are good, brainless fun."

He started the truck.

"Is there a place around here to go for coffee? or a piece of pie? or something?"

Emma smiled at him, as if relieved that he asked to continue the Welcome Wagon date past expectations.

"Sure. Head back east on Route 6—Second Street. There's a diner that's open until 11:30. Which is like four in the morning on Coudersport time."

When they arrived, they settled into opposite sides of a booth by the window.

Barbara Ann had always sat next to Jake in a four-person booth, leaving Jake a bit smothered, but he'd never told her. She was all elbows when she ate, which meant that Jake had to cede at least a quarter more of his rightful booth space. That was why he'd always asked for a table.

"They have good homemade pie. And by 'homemade' I mean they actually make it here. Not that they live here—but it isn't made in a factory."

Jake ordered cherry pie, not heated, with ice cream, and regular coffee.

Emma picked a triple berry pie with whipped cream and decaf coffee. "After I turned thirty, coffee after dark keeps me up until it's light again."

She's a little bit older than I am. A little bit. Although she didn't say how far past thirty she is. I guess it doesn't matter.

If she was watching her weight, Jake was glad it didn't spill into her dessert selection. She took a large forkful and declared her choice as "delicious."

Jake tasted his pie and nodded. "Good job. Good pick."

They didn't talk much as they ate. They exchanged a few comments about the movie, and Jake remarked how surprised he was that Coudersport still had a downtown movie house.

"I think it's a labor of love for the owners. I don't know them well, but I don't think they're getting rich off showing movies. They probably make more money off the popcorn than the tickets they sell. I sometimes just go in and get a box of popcorn without seeing the movie."

"It is good—especially with the butter."

Jake finished first and slid his plate to the side.

"So . . . you're a pastor?" she asked. Her tone was coy, lighthearted.

"I am," Jake replied.

"Did you always want to be a pastor?"

How do I answer this? Should I start being honest?

"Maybe," he said. "My father left my mother and me when I was like seven. I'm not sure of the whole story, but I haven't heard from him in more than ten years now. My mother raised me as a single mom—more or less. I don't think they ever officially divorced. My mother always wanted me to be a preacher. Her dream was to see me go to a seminary and be a famous preacher at a big church."

"Coudersport doesn't have any big churches, Jake. Or hadn't you noticed?"

"I know. But the Church of the Open Door is a legitimate church, and they needed a pastor. I needed a church."

"Your mother wanted that, Jake. But did you always want to be a pastor?"

"You want me to be honest? If I had my choice, I would be playing center field for the Pittsburgh Pirates. But that dream didn't happen. This one did."

Emma offered a knowing smile and looked like she wanted to push the question one more time, but didn't. Apparently, she would take his answers at face value.

"So, Emma, are you a 'churchgoing' woman?" Jake asked.

Emma shook her head.

"I grew up going to church. But I stopped going when I went to college. A lot of things happened, and I guess I lost faith in it all."

"What happened?"

"A lot of things."

Jake didn't push that question either.

"I'll change the subject," Emma said. "What's up with the young girl in the RV? My mother was talking about her. Tassy, right?"

"It is Tassy," Jake replied. He briefly related Tassy's story of how she came to the church and wound up living, at least temporarily, in Vern's RV.

"So he just threw her out on the side of the road? Her ex-boyfriend? A charming fellow, no doubt."

"That's what she said. And she is such an attractive young woman," Jake added. "And such a nice person. I just don't understand how someone would do that to her. She is not the sort of person who anyone would reject or abandon."

Emma almost winced, but didn't. If Jake noticed the pained look that swept past her eyes, he made no comment.

"So what does your faith say about that, Jake? I hope you don't mind me asking. As you might guess, I don't have a lot of intellectual friends in Coudersport. I have friends—good-time friends—but having an intelligent conversation? . . . Well, that doesn't happen all that much."

"No. I'm a pastor, remember? I'm supposed to handle questions like this."

He accepted a second refill on his coffee and added two sugars and cream.

"I know God is in control. Even when it seems like he isn't. Things don't always happen the way we want them to happen. But it doesn't mean God isn't there. Things happened in my life I don't understand. But it is not because God turned his back."

I hope that sounds like I believe that. I'm not sure I do. But that is the party line.

"So a pretty girl like Tassy being tossed out and abandoned is all part of his plan?"

Jake narrowed his eyes, as if in deep thought. "No. Maybe. Sometimes we do stupid things and have to suffer the consequences. But God is still there. We do have free will, and sometimes our free will gets us in trouble. We do stupid things. I know that has happened to me."

"You've done stupid things?"

"Some."

"Like what?"

Jake hesitated.

Should I be honest? Should I tell the whole truth? This is way too early, right?

He looked at his hands, wrapped around his coffee cup.

"Let's just say stupid things for now. Nothing horrible. Just stupid."

Emma let him off the hook by smiling.

"I guess that could describe all of us, right?"

At that moment, Emma's cellphone came alive, warbling. She grabbed it out of her purse.

"I should take this. It could be some sort of cat emergency," she said, explaining the unexpected interruption. "Hello?"

Jake could not help overhearing. She was sitting close and the person on the other end was speaking very loudly.

"Joanne talked to Arlene and then called Betty, and she said that Arlene's son—you know, Gary, the one with the lisp—well, he was at the movies tonight and he said he saw you with that new preacher fellow. Is that true? Or is he lying again? You know how those Pipers can be."

Emma closed her eyes, as if wishing to disappear.

"Yes, Mom. It is true. He saw us there."

"So, who did the asking—him or you? You aren't getting any younger, you know."

Emma shook her head, held her hand on top of the mouthpiece, and whispered loudly to Jake, "Do not do anything in this town that you don't want everyone to know about in like fifteen minutes. Don't do anything stupid. They will hunt you down like a rabid wolverine."

She returned to the call.

"Mom, we'll talk tomorrow. I have to go."

She snapped the phone shut and watched as a wide smile spread across Jake's face.

7

Jake felt good about his take on the first chapter of Ephesians. He would plow no new theological ground, but as a basic expository sermon, it was at least okay. And he had sprinkled in a few personal anecdotes throughout. He liked hearing personal anecdotes and hoped his new congregation would as well.

Verna played through the first two hymns, mostly in tune. Jake could not be sure if it was her or the organ that went wobbly on a few verses. Jake did not study music, so anyone who could decipher the black lines and squiggles was head and shoulders above him in musical ability. Apparently Verna also taught piano on the side, so Jake blamed the warbles on the organ.

Jake—Pastor Jake—walked up to the pulpit and cleared his throat. The pulpit was on the smallish side, so Jake had to lean forward just a bit when he grabbed both sides of it.

He started with a short prayer, then launched into his sermon. Perhaps fifteen seconds into the material, he noticed a few people staring at the door to the anteroom of his office. He had locked it the night before—just in case. Petey on the platform *once* was amusing; *twice* might be seen as an affectation, and he did not want to be known as the "cat pastor." An older lady whom Jake did not recognize pointed toward the door— and not a subtle pointing, her arm raised shoulder high. Jake tried not to be obvious about it, but he looked. A silver and black, furry paw scrabbled at the bottom of the door, trying to pull it open. The door, of course, would not budge. The cat tried three more times, then the paw disappeared. Jake took a deep breath and continued.

Maybe no one other than the lady and I saw it.

Why is this door locked? It wasn't locked last week. Jake! You must have made a mistake. I get it. You locked the door by accident. I know you didn't mean to lock the door. I need to hear your sermon.

Petey scampered from the small office into Jake's bigger office. The windows were closed.

He ran into the kitchen and tried the door, but even tugging with all his might didn't open it. The door did not budge. He looked at the windows in the kitchen. All were closed tight.

How am I going to get out of here?

He ran into the bedroom. Closed windows.

Wait. I know.

He ran into the bathroom. He didn't like the bathroom. He remembered once, as a small cat, he had jumped into a tub, not knowing it was full of water. He did not like being immersed, accidentally or not.

Took me two days to dry out.

But the window in the bathroom was open—sort of.

Jake had bought one of those sliding screens with the wood frame that pop in an out of an open window. Petey made his way to that window, jumped up, and pushed. It squeaked just a little. He pushed again, and the screen went clattering to the outside. The drop was only six feet and onto grass. Petey jumped and took off to the front of the church.

How do I open those doors? If I'm supposed to be inside, there'll be an open door for me. I'm sure of that.

He ran to the front of the church and up the steps. Neither of the doors was open.

Maybe I'm not supposed to be inside. Could that be possible?

Just then, as Petey stared hard at the double doors, one side opened. Charles Hild stepped out, reaching for a rumpled pack of Chesterfields in the breast pocket of his blue sport coat.

"Well, hello there. You're the pastor's cat, right?" Charles said.

Petey meowed, a tad annoyed at having to affirm the obvious.

"You want to go in?"

Petey meowed again.

"Okay, I guess. After all, you are sort of a church cat, right?"

Charles held the door open as he pulled a lighter from his pocket.

"Something about sitting in church this long makes me really need a cigarette."

Petey chose not to run, but walked, his tail held high, and slowly made his way down the center aisle.

Jake saw him first and closed his eyes in dismay.

Don't know why he's upset. Obviously, I'm supposed to be here. There was a door open.

The rest of the congregation noticed, of course, as Petey walked past them—especially those in the aisle seats. Petey walked slowly up the steps to the platform and jumped onto the center chair—the same one he had used the previous week.

Everyone in the congregation had laughed. And for a long time. Maybe it was the exasperated expression on his face, or the calm, serene look on Petey's face, or perhaps it was the tension between the two.

Jake waited until everyone had finished.

"I guess we have a visitor again. If it's okay with you, we'll just go on. Chasing a cat around the platform isn't on my order of service today."

Most everyone agreed with a chorus of "okays." A smattering of applause indicated general approval, Jake guessed.

Petey waited for the sermon to continue, still as a statue, his eyes flickering between staring at Jake in rapt attention and with bemusement at the congregation and their smiles.

"Okay, then, back to Ephesians."

Emma liked spring Sunday mornings. She had nothing pressing to do other than read the Sunday copy of the *Philadelphia Inquirer*, which she accomplished by 9:00. Finished with that task, she carried a cup of coffee out to the second-story porch. Winston followed her to the door but did not come out on the porch. Obviously, heights unnerved him. He realized she had not taken food with her, so he wasn't acutely disappointed. She did carry her small laptop computer with her, thinking she might catch up on e-mails.

She placed the computer on a small table and started it up. She typed in her password, then hesitated. Instead of opening her mailbox, she went to Google, and hesitated again for a long moment.

Then she shook her head and typed in: Barbara Ann Bentley.

I'm not snooping. I'm not. I'm just interested, that's all. Jake is a new friend, and I'm interested in his life before he came here. That's all.

Barbara Ann Bentley brought up more than a million hits.

Emma was not surprised. Type in "dancing pink hippos" and you'll find several million hits as well. She added "Butler" to the search and, on a whim, "beauty pageant."

Bingo.

Barbara Ann was the owner of a website that focused on beauty pageant tips and consulting on all things related to beauty pageants. Items for sale included a beauty pageant video and a book on pageant secrets, entitled, appropriately, *Beauty Pageant Secrets*. The site was very pink and very bejeweled, with many sparkles and diamonds.

It appeared that Barbara Ann no longer competed professionally but would be willing to help others in consultations, coaching and accompanying contestants with whatever pageant they entered. Barbara Ann included a picture of herself wearing a tiara and a sequined silver gown. She showed a great expanse of very white teeth.

"Well, Winston, our Pastor Jake dated a very pretty girl—if you like that style of pretty. A little artificial, if you ask me. But pretty."

Winston snorted in reply and remained standing, a few inches shy of actually crossing the threshold to the porch.

"And she has a lot of teeth."

Emma read some of the free hints provided on the site: "Always Smile—Even If It Hurts!" and some of the testimonials: "Without Barbara Ann I would have never won Miss Fayette County. From, Cindy Jones."

This is so unexpected. I never would have figured Jake as a man who would be with a woman like this. The two of them just don't add up.

She clicked on the heading of "Contact Me."

There was an e-mail and a mailing address. And there was a phone number.

Emma stared at it for a long time.

Probably an answering machine.

She looked out to the street and watched an old minivan rattle past.

Her fingers hovered over the keyboard, poised to leave the site and move on to a more intellectual news site—maybe the e-version of the *Wall Street Journal*.

Instead, she moved the cursor to the phone number, hit the copy key, and pasted the number into her contact list.

I'm not going to call her, of course. That would be wrong.

She stared at the number.

I should just erase it.

She stared a little longer. She didn't erase it.

That Sunday afternoon, Jake changed from his suit and tie and polished, uncomfortable preaching shoes into a pair of jeans and a Butler County Community College sweatshirt—"Home of the Pioneers." He once taught a course there: Comparative Religions of the World.

That seems so long ago right now.

Petey danced around him as he changed, purring and chirping and meowing.

"So, Petey," he said as he sat on the bed and laced up his sneakers, "did you enjoy today's sermon?"

Petey butted his head into Jake's shin and meowed loudly.

"You paid attention the whole time. That's a good thing. I only noticed a few sleepers today."

Petey jumped on the bed, then down again.

"So you think you're going for a walk with me? Who says I want to take a cat for a walk? And I thought cats don't do walks. Do they?"

Jake thought Petey tried to look offended and bemused at the same time.

"Well, I'm willing to try it. But you cannot run off and get lost. I already have invested a lot of money in you, between the food and the litter and the doctor's visits."

Petey lowered his head, as if he felt guilty for costing Jake actual, human money.

Spring had arrived, and then some. The breeze carried a hint of warmth, almost hot, and the trees had filled out in green during the last few weeks. Coudersport was much more rural than urban, so a walk in any direction took one into the country very quickly. The Allegheny River lay only a few hundred yards to the south of the church, though at this geographical point, was not much of a river but more like a large stream.

Jake grabbed an old Pirates baseball hat and stepped out onto the parking lot, breathing deeply. His shoulder had hardly bothered him for the past week.

No twinges, no omens. That's good. Omenless.

Tassy opened the door to the RV.

"Going for a walk? Could I come?"

"Sure. Just a short one. Down to the river."

The three of them crossed the road and headed south through an open field populated by tall grasses and milkweed plants and hundreds of butterflies that took flight as they walked.

"What kind are these?" Tassy asked. "I've seen them before, right?"

"Monarchs," Jake said. "They are pretty common. Did you know that they migrate all the way to Mexico?"

"Really? They can fly all that way?"

"I'm not sure. I think they do. Or maybe it takes a generation or two to get there. Anyhow, a place in Mexico gets hundreds of thousands of them. So many at once that they can break tree limbs."

"Really?

"Well, I haven't seen it. But that's what I've heard."

Petey, following them, meowed.

The headwaters of the Allegheny River lay only fifty miles upstream, so at this point, the river was not an impressive body of water. The spring thaw muddied the water and filled the banks to their upper limit, but the river still was no more than a swollen stream.

"This is really a river?" Tassy asked as they stared at the flowing water.

"It is. It picks up volume as it goes, of course. In Pittsburgh, it joins the Monongahela River and forms the Ohio River."

"That's a big river, right? I've heard of that."

"Pretty big. I've never seen the Mississippi. That's bigger."

Tassy sat on a large stone outcropping and folded her knees up. Petey jumped to join her.

"I wish I could follow the water. Just float away. Sometimes I would love to float away from everything."

Jake tossed a few pebbles into the water.

"I know what you mean. Life gets complicated sometimes."

Tassy nodded and reached to stroke Petey's back.

Jake said, "So, have you thought more about staying, Tassy? I know you said you don't feel like you belong here. But what would make some other place better? Couldn't you start your life from here? Begin it all again?"

Tassy shrugged. "That sounds easy. But it isn't, Pastor Jake. You might have everything figured out. Like faith and God and where you're supposed to be. But I don't. And I can't even see where I would go for answers."

"Tassy, I don't have everything figured out. I don't. Just because I preach doesn't mean I have all the answers."

She looked at him intently, as if she heard his words but did not agree with him, yet was too polite to call him on it.

"You can stay here, Tassy. You could find a job, I bet. Make new friends. Start over. Here is as good a place as any. Maybe better. You already have a place to stay for a while."

"Maybe. I don't know. Maybe if I had faith like you did, then it would be easier. I envy you, you know? God showed you a path and all you have to do is follow it. I would really like that. To be like you. You have a church and a job and a cat. I don't have any of that. I guess I'm a little jealous."

"Tassy, you have nothing to be jealous of. Really. You can find the way. You just have to have . . ."

"Faith? Hope? Pastor Jake—that's all I had when I left home. And now where am I? Broke and lost and . . ."

They both stopped talking. Petey looked first at Tassy, as if urging her to continue, to tell the truth, to get out whatever secret she was hiding. Then he looked at Jake the same way. But neither would speak. Both simply stared at the fast-moving water, filled with sediment, making the bottom of the river a mystery.

Emma picked up the phone a dozen times and almost dialed the number once. Then she laid it back down.

No, I can't do this. What would I say? Would she even tell me about Jake? If it were me—would I?

"Winston, what would you do?"

Winston didn't answer. He lay in the middle of the hallway and snored noisily.

Emma stared at the phone.

Then she picked it up and began to tap in numbers.

"So, Eleanor, what did you think of the new guy? Besides the cat, that is. Stupid animal. We're going to be the laughing stock around here. A pastor with a cat. That's what they're going to call us—the Cat Church."

Eleanor carried a pitcher of iced tea out to the patio and set it down carefully onto the metal table with matching metal chairs. The style would be considered retro in most settings, but these were original metal-tubed chairs from 1956. Vern religiously stored them in the garage each winter and cleaned them every spring, scraping off any rust and repainting the rusted areas with a coating of rustproof paint. They were now multicolored, but solid.

"I liked the cat being there. Did you see Irene Lindquist there? She said she would never come to a church ever again."

"She just came to laugh at the cat."

"So? She's at church. And she heard a good sermon. Maybe that's the way God works."

"With a cat?" Vern said, swatting away the idea like a pesky gnat. "God uses cats, now, does he?" He took a long swallow of tea. "Not enough sugar in this tea. Or lemon."

"Next time, fix it yourself, you old goat."

Eleanor had changed from her Sunday dress to an old housecoat. Vern didn't like her to wear a housecoat outside. "Looks like pajamas," he'd barked.

"It's just like a dress, that's all—but more comfortable," Eleanor had barked back.

They had had this discussion for more than twenty years and had not yet resolved the issue.

"Anyhow, I liked them both—the cat and the pastor. And besides Irene, I noticed a few other faces I haven't seen in years. Maybe the cat is a good thing."

"Over my dead body," Vern said. "No church I go to will start featuring a cat. Next thing you know, he'll want to have hootchie-cootchie dancers up front. That'll draw them in. What would you think about that?"

Eleanor picked up some grapes she had bought on sale at the Jubilee Foods in town.

"A cat is not a hootchie-cootchie dancer, Vern. And besides," she said as she chewed, "there's not enough room on the platform for hootchie-cootchie dancers. Maybe we could have one. What's one hootchie-cootchie called? Just a hootchie?"

Eleanor smiled to herself, knowing Vern would never find that amusing. She was right. He didn't.

"Well, he didn't talk enough about sin," Vern said with a scowl. "Needs to talk more about sin. That's what we need. Sin talk. Maybe that'll get a revival going."

Eleanor sighed.

"Sure, Vern. Let's talk more about sin. That will draw in the crowds."

"Worked in the old days. Big tent meetings. All they talked about was sin."

Eleanor was about to say, "And when was the last tent meeting in Coudersport?" but didn't. The afternoon was much too pleasant to spend arguing.

"Yes, Vern," she said quietly. "A big tent. That would do it. Crowds would come to a big tent."

Vern responded by smiling, staring at the apple tree in the backyard, and wondering when it would be the time to spray it for bugs. He enjoyed spraying things for bugs.

"NO. THE CAT WAS THERE. WITH THE PASTOR! HE CAME IN THROUGH THE FRONT DOOR."

Irene lowered herself into her plaid La-Z-Boy and raised the footrest as she listened to her mother's response. She wondered if she could teach her mother how to use e-mail. That would be so much easier and less taxing. A five-minute phone call, filled with shouting, wore Irene out.

For her first church service in decades (other than the service from the Vatican she watched on TV on Christmas Eve) this one wasn't all that bad. She had actually listened to the sermon, mostly, and had kept her eye on the cat that was paying attention to the pastor.

Verna's organ playing hadn't improved in the past years, but they had sung two hymns that she remembered from her childhood, and each brought back a tender memory of her father singing them wildly off key. Irene had managed to choke out most of the words.

"I LIKED IT. THE PASTOR IS A GOOD GUY. NO. NOT GOOD-BYE. A GOOD GUY."

And with that her mother hung up and Irene dropped the phone, nearly exhausted.

Maybe I'll go next week. Maybe. If the cat goes.

"Well," Big Dave said, smiling, "didya like it?"

Big Dave was still in his church clothes—a blue work shirt with a tie and newer jeans.

Carl swirled the coffee in his plastic cup. He was on his way home and stopped in after the service.

"Wasn't bad. The cat was pretty funny. Like he was trained to do that or something."

"Nope. Just a stray. He showed up the same day as the pastor. He came in here with him."

"Well, I gotta say I don't like sitting still for an hour like that, but it wasn't bad. Your new guy is okay. He didn't yell at all. And no lightning strike, either."

"You know, I did check the Weather Channel before I came. Just to be on the safe side."

It will be an answering machine. I'll just hear her voice and then I'll hang up. No harm in that, right?

Emma dialed half the numbers and hung up eleven times, stopping and staring at the phone, debating, and then on the twelfth attempt, she dialed all the numbers and let it actually connect and ring.

And no one answers a business line on a Sunday afternoon.

It rang once, twice, then the sound of a connection.

"Hello, this is Barbara Ann Bentley. May I help you?"

Good grief! She actually answered the phone! Who does that?

"Umm . . . uhh . . . Hello," Emma's heart raced.

"Hello. Can I help you? This is Barbara Ann Bentley, of Bentley Pageant Consultants."

Get a hold of yourself, Emma. You've operated on horses and wolves. You've held the insides of animals in your hands. You can talk to a pretty woman. Talk!

"Umm . . . hello, Barbara Ann, this is Emma Grainger. You don't know me . . . but we have a mutual friend. I think he's a mutual friend."

Barbara Ann was nothing if not pert, chipper, and super-polite and positive.

"And who might that be, Ms. Grainger?"

Neither Tassy nor Jake went further with the truth than they already had, much to Petey's dismay. He chirped, cried, churred, and meowed a hundred ways to Sunday, but neither of them continued to talk.

Jake thought Petey had seen some sort of larger animal— like a fox or a coyote—and was trying to warn them.

Tassy stood up hearing the word *coyote*.

"Do they eat people?" she asked, pivoting around, trying to locate the telltale movement of brush that would indicate a predator lurking nearby.

"No," Jake said, reassuring her. "They are more afraid of us than vice versa."

"I wouldn't bet on that. I've seen movies where a pack of wild dogs . . . or maybe it was wolves . . . chase these guys down and pick them off one by one. They're big animals with lots of teeth."

"I don't think we have any wolf packs in Coudersport, Tassy."

"Are you sure? This is like way out in the woods. I grew up in Philadelphia. This is like the jungle in comparison."

Jake could tell that she was more than a little frightened.

"You want to go back?"

"Yes. I do."

Petey kept hopping and chirping, as if he was trying to get them to stop walking and keep talking, but to no avail.

"Okay. Let's walk back. Petey can guard us, okay?"

Tassy offered a nervous giggle. "He wouldn't be any good at protecting me. They would eat him up in a minute. A wolf would, anyhow."

Petey offered one more meow, long and drawn out, as if expressing his resentment at being called an ineffectual guardian.

———— ✇ ————

If I am going to be a snoop, might as well be honest.

"Jake Wilkerson."

"Jake Wilkerson?"

Have I made a mistake? This isn't the same Barbara Ann? This is sooo embarrassing.

"Yes. Jake Wilkerson. He's a new pastor up here in Coudersport. I thought you knew him when he was in Butler. I must be mistaken. So sorry to have bothered you on a Sunday."

Barbara Ann remained very perky. "Oh, it's no bother. I often answer the phone myself on Sunday. A lot of pageants are held on Sunday afternoon. The smaller ones. Big ones are Saturday evening. But I have some up-and-coming clients. Sometimes they are in a crisis and need some advice. Like what color eye shadow goes with a magenta gown they have to wear because their original choice got lost or torn or something. Or do I really need double-faced tape if I'm not very big . . . you know . . . up there. I always had to use it. You know what I mean?"

Emma thought she sort of knew what Barbara Ann meant, so she agreed. "I do. I guess."

"Jake Wilkerson. So you know Jake. Are you two dating or something?"

What answer does she want? I think she would rather have him brokenhearted and never dating again. After her, who could come close?

"No. He's new in town. And he brought his cat into my office. I'm a veterinarian."

"A vet? I always wanted to be vet. I would love to take care of bunnies and kitties. But I found out there is a lot of math. I'm not real good at math."

"Well, there is not as much as you might think. You could still do it, I bet. Get a math tutor if you have a hard time with it. A lot of people in my class did."

"Really?" Barbara Ann said, brightening. "Wow. Maybe I could. Could I do this pageant consulting while I went to vet school? I really like helping girls be beautiful and win prizes and stuff."

"Well, I don't see why not," Emma replied. "Anything is possible."

Emma heard an atonal hum, then Barbara Ann said, "Jake Wilkerson. Yes, Ms. Grainger. I know Jake. Very well."

Tassy retreated into the RV, waved good-bye to Jake and Petey, and closed the door behind her. Jake heard the lock bolt securely.

Jake felt a little guilty about scaring Tassy, but he really thought Petey might have seen or smelled a coyote. Why else would the cat be making all that racket.

The two of them went into the parsonage. After preaching, even though it was only a single sermon, Jake went into what he called his "shut-down" mode. He put a disc in his stereo—some soft jazz music. He had a dozen such discs and he could never really tell them apart. He switched on the TV, found a basketball game between two teams he did not care much about, put it on mute, and laid down on the couch, with a scrunched-up pillow under his head. He would spend the next few hours there, alternating between watching and listening and napping. Such remains of a Sunday afternoon were the most delicious times of the week.

Petey sat in the middle of the room, keeping an eye on Jake, and watched him fall asleep.

So that's all he's going to do this afternoon? Petey thought. *I knew that being able to talk would come in handy sometimes. Like today by the river. They both need to open up. They should have figured out what I was trying to say. I made it as obvious as the noses on their faces.*

Petey sniffed loudly, licked his paw a bit, wiped off his face—both sides—and sauntered to his favorite chair.

If he can sleep, so can I.

In his thoughts, Petey smiled.

Jake is entitled to take a nap once in a while.

He circled the chair cushion several times until he found the most perfect spot in which to lie.

I shouldn't be hard on them. I don't like to think about my past either. I try not to think about it. I don't know why those humans acted like they did. Hurtful. And those people seemed like normal humans. But . . . God saved me from that, didn't he?

He lay his head down and closed his eyes.

Maybe I'll think about that some other time. Maybe.

"You do?" Emma replied. "Did you go to his church?"

"Yes. But it wasn't *his* church. He was an associate there. That's all. Not a senior anything."

Emma wanted to come out bluntly and ask the questions she really wanted answered, but was pretty sure that blunt would not work with Barbara Ann.

"So the two of you went to the same church."

"We did. Or he did. I was there first. My uncle—he's the senior pastor there. Has been there for years and years."

"Is it a big church? The church Jake is at now is really sort of tiny."

Emma thought she heard more than a note of smugness in Barbara Ann's reply, "I knew it. He didn't tell anyone where it was. I just knew it would be tiny. I figured the church would be a little desperate. And yes, my uncle's church is big. It is the biggest church in Butler. And has been the biggest for years and years."

"Barbara Ann, I hope you don't mind me being direct. But if you would, maybe you could tell me about the particulars. You know—what happened. Girl-to-girl, you know?"

Emma heard a long sigh.

"I will, Ms. Grainger. As a warning. Okay?"

"Sure."

"Jake and I dated for like forever. A year, I think. We even talked about getting engaged. Just talked about it. That's all."

"This was while he was on staff?" Emma wasn't sure why she was so intently curious, but she was, and having found a person willing to offer an explanation, she was determined not to let it go to waste.

"Yep. My uncle liked him at first. I did, too. Jake is a nice guy. Really he is."

"Did he do something bad? What?"

Another deep breath and a sigh.

"Not bad in a bad way. But bad enough. Bad for a pastor. We were taking this thing—a seminar or whatever—that my uncle taught for couples, on how to talk about stuff, how to be honest—all that sort of stuff."

"Sure, like premarital counseling."

"Except that we were definitely not premarital. We were dating, that's all. My uncle said it would be a fun thing to do as a couple. So we went. One of the exercises was to be totally honest about something we had hidden inside of us. I told him—and I am kind of embarrassed even now—that I used to touch up my hair color in high school. Not now. It's totally blonde all by itself now."

"Your picture on your website looks very pretty, Barbara Ann. Very pretty."

Emma could tell that Barbara was beaming.

"Why, thank you, Ms. Grainger. That's very kind of you. Anyhow, when it was Jake's turn, he started telling me some really disturbing stuff."

"Disturbing?" Emma braced herself.

"Yes. Disturbing. He told me he was having doubts about being a pastor. He even admitted to having doubts about God and faith—like maybe God wasn't always there helping us. Like maybe he's just watching and not saving us and doing good stuff for us."

"Really?" Emma replied, hoping that she sounded as shocked as Barbara Ann sounded, all the while thinking that such feelings of doubt sounded pretty normal to her.

"Yes. For a pastor to say that—that's just not right. So I told my uncle and my uncle confronted him and asked if it were true and Jake had to say it was and then my uncle had to fire him. He couldn't have a pastor who didn't believe in God."

"Did Jake really say he didn't believe in God?"

"Not exactly. But close enough. If you think God is just watching—that's like not believing in him."

"Wow," Emma replied, not really meaning she was surprised or shocked, but that she was just amazed at the whole incident.

"Wow, exactly. So I had to tell Jake that if he wasn't going to be a pastor, we weren't going to be a couple. I intend on marrying someone who can be the pastor of a church someday. That's important to me. I have an image to be concerned about. I couldn't go around dating an atheist, could I? Who would use a half-atheist beauty pageant consultant?"

"Nobody?"

"Exactly."

Emma inhaled deeply this time. After a moment, Barbara Ann posed a question. "You said Jake has a cat?"

"I did. Petey. A very special cat, if you ask me."

"Now, that is amazing," Barbara Ann said. "Him having a cat. I take it his mother doesn't know about it."

"I'm not sure. Maybe."

"She doesn't, Ms. Grainger. I am sure of that. She is a very controlling person. I am sure she would not go for him having a cat. Not at all. It's a good thing she lives all the way in Meadville. If she lived close . . . well, I am not sure what would have happened."

"Barbara Ann, I have to thank you so much for being honest with me. This explains a lot."

"So, you asked me for the truth—girl-to-girl. Now it's your turn to tell me the truth, Ms. Grainger: Are you two dating? Girl-to-girl."

"Okay. I'll be honest. We went out once. Just to the movies."

"At least now you're prepared. I don't know about you, but dating an atheist would be a big no-no to me. I talk about this in my video. If you don't believe you can win a beauty pageant, then you shouldn't enter. You have to have faith in yourself. If Jake didn't have faith, then he should have steered clear of the ministry—and me. Would have saved me a whole year of dating the wrong person."

"Well, Barbara, again, thanks so much."

"You're welcome, Ms. Grainger. By the way, Ms. Grainger, would you like a copy of my video? I have a lot of VHS ones. They don't sell very well these days."

"I would love one, but seeing how as my veterinarian job takes most of my time, I don't think I'll be entering any pageants."

"Oh, that's okay. It's got loads of good advice on beauty and self-confidence and all sorts of good, positive things. I'll send you one for free. Okay? Seeing as how we both know Jake. Okay."

"Okay, if you insist. That would be very kind of you," Emma said, wondering if she still owned a VCR that would play a VHS tape.

8

Jake walked out of Jubilee Foods with two bags of groceries. His cat food supply was already low. *Petey must be making up for lost time of not having enough food to eat for so long by eating a full can of tinned food every day, plus nibbling on dry kibbles all day.* Jake thought that level of consumption was a lot. He made a mental note to ask Emma about the proper amount to feed a cat the next time he saw her.

He loaded the groceries in the front of the truck. Petey had stayed at home this morning, barely raising his head from his morning nap position on the chair in the living room. It was his first stop on a standard rotation: morning nap—living room chair; midmorning nap—windowsill in office; after lunch nap—sofa in living room; predinner nap—the unused pillow on Jake's bed; and prebedtime nap—one of the kitchen chairs. The variety of sleeping spots Petey selected and how quickly he fell asleep and woke up fascinated Jake. And how varied his sleeping positions were: the prone cat, the cat on his back, the cat curled into an impossibly tight ball, the cat with his head upright and eyes closed, the cat with his head on his paws, the cat with a paw on his face, and the cat stretched out to twice his length.

As Jake walked around his car with his groceries, he spotted a tall, very thin, younger man walking toward him, with very long blond straight hair, worn well past his shoulders. A full beard flowed around his face and chin—a long beard, full and bushy, a bandana covered his head. He also wore torn jeans and a very tattered jean jacket. It appeared that he was coming straight at Jake. Granted, Coudersport was out in the country— well out in the country. And there were folks who lived even farther out in the country—miles away from even a small town and miles off any main road, and some, miles off even a bad, semi-paved road. Almost off the grid, if the truth be told.

One of these wilderness-looking men attended Jake's church. He heard him referred to as a "mountain man," a person who simply wasn't comfortable living in close proximity to anyone. He lived in a small cabin deep in the nearby Susquehannock State Forest, virtually hidden from view. His name was Mylon Fedders, and he slipped into church as it started and exited as they sang the final hymn.

The man approaching him was not Mylon but apparently went to the same barber and clothing store as the church's mountain man.

"Hey there, you the new pastor fellow, right?"

Jake extended his hand. "I am. Jake Wilkerson."

"Yeah, that's it. I saw you with Doc Grainger the other night."

"At the movies?"

"Naw. I got no use for movies. I was heading out of town and saw you walking. Me and Doc Grainger go way back. We went to high school together. She was real smart back then. Well, I guess she still is. Sorry. Let me introduce myself. Where are my manners? They call me Speedy Davis. Don't ask my real name. Doc Grainger may remember it, but I hope she don't. Anyhow, I hear tell you let a cat come to church. That right?"

If Jake was worried about becoming the "cat pastor," this may have confirmed it.

"I guess. The cat, my cat . . . yes, he did show up in church the last two Sundays. Apparently he likes to hear me talk."

"Don't that beat all? Animals—they do have a special sense, you know. They understand things. They know. I sort of live out there in the woods. Animals all around. Deer. Raccoons. A couple a bears, recently. Spiritual creatures, them bears."

Speedy pushed his hair behind his ears, using both hands, then shook his head to straighten the flowing locks on his shoulders.

"Anyhows, Pastor Jake, I was wondering."

Jake waited.

"I don't do church. I don't like being inside with all those people. Get real nervous, you know. Miracle I made it through school, you know?"

"I can understand that, Speedy. Really."

"But that don't mean I ain't interested in God and all that. But I was wondering. Maybe sometime you and I could talk. Not here in town. I'm sort of already itchy and I only been here a few minutes. Maybe you could come out to my place and we could talk. I got questions, and them bears—well, they do have a spirit, but they ain't much help with my questions."

He was asking for a pastoral visit?

"Well, sure. I could do that."

Speedy looked like he had just dropped a large weight onto the ground.

"Okay, then. I'll mail you a map. You couldn't find me without a map. Hey, even I have trouble finding home sometimes."

"Sure," Jake replied. "I would like a chance to talk. Anytime."

"That's righteous. Any man who preaches to a cat . . . well, that's a righteous man, you know?"

Jake didn't know, but for today, he took Speedy at his word.

Jake moved quietly in the kitchen. After years of apartment living, he kept his morning footfalls soft and the clatter of cups and coffeepots to a minimum. He knew he did not need to worry now—since Petey nearly always woke with him—but old habits and tendencies, deeply ingrained, are hard to ignore.

He stood at the kitchen sink, finishing his first cup of coffee, and saw headlights swing into the church parking lot.

"Maybe they're lost or turning around," Jake said aloud, as if Petey had been interested, which apparently he wasn't, being occupied by the half-filled bowl of kibbles at his feeding station. Jake had learned that Petey did not like his canned food early in the day. That meal should be served at lunch. Kibbles were enough for a morning snack.

But the car in the lot did not turn around or back out. The lights came closer to the church, the car stopped, the lights switched off. It was a truck, not a car. And the lumbering form that exited looked familiar. As it came closer to the light above the steps, Jake recognized his very early morning visitor.

"Jimbo Bennett," Jake said with some cheer as he opened the door. "What brings you here so early? Is there a predawn elders' meeting that no one told me about?"

"If there is, I make two people who haven't heard about it."

"Come on in. Want some coffee?"

"Sure. I pulled in just to see if your light was on. If it wasn't on, I wasn't going to stop. But I'm headed out to do a little fishing. No work today. One of the hydraulic lines on the drill unit we use busted yesterday and it won't be 'til tomorrow that we get the right part to fix it. I could have gone in and swept up the shop or something, but Lloyd—he's the owner, Lloyd Cummins—well, he said it was fine if I took off. So I've tossed my fishing poles in the truck and thought I would drown a few worms this morning. And the Missus is always saying how I don't have any men friends, so I thought I would ask if you wanted to come with."

Jimbo looked near exhausted after his dissertation. Jake had never heard him use that many words at one time before.

Jake ran through a quick mental calculation. He had never been fishing. He was pretty sure that he wouldn't like fishing. He was pretty sure that he would not like the feel of a real fish, slimy and flopping and jumping, in his hands. But he was also just as certain that this was probably a huge decision for Jimbo.

"Sure. If you have a pole for me, I'd love to go."

"Really?"

"Sure."

Petey looked up and meowed very loudly.

"You want to go, Mr. Petey?" Jimbo asked.

Petey meowed again, the same insistent tone.

"Can he?" Jimbo asked. "Maybe you don't want him to go with us."

"No. It's fine. He likes riding in a truck. Seems to like being by the river. We walk down there a lot. He sits and looks at the water. So, if you don't mind, he can go."

"Never had a cat in my truck before. Never had a pastor in my truck before. A lot of first times today."

Petey sat in the middle of the bench seat, though it was obvious he wanted the window seat instead. He complained loudly when Jake picked him up and plopped him down in the middle, moving a tackle box to make room for him.

Petey sniffed at the orange plastic box and wrinkled his nose, in obvious distress at the long-lasting odor of fish and worms and whatever else Jimbo handled when he picked up his tackle.

They drove a few miles past Big Dave's.

"There's a bend in the river here. Easy to get to. Lots of rocks for fish to hide in. Current isn't too strong. Usually a good spot."

Jimbo pulled off into the field and into the scrub grass and brush for one hundred yards or so, bouncing and rattling as they went. Even sure-footed Petey lurched back and forth a few times when the truck came upon bigger ruts.

"Right here. Shady spot, too. Should be good fishing today."

Jake accepted the pole Jimbo offered him.

"You want worms or a lure?"

Jake answered in a hurry. "A lure."

"I got a couple of Red Devils that always do well. I'll set it up for you."

"Thanks." Jake really meant it.

Jimbo showed him how to cast out, to hold the release just so and to let it go at the top of the cast, and where there might be fish beneath the silvery water.

"I'll use some fake worms. They say fish don't know the difference."

Petey climbed out of the truck with them, watched intently as Jimbo set up the rod and reels, and when Jake first cast into the water, almost made a jump after the lure.

"No, Petey. We're not playing catch. This is for fish."

Obviously disappointed, the cat sat glumly on a small rock at the river's edge.

The sun peaked above the small ridge that bordered the river valley, the water glistening red and gold.

For a long time, the only sound was the rippled water, and the occasional sounds of either Jake or Jimbo casting again, the whir of the reel and the hiss of the line and a small, indistinct splash when the lure hit the water's surface.

"Any bites?" Jimbo asked.

"I don't think so. I can sort of feel the lure move a little, but that's probably just the flow of the river."

"Probably. A fish bite is a sharp, little tug. Sometimes they hit it and spit it out. Sometimes they taste it first. That's what they say, anyhow. Never seen a fish eat, so I go by what they say on the fishing shows on TV."

"You do a lot of fishing?" Jake asked as he cast once more.

"Some. Not as much as some of the other guys. I like fish okay. I am not too crazy about chopping them up and all that. Most of the time I just toss 'em back in."

"I've heard that. Catch and release, right? The fun is the catching."

"Yep," Jimbo replied. "You know what kind of fish I really like to eat?"

"Trout?"

"Yuck. No. I really like them fish sandwiches at McDonald's. If I could catch those out here, I'd be here every day."

Jake laughed in reply.

After another longer period of silence, and after Jimbo cast out again, he spoke, his words measured.

"This is nice, isn't it? Gives you time to think. That's what I like about fishing. You don't have to pay attention all the time. Hunting, now, with a loaded gun and all—you have to be alert. Fishing, not so much."

"I have never been hunting. But I'll take your word for it."

"Yeah, I like fishing. I like sitting out here, by myself," Jimbo said. "Not that being with you is bad, Pastor Jake, but you know what I mean."

"I do."

"I can think about things out here. Like what's going to happen in the future. What we'll do when we retire. Stuff like that. Where I would want to go if I didn't have to work anymore."

"Where would you go?"

"Beats me. I like it here fine. The Missus wants to move to Florida. Or Hawaii. I don't think that would happen. Maybe Florida. I guess I could swing that for a week or two—but I'm not sure if I could move there."

Jimbo cast again. Petey flinched as he did, wanting to chase the worm.

"Where would you go, Pastor Jake? To retire."

Jake shrugged.

"Haven't thought about it. I have more than a few years until I need to answer that question."

"You pastor guys have all the luck," Jimbo said. "I know you're busy all week with sermons and meetings and visiting people and stuff like that—and everybody is happy to see you. You have a lot of connections. Us regular guys, not so much. I like the guys at work all right, and at church, but there aren't many that I would want to take fishing with me. I always feel like I'm being evaluated. Or judged. Like I'm not the smartest guy. I know that, but still."

"I don't think they're doing that, Jimbo. Not at church anyhow. Everyone seems to like you fine."

Jimbo brightened.

"Really? You think so?"

Jake could hear the insecurity in his voice.

"Sure. You're the church treasurer, right? That's a hard job. They wouldn't give that to you if they thought you couldn't handle it."

Jimbo tilted his head, considering the thought.

"I guess that's right. Maybe I'm just being . . . I don't know . . . too sensitive or something. Maybe it's because of the way I was brought up."

"How's that?"

"I was the last of four. Everyone had real good grades in school. I didn't. I couldn't seem to concentrate. So I got laughed at a lot. Funny, I don't think I ever told this to anyone before. Not even Betty."

Jake cast again.

"That's good. To talk about things. You ever want to talk, I'm here."

Jimbo stopped reeling in his plastic worm.

"Why, thanks, Pastor Jake. Thanks a lot."

———— ∞ ————

Wednesday found Jake polishing his second sermon from the book of Ephesians. Later on in that book there are problematic verses on submission and obeying and wives and husbands and slaves. Jake was pretty set on their meaning and implications, but many pastors regarded that section of Scripture as a live hand grenade. Regardless of the interpretation, somebody was bound to be a bit ruffled at the end.

Jake did not mind ruffling people when they needed ruffling, but as a realist, he knew that a few weeks into his position as a senior pastor—or only pastor—might not be the best time to start pulling the pins on theological hand grenades. *Time enough for that*, he thought. *Let me focus on the things we can all agree on first.*

The phone rang. Jake did not bother looking at the number on caller ID. He was a pastor, assigned to serve, and that meant answering the phone when it rang. It was the least he could do, rather than let calls disappear into a voice mail abyss.

"Pastor Jake Wilkerson here. How may I help you?"

Pastor Wilkerson . . . it is still hard to get used to answering that way.

"Well, Pastor Wilkerson, you could start by calling your mother more often than once a week. That's for starters."

Jake sat up straighter.

"Hello, Mother. You surprised me. You never call during the day. You always call in the evening. You say it's cheaper at night."

"Well, Mr. Smartypants, you are not the only one who is 'with it.' Your aunt said it doesn't matter when I call. They don't have evening rates anymore, with all these cellphones and crazy new gizmos. She said I can you anytime at all."

Jake winced, just a little.

"So, to what do I owe the honor of this call?"

"Jake, do not take that tone with your mother."

"I'm not. I just asked what you want."

"And I can't call just to talk to my only son? Is that so wrong now?"

"No, Mother. Not at all. It is not wrong to call. I'm happy you called. I am always happy to talk to you."

Jake's mother paused for a very long time before she responded.

"I am calling to let you know that your aunt has graciously offered to drive me from Meadville the whole way to Coudersport. That's a five-hour drive, Jakey. I offered to pay for gas, of course."

"Mother, the drive should only take three hours. I looked it up on MapQuest."

"MapQuest? That's smarter than your aunt now? Your aunt said five. She knows these things. You have to respect your elders, Jakey. She's been driving a long time."

Jake felt a small headache forming at the base of his neck, working its way up, tiny little fingers of tension clutching at him.

"Okay, Mother. Five hours."

Neither spoke for a long time.

"When were you planning to come?"

"Well, that's just it, Jakey. I would like to see your new church. Next week is just terrible, your aunt says. She has a hair appointment on Tuesday and a doctor's appointment on Friday, and I have my Lady's Circle on Thursday morning and I can't miss that, of course, and your Aunt Harriet doesn't like to drive that far on Mondays. She says there are too many trucks on the road trying to get back to work or something. So that doesn't leave us a lot of options. Saturday is out. And Sunday . . . well, of course, we cannot drive on Sunday. Other than to church, of course. And maybe to a restaurant. So, we don't have a lot of options, as you can plainly see. And the rest of the month is even worse. Next month, Harriet has a cruise planned—so it's out, of course."

"Yes, Mother, I understand."

"So we're coming tomorrow."

Jake shut his eyes. Hard. And pressed his thumb and forefinger on the bridge of his nose. He had hoped her first visit would not take place for a few months. This was early on Jake's radar. Very early.

"Okay," he replied. "Tomorrow is good. My sermon is almost done. I'll have plenty of time to spend with you."

"Well, won't that be nice," she said, though Jake did not believe she meant a word of it. "We can only stay for an hour or two. Your aunt doesn't like to drive after dark. So we'll leave at first light, get to Coudersport at noon. Is there a restaurant in Coudersport?"

"Of course there is, Mother."

"Then we can have lunch. We'll pay for our own meals, Jakey. You don't have to worry about that."

No sense in arguing about this now. Plenty of time for that . . . tomorrow.

"Sure, Mother. That sounds great. I'll expect you at the church at noon?"

"Okay, Jakey. Your aunt has one of those cellphones. So we will call when we're halfway there. Okay? So you can wait for us. Okay?"

"That would be great, Mother. Just great."

And Jake hoped that all traces of sarcasm were gone from his voice.

———— ∞ ————

Jake sat still for a long time. Petey looked up from his perch on the windowsill. He jumped off the sill, hurried to the desk, and jumped up into Jake's lap. He started to knead his paws against Jake's thigh, purring loudly.

"Thanks, Petey. Thanks for understanding."

Petey meowed in reply.

Jake looked around the room with a critical eye. *What do I have to do before she gets here? The parsonage is clean. I'll do all the dishes, of course. Make the bed. With tight corners. Sweep. Dust?*

Jake did not dust often.

I have coffee and half-and-half. I could buy donuts. Except she won't eat them. Too fattening, she will say. That is, unless she buys them for herself.

He sighed as he petted Petey's head.

What about Tassy?

A pained look came across his face. He narrowed his eyes.

Nothing I can do about that, short of driving the RV down to Big Dave's for the day.

Petey chirped loudly.

But I will have to warn her about my mother's visit. At least it gives me something else to think about. Worry about, that is.

———— ∞ ————

The clock ticked slowly, the last few minutes before noon seeming to take an hour to pass. His mother had called as they passed through Warren. There was no direct route from Meadville to Coudersport—no freeway, no single route. There were many ways to make the trip, all of them involving at least three route changes.

Maybe they'll get lost, turn around, and just go home.

The thought streaked through Jake's mind and he tried not to smile when it did.

At noon, he took his cellphone and walked outside. The church was not easy to miss; it was easy to find, but he would put nothing past his aunt or his mother. At ten minutes past noon, he caught a glimpse of his aunt's maroon Buick Electra slowly coming down the road, doing all of thirty-five miles per hour.

Maybe the trip did take a full five hours, Jake thought.

The car began slowing a quarter mile away, and Jake moved closer to the road so they would know they were in the right place. It kept slowing until it reached the driveway, traveling at perhaps three miles per hour, made a wide turn into the lot, and nearly circled it until it turned completely around, facing the road again. Jake was pretty sure his aunt did not like to go in reverse, so this circuitous parking procedure negated any requirement of backing up.

The car stopped and neither woman exited for at least thirty seconds.

I would ask why they are waiting . . . but Jake thought better of it and stood between the car and the church, a wide smile affixed to his face.

His mother exited the automobile first, dragging and pulling herself upright. "I thought we would never get here. This place might as well be on the moon, Jakey, it's so far away."

Jake's mother was a much shorter, older, feminine version of Jake—more wide than tall, with perfectly coiffed mousy brown hair and sensible shoes. She wore glasses, much larger than what was currently in style, in pale brown, that rode low on her nose.

"Hello, Mother, Aunt Harriet. Did you have a nice trip?"

Aunt Harriet held on to the car as she made her way forward. "Are we still in Pennsylvania?"

"You are. Almost in the middle of the state," Jake replied, hoping he could keep his vow of maintaining a level, calm discourse today. Even though he promised himself he could do it, he knew that he really couldn't. Not for a full two hours.

"This is in the middle of nowhere, Jakey," his mother said. "When you said senior pastor, I had no idea you meant it was so far away."

Jake didn't follow her logic. *But then, I seldom do.*

"Come on in. Let me show you around."

"And you live here, too? There's no separate parsonage?"

"I told you the living quarters are attached, Mother. It's a small church."

She harrumphed quietly and followed Jake to the front door of his house.

They both remained quiet as he gave them a quick tour of the kitchen, living room, office, sanctuary, and finished up by going back through the office and into the bedroom.

Petey was sitting in the middle of the bed. Apparently he had revised his nap schedule, given the coming of the special visitors. As they came in, he yawned broadly and meowed a greeting.

"Jakey! There's a wild animal on your bed!" Jake's mother said, retreating three steps back into the hallway.

"It's not a wild animal. That's Petey. He's a cat. He sort of adopted me on my first day here."

"Jakey! There's a cat on your bed. You have to get rid of it. You'll get a disease from it. He's on your bed. Where you sleep."

Petey lowered his head and offered a lower, rumbly growl-meow-growl. That was a new sound to Jake. Petey made dozens of different sounds, but his growl-meow-growl had been kept hidden until now.

"Mother, the cat is very nice. Very tame. And he was checked out by a veterinarian in town. He has a clean bill of health."

Petey made the same growl-meow again, as if perturbed at having his pedigree and health status discussed by strangers.

"And you plan on keeping it? A cat? Remember what I said about having wild animals?"

Jake sighed. "You did say Jesus never had a dog or a cat." Jake was sorely tempted to add, "As far as we know," but refrained.

"That too. But animals are cesspools of vermin and disease," his mother replied. His aunt covered her mouth, as if warding off some manner of infectious disease.

"Well, Petey's going to stay, Mother. He and I get along very well."

Petey meowed. Proudly and loudly, Jake imagined.

Jake's mother appeared stunned. "What?"

"The cat is going to stay."

My goodness. That felt so good to say. The cat stays. Wow.

"Jakey, I'm very sorry, but no. You have to get rid of the cat. You have to listen to your mother. The Bible says children have to obey."

Jake's aunt nodded vigorously, all the while eyeing Petey with suspicion.

Jake had read ahead in Ephesians. He'd compared at least six commentaries. "Mother, it says *children* have to obey. That means when a child is in their parent's house. Then it says to *honor* them. That's different than obey. Much different."

His mother narrowed her eyes. Her shoulders appeared to tighten and tense.

"Okay, Mr. Seminary Degree. That I paid for, may I remind you. Obey. Honor. To me, they are the same thing. Right, Harriet?"

"That's right. The same thing," Harriet added, taking one more step in retreat.

"Sorry, Mother. But they are not the same."

Goodness, that does feel good. Have I ever done that before?

His mother appeared on the verge of extending the argument. But Petey meowed loudly again, this time a friendlier meow, and jumped off the bed. Both Aunt Harriet and Jake's mother retreated farther and headed to the front door.

"I'm not agreeing with you at all, Jakey. But your aunt and I are hungry. I think we want to eat now, don't we, Harriet?"

"We do."

Petey must have had the good sense to stay in the bedroom, catching the morning sun on the floor. He did not follow them to the door as Jake thought he might.

Jake shouldered the door; it still grew balky on certain days. It squealed open. The three of them exited, blinking, in the bright noon sun.

At that moment, the door to the RV hissed open and Tassy made her way outside. She had been taking long walks each day. She said the exercise felt wonderful and she could not imagine why she had not done this before.

"Well, it was because of Randolph. He hated to do anything physical. Like walking," she had told Jake.

Tassy waved to Jake, smiling broadly. "Hey, Pastor Jake. Good morning."

Jake's mother stopped. Harriet almost ran into her.

"And who is that? And what is that monstrosity there?"

Might as well see everything at once, Jake thought.

"That's Tassy. She didn't have any place to stay, and a nice couple from church are letting her use their RV until she gets on her feet. She's looking for a job."

Jake's mother turned to face her son.

"And she lives there?"

"She does."

"And you live there?" she asked, pointing at the church.

"I do." Jake wanted to add, "with a cat," but he didn't.

"Jakey, that's not right. She has to leave. This doesn't look right. Not at all. You have to get rid of her. People will talk. They'll talk, won't they, Harriet?"

"They would talk in Meadville. That's for certain."

"Well, Mother, we are not in Meadville. This is my church and the elders are fine with her there."

Jake's mother drew in a sharp breath and held it for a long moment.

"Jakey, you have changed. I don't like it one bit. Do I, Harriet?"

"I don't think you do."

"God can't use you in this church, Jakey. It's too small. And you have a cat and a young woman living next door. God can't look past those things. And I would really tell you how I feel, Jakey, but Harriet is hungry. We need to eat lunch. Then we'll talk. When we all can think clearer. Right, Harriet?"

"That's right. We're hungry now, Jakey."

———❧———

Jakey—or Jake—survived lunch with his mother and aunt. Almost. Barely.

No one changed their minds or opinions about Tassy, the cat, or God, for that matter, but everyone ate their fill. Jake took them to Kaytee's Family Restaurant in the small downtown area of Coudersport. Kaytee's was not the most expensive place in town, nor was it the least expensive. They featured comfort food and real waitresses, and the owner went to Jake's church. Kaytee, the owner, extended a warm greeting to Jake and his party as they entered, made a fuss after finding out that he was with his mother and his aunt, and took them to their "best" table, which, in reality, was no different than any other table in the room. Perhaps it was being closer to the window that made it better.

Jake ordered the meatloaf platter special. His mother and Aunt Harriet debated for at least fifteen minutes the merits of the meatloaf platter versus the meatloaf open-faced sandwich versus a chicken salad sandwich, including a "free" cup of soup, versus the All-American KT Burger with fries and cole-slaw. Jake had given up being interested in the discussion and afterward was not able to recall what it was that either of his two guests actually consumed.

Kaytee had brought them each a piece of apple pie for dessert—"on the house."

Jake's mother had not been impressed with the church, but she was impressed with a free dessert.

Jake drove them back to the church in their car and Aunt Harriet insisted that they leave immediately because darkness falls quickly in the late spring in central Pennsylvania. Jake knew there was no scientific basis for such a claim but was not sad to see them hurry off so soon after lunch.

He stood at the edge of the road and waved until Aunt Harriet's car slowly disappeared into the horizon. He took a deep breath, felt the tension in his shoulder slowly unwind, and turned back to his new home.

Today was the first time I stood up to her—in any way. I know it wasn't that important—owning a cat. Or living with a cat, I guess. I don't think Petey would say I "own" him. And Tassy and the small

184

church and everything else. And you know what? It wasn't all that bad. She didn't collapse into tears. She was shocked. She would love to see Tassy and the cat disappear. But when she left it seemed like she might have actually been a bit resigned to them both.

He heard Petey howling on the other side of the door. The cat darted out when Jake shouldered it open, his eyes searching for the strangers, crying softly when he did not see anything other than Jake's old white pickup truck on the gravel of the church lot. Petey looked up at Jake and meowed loudly.

"They're gone, Petey. They went home."

Petey meowed again.

"No. They didn't like you. Or Tassy."

Petey offered his odd growl-meow in reply.

"But I told them . . . I told my mother that both of you are staying. She didn't like it. But I told her."

Petey meowed again, this time with his head tilted to the side.

"Yes, Petey. It did feel good. Really good. Healthy, almost."

Petey stretched up and put his front paws on Jake's knee. Jake picked him up and held him, sort of like a fullback holds a football. Petey meowed.

"I know. I feel good. I feel really good."

The two of them went back into the parsonage.

"And now I could really use a stiff cup of coffee."

9

The old Buick rattled and knocked as it came to a stop in the parking lot. Jake was outside, pulling weeds around the front steps of the church. One of the church members came in once a week with a large lawn tractor and cut all the grass but did not do weeding and primping. And Jake did not feel it proper of him to point out the weeds that he'd missed. Plus, he liked basic, manual labor. Weeding offered the opportunity to start a job, finish a job, and see the results of the job in short order.

Jake stood and waved to the driver, dropped the weeds he had just pulled into the large pile, and came over to offer his greetings.

"Vern, what brings you here today? On a Friday." Jake asked.

Vern clambered out of the car, fighting with the seat belt, muttering "Infernal contraption" under his breath. Once freed, he nearly tumbled out, and Jake made a move to stabilize him.

"I'm fine. I'm fine," Vern replied, all but brushing Jake away. "I have always hated this rattletrap of a car. I thought Buicks were good cars, but I'll never buy another one. General Motors, my foot."

Jake nodded.

The car is probably twenty-five years old. I think he's gotten his money's worth out of it.

Vern glared at Jake. Jake realized that this look was a permanent feature of Vern's and not to be taken seriously.

"I got food in the back for the girl. Eleanor had to get her hair done today. Why on Friday, I have no idea. Should be Saturday so it's all set for Sunday, but no, she says. Friday is her regular day and I got nothing to do all morning. So I went to Doug's and bought some food."

"You went grocery shopping?" Jake replied. There were four bags of groceries on the backseat.

"With the prices they charge, the owner should be wearing a mask and carrying a gun. Almost three dollars for a gallon of milk. That's just robbery. A young girl like Tassy can't afford that."

Jake thought he saw something in Vern's face, or his eyes, soften, but just for a moment. A very fleeting moment.

"So, Sonny, make yourself useful and carry some of this inside. She in there now?"

"I'm sure she is. Said that her stomach has been bothering her."

"Yeah, I heard. Bought some of that Eye-talian tea that's good for that. Made out of flowers—cammo something or other. Probably an old wives' tale. But it couldn't hurt, I guess."

Jake shouldered three bags, and Vern barely managed to lift the last one.

"She should be getting a job; that's what she should be doing. Can't live in the RV forever, you know. Eleanor wouldn't mind her staying, but come winter—well, she needs her own place."

"She's looking, Vern," Jake said. "I know that. Looking through the newspaper. Not much there."

"Maybe I'll ask around. People in this town owe me some favors."

"Well, Vern, that would be very kind of you."

Vern snorted.

"Just don't tell her, okay? I don't want any special thanks or nothing. Okay?"

Jake tapped at the RV door.

"Sure thing, Vern. Sure thing."

⸺ ◦◦◦ ⸺

Jake discovered a hidden talent in his new feline companion: Petey loved playing fetch. Jake had been in the office, and after a particularly troubling attempt at summing up the sermon, he'd snatched the last page of the sermon, wadded it up into a ball, and tossed it at the small trash can in the corner. Of course, he'd missed, and the ball had bounced back onto the floor. Petey watched this intently from his perch on the windowsill, then took off like a rabbit as the crumpled paper ball rolled toward the bookcases. He grabbed it in his mouth, shook it once, then trotted back to Jake and proudly dropped it at his feet, staring up at him with a great sense of accomplishment. Jake threw it again, and Petey chased it again and returned it to him just as promptly. They kept the game up for several minutes, until the phone rang.

This morning, Saturday morning, Jake sat on his front steps, enjoying the bright sunshine. He took a badly dented Ping-Pong ball he'd found in one of his boxes (how it got there he had no clue, as he had not played Ping-Pong since high school) and tossed it into the soft grass beside the church. Petey tore off like a cheetah, little clumps of grass kicking up from his rear paws as his nails dug into the turf. The dented ball had enough odd, flat surfaces that Petey could get his teeth on so it made retrieving easy. A dozen times, Jake threw the ball, and even though Ping-Pong balls don't travel all that far when thrown, Petey would watch the ball leave his hand and take off like a shot, following the arc as intently as a real cheetah might watch a fleeing antelope.

By the end, Petey began to pant a little, and at the last throw, he dropped the ball a few feet out of Jake's grasp, as if to say, "I'm done chasing for now. Let's take a breather."

It was at that moment that a car pulled into the church lot. Jake thought he recognized the driver, but the sun made it difficult to see.

"Hello, Pastor Jake, Petey. Just the two people I wanted to see."

"Hi, Emma . . . Dr. Grainger."

She wore her official doctor's coat and was carrying her official veterinarian's black leather satchel. The outfit and equipment may not have been actually official, but to Jake, they looked official enough.

"I know. It's Emma. But right now, you look like a doctor."

Petey ran up to her and rubbed against her leg.

"You know they do this to sort of mark the humans they lay claim to?" she said.

"Really? I just thought he liked me when he did that."

Emma smiled. "Well, that's what *The Big Golden Book of Vet Knowledge* said. What do books know, anyhow?"

Emma looked up toward the sky.

"You fix the steeple yet?"

Jake turned to look up as well.

"No. But it is crooked. That's been confirmed. A member of the church who said he knew all about steeples installed it twenty years ago. Turned out that he didn't, and no one wanted to offend him while he was still alive by going up there and fixing his mistake."

"How's his health now?" Emma said in a furtive whisper.

"Oh, he died seven years ago. But no one has formed the right committee to fix it. Money issues. Time. Energy. Now we're the church with the crooked steeple and the cat in the congregation."

Emma bent down and picked Petey up. He appeared to enjoy Emma's attention.

"I've heard. Someone said that the newspaper might want to do a story on it. You've got the town talking about your church, Pastor Jake."

Jake hoped his expression was that of happiness or surprise or glee, but that was not how he truly felt. His shoulder twinged again, sharply this time, as if he were expending a lot of energy to keep something hidden. He was used to that feeling. And he was getting used to the twinge.

"Well, I guess there are worse things that could happen. So, what brings you out here? On a Saturday. You don't have office hours on Saturday, do you?"

"Just in the morning. Some people can't get in during the week. But I came to give Petey a s-h-o-t. I completely forgot about it when I worked on his paw. No way of knowing what sort of vaccines he had before."

At the word *vaccine*, Petey squirmed a bit. Emma held on tight.

"Can we go inside? Just in case he knows what a vaccine is?"

Jake shouldered the door open. "The fellow who built the steeple installed the door as well."

Emma gave Petey to Jake, then opened her bag. She took out a small vial and a hypodermic. "He needs a rabies shot. And a booster shot. I'm nearly certain he would have had the standard vaccinations when he was a kitten."

She filled the hypodermic. Petey obviously saw what was coming and while he meowed loudly and pitifully, he did not try to squirm away. She poked once and injected the vaccine. She quickly grabbed the other and injected it into the other hip. Again, Petey yowled loudly but did not try to claw free.

"There. Now he is up-to-date. Legal and healthy."

Jake carefully put Petey on the floor. He looked up at both of them, meowed once more, in an angry tone this time, and stalked out of the kitchen, his tail held high, obviously more than a bit peeved at both humans.

"Both spots will be a little sore for a day or two. No playing tackle football, okay?"

"You said that he probably had shots as a kitten. How could you tell?"

"Shy of running elaborate blood work—and very expensive blood work—you can't. But Petey looks like a Siberian mix. Maybe with Maine coon. I looked it up to make sure, and he's got breed characteristics for both. Thick, nonshedding coat, right color, right body structure, right face. Siberians, even mixed, are not that common—I've never had one in my practice yet. Full blooded ones are still rather rare—and expensive. Around $1,000 a cat."

Jake whistled his surprise.

"Wow. I had no idea. You can get cats for free."

"Then you're lucky, aren't you? A thousand-dollar cat picked you. Oh, yes, and the breed is said to be almost dog-like in some of its behaviors."

"I could vouch for that. We were playing fetch-the-Ping-Pong-ball when you came. He loves retrieving things."

"Funny he doesn't have a microchip, though. Expensive cats usually do. But not all of them," Emma said. Then she looked around. "Nice place. I wouldn't have imagined this from outside."

Jake nodded. "It is nice. Very comfortable. And almost stylish."

Emma narrowed her eyes. "You know, this could be a wormhole in space and time and we've been teleported into another dimension. Somewhere far away from Coudersport."

"You're a science fiction fan?"

Emma picked up the two used hypodermic needles.

"I like some of it. I'm a sucker for the *Dr. Who* reruns on PBS."

Jake nodded again.

She is easy to talk with.

"Listen, Emma . . . if you're not busy . . . or don't have other arrangements . . . how about coffee or dessert or dinner or something . . . Sunday evening?"

Emma's eyebrows rose in surprise.

"This Sunday? Can you do that on a Sunday?"

"I'm . . . I'm pretty sure. The church hasn't had Sunday evening services for a decade. So, sure. I can go out on a Sunday evening."

Emma shrugged.

"Sure. I have nothing on my calendar. How about 6:00? Closing time in Coudersport on Sunday evenings is even earlier than during the week."

"Sure. That would be great. I'll see you then."

From the living room came the low, rumbling yowl from Petey, as if saying, "Good riddance."

"And tell Petey I'm sorry for the shots," Emma said as she walked out.

I do smell lilacs. Must be her soap. Or disinfectant. Or something.

The two elders, Bobby Richard and Rudolph Keilback, stood in the back of the church as the service started—the official ushers of the day. Ushers in a small church did not have many functions. They handed out bulletins that listed the hymn numbers, the sermon title and Scripture reference, the upcoming meetings, the year-to-date finances, and the weekly attendance figures.

Rudolph fanned himself with his stack of bulletins. The organist started to play the first hymn and most everyone who regularly attended were in their seats.

"You read this yet?" Bobby asked, his voice low and elderlike.

"Nope. Not yet."

"You see the attendance number?"

"Nope."

"Last Sunday, we were up twenty more than last year. That's as high as we been in . . . well . . . in years."

Rudolph wiped at his face with his other hand. The weather carried only a hint of warmth, and already, Rudolph was sweating. Summer and high temperatures were not kind to big men like Elder Keilback.

"I guess we made the right decision when we hired Pastor Jake."

"Think we did, too," Bobby added with a smile.

"The cat don't hurt, either. Got people talking."

Bobby craned his head.

"Is he here yet? Didn't see him come in."

"Yep. He's up there, sitting on his normal chair. Just waiting."

"Don't that beat all," Bobby replied.

"We made a good call on letting the cat stay, too."

"That we did, Brother Keilback. That we did."

"I guess it shouldn't matter why the new people are here, just that they're here is a good thing."

∽∾∽

Jake pulled into the drive and hurried out of his car. Emma called out from the second-story porch. "I'll be right down, Jake. Give me just a minute."

Jake leaned against his truck. He had washed it that afternoon—getting it mostly clean. He'd even vacuumed the interior, though it was already fairly clean. He was not one of those people who use their vehicle as a mobile recycling bin. The mats, however, had needed the cleaning, and he'd even taken Windex to the truck's windows—inside and out.

Emma came out in a rush and tossed a white sweater around her shoulders. She wore a simple blue blouse and jeans, but they looked nearly elegant to Jake.

The lilac smell is stronger now. Must be the soap. I like it.

Both settled in the truck.

"Where to?" Jake asked. "You have me at a disadvantage. I only know how to get from the church to Doug's Foods. And the movie theater. And maybe to Kaytee's."

"Oh, yes. Kaytee's. I heard about your mom and aunt visiting."

"Does anything happen in town that everyone doesn't know about the next day?"

"Nope. And remember that in Coudersport, you're almost a celebrity."

"What? A celebrity? Get out," Jake replied, surprised.

"No. Really. You'll be one of the better-known people in town. Already are, kind of. Me too. A sort-of celebrity. Not as much as you. I'm a doctor—of animals—so I'm a little lower than a real doctor. I'm a woman—makes the doctor thing unusual. I'm from here, so I have known many of the people in town all my life. I meet lots of people during the course of a week. It all adds up. We may not be the Hollywood sort of celebrities, but there's no escaping it. Like I said, don't do anything foolish here. They'll find you out."

Jake stopped at the stop sign at the end of the block.

Emma finally snapped her seat belt closed. "Are you hungry? Like let's-eat-right-now sort of hungry?"

Jake looked both ways and shrugged. "Not so much. A little. I don't know. After preaching, I stay sort of a little jangled the rest of the day. At home, I usually wind up just picking at things. Chips. Pickles. Popsicles. I don't know."

"You want to drive a little? Around town? I can point out the famous spots. And where people live. We have enough light for an hour's tour. Then, if we're hungry, we can split a milkshake at the malt shop."

"Really? You have a malt shop in Coudersport?"

"Of course not," laughed Emma. "Back in the fifties, we did—I think. Now we have McDonald's. Not the same, but it's what we have."

Jake liked being in the truck with Emma. He liked how easy she was to talk with. He liked that she laughed easily. That she was smart and witty. He recalled his time with Barbara Ann. It was so different. Even though he knew he shouldn't compare the two, and of course not this early, because he didn't really know if this was the start of a relationship or not (though he hoped it was), being with Emma felt better. Easier.

"Sure. Let's do the Coudersport tour. I'm up for that."

For the next hour, Jake and Emma drove slowly through town, and out and back again. She showed him the high school and the elementary school, and the homes of nearly all of his elder board, the organist, and the Sunday school superintendent. She showed him where she grew up and a good place to fish. She gave him the pros and cons of the supermarkets in town and told him which doctor—the human kind—she considered to be the best. "I'm still auditioning dentists. Haven't settled on one yet. But I inherited good teeth, so I don't have to rush."

She does have good teeth. Very nice smile.

When darkness came, Emma suggested that a trip to McDonald's might just be the proper end to an evening of cruising the town. "It's what we did in high school," she declared.

They both ordered Big Mac meals and sat inside the very bright restaurant and used too much ketchup on their fries. Jake ordered a small vanilla shake, Emma chose chocolate. They drank them as he drove back to her house. He pulled into the driveway.

He was about to turn the truck off.

"Leave it on, Jake. I'm going to run in and this way no one will see what I'm about to do. The porch light is too bright and I have curious neighbors." She held the shake in her right hand, undid her seat belt, and leaned toward him, closer and closer. Then she brushed his lips, cold from the vanilla shake, with hers, cold from chocolate. More than a brush, it was closer than that, and a little longer. It was a nearly chaste, chilly, longish peck, but earnest at the same time.

"I had a ball, Pastor Jake. We should do this again sometime."

He was still blinking as she slipped out and the bright dome light of the cab came on.

"See, too much light."

All he could say before she closed the door to the truck was, "Thanks. I had a great time, too." And she waved and disappeared up the stairs and into the darkness.

<hr>

Jake arrived home, after dark, and Petey sat in the middle of the kitchen floor, almost at attention, and meowed loudly when he came in, obviously upset at being left alone. His stare could be deadly.

"Hey, Petey, cut me some slack, would you?" Jake said as he tossed his truck keys in the blue porcelain bowl on the counter. "I was with Dr. Emma. You know, Winston's mom."

Petey narrowed his eyes.

She is NOT his mother. They cohabitate. Please. I am not stupid like that dog is. And tell her to give him a bath more often. Dogs are simply horrid at keeping themselves clean.

Jake walked over to his new coffeepot/machine, which used little plastic pods to whoosh out a single cup of coffee. Petey watched him as he stored away an armful of different boxes filled with pods and fussed with the machine, pressing buttons, seemingly at random.

He makes a big to-do about each cup—so he must like it. Still smells like an old raccoon, if you ask me.

Jake poured half-and-half into the freshly brewed cup of coffee and opened the kitchen door.

"You want to come out for a while? Get a breath of fresh air?"

He sounds downright chipper this evening. Why is that? And isn't chipper *an odd word? I wonder where that comes from.*

Jake took his usual spot on one of the lawn chairs. Petey sniffed about for a while, then joined him in the other lawn chair. Jake had found a round, metal table at a garage sale that he had placed between the chairs. That's where he put his coffee cup. The breeze carried the smell to Petey's face and the cat wrinkled his nose in reaction.

"We went for a long ride around town. We had fun. She is really easy to talk to—and funny."

Petey meowed in reply, a cautious meow.

"I know she is not a churchgoer. But we're talking about it."

Petey chirped.

"Well . . . we will talk about it. I bet she's open to discuss it."

Petey waited a moment, then replied with a low, rumbling meow.

"She's nice, Petey. She listens to me. And it's not serious. We're friends. That's all."

Petey looked the other way, thinking he heard movement by the back door.

"Well . . . "

Petey spun around and chirped again.

"She did kiss me goodnight. That was different."

Petey sat up straighter. He stared harder.

"Just an innocent peck. That's all. Between friends."

Petey narrowed his eyes. Even though it was dark, he was sure Jake could see his reaction.

"I'll be careful, Petey. I know. I know. I'll be careful."

10

Tassy put on her good sneakers and started to walk. This time, toward town.

Pastor Jake said he checked the odometer of the truck and from the church to McDonald's was only four miles. That's not so far. And he said Kaytee's was only a few blocks farther. He said their food was better. And not expensive at all. I'll see how long four miles actually is.

Staying inside the RV all day was making her a little claustrophobic. Tassy cleaned every morning, washed every dirty dish, made the bed, did not allow any clutter to form anywhere, but doing all of that did not take long. She read the employment ads in the paper and, so far, had found nothing she was qualified to do. And there were very few employment ads to begin with. A couple of them she asked Jake about—selling from home, working from home, and the like—and he had assured her that all of them were simply scams and would cost her money to sign up.

So, today she decided to wear her relatively good clothes, with sneakers for walking, and head into town to put in applications at whatever business would take them. She knew that Jake would drive her there, or she could call Vern or Eleanor, but she wanted to do this on her own. And Pastor Jake said a brisk walk is at least three to four miles per hour. So it would only take her an hour to get there. If she was really tired, she could always head back to Vern and Eleanor's house to arrange a ride back to the RV.

Four miles did not prove to be an insurmountable distance. Almost before she knew it, she was down the street from the McDonald's. She had eaten breakfast, a couple of crackers and some ginger ale, and the walk seemed to settle her stomach, which remained a little sensitive and a little nervous. She thought a single cheeseburger might be okay, with a Sprite or something clear. Maybe even a cup of hot tea. In the past few weeks, she had developed a fondness for tea laced with honey.

She ordered her food and looked around. There were no empty single seats or empty tables. The restaurant wasn't large and it was a bit too cool to try and sit outside. So Tassy held the bag in her hand, her cup of tea in the other, and waited off to the side.

Someone will get up soon.

In the corner, a tallish blonde woman, older than Tassy but not really old, motioned her over.

"You can sit here. No sense in waiting. Your food will get cold."

Tassy smiled. "You sure? I don't want to intrude."

"No. I'm by myself. It's fine. I'm Emma," she said, and gestured for Tassy to sit.

"And I'm Tassy."

Emma offered the most puzzled look.

"Tassy from Pastor Jake's church?"

Tassy removed the single cheeseburger and laid it on a napkin.

"I am. Well, I live right next to it. In Vern's big RV. Until I find a job. They're letting me stay for a while. They're nice people. Vern and Eleanor. And Pastor Jake, too."

Emma shook her head in what looked like amazement.

"And I'm Emma Grainger. The veterinarian. I fixed Petey's paw when Pastor Jake first showed up in town."

Tassy could not help from grinning. She leaned in closer and whispered. "He took you out on a date last night."

Emma whispered back. "I know. I was there."

Then they both giggled.

"Small world, isn't it?" Tassy said.

"Well, Tassy, I don't know how small the world is—but Coudersport is a very small town."

Tassy wondered if Emma would ask her if Pastor Jake said anything about their "date," but she didn't.

Maybe old people don't care as much.

"Did Pastor Jake bring you?" Emma asked, looking out into the parking lot, scanning for Jake's white pickup.

Tassy chewed slowly, making sure her stomach was ready for the food.

"No. He would have if I asked. But it's not a bad walk. Good exercise."

"Walk four miles for a McDonald's burger? You must be hungry," Emma said.

"You know, I'm not. But I want to look for a job. I thought I might put in applications around town. Maybe here, too."

Emma took a drink and appeared to be thinking something important. Tassy couldn't tell for sure. Older people often puzzled her. Like Vern, who always looked angry but was actually very nice.

"Tassy, what kind of job are you looking for?"

"Anything, I guess. I don't have much experience. I was in school before. The Community College of Philadelphia. I was just taking general studies. But now I'm looking for any sort of job. I don't mind working hard."

"Do you like animals?" Emma asked.

"I do," she replied, brightening. "I love Petey. He comes to visit in the morning if I don't feel good. He seems to want to take care of me."

"And you don't mind cleaning? Sweeping and mopping and that sort of thing?"

"No. I don't. I'm sort of a neat person. I like things tidy."

Emma looked away for a long moment. Her face grew serious.

"Would you consider working in my practice?"

"In a vet's office? That would be great. You mean it? What would I do?"

"I could use someone to do the cleaning, because I don't have the energy to do it at the end of a long day. Keep the supply cabinet up-to-date. Maybe answer the phone when I'm with a patient. Fill out patient charts. Send vaccination reminders. It's all on the computer. I could offer four days a week. I can't pay a lot, but it would be more than you would make at McDonald's. And it would all be daylight hours."

"Could I do all that? Is your phone system complicated?"

"Just two lines with one button each."

"I could do that. I could. I would love to do that. And be around animals all day. Wow. That would be super."

"Well, why don't we finish our lunch, then I'll take you over and we can talk about hours and pay and all of it. Does that sound good?"

"Doctor Grainger, it sounds like a miracle. It truly does."

⸻

Jake tapped at Tassy's door. She did not answer.

"Must be out for a walk, Petey. Did you see where she went?"

Petey chirped a reply and looked up at Jake with a quizzical look.

"Well . . . you want to walk by the river?"

Petey remained sitting, his tail wrapped around his rear paws. Usually whenever Jake said "walk," Petey was up and circling his legs, ready and excited to be walking anywhere.

"What about that way?" Jake asked, pointing to the west. The woods grew thick just past the church. Jake had yet to explore that part of the neighborhood. Petey just sat.

"You want to go for a ride?"

With that Petey jumped and ran toward Jake's truck, turning every few feet, looking back at Jake, making sure he was following.

"Okay, then. A ride. There's no one on the church's sick/must-visit list. I guess a ride would be okay. It gives me time to think, right, Petey? Being in charge of a church brings up a lot of things that I never had to deal with before."

Petey meowed loudly and scratched at the door on his side of the truck. Jake opened it and Petey hopped up, assuming his standard position. Jake drove toward town and then through town, waving at a few people he passed.

A celebrity. That's what she called me.

After the fourth honk and wave, Jake smiled to himself.

Maybe I am . . . a little.

He drove east until the town receded and only road and woods and fields remained.

Of course, they may be waving at Petey, and not me.

He drove on, not fast, watching the scenery roll past. North central Pennsylvania offered wonderful, natural vistas. Once outside of town, the landscape became nearly uninhabited. He drove east on Route 6 until he reached Denton Hills State

Park. He pulled into the large parking lot and looked up at the labyrinth of ski trails, now covered in green.

Petey meowed.

"We're not stopping. Just turning around, that's all. I could come here next winter. I could take up skiing."

Petey meowed loudly.

"No? You don't think I would be any good at it?"

He meowed again, as if to say, "No, you wouldn't be."

"Okay. We'll head back."

Midway between the empty ski runs and Coudersport, Jake saw a canted sign, the sun catching it just so, almost illuminating it, the sign almost lost in the foliage, covered with a tangle of vines. In a week or so, the sign would be hidden beneath the full greening of summer vegetation.

"Coudersport Ice Mine. Nature's Amazing Curiosity."

He pulled to the side of the road and stared at it.

"Petey, what's an ice mine?"

Petey chirped.

"Don't know, do you?"

Jake knew that farmers cut ice from lakes and rivers and stored the ice blocks under straw for the summer. But there were no large bodies of water nearby, from what Jake could see. A small stream lay on the other side of the highway, but that could not produce enough ice to furnish an ice mine, or to call it an ice mine.

He thought about taking a picture of it, but didn't have his good camera with him and his phone's camera would not do it justice. He looked around and tried to make himself remember the location, though much of the road looked like every other part of the road.

"Who would I ask about an old ice mine?"

Petey looked at him and chirped.

"Well, Emma might know. I could try."

He looked back to the road. There wasn't a car to be seen. He pulled out and headed back to Coudersport.

Ice mine? Ice mine?

He pulled into a service station.

"I need gas, Petey, okay?"

Petey sat, implacable, silent, and simply looked around at the other cars.

Jake went inside to pay.

"Have you ever heard of an ice mine around here?" he asked the clerk. "I saw an old sign along the road back a ways."

"The Coudersport Ice Mine? Sure. The road there is Ice Mine Road. Used to be famous, I guess. And aren't you that new pastor in town? The one with the cat? The cat that comes to church?"

"Jake Wilkerson," he said, and held out his hand. "The cat's waiting for me in the truck. Petey."

"Bailey Stewart. Don't go to your church, but I heard people talking about it. Mind if I come out and say hello to Petey? I'm more of a dog person, but cats are all right."

He followed Jake out to the truck. Jake opened the door on the passenger side.

"That's Petey."

"That's a pretty cat," Bailey said. "Can I pet him?"

"Sure. I guess. He doesn't get ruffled by much."

Bailey reached and stroked the top of Petey's head. Petey meowed softly in response.

"That's a handsome cat. Beautiful coat. And he likes going for rides?"

"Seems to," Jake said. "But what about the Ice Mine?"

Bailey stood there petting Petey. "Oh, yeah. It was the darndest thing. Been closed for, I don't know, years now. People say way back when, Indians had found a silver mine in these parts. That's the story. Some early settler or farmer thought he knew where it was and dug this mineshaft to get at the silver. Never found a trace of it. Wound up with a big hole in the ground. What happened was the mineshaft would be clear of ice all winter. But come spring and summer, giant icicles would form all along the roof. Like it didn't know what season it was—or like a hole opened onto the other side of the world or something. For a long time, they used to charge a quarter to go inside. But everybody is playing video games now, and hardly anyone came anymore, so they closed it down. The mine is just down this road, maybe ten miles."

"Ice in the summer—and not in the winter?" Jake said. "That doesn't make sense."

"Some professor from Penn State or somewhere came to look at it. Somehow the water in the rocks freezes during the winter, he said, and traps cold air in the rocks. When spring comes, the cold air gets loose and starts to freeze what water is dripping. He said it made sense. And he was a doctor of something or other."

Jake thanked him for the information.

"Say, there, Pastor. What time is your church? Maybe I'll take a Sunday and come see the cat. Would that be okay? Just to visit?"

"Sure," Jake said. "We would love to have you visit. Service is at 11:00. Petey would like to see you there as well."

"Okay, then. Maybe I'll see you some Sunday, then. Bye, Petey."

Petey looked at him and meowed a farewell.

"Don't that beat all?" Bailey said.

Jake headed back to town.

Freezing in the summer, empty in the winter. The exact opposite of how things should be. And there's always some logical explanation for those curious quirks of nature. Sounds like me—sort of. Full of faith when it didn't matter and now that I should have faith . . . I don't, really. Icicles in the summer. Paradoxical, isn't it?

The sun had turned velvet purple as Jake pulled into the church parking lot.

Quite the paradox.

———— ✦ ————

Jake stopped in at Kaytee's for a tuna fish salad sandwich. He liked tuna fish salad, but every time he tried to make it at home, it never tasted just right.

Easier—and better—to get it at a restaurant. They must use special ingredients.

Petey was at home this noon, so Jake had the luxury of a slow lunch, complete with coffee and pie afterward. He ate too many meals standing up in his kitchen.

The sandwich was great, the coffee was hearty, and the blackberry pie was more than delicious. He ate with deliberateness, slowly.

A man came and waved. His face was familiar—probably attended the church—but Jake could not put a name with the face.

"Dan Rummel, Pastor. I've been at your church. Once, anyways, since you've been here. Not a regular church person, I admit. I hope that's okay. I hope it's okay that you can be seen talking to a non-churchgoer in a public place."

Jake waved him to sit down.

"Of course we can talk. When a pastor can't talk to a person who doesn't go to church, well, that would be a sad day."

"Good. Thanks. Like I said, I'm Dan. Dan Rummel. I run Honest Dan's Used Kar Emporium on Sixth. That's *car* spelled with a K. People stop and tell me its spelled wrong."

"Do they really?"

"Well . . . no. Not yet. But they might. I've seen you drive by a few times. You've got a white pickup, right? A '87 F-150, right?"

"'86."

"Honest mistake. Not much difference between those two model years. You think of upgrading to a newer vehicle? I've got a couple of great late model truck deals just waiting for you."

Jake shook his head. "Not right now, Dan. The old truck is running fine. Maybe before winter. We'll see."

Dan pulled out a card from the breast pocket of his yellow sport coat.

"See, it's a magnet, too. You can put it on your refrigerator to hold shopping lists or pictures of the kids. Oh, wait, you're not married, right? Someone said that."

"No. Still single."

"Footloose and fancy-free. That's the way to be. Although for a pastor there may be a different definition of footloose and fancy-free, am I right?"

"I think you are correct. For me, anyhow."

Dan suddenly grew serious. The grin left his face. He pulled his chair closer to the table. Jake was glad he had finished his pie. If not, he would have faced the dilemma of eating in front of someone or not eating and waiting until they left.

"I've got a question, Pastor. You mind if I call you 'Pastor'? You're not exactly *my* pastor, but then again, you are *a* pastor, so the title should still be good, right?"

"'Pastor' is fine. Whatever you're comfortable with, really."

"Okay. I have a church sort of question. Been bugging me for years."

"Go ahead," Jake said, as he tried to put a studious, serious look on his face.

"So, when I was a kid, the family went to a loud church—lots of arm waving and shouting. Nothing wrong with it, I suppose. Baptized when I was ten. Like I really knew what I was doing at that age—sure. But here's the problem. Since getting out of high school, I don't go to church all that much. Couple of times a year. But I was baptized. So that should be enough, right? Do I still have to go to church? Should I feel guilty about not going? Because I really do, and I don't like feeling guilty."

Jake waited to respond.

"The Bible does say that we should not give up on gathering together."

"Does it give the number of times a year we have to do it?" Dan asked.

Jake had encountered such questions before.

"The Bible doesn't give you a calendar or a checklist of things you must accomplish. It does say that we need to be in fellowship, Dan. That's important."

Dan appeared to grow even more serious.

"But what happens if I stop having faith? Does my baptism make up for that? Because I can't say I believe much about religion anymore."

Jake drew in a breath.

"Dan, you need to have faith. Without it, there is no hope, no salvation."

I am such a hypocrite. I'm telling him what someone should be telling me. No faith means no hope.

"You sure about that, Pastor? Really sure?"

I should tell him the truth. But I can't.

"I am."

"Do you let people in church who don't believe? Isn't there some sort of test these days?"

"No tests, Dan."

"So it's okay to have doubts? You sure about that, Pastor?"

"Yes. I am sure, Dan. Tell you what. You think about it. And come see me in a week or so. Call me. We can meet here. Or I can come to the lot and look at the trucks you have."

"Really? You want to look at the inventory? Okay, then. I'll think about it. And you have to promise me that you'll think about a new truck. Okay?"

"Dan, we have a deal."

꧁꧂

Petey growled and stared at the door. Jake came out from his office. "Did someone knock?"

Petey meowed and stared at the kitchen door. This time, Jake did hear it. A soft rapping.

"Tassy," he said as he opened the door. "How are you today?"

She had her arms folded across her chest. The skies had been cloudy and gray since morning and a wind came down from New York, almost cold and biting. Tassy wore a black, hooded sweatshirt. Her nose was a little red.

"Come on in. Do you want some tea?"

She bent down, petted Petey, then picked him up and he began to purr loudly.

"No. Not today. I've had some. But I need to ask a favor."

"Sure. I'll help if I can."

"I need to buy a bicycle."

"A bike?"

"I need to be able to get to work."

"Tassy, I could take you. What about when it rains . . . wait, did you say you need to get to work? Did you find a job?"

Her face nearly disappeared behind her grin.

"I did. Or it found me, sort of. Emma—your Emma, the lady veterinarian—hired me to help clean and answer phones and stuff. It's only four days a week, but I can save up and maybe find a place of my own and a car and stuff. But I need a bike right now. It takes too long to walk to town from here."

"Emma . . . Dr. Grainger hired you?"

"I was waiting for a table at McDonald's and she invited me to sit with her, and we introduced ourselves and talked and she knew who I was, and I said I was looking for a job and she said she needed help with cleaning stuff, so we talked and now I have a job starting Monday morning. That's like a miracle, isn't it, Pastor Jake? A little miracle. Not like being cured of cancer or anything. But still."

"I guess it is, Tassy." *And why does the word* miracle *sound so hollow and false to me? It is the truth, right? Or it could be, I guess. A little miracle. Just not my miracle.*

"So I thought I could buy a used bike. Do they have, like, a resale shop in Coudersport?"

Jake squinched up his face.

"I . . . I don't think they do. But it's Friday. Most garage sales start today. There's always someone selling a used bike. We could go look."

"Can we? Do you have time? That would be super."

"Tassy, I can make time."

Petey stood by the truck's passenger side door and hopped up when Jake opened it. He took his normal position on the seat and then stared at Tassy as she attempted to enter, as if wondering where she was planning on sitting.

"Petey, move to the middle. Tassy has to sit down."

Petey meow-growled, one of his doglike behaviors, and reluctantly gave ground, edging over only a few inches to make way for Tassy.

Before Jake started the truck, he pulled Petey more toward the middle.

"It won't kill you to give up your spot, Petey. Be a gentleman, okay?"

Petey meowed loudly, in protest, but settled himself in the center of the bench seat, obviously unhappy at being usurped from his rightful seating choice.

They drove through downtown and headed off into the residential area. On the first block they saw two garage sales with cardboard signs and streamers announcing the sale. Jake slowly cruised past, waved at the people sitting in folding lawn chairs, looking for a bike in the assemblage of stuff displayed on the driveways.

"No bikes here," he said after looking at both sales. "We'll keep driving. I'm sure there'll be one."

Two blocks over, there was a giant sheet of cardboard with the badly drawn words BIG HUGE GARAGE SALE written with a fading black marker hung at an angle on a telephone pole.

"This looks promising," Jake said, and pulled to the curb. In the shade of the garage stood a tangle of used bikes. Tassy got out, excited, and Petey followed her, meowing the whole way.

Someone called out, "Hey! There's Petey!"

A woman in a very snug Coudersport Falcons sweatshirt bent down to the cat. "Aren't you the sweetest thing ever? I just love it when I see you in church. You're just so pretty."

She looked up to Jake. "I'm Millie LeGran. We come to church, on and off. Sort of mostly off, 'cause my husband says Sunday is the only day he gets to sleep in. But I've been coming since I heard about the cat. Really. He's such a cutie."

Petey sat back on his haunches, apparently drinking in the affection like a thirsty man.

"Well, that's good," Jake replied, trying to be sincere.

I am sincere. Aren't I? They're coming. Fellowship. Hear the word. What more could I ask?

"Do you have any bikes for sale? Tassy—you know, the young girl living in Vern's RV— is looking for one."

"I do. I do have bikes. When all five kids are grown and gone, they leave a lot of stuff behind. Like a dozen bikes of different sizes. I've been saving them, thinking that they'll come back and get them, but Bud says they're never coming back for an old bike, so I should just sell them along with all their other junk. He's not very sentimental, my Bud. So, they're all for sale. Tassy, what kind of bike do you want? A red one? The blue one is nice. I think this one has different speeds on it or something. Try it out. I had Bud pump up all the tires this week."

Tassy pulled out a blue one with gears, a girl's bike, that seemed to be her size. She climbed on top and road it down the driveway and began pedaling as she got to the street.

"I got helmets to go with that, too, Pastor Jake."

Petey watched Tassy ride away and meowed loudly. He ran to the end of the driveway, watching her. He called out again, a very loud meow this time, the loudest Jake had heard yet.

He didn't think Tassy heard but she turned around and pedaled back, coasting into the driveway. Petey ran and sniffed at her and then sniffed at the bike.

"What do you think? Does it ride good?"

"It does. Real nice. Fits me perfectly. This will be great."

Tassy got off the bike, put out the kickstand, and stepped back.

"How much?"

Millie sighed.

"I was going to ask $20 for each bike—and then, you know, haggle some. Bud said they're worth more, but this is a garage sale. But since you're with Pastor Jake and Petey . . . tell you what—I'll make this a donation to the church. Can I do that, Pastor Jake? I don't really care about the money. I just want to get rid of things. Just take it. And take one of these helmets. Try 'em on. Find one that fits. Okay?"

Tassy smiled like a child on Christmas morning.

"You mean it? This is so nice of you. But I should pay you something for this."

"Tell you what: you put a couple of extra dollars in the collection plate next Sunday and we'll call it even."

She picked Petey up.

"Especially since you brought Mr. Petey with you. I'm glad I had a chance to meet him personally. He's as nice as I thought he would be."

Jake could have sworn Petey's next meow smacked of smugness, as did his wincing expression as Mrs. LeGran gave him an extra special, long hug of farewell.

11

Emma, this is Jake. I don't want you to think that I do everything at the last minute—because I don't. Normally, I'm much more organized and scripted. I was supposed to join our Woman's Guild and Assistance Society meeting tonight, which has been cancelled since both chairwomen have come down with something and neither wanted the committee to meet without them. So I have the evening free. Rather than the two of us eating alone, would you like to share a table at Kaytee's?"

Emma, at that specific moment, was holding a frozen lasagna dinner that promised great taste with "only 375 delicious calories!"

"I would love to," she said as she stuffed the box back into the already overpacked freezer. "What time? And will this be formal?"

"Yes. I am wearing tails. And would 6:00 be too late? Or early?"

"6:00 is great. See you there."

Petey was staring at Jake during the entire conversation.

"Hey, Petey. It's just for dinner. No milkshake kisses after this meal, since we're driving separately."

Petey shut his eyes in response, as if trying not to think of what a milkshake kiss might be.

"I'll be home early."

Jake walked into the restaurant and saw Emma waving from a booth in the far corner.

"Hey."

"Hey, yourself. I bet the rest of the committee was disappointed that they wouldn't have you all to themselves."

Jake's face showed his total puzzlement.

"Jake, you can't be serious. You're a single fellow, reasonably attractive, and the talk of the religious circuit around here. Or the society circuit—at least as much as anything in Coudersport could be considered 'society.' Don't you think that the ladies-in-waiting would have wanted to have the meeting—regardless of the lack of leadership?"

"You think so?" Jake seemed both oblivious and surprised.

"Yes, really," Emma said, shaking her head in mock amazement at Jake's naiveté. "I thought pastors had to be perceptive."

"I am perceptive. Sort of. Maybe. Aren't I?"

"No, Jake, you're not. But that in itself is charming. It's why the ladies of the Women's Guild love you and are so disappointed."

A waitress came up to the table.

"Hey, Pastor Jake. Nice to see you tonight. How are you? How's Petey?" She turned her head toward Emma and added, dryly, "Dr. Grainger."

Jake saw something in Emma's eyes, and in the waitress's, but wasn't totally sure of what it was, except it made him a little uncomfortable.

"I'm fine. Petey is fine. And how are you, MaryBeth?"

Jake could have cheated and looked at her nametag, but MaryBeth went to his church and was the cousin or the niece or the next-door neighbor of the owner of Kaytee's.

"I'm fine, Pastor Jake. Thanks for asking. Since there's always a crowd around you on Sundays, I just wanted to tell you how happy I am that you came to our church. I love to hear you talk. And you make so much sense. And you're not old. And I really, really love little Petey."

"Why, thank you, MaryBeth. I'll be sure to tell Petey. He will be happy to hear it."

MaryBeth giggled in reply.

"You guys know what you want to order? Pastor Jake?"

Jake looked at Emma, who offered the barest hint of a shrug and an arched eyebrow.

Jake wasn't sure what that meant. He paused, then ordered. "The deluxe cheeseburger. Medium is fine. Fries are fine. A diet whatever-you-have would be fine."

MaryBeth turned, finally, to Emma, "And you, Dr. Grainger?" MaryBeth's words bordered on frosty.

"I'll have exactly the same. Makes it easy, right?"

"Sure," MaryBeth said, and spun away, heading toward the kitchen.

It was Jake's turn to shrug and offer a very sheepish expression.

"I didn't start that," he said, defending himself.

"I know," Emma said. "But that's why the Ladies Auxiliary is so disappointed."

"Women's Guild."

"Whatever. Just be assured that they are."

Jake took a long drink of water. "They never taught this in seminary."

"Just like they never taught me in vet's school how to deal with a pet owner who collapsed in tears—literally collapsed on the floor—when I suggested that an eighteen-year-old, blind, arthritic, half-paralyzed dog might be ready to go. Never touched on the human aspect of a vet's job."

"It is funny. Both of us have to deal with serious people problems sometimes—and we got very little training for it."

Emma rearranged the salt and pepper shakers. "Some people are good at it. Some aren't. I don't think it's a skill you can learn. Either you have it—empathy and understanding—or you don't."

Jake looked out the window for a moment.

"Jake, what is it you're good at? Knowing what a pastor does—really does during the week—is not something I'm too knowledgeable about."

Jake appeared pleased, for once, to talk about his role as pastor.

She really is interested. In me. I think.

"You know, the funny part of church and pastors is that a lot of people think all you have to do is really know the Bible. That's important, but what's more important is making what's in there understandable to people in the pews. And that's not easy. Some of it is confusing. Some of it will remain a mystery. So . . . making the Bible understandable—and keeping the church supplied with coffee. Those are the two most important things a pastor does."

MaryBeth brought the cheeseburgers and served Jake first.

"You guys enjoy. You need anything, Pastor Jake, just whistle, okay?"

"I will."

"One more church question," Emma said. "Then we can start complaining about the weather or something."

"Shoot."

"Okay—a pastor tells Bible stories. I get that. I did spend most of my youth in youth groups and Sunday school. So I have an idea of the general layout. Here's my question: Does a pastor, or do all pastors, or whatever, do they really and truly believe in everything they preach about? Or can they have some doubts about some of it? Is that something that never happens or sometimes happens or always happens?"

Emma took a very healthy bite of her cheeseburger and chewed thoughtfully as Jake scrunched up his face in thought.

How much do I tell her? And . . . why is she asking this? It almost feels like . . . like Butler revisited. Did someone call her? Or did she call someone? But she wouldn't do that. Would she?

"I'm sure it happens. And I think every pastor encounters things he can't explain. But doubts? Maybe some do."

"Do you?"

Jake looked out the window for a moment, trying to think of the right answer.

"No. Well, no. A few. A while ago. But everyone goes through ups and downs. It was just a down stretch."

Emma appeared as if she were about to offer a follow-up question. Instead, she just took another bite of her cheeseburger.

"This is pretty good, isn't it?"

Jake nodded. And he hoped his expression did not give away his anxiety.

⁕

Tassy practiced the bike ride to her new job on the Sunday before she started. She knew Pastor Jake would have given her a ride, but she did not want to ask him for help more than necessary. The bike ride took only fifteen minutes. It took even less on the way home, since there was a long stretch that was mostly downhill.

She washed her bike the day before, too, taking time to clean each wheel spoke individually. She washed her good jeans and her sneakers that Dr. Emma said would be acceptable to wear. She woke early that Monday and was on the road at least twenty minutes before she needed to be. She did not want to be late on the first day of her first real job.

Dr. Grainger had ordered several tunic tops with Tassy's name stitched on the breast pocket. Tassy had volunteered to help pay for them when Dr. Grainger asked her size, but Dr. Grainger assured her that a good animal clinic provided uniforms for their staff.

Tassy had just sat down behind the counter in the reception area when the front door banged open and a giant Great Dane lunged and clamored into the room, eyes wide, paws nearly akimbo, with a smallish woman clutching on to the dog's leash. Dr. Grainger must have heard the commotion and came out from the first examination room.

"Dangerfield, how are you?" Dr. Grainger said as she petted the very large dog, attempting to settle him down and only being partially successful. The small woman at the end of the leash put her hands on her knees and took a deep breath.

"Mrs. Linhart, how are you?"

"Desperate. Let's just get the shots done."

Upon hearing the word *shot*, Dangerfield looked back, with some nervousness, at the human at the end of his leash, but other than the anxious look, he did not react.

"All right, Dangerfield," Dr. Grainger said with firmness. "Let's go in here and I'll give you a treat."

Dangerfield perked up at the word *treat* and followed the doctor and Mrs. Linhart into the examination room.

Tassy waited and listened. She was pretty sure he was not supposed to come in to offer help but the dog was really, really big.

After a moment, Tassy heard one high-pitched yelp. She expected a deeper bass yelp. Then another, louder this time, and the door banged open, with Dangerfield semiwild-eyed, barging for the door, and Mrs. Linhart hanging on.

"I think he wants to go home now. Send me the bill."

Dr. Grainger followed them out to the porch and called out, "I will! And good luck!"

Tassy waited behind the counter.

"Vaccine and booster. Send the bill to Ruth Linhart on Niles Hill Road. She's in the database. The one I showed you. Remember?"

"I do, Dr. Grainger. And here it is."

Dr. Grainger shook her head and said, "Why she ever bought such an unruly dog, I will never know."

"Maybe her husband likes big dogs," Tassy volunteered.

"Maybe. But he also likes twenty-five-year-old secretaries. They divorced years ago. She lives by herself. Well, almost. With Dangerfield."

Tassy printed off the invoice, addressed the envelope, answered three phone calls, met two more patients—one an older man with a large, beautiful iridescent parrot on his shoulder—all before noon. She asked if she could pet the parrot, but the man explained that the bird—named Billy—wasn't the most pleasant parrot around. "He bites. And not little nips. Like cracking a Brazil nut."

Tassy wasn't sure if she had ever eaten a Brazil nut, but imagined they had pretty thick shells.

During the first morning of work, the unpleasant feelings in Tassy's stomach seemed to have diminished, but they returned, hard and sharp, on her second day.

Even Dr. Grainger noticed.

"You look pale, Tassy. Are you feeling well?"

Tassy had anticipated the question.

"I'm okay, Dr. Grainger. Just happens once in a while. Pastor Jake said it might be the water. He said some people are just very sensitive to changes in their water, and he said that Coudersport is on well water and I'm pretty sure we didn't have well water in Philadelphia. So I usually have tea in the morning—with honey—and that helps sometimes. Not always but sometimes."

Dr. Grainger looked concerned. Tassy felt it was very kind of her to be concerned.

"I do have a guest bedroom upstairs. Actually, I have several of them. If you ever feel ill, you can take a break and lie down for a few minutes."

"That's kind of you, Dr. Grainger. But I'll be all right. It passes."

The Church of the Open Door often lived up to its name and left the doors open during the service. Never a wealthy congregation—far from it, really—air conditioning was a luxury beyond their limited reach. Windows were opened when the weather grew hot. The quartet of ceiling fans was switched on when it grew very hot. One of the fans produced an almost inaudible, shrill whir, so using them was a last resort.

Spring in Coudersport could turn warm, and on this Sunday, the elders decided to lift the large windows, propping each of them up with a one-foot stick. During the summer, a basket in a far corner at the back of the church held an assembly of sticks of various sizes, all painted white. One-foot sticks were for warm days. Two-foot sticks were for slightly hotter days. Three-foot sticks were used only when a heat wave gripped the area.

Even Petey seemed affected by the heat. Normally, he remained in a seated position the entire sermon. This time he lay down, still paying attention.

The elders had placed the church's entire supply of hand fans in the pew racks. Some of them dated back twenty years, when the Jones Brothers Funeral Home was still in business. Some were simple, generic, green paddle-shaped fans. When Jake preached that morning, it was like gazing out on a field of corn dappled by a stiff breeze.

At least it is helping keep the air moving.

The elders informed Jake that when it got too warm, the pastor could preach without a suit coat. When it got extra warm, ties could be undone and top collar buttons unbuttoned. Jake wondered how warm it would have to be to wear shorts in the pulpit.

A few degrees less than hell, I imagine, Jake thought, then scolded himself for being petty.

The energy level in the congregation felt low, even sluggish—probably because of the heat. Even so, he thought the sermon had gone over well. Not too many people appeared to be dozing.

Jake dismissed everyone with a benediction, wished them a good week, and walked to the outside door to shake hands. He noticed that Petey had as many visitors as he did. There seemed to be, as of recent Sundays, a pool of people gathering around the cat, petting him, asking how he was doing, laughing at his inability to shed his fur coat in the summer.

Not everyone said much as they made their way outside. Sometimes it was "Good preaching, Pastor," or "Liked it a lot," or "Spoke to me today, Pastor." Today, he heard, five times, "Start up an air conditioning fund," and "Do it while it's hot," and "People will give more while it's hot outside."

Jake made a mental note to bring up air conditioning for discussion at the next elder's meeting.

The church had already grown some since he had become its pastor. Some of the faces could just be people coming back to their home church after such a long absence of a senior pastor, but some were entirely new faces—people who had never come to a church, and those who had not darkened the door of one for years.

If we want to keep them, we need to make everyone feel comfortable.

And it was at that moment Jake felt most uncomfortable.

Comfortable. Like that's what I need to work on. Like the Bible needs to have an air-conditioned audience.

Jake scolded himself again.

Just who am I to be so self-righteous Mr. Empty Inside.

One of the newer attendees at church, Glenda Davis, waited until everyone else had departed or at least had left the building. Usually, since Jake had been preaching, there would be one person, or a couple, or a family, who would hang back, waiting until everyone left. That's when they would come and present their problem or ask for a prayer or lay out an improbable, or unsavory, situation they hoped a pastor could deal with and make better.

Jake's seminary training now seemed terribly light and trivial considering the small number of interpersonal counseling classes required in a four-year course of study.

Maybe Emma was right. Some people are good at it. Some aren't.

Jake obviously did not consider himself a skilled counselor or mediator or problem solver.

Good problem solvers solve their own problems first.

"Pastor Jake, I'm Glenda Davis."

"Hi. I remember you. You introduced yourself a few Sundays ago. It is so nice to have you with us."

Glenda appeared flustered, as if she hadn't imagined that any pastor would have taken the time or effort to remember her name—an occasional visitor.

By this time, Petey had grown impatient, jumped down from his chair, and slowly walked down the aisle, chirping to himself, apparently complaining to himself about the heat.

"I love that Petey is coming to church. Gives me hope, you know?"

Jake waited. He did not know.

"I like the way you tell stories. And the way you listen, Pastor Jake. You listen a lot for a preacher. In the past, all they did was talk at me. But you seem to listen real good."

"Why, thank you, Glenda. I appreciate that."

"You met my son. That means a lot to me, too."

"Your son? Was he here this morning?"

Glenda's face showed happy and sad at the same moment.

"No. But he talked to you in town a while ago."

Jake screwed up his face, puzzled.

"Speedy Davis. He said you promised to talk to him. He told me in a letter. He doesn't have a phone."

"Oh, sure. I remember. I got his map in the mail yesterday. He asked if I would come next Friday. He didn't have a return address, but I plan on going."

Glenda put her hand on Jake's forearm.

"Thank you, Pastor Jake. Sidney—or Speedy—really needs help, Pastor. He's just . . . well . . . he's lost. His father was arrested ten years ago last February. He's in prison down at LaBelle. Attempted murder. It was the alcohol that did it. Since he left, Sidney went off the deep end. Lives out in the woods all by himself. Does odd jobs now and then. He might even be growing some weed for all I know. You know—marijuana. But when his father left, it was like a light went out inside, and he's been hiding out by himself ever since. I know you don't promise miracles, but the fact that he found you means a lot. Maybe he's coming back."

Petey circled Glenda's legs in a figure eight. She bent down to pick him up, obviously used to having a cat around.

"And thank you, Petey. I bet Sidney heard about you and figured Pastor Jake was a good man. Right?"

Petey meowed in the affirmative.

"Anyhow, Pastor Jake, I just wanted to thank you for listening. And for helping my Sidney."

Sometimes, more often than not, it seemed, Jake had nothing to say that fit the moment.

Petey spoke instead, offering a long, low, rumbling meow, followed by a loud purring.

Glenda's smile indicated that a cat's purr was enough.

<hr>

Emma clipped the leash on Winston, who did not to want to go for a walk.

"It's not that warm, Winston. You need the exercise."

And obviously Winston disagreed with her assessment, since once they were both on the driveway outside the house, he sat down heavily, with an audible "worf," and looked as if he had completed his required exercise by simply waddling down the stairs.

"No, Winston. Not enough. We're walking to the river. Maybe to Mitchell Park."

Winston groaned as he stood.

"It's no more than a mile. You can do a mile. Right?"

The dog snorted, not agreeing with the good doctor, not at all.

Emma walked slowly because of Winston's short legs, poor condition, and general aversion to anything remotely athletic.

Traffic in Coudersport on a Sunday remained light. The main road carried some traffic, but Emma and Winston stayed on the sidewalks and took three short breaks on their trip to the park.

Once there, she walked to the river's edge, found a nice grassy spot shaded by trees, and sat. Winston sat next to her, then rolled onto his side as if exhausted, his tongue lolling out, his eyes closed.

"Good acting, Winston. It was only twenty minutes. A dog your age should be able to run for an hour without problems."

Emma could have sworn that Winston closed his eyes even tighter, as if not wanting to hear what she just said.

"You can rest for a while. I don't mind sitting here. It's a nice day and this is a nice view."

The view featured a wide area on the yet-small river with smooth, clear water. The park was nearly empty and the flowing water produced a pleasant, calming sound.

I might as well spend some time thinking about it. Since I've been avoiding the thought all week. So here it is: I like Jake. I think he likes me.

Emma grinned at herself.

It's like I'm in ninth grade again, isn't it? I should start writing his name on the cover of my notebook.

"What do you think, Winston? You have a say in this as well. Remember Petey? The cat with the thorn in his paw? Did you like him? Think you could get along with him? Do you like Petey the cat?"

Winston responded with a snort. Emma thought it sounded dismissive, but Winston had never been a deep-thinking, intuitive dog. Some dogs were, Emma had discovered in her practice. And cats as well. Cats like Petey. If she asked Petey that same question, she would get an answer that was clear and decisive.

Some animals have a sense about things. You can tell what they're thinking. Winston, not so much. Of course, it might just be that he doesn't think at all.

She watched a duck glide down, quacking furiously as he landed, not very gracefully, on the river.

Winston is like a very young child. Sleep. Eat. Sleep. That's all he thinks about.

She stretched her legs out, kicked off her sneakers, and touched the water with her toes. Despite the warmth of the air, the water felt chilled—cold, actually.

"Winston, I know more about Jake than I should, I think. And what do I do with this information? It all has to do with faith, right? He doesn't have it. I don't think I ever had it. The big difference is that Jake probably had faith and lost it. I don't think I ever believed, and now . . . well, I guess I still don't. We both have questions. We both have doubts. That's a good reason to be together, isn't it?"

As she said the words out loud, she realized that it was a truly foolish reason to be together.

Having faith—or belief—would probably be a good thing. Maybe not having it will draw us together—both of us looking for the same thing. Maybe.

Emma reclined back, cradling her head in her arms crossed behind her, staring at the sky.

Well, he would be looking for it. Me, not so much.

"Do I tell him what I know? What Barbara Ann said about him? Do I tell him that I don't mind that 'he doesn't believe'? Would that make it easier for him?" Her face tightened in response to her own questions.

"Maybe that's it. We cancel out each other's doubts."

She closed her eyes.

That doesn't make sense either. But what do I do next? What do I do?

Jake had all but decided that he would buy a window air conditioning unit. But he would have to wait until tomorrow and take the drive to Bradford—the closest town with a Walmart Superstore, and the closest town with an inexpensive air conditioner.

"Hey, Petey, let's go for a walk."

Petey raised his head. He enjoyed being in a deep sleep on the living room chair, stretched out on his stomach, his back and front legs splayed out. He opened his eyes and blinked. *Give me a second to wake up, okay?*

He watched Jake lace up his shoes, and noticed that Jake would always carefully make sure the tension on each lace was the same as the other. He stood up and checked the fit and the tension.

"Okay, let's go. We'll go down to the river. It's cooler down there."

Once they entered the field, the air actually grew hotter, still, almost as if an invisible cloak of hot air had been drawn over the area. He listened and heard only the sporadic call of a bird or two. There were no avian squabbles this afternoon, no territorial battles. Jake forged ahead, Petey a few steps behind him, placing his paws down with care.

Once they arrived at the river's edge, Jake picked up a handful of smooth pebbles and began tossing them into the middle of the stream. The first time, Petey charged toward the edge of the water, giving chase to what Jake had thrown.

"No, Petey. These are not for retrieving. I just like to see the little splashes they make."

Petey stared up at him. *What? Watching splashes? What sort of fun is that?*

Petey sniffed at the water and gently nicked at it with his right paw. Then he splashed a bit deeper, drawing his paw back and licking at it, testing the water, as it were. He then retreated and jumped up on a smooth, flat rock, shielded from the sun by a large willow.

Jake remained until his handful of rocks was gone, tossing them in at random, his eyes set on the far southern horizon. He made his way toward the cat and joined him on an adjacent rock. He did not speak, just sat, with his legs extended out toward the river, leaning back on his palms, his face turned upward to the heavens.

Jake . . .

At these moments, and only at these moments, Petey wished he had been born with the ability to form words, to speak. He seldom wanted that ability during the course of any regular day, since he had discovered, early on, that speech often served only to get in the way of real feelings. People, and cats, for that matter, often did things they found hard to explain, and if they tried, they would simply use the wrong words to do so. Ask a guilty-looking cat why they shredded the drapes and you would not ever receive the real, truthful, soul-honest answer. And maybe there wasn't a real answer. Maybe they acted on pure instinct or pure impulse. But today, it was obvious to Petey that Jake had issues on his mind. It was obvious that Jake needed to talk things through.

Petey meowed, not loudly, not insistently, but inquiring, observant.

After a moment, Jake looked over.

"I don't know, Petey. Maybe it's just life that is bothering me."

Well, that worked pretty well. Maybe he's beginning to understand "cat."

230

"I know you don't understand, Petey. But it feels too good to imagine that you do."

I do understand. Most of the time, anyway.

"So, why do I talk to you?"

Because you need to.

"I guess when I say these things out loud, they get more real. They become . . . something I can deal with, rather than hide from. Maybe that's it."

Of course, that's it. People need to talk. Cats need to act. Good cats need to listen. And I am a good cat.

Petey meowed, hoping to sound quite understanding and aware.

"I know you would like to help, Petey. But maybe you can't."

I can, too. Why else would God have sent me? He did *send me. That's why I am here. To help you.*

"I'm a pastor of a church. Not as big a church as my mother wanted me to have. But I am a pastor."

I didn't like your mother, Jake. That may be terrible of me to say. But I don't think she was a very nice person. She thought I was a wild animal. Imagine that. Me. A wild animal. Preposterous, right? Is that the right word? Preposterous?

"When she visited . . . I don't know . . . things seemed to fall into place. Kind of. Maybe."

Things? What sort of things?

"When my father left, I was still pretty young. And it hurt, Petey. It hurt, even though my mother said we would be better off without him. I don't have many memories of him anymore. It's even hard for me to picture his face in my mind. It's like I see a form without a face. And he's always getting smaller when I think of him. He is fading away. The memories are. Disappearing."

That is sad, Jake. Cats don't grow up with fathers. And they don't spend a lot of time with their mothers, either. I remember my mother. She was very nice and very smart and she was a good hunter, and I bet she could catch more mice than anyone. She was a very nice mother.

Petey looked away from Jake and stared at the river, swallowing a few times.

"So my mother had my life planned out for me. Be a pastor. That's what she always wanted, Petey. And that's what I did. I became a pastor. She never asked me if I believed. Not really. I went to catechism and youth group and all that. I looked like I believed. And . . . even in seminary, deep down I was never really sure. Was I there for *me*? Or for God? Or did I go just for my mother? You know, Petey, I'm not sure anymore. My mother really struggled raising me. She always worked hard and we never had a lot and she always told me how much she sacrificed to raise me and send me to school. I felt obligated to pay her back. To do what would make her happy—to make her life have some shred of joy. And it worked. Me being a pastor gave her hope. I think it did, anyway. She was happy when she told other people I was a 'man of God.' That was the only time I remember her being truly happy."

You didn't want to be a pastor? I thought all pastors wanted to be pastors. Why else would anyone take the job?

"I wanted to do it—for her. Not for me. What does any seventeen-year-old know? Do any of them have any idea? Take Tassy. She's young. What does she want with her life? Get a tattoo? Find an apartment and a new boyfriend and start the whole stupid thing all over again? I don't know anymore. I just don't."

Petey meowed.

"I know you don't understand."

But I do.

"It's just . . . not having a dad . . . it's complicated. How do I have faith in something that I can't see? That's what I tried to tell Barbara Ann. And you can see where that got me. How do I have faith? In God the Father? What about *my* father? My mother never had a good word to say about him. It's not that she always said bad things, but she never said good things, either. It was like he wasn't even part of the equation. And then, I tell Barbara Ann some of my 'deep feelings' and that blows up. Better to keep deep feelings deep and hidden. Does no good to tell people what you really feel. That just gets you in trouble. I can do this job and not believe all of it. Right, Petey? Right?"

I never met that Barbara Ann person but I am sure I don't like her. I bet she had a bed full of stuffed animals, too. That is just creepy. You can have a real animal. Why bother with inanimate animals? Wait . . . you do need to talk about how you feel, Jake. That's important.

"So here I am, Petey. I am pastor of a church that is grow-ing—and it's because of you."

I can't take all the credit.

"I don't have faith. Maybe I never had faith. Maybe I never really believed. I've read that boys who grow up without fathers struggle with this. And I'm struggling, Petey. Just like the books say."

Petey looked at Jake and Jake stared back, almost as if they both understood.

"I don't know, Petey. I don't know if I can keep doing this. Being hypocritical like this. Not really believing what it is I'm preaching. Is anyone really being affected or changed? Or do they simply show up to see a cat in church?"

That seems a little . . . harsh, Jake.

"Who has really been changed by what I'm doing? Whose life is better because of me being here?"

And with that, without waiting for Petey's response, Jake got up in a hurry and started walking back toward church.

233

Petey waited just a minute, wondering what it was he should do now. Then he got up, stretched, and set out following him.

This is a hard thing. I don't know what it will take to get Jake to really see.

Petey heard a mouse rustle a few feet away.

Something big, I bet. I wonder if I can come up with something big. And soon.

12

Tassy set off for her second Monday on the job, the start of her second week. This morning had not been a good one. She had been awake for hours before dawn. She had a few crackers and the last of a large bottle of diet ginger ale that she bought at the Speedy-Mart in town. Neither ingredient seemed to do the trick, and during the entire bike ride she felt her stomach roll and twist as she pedaled.

The water here must really be horrible, Tassy thought. And I don't think I even drank that much. The water I did drink, I boiled for tea—so that should make it safe. That's what Jake said. He said he learned that in Cub Scouts. I can't see him in a Cub Scout uniform with a little yellow scarf and all that. He doesn't seem the type. And now that he's all grown and handsome, he seems so far from being a little boy.

Her stomach twisted again. She stopped pedaling for a long time, coasting to a stop until the curving and knotting in her gut stopped.

Good thing I left early. This trip is taking twice as long as usual.

She had planned to stop at McDonald's but didn't. The thought of a second cup of tea was nearly enough to make her stop pedaling again. Now she was down to seven minutes until

Dr. Grainger expected to see her come through the door. But when Tassy finally arrived—on time—and unlocked the front door with her key, she found herself in an empty waiting room.

"Dr. Grainger?" she called out softly. She went to the foot of the steps and called up again. "Dr. Grainger?"

She heard Winston scuffle about and saw his chubby face at the top of the stairs, with a grin, knowing that Tassy's presence meant a treat. He clomped down the steps in a furious snorling rush.

"Good morning, Winston. Want a treat?"

Of course Winston wanted a treat and tried to jump but mostly just raised his shoulders a bit.

Tassy gave him a dog biscuit as a reward, which he ate noisily.

"Is Dr. Emma up, Winston?"

She heard hurried footsteps on the hall upstairs.

"I'll be down in a minute, Tassy. I overslept. Can you believe it? The first time I've done this in years."

After a moment, Tassy heard the sound of water running.

Good thing we don't have any early appointments today.

Tassy rubbed at her stomach, hoping the nausea would soon pass.

A very good thing.

<hr>

On Monday morning, Jake decided against the air conditioner. He had a fan and that had been enough.

"I'm a bit worried that an air conditioner might be seen as excessive by some people in the church. What do you think, Petey?"

Petey chirped.

"I thought you would say that."

Instead of Kane or Bradford, which Jake had already visited or driven through on his day off, he decided to travel in a different direction. He pulled out his worn road atlas and peered intently at it while he had his second cup of coffee of the day.

"Emporium. Let's drive there."

Petey just looked at Jake, and it seemed as if he would have shrugged if he could shrug, but he couldn't.

Jake disappeared into the office but returned after a moment. "The Internet says that Emporium is a pretty little town out in the middle of nowhere. In a valley, I guess. It is supposed to be quite scenic. That sounds like a good ride, doesn't it?"

Petey stared. He did not seem to care one way or the other. Jake knew he simply liked riding in the truck.

With his nose close to the page, Jake peered at the atlas, muttering to himself. He traced one route with his finger, then another.

"I guess it doesn't matter how you get there—so I'll try this way. Come on, Petey. Let's take a ride."

Petey did not hurry to the truck but did not walk at slow cat speed either.

"See, Petey, we drive west a little bit and take the first road south. Regardless of what road we take, we'll get there. Sort of a metaphor for life, don't you think?"

Petey seemed unimpressed by metaphors and simply turned to stare out the passenger side window.

———— ∞ ————

As he drove, Jake noticed that the area between here and there became sparsely populated, a few homes and farms dotted the hills, bucolic, pastoral.

"This is nice, right, Petey? Pretty landscapes."

Petey chirped his response.

If you like this sort of thing. I think I like towns better. There's more to look at.

They drove in silence through several small clusters of houses huddled by the side of the road: Inez, then Austin, and Sizerville. In Sizerville, Jake saw a road sign that said: EMPORIUM 5 MILES.

"See, I told you all roads led to Emporium."

Jake drove into the small town, agreeing with the Internet's assessment of the picturesque nature of the place. And it was indeed "in the middle of nowhere," nestled in a bucolic valley, hidden, as it were, from the rest of the world. The Pennsylvania version of Brigadoon. That isolated part of the description began to appeal to Jake more and more, a place even further removed from the pressures of society and culture.

"Wouldn't it be nice to live out here, Petey? Far from the madding crowds. That's a title of a book or a poem or something."

Far from the Madding Crowd . . . by Thomas Hardy. It's about a shepherd. You know, I don't think I like sheep either. They stink, too. Not like foxes or skunks or dogs, but they do really smell. Anyhow, it's a book title.

Jake drove down the main street.

"You want some coffee, Petey?"

Not a disdainful cat by nature, Petey turned slowly to face Jake, with a tight, restricted look in his eyes.

Go ahead. You don't function all that well without multiple cups of the horrid drink. I'll be fine all by myself, left alone in the car. I'll be fine.

Jake pulled to the curb.

"Another nice thing about small towns is that you generally can find parking spaces. Where I grew up, you could drive around for an hour to find a free spot. See how nice this is?"

I have heard that before, Jake. You are repeating yourself.

———— ✺ ————

Jake rolled down both windows nearly halfway. The temperature had been predicted not to climb out of the 60s today, so Jake felt more than comfortable leaving Petey alone in the truck. He knew him well enough to know that he would stay put until he returned. And besides Petey, there was nothing of value in the truck to tempt a thief.

The Cabin Kitchen, a basic storefront restaurant, featured handwritten breakfast specials taped to the front window, along with signs for church bazaars, garage sales, rummage sales, bake sales, and free car washes—all bordering the bottom of the front window like an edging of mismatched flowers.

"A community place," Jake said to himself as he walked in. A clustering of patrons occupied the tables: some couples, some single gentlemen, all of them older, some with newspapers, all with coffee cups in front of them.

A waitress called out from the far end of the counter, "Sit anywhere. Take your pick. I'll find you."

Jake selected a stool at the counter. He liked stools at counters, perhaps since his mother never let him sit at a stool at any counter, in any restaurant, claiming that stools and counters looked too much like a tavern for her sensibilities. "What if Jesus came and saw you sitting on a stool like one at a bar and thought you were drinking a beer or a whiskey? He would pass you by, Jakey. You can't take that chance." Jake had always wanted to ask why, if Jesus were truly omniscient, he wouldn't already know that no alcohol was being ingested. But Jake, even at a tender age, knew better than to ask "foolish, devil-inspired" questions like that.

So he sat at the counter and slipped a menu out of the rack at its edge. Now seated, and noticing the smell of pancakes and toast, he decided that he might be hungry, as well as thirsty.

—∞∞∞—

Dr. Emma came down the steps in a hurry, her hair still wet. Winston had gone back up the steps and now followed her back down, lagging a full five steps behind, his back legs flumping on each step as he descended.

"So sorry," she exclaimed in a rush. "That's what having a back-up does to you, I guess. Makes you sleep in. I've never had that luxury before—having someone cover for me like this."

Tassy smiled back, or tried to. She was not successful.

"Are you not feeling well, Tassy? You look a little pale."

"No. I'm fine. I am. Just a passing morning thing. I think my stomach is still getting used to the water up here. Seems that I'm a bit sensitive, I guess."

She smoothed her hair from her face and hoped that she appeared healthy.

"Are you sure, Tassy? You can lie down for a few minutes . . . upstairs. I have four extra bedrooms, you know. Those old Victorians had a lot of kids, I guess. Or servants. When a single woman goes into a furniture store and asks for five mattress sets, you get odd looks, let me tell you."

Tassy tried to smile.

"Are you sure you're okay?"

Tassy grimaced, just a little, then nodded.

"I am. It will pass. It always does. And it only happens in the morning. That's the funny thing about it."

Dr. Emma stopped moving, stopped looking at the clip chart listing today's appointments, stopped looking at the order form for medicines that she had to sign, and stared at Tassy.

"Just in the morning?"

"Yes. Usually, if I have some tea and toast, or a couple of crackers, it goes away. By lunchtime, I'm good to go. Just getting used to the water. That's what Pastor Jake suggested. He said that some stomachs are sensitive. He said his mother was sick for a month when she moved to Meadville, and Meadville was only like an hour away from where she used to live. And Philadelphia is a lot farther than that. So . . . I'll be fine. It'll pass."

Dr. Grainger put the clipboard on the counter.

"And it is just feeling sick to your stomach? No other symptoms?"

Tassy pursed her lips.

"Yeah, that's it. Maybe . . . well, I'm thinking it's because of riding the bicycle and all . . . but there are some areas of my body . . . you know . . . that are more sensitive now than they have ever been. I don't know what the water would have to do with that. But I guess I'm just being overly dramatic. Right? A little neurotic, maybe. Or being a hypochondriac—that's what it's called, isn't it? When you always think you have some disease? Hypochondria?"

Dr. Grainger pulled up the chair next to Tassy and sat, putting her arm on Tassy's forearm.

"That's what it's called, but that's not what you are. I don't think you're being dramatic. And I don't think it's the water."

"Coffee, hon?"

Beverly, according to the nametag on her uniform, sidled up to the counter where Jake sat, carrying a half-full glass carafe of coffee.

"Sure. Regular."

"That's the only kind to drink," she replied as she sloshed the coffee into a thick mug. "Decaf is like drinking bad-tasting water. Seriously. Why bother?"

She took her order pad from a pocket.

"You ordering anything?"

Jake looked down at the menu in his hands.

"Do you have sweet rolls? I don't see them listed."

"We do. I have a couple of cinnamon rolls left, but if I were you," she said in a stage whisper, "I would order a toasted pecan roll. We actually make them here and they are very good."

"Okay. I'll have one of those, then."

"Wise choice."

Then Beverly stopped and stepped back a step or two, and leaned backward, as if studying an odd work of art.

"Do I know you?" she asked.

"I don't think so. This is the first time I've been to Emporium."

"No. Well, maybe that's true. I'm not questioning your veracity. But I have seen you somewhere."

Beverly turned to one of the couples seated at a nearby table.

"Dolores—doesn't he look familiar?"

Jake felt obligated to turn and look in return.

The woman who obviously was Dolores leaned forward and squinted at Jake.

"I don't think so. Henry? What about you?"

Henry lowered his newspaper. "Nope. Maybe you could just ask him who he is and how he got here and his Social Security number and his mother's maiden name so you could do a background check on him. How's that sound? Or get a skin sample for a DNA test."

Dolores dismissed her husband's caustic reply with a wave of her hand.

"Don't mind him. He's antisocial."

Beverly brightened.

"I know where I saw you. You're that pastor—the one with the cat. Right?"

Even though surprised, Jake had to nod in agreement.

"Jake Wilkerson. Church of the Open Door in Coudersport."

"That's it. My cousin e-mailed me a picture. Were you in the newspaper?" Beverly asked.

"When I first got to town. I think the church sent a notice to the paper. The *Potter Leader Enterprise*, right?"

Beverly shrugged. "Could be. I don't read newspapers anymore. I get all the news from the Internet. Dinosaurs like Henry—they still read the newspapers. But that's because he's too cheap to buy an iPad."

Henry lowered his paper and glared at her.

"Just because you're my older sister doesn't give you the right to criticize."

"Of course it does," Beverly replied. "Dolores said I could. Right, Dolores?"

"She is your only sister, Henry. You should be nice to her."

Jake watched as the family comedy unfolded before him. Beverly stopped, then turned back to Jake. "Where's the cat? You leave him home alone this morning?"

Jake figured the question was coming.

"No. Actually, he likes riding in trucks. He's in the truck waiting for me now."

"Get out! Really? Bring him in. Can we meet him?"

Jake hesitated.

"Oh sure, like the Health Department is waiting outside to do a sting operation on us for illegally serving cats in here." Beverly responded, noticing Jake's reluctance. "It's okay. For a minute. Anyone mind if the pastor brings his cat in?"

Weak choruses of "No" and "Okay with me" were the votes from the current pool of patrons.

"Okay. I'll get him."

Be careful what you do. You're a celebrity in these parts.

Jake went outside, walked to the truck, and opened the door. Petey sat up, obviously having been napping.

"You have fans who want to meet you. You want to do a meet 'n greet?"

Petey stood, stretched, arching his back, yawned, shook his head, as if clearing his thoughts, and then jumped down from the truck, almost like he was looking to see where his fans might be gathered.

"Over here," Jake said. "Follow me."

———— ⌒⌒⌒ ————

Dr. Grainger slid her chair closer.

"Tassy, I know I am an animal doctor, but I know a little about people medicine as well. Some of it transfers, I guess."

Tassy nodded.

"You're only sick in the morning? Nauseous, right?"

"That's about it."

"And it's usually gone by the afternoon?"

Tassy nodded.

"Tassy, I am not one to pry. And I don't have any right to ask—as an employer, and all."

"I know . . . I guess."

"I guess the only way to ask this question is to ask it: Do you think you might be pregnant?"

Tassy leaned back, as if she had planned on that specific reaction.

"No. No. I couldn't be. Really, I couldn't be," as if Tassy was trying to convince herself of the fact.

Dr. Grainger gripped Tassy's arm a little tighter—not hard, but firm, insistent.

"No. Really. I . . . Randolph has been gone for . . . It couldn't be. Really. It couldn't."

Dr. Grainger looked hard at her new employee, hard and long.

"No. No. No."

"Tassy, could it be true?"

"No."

"Tassy."

Tassy's face softened, her eyes went wavery, and her shoulders slumped.

"Maybe. I don't know. Maybe."

"Have you taken a test, Tassy? You know, the kind they sell at the drugstore?"

Tassy shook her head emphatically.

"No. I couldn't. I couldn't buy one because the man who runs the store knows Eleanor and if I bought one, he would find out, and then Eleanor would find out, and I couldn't do that to her. She has been so nice to me—letting me stay in the RV. Vern even bought me groceries. If they thought I was pregnant, what would it do to them? I just couldn't do that—disappoint them like that."

Dr. Grainger stopped. Her back stiffened. A harsh look came on her face.

"Jake . . . Pastor Jake isn't involved, is he? You're not protecting him, are you?"

Tassy appeared shocked—very, very shocked.

"Pastor Jake? No! No! Of course not. Pastor Jake, he's like a church person. He couldn't do that, even if he wanted to. And sure, he's cute and all that, but he's like, old. Not real old, like a grandfather or anything. But he's old. No, nothing to do with Pastor Jake. He's just been so sweet to me, too. He always asks if he can get me anything when he goes to town. Of if I need anything fixed. Or whatever. No, Pastor Jake. No."

Dr. Grainger appeared relieved.

"I had to ask, Tassy."

"I know. But, Pastor Jake? Heavens no."

She looked down at the floor, avoiding Dr. Grainger's concerned expression.

"I have been worried about this since I got here. Sort of. Like I've been nervous thinking that maybe I am."

Jake opened the door and Petey sauntered inside, sniffing and looking about, taking it all in with great deliberateness.

"He is just like she described him," Beverly said. "A perfect gentleman. She said he sits through the whole service like it's the most important thing he's ever heard."

"He is awfully cute for a cat—and I'm not a cat person," Dolores said. "But he does look like a good cat."

"He started coming the first Sunday I preached. I guess I was upset at first, but now, he makes it his business to be on the platform Sunday morning."

"And your church people don't mind?" Henry asked. "The elders or deacons or whatever you have?"

Both women turned to stare at Henry.

"I was just curious."

They pivoted back to Jake.

"No. The elders said that if Petey comes to church, it's okay with them. Actually, it turns out that more than a few new people have started attending since Petey's been coming."

Henry folded his newspaper and laid it on the table.

"Interesting. Sounds like you got an interesting church there. Pretty liberal, right? Gays and all that? Not that I'm being judgmental or anything."

Jake shook his head.

"No. If anything the church has a history of being very traditional, very conservative. Very. Fought for years over singing any hymn written later than 1890. So . . . it's traditional, more or less. We're traditional, and then some."

It took a long moment until Henry's face softened and a very small smile came, but a smile nonetheless.

"Might be worth checking out some Sunday. What do you think, Dolores?"

Both women pivoted back and stared at Henry.

Beverly spoke first.

"Henry here said that all church and God stuff is a bunch of hooey. He said that a lot. For a few decades, right? He always used a different word than *hooey*, but I have respect for having a preacher in here. This is *big*."

Dolores sputtered, "You mean it?"

Henry shrugged, trying his best not to appear anything other than normal.

"Sure. A cat in a church. That's interesting. Makes it more normal, I guess. More human—although that's a contradiction, isn't it? Down to earth. I don't know. Interesting, you know. I'd be willing to give up a Sunday morning to see that."

Beverly picked Petey up and held him in her arms. He meowed, enjoying the attention.

"Henry said it would take an act of God to get him to go back to church. Apparently, your cat, Petey, is an act of God."

Petey jumped down and walked to Henry, placed his front paws on his knee, and stared hard at the man's face.

"We have service at 11:00," Jake said. "It's a nice ride to Coudersport."

Henry patted the cat's head.

"Maybe. This Sunday. If the weather is nice. Or if I don't have anything better to do."

Petey the cat began to purr.

"I said maybe, cat. Not for sure."

⸙

"It's positive, Tassy," Dr. Grainger said as she examined the test. "We probably need to get a doctor to confirm that."

Tassy appeared to be at the edge of tears.

"I can't afford that, Dr. Grainger. I just started working here and if I do see a doctor . . . somebody will find out. I just couldn't do that to Eleanor. Or Pastor Jake. They trusted me."

Dr. Grainger and Tassy sat upstairs from her office, in her small, tidy, very modern kitchen. Dr. Grainger made whole-wheat toast and a cup of tea—the only food Tassy said she was capable of eating.

Tassy nibbled at one end of a piece of toast, like a mouse nibbling on a cracker, taking cautious, careful bites.

"We don't have to do anything today," Dr. Grainger said. "And I do mean 'we.' I won't let you go through this by yourself. Okay? I want you to know that, Tassy. You're not alone here."

Tassy managed a small smile.

"Thanks, Dr. Grainger."

"We have at least a month to handle this. You can't be that far along. We still have time. So we don't have to do anything today."

Tassy nodded, like a small child nods when dealing with something much, much bigger than she is.

"Okay. And thanks. Like a weight off my shoulders. Knowing for sure."

Dr. Grainger put her arm around Tassy's shoulder and squeezed.

"I know how you feel. And for now, Tassy, let's keep this a secret. It is nearly impossible to keep any secret in a small town, but let's keep this just between you and me. Okay?"

"Okay. Okay. Okay. Okay."

Each word grew smaller and softer until it was no more than a whisper escaping from Tassy's mouth.

"This is not something that needs to ruin your life, Tassy. You're young. You can start a new life. But not like this. This is not the way to do it. A child needs a family, Tassy. You don't want it to happen like this, do you?"

Tassy waited, then shook her head, signifying no, but a reluctant, hesitant no.

"One mistake does not have to ruin your life. And this would. You know it would. We can correct this. We can handle this, Tassy. Right?"

She mouthed the word *right*, but she produced no sound.

"Good. Then we'll think about it. But we know what we need to decide, right?"

Tassy nodded again, smaller this time, and she said not a single word, just nodded.

And for Dr. Grainger, that was enough.

For now.

Jake drove back toward Coudersport, the church, and his home. He did not speak for much of the trip. Petey sat, as was his custom, in the middle of the seat, staring straight ahead. Both appeared to be lost in their thoughts.

"Petey, I have to tell you that I'm really puzzled."

Petey faced him and meowed in response.

"If Henry said he was going to come to church because of me, I might feel good. Maybe. I don't know. But he didn't. He said he would come because of *you*."

Petey churred a reply.

"I know. It couldn't be because of me. I know that. I don't feel particularly close to God. And that's an understatement. I'm not even in the same county."

Petey chirped.

"Or the same country, for that matter. I'm puzzled because of what will happen when they show up. The people who are coming to see you are hearing me talk. And I feel like a counterfeit preacher up there. Am I really a man of faith? No. So that means then, that all of what I do is just some sort of show. Like a sideshow, or a carnival attraction. Is anyone really encountering the truth? Not from me. Maybe it's even worse than that. Maybe I'm even worse than a charlatan. Maybe this is all . . . not divine at all. Maybe it's all pretend. Maybe I'll wind up hurting a lot of people. Or damaging their faith. I don't know what to do now, Petey. What should I do? I've been lying to everyone since I got here. They think I have faith. I don't."

Petey did not like to walk about while the truck was in motion, but after hearing this, he stood up and tried to climb into Jake's lap.

Jake pushed him away, gently, but firmly.

"Dangerous to do that, Petey. But thanks for the support. What do you think? Do you think it could be a test to see if my faith comes back? Do you think it will happen, Petey? Can a person force faith to come back? Can I make it come back?"

Petey rammed his head into Jake's side, as if to tell him to stay with it, to keep searching, to keep trying, and to listen, to listen to that small voice calling for him to return.

———— ⚬⚬⚬ ————

Late that afternoon, after Dr. Grainger insisted on driving Tassy back to her RV, she hurried out of the church parking lot without stopping. She did not want Jake to come out. She did not want to talk to Jake. She didn't want to see Petey or Jake. She did not want to speak to anyone.

She drove past Big Dave's store, driving faster than she should have on the narrow, two-lane road. She snapped off the radio and drove in silence, the wind coughing in the open windows, loud, whining.

She stopped paying attention to where she was and just drove west, until the surroundings became more and more unfamiliar. She looked down at the speedometer and realized that she was not only breaking the law—by a lot—but also being really, really foolish. Even on straight, wide roads, with a clear head, Emma was not the best of drivers and became easily distracted.

Her thoughts were in a swirl, and she had never once envisioned her final moments on earth as flying off the road and slamming into a tree. She slowed down to the legal limit, and a few miles later, pulled off the road onto a wide shoulder overlooking a small valley and a rock-filled stream. She got out of the car and walked to the hood and leaned against it, wishing that she still smoked—a brief aberration in college— so that she had something to do with her hands at a moment like this. Instead, she crossed her arms, shut her eyes, and listened. The engine began to ping and creak as it cooled, birds called out, the breeze ruffled the branches. She heard her own breathing, coming faster than it should, as it always did when she was angry, impatient, and hurt.

She tried to fend off the flood of memories that the events of today had brought to the forefront. She knew, from the first moment of her encounter with Tassy, that those memories would come and it would be of no use to attempt to hide from them. Hiding would do no good. Drinking would do no good. She had tried that before and it just made for horrid mornings after. She knew she should simply let them happen, let them build and wash over her and then they would be forgotten—at least for a while. Not forgotten really, but put away. Hidden. For a little while.

This specific set of memories started during the summer between the end of her undergraduate career and the start of veterinary school. She was young, pretty, energetic, and vivacious in a way that drew attention from the most eligible of the eligible young men heading off to graduate school or medical school or to work in their father's companies.

Emma Grainger felt—no, knew—that she was at the center of many young men's desire.

And for Emma, Josh Cummings was her first and only choice. A premed student headed to Vanderbilt, Josh had met Emma in a math class during their junior year at Penn State. They were a cute couple, by all standards, and appeared destined to marry and have very handsome children.

But all of that would wait, of course, since medical school was in both of their futures.

And then it all changed when Emma discovered that she was pregnant, using a pregnancy test kit, much like the one Tassy had just used.

Emma squeezed her eyes tighter, hoping somehow the past would magically change and the path to today would alter and shift and become . . . different.

It did not happen today. It never happened. The past remains unchanged. Like always.

Josh had been sweet and supportive when she'd told him, almost excited. In retrospect, Emma saw his actions as practiced, as if acting out "this is how a man has to act when being told of an unplanned pregnancy: be supportive, be caring, but do not commit to *anything*." That is how it had seemed. For the first few days, he had held Emma and had whispered that everything would work out fine, that things were just a little confusing right now, and that they would soon deal with this after having thought it through, using logic and clear thinking.

A week after the announcement, that's when "the talk" occurred.

The question was: "Whose career gets put on hold for this?"

Josh had to become a doctor. It was his parents' dream. Emma had to become a veterinarian. It was her dream.

"A baby is going to make this very, very complicated. One of us will have to give up on their dream . . . if we go through with it. This . . . situation."

It had become a "situation" and not a pregnancy. Not a life, not a baby.

Emma had known what he meant. The thought had crossed her mind without his prompting. A baby would create a massive upheaval in their well-crafted plans for the future. It would add one more hurdle, a huge hurdle, to achieving their dreams.

"We need to think this through, that's all. It doesn't affect the way I feel about you. But we have to face reality. We have to think of our careers. Don't you agree?"

Emma had agreed. What choice did she have?

And Josh had driven her to the facility to "handle it." He'd driven her home afterward. He'd stayed with her that night, bringing her hot compresses for the cramps, and brewing herbal tea. He'd stayed part of the next day.

And life went on. For Emma, the colors of her world had changed. They had become muted, burnt sienna instead of red. Life was a bit askew. Sounds were different. Every smile felt forced.

And one month, to the day, after Emma had "handled it," Josh had sat in the driver's seat of his Volvo, after a dinner of pizza and beer, and had told Emma, dispassionately, "This just isn't working for me. I think we both need some space here. We both need to find our own way. You feel it, too, don't you, Emma?"

Emma had not felt it but had seen her new reality in Josh's hopeful face, only hopeful because he was jettisoning unwanted baggage from his life.

Emma was that baggage.

The rest of the summer, and for much of her first year of veterinary school, Emma simply had gone through the motions. She did not hear from Josh at all that year, though a friend said he was dating again—a perky, red-haired, second-year medical student from Syracuse. Emma had felt nothing. She had felt empty.

And during a routine medical checkup some nine months after "handling it," the doctor had become more interested than usual in certain things, and had ordered more tests than usual, and afterward, had given her the news that it looked like, to him, at this date, that Emma would probably not be able to have children in the future. Something about scarring. Something about seeing this with some regularity in women who had "handled" things.

And since then, Emma did her best to hide the guilt and the shame and the anger that "handling it" had caused. For the most part, she was successful. She was not often reminded of the past. Her friends who married and had children were no longer her closest friends, really—drifting apart because of different interests, of course, so her chance of seeing a happy mother and child had grown increasingly slim with each passing month.

And Emma went on with her life.

She seldom thought of the word *murderer*.

It was not murder.

It was simply handling a problem.

She had "handled it."

She got her life back. Josh went on with his life.

No one murdered anything.

She'd pursued her dream, achieved it, and in that she could take cold comfort.

And her life went on.

And she told herself the decision had been correct, even it was painful. And it had been.

Painful but necessary.

Not murder. Not murder at all.

And Tassy would see the truth in that. Eventually. She would.

13

Jake picked up the phone in his kitchen and dialed a now-familiar number.

"Hey, this is Jake. You up for a ride to Port Allegheny? One of the church folk said there is an Italian restaurant there that's actually pretty good. And I haven't had good Italian food for weeks. Want to go for dinner? My treat."

The phone had rung a number of times, almost to the point of the call automatically going to voice mail. First, Jake wondered if Emma was home, and then he wondered if she had been debating on whether or not to answer his call—based on the caller ID, of course. Jake looked at the caller ID and made those "answer/don't answer" decisions all the time.

"Jake, thanks so much for thinking of me, but can I take a rain check on this? I'm . . . I guess I'm just not in the mood for it right now. Maybe some other time, okay?"

Obviously, her answer took him by surprise, at least a little.

"Oh. Okay. Maybe some other time, then."

As he hung up, he wondered if "some other time" meant something more than just "some other time." Was Emma trying to tell him that she no longer wanted to see him? Or that she had better things to do than go out to dinner with a pastor who didn't believe that he should be a pastor? Or that she simply did not really like him at all and was trying to find an easy, safe, nonconfrontational way to let him know?

———❧———

Petey sat on the desk and watched as Jake dialed the phone and held it up to his ear, with an odd, nearly goofy look on his face. He stared intently as Jake spoke, and noticed Jake's eyes as he hung up the phone. The expression had changed. Dramatically.

He meowed as if to ask about the problem.

"She said she wanted a rain check."

Petey tilted his head.

"That's a nice way to say no."

Petey meowed again.

"Hey, she's allowed to say no. We've only been out a few times. No one said anything about long-term. No one is suggesting that we're . . . you know . . . dating. It's okay, Petey. She's nice, but she isn't the only person in the world, you know."

Petey simply stared back, watching Jake's eyes.

"Yes, I know. But I don't think God has anyone preordained for another person and we have to search until we find that one person. It doesn't work that way."

Petey remained silent.

"Okay. I get it. I shouldn't be talking about God's plan for my dating life, since I'm pretty sure he doesn't have plans for my spiritual life. Right? That is what you're thinking, isn't it? Why would he want me to find a special person when I'm lost myself? That's it, isn't it?"

And with that, Jake stood up quickly, nearly tipping the chair over, and stomped, or almost stomped, out of the room.

Petey watched him go.

I just wanted to know what a rain check meant. I never heard that before. Why do they say a "rain check" when they mean "no"? Wouldn't a "no" be much simpler and easier?

He licked his paw and wiped his face three times on both sides.

Human are so confusing, aren't they?

The tattered envelope, apparently a reused direct mail solicitation for a credit card, with a new address taped over the old, had arrived in the mail to the church. Jake almost threw it away, but took a second and a third look at it and realized what it was and who had sent it.

Speedy had sent the map, an intricately drawn map, complete with an index and a map key in the bottom right corner. He had labeled route numbers and street names, indicated Jake's church, Dr. Grainger's office, the movie theater, Kaytee's, and the route to take out of town heading east into the Susquehannock Forest. He had drawn the road to turn off into the forest, and the road to turn off the road that he turned off on, and what stand of trees to look for, and the exact mileage between forks in the road, and included the notation "Rough road, drive slow and watch for badgers."

On the top of the map was a handwritten note, done in tiny, precise letters, all capitals, in blue ink.

Can you come to visit on the twenty-first? I will be home that morning. Until noon. Then I will be gone until three. (I don't have a watch, but I am pretty good at telling the time from the sun.) Promptness would be appreciated. If you are not there, I will assume that you are not coming. Perhaps if that happens, we can set another time. If you are not there, I will write again. But please save this map. You can use it if you come at another time. Thank you. Speedy Davis. (Dr. Grainger did not tell you my real first name, did she? Did she remember? It is Sidney. Isn't that a horrible name? I have never liked it. Speedy is much better. Thank you again. Speedy Davis.

Jake took Speedy's map and compared it with his well-used atlas. The route would be easy to follow. Speedy was a competent, if obtuse, cartographer.

He placed the atlas and the hand-drawn map on the truck seat. He had asked if Petey wanted to accompany him, but the cat did not budge from his chair that morning, only raising his head in response, and blinking his eyes, as if not willing to be roused.

I can't go today, Jake. I can't. Something tells me that I have to stay here and protect things. I'm not sure what I have to protect or from what.

But I sure hope it is not from foxes.

I am hoping, and praying, that if I am asked to protect Tassy I can do as asked, and I will be successful.

Just no foxes, God. I don't think I can win against a fox.

Petey stood up and stretched.

But you know I would try my best, whatever happens, right? I would try my best to do my job.

Whatever that job might be. Whatever the task. I will try.

Jake left Petey at rest and drove through town and out again, heading east, deeper into the dark green forests of north central Pennsylvania and the stands of century-old lumber and moss and deep, almost nighttime shade, and clean mountain streams filled with bears and badgers, apparently.

He spotted his first turnoff easily. He stopped the truck and looked carefully at the speedometer.

"4.3 miles."

He did the math in his head and drove south, along what must have been a former logging trail, filled with ruts, rocks, and small fallen trees. Rough, but not impassible.

At 4.2 miles he slowed further, and scanned the east side of the road for the second cutoff and the stand of old pines that formed an "X" of sorts, flanked by a grove of black cherry trees.

"That must be it there," Jake said as he slowed and then turned into a thickness of brush—brush that all but covered a set of tire tracks. The truck protested a little but climbed and bounced and rocked and then came out on a small meadow filled with wildflowers and Queen Anne's lace. The rough track led around the meadow. At the far end was a small cabin with a tin roof and a curl of smoke coming from a stone chimney. As Jake got closer, he saw a figure come out of the house, waving.

"Hey, Pastor Jake, you found me! Good job. Not everyone can follow a road map that well. You know, you gotta trust the mapmaker when you go off road. If you don't trust the mapmaker, then you're just lost, right? And you must have trusted me. That's a good thing. Reassuring."

Jake stopped, felt his kidneys settle back into their proper place from the jostling of the washboard road, and stepped out.

"It looked like you've drawn the map before. I figured you had directed people here before me."

Speedy looked alarmed.

"Good heavens, Pastor Jake. No. I never did. You're the first person I ever invited here. The very first. You won't tell anyone where I live, will you? I'm pretty sure I'm on state land here and they might not take kindly to me living here, rent-free and all."

Jake extended his hand.

"Speedy, no one will ever ask. But if they do, I will have forgotten all about the map. I promise."

Speedy looked greatly relieved. His face relaxed. He let a smile return. He wiped his hands on his shirt, then looked around as if expecting a few more people to show up.

"You hungry, Pastor Jake? I got some awesome squirrel jerky. And I got a pitcher of cool sassafras tea. And it's sweetened with real honey that's from a hive 'bout a mile from here."

Jake followed Speedy up onto the porch and took a seat on what looked like the middle seat from an old VW van.

"The tea sounds good, Speedy. I'll pass on the squirrel. I had a big breakfast."

"Sure thing."

Speedy returned after a moment with two metal cups filled with amber liquid.

"I like these metal glasses, 'cause they can't break. I don't wear shoes inside the house, so glass slivers can be dangerous."

Jake tried not to hesitate when he took his first sip. The tea was cool, not cold, and tasted earthy and sweet and healthy and not poisonous at all.

"Good," he said.

Speedy beamed as if he had just been given an award.

"Music to my ears, Pastor Jake. I like a man who likes his sassafras tea."

—⁂—

Emma tapped in her request for information on the Internet. She waited a fraction of a second and the result popped up.

She scanned down the first page and saw the link she needed. Another tap and the website popped up. It posted the hours. Then a list of frequently asked questions. She scrolled down the list. Answers to her three questions were there within the first ten. She slowed and read them carefully.

"We'll have everything we need. No problem there."

She looked at her watch.

"Plenty of time."

She turned the OPEN sign on the front door of the clinic to CLOSED and called up the stairs.

"I'll be back in a few hours, Winston. You're in charge until then."

She heard a muted "worf" in response.

She drove out of town, pulled into the parking lot of the Church of the Open Door, and stopped close to the front door of Vern's RV. She tapped at the door.

Tassy appeared, a little pale, and let Emma inside.

"Hi, Dr. Grainger. I'm sorry I'm not at work. But I just don't think I could make the bike ride today."

"Tassy, like I said before, that's not a problem."

She laid her car keys on the coffee table and sat on the couch opposite Tassy. They both turned to hear a scrabbling at the window. Tassy smiled weakly, rose, and slid the window open. Petey jumped down and meowed loudly, looking at Tassy first, then turning his stare to Dr. Grainger.

"Petey, I'm not here for you today. I'm here for Tassy. Don't have to worry at all. Okay, buddy?"

Petey chirped a reply.

Dr. Grainger looked small and tight, her arms almost folded in front of her, her hands clasped together.

"I know we've both been thinking a lot, right? About what we discovered. About your condition."

Tassy nodded, glum and unsmiling.

"And I think we probably have come to the same decision."

"I don't know. Maybe," Tassy said, her words small, snaillike.

"You don't have to go through this, Tassy. You're young and this is not the time for a burden like this. It's unplanned, right? You don't want to complicate your life anymore than it already is."

Tassy looked up. Petey walked into her lap.

"You're right, Dr. Grainger. You're right. I'm sure you're right."

The cat appeared confused, or concerned. He looked at Tassy, then Dr. Grainger, and then back at Tassy.

"We can handle this today. There is a clinic just across the state line, up in New York. It will take us forty-five minutes to get there. It's the closest clinic—other than driving to Philadelphia. The procedure is short—maybe thirty minutes. We can be back here by dinnertime. And then your life will start over—from that point. You can make a fresh start that way. It's . . . it's really the only logical way. And we have to look at this logically."

Had Tassy been more intuitive, more sensitive to the subtle nuances of long-delayed guilt and anger, she might have picked up on why Dr. Grainger was so sure. She might have understood that by following the path already walked on by a young Emma Grainger, it would somehow alleviate, or ameliorate, the pain Emma carried inside, carried every day, the secret carried and hidden. Pain is manageable when divided and shared. With this decision, neither Tassy nor Emma would feel totally alone—ever again. They would be connected by this shared pain. Emma would not be unique or alone or the only woman she knew that carried this sort of secret burden, this invisible pain. Pain shared is pain halved. Emma did not want to see another woman follow a different path and make it through unscathed.

JIM KRAUS

No.

No, Emma knew that for her to heal, the pain had to be shared. Tassy must endure what she did. Theirs had to be a shared story, a shared history.

It was the only way. Blood for blood. Sacrifice for sacrifice. Biblical.

"So, you believe in God—right, Pastor Jake?"

Now is not the time for total self-disclosure.

"Yes, I do, Speedy. I believe there is a God."

Speedy looked at his hands.

"I been thinking about one thing, Pastor Jake. Could you call me Sidney? Just for today? I don't think that Speedy is the right name to use when God is listening. Like I'm trying to hide something. And I don't have anything to hide. I want to make sure God knows that. Okay?"

"Sure. Sidney it will be, for today, if you want. But I think that both names would be fine with God. I am certain he doesn't spend his nights worried about our nicknames, no matter how inappropriate."

"You think?" Sidney replied. "That's a relief."

"So Sidney . . . you said you had questions. I am not sure if I am the person who has all the answers, but I will try. I will try my best."

Sidney took a deep breath as he closed his eyes.

"Man, that's all I can ask, right? Try to find the answer. Try to find the truth. That's righteous."

"Can I pray for you . . . and us, to get us started?"

"You sure can. Don't think anybody's ever prayed for me before, 'cept maybe my mom."

Jake folded his hands together. He bowed his head. He closed his eyes.

"Dear Lord, I'm asking for your help today. For Sidney. For me. Help us find you. Help us find faith again. Help us see you. It's a simple prayer, God. It's a simple request."

Jake sniffed loudly. His throat had grown tight, but he coughed and continued.

This prayer might have been the first prayer—ever—in which Jake had actually asked God to help him find his faith, his belief, his center. Up until this moment, Jake knew it was up to him, and him alone, to find his faith. As he'd heard all his life, he knew God rewarded those who were seeking faith.

"I don't know what questions Sidney has for you. But I know the questions I have for you, God. Questions like . . . why did you abandon me as a child? Why did my life turn out the way my mother wanted and not the way I wanted? Why did I pretend to have faith all my life . . . when it was never really there?"

Now Jake felt the tears form behind his closed eyes.

"Lord, help Sidney. Help me. Please help me, God. Help me find faith . . . help me know what faith is. Help Sidney find faith, God. Help him right now. Enter his heart, God. Give him the gift of faith. Fill us with your Spirit. Fill us with faith. Help us know, without doubt, that you will never abandon us. You have never abandoned us."

He took a deep breath. He opened his eyes. He looked up.

"Amen."

He looked at Sidney, who had fallen to his knees while Jake prayed, and whose face, too, was wet with tears.

"Amen, man. Amen. It's like you looked inside me and knew what I needed. Faith. And then there it was. God heard you, man, loud and clear."

Petey's meow turned into a soft, gravely growl as he stared at Dr. Grainger, his eyes narrow as if he were facing some loud, hidden, dangerous noise.

"Today?" Tassy asked.

"We don't have much time, Tassy. If we wait, they won't be able to handle it. It will get more complicated. There is a time limit. Let it go too long and it becomes much more difficult. It might even be impossible then. And we don't want that, do we?"

"Today?"

"Yes. Waiting will only make it harder."

The fur on Petey's neck began to grow stiff and expand, making the small animal appear bigger, more ferocious, more protective. He growled again, low, rumbling, threatening.

"Petey," Tassy said sharply, almost scolding him. "Settle down. There's nothing for you to be angry about."

He jumped from her lap and stood between Tassy and Dr. Grainger. He arched his back.

"Petey!" Dr. Grainger snapped. "Enough. Stop it or get out."

Protect her. That's what I have to do. I'm not sure what they're talking about, but Tassy has to stay here. Nothing good can happen if she goes to New York. I don't know where that is, but it is not where she should go. Right? Right?

His breathing quickened, his ears folded back, his fur on edge, his back arched.

This is why I'm here, isn't it? To protect someone who is helpless? You sent me to do this, didn't you? You did, right?

He took a step forward, toward Dr. Grainger, keeping his eyes locked on hers.

That's what you do to danger. You stare it down. You can't let them look away.

That's what my mother taught me.

He arched his back higher and for the first time in many months, Petey hissed, as loudly as he could and with his right paw, the one that Dr. Grainger had repaired, he swung out, claws extended, swiping at the air, letting everyone know just how serious and dangerous he could be.

Especially when called on to protect someone helpless.

"Is that what you need, Sidney? To find faith?"

Sidney pushed his long hair behind his ears and shook his head as if to clear his thoughts.

"No. I mean, yes. But, like, Pastor Jake, I think I've found it. No. That's not it. I *know* I found it."

"You mean now?"

Sidney shrugged, sheepish.

"Yeah, I guess."

"Just like that?"

Sidney shrugged again. He shrugged a lot, Jake observed.

"How long should it take?"

Jake had no quick answer for that.

"I'm . . . I'm not sure."

"Ain't faith like a switch—on . . . or off? Not much in between, is there? And you asked God, and he . . . I guess he gave it to me. Or let me see it. And let me know what it felt like. It got switched from off to on. Inside me. Faith. It's on now. That faith switch. It's on. I can see."

That's it? That's all it took? All that seminary training, and all it took was a thirty-second prayer? And not a very good prayer at that.

Sidney sat back on his rickety wooden chair with fingers of the frayed wicker seat poking out under his jeans. He looked about, as if seeing his world for the first time, smiling, beatifically, graciously accepting whatever it was Jake helped him find.

"You want to pray, Sidney?" Jake said, almost secretly hoping that Sidney had not found faith—because if he had, and if it were that simple, then Jake's wandering in the wilderness for these past years would have been rendered implausible and self-indulgent and foolish and childish—and more—and worse . . .

Sidney doesn't understand faith. I'm betting he has no idea what he's talking about. A person who is lost does not get found just like that. It takes time. It takes effort . . . a lot of personal effort. It takes . . . work. And Sidney has not worked at all. Faith does not snap on like a light switch. It doesn't work that way.

He waited, the crickets or spring peepers or katydids chorusing at the far edge of the meadow.

If Sidney can find faith like flipping a switch . . . then what about me? What's wrong with me?

Sidney closed his eyes.

"Hey, God. Thanks. I guess it took Pastor Jake to help open my eyes. Thank you for sending him to me. Thanks for giving me faith. I can feel it. Like I know that everything comes from you and that I came from you and I owe everything to you. I have that faith. I do. And like, God, if Jake needs something, could you show him the way? That would be righteous, man. I guess . . . amen. Amen. Is that right? Amen."

"Yes, Sidney, that's right. Amen."

Petey appeared to quickly cycle through all the alternatives and choices he had before him. He could attack. He could defend. He could do battle. He was obviously ready to do any and all of them.

But at the moment, when his back was arched highest and his ears laid flattest, he saw the glint of shiny metal, a glistening of a key.

He knew that those metal things, keys, started cars and trucks.

Without them, no one could go to New York.

Houses on wheels, he was not sure of. Perhaps it was a different system. But he did not think Dr. Grainger would drive the house with wheels.

From the couch, he launched himself at the coffee table, sliding when he landed, his head down, his mouth open, growling as he bent down, close to the surface, and closed his jaws around Dr. Grainger's keys—all on a ring with a short but thick leather lanyard. He grabbed the lanyard in his mouth and launched himself toward the open window. There was not a large landing space there, on the inside, but there was the merest hint of a ledge, of a sill. The weight and the heft of the keys almost took him off balance, but his front paw landed just right, and rather than perch there for a second, he just pulled harder on the thin ledge of the window and propelled himself through the still-open window and down to the ground.

The drop was at least six feet onto hard, sharp gravel.

The keys jangled and fell when he hit the ground.

The RV door slammed open.

"Petey! Petey! Put them down! Now!"

Dr. Grainger ran at him.

Though his paw hurt, a lot—the one that had been fixed—he still scrabbled as fast as he could, as efficiently as he could, and got hold of the leather lanyard just as Dr. Grainger reached him. He jumped to the left and ran, with the keys in his mouth, banging against his chest with each step, running as fast as he had ever run, straight toward the open field beyond and then to the tree line beyond that. He ran, hearing the heavy footfalls of Dr. Grainger behind him.

"Petey! Drop that! Now! Drop it!"

He ran harder and faster, darting to the left, around and under a thickness of brambles and blackberry bushes, and then under a pine that had branches low to the ground. He ran farther. Dr. Grainger's voice became quieter, but no less urgent.

"Petey! Come back here with those! Now!"

He ran into the cool shade of the trees and did not stop running until he jumped a half-rotted fallen tree. There he turned around, panting.

There was no one following him. Then he saw Dr. Grainger at the edge of the woods, the field and the church behind her. She looked small from that distance.

"Petey? Petey? Where are you?"

Petey let the keys drop. The leather hurt to bite. It felt as solid as wood and tasted of salt and grease.

He tried to still his panting. He knew it was loud and he knew he could have heard it if he were the one doing the looking.

But Dr. Grainger did not see him. She obviously did not hear him. He flattened himself as much as he could, only a thin sliver of his eyes visible from behind the fallen tree.

Tassy joined Dr. Grainger and they both called out to him.

It hurt not to answer, because he was a good cat, after all, but he had done what he had to do. He was not sure why he had done it. All he knew was, in that moment, it had to be done, and he was the only one left to protect Tassy. He was the only one available. He had to act. He knew that beyond the shadow of any feline doubt.

Sometimes a good cat has to do a bad thing.

The two women called and tromped about at the edge of the woods for several more minutes. Petey watched as they both turned and headed back toward the church and the big house on wheels where Tassy lived.

He looked down at the keys. He looked at the trees around him and paid close attention to what this smelled like. He stood up and looked about, carefully and slowly, breathing in the environment carefully.

He would remember this. He would.

And then he began to walk back to the edge of the woods. He would remain in the shadows until Jake returned. Jake would know what to do. Then he would bring the keys back.

He would wait.

After all, he was a good cat. He was a smart cat.

14

Listen, I know it's a smart key. Do you have another one at the dealership?"

Emma paced in the small living room of the RV, holding her cellphone to her ear.

"Well, when is Frank coming back from lunch?"

She pivoted on her heel, obviously becoming more upset and anxious by the minute.

"Could you call his cellphone, please? This is important."

She lowered her head and half-cradled it in her free hand, her eyes shut tight.

"Well, then, do you know where he went for lunch? Come on, this is not that hard, Marjorie."

She stopped, tapped her foot, then shook her head.

"Okay. Okay. He's incommunicado for the moment. Okay. I get it. But he will be back by 1:00? Are you sure?"

Dr. Grainger snapped her phone shut.

"Only one person at the dealership who can access the records needed to program new keys. That is, if they have any spare keys on hand. What I wouldn't give to live in a city inhabited by people other than incompetent bumpkins," she hissed.

Tassy sat on the couch, holding herself tightly, making small rocking motions, almost imperceptible.

"Tassy, you don't know where Pastor Jake is, do you?"

"He didn't stop by when he left this morning. He usually does. But he didn't today."

Emma stabbed at his cellphone numbers again.

Even Tassy could hear the automatic "No Service" recording.

"Okay. Okay. What now?" Emma said, as if there was no one else in the room.

Dr. Grainger drew in a deep breath and exhaled loudly.

"Okay, I know," she said, answering herself.

Dr. Grainger slipped her cellphone in her pocket. She zipped up her light jacket.

"Tassy, how long does it take you to bike to town from here?"

"Fifteen minutes. Maybe a little longer, if I don't push as hard."

"Okay. I'm taking your bike. I'll ride into town and to the dealership and I'll be there when Frank gets back from lunch, and he'll get me a new key and I'll be back by 1:30. That still leaves us enough time. Okay?"

Tassy looked up, her eyes only a few moments from tears, and nodded.

"Okay, Dr. Grainger. Okay."

She did not say thank you as Emma thought she might.

Emma got on the bike and wobbled out of the parking lot. She began pedaling as fast as her legs would allow. It had been a number of years since she had been on a bike, and she knew that she would pay for it with stiff and sore muscles the following day.

"Well, can you hot-wire it—or whatever they do on TV? Seems like a pretty simple operation."

Frank, a short man in a formerly white short-sleeved shirt and a short tie, shook his head. He appeared to be sad.

"No, Dr. Grainger. I bet Harlan in the back could do it. He's from up toward Shinglehouse—and I think they teach that in shop class up there."

Frank smiled as he said that, then frowned again.

"But that would void your warranty. And since I know about your predicament, well, I would have to hold you to it. Voided. That's not good. Not good at all. And you don't want to void a warranty. Your car is only a year old. Not worth it at all. We'll have a new key tomorrow morning, Dr. Grainger. Of course, if you have a dog or cat emergency, I'd be happy to drive you there."

Dr. Grainger inhaled, obviously exasperated.

"And no loaners? No rentals?"

Frank shook his head.

"What if I take a test drive in a new car and bring it back by dinnertime?"

Frank's laugh was short, choppy, and hacked.

"Dr. Grainger, you are a kidder, aren't you? Like I said, I'll be happy to take you anywhere now. But our two loaners are out. And the owner of the dealership is gone until late—some sales meeting in Kane. Or was it Bradford? I'm not sure. I could check. Anyhow, so I don't have anything available right now. This evening, I'll have one of them loaners back. Six, I think he said. Would that help?"

Emma shook her head no.

"I wish them smart keys never got invented," Frank said. "People lose 'em and it's real expensive to replace 'em. Can't just go to the hardware store to cut a new one anymore."

Dr. Grainger had misplaced one set of keys already. The set that Petey made off with was her second, emergency set. Her mother didn't own a car anymore. She could call a friend, or one of her cousins—but how would she explain that she needed to take Tassy to New York and why they were going? No . . . that would not work. Anything other than using her own car would simply be too risky and too fraught with someone insisting to hear the reason for the trip. That would mean one untruthful explanation piled onto another, and Emma was certain that it would all fall apart. It would force her to tell her secret, which was something she vowed never to share with anyone.

"Can't you take your trip tomorrow, Dr. Grainger?"

Her shoulders slumped.

"Maybe. Maybe I can. You're sure the key will be in tomorrow morning?"

"Yep. I just called the parts warehouse and the key will be in our shipment. Stanley always gets here by 9:00 in the morning. He comes all the way from McKeesport, but he leaves real early. He'll be here, all right."

Well . . . if we have to wait one more day . . . we can do that. One more day won't change anything.

Petey remained hidden under a thick laurel bush. He would wait for Jake to return. Jake would know what to do.

While he waited, he remembered.

He had hidden beneath bushes before.

It was a time he did not want to recall.

His first memories were pleasant. He remembered his mother and how sweet she smelled. He remembered a young woman with blonde hair selecting him and taking him to live

275

with her. He remembered her name but refused to bring the name into his awareness. It was better not to remember. Petey was happy there. He had another name then, but he chose not to remember it, even though he could if needed.

She was a nice person. When she left for work in the morning, she left the radio on for Petey. Sometimes she left the television on instead. That was the reason—one of the reasons—that Petey was now so smart. He watched the house from the windows. She did not let him outside. Petey did not mind not going outside. He did not like the birds that flittered about in the trees. He did not like the squirrels; they seemed to be rude and inconsiderate. But those problems were not insurmountable. Petey imagined that every cat had some problems in their life. His did not seem that bad.

The woman really, really liked Petey and let him sleep on her bed every night. He made sure there were no birds or squirrels in her room.

When that man came into their lives, everything changed.

Petey did not like him, even at the first meeting. He seemed harsh, tall and harsh.

The man and the woman seemed happy at first, but some time later they began to argue and fight. The woman would cry sometimes, and Petey tried his best to cheer her up. This was before he knew about God. He learned about God on the radio.

One time they were arguing, and the man kicked Petey. He hit the wall—hard. The woman ran to pick him up. He was fine, but very, very sore. The man never apologized.

It happened again. But this time, the man hit the woman and threw her against a wall. When Petey tried to step in between them, the man kicked him again.

Three days later, the woman took Petey in her car and they drove for a long time. She stopped the car, opened the door, and pushed Petey outside. She was crying. He did not hear what she said, but she was crying very hard.

Then she closed her door and drove away.

Petey spent two days at that spot, waiting for her to return. She did not return.

He knew now he had to fend for himself. God helped. Petey found mice and water and safe places to sleep. He walked and walked. He lived on his own for a long time. He could not remember how long it was. But it was a long time. And then, one day, he heard where he must go and who he must find.

And that's when he found Jake. And Tassy.

It seems we all are abandoned.

Except by God.

⚬⚬⚬

Petey must have dozed off. He awoke to see Tassy and Jake in the parking lot. Tassy was speaking, then she gestured in Petey's direction. Jake stared and squinted. Petey felt sure Jake could not see him, but Jake started to walk toward him.

And he began to call out his name.

When he was a few dozen yards away, Petey came out from under the bush, meowing loudly. Jake stopped.

"What did you do, Petey?" His words were very harsh. He sounded like that man who Petey did not like to think about.

Petey stood and walked away from Jake, very deliberately, into the woods—not running, but walking fast, looking over his shoulder, making sure that Jake was following, making sure that Jake saw where he was going, keeping yards between them.

He came to the fallen tree and jumped, and turned to face Jake, sitting just behind Dr. Grainger's car keys, his front paws almost touching the thick, leather lanyard.

277

"Petey! What are you . . ."

Jake stopped talking when he saw the keys.

"What? Why did you bring them here?"

Petey meowed, trying to explain. It was obvious that it was a more complicated situation than a cat could easily talk through.

"You brought them here?"

Petey chirped. That usually meant yes.

"You hid them from Emma?"

Another chirp.

"Why?"

Petey remained silent.

"Does Tassy know why?"

Petey chirped once, then once more, then one final time. Then he got up, waited until Jake picked up the keys, and started walking back to the house with wheels on it.

Of course, as Petey imagined he would, Jake followed, walking fast. Muttering to himself.

Tassy was waiting outside the RV, her arms crossed over her chest, a worried look in her eyes, her hair pulled back into a severe ponytail.

"Tassy, what happened here? Where is Emma? Where is Dr. Grainger?"

"We . . . we were talking and Petey came in and stole her keys, and then she had to take my bike to town to try and get a new car key."

"Petey took her keys? Why?"

Tassy shrugged.

"I don't . . . I don't know."

Jake looked down at the cat.

"Why did you take the keys, Petey?"

Petey meowed and stared back at Jake. Then he looked at Tassy and refused to look away, even when she looked away and even when she stepped backward a step. His eyes followed her as she turned and walked back inside the house with wheels.

"Petey?"

⸺⸺

"Jake!"

Jake looked up and watched as Emma coasted the bike across the parking lot. She came to a stop and simply let the bike fall to its side.

"Did you hear what your stupid cat did? He stole my keys. My very expensive-to-replace keys."

Jake held out the keys Petey had led him to.

"These keys?"

Emma snatched them from Jake.

"Where did you find them? He took off like a rabbit into the woods. We didn't even see what direction he took once he hit the tree line."

"He led me right to them," Jake answered. "Like he was proud of having taken them but didn't know what to do with them once he had them."

"Stupid cat. You should really train him better. Or keep him out of Tassy's place. It was like he was possessed or something."

Emma thumbed through her keys, counting them, as if she thought maybe Petey took one off the ring and hid it somewhere else in the woods.

"What were you here for, Emma? I thought Tassy wasn't feeling well today."

Emma glared back.

"That's really none of your business, is it?" she said, her tone sharp and brittle.

If Jake had been surprised by her attitude, he did not show it. He had learned how to stand up to his mother. He could stand up to Emma.

"It is my business. A little. She goes to this church. I'm her pastor. I'm concerned about her, that's all."

Emma's face went cold, like ice forming on a pond.

"Yeah, you're a pastor, all right. You're a pastor."

Jake stepped back a half step.

"What do you mean by that? What brought this on?"

Emma stepped forward, leading with her chin.

"Listen . . . Jake. I talked to your ex-girlfriend. Your former fiancée, Barbara Ann Bentley. Remember her? You never said anything about her, did you?"

Jake did not retreat. "What does she have to do with any of this?"

"I called her, Jake. I was interested in how you wound up in this backwater, here in isolated Coudersport. Well, Jake, she told me that you were fired from your church in Butler. Something about not having any faith. That ring a bell?"

"She called you?"

"She didn't call me, Jake. Come on, now. I called her. I wanted to know more about you. Why you're here, for one."

"And she told you?"

"She did. And you call yourself Tassy's pastor? Please, Jake. Let's not kid ourselves. You say you don't even have faith in God. How can you be anyone's pastor? Really, now."

"You don't know what you're talking about, Emma."

"I do, too. My question is what are you doing—pretending you're a pastor if you don't believe any of it? Petey probably has more faith than you do."

And with that, Emma ended the argument. She jumped into her car, slammed the door, and started the car. Tassy must have heard them arguing and stepped out of the RV.

"I'll send you the bill for my new keys I had to order because of your stupid cat. And no clergy discount this time, Jake."

Her tires spun and roared and a cascade of gravel bounced off the side of the RV.

∞

The three of them—Tassy, Jake, and Petey—watched Emma drive off, watched her fishtail out of the parking lot with squealing tires, and speed onto the two-lane road back toward Coudersport. No one said anything for a few moments. Petey was the first. He meowed loudly.

It was obvious, to Jake at least, that he was confused.

"I don't know, Petey."

Jake turned to Tassy.

"Do you have any idea of what's going on?"

And with that, Tassy ran back into the RV, leaving the door open. Jake was fairly sure she was crying as she ran. They both followed her inside. She had collapsed onto the couch and curled herself into a ball, her head hidden in her knees, her arms wrapped around her legs.

She was crying.

Petey jumped on the couch and butted against her side, chirping and meowing. Eventually, she uncoiled, and he climbed into her lap, purring so loudly that Jake could hear him. Jake sat in the chair opposite.

"Tassy," he said with care, "something is going on. I would like to be able to help. Please let me help."

"You can't help, Pastor Jake. It's beyond anybody's help. Really."

Petey meowed, loudly, as if he understood, but disagreed with her.

"Tassy, Petey is right. Nothing is beyond God's help."

She sniffed loudly and wiped her face with her sleeve. She stared at Jake, not in anger, exactly, but more in supplication. Angry supplication, perhaps.

"I'm pregnant. Can you help that, Pastor Jake?"

Her words were indeed tinged with anger.

Jake resisted the urge to answer right away, to say the first thing that came to mind, to be blunt or bold or inconsiderate or unfeeling. He waited. He tried to allow the meaning of the words to sink in, to be assimilated fully before he spoke.

Petey spoke first, with a long, low, rumbly meow and purr combination.

Jake had not heard that before.

He tried out one response in his head, and then another, and another, and none of them sounded correct, sensitive, or pastoral enough. Then he remembered Sidney's smiling face.

"First, Tassy, you have to remember that no matter what— God loves you. He will always love you. You cannot do anything that will change his love for you. I promise."

Jake was now talking to her as well as himself.

"God is constant. We may change and get angry and make mistakes . . . but God will always be there, waiting for us, with open arms."

Tassy stared back at him. Jake was not sure if she believed a word of what he said. But the words had to be spoken.

"And it doesn't matter if we understand it or not . . . it's true. That's where faith comes in. We just have to believe in the truth. It's pretty simple, actually. Just believe."

Jake listened to his own words. Most of the time, he didn't. But this time he did—and he found himself thinking, *That makes a lot of sense. Just believe. Don't complicate it with how it should be or how others think it should be—just believe. Faith. Belief. Just accept it.*

"Maybe," Tassy said.

She did not look convinced, but she appeared less angry.

"Why was Emma here?" Jake asked.

Tassy shook her head and said nothing.

"Tassy . . . why was Emma here?"

Tassy began to pet Petey.

"We were . . . we were going to . . . 'handle it.' You know. Take care of it. She said that having a baby now would complicate my life too much and it wouldn't be right and if I handled it, I could just start over again. Sometimes things happen and you have to take care of it. This was a mistake I needed to fix. That's all. I was going to take care of it."

She started to cry again halfway through, and the tears began to course down her cheeks and fall on Petey's head and back. He did not attempt to move away.

"That's when Petey took her keys. That's when he ran off with them."

Jake waited a long time until he spoke again. "Tassy, I know that things seem dark right now . . . but what you were considering . . . well, that wasn't the answer. If you had done that, you would live with that regret and that pain, every single day, for the rest of your life."

She nodded.

"Whatever happens from here on in . . . I'll support you however I can. The church will support you. I know they will."

She nodded. "Do I have to go to church every Sunday?"

"If you want to, yes. If you don't, then no."

Her voice grew small. "I'll probably go. But not if I don't feel well."

"I understand."

"But I'll probably go. Petey goes all the time. I guess I can go, too."

Jake sat with Tassy and Petey until they both fell asleep on the couch, and then he silently slipped out. He knew where he had to go and what he had to say. He didn't want to have to ask, but he knew he had to. The church was bigger than he was. He did not want people hurt. He did not want new faith damaged.

He would ask. But he remained unsure of what the answer might be.

He carefully got into his truck and closed the door as silently as he could. He let it roll to the edge of the parking lot before he started it up. He drove to Coudersport, always keeping the truck well below the speed limit.

He pulled up to Dr. Grainger's office and drew in a deep breath. He closed his eyes, still trying to come up with what he might say that would help to keep others from peril, or damage.

He rang the bell on the side of the house. He heard foot-steps and a series of rumbling barks. He waited. After a long time, he saw Emma's feet first, descending the long staircase.

There was no welcome in her eyes as she propped the door open halfway, then crossed her arms over her chest.

"What?"

Jake threw away whatever practiced words he had formu-lated. "Listen, Emma. I . . . I want to apologize to you. I should have been truthful from the very beginning. And I wasn't."

"Okay. You're sorry. Good. You're still a fraud."

Obviously, looking at Jake's face, one could tell that the words stung.

"Maybe. Maybe I was. But not now."

Emma offered a twisted smile in reply. "Just saying it doesn't make it so, Jake. Words are cheap."

Jake stood firm and did not look away. "You're right. They are. Coming here, I was thinking how I could ask you not to say anything about Barbara Ann to anyone. And not to say anything to anyone about why I was fired from the church in Butler. But right now, this very minute, I decided that I couldn't do that. It would be a lie. And I'm tired of lying—to others, as well as myself. So . . . I just want to say I'm sorry. For everything, I guess."

"Good. You're sorry. Anything else?"

Jake took a deep breath. "Emma, I am going to stand by Tassy. Whatever she needs to have this baby and to raise this child, I am going to do my best to supply that. Whatever it takes. I am not going to abandon her."

Emma smirked. "Listen, Jake, we have all been abandoned. Me, you, Tassy, Petey. We are all abandoned. By someone. God, former boyfriends, parents—whomever. All abandoned. It's the way of the world, Jake. You should be the first to realize the truth of that."

Jake shook his head. "That's where you're wrong, Emma. I just found out this morning. God never left me. He was always there. I may have moved away, but God did not abandon me. And he sent me Petey. God must have done that."

Emma's caustic, brittle laughter gave every indication that she considered Jake to be delusional.

"No. I am serious. If Petey had not been there, you and Tassy would have 'handled it.' And that would have scarred her, Emma. She would have to live with that forever. God knew what Petey was doing. God was saving me—and protecting an unborn life."

"Okay, Jake. Sure. I believe that. God sends cats to save people. Right. And we're done here, okay? We're done."

Jake saw in Emma's face something hidden and painful and lost. "Emma?"

"We're done. See you around, Pastor Jake. Maybe. See what happens this Sunday when people find out what sort of fraud you are. See what happens then. Abandoned? You'll see, Jake. You'll see."

Emma closed the door.

"I'll be back, Emma. God did not abandon me. I won't abandon you, either."

She spun around on her heel.

"Hey, don't bother with any special treatment for me, okay? Once people find out, you won't be around anymore. So don't bother."

And all Jake saw was the heels of her feet, hurrying up the steps and out of view.

15

Jake spent all of Friday and all of Saturday in his study.

He stopped at the RV several times, checking. Tassy did not work on Fridays and she said she felt a little better. Jake insisted she make an appointment at the county health department in Coudersport for a prenatal checkup, which she did.

Other than making coffee in the morning, Jake spent the majority of both days working on his message. By Saturday evening, he thought that his sermon was in good shape. Not spectacular—but good.

On Sunday morning, he woke up at 4:00, well before the sun rose, and walked into the office. He picked up his packet of sermon notes. By the time he read through the second point, he realized, beyond a shadow of a doubt, it was a sermon he could not deliver. Not now. Maybe not ever.

He tossed the notes back onto his desk.

Petey walked in, meowing to himself.

"What do I say, Petey? What do I say? Emma must have said something about all this to at least one person . . . so the whole town knows about everything, by now. So what do I say?"

Petey jumped up on the desk in one fluid motion and then flopped onto his side, purring loudly. Jake petted his side.

"I don't know what you want," he said.

Petey purred louder.

"Lord . . . what do I say? What do I tell these people? How I betrayed them? How I found you? What?"

—⁂—

Jake held the hymnal for the first two songs of the Sunday service and pretended to sing, just mouthing the words, just moving his lips. Elder Keilback presented the announcements for the day—the upcoming all-church picnic, the status of the steeple fund. There might have been others, but Jake hardly heard a word of it.

He glanced down at the bulletin. The sermon would immediately follow the announcements.

Jake swallowed hard, stood up, and walked to the pulpit.

Petey was already in his usual chair, sitting, precise and attentive. The church was full. Jake had read all the studies that indicated if a church wanted to grow in attendance, it needed to have 10 percent of its seating capacity unfilled. Fewer open seats than that meant newcomers would feel uncomfortable and not return. Perhaps another ten people could fit in the church, if others scooted down a little bit. They had enough room to place folding chairs in the aisles, something the elders had talked about but had not yet scheduled. It would add another thirty spots.

"We're always down a little during summer anyhow," one of them said. "Let's table the extra chair discussion until the fall. Then we'll see."

A building program . . . well, there had never been a building program at the Church of the Open Door, so none of the elders had experience holding on to the idea. They had never once needed to consider an expansion of their facilities.

Until the cat showed up, that is.

Along with Pastor Jake.

Jake took hold of both sides of the pulpit. They had raised it six inches a few weeks earlier, at Jake's request. The carpentry work was not elegant, nor seamless, but the pulpit now stood higher and was more comfortable for the pastor.

Jake normally took his notes, which he always folded precisely, lengthwise, out of his breast pocket.

This morning, he did not take out his notes. He had no notes. This morning, he realized, something different would be required. There was no need for a prepared sermon.

Jake took off his sport coat and laid it on one of the chairs next to Petey.

That was not unusual. When the temperature rose, the church people cared less about style. The pastor could preach in a shirt, without a tie, when the thermometer rose past eighty degrees.

But today, the temperature hovered in the mid-seventies, with low humidity.

Jake looked out on the congregation. He knew almost all of them, at least by first name, maybe not all intimately yet, but he knew them all. And they knew him. He could not go to downtown Coudersport without running into someone from the church, or someone related to someone from the church.

Coudersport was a small town, but people already knew Jake . . . and perhaps even respected him, a little.

He looked at their faces. He tried to decipher what they were thinking. He attempted to gauge how many had heard the secret Emma held—the secret Emma said she was going to unleash on Coudersport.

He did not see incredulity or anger or disbelief or suspicion.

He saw the same earnest, hardworking, honest (for the most part), genuine people he saw the very first time he spoke in this church. He saw Jimbo and his wife. He saw Eleanor and Vern. He saw Tassy sitting next to them, her face more radiant today than ever before. He saw Sidney's mother, beaming. He had told her about his meeting and prayer with Sidney. He saw people expecting to hear from God that day—not hoping, not wishing but expecting. This is the day when God would speak to them most clearly.

They knew God was everywhere, and all the time. They knew that. But they also knew—no, felt—God spoke to them most clearly and directly in church. That is how it worked in their lives. God speaks most clearly when they are behind the church doors and under the cross on the steeple.

Jake cleared his throat.

He said a very short and very concise prayer—silently, to himself.

Help me.

And he concluded it very concisely.

Thank you.

He cleared his throat again. It was a nervous tic, and he knew it, and he did his best to keep the throat-clearing under control. He did not want to be that pastor who every teenage boy in the youth group could imitate with startling clarity, and all they would have to do is clear their throats a few dozen times before speaking.

"Friends," he began.

And they are my friends. For the first time in my church career, I have friends in the church.

"I have to share something with you today. I never intended on sharing this with you. But I have to. I always knew, eventually, the truth would come out. And the truth will be better now than waiting until later. That's when truth turns bitter."

Now he noticed a shift in the attitude of those listening. They had noticed he had not started off the sermon with a joke or a personal story, or something he had read in the newspaper.

Today felt real and serious.

Several people leaned forward. Some people appeared to be bracing themselves, as if they were about to embark on some roller-coaster thrill ride at Kennywood Park.

"I am going to tell you something about myself that I hoped I would keep forever hidden. But there is no secret that can remain a secret forever. All secrets get told, eventually. No confidence is forever confidential."

Now, everyone was listening—even the few older men who always fell asleep during the first two minutes of Jake's sermons.

"When I came to this church, when you invited me to this church to become your pastor . . . I am sure—no, positive—you all expected me to have this strong faith and a resolute, bedrock trust in the Almighty. You expected me to have no doubts as to the center of the Christian life. You expected, and you deserved, a man who had a solid, sure, positive, longtime, deep-seated, forever sort of faith."

He took a breath. The rest of the congregation seemed to breathe in with him. A great deal of fresh air left the sanctuary with one assembled breath.

"I was not that person. I had doubts. Serious doubts. When I was a pastor in Butler . . . at the church where I served before I came here, I told a woman I was dating I just wasn't sure about my relationship with God. I told her I wasn't sure if God was really watching me and directing my life. I was honest when I told her I just didn't have . . . I didn't have faith anymore."

Jake stopped for a moment.

The congregation did not seem to be incensed or angry or to be thinking about getting out their pitchforks and torches.

They did seem as if they were intent on hearing this story play out, however. Very intent.

"When I told her, this woman I was dating, that information, that secret was no longer a secret, and it got back to the senior pastor of the church. I know. I know. It was bound to happen. That's why I said that no secret ever stays a secret long if more than one person knows it."

Jake walked away from the pulpit. There was a microphone on the pulpit, and a small amplifier, but the sanctuary was not large. Anything spoken aloud, with some power, even a little power, was loud enough for everyone to hear. Jake made sure he spoke loudly and clearly.

"So my boss, the senior pastor, asked me if it was true—me admitting to this woman that I had lost my faith. I could have lied and said she had been mistaken."

Jake paused.

"Did I mention this young woman was the senior pastor's niece?"

There was a smattering of nervous laughter, and those who laughed quickly realized it was not a laugh line and immediately ended their smiles and laughter.

"I could have lied and blamed this woman for 'misinterpreting' what I had said in confidence. But even I couldn't do that. I told him it was the truth. That what she had said was true."

Jake sat down in the chair next to Petey. Petey meowed as Jake sat, as if to say his actions were most unusual and did he really know what he was doing this morning?

"He fired me. He had to. He had no choice. You can't have a pastor—someone in charge of the spiritual well-being of hundreds of people—who doesn't have faith. An oxymoron."

Jake wasn't sure if a majority of people sitting in front of him knew what an oxymoron was.

"Like jumbo shrimp. That's an oxymoron. Is it jumbo or is it small?"

He grinned at them. "He fired me and I can't blame him one bit for doing that. A pastor who no longer has faith may be acceptable in some churches, but not a church that really believes in the Bible and everything it teaches. A pastor without faith."

He stood. "An oxymoron."

He walked back to the pulpit, carefully choosing each step.

"So I started here as a pastor without faith. And I think I was doing okay. Even though I thought God had abandoned me. I've told you about my childhood. I've told you my father left us. He abandoned us. I intimately knew that feeling—the feeling of being alone. What I felt about my father's leaving, well, I thought God had done the same thing to me. And when my father left, I pretended to be brave and strong. I thought if I did everything right and went to seminary and became a pastor, then everything would be fine and dandy. It wasn't. It caught up to me. A few days ago, I was praying with a young man who was looking for faith. And he found it—just like that. He was filled with faith and the Holy Spirit. Immediately."

Jake snapped his fingers. It sounded loud in the still church. He looked out and saw Glenda Davis, near the back, tears in her eyes.

"Just like that. Amazing. Here I was struggling and working and striving to regain my faith—and this young man just lays down his arms, stops battling, and accepts. And there it was."

He walked to the other side if the platform.

"This is what I discovered. This is what I learned. God never left me. He was always there. I wandered off. God didn't. And he sent me a cat. He sent this church a cat. Petey. How many people are here today because Petey is here?"

A number of people—a large number of people—raised their hands.

"God cares about you. Enough to send a cat—because He knew that is what would work. That is what would draw you inside a church. He brought you all here."

Jake sat down on the steps of the raised platform.

"But I've lied to you. I have been a fraud. I have said I was a man of God . . . but until a few days ago, I was lying. I'm sorry. So, so sorry. You need someone better. You deserve someone better. You do. This church deserves the truth."

Jake clasped his hands together, loosely, and sat still for a moment, not speaking.

What happened next surprised Jake. Really, really surprised him.

The massive elder, Rudolph Keilback, stood up in the pew. He made his way to the center aisle, people parting to let him pass, like Moses and the Red Sea. He turned to face Jake and marched up the center aisle. Jake looked up at his face. Rudolph wiped his cheeks with the back of his hand. He might have been crying.

"Listen. I don't want to be up here. I don't do well in front. You all know that. But . . . Pastor Jake . . . you can't leave us. I . . . said I believed when I was a little kid. But you want to know the secret I kept for the past forty years? I never did believe. I don't think I did. I went to church. I went to church for years. I'm an elder. But I never knew . . ."

He held the pulpit with both meaty hands and gripped it so hard Jake was sure he'd hear wood splintering.

"Not until Pastor Jake showed up did I know what it was to believe. And not until today did I ever think anyone else had that problem or that secret. If you think you have to leave, Pastor Jake, then so do I."

Quiet filled the sanctuary like a tidal wave.

After at least a full two minutes of silence, with Elder Keilback at the pulpit and Pastor Jake sitting on the platform, another man rose. He was in the middle of the row, seven rows back.

"I never believed either. Until right now. I've been pretending. Thank you, Pastor Jake, for making it okay for me to . . . cry with you. And to find faith with you."

A woman stood up on the other side of the aisle.

"I've been head deaconess longer than a lot of you have been alive. Today I believe. Today I have faith. Today it all became real. Today my real life with God starts."

Jimbo stood up. His wife, at his side, was in tears.

"I know I could be a better husband. I could listen more. I don't know what I would do without . . . Betty here. I would be lost—totally and utterly lost."

Jimbo had begun to tear up as well.

"Family. That's what matters. This family."

Tassy stood up. She was holding on to Eleanor's hand. Jake could see that their grips were tight, white-knuckle tight, perhaps.

"You here are all my family. This church is my family. And I have a secret I need to share with you all. I'm going to have a baby. And before today, I was planning on running away because I felt like you would all be disappointed with me. I almost had an abortion. I came within minutes of it. Petey saved me. It's a long story. God led me here—to this church and to Pastor Jake and to Petey. He has protected me. And now you're my family. And I promise I will do my best to make the faith you have in me worth it. I promise."

Eleanor stood up and put her arm around the young girl's shoulder. Vern stood up as well, his eyes and face wet, and embraced them both.

And people began to cry and to pray and to hug and to embrace.

Jake saw a few people standing in the back. One of them was Speedy . . . Sidney Davis. His mother was crying harder now.

And that's when the church organist, Verna Ebbert, walked up to the platform, switched on the organ with an audible pop, and began to play a warbly, off-tempo rendition of "Just as I Am."

Just as I am, without one plea,
but that thy blood was shed for me,
and that thou bidst me come to thee,
O Lamb of God, I come, I come.

Just as I am, and waiting not
to rid my soul of one dark blot,
to thee whose blood can cleanse each spot,
O Lamb of God, I come, I come.

Just as I am, though tossed about
with many a conflict, many a doubt,
fightings and fears within, without,
O Lamb of God, I come, I come.

Just as I am, poor, wretched, blind;
sight, riches, healing of the mind,
yea, all I need in thee to find,
O Lamb of God, I come, I come.

Just as I am, thou wilt receive,
wilt welcome, pardon, cleanse, relieve;
because thy promise I believe,
O Lamb of God, I come, I come.

Just as I am, thy love unknown
hath broken every barrier down;
now, to be thine, yea, thine alone,
O Lamb of God, I come, I come.

To Jake, it was the most beautiful song he had ever heard, better than a celestial choir of a thousand angels.

Much, much better.

———

Sunday service ran long that day.

There was a lot of singing. There was a lot of sharing, a lot of asking for forgiveness. There was more hugging in the church this Sunday than there had been in the last decade. Perhaps two decades.

At a few minutes past 2:00, a few people decided they were really hungry, or they had children who were really, really hungry, so the crowd started to slowly disassemble. By 3:00, the sanctuary was empty, save for Pastor Jake and Petey.

Jake could not help smiling. It was not a smug smile, or a self-satisfied smile, but a smile warmed by gratitude and amazement.

"God showed up, didn't he, Petey?"

Petey meowed contentedly.

"I know you thought you had it all figured out . . . but I sure didn't. I never expected any of this to happen. Never in a million years."

Jake was sitting on the platform steps, and Petey lay down next to him and rolled on his side. Jake petted his stomach and Petey rolled his head back and forth, purring loudly, content, happy.

"There is probably one more person I need to deal with today."

Petey looked up.

"Emma. Dr. Grainger."

Petey meowed in agreement.

"I should go now. She might think she destroyed my career. But in reality, she started it."

Jake stood and pulled out his truck keys.

"Want to come?"

Petey stayed exactly where he was.

"Okay. I'll leave the office door open. Okay?"

The cat chirped a reply.

A few minutes later, Jake stood outside Dr. Grainger's door— the side door, her private entrance. He was not frightened or anxious or nervous or intimidated. All that had apparently disappeared with a number of Jake's other fears and phobias.

He saw the curtain move in an upstairs window. She had to have seen his truck in the drive. A moment later, he heard footsteps—slow, methodical, as if each step down was a harder step to take.

She turned the inside latch and opened the door, only a quarter of the way. Jake was pretty sure he saw fear in her face.

"Emma, I want to apologize to you again. I should have been honest with you from the very beginning. I wasn't. I led a lot of people to believe I was something much more good and noble than I really was. But all that has changed."

Emma's face did not show a smile or a frown or any emotion at all. She had become a cipher, neutral.

"I spent all of Friday and Saturday trying to figure out how to spin what happened, how to make people believe that what happened didn't happen the way it happened. But then, this morning, I realized I could no longer pretend. I stood up and confessed everything to the church. And no one condemned me. They forgave me."

Now Emma looked surprised.

"Others stood up alongside me and confessed to have the same doubts. People began to cry and hug one another and forgive one another for past transgressions. It was the most amazing church service I have ever been part of. And you know . . . when I was praying with Speedy—rather, Sidney—Davis, praying for his faith . . . that's when my faith welled up inside of me. I had spent so much time working, trying to find it and to cultivate it . . . and all I had to do was accept it. You taught me a valuable lesson, Emma. And I want to thank you for that."

Emma remained surprised. Her eyes were wider than they had been.

"You're . . . you're welcome, I guess," she said.

"Thanks for helping me finally see the truth. Thank you so much."

Jake left her standing in her doorway and walked back to his truck, feeling lighter and clearer and more solid than he had ever felt in his entire life.

16

Three weeks later, Jake had a meeting with Wilbur Brookings, the head of the elder board. The meeting was a small one—just Jake and Wilbur—with coffee and donuts at Kaytee's. Several donuts, actually. Kaytee's made very good donuts.

Wilbur wanted the meeting to stay confidential, at least temporarily.

"You said it yourself, Pastor. A secret is compromised the second another person hears it. So I'm trusting you to hold this one under your hat for a while. Since you're an honest man and all."

Jake promised that he would, and then braced himself for what might be coming.

"We need to start a building committee," Wilbur said in a whisper. "The church is packed and it's summer, and no one comes in the summer. We're putting chairs in the aisles and that's not enough—or comfortable. So my question is, how do you go about starting a building committee? We've never done this before. I've never done this before."

Jake was taken aback, for a little bit. He was expecting something darker, more personal. Building onto the church was neither of those. Jake had never started a building campaign either but had a shelf of books in his office that described the process and the parameters and the pitfalls.

"I'll look at them and get you the two best ones. That will be our start. And I promise not a word will escape my lips until you say so."

Wilbur sighed deeply, and it was a happy sigh, if sighs can have happy connotations.

"I blame that stupid cat, you know. And you, too, Pastor Jake. We could have stayed small and happy if it weren't for you two."

He paused for effect, then smiled.

"I'm kidding. But you knew that, right?"

———— ∞∞∞ ————

Jake sat at Kaytee's by himself after Wilbur left.

He was simply happy to sit there with his coffee and one more small chocolate donut . . . until Emma Grainger walked in. She saw him and hesitated, then seemed to shrug to herself, and walked to his table.

He was pretty sure that the waitresses knew what had gone on between them. No—he was not just pretty sure. He was positive. News that delicious does not remain untasted, especially in a town this small.

"We should probably talk, Jake."

Jake bore no anger or grudge. He liked Emma. He liked her a lot. And he was willing to let her walk away from a relationship with him if that was her choice. And it certainly appeared to be her choice.

"Sure," Jake replied. "Anytime."

Emma pulled a chair out and sat down.

"How about now?"

"Now is fine," Jake said. *Now* did surprise him a little. He thought she might give him some time to prepare. Or give herself time to build up courage or whatever she needed. But no, it would be now.

"First off, I need to tell you that I didn't mention your . . . 'situation' with Barbara Ann to anyone in town. I wanted to. I really wanted to hurt you badly. But I didn't say anything."

Jake wanted to take her hand and squeeze it in a reassuring way but did not.

"I know," he replied. "Some of our more . . . attentive church members, the ones that are more plugged in, if you know what I mean, asked me later why I'd said anything at all. And I told them I figured they had all heard about Barbara Ann and what happened. But no one had heard a word before I brought it up that Sunday. I see now I easily could have kept that secret a secret. But I am so grateful I didn't. And I'm glad you didn't say anything to anyone. That's a lot to feel responsible for."

"I wanted to tell everyone, Jake. I did. More than you can imagine."

Jake nodded to the waitress who came by with a coffeepot. He waited until she poured the coffee and left.

"Emma, you don't owe me any explanation. And I may be out of line for asking. But . . . I'll ask anyway. Why? Why did you want to see me hurt?"

Emma looked pale and drawn, as if she had not slept well the past few weeks.

"You talked about honesty. I suspect I need be honest about this as well. Hiding it all these years hasn't done me much good."

Jake waited. Tassy had suggested a possible reason for Emma's anger, but Jake wasn't sure. For the last few weeks, Tassy said Dr. Grainger had been strictly professional in the office. Not cold or hostile or angry, just a chilly sort of professionalism. Tassy did not mind, but she did feel bad for Dr. Grainger. It appeared to her that Dr. Grainger was not enjoying anything.

"It started just before I headed off to vet school. The summer before."

Emma looked down at her hands, folded in her lap.

"Do you want some tea, Emma? or coffee? or toast?" Jake asked.

She looked up, offered him a weak smile.

"No. Maybe water. I'll drink yours if I need it. You've had your shots, right?"

They both smiled.

"I have my papers," Jake said. "Me and Petey both."

He waited.

"I got pregnant," Emma said. "He said he would take care of me. He made it sound like everything would work out. I loved him. I loved him a lot. We were perfect for each other. He would be a doctor and I would be a vet. Perfect."

She looked out the window and watched a TrueValue hardware truck make its way, carefully, down the narrow street.

Jake had learned that being attentive and silent was often all that was required of a good listener.

"Then he said one of us would have to give up their dream. If I 'went through with this.' He said we had to be adult about it. He said we needed to 'handle it.' He said nothing would change afterward. He promised me nothing would change— after we handled it."

She took in several deep breaths, trying not to choke up, trying not to cry.

"He promised."

She looked down, away from Jake's eyes.

"We handled it. It was hard, but he was with me. It would be okay. He promised. And then he left. He never talked to me again. He's married now, to another doctor. They live in Dallas. I handled it for him. So we could both keep our dreams. No one would get hurt."

Jake waited. Emma did not cry. But she did not look up, either.

"I murdered my first child," Emma said. "My only child. I live with that every day, Jake. There's not a day that goes by that I don't think about my baby, a baby I had killed. It's hard. It is very, very hard. Some days I just do not know what to do with the truth."

She looked away for a long time and Jake let the silence be.

"And when Tassy found out she was pregnant—all that anger came back. Here was a young girl who was in the same situation I was in. I was cheated, Jake. I was cheated out of a child. And abandoned. I'll never have children now. That's what the doctors have told me. And I didn't want anyone else to have what I can't have anymore, either. That's why I tried to get Tassy to an abortion clinic."

Now she started to cry.

"I am so sorry, Jake. I am so sorry for what I almost did to her. I feel like the worst person in the world. She comes to the office in the morning, and I see her all radiant and growing and happy—and I don't know how I will get through the day without being reminded every second of what I almost forced her to do."

She grabbed a thickness of napkins from the chrome dispenser on the table. She wiped her eyes and her cheeks.

"How do I do this, Jake? How do I move on from here? How do I move on from murder?"

This time, Jake followed his instinct and took one of her hands. From the corner of his eye, he could see the waitress in the far corner, by the coffee service, put her hand up to her mouth as he did that.

There are no secrets, especially in a small town.

"Emma. We can start over. Your life can start anew right now."

Emma sniffed.

"What I tried to do was horrible. To her. To you."

"You want it to be forgiven? I forgive you. Tassy loves you like she would love an older sister. She would forgive, even though she knows there is nothing to forgive. You acted out of pain. And what is bigger than her or me is the fact that God loves you, Emma. And he will never leave you. There is nothing we can do that will strip God's love for us. Nothing, Emma. That is true. And that is faith. He will never leave you."

She looked up, tears streaking down her face.

To Jake, she looked beautiful.

"Can you show me what I need to see? What I need to feel? Can you show me this faith you have?"

"I can try," he said. "I can try."

Tassy handed the keys to the RV to Jake.

"I'll miss living here. I'll miss having you to talk to. I'll miss Petey."

Petey stood at Tassy's side, meowing, rubbing his face against her shin, then meowing again. There was a suitcase on her other side, and Petey knew what suitcases meant. They meant good-byes, and Petey did not like good-byes.

No one said anything about her leaving.

He jumped up on the suitcase and stared at them both, Jake and Tassy, with defiance in his eyes.

*She can't leave now. Not with me on the suitcase. She'll have to
stay here forever and ever.*

Tassy leaned into Pastor Jake and hugged him with a
fierceness.

"I'll be here for you. Anytime you want me, I'll be here.
And I know you won't have Petey to talk to—but you'll have
Winston."

What!? Winston is leaving, too? That doesn't make any sense.

"I'm happy for you and happy for Emma. She does have a
lot of spare bedrooms. One will make a great nursery."

"That's what she said. She wants it all pink and frilly. I was
thinking something a little more hard rock and edgy."

*She's moving in with Dr. Grainger? Why doesn't anyone tell me
anything important? First, I find out the house with wheels has to
be moved. Then they tell me a new building is going to start soon.
And now Tassy is leaving. You take a few naps, and the world passes
you by. I don't get it.*

"And I guess I'll see you there as well . . . sometimes. Right?"
Jake tried not to grin.

"We are taking things very slow. Emma needs to let her faith
grow without me holding her hand. So we're moving slow."

"But steady."

"Okay—slow but steady. No heavy lifting at the moment."

Tassy laughed. "Speaking of lifting, how's your shoulder?
Dr. Grainger said she knows a great chiropractor. She knows
the best of everything around here. She knew the best obstetri-
cian—and Dr. Hallis has been so sweet to me."

"My shoulder is fine. For the most part. That's just me getting old in front of your eyes."

An old Buick with dented front fenders bounced into the
parking lot.

"You're not getting old. Now, Mr. Waldorf—he's getting old. But he's my ride today. He and Eleanor insisted."

Jake waved. Vern almost waved back. Eleanor did.

Tassy stood on her tiptoes and kissed Jake's cheek.

"I love you, Pastor Jake."

Hey! What about me? I'm the one who saved you. Petey meowed and nearly stood erect, swatting at Tassy's side.

"And you, too, Petey," she said as she gave him a dainty kiss on his forehead. "I love you most of all."

Epilogue

Early autumn is a most beautiful time in Coudersport. The oaks and cherry trees start to redden and yellow and the hills are aflame with fall colors, the sort of colors an artist could never hope to truly capture.

The air grows neat with a chill, just the hint of chill, and a scent of apples and of harvested corn and pumpkins fills the valleys.

Petey took to lying on the concrete steps to the old sanctuary, catching the afternoon sun.

He sat up, adjusted himself with great care, and looked up at the heavens.

This was where I was supposed to be. Jake was the man I was sent to help. This has happened like it was supposed to happen. Like I said on that first day. I am really pretty certain I am the only cat that could have done this. I am a smart cat, aren't I? I am a good cat.

While he sat, still as a statue, he heard a rustling, then saw a nervous dart of gray and brown. A field mouse scurried across the bottom step, oblivious to Petey, since he had not moved in some minutes. Petey flinched, just the merest fraction of an inch.

No. No one here needs a mouse right now. Maybe later. But I don't need one now. Not today. I have too much already.

He watched the mouse disappear under a thickness of dried leaves.

I am a good cat, aren't I?

A good cat and a smart cat.

Discussion Questions

1. Come on now, a cat? Really? A cat who thinks he talks to God and is following God's instructions? Seriously though, do you think that God could, or would, use such a method as that to reach a person who is lost?

2. In a sense, Jake Wilkerson assumes the position of pastor of the small Church of the Open Door under false pretenses: he is pretending to have faith and be spiritually mature. Do you think God can use a broken person in such a way, or do you think Jake was being deceptive? Why would God choose such a person to lead others?

3. Besides his feeling lost, what other obstacles does Jake face in his return to the pulpit and to faith?

4. Perhaps Vern Waldorf is simply being honest when he grows angry over the idea of letting Tassie live in his RV. Perhaps he is simply mirroring the views of some of the "upstanding Christians" in the community. How might we be guilty of the same sort of attitude if we try to separate ourselves from someone who seems to be sinning?

5. Suppose Jake is only thinking that Petey is manipulating him into certain situations? In what ways can that sort of "perceived manipulation" be the sort of nudge we need to turn back to God? And could the nudge from a manipulating cat be of a divine nature?

6. Dr. Emma Grainger lets her past actions define who she is—even if she is not aware of it. Do you agree with that statement? Are there things in your life that are defined by what you have done in the past? Is that always a bad or negative thing?

7. Tassie is nearly convinced to have an abortion because of the strident urgings of Dr. Grainger, a person she

greatly respects. The doctor uses her position to attempt to get Tassie to do what she says. Is using our position to get people to act in a certain way or to do certain things always a negative? Have you ever used your position or standing to get someone to conform to your way of thinking?

8. Many people get stuck in a situation or an emotion because of a tragedy or dramatic event in their life. What sort of advice would you have given Emma? Would that advice change over time—would the advice you offered a month after the abortion be dramatically different than the advice offered a year after the abortion?

9. As an outsider, and a stranger, and an unwed mother-to-be, Tassie faces some immense challenges in her life. Do you think she handles them well? Do you think she listens to others too much? What would you have done in the same situation?

10. Petey the cat seems to draw a lot of people to the church—perhaps only because of the novelty of it all. Do you think it is wise of the elders to condone such an action? Do you think that simply preaching the word should have been enough? Do you think that the cat on the platform with the preacher is simply a gimmick—and that God never uses "gimmicks" to attract people to the truth?

11. When Dr. Grainger learns the truth about Jake's past church experience and his past relationship experience with Barbara Ann Bentley, she truly wants to use that information to damage Jake's reputation and to hurt him. Has anyone ever hurt you using "the truth" as a weapon? When is it okay to leave secrets secret? Is it always necessary to tell the "whole" truth?

12. Jake's mother is terribly controlling—or at least tries to be—all with good intentions. She wants Jake to do well, wants him to be free of scandal, she wants the best for her son. Have you ever felt overwhelmed by the crush of "good intentions" from someone who was just trying to do good? Is there a way to gently tell people that they have gone too far in their efforts at helping you?

13. Do you think that Jake and Dr. Emma eventually get married? Do you think the story would be satisfying if they didn't? Why or why not?

14. Do you think that Emma will eventually find faith? Is it proper for a pastor to "see" someone who is not a believer—yet—but seems to be well on their way to finding faith? How would that be received at your church?

If you missed Jim Kraus's first adventure, check out this sample chapter

———∞∞———

The Dog That Talked to God

1

Born in the wealthy enclave of Barrington, Illinois, in late autumn, Rufus was the smallest pup in a litter of four—black with white highlights, white eyebrows and chest. The breeder, a precise woman with a lazy eye, said that as an adult, he would most likely remain on the smallish side. That's a good trait for a miniature schnauzer. He had the look, even as a seven-week-old, of a polished, professional dog, holding a practiced dog show stance—legs back, chest forward, eyes alert—all inherited traits, genetics at its best.

But she said nothing about Rufus talking. Not just talking, but talking to God. In dog prayers, I imagine.

Though, in her defense, I would guess that she was unaware of this unusual talent.

And, also in her defense, if she knew of his abilities and had mentioned, "Oh yes, Mrs. Fassler, and the runt of the litter—the dog you want—well, he talks, and he claims he talks to God." I mean, honestly, if she had said that, or anything remotely

313

like that, then odds are that the good dog Rufus would not be sitting in the chair opposite me right now, watching me type.

Perhaps if Rufus had been adopted into another home—a home with an owner who wasn't lost and confused and didn't need to be returned to the awareness of the existence of God—he would not have bothered speaking at all, except to bark at the door to be let out. Even Rufus is not sure of that possibility.

"I don't ask foolish questions, Mary," Rufus answered when I asked him about the odds of him spending his life with me, rather than some other, more spiritually healthy person.

But I digress.

———— ⨯⨯⨯ ————

I did not mean to cavalierly hurry past the most compelling element of this story: the fact that Rufus talks to God. And he talks to me—Rufus, that is, not God. Sometimes.

It's hard to be nonchalant or blasé about such an ability, I know. But I cannot leap into this tale without returning to the beginning. You need to know how all this came about. You need to know the origins of the story. After all, what would the Bible be without Genesis and the garden of Eden? Confusing, to say the least, and most likely incomprehensible. Imagine the Bible as a movie you walk into during the middle. You can make up your own backstory, but it would all be just a guess. Admit it: without that opening scene, not much of the rest would contain any internal logic.

As a child, I used to do that—walk into a movie theater whenever, and watch the film, sit through the ending, and wait for the opening reel to start again until I would say to myself, "This is where I came in." It was easier years ago, before the age of googolplexes and corporate theater chains. Back in the day, each theater had one screen and would play the same movie over and over, with only a cartoon and previews to separate one screening from another. Once I got to that point of having seen a particular scene before, I would leave, satisfied that I had seen the entire story. I remember doing that to *The Time Machine* with Rod Taylor, a movie star without much reason to be a star. Seems ludicrous to me now. I had constructed my own narrative as to how Rod got to whatever point in the future he started at, which then altered my imagined story as the true narrative unfolded. With that movie, I was close to guessing the actual story and plot. Close, but, as they say, no cigar.

As a child, reconstructing a complicated narrative was child's play.

It is not so easy today.

———— ∞ ————

Throughout my youth, my family owned pets. Owned, I suspect, is now a pejorative term. I mean, do we really own a dog? Or do we merely cohabit in the same spaces? The latter, I am now certain. My father, an impetuous man with a generous heart, once bought a squirrel monkey from Gimbels Department Store in Pittsburgh, Pennsylvania—when department stores, I surmise, could sell squirrel monkeys.

A monkey proved to be a pretty interesting pet, but if you fed it something it did not like, it would simply heave it out of the cage. Neatness is not any monkey's most endearing trait.

I remember growing up with a mutt, the family dog, a loyal animal who became as much a member of the family as I. As a teenager, I stood beside her in the vet's office when he administered the oh-so-humane and oh-so-lethal injection to a lame, sick, dying dog. I remember her eyes, just as they went dark. I remember weeping all night over that loss.

In my forties (midway, if I am feeling honest) I found myself alone again. I was pretty certain I needed a dog. Christmas was coming and I did not want to be alone.

Before—well, before my current losses and tragedies—the parameters of a dog purchase became the topic of long conversations among Jacob, John, and me. It had been decided that hypoallergenic was a necessity; preferably nonshedding, small, with minimal genetic health concerns, loyal, good with children, non-nippy, benevolent, artistic, and kind. Just kidding about the last three, but we did have a pretty substantial list of preferences. The miniature schnauzer breed met all of our qualifications.

But we, as a family, never had a chance to fulfill that dream.

Alone, now, I decided to take action—and taking action was something I did not do lightly. Unlike me, the schnauzer, according to the breed books, had decisiveness bred into its genes. A good watchdog, the books insisted. A barker, but not a biter. Since I live in a relatively safe suburb, a barker would be sufficient.

I made a few calls; I looked on the Internet.

A friend advised against getting any dog. "They're all the same—stupid, hairy, and only interested in food. Trust me," she had said. "You will get companionship, but it will be stupid companionship. Like a blind date who you find out later cheated to get his GED, and who is five inches shorter than he claimed."

She owned an Irish setter, a truly small-brained animal. I say she owned it since she did all the dog upkeep in her family—feeding, walking, feeding, letting out, letting in, feeding, washing the muck off of it. The rest of the household liked the dog, but as is often usual for families, the mother remained stuck with all the dog duties. And to complicate things, her dog could not be described as smart—not even close to smart.

It ran into the same glass sliding door every morning of its life. Like a chicken, it appeared to wake up to a new world every dawn. A pleasant dog, for certain, but, as noted, not very smart. And it often smelled wet. Most of us know that musty, yeasty, heady, nearly unpleasant aroma of a wet dog. Like wet newspaper. What they have in common is beyond me.

"But I'm looking at a smaller dog. Something that I can pick up if I have to," I told her.

It took two people to lift my friend's Irish setter, or a single person using a hospital patient lift—and where was one of those when needed?

"Jacob always wanted a schnauzer. Sort of like fulfilling a promise, you know?" I added.

My friend shrugged, apparently resigned to my choice, to my fate.

After all, how do you argue with one of the last wishes of a dead man?

There were a few AKC breeders near where I live who specialized in miniature schnauzers.

And when I was ready, only one breeder—the precise lady in Barrington with the lazy eye—had a litter with an unspoken-for puppy.

"I have a litter of four. The two females are spoken for. The larger male is going to another breeder in Florida. That leaves one male puppy. He's the runt of the litter. But he's healthy."

I attempted to make arrangements to complete the purchase.

"It's not that simple," she said, a slight note of caution in her voice. "Before you come, I have some questions. Save you a trip. I don't sell my dogs to just anyone."

"Of course not," I said, thinking it was a poor method of marketing puppies, but I played along. "I completely understand."

"Do you live in a house or an apartment?"

"A house. It's too big for me," I said, telling this stranger more than she needed to know. "I plan on selling in a year or two, and moving to a smaller house. More manageable. But a house. A house, yes, not an apartment or a condo. I don't think I would do well in an apartment anymore. Odd noises and someone is always cooking with too much curry. So, yes, I have a house. I will have a house. Now. And in the future."

"Does the house have a yard? Will the new house have a yard?"

Don't all houses have yards?

"It does. And the back is fenced. It's pretty big. The land-scapers bill me $40 a week to cut it . . . so there's a lot of room for a dog to run. And if I do move, that house will have a fenced yard. Keeps out the riffraff dogs, if you know what I mean."

Her silence probably meant that she didn't.

"Do you work?"

No . . . I thought I might pay for the puppy with food stamps.

Sorry. That's just me being snarky. Sorry.

"Yes."

"Are you gone all day? Will the dog be alone all day?"

Oh . . . now I see why you're asking.

"No. I work from home. I write books. And I edit some. And I publish a newsletter for writers. But I'm home 95 percent of most weekdays. I do go out to Starbucks sometimes to write. There's something about having to block out other people's conversations that makes me concentrate more effectively. But that's only once a week. Maybe twice, if I'm stumped by something."

The precise lady waited, then spoke carefully.

"I wouldn't sell this dog to a single person who worked outside the home all day. These puppies need companionship.

They'll get neurotic without a person—or people—around. Nothing worse than a neurotic dog."

She said nothing about dogs that had delusions of grandeur. Would I describe Rufus as . . . delusional? Or would that just be me?

"Any small children in the home?"

I waited a heartbeat, as I have done now for these last few years, until that small scud of darkness passed.

"No. No one else. It's just me."

The precise lady must have been thinking "divorced," or "widowed," or "never married." I did not volunteer further information. She did not ask. Often, when even thinking about the past, even to myself—still—I would get teary. Buying a dog is no time to get teary.

"Well, why don't you come up this Saturday? The puppy won't be ready to leave for at least another three weeks. You can see how you'll get on with him. We can talk."

I hung up the phone thinking that I need to make a good impression on this woman, or else I'll have to find another breeder and the next closest—with puppies available—was in Ohio. I did not want to drive to Ohio. Not just yet. Maybe not ever.

I arrived at the breeder's home early—a lifelong trait. To me, being on time is fifteen minutes early. The setting was not exactly rural, but I estimated that I was a good ten minutes from the nearest Starbucks—or a Texaco station selling chilled bottles of Starbucks Iced Coffee. So I sat in the drive and waited. I would have really liked a coffee. Caffeine settles my nerves.

I rattled in the car, more than a little nervous.

The breeder was exactly as I had pictured: precise, wore her hair short, trim, with practical glasses clipped to a gold chain around her neck; with that one eye slightly off-kilter to the other. She may have been wearing Earth Shoes. I was unaware if they had made a comeback; hers looked sensible and organic with a leather strap. I admit that I am far from being style-conscious. I buy good clothes, good outfits, designed to last. I haven't purchased a new outfit in years . . . well . . . since before the accident, I guess.

She extended her hand for a firm handshake, and escorted me to the basement. I could hear scuffling and yipping as we descended. In a large, airy room, with French doors leading to the outside, now closed, two adult schnauzers were in a large pen with what appeared to be a large, single mass of wiggling puppy. The room smelled of dog—but that inviting new-dog smell.

"Sit down," she said, and for that second I was not sure if the breeder meant me or the dogs. I realized that I should sit.

I sat on a plastic chair—one of two in the enclosure.

The two adult dogs sniffed the air, not in fear, but in exploration, in greeting. The larger one trotted over to me, placed its front paws on my knees, and stared hard into my eyes.

Schnauzer eyes are dark, or mostly dark, so the iris in their eyes is all but indistinguishable. They are like cartoon eyes—all one color—so it is difficult to see emotion in them. And schnauzers are not smilers. Some dogs—like labs, for example—can pull their lips back and offer a grin, with a lolling tongue. (I have since discovered that labs aren't that happy. They are simply manipulative.)

The larger dog, apparently satisfied with what it was looking for, hopped down.

The smaller dog walked toward me, with what I took to be deliberate steps. It too placed its paws on my knees and stared.

"That's the mom," the breeder said, not using the word *mom*, but the breeder word for a female dog—a word, incidentally, that I have never liked using, either in anger or in scientific dog-calling. She was Rufus's mother after all, though the name Rufus would not be decided for a few weeks.

She stared deeply, as deeply as a dog can stare, without being distracted by the yelping of one puppy or the whine of another. She stared, just stared, for the longest of moments. Longer than most dogs stare at anything, with the possible exception of an empty food bowl. (This I have learned recently as well.)

I didn't know what to do, so I gently covered her paws with my hands—like offering a manner of assurance that I was a good person who would treat her offspring well.

After what seemed to be a long time, she sort of gave a nod, like she approved, or found me acceptable, or knew her one special offspring was exactly the puppy I needed, then dropped back to the ground, sniffed my leg and shoe for a moment, and walked back to the big ball of puppies in the corner. This was not her first litter, so she obviously knew the routine. Puppies grow up and move on in the wild, and they do the same if they reside in urban domesticity.

The breeder walked over, reached in, and extracted a small furry lump of wiggle, mostly black, with some white. She handed it to me.

"This one will be yours if you want."

I held the small wriggling bud of puppy cupped in my two hands with plenty of room to spare.

"The pup can't see real well yet, so all it sees is your hands."

I stroked the little face with a finger, gentle, but not overly gentle. It was a boy puppy, after all. The puppy seemed to like that and promptly fell asleep in my hands.

"That's a good sign. Some dogs just stay all riled up—being picked up, carried, strange scents—they'll struggle to get away. Apparently, he thinks you're a safe place."

He was the most beautiful puppy I had ever seen.
And he fell asleep. My heart began to sing, just a little. After such a long silence, it startled me at its ability to do so.
This was indeed the puppy that I needed to have in my life.
More surprises came later.

———

The breeder gave me a list of things to do, and to have them all accomplished in the three weeks between the initial meeting and the final handoff—Rufus's adoption, as it was. The list was not extensive, but it was twice as long as I had anticipated.

"I can't visit your house, so you have to give me your word that all of it gets done. Okay?"

It was a command that I could not say no to.

"Of course."

I could see why she was good at training dogs. I really wanted to please her.

A dog crate; dog carrier for the car ride home; puppy food—one of two preferred brands—a water dish; collar, two leashes; one retractable, one a strong tether; the name of the dog's veterinarian; a picture of the fenced yard; an appointment set for a puppy class. The list ran on for nearly a full page.

Obtaining all the necessary documentation and supplies was not that difficult. The cage—sorry, the *crate*—fit into the alcove of a desk built into the kitchen layout. (I had been told that *cage* was pejorative, crate was preferred by most breeders.) I never used the kitchen desk, except as a temporary storehouse for receipts, mail, and magazines waiting to be evaluated before becoming recyclables. The top drawer held in the neighborhood of a thousand pens and pencils, all halfway to being thrown away because none of them worked, forcing me to take telephone notes with a huge felt-tipped sign marker on legal pads, the ink soaking through four sheets at a time.

I have to get better organized. I mean it this time.

The cage—rather, the crate—fit snugly in the kneehole of the desk. I added two sleeping pads, the top one a leopard print, to ensure a soft rest. I took a picture of it. I would show the breeder all my preparations.

No one prints pictures anymore. All they do is show others the back of their camera or cellphones. I miss passing actual snapshots around, but I didn't think I needed a permanent record of a dog crate and food bowls and the like, so I carried my camera with me.

I'll probably never delete them from the memory stick, though.

I wasn't sure about the crate situation. I never had a crated dog before. The family dog had the run of the house. Looking back, I don't remember where the dog slept. Did we have a dog bed somewhere? My mother, the sole surviving parent, resided in a nursing home, and while she had only begun to wade into the shallow, yet troubled waters of dementia, for now she would resent being asked inconsequential questions like "Where did the dog sleep?"

She would become agitated a little, and wave the question off as if it were a pesky mosquito. "How I am expected to remember foolish things like that?" she would snap, prickly as she had ever been. Some things do not change over the decades.

I would want to say that I did not expect her to recall the details, but that we were simply making conversation. Instead of asking a follow-up question about how the family had decided on a dog name, I would instead sit back, and watch

Wheel of Fortune with my mother. She could not hear worth beans and had no use for gadgets like hearing aids, so the volume would be turned up to a painful level. Virtually every television in the Ligonier Valley Nursing Unit remained turned to the same level. I don't understand how the nurses and aides tolerated it. It would be like working in a tavern that featured heavy metal music. Or working in a steel mill. Here, all televisions, except the one in the main visiting lounge, had to be turned off by eight in the evening. Then silence rolled down the halls like a tsunami.

The breeder said that the prehistoric dogs lived in dens, so a crate, which she was careful to call a crate, fulfills their ancestral urges of being covered, protected, and easily defended. I draped a thin blanket over the top and sides. I planned to swap the thin one out for a heavier one in colder weather. The door latched easily. The crate provided plenty of turnaround area. The padding looked, and felt, pretty comfortable as well.

I had not purchased the Kuranda Dog Bed—patented, orthopedic, and chew proof. It certainly looked comfortable in the pet store, nearly as expensive as the new mattress I had purchased for myself eighteen months earlier. That was a necessary purchase; a deluxe dog bed could not be considered in the same category.

I had an assortment of puppy food, puppy chews, puppy toys, and assorted puppy diversions.

Even before I handed the breeder a check, this dog purchase had become expensive.

Do friends ever give puppy showers? My initial reaction was a strong no, with a wishful yes right behind.

I was ready. I was prepared.

Yet nothing could prepare me, really and truly, for what was to happen in a few short months.

—⦾⦾⦾—

The breeder actually looked at every picture I took of my purchases, my preparations, my supplies, my complete photo essay of my backyard. She even checked the photocopy of the medical license of my intended veterinarian.

"I've never heard of him," she said, "but he went to Cornell. Best vet school in the country."

"She. She went. The B. T. stands for Barbara something or other," I answered.

The breeder brightened.

"Good. I've always found female vets to be more compassionate—and intuitive. Good choice."

I felt proud of what I had accomplished. It was a feeling I had missed in recent months.

She presented me with the puppy's papers and AKC registration—a thick packet of documents that displayed his lineage back to the *Mayflower*, apparently. I had assured her that I had no interest in showing the puppy, or dog, as it grew. I promised to have him neutered; perhaps breeders do not want more competition from unskilled amateurs like me. "Neutered makes for better pets," she declared. I knew, for certain, that his papers would be filed in my office at home, and then lost in less than six months.

I'm not going to sell the dog for a profit, like flipping a foreclosed house. He's not going to procreate. Why would I need to know his great-great-great-grandfather?

I handed her the check. The dog was now mine.

"What are you going to name him?" the breeder asked.

I shrugged, apologetically.

"I'm not good with names . . . or book titles. I let my publisher pick titles. But with the dog, I thought I might see what sort of name fits him after a day or two."

"Don't wait too long. Puppies get imprinted with whatever you call it—especially if you use it a lot when they're young."

He lay down in the middle of the pet carrier, not frantically trying to escape or cowering in the corner. But in the middle, like that is where he was supposed to be. It did make it easier to carry, since the weight was evenly distributed.

I had been nervous concerning the ride home, worried about a whining, yelping puppy carrying on so much that I would have to stop. I'd imagined him chewing wildly at the door, scrabbling to escape his new and probably evil owner. But there were no histrionics, no puppy on the edge of puppy craziness. Just a very calm puppy, supine, staring out through the wire mesh door.

I pulled into the garage, stopped the car, and carefully took the carrier from the car.

"Show him his bed, his food, and the door you'll use to take him outside. Take him out on a leash right away and start his bathroom training," the breeder instructed, touching on the three most important elements in a puppy's small world.

I followed her instructions to the letter.

He dutifully sniffed at his crate, stepped inside, sniffing, looking at the cushion, then up at the top of the crate—like people do on all the HGTV shows when they enter a new room. I have noted that potential homebuyers invariably look at the ceiling, as if to make sure the house has one. Why do people do that? It's a plain ceiling. Look to see how big the closets are first, and if you have good water pressure. No one checks the water pressure on those shows. I have yet to see a single buyer flush a toilet. There might be a lot fewer home sales if people flushed toilets or ran showers.

The puppy completed his examination of the crate. I led him to his food dish and water bowl—both filled with fresh supplies.

He sniffed at both.

I snapped a leash onto his collar and led him to the . . .

Wait. What door am I going to use?

The back door led to a back deck, a second-story affair. A puppy this small would not yet be able to climb stairs.

I'll have to use the front door.

We stepped outside through the main door, and his sniffing became a bit more earnest. It took him fifteen minutes to sniff his way around the front yard. I was cold by the time he completed his inspection. There were other dogs in the neighborhood, so he took some time getting acquainted with their calling cards.

I am told that dogs can tell the size and sex and temperament of other dogs by the scent they leave. Seems a crude way of doing it—but if you can't talk or write, I suspect it is the only way.

He actually relieved himself out there, by a bush toward the side of the house—a bush I didn't really like, so if his ministrations killed it, I would not be upset. It was some sort of weedy looking shrub that had been billed as the bearer of fragrant flowers. The flowers lasted all of three days; the rest of the time it simply looked weedy. I praised him, as I had been told to do.

We walked back into the house. I unclipped his leash.

"Keep him in the kitchen at first. He'll be overwhelmed if he has too much space to explore."

Two doorways led into the kitchen: one a pocket door to the dining room, easily closed off; the other archway could be cut off by opening the basement door, leaving a gap of only an inch or two. The bigger problem was the wide arch between the kitchen and the family room.

The puppy seemed to be a cautious type, so my initial solution employed two lengths of white clothesline rope, strung at two inches off the floor, and the other at six inches, and affixed to the molding with adhesive-backed Velcro. If the puppy ran into them at full force, which he gave no indication of doing, the ropes would give way. More important, if I ran into them, stumbling toward the sunroom with the first coffee of the day and with my typical morning slit-eyes, then I would dislodge them as easily, without tumbling down and scalding myself with hot coffee.

The puppy sniffed the ropes, and made no attempt to cross the barrier.

It appeared effective. Maybe I could market this idea.

The puppy stared up at me.

No. How hard would it be to duplicate this? Not very.

I sat on the floor, my back to the wall, and invited the puppy to play. He slithered over with a wiggle. I imagined that he looked happy. I couldn't tell. This was the start of a long process, learning how to read the moods of this small animal.

He crawled into my hands and began a gentle nibbling on my fingers. His breath smelled healthy, like milk.

"Don't let him bite you," the breeder had scolded me. "Bad habit for a dog to have—biting."

But chewing is what a puppy does. As long as he did not bite in anger, I would tolerate a dog-to-owner chew every now and again.

After thirty minutes, the puppy crawled down from my leg and sat on his haunches, looking as tired as a . . . well, a puppy.

"Go into your crate," I directed and pointed at the open door to his den.

The puppy stared at my finger for a moment, as if my finger was the object he should focus on. "No," I said, as I pushed my finger forward into the air, gesturing toward the door. The puppy appeared to scowl, or furrow his brow as if in thought, then turned his head toward the crate. He lifted himself off the floor and walked with a surprising deliberateness toward his den, his crate, climbed over the two-inch frame, walked in, circled three times, then lay down, his head on his paws, his eyes facing me.

"Tired?"

He blinked, and let his head fall farther onto his paws.

"Can I get some coffee? Will I keep you awake?"

He did not answer. I am not sure, in the retelling of this episode, if he understood me at that young age, and simply waited to speak until the right time, or if he was in the process of trying to understand my speech. I think the latter, though I have not asked him. It doesn't seem to be that pertinent a question, in retrospect.

I sat in the upholstered chair in the bay window in the kitchen, sat with my coffee, watching The Weather Channel with the sound muted, sipping as quietly as I could manage, watching the puppy fall into a deep, untroubled sleep.

Want to learn more about author
Jim Kraus and check out other great
fiction from Abingdon Press?

Sign up for our fiction newsletter at
www.AbingdonPress.com
to read interviews with your favorite authors, find tips
for starting a reading group, and stay posted on what
new titles are on the horizon. It's a place to connect
with other fiction readers or post a
comment about this book.

Be sure to visit Jim online!

www.jimkraus.com

What They're Saying About...

The Glory of Green, by Judy Christie
"Once again, Christie draws her readers into the town, the life, the humor, and the drama in Green. *The Glory of Green* is a wonderful narrative of small-town America, pulling together in tragedy. A great read!"
—Ane Mulligan, editor of *Novel Journey*

Always the Baker, Never the Bride, by Sandra Bricker
"[It] had just the right touch of humor, and I loved the characters. Emma Rae is a character who will stay with me. Highly recommended!"
—Colleen Coble, author of *The Lightkeeper's Daughter* and the *Rock Harbor* series

Diagnosis Death, by Richard Mabry
"Realistic medical flavor graces a story rich with characters I loved and with enough twists and turns to keep the sleuth in me off-center. Keep 'em coming!"—**Dr. Harry Krauss, author of** *Salty Like Blood* and *The Six-Liter Club*

Sweet Baklava, by Debby Mayne
"A sweet romance, a feel-good ending, and a surprise cache of yummy Greek recipes at the book's end? I'm sold!"—**Trish Perry, author of** *Unforgettable* and *Tea for Two*

The Dead Saint, by Marilyn Brown Oden
"An intriguing story of international espionage with just the right amount of inspirational seasoning."—*Fresh Fiction*

Shrouded in Silence, by Robert L. Wise
"It's a story fraught with death, danger, and deception—of never knowing whom to trust, and with a twist of an ending I didn't see coming. Great read!"—Sharon Sala, author of *The Searcher's Trilogy: Blood Stains, Blood Ties,* and *Blood Trails.*

Delivered with Love, by Sherry Kyle
"Sherry Kyle has created an engaging story of forgiveness, sweet romance, and faith reawakened—and I looked forward to every page. A fun and charming debut!"—Julie Carobini, author of *A Shore Thing* and *Fade to Blue.*

Abingdon Press fiction
a novel approach to faith

AbingdonPress.com | 800.251.3320

BKM112220003 PACP0103464-01

Conversations with
St. Bernard

Other Abingdon Books by Jim Kraus

The Dog That Talked to God
The Cat That God Sent

Conversations
with **Saint**
Bernard

A NOVEL

JIM KRAUS

a novel approach to faith

Nashville

Conversations with St. Bernard

Copyright © 2015 by Jim Kraus

ISBN-13: 978-1-4267-9160-4

Published by Abingdon Press, P.O. Box 801, Nashville, TN 37202

www.abingdonpress.com

Macro Editor: Teri Wilhelms

Published in association with MacGregor Literary Agency

Library of Congress Cataloging-in-Publication Data has been
requested.

Printed in the United States of America

1 2 3 4 5 6 7 8 9 10 / 20 19 18 17 16 15

To Terese and Elliot—
who are my source of daily inspiration

Prologue

Lewis snorted loudly as George let the RV rumble to a gradual stop.

"Too windy?" he asked. "Sorry."

George glanced at the GPS system on the dash and scowled. Then he pulled out a map—a real paper and print map—carefully sliced out of a large road atlas and folded into sixths, so it would fit neatly under the visor on the driver's side. He looked at the first fold, scowled again, then flipped it over.

He glanced in the rearview mirror. The road behind the RV remained empty. He had time to survey his options. There had been little traffic on Route 6 as he navigated his not-so-large RV through the north central portion of Pennsylvania. He looked at the GPS again. An arrow, which George found annoying, pointed to the left. It also flashed every five seconds.

"Stupid GPS."

George brought the map close to his face. At sixty-eight, his visual acuity was not what it had once been.

But then . . . nothing is as it was once, he thought, and his scowl was briefly replaced by a more curious expression, an almost smile, but not truly a smile, just a degree or two distant from a smile. When he almost smiled, from a distance, one might think of an aging Jimmy Stewart. Handsome, but unaware of the depth of his own appearance. Someone recently mentioned his cogent look, most of the time, aware, trim, and well-maintained.

Might be talking about shrubbery . . .

George looked up and tapped at the compass he had glued to the ceiling of the RV, next to the rearview mirror. Evaluating both the map and the compass, he realized the GPS unit was pointing in the right direction.

"Rats," he whispered to himself.

George had hoped he'd caught the electronic gizmo in a mistake.

He had not.

For the past three days, since departing from Massachusetts, he had not once proved the GPS wrong.

"There is always a first time, isn't there, Lewis?"

Lewis, in the passenger seat, did not reply. He had most of his head and right shoulder out the window, leaning heavily to the right side, breathing deeply. It was obvious Lewis had thought he had seen a squirrel in the tree next to the stop sign, but it must have been a leaf quaking in the breeze.

Lewis, like most dogs, appeared to be fascinated by squirrels. However, if the truth be told, he was more aggravated than fascinated. Scampering and chattering, with their scolding, imperious attitude, a squirrel could simply disappear from a dog in the blink of an eye. And Lewis, like all dogs, found it both perplexing and exasperating. That was the truth of squirrels and dogs. And Lewis was a dog who had great regard for the truth. Everyone who met him soon discovered Lewis was a dog who had a supreme reverence for the truth, and he appeared to tolerate nothing less from those circling his life.

The large dog wore a sturdy nylon harness attached to the seat belt, and which gave him mobility in the seat, yet would keep him mostly protected in the event of any traffic mishap. Lewis pulled his head back inside and looked over at George, his traveling companion. George tried not to smile at the dog's naturally wise, avuncular expression. It was clearly apparent Lewis loved traveling—or at least riding in the RV, or perhaps in any sort of vehicle. Obviously, George imagined the dog's fondest dreams had come true as they began to make their way across America.

The pair of them, as odd as they were at the moment, were headed toward Towanda, Pennsylvania, and Riverside Acres, an RV park on the south side of the Susquehanna River, just across from Towanda, their planned stop on the third day of their trans-continental journey.

But Lewis's journey began just a year prior to this day. And George's journey started many, many years before—more than a lifetime, it seemed.

PART ONE

1

Lewis had not been the largest of his litter. St. Bernard puppies are never small, yet Lewis was "smallish." Lewis's mother had been on the smaller side of the breed, as well, weighing in at no more than 125 pounds or so.

Lewis earned the name Lewis because of the Burden family—the family who had adopted him.

Alex Burden, the singular offspring of Trudy and Lyle Burden, sat on an old, modestly shabby couch in the basement of the breeder's house, the upholstery covered with a thin veneer of dog hair. A slight boy, of average height, with a shock of brown hair with a mind of its own, Alex also had brown eyes, penetrating brown eyes, making him look older and wiser than his years.

Alex's parents remained at the doorway, watching their son watch the puppies. Alex was a deliberate and careful child, observant to a fault. Six yelping, growling, jumping, tussling, happy puppies were among his choices. The Burdens had been promised the first pick. And his parents had declared Alex, and Alex alone, would make this decision, this puppy choice.

"After all," they said quietly to each other the night before, "they are all St. Bernard puppies with a good bloodline. Alex can't make a bad choice."

So they agreed.

Alex had been a child with more than his share of troubles in his first eight years of life. There had been open-heart surgery, almost as a newborn. There had been a repaired heart valve at age three. There was the coarctation—a serious narrowing of the aorta—at age five. Other maladies had plagued his childhood. Surgeries and doctor visits had pocked his first years of existence.

But for the past three years, his health had improved, and his doctors claimed the most obvious dangers had passed and happily declared Alex to be a normal, healthy child, with no limitations on his activities. Mostly.

Just be careful. And observant, the doctors said. *Once burned, you know . . .*

"Normal kids have dogs," his father stated. "I had a dog. We have twenty acres of woods behind us. Our house is big. We can handle a big dog. Alex would like a full-sized dog."

So the three of them came to Clairvaux Kennels just west of the port of Gloucester. The breeder, Penny McAlister, a kindly woman of scattered attention, hovered behind the Burdens. She swatted at an errant strand of hair. Most of her hair was in strands, and most were errant. A personal style, but it fit her like a cold hand in a warm mitten.

"I know which one he'll pick," she whispered.

Trudy turned her head, just a bit.

"Which one?" she whispered back.

One puppy, the smallish one, the smallest of the litter, not actually called a runt, for no St. Bernard can truly be called a runt, the one who stood at the edge of the enclosure, his front paws at the top of the small solid partition, his eyes showing a fierce determination to scale the wall, to explore what none of his brothers and sisters had yet explored—or wanted to, apparently. The remaining members of his litter had been content to squirrel about in a large furry ball near their sleeping mother.

"Him," Penny said with finality. "He will want the one who will try to do all the things he couldn't do as a small child. He'll pick it."

Penny had been advised of the rudiments of Alex's extensive medical history.

Trudy, wearing her most sensible sweater and Danish clogs, did not think he would pick the one at the edge.

A dog who likes to explore, his mother thought, *and it could be dangerous. And Alex knows too much about danger.*

12

"This one," Alex said, pointing to the puppy who now had his rear leg almost to the edge of the partition, almost gaining a foothold, then slipping back and falling in a heap, only to scramble to his feet and try climbing the fence one more time.

Penny arched her eyebrows in celebration as she passed Trudy and retrieved the adventuresome puppy, then placed it in Alex's arms.

The puppy did not squeal or squirm or attempt to get away. He seemed most content to stare at Alex, stare hard, as if he were memorizing his face, and sniffing hard, to memorize his scent. Alex stared back. He did not speak. He did not introduce himself or tell the puppy he was a good puppy.

There was no giggling. There was no whimpering. There was no nipping and no petting—not yet, at least. None of it occurred. The puppy and the boy just absorbed each other, silent, and nearly still.

After a long serious moment, Alex finally spoke.

"His name is Lewis," he said.

"Lewis?" his mother asked. "Why Lewis? Do you know anyone named Lewis?"

She had read somewhere, in a newspaper, perhaps, young boys of Alex's age would often try to name a pet after a friend in school. The experts said it was the equivalent of awarding a high honor.

"No," Alex replied. "Other than . . . like in Lewis and Clark. You know, those guys I read about who explored America. Seems like a good name for an explorer. And there's a Clark in my class. He wouldn't like it if I named a dog after him."

And what do the experts know? his mother thought, smiling.

This is how Lewis was named Lewis.

His more unusual abilities showed up later. Much more unusual than simply being adventuresome.

Lewis expected the truth.

And often got it.

Not always, but often.

2

George locked the front door and stepped back. He looked at the house, trying to see it as dispassionately as he could. There were memories inside—some good and, during the last years, not so good.

And now . . . maybe I'll be able to get a good night's sleep . . . away from here . . . and the memories.

The house had been completely empty for nearly two weeks. George had sold much of the contents in an estate sale, run by a quartet of too-chatty ladies who had bustled about the house for over a month in preparation. What did not sell in the estate sale, and was in good condition and usable, went to a local church charity resale store. What George felt guilty about donating to charity went unceremoniously into a trash bin. Old metal shelving, still serviceable, perhaps, a little dented and rusty—those went to the trash bin. A stack of *National Geographic* magazines. (George felt more than a little guilty when he threw them into the trash bin.) Box after box of cheap—inexpensive—paperback books George read while waiting. In the span of a year or two, the pages had already turned yellow and brittle. Even the local used bookstore had turned them down. An upholstered sofa that had seen better days. Odds and ends. Broken things. A ten-year-old computer. Two old analog TVs.

And now the house stood empty and broom-swept and ready to have the next family occupy it and make a life within its walls.

For George, his time was over.

It had been three years since Hazel had . . .

George did not like thinking about the last decade. Life's final descent, for Hazel, had been a long and arduous and painful path.

No one should have to spend so much time and energy dying.

George knew it was coming, her ultimate end, and so had everyone else in their small circle of family and friends. He had waited almost two years before putting the house on the market. It had sold in two months, and for his asking price. He had rented a small apartment in Gloucester and installed the bare minimum of necessities.

His one major purchase since Hazel died had been a used RV—a recreational vehicle.

We always wanted to travel. And for the last ten years or so, we couldn't. So I will go in her stead. Recreation? Maybe. Honoring a promise is more like it. A promise. A plan fulfilled.

Their one daughter, George's only daughter, only child, Tess, lived in Phoenix with her husband, Gary. She called once a week, but with her mother gone, his wife gone, they had less to talk about than before.

She had been enthusiastic about her father's plans for a trip across country.

"It will do you good to be busy and meet people."

She sounded relieved. No decisions to make regarding his care. If he was able to drive across America, he was more than capable of taking care of himself.

George walked to his car and did not look back as he drove away.

"One chapter closed," he said to himself. "And one chapter begins."

He came to the stop sign at the end of Sumner Street, the street where he and Hazel lived for forty-five years. His heart hurt, just for the moment, upon realizing some chapters are more final than others.

Ain't it the truth, he thought to himself.

If he had any idea of how the concept of truth would change his life in a few short months, he gave no indication. He simply nodded to himself, agreeing with his own sage comment, and turning left, he headed to the west side of Gloucester and his new home on the second floor of the far west building in the Gloucester Arms Apartments and Condominiums complex.